MW01133956

Love & bless
Debbie Aly

A Forever Kind of Love

by
Debbie Alferio

authorHOUSE™

1663 LIBERTY DRIVE, SUITE 200
BLOOMINGTON, INDIANA 47403
(800) 839-8640
WWW.AUTHORHOUSE.COM

First published by AuthorHouse 05/26/05

ISBN: 1-4208-5123-3 (sc)

Printed in the United States of America
Bloomington, Indiana

This book is printed on acid-free paper.

This book is dedicated with love and thanks to God

for giving me the dream, and to all those who believed

in me enough to help me make it a reality.

1

October 4, 1987. That date is one that I would rather forget, and yet, never want to.

I sat alone at a corner table at Gartano's, a fabulous little Italian bistro in the heart of downtown Philadelphia. I loved everything about the place—the food, the atmosphere, and the friends I had made since I started going there four years ago. One friend in particular, a waitress named Kayla, and I had become like sisters. Kayla was much older than I, but she was always there for me, and until that night, I didn't realize just how much.

My first visit to Gartano's was with Eddie Williams, my high school sweetheart, and it was Eddie that I waited for that night. He had taken me there on our first "official" date after we moved to Philly, and it had become our favorite spot for dinner, or just to have coffee and dessert. Tonight I waited anxiously for Eddie to arrive, and my palms were so sweaty I could hardly grip my coffee cup. I had loved Eddie for five long years, loved him with everything I had, and I decided I couldn't wait any longer. I was more than ready to become Mrs. Eddie Williams. And I was going to ask him to make it official.

"So, girl, when's this man of yours going to show up?" Kayla asked as she filled my cup.

"Don't you worry, he'll be here," I replied as I nervously looked at my watch. "He's coming straight from work. I told him not to be late."

"Well, I know it'll all be just fine." Kayla said soothingly. "You have a lot of guts asking him to marry you. I never heard of the girl doing it, but why not? This is the eighties!"

"Hey, Kayla, your order's up!"

I turned to see who the unfamiliar voice belonged to. Behind the counter dressed all in blue was a man I hadn't seen in Gartano's before. He was very handsome, tall with wavy black hair cut neatly, and silver rimmed glasses that made him look even more distinguished. He was slender, but even through his shirt sleeves I could see he had a muscular frame. I guessed him to be about my age, if not just a little older.

"That's Mitch Tarrington, he's new, just started a week or so ago. He's helping Jimmy manage the place, being that we're getting so busy now. And yes, he's single, AND very handsome, but aren't you here for another boy?" Kayla chuckled.

"Oh, please, Kayla, I just didn't recognize him, that's all. You know my heart belongs to Eddie!"

"Uh, huh, but it doesn't do any harm to look!"

As if on cue, Eddie walked through the door, waved, and headed straight for my table. Kayla gave me a quick little hug for luck and went back to work, taking care of the other customers who were quickly filling up the surrounding tables. Eddie kissed my cheek softly, and sat down. I could immediately tell something wasn't right, but I didn't know just what.

"So, what is it that's so urgent?" Eddie beckoned Kayla, and she poured him a cup of coffee.

"Well, Eddie," I started nervously, "I don't know how else to say this, except to come right out with it." I glanced at Kayla, who was nodding approvingly.

Eddie looked at his watch, and took a sip of coffee. He seemed distracted.

"You and I have been together for five years now....." I began, but Kayla interrupted.

"Eddie, you have a call." She said. I looked at him as he excused himself and went to the phone. I noticed Mitch watching him as well. I watched as Eddie seemed to end the call quickly, glancing my way as he spoke. He came back to the table and sat down.

"Who was that?" I asked curiously. "Who would be calling you here, Eddie?"

"Look, Dana," Eddie sighed heavily. "I gotta be straight with you. That phone call, well, it was from a friend that I'm meeting tonight.....a female friend." He paused and sighed nervously. "Actually, she's more than a friend." Eddie dropped his eyes from mine. "Dana, I never meant to hurt you......"

I looked at Eddie, and my heart sank to my knees. "Eddie, what are you trying to tell me?"

"Dana, I've met someone, and I've been seeing her, secretly, for a while now. I meant to tell you, but I just didn't know how." Eddie reached out for my hand, but I pulled it away.

The tears began to roll down my cheeks, and my hands were shaking as I placed the cup back on its saucer. I looked into Eddie's eyes for some sort of sign, something that would tell me I hadn't heard him correctly. But looking at his face I knew he was telling me the truth.

"Eddie, how, why, I don't understand......"

"Dana, I'm so sorry, I honestly never meant to hurt you, I never meant for this to happen....." Eddie once again reached out for my hand, but I folded my arms tightly across my chest.

"Do.....you love her?" I could barely choke out the words.

Eddie didn't answer, but his face told me what the answer was. "I'm so sorry Dana, please forgive me." Eddie rose to his feet, took his gloves from his pocket and looked at me once more. "I had better go. Will you be ok? Can I call someone for you?"

"Eddie, how could you? I loved you, I do love you....."

Eddie touched my cheek, and without saying a word, turned and walked out of Gartano's into the chill of the night. But the chill I felt was much deeper than that of the autumn wind.

Kayla looked at me in disbelief, and came to join me at the table. Sitting down, she took my hand in hers. "What happened girl? Did he say no?"

Tears of pain were still streaming down my cheeks. "Oh, Kayla, it's much worse than that. He broke up with me!"

"What? Broke up with you? Is he THAT afraid of commitment?"

"He's met someone else, Kayla, and he's in love with her. He didn't tell me who, and I don't want to know. I just don't understand. How could he do this? How, after all we've been through!"

Kayla stood up and helped me to my feet. "Come on, girly, I'm going to take you home with me. You don't need to be alone tonight."

As we walked toward the door, I felt as if someone's eyes were upon me. I turned toward the counter and caught Mitch's gaze, his eyes full of wonder and concern. I paused just for a moment to look at him, wondering why he would care, and then followed Kayla out into the night. I wouldn't find out until much later that he had been watching the whole incident with Eddie, and just how much he really did care.

Kayla's home, as always, was warm and inviting. Laughter streamed toward us as we entered, and I looked to see her husband and two children playing a game on the family room floor. Joseph got up and greeted Kayla with a kiss.

"Hey baby, how's my favorite gal?" Joseph quipped. Then he turned toward me. "Well, how are you, Miss Dana?" Joseph's look grew somber as he noticed my tear streaked face. "Oh my, it looks like you're feeling a little blue tonight."

"Yes, she is, Joseph, and I told her she could stay here with us tonight. I don't think she needs to be alone, upset as she is." Kayla placed her arm around my shoulders and gave me a quick hug. "I'll let her borrow some of my things tonight. They may be a little big, but they'll be ok. Then she can go home in the morning for some fresh clothes."

"Isn't any of my business," Joseph began, "but I'm guessing there's a man involved."

"Well, there was," I sniffed, "but not anymore."

"Oh, I'm sorry, Dana," Joseph said sympathetically. "But let me tell you, he can't be very smart to let one like you get away."

I managed a smile as Riley and Joanna came toward their mother. Kissing them both, she sent them quickly on their way, and then beckoned me into the kitchen. "Let me fix you something to eat. Some chicken soup and a cup of hot tea cure anything!"

"Kayla, I'm not sick." I commented.

"But you *are* heartsick." She replied. "And this will make you feel much better. Then, you can go take a hot bath and I'll give you some sweats to slip on for the evening. After that, we can talk, if you feel up to it."

"What would I do without you, Kayla?" I asked.

"Well, you just let me take care of you tonight, and by tomorrow, you'll be feeling much better."

Later that evening, Kayla and I sat in their quiet family room, Joseph and the children long since in bed. We were curled up in front of a cozy fire Joseph had started for us, sipping hot chocolate and talking about how awful men could be.

"You know," Kayla started, "not ALL men are awful. Take that Mitch, for instance....."

"Now wait just a minute," I quickly responded. "I have a feeling I know where you're going and I'm NOT going with you!"

Kayla chuckled. "Girl, come on, I was just going to say that Mitch is a nice guy. Acts like one who would know how to treat a lady right."

"And just how would you know that?" I asked.

"Well, I don't, really. I just think so. He never says an unkind word to any of the ladies at work and you know, he talks really kind about his mama, too."

I couldn't help but laugh at the thought that last comment provoked. "His *mama*?!? Is he a mama's boy?"

"Now, don't go bashing like that, you know that isn't what I meant!" Kayla couldn't help but laugh, too. "He just seems like a very nice fellow, that's all!"

"Well, nice or not, you can forget it!" I retorted. "I'm not interested in Mitch or anyone else of that gender! As far as I'm concerned, men can't be trusted. They're all pigs!"

"Right now they may be, but you'll change your mind, and when you do, you'll be looking for one like him. Just mark my words, you will!" Kayla winked.

"Listen, I will give you one thing," I confessed, "he *is* awfully cute!"

Giggling like a couple of schoolgirls, we talked deep into the night.

Morning came too soon, and a note from Kayla greeted me on the nightstand next to the bed. She had already gone off to run errands before work, and I was instructed that there were fresh cinnamon rolls and hot coffee waiting for me in the kitchen. Joseph had gone to work, and Riley and Joanna were already at school, so I was left alone to "make myself cozy" in Kayla's home. She had even taken the liberty of calling me off sick from work. "You deserve a day for yourself," the note said.

After breakfast and a quick shower, I dressed in yesterday's clothes and decided I'd better head home. The day was sunny and bright, and although the air was chilly, I didn't feel the need to catch a taxi. I started the walk to my apartment, about ten blocks or so from Kayla's house. As I walked, I tried to sort out the events of the night before. The pain and disbelief of Eddie's words were slowly being replaced by anger and resentment. How could he do this to me, after five years together, and especially, after saying he loved me? I never saw it coming, and that angered me even more. Was I really that naïve, that I couldn't see the signs? Or was Eddie that sly, that he never gave me any?

As I approached my apartment, David, the doorman, greeted me. "Good morning, Miss Walker! Fine day, isn't it?"

"Good morning, David." I replied. "Yes, it is a fine day, I guess." David held open the door for me, and I made my way up to the third floor where my apartment was. I fumbled to open the door, stepped in and closed and locked it behind me. My answering machine was beckoning me with a blinking light, so I quickly walked toward it, and then paused before I pushed the button. Maybe it was Eddie, calling to apologize. Maybe he would say that it was all a mistake, that he still loved me, and wanted me back. Then again, it might be someone else. I decided that I should find out, so I swallowed hard and pushed the button.

"Dana, it's Eddie." My heart skipped a beat. Could he want me back? I sat down to listen to the rest of the message.

"Dana, I feel that I owe you an explanation. I know you probably don't want to listen to this, but please hear me out. See, well, remember several months ago when we hired those temps to help out during that big audit we did?" Eddie worked as a corporate accountant for one of the biggest firms in the city. "Well, Kathleen was one of those temps. We hit it off right away, and I never meant for it to go this far, but I was caught up before I knew it. I really do care for her, Dana, and well, I may even ask her to marry me. Dana, I'm sorry, but I gave it a lot of thought, and this wasn't easy for me, either. I just couldn't bear not telling you the whole story, the truth. Please know that I never meant to hurt you, and I hope someday you can forgive me. Take care of yourself." The phone went to a dial tone.

I couldn't believe what I had just heard. Marry her? How ironic, Eddie, I thought. That's precisely what I was going to ask you to do. I couldn't hold back as the feelings rushed upon me, and I began to cry, long and hard.

The next few weeks were nothing more than going through the motions, or so it seemed, but each day seemed to bring me closer to moving on, and closer to letting Eddie go completely. Sometimes at night, I would still take his picture from the drawer and have a good cry, but I felt the need to do that less and less as time went on. I found that the best way to keep Eddie's memory from creeping up on me was to stay away from anything that reminded me of him, including, and especially, Gartano's. It was just too painful to be there. If I met Kayla after work, I would only step inside the door, just as she was leaving. Being such a wonderful friend, Kayla felt the need to nurture me through this time, and would call me at work during the day, and often at night I would join her and Joseph and the kids for dinner. They welcomed me into their home and made me feel special. Kayla was always there when I just wanted to vent, or cry about Eddie. Finally, around the first of November, Kayla decided that the best way to help me forget Eddie once and for all was to have me revisit Gartano's for dinner.

"Just come in tonight, eat, and relax. I'll tell Mitch to watch for you....." Kayla teased.

"Oh, Kayla, don't you dare!" I pleaded. "I don't need any man messing up my life again! I'll only come," I agreed, "if you promise to leave him out of this!"

Later that evening as I stepped into Gartano's, the warmth and charm were almost too much for me to bear. I had to do this, though. Kayla was right. I couldn't spend the rest of my life avoiding things I enjoyed, just because they reminded me of Eddie. I needed to find something else to identify Gartano's with, and much to my surprise, I did the minute I heard his voice.

"Kayla, your order's up!"

Kayla greeted me with a smile and a wave, and her gesture caught Mitch's attention. He stood motionless for what seemed like forever, just staring at me, before Kayla nudged his arm and drew his attention away. There was just something about the way he looked at me, but what surprised me the most was, I didn't mind it the way I thought I would.

Kayla hurried over to my table. "You need to just go up and talk to him, girl." She said. "It isn't hard to see that he noticed you."

"Look, Kayla, if I've told you once, I've told you a million times, I'm NOT interested! Now, could you just bring me a nice plate of lasagna?"

"Suit yourself." She quipped as she poured my coffee.

Kayla stopped by the table now and again for some small talk as I enjoyed my dinner. This wasn't as difficult as I had imagined. In fact, I didn't think of Eddie at all. I didn't think of Eddie because, well, I was thinking of Mitch.

I found it somewhat strange at first, because, after all, I had only been apart from Eddie for about a month. I just couldn't get out of my mind the way Mitch had looked at me that night Eddie broke up with me. Eddie. There were times I still missed him, yet more times now that I cursed him for what he had done to me. But, somehow I believed there was a reason for everything, and I knew deep inside that there was a reason for this, too. Maybe the attraction to Mitch was a purely physical thing, I thought. He *was* very handsome, and seemed to get along well with everyone around him. The regular customers seemed to adore him, particularly one older gentleman everyone knew as Joe. Joe was always at Gartano's, or so it seemed, and would sit at the counter for hours sipping coffee and making conversation with the employees who floated around the bistro. But it was easy to see that he had taken Mitch under his wing, so to speak, and Kayla said that he once told her Mitch reminded him of his own son who lived hundreds of miles away. Now I sat and watched the two, engaged in conversation. I was too far away to hear what they were saying, but unless I was just being paranoid, I had a feeling I might be the subject of the discussion.

"Pretty little thing, isn't she?" Joe asked Mitch as he shot a quick glance at Dana.

"Absolutely." Mitch replied in a dreamy tone, fixing his eyes upon her once again.

"Well then, son, go and talk to her. If you just keep staring at her, she's going to think you're some kind of stalker or something."

"Oh, Joe, I can't do that right now. I'm, uh, well, I have work to do."

"Nonsense!" Joe retorted. "Go refill her coffee cup or something. Ask her how she liked her dinner. Anything!"

"No, now can we just drop it, please?" Mitch seemed to be getting agitated. "Besides, Kayla's taking care of her!"

"Well, now, there you go!" Joe said. "Have Kayla tell her you're interested. They seem to be pretty good friends. She can do the dirty work, and you can move in for the kill!"

"Joe!" Mitch chuckled. "She's not the 'prey' and I'm not a lion moving in for any 'kill'. Besides, a girl like her wouldn't give me the time of day!"

"Well, if you're not a lion, you sure are drooling a lot!" Joe chucked Mitch under the chin.

"Oh, gee, I have work to do. I'm just wasting my time talking to you anyway!" Mitch started to turn away.

"Now look, Mitch," Joe started again. "Every time that girl has even popped her head in this place, you've acted like a little lovesick puppy dog, just standing there staring at her. It's very obvious to see you have a crush on her....or more." Joe took a sip of coffee.

"You're crazy!" Mitch was losing his temper. "Now I'm not even allowed to see who's coming in and out of my restaurant? She's nothing more than a customer, that's it! I look at her, yes, I look at a million people a day, and *some* of them just *happen* to be female. Just because I find her attractive doesn't mean I have a crush. I.....oh, forget it!" Mitch threw the towel he was holding down on the counter and stormed into the manager's office.

Closing the door partway, Mitch sat down on the couch there and placed his head in his hands. What was going on inside him? Joe was right—Dana was a beautiful girl. And maybe, just maybe, he did have a crush on her. He felt like a fool just staring at her all the time, but what else could he do? Well, he could try talking to her, but why bother? A guy like him didn't stand a chance with someone like her. She seemed to have it all together. What could he offer her? He'd witnessed the night Eddie broke up with her, and it broke his heart to think of anyone hurting her. But she had Kayla to lean on for that, and what could he have done, anyway? He didn't know her, after all. And what would she see in a restaurant manager? Eddie obviously looked like the type of guy who could offer her so much more, the type of guy she would go for. Ok, then, with this wealth of knowledge, why couldn't he get her off his mind? His thoughts were interrupted by a knock on the door.

"Mitch, are you ok?" It was Kayla. "You seem a little bit upset."

Mitch smiled. "Thanks, Kayla, but I'm fine. Really." His voice couldn't hide his feelings very well.

"Look, I know what this is all about." Kayla said as she joined Mitch on the couch. "Every time you see her, boy, it's written all over that handsome face of yours. You're smitten with her."

"No, Kayla, I'm NOT, and I really wish everyone would quit telling me how I feel!" Mitch got up and started toward the door of the office. He placed his hand on the knob, then stopped and turned back toward

Kayla. "Ok, I do think she's attractive, but I swear THAT'S IT!" Mitch started to open the door.

"Mitchell, you can't fool me. This is Kayla you're talking to now!" Kayla stood up and pushed the door closed again. "Come back here now and sit down, I want to talk to you."

Mitch pushed his hands into his pockets and walked back to the couch. But he didn't look at Kayla. He knew she could read him like a book, even though she had only known him a short time. And he also knew he wasn't very good at hiding things.

"You know, Mitch," Kayla started, "every time you see her you just stare. I notice, Joe notices, everyone else notices, and you don't think *she* notices?" Kayla placed her hand on Mitch's arm. "If you don't talk to her soon, she's going to think you're some kind of stalker or something!"

Mitch shot her a quick look. "Have you been talking to Joe....?"

"No, but I've been reading your face, and, well, I've been reading hers, too. She's smitten too, but 'course she'll never admit it, either. Two of the most stubborn youngsters I've ever seen!"

Mitch sat silent for a minute, took off his glasses and rubbed his eyes. Kayla had to be insane. Dana wasn't 'smitten', or anything else, with him, for that matter. Every time he did catch her eye, she would turn away. No, there was nothing there. Couldn't be.

"Look, Kayla, I've had enough of this conversation, and I've had enough of everyone butting into my business." Mitch calmed the tone of his voice. "I appreciate what you think you are trying to do, but it's over as of now, got it?" Mitch replaced his glasses and started toward the door once more. "Now, we both have customers to take care of, and we better go and do that."

"Ok, but you know, I still don't...." Kayla got up and started after him.

"It's OVER, Kayla, please!" Mitch went back out into the bistro.

"Not 'til the fat lady sings, and I'm that fat lady." Kayla said to herself.

Later that night as Mitch walked home, his thoughts turned back to his conversation with Kayla. She seemed to know Dana very well. Could it be true, that she was attracted to him too? Impossible. He thought about Eddie once again, and the look in Dana's eyes as she left that night with Kayla. He had felt a connection, or at least he thought he had. Maybe it was just Dana needing some sympathy. Or maybe it was just him wanting her to feel something. Or maybe, it was all just crazy.

Once inside his apartment, Mitch kicked off his shoes, loosened his tie and fell onto the couch. He fell asleep to the sound of the TV, and thoughts of Dana.

On the other side of town, my apartment was quiet as I sat in my favorite chair, sipping a cup of tea, and glancing at the newspaper. What was that I just read? I just couldn't concentrate. For some reason, all my thoughts kept going back to Mitch Tarrington. What was it about him? And why on earth did he keep staring at me? This was ridiculous. It was late, but I decided to call Kayla, thinking that would get him off my mind. Little did I know what I was headed for.

"Hi, Kayla, it's me, Dana." I started. "Sorry to be calling so late."

"It's only ten thirty." Kayla replied. "It's not too late. Is something wrong?"

"Oh, no, I'm fine." I lied. "Just wanted to chit chat. There's nothing worth watching on TV, newspaper's depressing, so here I am!"

"So, I'm your boredom breaker, huh?" Kayla laughed. "That's ok. I can handle that."

As always, Kayla and I commenced into a whirlwind conversation of subjects, touching on everything from her family to the sale at Marlo's Dress Shop in town. It was Kayla who steered the conversation to Gartano's, and finally, to Mitch.

"It was good to see you in the bistro tonight, girl. We've all been missing you." Kayla paused. "I think Mitch missed you, too."

"Now listen, Kayla," I began. "Please don't get going on that again. I told you before….."

"I know, you "aren't interested"." Kayla's voice changed to sound very matter-of-fact. "Well, that's just a bunch of hogwash, and I wish you two would admit you want to get together!"

"Just where are you getting this information?" I snapped. "You know, Kayla, for weeks you've been trying to fix me up with this guy. Have you *seen* the way he looks at me? It's as if he's trying to figure out what I am or something. Like, oh, I don't know, he's *stalking* me!"

Kayla burst into laughter, thinking back to her conversation with Mitch, and the fact that she had made that same comment to him. "Baby girl, you're seeing a man who wants to be with you! He stares because he thinks you're so beautiful, and you are. His eyes are taking in what he wishes his hands could hold!"

"Kayla, really, I just can't believe you!" I shot back. "Has he actually *told* you he wants to be with me? Or is this just another one of your little ploys to take care of me? I appreciate it, but I am a big girl now. I'm over Eddie, I'm moving on, and I DON'T need any man to help me with that!"

"I'm sorry." Kayla's voice softened. "I didn't mean to upset you. But, let me just tell you something, and you need to hear me out. Tonight, Mitch went into the office at the bistro, and I joined him there. He told me he thought you were attractive....."

"Ok, so he thinks I'm attractive. That's a long way from "wanting to be with me!""

Kayla continued. "I'm a pretty good judge of character, and I've come to know that boy pretty well in the short time he's been there. Beautiful women come and go all the time down there at the bistro. He doesn't notice them. Doesn't pay one second of heed to *any* of them, *except* you. He's got it, and he's got it bad!"

"Well, I certainly hope "it" isn't contagious, because I don't want it!" I quipped back.

"Oh, honey, it's much too late for worrying about that!" Kayla replied. "The bug has bitten you, too. And it bites hard!"

Before Kayla would let me hang up, she made me promise I would come into Gartano's again the next evening. I would go, I decided, if nothing else, to prove to her that Mitch Tarrington had no attraction to Dana Walker. Or vice versa.

On November 4 at eight o'clock sharp, as promised, I once again found myself stepping into the warmth and comfort of Gartano's. As usual, the place was buzzing with laughter and conversation, and Kayla was floating from table to table, filling cups and bringing orders. The only table I could find, much to my dismay, was close to the counter. I decided I had no other choice but to sit there, so I did.

Mitch hadn't seemed to notice me tonight as I walked in, and was busily filling orders and giving instruction to the cooks and waitresses who seemed to be running from here to there. It was my turn to stare this time. As much as I tried to fight it, I couldn't help it. Something about him just made me feel funny inside. Kind of the way I felt the first time Eddie had kissed me back in high school. Odd, I thought. I'm not a little schoolgirl anymore, and besides, that was much different. I was just admiring Mitch for his appearance, I told myself. I knew nothing about the man beneath all that. And I didn't want to. Or did I?

Kayla poured me a cup of coffee. "Well, I'm glad you made it here.' She said, smiling. Then she got close to my ear, and poked me teasingly. "*Now* who has the staring problem?"

"Kayla, oh, you make me so mad!" I had to laugh at the smirk on her face.

"I know, I know, you "aren't interested", but he sure is fine, isn't he?"

I looked up again, and this time, Mitch was looking back. And, then, it happened. He smiled at me. Embarrassed, I dropped my head and picked up the menu.

"Now, you see, I'm not so crazy, am I?" Kayla was still looking at Mitch, who was still looking at me. "He's definitely got it for you!"

"I would like the spaghetti, please!" I refused to look up as I placed my menu back on the table. "And, please tell me he's not still staring at me!"

"Ok, he's not still staring at you." Kayla said smugly. But when I looked up, Mitch smiled again. Once again, I looked down and, picking up my purse, pretended to search for something.

"I think you're supposed to smile back." Kayla said, smirking again. "It's easy, just bring up the corners of your mouth, and do it."

I looked up at Mitch again, and I fixed my gaze on him for just a moment. He was so handsome. And he had a smile that would melt any girl into putty. Wait, was that a dimple on his cheek? Oh, great, I'm falling for this, I thought. I'll just smile back and get it over with. I managed to crack a small smile, and returned to my purse expedition.

"Ok, now, don't you feel better?" Kayla mused.

"Hey, I smiled, now would you please leave me alone?" I put down my purse and began to sip my coffee.

Kayla left the table and went back to work. Several moments went by, and I looked at my watch. What could possibly be taking a plate of spaghetti so long? The longer I sat, the more I noticed people leaving the bistro. What was going on? I called for Kayla.

"Why is everyone leaving?" I asked. "And where is my food? I'm starving!"

"Well, the food's on its way, dear." She replied. "And we're closing up early tonight, didn't I tell you? We've got a little inventory to do, so Mitch thought it would be a good idea to get going on it."

"Well, then, I guess I better be going, too. I can always make a sandwich at home." I started to stand up, but Kayla pushed me gently back into my chair.

"I have that order in and you're not leaving until it's finished." She said sternly. "And besides, you promised my kids you'd stop over tonight, remember? I won't be leaving for a little while, so you just sit tight. It's Friday, so they'll be up late."

I couldn't argue with Kayla, so when she finally brought my food, I took my time eating it. Before I was finished, the bistro was empty of customers, except for me and old Joe. Mitch was busily helping a few of the cooks count things in the kitchen, and Kayla finished cleaning tables. Soon, Mitch appeared carrying a huge bowl covered in plastic wrap, but I couldn't see exactly what was inside. He sat it on the counter, and called for Kayla.

"Just what is this?" He asked her, pointing to the bowl.

"Oh, that." She replied. "That would be a bowl of whipped cream."

"And why do we have a huge bowl of whipped cream? What happened to the canisters we usually use?" Mitch began to take the cover off the bowl. "Is this even fresh?"

"The canisters, well, that's a long story." Kayla said. "And yes, honey, it's fresh. Want to see for yourself?" Kayla picked up some of the whipped cream on her finger and smeared it on Mitch's cheek, giggling playfully.

"What did you do that for?" Mitch appeared dumbfounded, but not upset. He was smiling now, and a playful look came over his face. "Since you did that, I guess the only thing I can do is this!" He scooped up a handful of the cream, and flung it at Kayla, hitting the front of her apron. He laughed an ornery sort of laugh, which drew my attention to the event at hand.

"I think I don't want to be a part of this!" Joe started to get up from his stool. As he turned, Mitch flipped a spoonful of whipped cream in his direction, hitting him on the arm.

"Now, listen here, sonny boy!" Joe smiled at him. "I'm an old man, and I don't take too well to these childish antics!" Mitch was still laughing, that is, until Kayla hit him full face with a handful of the whipped cream.

"You best respect your elders, boy!" Kayla snapped. "How dare you pick on Joe!"

With that, the two of them were engaged in a full force whipped cream battle, dodging each other's shots like a couple of playful children. The laughter brought the attention of the other employees who were standing out of range of the flying confection. I was content to watch the whole spectacle from the safety and comfort of my table, that is, until Kayla noticed me laughing hysterically.

"Oh, you think this is funny, huh? Seeing this little bit of a boy take on this big mama?" The next thing I knew, I had whipped cream in my hair.

"Kayla!" I squealed. "I'm not a part of this!"

"Are now!" she laughed, and threw another handful in my direction. Before I realized what was happening, I had a handful of whipped cream and was chasing her around a table. Within a matter of seconds, both of us were splattered from top to bottom. The sight of us seemed to amuse Mitch beyond words, as he removed his glasses to wipe the tears of laughter from his eyes. Kayla and I paused and looked at him, then at each other.

"You thinking what I'm thinking?" Kayla asked.

"Oh, yeah!" I chuckled. Before Mitch could put his glasses back on, Kayla and I hit him simultaneously with whipped cream, right in the face. The crowd cheered as we slapped a high five.

"That was *not* funny!" Mitch clamored. "Especially when I had a disadvantage!"

"And what would that be?" Kayla inquired. "That we're just better shots than you are?"

"No, that I couldn't see!!" He wiped his face, replaced his glasses and dipped both hands deep into the bowl. "But I can now!" I ducked just in time to avoid a handful of whipped cream hitting me right in the face. Kayla wasn't so lucky.

By this time it was Kayla and I who were dodging Mitch's well aimed shots, but it seemed for some reason that his attention was more focused on me. I armed myself with another handful, and when he turned his back just for a moment to see where Kayla was, I threw it, hitting him in the back of the head. He swung around and took off after me, his eyes shining with mischief. Not knowing what else to do, I ran past the crowd and into the safety of the office, slamming the door behind me. I dropped to my knees and pushed all my weight against the door. In less than a second or two, I could hear Mitch's footsteps stop on the other side of the door, and the sound of him catching his breath.

Now what do I do, I thought. I can't open the door with him right there like that. I would just have to wait it out. He would have to leave eventually, and then I could escape unnoticed. A few days away from Gartano's would be more than enough to put that comfortable distance between us again.

Mitch knocked on the door. I didn't say a word, and held my breath. He knocked again, and this time, tried to turn the knob. I looked up, realizing that the deadbolt was too high for me to reach from this position, and I had forgotten to lock it when I came in. I heard him sigh deeply, and then he tried to push the door open. I pushed back with all my strength. He chuckled, and pushed again, this time a little harder. Still, I did everything I could to push the door closed again. He sighed once again, and pushed harder still, this time managing to get his hand around the inside of the door. I couldn't resist any longer, both because he was too strong, and because I didn't want to hurt his hand. I moved back, and in an instant, I realized he was there, looking down at me.

I didn't want to look at him, but I couldn't help myself. Slowly, my eyes made their way up and soon I was staring right into the face of the most handsome man I had ever laid eyes on. There was something about the way he was looking at me. He wasn't smiling, but his eyes were shining with a sort of soft affection, and I never realized before how beautiful and blue they were. Suddenly, he extended his hand to help me to my feet. Without saying a word, I took hold, and stood up before him.

"You may need this." Mitch said softly, handing me a towel. Until that moment, I hadn't realized I was still holding on to his hand. I took the towel and wiped my face and hair.

"I'm sure I look a mess!" I dropped my gaze from his face.

"No, not at all. Not to me." He was speaking very softly, almost as if he were nervous.

I could feel my knees starting to shake. "Well, I guess I'd better get going, Kayla's waiting for me." I said, starting to move past him. Mitch didn't move.

"Can we, uh, sit down for a minute?" Mitch asked, pointing toward the couch.

I wasn't sure why, but I nodded and sat down. Mitch closed the door halfway and sat down beside me. I didn't look at him. I couldn't look at him. My insides felt like a bowl of jelly. What was happening to me, and why was I here? I felt like running, but yet, I knew I wanted to stay. Mitch's soft voice broke the silence.

"You sure have a heck of a way to get a guy to notice you." He said, teasingly. "I've never had whipped cream thrown at me before by a girl—or anyone else, for that matter."

I couldn't hold back the smile that was forming on my lips. I looked up at him, and he smiled at me sweetly.

"Mitch, I....." I started to speak, but I was so caught up in the moment, the words wouldn't come. Mitch said nothing. He sat patiently waiting for me to continue.

I didn't understand why, but I felt the need to tell him what was on my mind. "Mitch, I've been coming to Gartano's for a long time now. Four years, to be exact. I feel like this is, well, kind of a second home for me. It holds a lot of memories, some good, some not so good."

Mitch still sat silently, folded his hands in his lap, and turned more toward me. He was looking right into my eyes, and again, I dropped my gaze. I just couldn't look at him for some reason. Every time I did, I felt my heart skip a beat.

"There's something I need to tell you, something I need for you to know." I stopped talking and looked at Mitch. His face was full of concern, but still he sat silently. I wasn't used to anyone listening to me so intently. Eddie had always had a way of trying to solve all my problems midstream, never letting me completely get a thought out of my mouth. I had always thought it meant he cared, until now. All it had meant is that he didn't want to listen to me, that he needed to feel superior. Mitch wanted to listen to what I had to say. I decided I would just come out with what was on my mind.

"That guy you saw me here with a while ago, well, that was Eddie. Eddie was my boyfriend, and for five long years, my entire life. I loved him, Mitch, loved him very, very much. But that night he was here, the night you saw me leave with Kayla, he told me he loved someone else."

Mitch turned away. "I'm sorry." He said softly.

"Actually, that night I came here with a plan. I was going to ask Eddie to marry me. But it never happened. He never knew how I felt, he never knew how much I really loved him, and he never will."

I could feel a tear starting to drip down my face, and I began to feel a twinge of that old familiar pain, the pain I thought was gone from my life. But, it was Mitch's words that shocked me more than what I was feeling. And they were so soft, I could barely hear them.

"Dana, I'll never hurt you like that."

I turned toward Mitch. "What did you say?" I wanted to be sure I had heard what I thought I had heard.

Mitch turned to face me once again. "I won't ever hurt you, Dana." He paused for a moment, and then continued. "I know that you don't know me at all, and you may not want to. But, I've watched you each time you came here. I've wondered about you, I've thought about you, I've even dreamed about you." Mitch swallowed hard. "I don't even know why I'm telling you this, except for something my mom once said to me."

"And what was that?" I asked. He had caught my curiosity.

"Well, she told me a long time ago that if you really......care....about someone, that you should never keep secrets from them. "Mitchell, no secrets." She would say. So, I've always tried to follow that rule. I guess....I guess that's why I had to tell you."

My emotions were speeding in ten different directions, and I wasn't sure what I should feel at that moment. Here I was, with this wonderful, beautiful man pouring his heart out to me, telling me he cared and I was on top of the world. But, at the same time, I was scared to death. Something was happening here, and I had a feeling I knew what it was, and I couldn't fight it anymore. Not answering Mitch, I took my turn, just listening.

"Dana, I know this is awkward, well, for both of us." Mitch wrung his hands nervously in his lap. "But I really would like to get to know you better. But, I'll understand, if you say no. Like I said, no secrets. You can just tell me and I'll leave you alone. I mean, I don't have much to offer, anyway....."

"Mitch, stop!" I pleaded. "How can you say that? You don't know this, but....." I stopped again. Then I remembered, no secrets. "Mitch, truth is, I noticed you, too, the night Eddie broke up with me, and every time I've been here since then. I've thought about you too, but I just wasn't sure......how you felt about me."

Mitch smiled, and reached out for my hand. This time, I took it willingly, and he placed his other one on top of it. His hands were warm and strong. He looked deep into my eyes, and I could feel myself melting once again.

"I would like to get to know you better, too, Mitch. I really would." Mitch moved closer to me, as if he were going to kiss me. Then he stopped.

"Wait a minute." He teased. "I've never 'formally' introduced myself to you. I think that would only be the proper thing to do, under the circumstances." I chuckled as he extended his hand for me to shake. "I'm Mitchell Jacob Tarrington, the third. Blame that on my mother. But you can call me Mitch!"

"Well, that is an awfully long name," I teased back, "so Mitch will be just fine. And, I'm Dana Patrice Walker. The Patrice is after my great-grandmother. But, you sir, can call me Dana." We laughed softly and shook hands. Mitch's face grew serious again, and he gazed into my eyes.

"Mitch, uh......" the words stuck in my throat. "I can't say it, nothing, just forget it."

"Remember, Dana, no secrets. It's me you're talking to. You can say anything to me." Mitch took my hand once again.

"Mitch, do you believe in love at first sight?"

He smiled. "Absolutely!" he quipped.

"Well, has it ever happened to you?" Mitch was drawing closer to me now, and his eyes were shining.

"Yes, Dana, it has. About a month ago." He leaned over and kissed me, the sweetest kiss I had ever known.

Mitch smiled sheepishly. "Well, now you've forced me into a very sticky situation."

"I have? What's that?" I answered anxiously.

"I have to decide, do I stay here and finish up the inventory, and know I have a job tomorrow or do I walk you home and risk it all?"

Mitch cupped his hand on his chin, as if in deep thought. Then he stood up, turned back to me and extended his hand. "Ok, where do you live?"

"No, now, Mitch, I think you should stay, really. I don't want Jimmy to get upset with you. Besides, I promised Kayla I'd go home with her this evening."

He looked disappointed at first, but then shrugged it off. "Oh, well, ok then, if you already have plans."

"But it's nothing we can't do another time!" Kayla stood in the doorway, and the sound of her voice startled us both.

"Just how long have you been there?" Mitch asked her suspiciously.

"Oh, I'd say long enough to know you two have finally gotten your act together!" Kayla threw on her coat and hat. "I'll be going now, Mr. Tarrington, and Dana, I'll be talking to *you* later!" She winked at me and walked away.

"Come on, we'd better get going, too." I said to Mitch. "We don't want to give anyone the wrong impression, you know!"

As we walked back into the bistro, most of the crew was still there, finishing things up. The mess created by our little battle had all been scrubbed away, and everything looked top notch. One of the cooks noticed us first, and started a round of applause, followed by the others. Mitch turned five shades of red, and I buried my face in his shoulder. Finally, he held up his hand to silence them before he spoke.

"Ok, everyone, I know what some of you are thinking," We heard a few chuckles here and there, "but everything is really quite innocent. Dana and I had a nice discussion after our little fiasco, and well, we have decided......." Mitch stopped and looked at me, as if for approval. "Ok, I guess I have decided........" Mitch looked at me again.

"What's wrong, Mitchell, cat got your tongue?" I said quietly. Then I turned to the crowd. "We've decided to start seeing each other!" Applause filled the room once again, and Mitch just looked at me, shaking his head.

"Are you always this assertive?" He asked teasingly.

"Yes, and is that ok with you?" I teased back.

"Absolutely!" Mitch pulled me into his arms and gave me a quick peck on the forehead.

The crew finished up the work at hand and as if they knew we wanted to be alone, they all left together. Mitch helped me with my coat, then put on his own. He started to put on his gloves, thought twice, and put them back into his pockets. "I have a better way to keep these warm." He said, grinning at me. Once outside he locked the door behind us, took my hand in his, and placed it into his coat pocket.

As we walked along, I couldn't help but feel like I was walking on air, and I wondered when I would wake up from this dream. I glanced at Mitch and wondered what he was thinking about just then. Was he feeling the same thing I was? I didn't want to ask. I just wanted to believe that he was.

Mitch was the first to break the silence. "So, Dana, I don't know if you would be interested, but I was just thinking, unless you think it's too soon, I mean, I know we really just met......"

"Well, I won't know until you ask me." I replied.

He took a deep breath. "Yeah, well, I have this little problem and it's called my mother. See, she's having the family over for dinner tomorrow night, and well, she's been wanting to meet you."

I stopped dead in my tracks. "She's been wanting to *meet* me? How does she even *know* about me? And just *what* does she know about me?"

Mitch placed a hand on each of my shoulders and turned me toward him. He bit his lip nervously. "I told her about you after you came in the first time, the night Eddie broke up with you. I told her how he made you cry, and that if I knew you, or him, better, I probably would've decked the guy."

I looked at him, astonished by what he had said. "Mitch, you didn't even know me, and you said that?"

"I know, but it really made me mad to see him just walk out on you like that. I couldn't believe anyone could do that to someone like you."

"But you didn't know anything ABOUT me!"

"I know, Dana. I didn't understand why it bothered me, either, but it did. My mom has this way of being able to tell when something's wrong, so I had to tell her how I felt. You know, no secrets."

"Ah, yes, no secrets. So, anything else I should know, or should I say, anything else I should know that she knows?"

"Just that I think you are the most beautiful woman I've ever seen, that I feel amazing just being near you, and that ever since that night, I haven't been able to do anything, not anything, without thinking about you. As Kayla would say, I guess I'm quite smitten with you!"

"And I with you, Mr. Mitchell Jacob Tarrington, the third!" He took my hand once again.

"One more thing," he started, "just *where* do you live?" We both laughed and I pointed him in the right direction.

David greeted us and held open the door. We stepped inside the lobby and out of the cold of the night. Mitch's glasses began to fog up from the temperature change, and he took them off to wipe away the mist. "Man, I hate this." He grumbled. "I wish they made defrosters for these things."

I chuckled. "Don't you ever go without them?"

"Can't." he replied. "I can't see a thing without them, not clearly, anyway. Everything becomes a big blur the minute I take them off. Farsighted, since I was about, oh, ten years old or so."

"What a bummer that must be." I stated. "It's a shame, because you really do have such beautiful blue eyes."

"Sorry I have to hide them from you." Mitch apologized, and I realized I may have hurt his feelings.

"Oh, no, Mitch, I think the glasses make you look very, well, very distinguished."

"Thanks, I guess," He replied.

We both stood in the silence for a moment. Then Mitch spoke. "So, you never gave me an answer about dinner tomorrow. Would you like to join us?" He looked eager for my answer, almost like a child asking his mother for a treat. I had to smile.

"Well, ok, but just one thing."

"Sure, anything!"

"What do I do if they don't like me? Will you stay with me, and if I get too nervous, will you bail me out?"

Mitch chuckled and reached out for me, smiling with affection. "Listen to me, now," he started soothingly. "I'll stay right by you, and not leave your side, not even for a minute. Promise." He raised his hand as if to make a vow. "And as for them not liking you, that's just crazy. How could they not like you?"

"Well, I don't know." I looked down from Mitch's face. "I don't always make a great first impression on people."

"What are you talking about? You made a great first impression on me! Heck, I was head over heels the first time I laid eyes on you! And the whipped cream? Well, that was just the thing that clinched it for me!" He chuckled again, his eyes shining.

"Come on, Mitch, I'm serious. What if they don't like me?"

"Look, Dana, they're going to love you, guaranteed. There's no way they can't."

"And tell me, Mr. Wise-guy, just how you can be so sure they're going to "love me?""

"Well, that's easy." Mitch said, pulling me even closer. "Because I do."

I can't remember how I got up the stairs to my apartment, but somehow I managed to get inside, lock the door, and flop down into my chair before I even realized where I was. I was still reeling from all that had happened that evening. Mitch was amazing. I didn't have to wonder anymore how he felt about me because now I knew. He was in love with me. And something deep inside me told me that I was in love with him, too. I thought about that for a moment. How could love, real love, happen so fast? I didn't have an explanation. I had heard of it happening to other people, but not once had I ever imagined it happening to me. But now it had, and I couldn't have been happier. My bubble burst, just slightly, by the ringing of the phone.

"Hello?"

"Girl, you sound out of breath! Are you and Mitch 'busy'? Should I leave you alone?" It was Kayla.

"Kayla, for heaven's sake!" I couldn't believe my ears. "He isn't even here. I just ran to the phone, that's all!" Then I thought about what she had said, and laughed. "Besides, what kind of girl do you think I am?"

"Oh, honey, I was just teasing, I know you're a good girl!" Kayla continued. "So, do you still think I'm crazy?"

"No, and yes, I mean, no, I don't think you're crazy. And yes, you were right. About Mitch, I mean. Kayla, he's really terrific!"

"I know, and it seems he's a good kisser, too. Planted one on you tonight, didn't he?"

"Kayla!" I said, surprised. "Were you spying on us in the office tonight?"

"No, now, you know I wouldn't do that, not on purpose anyway. I just came back there to make sure you were alright, and, well, I just happened to arrive at that moment. Girl, you looked like you were just going to float away!"

"Oh, Kayla, it's all happening so fast!" I replied, sinking into my chair once more. "The kiss, the words, just the way he looks at me, I just don't know. What if he gets home and thinks it's all a mistake? What if it's just infatuation?"

"Now, Dana, why on earth would you even entertain a thought like that?" Kayla put on her know-it-all voice again. "That boy's crazy about you, has been from the very first time he saw you. I know that look, and the way he kissed you, oh wee, girly, that man is in love!"

"You really think so? I mean, he kind of said that to me......."

"Honey, that's something you don't kind of say to anyone. It either is or it isn't. And if he said it, well, he's the kind of fellow that wouldn't say it unless it was so!"

"Oh, Kayla, I hope you're right!" Then, suddenly, something hit me. "Oh, no!" I exclaimed.

"What is it, Dana?" Kayla asked.

"Well, Mitch is having dinner with his family tomorrow night, and he asked me to join him. I said I'd go, but he never told me what time, or if he was picking me up......"

"Now, just calm down, missy, I'm sure he'll call you." Kayla soothed.

"He doesn't have my phone number. I never gave it to him, and I don't have his, either."

"Oh my, that is a problem. Well, don't worry your pretty little head about it, now. Mitch is a smart man, he'll figure it out. Maybe you should just stop by the bistro and ask him what time." Then she paused. "Uh uh, that won't work either, he's not working tomorrow. Jimmy gave him the day off. I guess he was planning to spend the whole day with his family."

"Kayla, what am I going to do? I don't know how to get in touch with him!"

"Tell you what—maybe Jimmy will have his number. We can find out in the morning. We'll get you there, don't you worry."

"I can't believe I didn't give him my number. How stupid of me! But, let me tell you, Kayla, looking into those eyes, I think I may have even forgotten my own name!"

I could hear the smile in Kayla's voice. "I'm so happy for you, Dana, so very happy."

2

I turned over in bed and looked at the clock. Oh, my gosh, ten a.m.! How could I have slept so late? I had so much to do today. Since I had no idea what time I'd be meeting Mitch......Mitch. Just the thought of him sent chills up my spine. I still couldn't believe this was happening to me. But, I didn't have time to sit and daydream now. I had to get dressed and get downtown to do some shopping. Maybe have my hair done, too. I wanted to be sure I did make a good first impression on Mitch's family.

I threw on my robe, and headed to the kitchen to start a pot of coffee. Then I slipped into the bathroom and turned on the shower to let it warm up. I was just about to get undressed and step in, when I heard a knock on my door.

Who in the world could *that* be, I thought. Maybe I should just ignore it—probably just one of the neighbors wanting to borrow something. If I don't answer the door, they'll think I'm not home and go away. I just had too much to do. I took off my robe. Another knock, this time a little harder. Then I heard a voice. An all too familiar voice.

"Dana? Are you in there?"

I shut off the water, put my robe back on and went out into the living room. Another knock, even harder this time.

"Ouch, oh, great!" I heard. "Dana, it's me, Mitch. Sweetheart, are you there?"

Sweetheart! He called me sweetheart! I rushed to the door to let him in, but stopped just as I reached for the chain lock. He couldn't see me like this! What could I do?

Mitch must have heard my footsteps from the other side of the door. "Dana? Is that you? Ow, oh, man that hurts. Let me in, please."

I just couldn't let him see me without any makeup, without my hair done, and especially, in my pajamas and robe! I thought fast, especially since he now knew I was here. "Hello, Mitch, what are you doing here?" I called through the door.

"Why am I here?" he repeated quietly to himself, as if he needed to analyze the question. "I thought we were going to my parents' house, and well, I realized I didn't give you any of the details, and ...... sweetheart, please, why won't you let me in?"

"Well, Mitch, truth is, I just got up."

"So?"

"So, silly, I'm not dressed and I was just going to take a shower. And I have a lot to do, and....."

"And you don't want to see me, is that it?" Mitch sounded a bit irritated. "Ouch." He said again.

"Oh, no, no, that's not it at all!" I quickly replied. "I just don't want you to see me like THIS!"

"Like what?" he asked, now sounding a little more irritated. "It's a little hard to see ANYTHING from this side of the door!"

"I'm sorry, Mitch, I'm not meaning to be cruel. It's just that if you saw me right now, you might run away!"

"Oh, good grief! Why don't you open the door, and let me see for myself? Ow!"

"Mitch, why do you keep saying "ouch"? Did you hurt yourself?"

"Usually, that has something to do with it," I heard him sigh deeply. "Dana, I'm not going to go away, so it's either you open the door, or I just stand out here forever, getting louder and louder and irritate all your neighbors."

"But Mitch, I really would like to get dressed first. And I can't do that until I shower, and if you come in, you'll see how awful I look right now, and ......"

"Dana, you're being ridiculous. I don't care how you look, or how you think you look. OPEN THE DOOR PLEASE!"

Mitch's tone told me he didn't care about anything but getting out of the hallway. I sighed deeply, quickly tousled my hair, wiped my eyes, and opened the door. He stood there, holding his hand with the other, and looking not the least bit happy.

"Good morning, handsome." I said sweetly, trying to break a smile from him. I stepped aside and let him come in, closing the door behind him. Mitch turned, looked at me and started to laugh.

"What's so funny?" I asked. "Do you find something about my appearance amusing?" I knew I looked rumpled, but I had warned him, and now his laughter was upsetting me.

"You....look.....nothing like I thought you would in the morning!" He was still giggling, and had leaned back against my counter, folding his arms across his chest. Suddenly, his stare caught me, and began to make me a little uncomfortable.

"Just how did you think I would look? Is it that much worse than you thought?" I paused. "And just why were you thinking about what I'd look like in the morning anyway?"

"I'm a guy, remember? I'm allowed to at least *think* about such things, aren't I? And as for how I thought you'd look, it's just the opposite." Mitch smiled. "You look incredible!" He gave me a slow once over, shaking his head as he went from head to toe, and back again.

I smiled, but then had a second thought. "Wait, what do you mean?" If how you're seeing me is *better* than what you thought, then you must've thought......."

Mitch walked toward me, but I backed away, and folded my arms sternly, as if to resist him. He stopped, and reached out for me.

"Dana," he cooed. "You know that's not what I meant. I'm sorry. Nobody looks good when they first get up, that is, except you. It's just that you're always so put together, everything in it's place. It's nice to see you aren't like that all the time, that you can be, well, natural."

He wasn't scoring any points with me at that moment. "Oh, so am I too 'perfect' for you, Mitchell Tarrington? I'm sorry I take pride in my appearance. I'll be sure to stop taking care of myself, just to please you!"

Mitch bit his lip. "Wait a minute." He replied. "Don't put words into my mouth. You're the one who wouldn't open the door, who was so worried that I might see you when you weren't all dolled up!"

"Oh, so now I'm too 'perfect' *and* too 'dolled up' for you! Why did you come here? To insult me?"

"I'm NOT insulting you! If you would just listen, you MIGHT realize that I'm trying to compliment you!"

I sat down on my couch, arms still folded, and turned away from Mitch. I could hear him walk toward me, and he sat down, looked at me, and cracked a half smile. "Was this our first argument?" He asked, quietly.

"Was....or is," I replied

"Well, you know," he said moving closer, "I like to argue, because when you're done, you get to make up."

"And just what makes you think I'm ready to make up?" I said, still being stubborn.

"Because I'm just too hard to stay mad at!" Mitch grinned and came at me full force, burying his face in my neck, and nibbling me playfully, making me laugh. Then, he kissed me lovingly. He was right. I couldn't resist such a charmer. Especially when he called me sweetheart.

"You're terrible!" I laughed, playfully pushing him away.

"Oh, but you love it, don't you?" He started toward me again, but I put up my hands.

"Didn't you say you hurt yourself? Let me see." I took his hand to inspect the damage. "You did cut it, didn't you? Come with me, and I'll put something on it."

I led Mitch into the bathroom and took some first aid supplies out of the medicine cabinet. "Now, just sit down and let me take care of that for you." I began to apply some iodine, and he winced. "What did you cut it on, anyway?"

"There was a nail sticking out of the door frame and I got a little too close to it when I knocked. Ouch!" He exclaimed, pulling his hand away. "It's ok, really, it'll be fine." He started to get up, but I pushed him back down.

"Remember, I'm the assertive one here." I smiled at him. "Let me take care of it. I don't want you to get an infection."

I took his hand once more and before long, had it all cleaned and doctored up, complete with a bandage. "Now, doesn't that feel better?"

"Yes, Dr. Dana." He replied. "Now, are you ready to go out with me?"

"Of course I am!" I answered happily.

"Well, what makes you think I'd take you anywhere looking like that?" Mitch got up and began to laugh again, wholeheartedly.

"Oh, you!" I pushed him out the door and could still hear his playful laughter as I closed it behind me.

After I showered and dressed, I found Mitch waiting patiently for me in the living room, sipping a cup of coffee and reading the morning paper. I stopped before he realized I was there, and just looked at him for a moment. He looked as if he belonged there, and it was nice to see him in a "natural" state, too. He wasn't dressed up today, not the way he did for work. There was no tie, no dress shirt, and no dress pants. Today it was jeans, a sweater, and hiking boots. I thought he looked adorable.

"Sorry I kept you waiting." I announced as I stepped into his line of vision.

"Oh, not a problem. I hope you don't mind me kind of making myself at home."

"No, that's fine, I'm glad you did!" I replied. "So, what's the plan? Are we going to your parents' house now?"

"Well, I called my mother this morning, and she said dinner is set for around five or so, so I thought you and I could just spend some time together today and head out there around four. I thought it might give us a chance to get to know each other a little." Mitch looked at me for approval.

"That's fine, but I really did want to go downtown for a few things first." I stated.

Mitch stood up. "Look, I'm sorry. I shouldn't have just assumed you'd be free, or that you'd want to be around me all day. How about I go, let you do what you need to, and I'll pick you up later."

"Don't be silly!" I said. "I was just going to pick up a new outfit to wear to dinner tonight. I'd love to have you come along, if you don't mind going shopping."

"What's wrong with what you have on?" Mitch asked, giving me the up and down look.

I glanced down at my jeans and sweater. My hair was pulled up in a ponytail and my favorite boots were showing signs of wear. "I can't meet your parents looking like this!"

"I really do wish you'd stop that!" Mitch came toward me. "You're beautiful, just the way you are!" He cradled me in his arms and put his chin on top of my hair, sighing deeply. "But, if it'll make you happy, then I'll go shopping with you. But, you have to let me buy you lunch."

"Deal!" I sealed it with a kiss.

We headed out into the morning, and once on the sidewalk, I pulled on my gloves and hat, preparing for the walk downtown. Mitch caught me by the arm.

"Oh, no, my dear, your chariot awaits!" He said, pointing to a sporty blue Mustang convertible. I noticed it had personalized license plates that said "MJT III." Cute, I thought. I looked at him, puzzled.

"You have a car?" I asked

Mitch chuckled. "Yes, I have a car, and believe it or not, I do know how to drive it. I just usually walk to work because it's much more, well, economical for me, considering I only live three blocks from Gartano's." He opened the door for me and I got in, fastened my seatbelt, and waited for him to get in. "So, where are we off to?" He asked.

"Well, let's see, I love Carlson's Department Store. I can usually find what I need there. Is that ok with you?" I touched Mitch on the arm.

"Carlson's it is!" And we headed off.

The morning gave way to early afternoon, and Mitch was the best shopping companion. He sat through dozens of outfits, countless pairs of shoes, and even a manicure. Despite his patience, I didn't want to push it too far, so around one p.m. I asked if he was ready to wrap it up and have some lunch.

"I thought you'd never ask!" He teased. "What are you hungry for?"

"Anything is fine." I replied.

"No, now wait." Mitch stopped. "When a girl says anything, she usually means she has something in particular on her mind. I have sisters, I know these things."

"Just sisters, huh? Never had another girlfriend? I'm sure a gorgeous man like you has had his share of the ladies!"

Mitch seemed surprised that I would ask that question. "Hey, I learned a lot from my sisters. And as for the other, yes, I've had a few."

"Just a few?" I prompted.

"Yes, Dana, just a few. I'm not the big ladies man everyone would make me out to be!"

"I just wondered, that's all. I just want to know everything about you, but you don't have to tell me anything you don't want to tell."

We were sitting in Mitch's car now, and he put the keys in the ignition. Then he turned to face me.

"Ok, yes, I did date a few girls in school, but only one seriously. Jessica Radcliff. We went out for a long time, and I thought, well, that there was a chance we might be together forever, but it didn't work out. She went off to college and met someone else, and well, end of story. About three years ago."

"That must have been very difficult for you, Mitch." I touched his hand.

"Well, it was, for a while. But, that's all in the past, and it worked out for the best. I honestly haven't even thought about her since then."

I looked at Mitch's face, and I could tell that perhaps I had stirred up an emotion in him that he hadn't dealt with in a while, and I felt badly for him. I knew that pain, because it was the pain I had felt losing Eddie. But, like I had always said, things happen for a reason. I realized just then that the pain we had both felt was the only way we could ever get to the joy of having each other.

Mitch broke the silence. "So, what else can I tell you?" He inquired.

"Well, I am going to meet your family. Tell me about them. I want to be prepared."

"Ok, let's see. First of all, I'm the baby of the family. There's Julia, Christopher, Angelina, and me. They're all married, with kids, except for Julia, and they will all be there today."

"Oh, fantastic." I said sarcastically. I didn't realize I was facing the entire Tarrington lineage!

"Hey, don't worry, they're harmless. Except for Chris. He likes to crack on me, but he doesn't mean anything by it. Just the sibling thing." Mitch started the car. "I told you, I'll be right there with you. I won't let you down." And somehow, I knew he wouldn't.

After a fabulous lunch at a corner café, Mitch took me back to my apartment to change. I was all for just getting dressed and leaving, but he had other ideas. Once inside, he started putting the moves on me once again, but I pushed him away.

"Mitch, as much as I would love to sit here and neck with you all afternoon, I don't think your mother would be too happy if we missed her dinner. What would I say to her?"

"She knows me pretty well." He replied, playfully. "Just tell her I had you in a permanent lip-lock, and we had to call the paramedics to pry us apart."

"You really are something else, you know that?" I grinned. "Now, let me go and get ready. I promise I won't take long."

Mitch sighed heavily, picked up the TV remote, and turned it on. "Have it your way." He replied with a smile. "But, when you get back, just know I will still be here!"

"That's precisely what I'm hoping for." I said, and disappeared into the bedroom to change.

After about fifteen minutes or so, I reemerged, only to find Mitch sound asleep on the couch. Poor baby, I thought, all that shopping must have worn him out. I stood for a minute, just watching him sleep. He looked like an angel. My angel. I wanted to just leave him alone there, but it was already 3:30 and I didn't know how far away his parents lived. I slipped up behind him and ran my fingers gently through his hair. Slowly, he opened his eyes, took off his glasses and rubbed them sleepily.

"Tired?" I asked, still running my hands through his hair.

"I guess I must've been." He stretched and caught me around the waist. "Can I have a kiss now? I've been waiting."

I leaned over and kissed him. "That's all you get for now. We need to get going, or we'll be late."

"Very well, you're the boss." Mitch stood up and put on his coat.

"Good thing you're learning that early on." I teased. "It'll make things much easier later!"

Mitch grinned and shook his head. He opened the door and beckoned me out into the hallway. For some reason, the anxiety of what was to come hit me, and I suddenly felt very nauseous.

"I need to go back in, Mitch. Quickly!" I raced back through the door, and sat down on the couch, as if to catch my breath.

"Dana, what's wrong?" Mitch was startled.

"I don't know, I just got very queasy. I'm starting to feel better now."

"Are you sure? Can I do anything?" Mitch was crouching down in front of me now, his face full of concern.

I sat still for a moment. "Mitch, I'm scared to death!" I could feel a tear starting down my cheek.

Mitch touched my cheek lovingly. "Why are you so nervous, Dana? It's just my family. It's not like we're going to meet Frankenstein and his bride or something!" I knew he was trying to make me laugh, but it wasn't working.

"It's just that I can't help remembering something from my past."

Mitch sat down on the floor. "Tell me about it."

"Eddie's family hated me. They hated everything about me. I wasn't good enough for their son, and they didn't have any qualms about telling me so. That's why, after graduation, Eddie and I decided to move here, to get away from them. We each got our own place, and it was all perfectly innocent, but they knew we were still seeing each other, so they would make things up that just weren't true. I heard that there were some awful rumors going around back home, even that I was pregnant, and that it wasn't Eddie's baby. That hurt me more than anything, Mitch, that they could say something so terrible about me. They always told Eddie that he could do better, that he could find someone who wasn't so plain, someone who wasn't so...." The tears were coming harder now.

Once again, like the night in the office at the bistro, Mitch sat silent, just listening.

"I can't go through that again, Mitch, I can't. I'm so afraid they won't like me!"

Mitch wiped a tear from my cheek. "Well," he sighed heavily, "that explains why you were so uptight about all this." Then, he softened his voice and turned back to face me. "Sweetheart, these people are *my* family, not Eddie's." Mitch turned my face toward his. "And I'm Mitch, remember? It's going to be ok, I promise. I wouldn't ever lie to you, Dana. You don't have to be afraid anymore." He reached out to hold me. "Now, dry your eyes, and let's try this again, ok? For me?"

I looked up at him and nodded. "I bet you think I'm being really silly about now."

Mitch's face went serious. "Dana, don't tell me what I'm thinking." He said firmly. "I understand. You had a bad experience, but it's over now. I want you to forget about it, ok? It's my turn to be assertive."

Once inside the car, Mitch held my hand reassuringly. We didn't talk for the first few minutes, but the silence between us seemed comfortable. I looked over at him. Funny how, even though I had only known him a few days, it seemed like I had known him all my life. Even after five years with Eddie, I didn't feel I had known him as well as I felt I knew Mitch right now.

"I know you're looking at me." Mitch said, not taking his eyes off the road. It was beginning to snow, and the roads were getting slippery. "Having second thoughts, now that you've had a chance to really inspect me?" I could see him smile.

"I was, I mean, looking at you, that is." I said softly. "And no, I'm definitely not having any second thoughts. I was just thinking how it seems like we've known each other forever, and really, we haven't."

"I would think that's a good thing, myself." Mitch replied. "I think sometimes people get too caught up in time tables. You know, can't kiss on the first date, can't hold hands, and can't ever, not ever, possibly fall in love that quickly. Not a forever kind of love, anyway. Why, that would just be out of the question, now wouldn't it?" He smiled. "But, you know, I've never really been one to play by the rules." He squeezed my hand. He must have noticed I still looked uptight. "Dana, I can take you back home, if you really don't want to do this."

Although the offer was tempting, I decided I didn't want to let Mitch down. "No, it's ok," I replied softly.

"Still nervous?" He asked sympathetically.

"A little." I replied

"Don't be. I'll tell you what. How about if I give you some pointers on how to score brownie points with the crew? Would that make you feel any better?"

"It can't hurt, I guess." I said.

Mitch put both hands on the wheel. "Ok, first is my dad. Mitchell Jacob Tarrington, Jr. But he goes by Jake, to avoid any confusion, you know, since I share the name. Dad's just an easygoing kind of guy, and he likes everyone."

"That's good to know!" I said, letting out a sigh of relief.

"Next would be Mom. She hates to be called Mrs. Tarrington, says it makes her feel old. So, you can start off there, but when she says to call her Olivia, do it. Chris can act like a real know-it-all sometimes, but he's really a good guy. And as far as Julia and Angelina, they love everybody, too, so that should be an easy one. But, they like to talk, so if they get off on a tangent, I'll bail you out."

"My hero!" I sighed.

Mitch smiled again. "Absolutely!" he quipped merrily.

"You like to say that don't you?"

He laughed. "Absolutely!"

A few minutes later, we approached the Tarrington's home. "Ok, Mitchell, spill it!" I exclaimed, as my eyes were fixed upon the biggest house I had ever seen, on what must have been a hundred acres of land. The setting was beautiful, surrounded by trees and rolling hills. But I could immediately tell that there was at least *one* secret that Mitch hadn't told me. His family was loaded!

"What are you talking about?" He pretended he didn't understand.

"Why didn't you tell me you had all this?"

"I don't, my *parents* do." He replied. "Besides, what's the big deal? It's just a house!"

"For the love of......" I started. "Mitchell THAT is not JUST a house. That's a doggone MANSION!"

"And you've never seen one before?" He was agitating me with his nonchalant attitude.

"As a matter of fact, no, I haven't! Why didn't you tell me, Mitch? I thought you said no secrets!" I was becoming more irritated.

"Ok, you got me." He stopped the car and put it in park. Then he turned to face me. "Dana, my family does have money, you can obviously see that. You may have heard of Tarrington Industries? You know, the medical products?" He held up his bandaged hand, as if I needed a visual to get the point.

I thought for a moment, and didn't know why it had never connected before. "So, you're *that* Mitchell Tarrington!"

"No, my *dad* is *that* Mitchell Tarrington. I'm just the kid, nothing more."

I stared at Mitch in disbelief. "Mitch, I don't get it. Why didn't you say something before?"

"Why, Dana? Would it have changed anything between us? Would it have made any sort of difference, if you knew.....if you knew I was a rich kid?"

"Of course not!" I exclaimed. "It's just that, well, I don't think you should be ashamed of where you come from, that's all!"

"What makes you think I'm ashamed? Just because I didn't tell you? Man!" He hit both hands on the steering wheel, and I knew I had upset him.

"Mitch, I'm sorry." I said. "I just don't understand why......."

"Why I didn't tell you?" He turned toward me. "I didn't tell you, Dana, because I chose, much to my father's dismay seven years ago, to walk away from all this. He offered me a job at Tarrington Industries just after I graduated, but I turned him down. He offered to pay for everything I own, and I turned him down on that, too. I chose *not* to be the one to follow in my father's footsteps. I wanted to live my own life, to be what I made of myself, not what somebody else made of me. I'm perfectly happy with my life. I may not have much, just being a manager at Gartano's, but I am happy. Happier than I would be working at Tarrington Industries, in a job my father handed to me." His voice calmed. "I didn't tell you, Dana, because I wanted to make sure that it was me you wanted, not my family's money."

I sat in silence beside Mitch, taking everything in. Mitchell Tarrington. He was probably the biggest name in medical products in this part of the country. I never connected it. Maybe it was because Mitch didn't act like a rich kid. But, then, how did a rich kid act? I guess I was stereotyping, and I didn't want to do that, with Mitch or anyone else.

I grabbed his hand, and leaned toward him.

"Is there anything else I should know?"

"No, I don't think so. Oh, wait. I will be getting a huge inheritance someday, but I'll probably just pay off some bills, put some in the bank, and donate the rest to charity. Pretty boring, huh? Or, should I say, pretty common." He was still irritated, and his attitude was coming out.

"Look, if you want to escalate this into an argument, that's fine. But, there's something you should know first."

He looked at me, expressionless. "What would that be?"

"That none of this, though it is very nice, matters one bit to me. It doesn't make a difference to me at all. You are who you are. And......... Mitchell Tarrington.....I love you!"

Mitch smiled brightly. "What if I told you I loved you too?"

"Now that would make me very happy!"

We finally came to a stop in front of the house, and Mitch looked at me lovingly. "Are you ready to do this?" he asked.

"I think so." I replied. "Remember, you promised you'd stay with me!"

Mitch laughed. "Yes, I will. Now come on before they start gawking out the windows. I hate being spied on." Mitch walked around to open the door for me, and tucked his arm around my waist. "Now, don't be nervous." He opened the front door, and his mother and father came toward us, just behind the butler.

"Dana, this is Alexander, my parents' butler. Alexander, this is Miss Dana Walker, my....."

"Oh, it's alright, Mitchell, go ahead." I giggled. Mitch shot me a look and rolled his eyes.

"....my girlfriend!"

"Very nice to meet you, Miss Walker. May I take your coat for you?" Alexander extended his hand. I looked to Mitch for a clue, but he just stood there, smiling.

As Alexander took my coat and walked away, I leaned toward Mitch and tugged on his shirt sleeve. He bent down so I could whisper in his ear. "Mitchell, they have a BUTLER!" I whispered excitedly.

Mitch leaned toward me, and whispered back. "Yes they do, and why do you keep using my proper name? Stop being so uptight!" He laughed and kissed me on top of the head.

His mother and father stopped in front of us, and I dropped my eyes. I was so nervous I couldn't feel anything. Mitch's mom came close and greeted him with a hug.

"Hello, honey, did you have a nice drive up here today?" she asked.

"Hey, Mom." Mitch kissed her on the cheek. "The roads are getting a little slick, but we did just fine."

Mrs. Tarrington noticed the bandage on Mitch's hand and brought it up for closer inspection. "Oh, Mitch, honey, what did you do to your hand?" She inquired with concern.

"Oh, it's nothing, Mom. Anyway, Dana took care of it for me!" He gave me a little smile.

Mitch's dad shook his hand, and pulled him into a bear hug. Jake Tarrington was a distinguished looking man, not as tall as Mitch, with sandy blonde hair and shining hazel eyes. He was built slightly larger than Mitch, and his voice was deeper, yet pleasant. "So, son, aren't you going to introduce us to this attractive young lady you brought along?"

Suddenly I felt even more nervous as I felt their eyes upon me. I moved closer to Mitch, and wanted to grab his hand, but I didn't know if I should. Just at that moment, he must have read my mind, and I could feel his fingers wrap around mine.

"Mom, Dad, this is Dana Walker. Dana, my mom, Olivia, and my dad, Jake Tarrington."

"So wonderful to meet you, Dana." His mother extended her hand. "Mitch has told us a lot about you."

I glanced up at Mitch, and he looked away, a guilty sort of grin on his face. He looked like a little boy who had gotten caught with his hand in the cookie jar.

"Oh, well, it's very nice to meet you, too." I said back, shaking their hands. "You have a beautiful home here."

"Would you like me to show you around, Dana? I'd be happy to take you on a little tour." Mitch's mom smiled sweetly.

"Sure, that sounds great, Mrs. Tarrington." I replied, trying to sound confident.

"Oh, dear, please, call me Olivia!" Mitch once again smiled impishly, an I-told-you-so look in his eyes.

It was at that moment that I remembered Mitch had a hold of my hand. "Well, let's go have that tour, Mitch!" I said, reassuring myself that he was going to stay true to his word and not leave my side.

"Now, Mitch, you can trust me with her, I don't bite." His mom laughed, placing her arm around my shoulders. She noticed he was holding my hand, and smiled sweetly. "Now, let go and you go on and visit with Dad. You can have her back in a little while." I must have looked terrified at that moment, because Mitch chuckled again.

"Well, I guess I'd better listen to my mom, huh?" He sighed. "I'll see you a little later, Dana. Have a good time!" He turned and walked away, chuckling and grinning from ear to ear.

"He's a character, isn't he?" Olivia smiled at her youngest child. I just nodded silently. She led me into the kitchen, where Alexander was putting the finishing touches on the meal.

"This is probably the place I spend most of my time." She told me. "I actually do most of the cooking myself, but I decided to let Alexander help a little more today. I wanted the chance to get to know you, Dana. I thought we might talk a little before the others arrive."

I didn't know just how to respond, so I just smiled.

"Alexander, would you excuse us for a few minutes?" Alexander nodded and left the room. Olivia pointed to a chair and asked me to sit down, so I did.

"So, Dana," she started, her blue eyes soft and kind. I saw clearly that it was from her that Mitch inherited his good looks. Her hair was dark, about collar length, wavy and neatly styled to show off her face. I guessed her to be close to sixty, but she appeared much younger.

"Mitch and I are very close, we always have been. I told him as a little boy that he shouldn't keep secrets from those people he cares about. I have always taught him that being honest and open is best, no matter what."

"Yes, he told me that." I replied. But I couldn't help thinking about Mitch not telling me about the family fortune. No sense digging that up again, though. I waited for Olivia to go on.

"Another thing about Mitch is, he doesn't hide his feelings very well. When he's upset, I know it. When he's happy, or angry, or anything else, I know it. Dana, that first night he saw you at Gartano's, and came here after work, I knew something was bothering him. And I also knew something else, even then. And even more now, now that I've seen the two of you together."

I looked at her curiously, and waited for her to continue.

"He told me about that boy that broke up with you….."

"Eddie," I said, as if I needed to fill in the blank.

"He told me about Eddie and how, for some reason, that it really angered him that he treated you the way he did. He also told me that it hurt him to see you cry. He didn't understand his feelings at that time, Dana, but I did. Mitch fell in love with you that night, and he loves you even more today."

I didn't know what to say so I just sat there, looking at her. How could one person know another so well? Perhaps it was just the connection between a mother and her son. Or maybe, it was the connection between two people who loved each other completely.

"Dana, I don't mean to make you uncomfortable at all." Olivia continued. "Mitch is a wonderful boy, a wonderful man. It's so easy to see the way he lights up when he speaks your name, and to see him with you, even just this one time, there's no doubt about how deep his feelings go. He isn't always perfect, no one is, and he can have an attitude at times. Even a bit of a temper."

I had to laugh. "Oh, yes, I've already witnessed that, first hand."

Olivia smiled and patted me on the hand. "That's ok, it just means he isn't afraid to be himself around you. He's comfortable with you already. I know it seems like it's happening so fast, but don't let that scare you. Time doesn't mean a thing when you truly love someone. Love at first sight really *does* happen, Dana."

I thought about her words, and the fact that Mitch had said almost that exact same thing to me on our drive here earlier. She stood up.

"Dana, Mitch will take care of you. He isn't one to do anything halfway. If he says something, he follows through, 110%. So, if he's told you he loves you, Dana, and I'm sure he has, don't ever doubt it."

I smiled at her. "Thank you, Olivia, and I won't." I hesitated, then figured I didn't have a need to hide anything from her. Somehow, we had made a connection of our own, and I decided I would tell her what I was sure she already knew.

"Olivia, can I say something?"

"Certainly, dear, go ahead."

"I love Mitch, too, very much! It seems funny to be saying that, after only one day, but I really feel that it's true."

She smiled and grabbed my hand, leaned over and hugged me. "Yes, dear, I know you do, I know you do."

I heard the sound of footsteps and turned to see Mitch and his father coming into the kitchen. "Is it safe to come in here?" Mitch asked, coming to stand behind my chair.

"Of course!" his mother replied. "I was just filling Dana in on the last twenty five years of your life, that's all!" Olivia laughed as Mitch pretended to grimace.

"Well, now that you know my history from day one, considering I *am* only 25, I guess you really know just how awful I am!"

"Oh, I don't know." I replied. "I think there may still be some things I need to find out for myself!"

Jake smiled. "The others should be here soon. Chris and Trudy had a few errands to run today and your sisters, well, you know they can never get anywhere on time!"

Mitch nodded. "That's the truth!"

"Well, son, why don't you go ahead and show Dana the rest of the place, that is, if she's interested."

Mitch looked down at me. "Well, are you game?"

"I am!" I replied. I was anxious not only to see the rest of the estate, but also, to have some time alone with Mitch before his family arrived. He pulled out my chair and I followed him into the family room.

Jake put his arm around Olivia. "Suppose we're looking at our next daughter-in-law?" Olivia asked.

"Could be, dear, but give them time. They need to get to know each other a little more. Mitch is smart, he won't rush things."

"Jake, it's too late for that. They're in love!"

"In love?" Jake looked shocked. "My word, dear, they just met!"

"Jake, do you remember another couple, oh, about forty years ago?" Olivia asked. "Married just a month after we met, and here we still are!"

"Yes, I do, dear, but that was different. Times have changed."

"But certain things stay the same, Jake. Mitchell loves that girl, has for a while, even before she ever knew. And she told me she loves him, too. Just look at the way they get along, it's so easy to see. It doesn't matter that they just met, Jake. It didn't matter with us, and it doesn't with them, either."

Jake lifted his eyes from Olivia to the next room where Mitch and Dana stood looking out the window. He watched his son draw her face to his and kiss her once, then again. He turned back toward his wife.

"Call the caterers, I think we may be having a wedding soon!"

Olivia laughed and went off to help Alexander finish dinner.

"Hello, we're here!"

The sound of several voices suddenly filled the air, and I concluded that the rest of Mitch's family must have arrived. Mitch quickly headed for the door, just behind his mother and father, and of course, Alexander leading the way. In his excitement, I didn't think Mitch even realized he had left me behind.

"Greetings everyone!" Alexander said gleefully, quickly gathering up coats and hats and heading down the hallway with them.

I stood back, watching the scene as everyone exchanged hugs and kisses. I could just see the love these people shared, and I understood why Mitch was so loving and kind. I especially watched the way Mitch interacted with them all, and the children seemed to hold a special attraction to their uncle. One in particular, a petite little girl with golden blond hair, seemed to draw most of his attention.

"Hey, Meggie, how's my best girl?" Mitch caught her up and kissed her on the top of her head.

"I'm fine, Uccle Mish." I chuckled at the way she mispronounced his name. She noticed the bandage on Mitch's hand. "Did you hurt your hand?" She asked, seeming concerned.

"Oh, I did, but it's ok now." He replied, holding it up for her to see.

Then she caught my image, and pointed. "Who's that?" she asked innocently.

I had been content where I was, until suddenly, everyone's eyes were upon me and they fell silent.

"Oh, man, am I dumb or what?" Mitch exclaimed, hitting himself lightly in the head.

"It took you twenty five years to finally figure that out, huh?" Mitch shot a glance back at a man I quickly concluded to be his brother, Christopher. The others laughed.

Mitch put the little girl down, then walked up to me and took me by the arm, as if to lead me toward the masses. "I'm sorry, Dana." He apologized. The he leaned toward me . "It's ok, don't be nervous." He whispered. "I'm right here."

"Everyone, I'd like you to meet......" Mitch didn't get a chance to finish his sentence.

"You must be Dana!"   A petite, dark haired woman stepped forward and extended her hand. Her hair was pulled back, showing her beautiful, smooth skin. She was attractive, and looked somewhat like Mitch, except that her eyes were brown.

"I'm Angelina, Mitch's sister."   I shook her hand.   "This is my husband, Jim, and my daughter Megan."

"Hello." I said, trying not to sound too nervous. I could feel Mitch's hand on my back now, gently prompting me forward. I tried to resist, but he pushed a little harder, so I stepped more into the midst of them all.

"Hi, Dana, I'm Chris." Mitch's brother shook my hand. Although very attractive as well, he really didn't look like his brother or sisters, but held more of a resemblance to Jake. He was almost as tall as Mitch, but not quite, with sandy blonde hair and hazel eyes. I noticed right away that he had a sweet smile, and his eyes lit up each time he flashed it. "And this is my wife....."

A very pregnant lady stepped forward, her face glowing in a radiant smile. "Trudy," she said extending a hand, "and this is Kyle, Michael, and Alexis." She patted her swollen stomach. "And this is, Diana!"

"Another girl!" Chris said proudly, and pulled her to him.

"Congratulations!" I said, just before they were nudged aside by another member of the family.

"Dana, I'm Julia, Mitch's other sister, and I'm so happy to finally meet you!" She gave me a little hug, which caught me slightly off guard, but I hugged back. Julia was tall and curvy, and held a resemblance to both her parents. She, too, was very pretty, with sandy blond hair and blue eyes. "This is Paul, my husband." I smiled at them. "Mitch has told us so much about you!"

I glanced up at Mitch, and gave him a glare. I just wondered what other little facts I would find out today, and just what he had told them. Mitch bit his lip and rocked back on his heels. Angelina caught his action and laughed.

"It appears that Dana wasn't aware we all sort of know her already, am I right Mitch?"

Everyone laughed and began to head toward the dining room. I grabbed Mitch by the arm, stopping him and pulling him aside.

"Something wrong, my love?" He asked playfully. He bit his lip again, and I surmised that it was just another little "Mitchism", something he did when he was feeling a little guilty, or nervous.

"Mitchell," I began, "just what have you been telling your family about me?" I paused, and took a deep breath. "I don't get it, Mitch, we've only known each other a few days! There couldn't have been *that* much to tell, unless...." I stopped, mid-sentence. "You've been making up things about me!"

Mitch looked stunned. "That's what you might want to think, Dana, that it's only been a few days. Maybe for you, but I've known you since, well, October 4th!"

I just looked at him. He remembered that date! It was just one thing after another with this man and he continued to amaze me.

"I still can't believe you!" I said, pretending to sound a bit miffed.

"Well, that's because I'm so unbelievable!" he teased, kind of telling and asking at the same time.

"No, your just impossible!" I teased back, poking him in the stomach playfully.

"Oh, is that so?" Mitch pulled me close to him and began to tickle me. I started to laugh and tried to squirm away, but he held me tighter. "So, you *are* ticklish! I was wondering about that!"

"Mitchell, let me go!" I squealed.

"Only on one condition." He bargained. "That you stop calling me by my proper name, and that you kiss me."

"That's two conditions." I giggled.

"Well, I never was very good at math!" He stopped tickling me and leaned down to kiss me, but we were interrupted.

"Come on you two lovebirds, you'll have time for that later!" It was Trudy. "Dinner's waiting."

The dining room was filled with laughter and conversation, and the busy activity of mothers helping children prepare plates and get them situated at a small table in the corner of the room. Alexander and Olivia were placing baskets of bread and salads on the table, as Jake was retrieving condiments from the pantry. Our entrance seemed to go unnoticed, so we just stood in the doorway for a moment, taking it all in.

"Are you still nervous?" Mitch asked.

"Well, just a little, I guess," I replied. "It's just that I'm not used to so many people in one house, all at the same time!"

"It's just my family, and I told you there were a lot of them before we got here today." He conceded. Then he turned to me. "Doesn't your family ever get together like this?"

The question stung and my face grew serious. "I don't have a family."

Mitch took a step back, a look of shock and surprise on his face. "What do you mean, you don't have a family? Everyone has a family. Everyone has to come from somewhere!"

It was easy to see Mitch was having difficulty understanding, especially when his situation was so different from mine. "I do come from somewhere." I replied quietly. "But my parents were killed in a plane crash when I was twelve. Dad had a pilot's license—he had flown in the Army—and something just went wrong that day. My grandma took me in and raised me, until I moved out here, and when she got sick, I tried to make it home, but I didn't get there in time......" The emotion overwhelmed me, and the lump in my throat prevented me from speaking. I swallowed hard, and tried to continue. "I don't have anyone Mitch, not like you do. I'm all alone." I could feel the tears starting to fill my eyes.

Mitch's face still held a puzzled look, like he was trying to comprehend what I had just told him. He stepped back toward me again.

"Dana, I....." He took off his glasses, as if to wipe a tear from his own eye, then replaced them. "I wish you had told me this sooner. I had no idea that...." He touched my cheek softly. "I'm sorry, Dana."

I wiped my eyes and managed a smile. "It's ok." I said. "I've learned to get along, and I do fine."

Mitch put his arm around my shoulders and hugged me to him. "I know you do, and you know what else? You aren't alone, not anymore." He kissed the top of my head.

Just then, Julia noticed that we were there. "Come on you two, we've saved you a spot right there." She pointed to two empty chairs and we both sat down. I could feel Mitch's hand touch my leg, and I placed my hand on top of his.

Jake silenced the room, said grace, and then it seemed everyone started talking at once. I just sat for a few moments trying to take it all in, and Mitch noticed me and smiled. He leaned toward me and whispered in my ear.

"See that metal thing right there, honey? That's called a fork. Feel free to use it." He chuckled.

I just looked at him and stuck out my tongue. He raised his eyebrows playfully and smiled.

"So, Dana," Angelina started, "are you from this area?"

"Well, not originally." I replied. "I was born and raised in Iowa. I moved out here after graduation, about four years ago."

"So, what brought you to this part of the country?" She inquired further.

I put down my fork and looked at Mitch, as if not sure how to answer her. He didn't say anything, and started to bite his lip again. I believed that Olivia and Jake knew the truth, but I wasn't sure I was ready to share those details with the rest of the family.

"Well, actually, I thought there would be more opportunities for me here to further my career. I'm a kindergarten teacher."

Angelina smiled. "Oh, that's so wonderful, Dana! I'm sure that's very fulfilling."

Mitch put down his fork, wiped his mouth and looked at me again with a half smile. His eyes were full of wonder, and what I thought might even be a little bit of disbelief.

I decided to let him compute that for a while. I turned toward Olivia. "Everything tastes just wonderful, Olivia." I complimented.

"Thank you, dear, I'm glad you're enjoying yourself."

"Oh, I am, very much." I replied.

It was Julia's turn to ask questions now. "Since no one else has asked this yet, I will." She began. "I understand you know Mitch from Gartano's. How did you two actually hook up?"

Mitch was taking a drink, and the question must have brought back memories of our whipped cream battle. He started to laugh, and choked on his drink. I decided to be a little nasty myself and put him on the spot.

"Why don't you tell her, Mitch?" I smiled impishly at him and took a bite of my salad. He shot me an I'll-get-you-for-this sort of glance, and coughed again.

"Well, Mitchell?" Julia smiled and looked at Mitch curiously. "So, how did you two hook up?"

Mitch decided to be ornery. "Let's see now." He looked up, placing his thumb and forefinger on the side of his face, as if in deep thought.

"I think it had something to do with a late night spaghetti dinner, some whipped cream, and the couch in the manager's office!"

Everyone grew silent, looked at Mitch, and I caught Chris and Jake smiling at each other. Chris cleared his throat and looked down. Mitch smiled and took another bite of his salad. He knew not to look at me. I smacked his leg under the table.

"Ouch, that hurt!" he responded, quietly. Then he looked at me and formed the word "Gotcha!"

After dinner, everyone gathered in the family room to visit further. Mitch directed me to a chair next to a beautiful baby grand piano, and he sat down on the bench next to me. Everyone seemed to be busily nursing their own conversations, so Mitch turned to me and took my hand.

"You never told me you were a teacher!" he said. "What else don't I know about you?"

I pointed toward the piano. "Well, I've always wanted to learn how to play one of those."

He cracked a small smile again, just enough that his dimple showed. "What, the piano?"

I giggled. "That is what you call it, last time I checked!"

"Not a problem—I can teach you." He answered confidently.

I laughed. "You know how to play the piano?"

"Absolutely! What's so surprising about that?" Then he added, "Mom made me take lessons as a kid. We're the only ones in the family that know how."

Julia and Trudy must have read my mind at that moment. "Mitch, if you're sitting there, you have to play for us!"

Mitch looked embarrassed. "No, that's ok, we'll skip it today."

"Come on, little brother," Chris teased, "impress that girl of yours!"

"Go ahead, Mitchell!" Julia prompted. "Play something for us."

Just then, little Megan ran up to Mitch, and he bent down toward her. She put her arms around his neck and pulled him forward even more. "Uccle Mish, I will kiss you if you play a song!" She pecked him on the cheek and ran back to her mother's arms.

"I'll bet Dana will, too!" Chris smirked.

Mitch blushed, stood up and pulled out the bench. Sitting back down, he flexed his fingers over the keys. Then, snickering softly to himself, he began to play chopsticks. Everyone laughed.

"That's not fair, Mitchell!" Julia laughed. "We all know you can do better than that!"

Mitch's face suddenly turned very serious and everyone got quiet. Without even opening a music book, Mitch began to play a beautiful classical piece. I was amazed at the ease with which he played, and the way he seemed to lose himself, and everyone else, in the music. As he ended the song, everyone applauded.

"Mitch, you play beautifully!" I exclaimed, still in awe.

"Don't let him fool you." Chris teased. "Took him years to develop that talent. But, that's not all the amazing Mitchell Tarrington, the third, can do." I turned to Chris with a questioning look, and he continued. "He can sing, too!"

"And dance, very well." Angelina added.

Mitch dropped his head, shook it and laughed. "I really wish you hadn't said that, especially you, Chris."

I turned to Mitch. "You've got to be kidding me, right?"

"Yes, yes, that's all it is, we're just kidding you, isn't that right Chris?" Mitch shot a glance at his brother. "Right, huh, Ang, just kidding."

By now all the others were chuckling, too, enjoying Mitch's embarrassment.

"Why don't you show her, Mitch, old buddy?" Chris prodded. "I'm sure she'd love to hear you sing!"

Mitch was turning red. "I am not going to sing. I played the piano for you, that's enough!"

"Oh, come on, just one song!" Angelina pleaded.

Mitch was a quick thinker. He looked at his watch, jumped up off the stool, and turned to me. "My, but it's getting late, we'd better start heading back." He turned back to everyone else. "Gee, folks, but I guess the show is over for today!"

"Chicken!" Chris laughed. "Ok, little brother, you're off the hook this time." Chris walked over to Mitch and patted him on the back. "But Thanksgiving isn't far away, and we'll be back!"

After saying our goodbyes, we started down the long driveway toward the main road. Mitch stopped just out of sight of the house and put the car in park.

"Something I need to know, Dana." He started. "How did I get so lucky?"

"I don't know what you mean, Mitch. Lucky in what way?"

"Two days ago, I was just an average guy, working hard to get by, and then you came along and I feel, well, I feel like I could take on the world!"

I moved closer to Mitch and wrapped my arms around his neck. "Oh, I don't know," I replied, staring deep into his eyes. I kissed him softly. "Maybe it isn't luck. Maybe it means God wants us to be together."

The drive home was pleasant, and most of the time we just sat in the silence, simply enjoying the fact that we were together. My mind reviewed all that had happened in just two short days. I looked over at Mitch. He continued to amaze me, and every moment with him made me love him even more. Fate has a funny way of doing things, I thought. A month ago I wanted to be with Eddie forever. Now I wanted nothing more than to be with Mitch.

Finally, we pulled up in front of the apartment building and Mitch stopped the car. He came around to let me out, then took my hand and led me through the door David held open for us. This time, I reached up, took off his glasses, wiped away the mist and replaced them. He smiled.

"Thank you." He said. "Not just for that, but for a perfectly wonderful day!"

"You're welcome." I replied. Then I had another thought. "Mitch, I'm sorry."

He looked confused. "Sorry about what?"

I continued. "I should have told you about my family," I said. "And about my job. I don't want to keep any secrets from you, Mitch. I guess I'm still afraid....."

"Afraid of what?" he asked "Afraid I'll find something out that will make me change my mind about you?"

I nodded. How could this man read me so well already?

"That will never happen, Dana!" Mitch said firmly, yet gently. "In case you haven't been paying attention, I am madly, hopelessly, and completely in love with you. I know it sounds crazy, and it's all happened so fast, but like I told you before, time doesn't matter. Not to me."

I hugged Mitch so tightly it felt like we were one person. "I love you so much, Mitch!"

"See you tomorrow?" he asked "I mean, if you don't mind spending more time with a spoiled rich kid." His eyes were shining.

It was my turn to use a Mitchism. "Absolutely!" I quipped. "But just one thing."

"And what's that?"

"I'm giving you my phone number this time. I don't want you to see me in my pajamas and robe again......at least, not yet!"

Mitch smiled and laughed. "I kind of enjoyed that, but ok, I guess I can call first, if you insist." He took the piece of paper I had written my number on and tucked it into his pocket. Then he jotted his down and handed it to me. "Just in case you want to call me sometime," he said. Then he got a mischievous look in his eyes. "I'll be looking forward to the next time, the next time I see you "au natural", that is!"

He kissed me again and headed back into the night. I watched as he drove away, and I realized, I missed him already.

Once inside my apartment, I kicked off my shoes, hung up my coat, and decided to make a nice hot cup of tea. It was then I noticed the light flashing on my answering machine.

Probably Kayla, wanting all the details of the day, I assumed. I walked over and pressed the button, then turned to make my tea.

"Hello, beautiful!" I couldn't believe it. It was Mitch! How could he have called me so quickly when he had just left? I turned my full attention to the message.

"Ok, I know that you are probably wondering how I could get home so quickly, and call you, but I realized something earlier today. When I have my car, it only takes me about three and a half minutes to get from my place to yours."

I chuckled because, knowing Mitch, he probably actually timed that trip! I sat down to listen to the rest of the message. I never realized before just how sexy his voice was, and how it made me feel.

"Anyway, the reason I am calling you is, because, well, there was one more thing I didn't tell you today. See, my family all go to church together on Sundays. So, I wanted you to know that I'll be picking you up at 9:30 in the morning, sharp. Afterwards, I'll make you a wonderful brunch, at my place."

That little sneak, I thought. He left the message so I couldn't tell him no! Not that I would have, anyway, but I guess he wasn't ready to take that chance. And *make* me brunch? Unbelievable!

"Ok, well, yeah, I also wanted to say that I love you. Sleep well, Dana. I miss you already."

My heart was pounding a mile a minute. Then I smiled. He really is all that, and more. My thoughts were interrupted by the ringing of the phone.

"Hello?"

"Ok, girl, all the details! Start from the beginning!" It was Kayla, calling to interrogate me.

I laughed. "You know, there was a message just now when I got home, and I thought it was you, but guess what? It was Mitch!"

"Mitch?" Kayla sounded surprised. "Weren't you with him all day?"

"Yes, but he asked me to go to church with him and his family tomorrow morning." Then I rethought what I had just said. "Well, actually, he told me I was going to church with him and his family, and then to brunch with him and then, well, whatever!"

"Church, well, my oh my!" Kayla sounded impressed. "Told you he was a good boy, didn't I?"

"Oh, Kayla, he is so much more than that! Get this," I started excitedly. "We drove up to his parents' house, and like, this thing is not just an ordinary house, like yours and Joseph's. Kayla, his parents live in a mansion! They have a butler and everything!"

"Get out, girl, a mansion?" Kayla sounded shocked.

"That's what I said." I replied. "Kayla, his dad is the Mitchell Tarrington that owns Tarrington Industries. You know, the medical products."

"Uh, uh, uh, that boy's loaded, Dana!"

"Well, yes, and no." I continued. "He told me that seven years ago, his dad offered him a job in the company, but he turned it down. He doesn't want the money, doesn't care about the money, Kayla. He wants to be just who he is, and he says he's perfectly happy!"

Kayla didn't say anything for a minute. "You know, I can see that from Mitch. He certainly doesn't seem like one who would go for that sort of thing."

"I couldn't believe it, Kayla. I mean, none of his family acted like it was a big deal. They were all so nice and treated me like they had known me forever!"

"That's good to hear you got along ok, dear," Kayla said soothingly. "So, what else happened?"

I started from the beginning of the day, when Mitch showed up at my door unannounced, how he went shopping with me, and how he was so supportive of me the whole time we were at his parents' house. Then I laughed and told her how he answered his sister when she asked how we had gotten together.

"I sure hope you smacked him for that!" Kayla laughed.

"Oh, you know it! Made sure it hurt, too, well, a little anyway!"

I went on, telling her how he played the piano. "And, from what I gather, Kayla, he can sing, too!"

"My oh my, girl, you got you a good one, now didn't you? All that, and a bag of potato chips, that boy is!"

"Oh, Kayla, I feel like the luckiest girl in the world!" And somehow, I knew I was.

3

I fell into bed that night, eagerly anticipating tomorrow with Mitch. Although I didn't remember falling asleep, I was startled by the sound of the alarm clock the next morning. I turned over and smacked the snooze button. Only eight a.m., too early to get up. Then I remembered—Mitch was coming at 9:30. That only gave me about an hour to get ready. I wanted to make sure I looked perfect for him.

After starting my morning coffee, I decided I would dig through the closet to find the perfect outfit for church. I finally chose a skirt and top, conservative, yet appealing. I assumed it would be something Mitch would like, so I laid it out on my bed and went to start a shower. Just then, the phone rang. I turned off the water, and grabbed the phone on the nightstand.

"Good morning, beautiful!" Mitch chirped into the phone.

"Mitch, hi!" I said back. "I thought that you were picking me up at 9:30. Why are you calling?"

"Can't I call and say good morning to my best girl?" He inquired.

I laughed. "I thought Megan was your best girl."

Mitch laughed back. "Oh, well, I have to tell her that. Keeps her idolizing me, you know. Reputation is everything!"

"You are such a goof!" I teased. "What did you really want?"

"Well, I just wanted to hear your voice, that's all." Mitch fell silent. "I miss you. I hardly slept all night just thinking about you."

I smiled at the thought of Mitch being lonely for me. "That's sweet, Mitch." I replied. "I miss you too, honey, but we'll be together in an hour! That is, if you let me get ready."

"Oh, alright, but I wouldn't mind seeing you in your robe and pajamas again. Although I don't think that would be very appropriate for church!"

I laughed. "No, and I might scare away the congregation if I showed up like that!"

I heard Mitch's voice soften. "I don't believe you could scare anyone. See you in an hour. Dana....."

"Yes, Mitch?"

"I love you!"

"I love you, too."

I quickly got ready, and anxiously awaited Mitch's arrival. As promised, precisely at 9:30, he knocked on the door. This time I didn't hesitate opening it for him. My heart skipped a beat when I saw him standing there. I had seen him dressed up dozens of times at Gartano's, but something about the way he looked today took my breath away.

"Dana, let's not have a repeat of yesterday." He mused. "Let me come in, please".

I giggled. "I'm sorry. It's just that, wow, you look so good!"

"Oh, do I? You don't look too bad yourself!" Mitch started toward me, and in one motion both pulled me to him and closed the door. He began to kiss me, and then nibble on my neck.

"Dana?" He said softly, in between kisses.

"What, Mitch?"

"Let's skip church and stay here. I really want to stay here."

I let him kiss me a few more times and then gently pushed him away. "I really think we should go, Mitch. I don't want anyone to get the wrong impression." I smiled at him.

"Why do you always have to be so logical?" He sighed deeply. "Can't you ever just have fun?"

"What, are you saying I'm not fun?" I teased.

Mitch started kissing my neck again. "Oh, I'm sure you could be," he answered.

"We... had better go, Mitchell." I giggled. I pulled away and handed him my coat. "Now, help me put this on....and no funny business!"

Mitch sighed and helped me on with my coat. Then he turned to me again, pulled me to him, and got close to my lips, as if he were going to kiss me. "Are you sure we have to go?" he whispered, lifting his eyebrows impishly.

"Out the door, Mitchell Tarrington!" I laughed as I pushed him into the hallway.

We drove to a beautiful country church just outside of town, and found Mitch's family already waiting.

"What took you two so long?" Chris asked. "I was beginning to think you weren't coming!"

Mitch smiled a mischievous smile at me. "Well, I was hoping we weren't, but Dana insisted."

Chris smiled a knowing smile and patted Mitch on the back. The beauty and peacefulness of the sanctuary drew me in, and I stood still for a moment . The sun was pouring in the huge windows on each side, and the lights reflected what looked like images of angels on the wooden beamed ceiling. At the front, hanging behind the pulpit, was the biggest wooden cross I had ever seen. We found two pews big enough to hold all of us, and we sat down. Mitch took my hand and smiled.

The minister greeted everyone with a smile, and instructed that we should stand for some hymns. Mitch took a hymnal from the pew, opened it to the page, and held it over so that I could see it. The music began, and everyone started singing, but I didn't. I was too overtaken by the voice of the man standing next to me. The man that I loved.

Chris was right. Mitch *could* sing, and he sang like an absolute angel! I stood listening to him, and for a moment, it was as if no one else was there. With that talent, why wasn't he doing this professionally, I thought. Mitch must have realized I was staring at him, because he stopped singing and leaned close to me.

"What's the matter? Why aren't you singing, too? That's what you're supposed to be doing."

"It's just that you have a beautiful voice!" I exclaimed softly. "Chris was right, you really do know how to sing!"

"And you doubted my brother's word? How dare you!" Mitch smiled and began to sing again, prompting me to join in this time, so I did.

Chris leaned forward and tapped me on the shoulder. "Didn't I tell you?" He whispered. "The guy has talent."

I smiled and nodded. He certainly did, but I somehow knew he'd never admit to that.

The service was wonderful, and afterwards, we joined Mitch's family at the back of the church.

"What are your plans today, dear?" Olivia asked Mitch.

"Well, I promised Dana we would have brunch, and then, well, I guess just hang out for a while." Then he turned to me. "You know, if you feel up to it, I really should start doing some Christmas shopping."

I laughed. "Well, at least you don't like to wait until the last minute." I told him. "Shopping is one thing I'm always up for!"

"Well, then, you kids have fun!" Olivia smiled, and kissed both of us on the cheek. With a few more goodbyes, the family was on its way.

Mitch tucked me into his car, got in himself and put the keys in the ignition, but didn't start it. "Dana, I owe you an apology."

"What for? What have you done wrong?"

"Well, I was just thinking about the way I told you that we should have no secrets, and well, there is one more thing that I haven't told you about me."

I looked at him curiously. "What is it, honey? You can tell me. Go ahead."

"Well, about that brunch thing. Would you mind much, if, well, we actually went somewhere to eat? Other than my place, I mean."

"I don't get it. I thought you actually wanted to cook for me."

Mitch almost looked embarrassed, and dropped his eyes. He chuckled. "You know," he started, "I knew the minute I said that on your machine that I should have taken it back. Dana, truth is, I'm really not much of a cook, and I wouldn't have a clue even what to make, let alone how to make it!"

I laughed and kissed his cheek. I could see his dimple starting to form, and then his smile.

"You silly boy!" I replied. "Then why did you even say that to begin with?"

"I guess I wanted to impress you." By now Mitch was starting to chuckle, too. "Guess that backfired, huh?"

Then I had a thought. "Mitch, I'm curious about something."

He looked at me as if confused. "What's that?" He asked.

"Well, you've been out on your own now for, what, about six or seven years? If you can't cook, how have you survived this long?"

Mitch laughed. "Well, now let's see....I eat out a lot, bum a meal off Mom whenever I can, and well, I guess I can cook a little bit, if you count TV dinners and stuff like that."

"Oh, you are so insane!" I leaned over and kissed him, but as I started to pull away, Mitch pulled me back and kissed me again.

"Tell you what," I began, "How about if you take me home, I'll change, make us both brunch, and then we can go shopping?" I waited for Mitch to answer.

"I don't know, Dana." He replied.

I looked confused. "Why not?"

He smirked. "What if you can't cook either and I get, like, food poisoning or something?" Mitch shied away as if he knew I was going to smack him, which I did, lightly on the arm.

A few minutes later we were back in my apartment, and I announced I was going to go change into some more comfortable clothes.

"That robe and pajamas would be real nice!" Mitch smiled and raised his eyebrows.

"I don't think so, sir!" I wagged my finger at him. "Why don't you get the eggs and some cheese out of the refrigerator, the frying pan is in the cabinet there, and I'll be back in a jiffy."

"Yes, ma'm!" Mitch replied, and gave me a salute.

I quickly changed, did a quick fix of my makeup, and reappeared to find Mitch waiting for me in the living room. He was standing in front of my bookcase, and I could see he was looking at something, but at first, I couldn't see what. As I moved closer, I noticed that it was a picture of me with my parents, taken when I was only about ten.

Mitch smiled and reached out for me. "Is this your family?" He asked soothingly.

"Yeah, that's Mom and Daddy." I replied softly. "And, that's me."

"Beautiful, even then." Mitch said as he kissed the top of my head. Then he picked up another picture. "And who might this be with you? Your grandmother?"

"Yes, that's Grammy," I replied. "I really loved her, Mitch. She was a saint." I felt a tear forming in my eyes, and knew I needed to walk away before I started to cry.

"I'm sure you did, sweetheart." Mitch replied softly. "She did a great job raising you."

I smiled up at him, and he noticed the tear. "I'm sorry, I didn't mean to make you cry."

"You didn't, Mitch, the memories did. I still miss them sometimes."

"I don't think that will ever change, Dana. But, don't forget, you are never alone. You have me, and I'm not going anywhere. Promise." I looked into his eyes, hoping he meant what he said.

We stood together in the silence for just a moment before I spoke. "Come on with me, and I'll teach you how to make an omelet!"

Mitch grimaced, but followed me willingly. He folded his hands and stood back, pretending to intently watch everything I was doing, but I had a feeling he was really watching me and not my actions. After a few minutes, we sat down at my table, and I served him a ham and cheese omelet, complete with hash-brown potatoes and toast. Mitch took a bite.

"Not bad!" He nodded approvingly. "I guess you can cook, after all!"

"Glad you think so!" I smiled back. "You know what they say, the way to a man's heart is through his stomach."

Mitch looked at me, a smug little smirk on his face, and chuckled. "I can think of a few better ways to get there myself."

For some reason, I noticed just then that his hand was no longer bandaged. It still looked painful, even from where I was sitting, so I decided to ask.

"How's that hand? I noticed you took off the bandage."

"I guess it's ok." Mitch said, between bites. "It was a little hard to shower with a bandage on it."

"Why didn't you wrap it back up after?" I inquired. "It still looks a little red."

Mitch shrugged nonchalantly. "Well, dear, first of all, I don't keep a lot of first aid supplies around my place," he smiled, "even if my dad is a tycoon in that arena. Second, I didn't think I needed it to be bandaged anymore."

"Well, dear," I mocked, "you should keep some things like that around, just in case you ever need them. And it does still need to be bandaged, so when you're finished, I will fix it back up for you."

"But...." Mitch started to resist, but I put up my hand.

"Don't argue with me, Mitchell. It's a done deal." I took another bite, and gave him a stern look.

"Why is it, whenever you are yelling at me, you use my proper name? My mom and sisters always did that, too. Is that like, a girl thing or something?" He took a drink of his coffee. "I like to be called Mitch, you know."

"I didn't realize I did that, but I also didn't realize it bothered you so much." I replied smugly. "But then again, maybe that's why I do it to begin with. It's at those times I want you to know I mean business."

Mitch picked up his napkin, wiped the corner of his mouth, and placed his fork on his plate. "So, think you can boss me around, huh?"

I continued to eat, not looking at him. "No, Mitchell, I *know* I can!" I smiled, and giggled softly.

"Oh ho ho, really now?" A hash-brown hit me on top of the head, and bounced onto the table. I looked up slowly to see Mitch grinning from ear to ear, armed and ready with another potato.

"Don't go there, Mitch Tarrington. I'm warning you, don't do it."

"And if I do?" He smirked.

"You'll be cleaning up the kitchen, by yourself!"

We finished our brunch, tidied things up and I headed to get the things I needed to re-bandage Mitch's hand. I sat him back down at the table, and within a few minutes, had it all done up again.

"There now, my little patient, all better once again. You were such a good boy this time, I'd give you a lollipop if I had one!" I teased.

"Thanks," Mitch grumbled. "But I still don't think I need it bandaged."

"Oh, stop being like that, Mitchell." I said. Then I realized I had used his proper name again. "Sorry, I mean, Mitch."

He smiled and offered his arm. "Are you ready to go shopping now, beautiful lady?"

"Lead the way!" I said merrily, taking hold.

The sunny day had turned to where there was a threat of snow, so we decided to drive to a little shopping mall on the other side of town instead of walking around in the city. I decided it might not be a bad time to find out a little more about my Mitch.

"I was thinking about something earlier, Mitch." I said.

"Oh, what's that?" He inquired, glancing at me.

"I've learned a lot about you in the last few days, and I feel I do know you well, but there are still some things that I don't know about you that I think I should."

Mitch had a puzzled does-not-compute look on his face. "Like what?"

"Well, when your birthday is, your favorite color, your favorite food, where you went to college, what kind of music you like, wh.....'' Mitch laughed and cut me off mid-sentence.

"Whoa, now, sweetheart. I'm a guy, remember? We don't comprehend more than a few things at a time."

"Sorry." I said. "Just answer what you can remember!"

He smiled. "Ok, let's see." He started. "First, my birthday is, believe it or not, December 24. So, that means I will be twenty six on Christmas Eve."

"I'll bet you always clean up on gifts!" I teased.

Mitch smiled again. "My favorite color, I guess, would be blue, and I love Italian food, so I guess that may be why I chose the job at Gartano's. College, well, that was the University of PA, right here in Philly, and....what was the last thing you asked?"

"Music." I replied.

"Hmmm, music. I really guess I could say I like all kinds. I have a very diverse music collection at home."

I laughed. "All kinds, huh? I just can't picture you being into heavy metal. Mitch Tarrington, the head banger!"

Mitch laughed back. "No, I guess not." Then he turned to me. "So, what about you? Tell me about Dana Walker."

"Well, I was born on January 4, so our birthdays aren't that far apart, but I will be just twenty three on mine. So, that makes you the older man!"

"Hey, call me a cradle robber if you want!" Mitch teased.

"I love blue also, and pink and yellow. I love Italian food, and big, fat cheeseburgers with all the trimmings! And, of course, what girl doesn't like chocolate!"

"So, that means I'm in trouble if I forget Valentine's Day, huh?" Mitch shot me a glance.

"You learn fast!" I teased. "Now, let me see, what else? Oh, I went to college here in town, at La Salle, and as for music, I like a lot of different things, too. It just depends on what kind of mood I'm in."

"Interesting!" I could see the wheels turning in Mitch's head. "What did you like to do when you were a little girl?"

"I was actually quite a tomboy." I replied. "There weren't a lot of girls in my neighborhood, so I learned to play football, and baseball, and a little basketball, too, with the boys who lived nearby. Of course, I did some of the girly things, too, like dolls and tea parties. I would just make one of the boys play tea party with me, if Grammy was too busy."

Mitch looked as if he was trying to picture me playing tea party with a boy. "So, I can see this assertiveness thing isn't something new."

I ignored that comment. "What about you? What did you like to do?"

"Well, it was always pretty interesting at my house, seeing as I had two older sisters and a brother. We would play all sorts of games, of course baseball and football and all that. We also had horses, so we went riding a lot, we'd sled in the winter, and ice skate."

"I can see where that would be the perfect place for sledding," I replied

"Absolutely!" Mitch's face lit up and he got excited, as if he were reliving his childhood in his mind. "Chris and I would go to the bottom of the big hill behind the house, and we'd build a wall out of snow. Then we'd make dozens of snowballs and when the girls came down, we'd nail 'em every time!"

Both of us were laughing. "Mitch, that is so mean!"

"No, Dana." Mitch reached beneath his glasses and wiped his eye. "It was so much fun, because they knew we were there, but they were still silly enough to keep falling for it, year after year!"

"So, that's where you got your arm from, throwing snowballs. I wondered why you were such a good shot with that whipped cream."

"Well, that and the fact that I was a varsity pitcher on my high school team."

"Wow, I've never dated an athlete before!" I laid my head on his shoulder and batted my eyelashes at him.

Mitch blushed. "Really? I was thinking," He looked over at me, his eyes shining, "with a body like that, you must've been a cheerleader or something!"

I blushed as well. "No, not me. I was pretty shy, so I really didn't do anything in high school. Well, I did help with senior yearbook." Then I paused, thought twice, and said it anyway. "That's actually how I met Eddie."

I could see Mitch take a deep breath, and he bit his lip. "Dana, do you still care about him?" I could see the questioning look in his eyes.

We were at the mall now, and Mitch found a parking spot, pulled in and shut off the car. I took his hand.

"Eddie is no longer a part of my life, Mitch. All that's in the past, and the only thing I care about is today, and my future, with you."

"I guess I just needed to know." Mitch pulled the keys from the ignition, and closed them tightly in his hand.

"Well, don't ever wonder about that again, ok?" Mitch was looking down at his fist, enclosed around his car keys. "Mitch, look at me." I prompted. "I love you, not Eddie, not anyone else, not ever again. Just you."

Mitch smiled and nodded. "I believe you, Dana."

"Let's go shopping then, my little head banger!" I laughed as Mitch let me out of the car, doing his best imitation.

The inside of the mall was warm and inviting, decked from top to bottom with the sights and sounds of Christmas. Everywhere we turned there seemed to be people rushing here and there, some with bags full of gifts and others pushing tired children in strollers. Mitch once again wiped the mist from his glasses, giving me that I-hate-this look, and unzipped his jacket.

"Where do we start?" I inquired. "Do you have an idea of what you may be looking for?"

"Ah, yeah!" Mitch reached into his pocket and withdrew a folded piece of paper. He opened it up. "This is my list," He replied. "Everyone is on here, and what I want to buy for them."

"Oh, my, aren't we organized now!" I squeezed his arm. "Mitchell, I'm impressed!"

"I'm really not...organized that is. I just try to listen whenever we get together and if someone mentions something they want, I jot it down. Then, when the time comes, I usually have a list done up already."

I was truly impressed with Mitch's logic. "That's a great idea!" I said. "Can I see the list?"

Mitch started to hand it to me, and then drew it back quickly. "Wait," he said, "give me a minute." He walked over to a bench, sat down, and taking out a pen, jotted something down. Then he ripped off the bottom of the sheet, and placing it in his coat pocket, returned to me.

"What was that all about?" I inquired.

"Oh, nothing," He smirked. "Ok, you can have the list now."

I pretended to try to reach into his coat pocket. "I want that part, too!"

He grabbed my hand and wrapped his fingers around mine, laughing. "Oh, no you don't! That is off limits to you, young lady!"

We started at the toy store, and I realized Mitch was probably more of a child than the ones we were shopping for. He seemed to get a kick out of seeing what everything did, and matching up the toys to fit the kids' personalities and interests. Thirty minutes and two shopping bags later, we were heading to the next store.

"Ok, all the kids are done." I said, looking at the list. "Let me have your pen and I'll mark them off for you."

Mitch handed me the pen and I crossed the kids' names off the list. "Now, how about we go to the sporting goods store? We can pick up the things for the guys." I suggested.

"Sure, lead the way!" Mitch replied.

We made our way into the sporting goods store, purchased two shirts for Mitch's brothers-in-law, and headed back out into the mall. We decided our next stop would be Jacy's Department Store. He remembered his mother mentioning that she wanted a new set of baking dishes, and he figured that would be the best place to get them. Thinking twice, I stopped him just before we entered the store.

"Mitch, I know that you may think baking dishes are an appropriate gift." I started, trying not to hurt his feelings. "And it's not that I mean to cut on your selection or anything, but, well, don't you think it would be nicer to get her something more personal?"

"But Dana, my mom loves to bake!" he protested. "What's wrong with getting her baking dishes?"

I thought for a moment before I answered. "Nothing's exactly wrong with it, I guess, but why not get her a cookbook, also? Or maybe an apron, and then we can have her name stitched on it. The gift should be personal, Mitch."

Mitch took in what I had said. "A personalized apron, huh? I kind of like that idea, and I think she might, too!" He squeezed my hand. "I knew there was a reason I brought you along."

I smiled. "Let's go pick one out for her, then."

Although I had some of my own ideas about which apron I thought Olivia would like, I let Mitch do the deciding. After all, it was his mother, I thought. He picked a pretty Kelly green one trimmed in white, and we took it to the checkout area. But by the time we paid for it, the apron wasn't the only thing that was green. So was I.

"Hello." The salesclerk smiled sweetly at Mitch. I noticed that she was very pretty, with sparkling blue eyes, and perfect long, golden hair. She was dressed in a smart looking blue dress, Mitch's favorite color, and although somewhat conservative, it showed off her Barbie doll figure in a way that left nothing to the imagination. I was suddenly aware that as she was checking out the apron, she was also checking out Mitch. But the one thing I noticed even more, looking into his eyes, was that he seemed to be checking her out, too!

"Doing some Christmas shopping today?" she asked.

"Yeah, something like that," Mitch replied, smiling and glancing just for a moment at the four bags full of gifts. "My credit card is really taking a beating today."

The girl gave a very fake little giggle. "Well, I'll try to go easy on you, uh, I mean, it!" I could feel my blood beginning to boil.

Without saying a word, Mitch handed me the two bags he was holding and reached for his wallet in his back pocket. The salesclerk gave him a total and he pulled his card out and handed it to her, looking all the while right into her eyes. That made me even more angry, and I felt myself clenching my jaw as I glared at him. She hesitated for a moment as she took the card from his hand and smiled again, looking at the name.

"My, but that is a very official sounding name, Mr. Mitchell J. Tarrington, the third." Then she giggled again. "You'll have to write small, the signature line here is not very long." She handed him a pen and again, hesitated as he took it from her. He was blushing. He looked back up at her and handed back what he had just signed. I had stepped away but could still see the flirtatious little smirk on his face.

"Looks like you were able to get your whole name on that little line after all." She said in her best Barbie voice.

"Well, I've been writing it for years." Mitch said in a sing-song kind of way. At that moment, I actually wanted to punch him.

"Oh," she giggled, "I see why, you cheated." She teased. "It just says Mitch Tarrington." Then she smiled at him again, and this time, I wanted to punch her.

The girl handed Mitch his package, and smiled again. "Have a wonderful day, and please......come back again."

"Thanks," said Mitch, giving her his best smile, "I will."

I had moved further away from Mitch, not that he'd noticed, and was standing next to a display of pots and pans. I toyed with the thought of throwing one at him, but decided I really didn't want to spend Christmas in jail for murder. He looked around for a minute, then saw me and started over.

"Got it!" Mitch said, holding up the bag.

"Did you get her phone number, too?" I said, under my breath.

"I'm sorry, what was that you said?" Mitch asked. I didn't answer. Then he smiled and took a few bags from my hands. "I wondered where you'd gone off to." He said, cheerfully. "I thought maybe you'd left me!"

"Thought about it." I grumbled. "Don't know why I didn't."

Mitch turned and gave me a puzzled look. "What did you say?"

"I said nothing I care to repeat, not to you, anyway!" I thrust the last bag into Mitch's arms and started to stomp off.

Mitch hesitated for a moment, and shook his head, still holding a very puzzled look on his face. Then he caught up with me. "Dana, are you mad at me for something?"

I stopped and looked up, as if talking to someone imaginary. "Gee, he's handsome, talented, *and* smart, too! Oh, what a *lucky* girl I am!"

Mitch was still looking dumbfounded as we reentered the mall. "Could you please help me with these bags? They're getting a little hard for me to carry." He tried to hand a few back to me, but I folded my arms tightly across my chest.

"I don't understand, Dana, what did I do? You weren't angry with me before we went into that store, or before.......we.....picked out the apron....," Mitch sighed heavily, as if it was finally starting to compute. "Oh, I get it." He said slowly. Then he chuckled. "Dana, you're thinking I was checking her out, aren't you?"

I wheeled around and glared a hole right through him. "No, I don't THINK anything!" I said angrily. "You WERE checking her out, Mitchell! I was watching you the whole time!"

Mitch put down the bags on the bench he was now standing next to, and placed a smug look on his face. "I didn't do anything wrong, Dana. Why are you acting like this?" He started to take a step toward me, but the look on my face made him think twice. "I was just making small talk while she rang up my gift, that's all." He was trying to look perfectly innocent, but I wasn't buying it.

"Small talk?" I asked, still fuming. "Mitchell, you were flirting outrageously with her! And enjoying it too, I might add!"

Mitch suddenly found something amusing about this whole thing, because he began to laugh. So hard, in fact, that he had to take his glasses off. A few people walking by actually looked around to see what it was that he found so funny. But then he put his glasses back on and noticed I wasn't laughing.

He dropped his eyes and the smile faded from his face. "I can't believe you would actually think I could go for someone like that, Dana." He sighed heavily again. "Why would I want her when I have you?"

"You tell me." I said softly, yet sternly. "Maybe you wish I looked like that!"

Mitch smiled and started toward me again, this time trying to place his arm around me. I moved away and he pulled back his arm, and folded them across his chest. Then, he rocked back on his heels and bit his lip, just like he'd done at his parents' house that day.

"I honestly don't believe you, Dana." He began. "I was just trying to be polite. I don't think it would have been very nice not to acknowledge her at all."

"If that was *just* being polite, I would hate to see what you do when you're trying to be a gentleman!"

Mitch got a mischievous look in his eyes. "How about if I show you?" He reached out for me again.

"No, thank you!" I said firmly. "What I would really like is for you to take me home now."

"Take you home?" Mitch questioned. "Had enough shopping for one day?"

"No, Mitchell, actually, I've had enough of you for one day!" I could see in Mitch's eyes that my words had stung, but I was too angry at that moment to really care. Mitch dropped his eyes, turned to pick up the bags and started to walk toward the mall exit with me. But I noticed instead of walking beside me, he stayed just a few steps behind.

He held the door open for me as best he could with an armload of bags, and once he had loaded everything and we were back in the car, he tried to talk to me again.

"Dana, sweetheart..." he started, "I really don't like this silent treatment. We were having so much fun when we got here today. Can't we just forget about this?"

I toyed with the thought for a moment, then decided I wasn't ready to do that just yet. Then I wondered just why the whole thing had bothered me so much. Was it really what he did, or was it my own insecurities creeping back in, my lack of trust in men in general? I surmised it may be a little bit of both.

I looked at Mitch, my arms still folded tightly across my chest. "Can we please go now?" I asked. Then I added sternly, "And don't call me sweetheart!"

Mitch sighed and started the car. I stared out the window at the snow that was starting to lightly drift to earth. I didn't look at Mitch and I didn't say anything to him, either. I was far too upset, and didn't feel like arguing anymore. Mitch must have decided it was better not to say anything else, either, and just remained intent on his driving.

As we approached the city, I felt almost a relief as I knew that soon, I would be back in the comfort of my apartment where I could let the events of the afternoon escape me. But Mitch had other ideas, and instead of heading toward my apartment building, he headed in the opposite direction.

"Mitchell, where are you going?" I asked, still holding an attitude in my voice.

"I thought we might go to Gartano's for a nice dinner. It's usually closed on Sunday's, but Jimmy decided to open today since we closed early the other day for inventory. And I figured since he was good enough to give me the whole weekend off, least I can do is give him some of my money." He glanced over at me.

"I don't want dinner, Mitchell, I want you to take me home!" I said firmly.

"Maybe I don't want to take you home yet, and since I'm driving, you have to go where I take you!" Mitch's tone was very authoritative, so I decided I had no other choice but to go along. But, I decided, I didn't have to like it.

Mitch pulled up in front of Gartano's and before getting out, he turned to me again.

"I don't want any dinner, Mitchell." I said again, being stubborn.

Mitch smiled. "Well, fine then, but I do, so let's go in. You can watch me eat."

"I would much rather just stay here." I said softly. "That will make it easier for you to flirt, should the occasion arise."

"Honestly, I don't believe you." Mitch was smiling, and much to my dismay, he leaned over and kissed me on the cheek. I pretended to wipe it off, but he was starting to melt me.

"Ok, that's alright." He said. He opened his door, and turned to get out, then stopped. As he tucked the keys into his pocket, he leaned close to me again. "But you can't stay mad at me forever."

"Watch me!" I answered stubbornly, and I could hear the sound of Mitch's laughter as he came around to open my door.

As always, Gartano's was warm and familiar, and I could feel some of the tension falling away as we entered the door. Kayla saw us and came quickly over to greet us. Giving me a hug, she stepped back, noticing I wasn't smiling. Mitch was smirking and he rolled his eyes at me, which must have clued her in that we were fighting.

"Oh, oh, trouble in paradise?" She asked, looking first to me, and then up to Mitch.

"Something like that." Mitch said, nodding toward me and smirking at Kayla again. "But one of us has no clue why!" Once again, I felt like punching him.

"Well, now, how about we just sit you right over here, and I'll bring you some hot coffee." Kayla led us to a little table in the corner and walked off toward the counter. Mitch held my chair for me and I sat down.

"Dana, please stop this nonsense right now." He said, softly. "You've really carried this too far!"

His words rekindled the anger. "Why don't you go find someone else to have dinner with?"

Mitch sighed again. "I'm going to go talk to old Joe for a moment." He got up from the table, came around and kissed me on top of the head. "Please don't leave while I'm gone, ok?"

"I'll think about it." I fussed. Mitch chuckled as he walked away.

Kayla watched Mitch walk up to Joe, and once he was gone, she joined me at the table.

"What's going on, girl? That boy looks like he's been stung by a bee, and I think you're it!"

"I don't think he's happy with me, Kayla." I sighed. "See, we went shopping today, and there was this salesgirl who was really pretty. You know, a regular Barbie doll. She could've been a model."

Kayla smiled knowingly and took my hand. "I know where you're going with this, Dana, but you go on now and tell Kayla all about it."

"He bought his mom an apron for Christmas, and when he went to pay for it, this salesgirl started flirting with him, and he was flirting right back. And, I might add, he was really enjoying it! He didn't even notice when I wasn't standing next to him anymore, Kayla. Then, he had the audacity to say he didn't do anything wrong!"

Kayla smiled. "Well, actually, Dana, and I know this isn't what you want to hear," she paused,"to him, he didn't do anything wrong. See, honey, men don't see things the way we do. Maybe he did think she was pretty, but I'm sure that's as far as it went in his mind."

"I don't know about that, Kayla, he was really checking her out. Why, he was practically undressing her with his eyes!"

Kayla smiled and gave a chuckle. "Oh, now come on. I know it seemed that way to you, but girl, you need to realize something."

"What would that be?" I said smugly. I thought Kayla was supposed to be on my side.

"You go on now, and just take a look at Mitch. He's a beautiful, handsome man, and you're going to have to expect that other ladies are going to give him the eye now and again. But when you see that happening, dear, you just tell yourself they're all jealous because it's you he's with, not them, and be proud." Kayla paused for a minute in thought. "Truth be known, Dana, that girl was probably trying to annoy you, and it worked, now didn't it? I can't judge, and I try not to do so 'cause it's not right, but sometimes girls like you described her just want to have a little fun. It's a game they play because they know they can't actually get the man."

"Why couldn't he just say hi and leave it at that? Kayla, you should have seen the way he was looking at her. I just know he was comparing her to me!"

Kayla nodded her head. "I'm sure he was too, dear, but not the way you think."

I was confused. "What do you mean?"

"If I know Mitch at all, and I think I do, he was probably thinking how much better you looked than her. And how fake she was. He's got the real deal, honey, he doesn't want anything like that." Kayla patted my hand again. "Dana, like I told you before, that boy adores you. Now, why don't you trust in that, make up to him and stop all this fussing? Life's too short."

I thought about what Kayla was saying. Mitch did ask me why he would want someone like that girl when he already had me. And she was right about another thing, too. Mitch was a handsome man and I guessed I would just have to get used to other women admiring him.

"Remember one more thing, Dana," Kayla said as she stood to leave the table. "One's like him only come along once in a lifetime. Don't mess that up, ok? He's heaven-sent."

I smiled. "Kayla, you are really special, you know that?"

She smiled and bent down to give me a hug. "You are too, baby. Now make up to your boy and enjoy your evening together."

Little did I know, while Kayla and I were talking, Mitch and Joe had been carrying on their own conversation.

"Hey, Mitch!" Joe patted Mitch on the arm as he sat down beside him. "How's it going with that little girl of yours?"

"Well, I thought we were doing alright, Joe, but now I'm not so sure. She's really mad at me." Mitch picked up a coffee cup and the waitress standing there filled it. He nodded to her, then turned back to Joe and took a sip. "The thing is, I can't figure out what I did wrong!"

Joe smiled. "Is it really, son, that you can't figure out what you did wrong, or that you can't figure out why she thinks what you did was wrong?"

Mitch thought for a moment, then took another sip of his coffee. "I guess a little of both. I mean, all I did was have a little small talk with a salesgirl at the mall, and she practically accused me of wanting to go home with her!"

"Well, now, Mitch, let me tell you," Joe started, smiling in a fatherly sort of way. "When a woman loves a man, she becomes somewhat like, well, a tigress. That man becomes her territory, so to speak. When anything threatens her territory, she becomes defensive."

"Ok, I think I'm following you." Mitch looked at Joe thoughtfully. "So, your saying, Dana felt threatened by me talking to that girl?"

"Exactly!" Joe made a fist and tapped Mitch lightly on the arm. "She was just protecting what she doesn't want to lose."

"But all I did was talk to her, Joe. Dana said I was flirting, but I wasn't!" He took another sip of his coffee. "Does this mean I can't ever talk to another female as long as I live?"

Joe laughed. "You know, son, here's something funny. Women have different views of things than we do. What you saw as idle conversation, Dana saw as flirting. Maybe it was the way you looked at the girl, or the way you said something, I don't know. Chances are, you didn't think a thing about it. But she did."

Mitch let that sink in for a moment. Joe continued. "Let me ask you this, Mitch, was the girl pretty?"

Mitch shrugged. "I guess, you know, the kind that other men might find attractive, but I find kind of fake. Too much like a Barbie doll." He looked across the room at Dana, and his heart melted just at the sight of her. "There's only one girl I find attractive, and she's sitting over there." He pointed, and dropped his eyes.

Joe smiled. "Chances are, she thought you saw something there you preferred over her, and it made her second guess your feelings."

"I tell her she's beautiful all the time. Why would she think that?" Mitch seemed surprised at the thought.

Joe paused and turned toward Mitch completely. "Well, you know, here's something to remember. All this thing between you two, well, it's all happened pretty fast for her."

Mitch interrupted. "But not for me, Joe. I fell for her that first night she came in here, and that hasn't changed!"

"Now, I know that, and you know that, but you need to make sure she knows that!" Joe smiled and shook Mitch's arm. "She needs that reassurance. Give it to her." He took another sip of his coffee. "Go on back over there, now, and join your girl."

Mitch looked at Dana again. She was tracing the outline of her coffee cup. He couldn't help but smile.

"Thanks, Joe." Mitch cupped Joe's shoulder and patted him on the back. Then he walked slowly back toward the table where Dana was sitting.

"Can I sit down?" He asked softly.

"Yeah, I guess," I said, still tracing my cup.

"Dana, look, I'm sorry. I didn't realize that I had done anything to upset you today. I guess I just don't understand women very well."

"No, I guess you don't." I replied. "But then again, I guess I don't know men very well, either."

Mitch smiled and reached out for my hand. "I suppose we'll have to learn together, huh?" He rubbed the top of my hand with his thumb. "Sweetheart, I want you to know, I didn't see anything in her, nothing at all. That's the truth."

I looked up at Mitch, and could see the tenderness in his eyes as he looked at me. "From where I was standing, Mitch, it didn't look that way. I was afraid......"

He was doing it again. Just looking into my eyes and listening. Then he broke the silence. "What? That I saw something there I wanted? That maybe I liked better than I already have?" I nodded. "Dana that will never happen. I promise you that, please believe me." Then he got up and came around to my chair. Crouching down next to me, he brought my face to his and kissed me. "How could I ever find something better when I already have the best there is?" Mitch stood up. "Tell you what," he said, still holding onto my hand. "What do you say we skip dinner? I have a better idea."

"What's that?" I asked curiously, watching as the mischief danced in his eyes.

He bent down close to me again. "Hmm, let's just say it involves necking on a couch in the manager's office!" He raised his eyebrows and smirked at me.

"You're terrible, Mitchell Tarrington!" I exclaimed as he laughed playfully. "Just for that, I'm making you buy me dinner now!"

Still laughing, he noticed that Kayla was standing behind him, smiling at our little making up ritual. Turning to her, Mitch exclaimed, "She's so sexy when she's being assertive!"

I smirked right back at him and pointed to his chair. "Sit!" The love in Mitch's eyes said everything at that moment. I knew I had nothing to fear.

We enjoyed the rest of the evening, and Mitch was the perfect gentleman throughout it all. I don't think he took his eyes off me one time and our conversation was fantastic and lighthearted. After finishing dinner and splitting a piece of apple pie, we decided it was time to call it a night.

Kayla stopped by our table as we prepared to leave. "Now, look here, you two." She said. "You better keep that look for each other you have right now, because I don't want to see any more of this nonsense you came in with tonight." She had her hand on her hip, looking like she meant business.

Mitch and I looked at each other, and he put his arm around me. "I think she means it, honey." He said.

"Darn right I do, little boy!" she said, sounding very matter-of-fact.

"Trust me, Mitch, you don't want to mess with her!" I laughed.

As we approached the door, Mitch stopped and turned to me. He grabbed my hand, pretending to pull me in the other direction.

"What are you doing?" I asked.

"I was thinking about that couch in the manager's office again." He teased. "Wanna join me?"

I opened the door and pushed him onto the sidewalk. "You're something else!"

He was laughing and wincing away from me. "You don't have to be so rough do you?"

I laughed. "Take me home, Mr. Tarrington!" I said.

Just then, Mitch spun me around to face him. His face grew serious. "Dana, I promise, I will never hurt you, not ever again."

I hugged him tightly. "I know." I said softly.

4

The next few weeks were filled with excitement as Mitch and I went back to our routines. Our days were filled with work, and our evenings were filled with each other. Sometimes we would even call each other and leave loving little messages, just to say we missed each other. We were next to inseparable on weekends, and every Sunday I joined him for church, sometimes going to his parents' house afterwards for lunch. I was becoming more and more comfortable with Mitch's family, and instead of nervousness, I now felt comfortable there. I joined them for Thanksgiving, and I felt almost as if I had been doing it for years. December had come, and our thoughts were turning toward Christmas. Early on a Sunday morning, Mitch called me.

"Good morning, beautiful." He said cheerfully.

"Hi, handsome. What's up?" I replied

"Well, I was just looking at my Christmas list, and realized, I still have things to buy. I was wondering, would you like to do a little shopping today, after church?" He asked

"Sure, but only on one condition." I said.

"And that would be?" Mitch inquired.

"That we don't buy anything at Jacy's". I said.

Mitch laughed. "Anything for you, sweetheart." He replied.

An hour or so after church, Mitch and I were arriving at the mall. He took me by the hand as we entered, once again grumbling about his glasses steaming up. I just smiled this time, and waited for him to wipe them off. Replacing them, he turned to me.

"Let me see what else I need to do here." He said, taking out the list. "Not too much, just a few things. We should be able to knock that out in an hour or two." He handed me the list. "You get to be in charge of this, ok.?"

"I think I can handle my assignment." I said happily, taking Mitch's hand once more.

After jumping in and out of a few stores, we were well on our way to completing our little expedition. Stopping for just a moment, I decided to go ahead and mark off the list the things we had already bought.

"Mitch, do you have a pen I can use to mark this off with?" I asked him.

Mitch didn't answer, and it suddenly struck me that he seemed a little distracted with something behind me. I glanced around and noticed we were stopped next to a jewelry store window. I didn't see how anything there would interest him, but he was still staring.

"Mitchell!" I exclaimed a little louder, drawing his attention back to me. "Honey, your pen, please."

"Oh, sorry, I was just looking….."

"Yes, what *were* you looking at?" I asked.

Mitch seemed lost for words. "I, uh,…I thought I saw someone I knew, that's all."

"Oh, really, who?" I inquired further.

Mitch bit his lip. "Uh, just a guy I went to college with. Can't remember his name, though."

I nodded. "Well, ready to move on then?"

"Absolutely! Where to next?" Mitch was starting to stare again, but I decided I would just try to ignore it.

I tucked the pen into my purse, and scanned down the list. "How about the sporting goods store? We can pick up that sweatshirt for Chris." I noticed Mitch was ignoring me again. "Mitchell!"

"Oh, yeah, ok sweetheart, that sounds good." We hadn't walked three feet before Mitch stopped again. "I'm sorry, what did you say?"

I gave him a funny look. "Is something bothering you, honey?" I asked

Mitch shook his head and smiled. "No, why?

"Well, you seem distracted."

He bit his lip, and I knew he was lying. "I told you, I thought I saw someone I knew. That's all."

"Mitchell, you aren't telling me the truth. I can tell." I prodded.

Mitch looked at me in disbelief and tried to put on an innocent face. "Dana, why would I lie to you? There's nothing going on, really." He smiled and put his arm around me. "Now, come on, let's go shopping."

The rest of the day Mitch did his best to keep his mind on shopping. But he couldn't help thinking about what he'd seen in the jewelry store window, and especially, what it meant.

Over the next few weeks, Mitch and I seemed to be falling deeper and deeper in love. I couldn't even remember what my life had been like before he was in it. At work, I talked about him constantly and the other teachers knew him as a household name. On the last day of school before vacation, Carrie, our school secretary, surprised me with a knock on my classroom door. The children were gathering up coats and hats, preparing to leave, as she poked her head inside the door.

"Dana, there's someone here to see you." She smiled.

I looked at her curiously. "Who is it?" I asked.

"Your worst nightmare!" Mitch smiled as he squeezed past her and stepped into the classroom. All the children stopped to see who the stranger was. Suddenly realizing they were all looking at him, he smiled. A little girl raised her hand.

"Miss Walker?" She asked.

"Yes, Melissa?" I answered. "What is it?"

She pointed to Mitch. "Is that your boyfriend?"

Some of the other children giggled, and I looked at Mitch. He had dropped his head and was shaking it back and forth, blushing from ear to ear.

"Are you going to answer her?" I asked him. He shot me an embarrassed look. "She's waiting." I teased.

Mitch lifted his eyes just enough to look at her. "Yes, I am." He said slowly.

I heard a few more children giggle. Another little girl raised her hand this time.

"What is it, Judy?"

"Are you going to......" she giggled, "kiss him?"

All the children giggled and Mitch dropped his head again, bit his lip, and blushed. "I think I'll just wait for you out in the hallway." He said. He looked so cute, and he shook his head and chuckled as he closed the door behind him. I couldn't help but smile.

"Alright children, let's get our things together and get going now." I said. I looked out through the classroom window into the hallway, and I could see Mitch watching the children as they excitedly left for Christmas vacation. I dismissed my own class into the care of the teacher's aide, and Mitch popped his head back in the door again.

"Is it safe?" He asked, looking around the room.

"Yes, I think so." I said. "So, to what do I owe this honor?" I asked as I turned to erase the chalkboard. Mitch walked up behind me and put his arms around me.

"Sweetheart, I have some exciting news, and I couldn't wait to tell you about it!" Mitch had turned me around to face him. He looked like a child who had just received his favorite toy.

"Really, what is it?" I asked excitedly.

Mitch bit his lip, then smiled a big smile, holding me out at arm's length. "You are looking at the owner, operator, and head manager of Gartano's!"

I stepped back and my mouth fell open in astonishment. "What are you telling me, Mitchell?"

"Well, Jimmy approached me a few weeks ago, and said he was ready to step down, you know, sell his share, so he wanted to give me the first opportunity to buy him out. So, I thought about it for a week or so and well, I decided to go for it! He's still going to stay on and help me out, but for all intense purposes, the place is mine!"

I stepped back and looked at him in amazement. "Why didn't you tell me about this, Mitch?" I asked him.

His expression changed and he bit his lip. "Aren't you happy for me, Dana? I thought you would be....." He was searching my face now, as if looking for approval.

I hugged him tightly. "Yes, I'm ecstatic for you, honey!" I exclaimed. "It's just such a surprise, that's all. I wasn't expecting it!"

"Well, that was the whole idea." He replied. "I wanted to make sure it all worked out before I said anything." Mitch placed both his hands on my shoulders and looked directly at me. "You know what this means, Dana? This means we'll never have to worry!"

I looked at him curiously and wondered why he said that the way he had.

"And the best part is, I did it, financially, that is, all on my own! No help from my parents, no help from anyone!" I could see that he was most proud of that fact over everything else. "Now, just one thing." Mitch started, and he lifted me up onto my desk, taking both my hands in his. "For a little while, it means I may have to work more. Just until I get a feel for everything, that is. But, you can come down there and be near me. You'll do that won't you?" Mitch once again looked as if he needed my reassurance.

I smiled. "Of course, I will! I'll take up permanent residence if I have to!"

"Oh, Dana, I'm so happy I could burst!" He took my face in his hands and gave me a quick kiss.

"Have you told your parents yet?" I asked.

"Nope, just you. I figure I can let everyone else know on Christmas Eve, you know, kind of make it an announcement of sorts!"

"Good idea!" I said. I jumped off the desk and put my arms around his neck. "Well, I think this calls for a celebration, don't you?" I looked at him and once again, his expression changed.

"Ah, baby, I'd love to, but.....gotta go to work. I'll be pulling a late one tonight, too. Jimmy is going to run through a bunch of stuff with me. But, you can come down later, if you want. I'm sorry." Then he smiled again. "We can celebrate right now, though. No one's watching."

"Mitchell, I'm at work!" I said.

"Class dismissed." He said and leaned forward, kissing me passionately. He sighed deeply, letting me go. "Well, I'd better get going. Will I see you later?"

"Sure!" I said.

He smiled and waved as he walked back to the door. "Until later, then." He blew me a kiss and I watched him walk out.

I was putting on my own coat and hat when Carrie popped back into my room.

"Dana, was that him?" She asked excitedly. "Was that Mitch?"

"One and the same!" I smiled.

"Oh, Dana, he's a dream!" Carrie pretended to swoon.

"You don't have to tell me that!" I replied. "He came by to tell me he just took ownership of Gartano's!"

"No kidding!" Carrie sounded impressed. "That's really exciting, Dana."

"I know," I replied. "And the little sneak never breathed a word of it to me until just now, can you believe it?" I grabbed my bag off the desk and headed out the door, Carrie close behind. "I have to go do some shopping, now!" I said. "Have a great vacation, Carrie."

"You, too!" she called.

I caught the bus to downtown, and decided I would hit a few stores there. I wanted to finish up my Christmas shopping, and get something special for Mitch. Unbeknown to him, I had already been stopping every day after school to pick up gifts for his family. It was fun to finally have people to buy for, and, like Mitch had the day in the mall, I had an especially good time picking out the gifts for the children. But until now, I still hadn't found just the right thing for him.

Glancing in a jewelry store window as I passed by, I suddenly saw a beautiful pocket watch sitting there on display. It had a shiny silver case, and an almost iridescent blue face. I decided to go inside and ask about it.

"Hello, miss, how can I help you today?" The store clerk asked merrily.

"I'm interested in the watch you have there in the window, the one with the blue face."

The clerk went to retrieve the watch as I waited at the counter. He returned and handed it to me. It was stunning.

"It's going to be a gift for my boyfriend." I told the clerk. "Can I have it inscribed?"

"Certainly." The clerk replied. "We can do that for you right now. You'll just need to tell me what you would like on it."

I gave the clerk my instructions and found a seat on a little bench they had placed in the corner. A few minutes later the clerk returned with the watch for my inspection, I paid for it, and went on my way.

After a few more stops, I decided to take the bus home since I was bogged down with packages. At my stop, I got off and made my way up to my apartment. I eagerly tossed everything down and fumbled for the watch. Taking it from the box, I looked at the inscription once more. On the outside of the case, I had inscribed his initials, MJT. On the back, I had written, "I will always love you. Dana." I placed it back in the box.

It was still somewhat early, so I wrapped the rest of the gifts and decided to take a quick shower and change before heading to Gartano's. My thoughts drifted back to what Mitch had said in the classroom. We would never have to worry. We. I wondered why he had used that expression, and thought perhaps he just said it for my benefit. Not worth worrying about, I guessed.

As I reached for my coat and hat on the rack, I once again noticed the package containing the watch on the table. I hope he likes it, I thought. Then I had an idea. It was a special day for Mitch, and I wanted him to know how happy I was for him. I decided to give him the watch then instead of waiting for Christmas. I tucked it into my coat pocket and headed on my way. Then I had another idea and stepped back into the apartment. Picking up the phone, I dialed Gartano's number and got Kayla on the line.

"Hello?" Kayla answered.

"Hey, Kayla, it's me. Don't say anything, I don't want Mitch to know I'm calling."

"What's going on? Is something wrong?" Kayla sounded concerned.

I laughed. "No, everything's fine, but I need your help with something. Kayla, Mitch is so excited about his new role down there, and I want to surprise him."

"That sounds nice! What did you have in mind?" She asked.

"Well, I'm going to stop by the bakery on my way down there, in just a few minutes. I'm going to pick out a cake and have them put it aside. Do you think you could make up an excuse, and then slip out and pick it up for me? I already called, and they'll be open late tonight, for Christmas orders, you know."

"Sure, I can do that for you, dear. I'll think of something good, don't you worry. Consider it done."

"Great, let the others in on it too, ok? But please make sure no one mentions a thing to Mitch. I want him to be surprised! Oh, yeah, make sure you get Joseph and the kids down there, too."

"No problem, I can handle my mission!" Kayla laughed.

"Thanks, Kayla, you're the best!"

"That's what they say anyway!" she teased.

The evening was crisp, with a dusting of newly fallen snow. The sky was filled with a million stars, sometimes hard to see with all the lights from the city, but I still knew they were there. I stopped by the bakery and picked out a huge cake, and had them write "Congratulations Mitch" on the top. I paid for it and told them who would be picking it up, then continued on my way to Gartano's. I stepped inside and Mitch's face lit up.

"There's my girl!" He called out. He put down a towel he had been holding and headed toward me, smiling brightly. I could tell he was still happy about everything that had transpired today, and wanted me to share his joy, which I did. He greeted me with a kiss.

"Welcome to my place!" He said excitedly.

Leading me to a table, he pulled out a chair and sat down on the other side. He took my hands in his and then sat back in his chair with a sigh, his smile never leaving his face.

"You know, Dana," Mitch started, "I've only been here a few hours, but I'm exhausted! I didn't realize there was so much that went into all this. I mean, I know I can handle it and all that, but it's gonna take some getting used to. I had my things to do, and I know how to do them, but now I'm learning all the things Jimmy had to do. I guess it's kind of like a role reversal."

I looked at Mitch and he did look tired, but as he looked around Gartano's, I could still see the pride and excitement.

"I don't doubt that you'll keep this place humming like a fine tuned engine!" I said. "You'll just have to learn to pace yourself, though. I don't want you getting too exhausted and getting yourself sick."

Mitch smiled. "Oh, my Dana, always taking care of me, aren't you?"

"That's my job," I replied, "and I enjoy doing it."

Mitch jumped up and pointed toward the counter. "I need to go talk to Jimmy for a minute, but you stay right here."

I giggled at his childlike manner. "I promise I won't move." I replied.

I watched as Mitch placed his arm around Jimmy's shoulders and engaged in conversation with him, still not taking his eyes off me. He patted Jimmy on the back and, still smiling, returned to our table.

"You know, sweetheart," he started, "I haven't eaten yet and I'm starving! How about we have dinner together, would you like that?"

"Don't you have things to do, Mitch?" I asked with concern. "I know you're busy and I don't want to distract you."

"That's what I just talked to Jimmy about." He replied. "I told him I was taking a dinner break, so it's all cool." Then he patted my hand. "Besides, your not a distraction, baby, you're a blessing."

I could feel the blush rising in my cheeks, and I looked down. Mitch let go of my hand and handed me a menu. "Not that you need this," he said, "because I'm sure you know everything on there, but take a look at it anyway."

"Well, ok, I guess it wouldn't hurt......" Suddenly, I noticed why Mitch was so anxious to have me look at the menu. At the bottom of the page, in bold black print, it read, "Mitchell J. Tarrington, III, Owner and Proprietor." I looked up at him and his eyes were shining with pride..

"I'm impressed!" I said excitedly. "Honey, that's really wonderful."

"Yeah, pretty neat, huh? Just got those in this afternoon!"

Just then, Kayla came in with Joseph and her children. I smiled and waved, but I noticed she wasn't carrying any cake. I shot her a curious look, and she must have read my face because she pointed and formed the words, "In the office." I nodded to her and turned back to

Mitch. He hadn't noticed her arrival, as he was still studying his name in print.

Kayla sat her children down at a table, and instructed Joseph to come over and say hello. A moment later, he was standing next to our table. Mitch didn't even notice him—he was still looking at the menu.

"Mitchell, put that down." I laughed. "You act like you've never seen your name before. Besides, we have company."

Mitch lowered the menu to look at me, and then noticed Joseph. He stood up and shook his hand. "Hey, Joseph, what are you doing down here tonight?" He asked. "It's good to see you!" Then his face grew serious. "Is everything ok? I mean, Kayla left here pretty quickly earlier. She said you called and needed her at home."

Joseph thought fast. "Oh that, well, I, uh, I lost my car keys, and I needed them. She's real good at finding things. I hope you don't mind me taking her away for a little while."

"Oh no, that's fine. Did you find them?"

"Yeah, we did." Joseph decided he would make it more legitimate by adding, "I was going to take the kids out for some pizza, but Kayla suggested we just come down here."

"I'm glad you did." Mitch replied, sitting back down.

Joseph's face brightened. "So, Mitch, I understand some congratulations are in order here! That's really something, you taking on this place."

Mitch's face lit up again. "Thanks, Joseph!" He said. Then he shrugged and tried to act nonchalant. "But it's really not that big of a deal."

I shot him a glance across the table. "Don't let him fool you, Joseph. He's like a kid in a candy store!" Mitch smirked at me and chuckled.

"I figured that." Joseph said. "You have a right to be proud."

Just then our dinner arrived and Joseph returned to his children. When we had just about finished our meals, I reached into my coat and retrieved the box containing the watch. Mitch had picked up the menu again to study his name. Smiling, I took it slowly out of his hands, and handed him the box.

He looked up at me curiously. "What's this?" He asked.

"I was going to give it to you for Christmas, but I just can't wait. Since this is a special day and all, I thought you might like it now."

"What is it?" He asked again.

"Well, silly, you won't know unless you open it. Go ahead."

I watched as Mitch carefully untied the ribbon and slowly loosened the ends of the paper. Even though I knew what was inside, he was driving me crazy with how slowly he was unwrapping it.

"Oh, Mitch, just tear it open!" I finally said.

"I like to take my time." He said impishly. "Makes the fun last longer." He raised his eyebrows at me and smirked.

"Would you PLEASE just open it?" I said back.

Mitch chuckled and tore the rest of the paper off the package. He slowly removed the lid and his face grew serious. Taking the watch from the box, he placed it in the palm of his hand.

"Dana, it's beautiful." He said. Mitch pushed the button on the top to open the watch. "Blue, nice." He added. He carefully closed the cover, then turned the watch over and read the inscription. His face was overcome with emotion, and he closed his hand around the watch, bringing it up to his chest.

"Do you like it?" I asked. "I hoped you would."

Mitch got up and came around to my chair. He crouched down beside me and took my hand. "It's the best gift I've ever received." He said, his voice soft and full of love. "No, I take that back." He said, looking at me. "You are the best gift I've ever received. Thank you, Dana." He smiled and kissed me, then without pulling away, kissed me again, this time longer.

Just then, our moment was interrupted by Jimmy's loud voice. I turned to see the crew gathered around the counter, Mitch's cake sitting on top.

"Can I please have everyone's attention, just for a moment?" He said. The place grew quiet as Jimmy held up his hand.

Mitch stood up. "What's going on?" He asked me. I grabbed his hand and smiled.

"Today is a very special day in the future of Gartano's." Jimmy continued, pointing toward Mitch. "Those of you who come here often have probably noticed this guy around here a time or two. And I'm sure most of you ladies have noticed him!" Jimmy teased. Everyone chuckled.

I decided to get in on the fun. "But, sorry gals, he's taken!" I said, matter-of-factly, and hugged Mitch's arm. Everyone chuckled again.

Mitch was smirking, still not sure what was happening, and he leaned down toward me. "Did you have anything to do with this?" He asked. I just smiled at him and turned back toward Jimmy.

Jimmy went on with his little speech. "After many years of hard work, I've seen Gartano's become an institution of sorts in this part of town. But, over the last few months, it's become even better, thanks to him." Jimmy turned back to the crowd. "I want to thank all of you who have been there for me over the years. But, I have decided that it's time to take a step back, take on some other duties here and trust someone else with the starring role. And I couldn't think of anyone better to do that." Jimmy beckoned Mitch to come and stand next to him. He placed his arm around Mitch's shoulders. "Ladies and gentleman, I would like to introduce to you Mr. Mitchell Tarrington the third, the new owner and proprietor of Gartano's."

The room broke into a loud round of applause and Mitch's face was bright, yet full of emotion. I was hoping he wouldn't cry, because I knew it would embarrass him. Just at that moment, I saw him take off his glasses and wipe a tear from his eye. He bit his lip, replaced his glasses, and gave Jimmy a hug and a pat on the back. As the applause was dying down, I heard one of the cooks speak up.

"Hey, boss, how 'bout a speech?" The others joined in agreement, and Mitch stepped forward. Everyone applauded and Mitch waited until everyone got quiet again. He bit his lip nervously, and put his hands into his pockets, rocking back on his heels. Another Mitchism. He looked adorable to me.

"Well," Mitch started. "I'd like to thank everyone, I was certainly not expecting anything like this." He turned to the crew, then back to the crowd. "I'm not much for speeches, so I'll make this short. I appreciate the part all of you have played in making Gartano's what it is today, and I just hope that I can do as good a job in the future as Jimmy's done in the past." Everyone applauded again, and Mitch got an all too familiar twinkle in his eyes. "One more thing." He started, and everyone grew silent again. "There is one person here tonight that you may have noticed in here a time or two as well, and I'm very proud to say, sorry, guys, she's taken, too!" More laughter filled the air. Then everyone got quiet again, as Mitch walked over to where I was sitting and pulled me up by the hand, making me come and stand next to him.

"Folks, I had my doubts and fears about all this, I'll kid you not, and a lot of prayers went up. But, besides God, even though she knew nothing about this until today, this is the person who gave me the confidence to go for it." Mitch turned to me and smiled, a warm loving smile. It was as if at that moment, he felt we were the only two people there. "Dana, I want to thank you for making me more than I ever thought I could be. I love you!" I could hear everyone's, "Ahhh" as Mitch kissed me. A tear fell down my cheek, as they applauded again.

"Save room for dessert, 'cause we've got plenty of cake for everyone!" Kayla called out.

The customers returned to their chatter and Mitch held me tight. "You really are something else, you know that?"

"Yeah, well, let's go have some cake!" I took his hand and we joined the others for the celebration.

After some cake and coffee, Mitch informed me, much to his dismay, that he needed to return to work. "You can stick around as long as you want, just hang out here and be near me." He said.

"As tempting as that sounds, I really should be heading home. It's getting late and you have things to do." I replied. I knew if I stayed I would only be a distraction to him, and it was important to me that he learn everything he needed to know about Gartano's.

Mitch smiled. "Well, ok, you go on then, but be careful. I'll probably be pretty late tonight, so I'll just see you in the morning, alright?"

I kissed him as he helped me on with my coat. "That's fine, Mitch. Don't get yourself too exhausted now!"

"Too late for that, I'm already beat. But, I'll be fine." Mitch was trying to sound reassuring, but I couldn't help but worry a little anyway. He held the door open for me and kissed me again as I was walking out. As I started down the sidewalk, I could feel his eyes looking at me through the window, and I turned to see him there, just smiling at me. I smiled back and waved, then turned and started to walk home. As I looked up, I noticed the stars again, but there was one in particular that seemed to shine brighter than the others. I paused for a moment and closed my eyes, sending up a prayer of thanks. Luck wasn't the reason I was with Mitch, and I knew that. I believed he was sent from Heaven for me to love.

About 11:30, Jimmy could see that Mitch was dead on his feet. "We've done enough for one day, boss." Jimmy said. "I can finish things up here, won't take me very long. You go on home and get some rest. Tomorrow's another day."

Mitch yawned and stretched. "I'm ok, Jimmy, really. I can stay and help out."

Jimmy laughed. "And what, fall asleep on your feet? Go home, Mitch. I'll see you tomorrow afternoon."

"Ok, then, but I'm only going because you're making me. Don't go coming back and saying I'm slacking on the job!" Jimmy laughed as Mitch put on his coat. "Good night, Jimmy, and hey, thanks again for everything today."

"My pleasure, and hey, Mitch....you're gonna do just fine."

Mitch smiled and nodded at Jimmy, then opened up the door and headed for home. He couldn't remember when he had felt so tired before, but still his mind was racing. So much had happened in just a few short weeks. First Dana, now Gartano's and still he knew, the best was yet to come. That thought captured him. Dana may not have known it right then, but she was soon to find out that the real reason Mitch decided to take over Gartano's had nothing to do with the fact that he wanted to own a business.

Mitch dragged up the stairs to his apartment, unlocked the door and tossed his keys on the table. He noticed a small scrap of paper lying there, and not recognizing it at first, he curiously picked it up. Then he remembered. It was the piece he'd torn off his Christmas list the day he took Dana shopping. He smiled at the thought and remembered how she had tried to see what it said. He looked at it again. "Buy Dana something special." He had gotten her a pretty silver heart necklace, inscribed with her initial, remembering that she had told him gifts should be personal. But now, his heart was telling him that gift wasn't going to be enough.

Sighing, he poured himself a glass of soda, then went and sat down on his couch, kicked off his shoes, and put his feet up on the coffee table. He was so very tired, and taking off his glasses, he closed his eyes and thought he might go to sleep. But he knew what he needed to do, and his thoughts were keeping him awake. He replaced his glasses and dialed the phone.

"Hello?"

"Hey, Chris, it's Mitch."

"Hey, little brother, it's kinda late. Is something wrong?" Chris asked with concern.

"No, not really, I just needed to talk to you about something." Mitch replied.

"Must be pretty serious if it couldn't wait 'til morning. Go ahead, buddy, I'm listening."

Mitch thought for a minute. "Well, actually, I hate to ask, but, could you possibly come over here? I'd rather talk in person."

He heard Chris sigh. "Yeah, sure, Mitch, I'm in my sweats, but I can throw something on and I'll be there in a few, ok?"

"Thanks, Chris."

Mitch hung up the phone and decided a shower might wake him up a little more. He took a quick one, threw on some sweats himself, and sank back down into the couch. Now he was wide awake, and was formulating his plans when Chris knocked on the door. He jumped up and unlocked the door for his older brother.

"Ok, Mitchell, this better be important if it was worth dragging me out at midnight for." Chris smiled teasingly as he entered and sat down.

"I'm sorry, Chris, I know it's late, but........" Mitch sat back, took off his glasses and rubbed his eyes.

"Buddy, I can't read your mind. You have to tell me what you're thinking about. What's going on?"

Mitch put his glasses back on and smiled at him like the cat that had eaten the mouse. "I've decided to ask Dana to marry me!"

Chris looked at him with astonishment. "Wow, Mitch, that's a big step! Are you sure about this? I mean, you two haven't been together that long."

Mitch leaned forward and looked Chris directly in the eyes. "I know that, and it might seem that way to you and to everyone else, too." Mitch continued. "But, Chris, what you may not know is that the first night Dana came into Gartano's, I took one look at her and fell in love. Completely, totally and madly in love. I didn't understand it then, not at first, but I do now. And I want to do something about it."

Chris sat back, collecting his thoughts. He reached for Mitch's soda and took a drink himself. Then he sighed heavily and decided to give some brotherly advice.

"Mitchell, everyone on this earth knows that you're in love with her. Anyone that looks at you can see that. I just don't know if you should rush things, that's all. Why not give it a little more time and be sure?"

Mitch clenched his jaw and looked at Chris again, squarely in the eyes. "I appreciate your concern, Chris, but I'm not a kid anymore. You don't have to look out for me. I am going to be twenty six years old in just a few days. I love her, Chris, and she loves me. I've never been so sure about anything in my entire life. I want to do this more than anything I've ever wanted to do since the day I was born!"

Chris smiled at his little brother. He had given him the answer he wanted to hear. Now he knew that Mitch was not making a mistake, and that his love was real for Dana. He decided to tell him just that.

"Mitchell, I wanted to hear you say that. I wanted to hear you tell me that you were sure. I believe that you are, buddy." He stopped for a moment, as if bringing up a memory. "You know, Mom and Dad only knew each other a month before they got married, and they're still together forty years later. Guess it just runs in the family!"

Mitch laughed. "Yeah, well, like I told Dana, time doesn't matter to me. I feel like I've known her forever." He sank back on the couch again and sighing deeply, he closed his eyes and put his head back. "Chris, she is just so incredible! So smart and sexy and beautiful. Oh, she is so beautiful."

"You need to remember, Mitch, beauty doesn't last forever." Chris warned, still testing his brother.

"No, you're right, Chris, but true love does. I love Dana. I wouldn't care if she gained 500 pounds and all her hair fell out. She would still be Dana and I would still love her just as much, even more!"

Right again, Chris thought. He thought he would go further with his little test. "I don't mean this to sound bad or anything, Mitch, but will you be able to make it on your salary? I mean, you do alright for yourself, but you'll have someone else to worry about."

Mitch was ready for the question. "Ok, Chris, I was going to tell everyone on Christmas Eve, but I'm going to tell you now, just to answer your question. But first you have to promise you won't say anything to the family, not even Trudy."

Chris laughed. "Is this like when we were kids, and you made me promise not to tell Mom you had broken her favorite vase?"

Mitch laughed at the memory. "Well, no, this is much bigger than that." Mitch's eyes filled with excitement again. "I bought Gartano's!"

Chris couldn't believe his ears. "You *what*? How on earth did you......" Then he had a thought. "If Mom and Dad don't know, Mitch, where did you get the money?"

Mitch's face took on a somber, yet prideful, look. "Chris, first of all, you should know that I don't ask Mom and Dad for money. I want to do things myself. That's important to me." He looked at Chris and Chris nodded at him, still listening. "Most of it, well, the bank still owns. I'll pay that off by working there. The rest of it I paid for with my savings, well, you know, the one they set up for us when we were kids."

"You mean your trust fund?" Chris asked. "I thought you used that for college."

"Yeah, the trust, that would be it." Mitch answered. "But, unlike you and the girls, I was cursed, so to speak. When I turned 18, just after graduation, Dad offered me a job at Tarrington Industries, but I turned him down."

"Yeah, I know that, Mitch, but Dad never held that against you. He was actually proud of your decision to make it on your own."

"Well, Chris, that may have been what he told you, and everyone else, but he was actually pretty upset with me. So upset, in fact, that he had my trust rewritten and wouldn't release it to me until I turned 25."

Chris shook his head in disbelief. "Wow, that really stinks. I can't believe it!"

"Well, it bothered me at first, but I guess it all worked out for the best. I may have used the money foolishly when I was younger, but I used it wisely when I could finally get it. Not only did I put a good chunk toward Gartano's, but I bought my car and also paid off my college loans. That pretty much wiped out that money, but I also have a savings outside that, too."

Chris was truly impressed with his little brother. He definitely wasn't a little kid anymore. He was a responsible man.

Chris was curious. "Why did you start another savings account, Mitch, when you had the trust?"

Mitch sighed. "Well, with Dad so upset about the job thing, I decided that when I began working, I'd put so much of each check aside just to be safe, so that's what I've done." Mitch picked up his bankbook off the table next to him, and waved it at Chris. "I have around $3, 000 in there, Chris, and that should more than take care of a ring for Dana and start a little nest egg for the two of us."

Chris sat back and smiled. "You seem to have it all together, little brother." He said. "So, now tell me, why did you want to share all this with me?"

Mitch smiled a bright smile and bit his lip. He leaned back on the couch again and placed his hands behind his head. "Well, I need you to help me propose to her."

Chris laughed. "Now, wait a minute, guy, I think you're supposed to do that yourself."

Mitch chuckled, too. "No, man, I'm serious. I have a plan and I want you to help me with it."

Chris rubbed his hands together, as if he were being let in on a government secret. "Do tell, little brother, do tell!"

After Mitch explained everything to Chris and sent him on his way, he decided that he had better try to sleep. He took off his glasses, turned off the light and crawled into bed. He never realized before just how cold, empty and alone it felt. Then he smiled. Before long, he hoped, he wouldn't have to worry about that anymore. He grabbed the pillow next to him and hugged it. Imagining it was Dana he was holding, he drifted off to sleep.

The next morning my phone rang early. It was Mitch.

"Hi, sweetheart, did you sleep well?" I asked him.

"Well, it took me awhile to fall asleep, but when I finally did, I don't think I heard a thing again until this morning."

"That's good, I know you were really tired. Are you working again today?" I asked.

I heard Mitch clear his throat. "Well, uh, yeah, but not until later."

"Good!" I replied excitely. "Will I be seeing you soon?"

Mitch grew strangely quiet. "Sure, uh, oh darn, I forgot."

"Forgot what?" I asked.

Mitch didn't like to lie to Dana, but he couldn't tell her he was going to go buy her a ring. He thought up the best excuse he could.

"Jimmy asked me to look over some things down at Gartano's before we open today. He's meeting me there, but it shouldn't take more than, oh, an hour or two. Ok?"

I was disappointed, but I wanted to be supportive of Mitch. "Oh, ok, Mitch, that's fine." Then my voice brightened. "Hey, I know, I could meet you there, if you want."

Oh, great, Mitch thought, just like a woman to make things complicated. Afraid she would show up at the bistro, he decided to give her something to keep her occupied at home. "Honey, that would be wonderful, but I'm gonna be pretty wrapped up, and you know I hate to neglect you." He tried to put some lightness in his voice so she wouldn't suspect anything. "Dana, you know what I'd really like? Do you know how to make chocolate chip cookies?"

I was puzzled. "Chocolate chip cookies? Yeah, I can make those. Why?"

Gee, at this rate, he thought, he'd never get to the jewelry store! "Well, my mom never makes any regular kinds of cookies at Christmas, just all that fancy stuff. And chocolate chips are my favorite. Would you make me some? I'll bring some hot chocolate and we can have those cookies when I get there."

I was silent, and Mitch held his breath. "Ok, Mitch, if that's what you really want me to do, I'll make you chocolate chip cookies."

Mitch exhaled a sigh of relief. "Sounds great, see you soon. I love you!" Then he looked up. "Forgive me for that, please." He said, softly.

I still wasn't sure what I had just agreed to. "I love you too, Mitch."

Chocolate chip cookies? Oh, well, I thought, could be worse. He could've asked me to clean his apartment or something. I had never seen it, but the idea of what a bachelor's apartment might look like somewhat frightened me.

I set to work getting the ingredients together for the cookies, and decided to call Kayla to chat while I was working on them.

"Hi Kayla, what are you doing this morning?" I asked lightheartedly.

"Why, hi there, girl, didn't expect to hear from you!" Kayla said, surprised. "Aren't you with Mitch today?"

"No, he said he had to meet with Jimmy before work. So, he went down there, but Kayla, he was acting awfully strange when we talked."

Kayla knew that Mitch had lied to Dana, but figuring he had a good reason, she decided not to let the cat out of the bag. Jimmy had told her the night before that he was taking his children ice skating this morning. She thought it best to just play along.

"How do you mean, Dana?" she inquired.

"Just that, well, he asked me to make him chocolate chip cookies while he's gone."

Kayla laughed. "Why honey, what's so strange about that?"

"He told me his mom only makes fancy Christmas cookies, and he wants chocolate chip. That just sounds strange to me. As I understand it, she bakes for two straight weeks before Christmas. There's got to be some chocolate chip in there somewhere!"

Kayla teased. "Now come on, Dana, don't go reading something where there's nothing. He just wants you to make him some cookies." Then she thought fast. "Maybe he thinks that will keep you from missing him while he's working."

"I hadn't thought of that." I replied. "You're probably right. Well, I'd better get started on these. I'm not sure what time he'll be getting here."

"Ok, I'll talk to you later." Kayla said. "Bye."

"Bye, Kayla." I hung up the phone and busily began the task Mitch had assigned me.

Mitch was waiting anxiously for Chris to arrive. He had asked him to go along to get Dana's ring, for moral support more than anything. Finally, he heard the knock on the door.

"It's about time!" Mitch said anxiously. "I can't stall her forever, you know!"

Chris laughed. "Let me guess, she wanted to know what you were doing."

"Oh, man, worse than that. I told her I had to go into work for a little while, to go over some things with Jimmy. So, she wanted to come down there and meet me!"

Chris looked anxious. "You don't think she'll show up there, and find out you lied to her, do you?"

Mitch laughed and bit his lip, an ornery smile covering his face. "Nope, I have her making chocolate chip cookies for me. I gave her this little sob story about how Mom never makes them at Christmas, and they're my favorite."

Chris laughed and patted his brother on the back. "Very good, little brother. But, you know she'll catch on if she sees all the ones Mom actually does make!"

"Well, I'll just have to worry about that when the time comes." Mitch said, putting on his coat. "Come on, let's get this over with."

Chris smiled knowingly. "It's all gonna be fine, little brother, trust me. Save the butterflies for tomorrow night!"

Mitch decided to drive, so they got into his car and headed toward the mall. Chris broke the silence first.

"So, any idea what kind of ring you're going to get for her? Has she mentioned anything that she might like?"

A funny expression came over Mitch's face, as if something just registered with him. "You know, Chris, come to think of it, we've never even talked about getting married!"

"Really, now?" Chris sounded surprised, then he laughed. "That's probably a good thing, Mitchell. It'll make the surprise that much better. She'll never see it coming!"

Mitch smiled. "Hey, that's good! I really do want her to be surprised!" Then his face grew serious. "I just hope she says yes."

"Why would she say anything else, buddy? Come on, don't even think about that. Dana adores you. Everyone knows that, and you more than anyone."

Mitch took in his brother's words. "You're right, I'm just uptight. I hope I don't blow it."

Once at the mall, Mitch led Chris to the jewelry store he and Dana had stopped in front of the day they went shopping. He put his hand on Chris' shoulder and his finger on the glass. "That's the one!" he said excitedly, pointing to the ring. "A few weeks ago, we came shopping, and for some reason, we stopped right here. I saw that ring and that's when it hit me, Chris. I could picture it on Dana's finger, and that's when I knew I wanted to marry her." Mitch smiled. "Girls sure can do funny things to you, can't they? Or, make you DO funny things!"

Chris laughed and led his brother into the jewelry store. "Buddy, you just wait, you just wait!"

The saleslady approached them and smiled. "Good morning, gentlemen." She said pleasantly. "Is there something in particular you're looking for today?"

Chris looked at Mitch, and he had suddenly taken on the deer in the headlights look.

He decided to help him out. "He is." Chris replied, patting him on the back.

Mitch shook his head, as if he were trying to come back to reality. "Yes, actually, uh, I'd like to purchase an engagement ring."

The saleslady smiled at Mitch. "Wonderful! Did you have anything in particular in mind, or would you like to see what we have available?"

Mitch pointed. "I really like the one you have on display there in your window. I saw it a few weeks ago and thought it would be perfect for my girlfriend."

Mitch showed the lady which ring, and she brought it to the counter for him to inspect. His hands must have been shaking when he reached out for it because the saleslady smiled sweetly and her voice softened. It was almost as if she knew what Mitch was thinking at that moment.

"No need to be nervous, I'm sure she'll say yes!"

Mitch was still staring at the ring. "I sure hope so." He said.

"Oh, now why wouldn't she say yes to such a handsome fellow?" He knew the saleslady was just trying to be nice, but he mustered up a nervous "Thank you" and handed her back the ring. Then he smiled. He wondered if Dana would think she was flirting with him, too..... even though she was old enough to be his mother.

"Now, this is a size six." She told him. "Is that the size you need?"

Mitch looked at her and his heart sank. He hadn't even thought about that! What if the ring didn't fit her?

"Gee, I'm not really sure. I mean, we never even talked about it. I wanted to surprise her."

"Well, let me see now?" the saleslady thought. "About how big is your girl, her hands, I mean?"

Mitch clenched his jaw. "She's small, I guess you'd say petite." Mitch tried hard to conjure up a picture in his mind of Dana's hands. He took the ring back from the saleslady and looked at it again. "I think this will work, I really do." He sighed.

Chris decided it was time to move things along. "Mitch, are you going to buy the ring, or just bring Dana down here to visit it once in a while?"

They all chuckled and Mitch asked the lady to go ahead and ring it up for him. He pulled his checkbook out of the inside pocket of his coat, wrote the check and handed it to the clerk, along with his driver's license. Recognizing the name, she smiled.

"Mitchell Tarrington, of Tarrington Industries?" she inquired.

Chris knew what Mitch was thinking and decided to bail him out again. "No, ma'am, our father is that Mitchell Tarrington. We're just the sons."

She handed Mitch the little bag with the ring and his driver's license. "Well, Mr. Tarrington, congratulations."

"Thank you." Mitch smiled and tucked the ring inside his coat, right next to his heart.

Back at home, Mitch handed the ring box to Chris. "You know what to do." He said. "Just don't let anything happen to that, ok?"

"You can trust me, little brother. Don't worry, it'll be safe with me."

Mitch laughed. "Well, remember, I know where you live if anything does happen to it!" Mitch turned to his brother and extended his hand. "Thanks for going with me today, Chris, and for, well, just being there."

Chris pulled his younger brother into a bear hug and patted him on the back. "Any time, little brother, any time."

5

Mitch said goodbye to Chris and decided to head to Dana's. Just before walking out the door, he remembered, and pulled two packages of hot chocolate mix from the cupboard. Once on his way, he decided to try his best to forget about everything else, and conjure up a story to coincide with where he had told Dana he would be. He didn't want her to suspect anything.

Once outside Dana's door, he paused before knocking and inhaled deeply. He smiled. Chocolate chip cookies. His little plan had worked. Mitch knocked on the door, and Dana opened it up to him. He snickered, noticing she was holding a half eaten cookie in her hand.

"Couldn't wait, huh?" he asked. He snatched the rest of the cookie from her and popped it into his mouth. "Hey, not too bad!" Then he teased, "Note to self, Dana can cook *and* bake!"

"Note to self," Dana teased back. "Mitchell is a wise guy!"

Mitch patted his coat pocket. "Got the hot chocolate, should I put on some water?"

"Sure," I replied.

Mitch took the teapot from the stove, filled it up, and placed it back, lighting the burner beneath it. "See, I can cook too, smarty pants!" He snickered.

I looked at him and rolled my eyes. "That hardly qualifies as cooking." I said snidely. I took the plate of cookies into the living room and placed them on the coffee table.

The teapot whistled and after making our hot chocolate, Mitch joined me on the couch and snatched a cookie from the plate.

"I mean it, Dana, these really are good!" He smiled approvingly.

"Glad you like them." I said. "Now, see, what would you do without me?" I teased.

Mitch's face grew serious, and he thought about that question. He didn't want to know the answer. He never again wanted to know what life was like without Dana by his side.

"Mitch, honey, is everything ok?" I asked.

"Perfect." He replied, coming back to reality. He put down his cup and picked up a cookie, this time breaking off a bite to feed me, and eating the rest. "So, did you miss me this morning? I missed you."

He had his feet on the coffee table now, and one arm on the back of the couch. I smiled at the way he was so comfortable around me now. It pleased me to know that he felt he could be himself. I put down my cup and scooted closer to him, laying my head on his chest. He kissed me lightly on the forehead.

"I always miss you when we aren't together." I said. I could hear the sound of his heart beating and it was very soothing. I closed my eyes and took in the scent of his cologne, as I always did. "Mitchell," I started. "Can we just stay like this, forever?"

Mitch smiled at the thought of that and hoped that they would. "Sure, baby, anything you want." He replied. He brought his hand down and began to stroke my hair.

We sat in the silence, just enjoying each other's company. Finally, Mitch spoke.

"It's snowing, Dana, look out the window. Isn't it pretty?"

I opened my eyes to see what he was looking at. The snow was falling lightly, and it had gathered on the window sill, sparkling in the soft sunlight.

"Yes, it is, Mitch. Would you like to go out and take a walk?"

Mitch thought for a minute. "It's nice and cozy here. Why don't we just stay here and watch it fall through the window?" Mitch picked up his cup again, took another sip, and placed it back down. Then he scooted down and maneuvered so we were laying side by side. He smiled sweetly and looked into my eyes, tucking a strand of my hair behind my ear.

"Have I told you today how beautiful you are?" he asked.

"Not today," I replied.

"Have I told you how much I love you today?" he then asked.

"I don't think so," I replied softly.

"Well, then I'd better." He said. He turned himself a little more to face me. "You are the most beautiful woman I have ever seen, and I love you more than anything in the world." Mitch began to kiss me and I couldn't help but lose myself in his love.

After a few minutes of his kisses, Mitch sat up and put his feet back on the floor. He pulled his new watch from his pocket and opened it to see the time.

"This really is a wonderful gift." He said. "Notice where I keep it? In my shirt pocket. That way, it will always be close to my heart."

I smiled and sat up myself. "And what if you aren't wearing a shirt with a pocket?" I asked. "Where would you keep it then?"

He chuckled. "Uh, probably in another pocket." He said slowly, almost asking instead of telling.

"Smart alec." I giggled.

He pulled me toward him once again. "I have an idea." He said cheerfully.

"What kind of an idea?" I asked suspiciously, moving away from him a little.

Mitch laughed. "What I was thinking is, it really is a shame to waste all that perfectly good snow. I don't have to be at work until 5:00 today. How about we go ice skating after lunch for a little while? What do you say?"

"Mitch, I haven't ice skated in years!" I exclaimed. "But it does sound like fun."

"Great!" he said, propping his feet up once more. "I have another idea. Let me make us some lunch. You can sit here and relax."

"But Mitch, I thought you said you couldn't cook!"

"Well, that might be a problem, then, huh?" He looked as if he were in deep thought. "Got any macaroni and cheese?"

I smiled. "Yes, I think so."

He stood up and stretched. "I used to live on it in college. Learned fast that it's not that easy to mess up." He gave me his best puppy dog eyes. "Will you settle for that?"

"Sounds wonderful, but why don't you let me help you?"

Mitch took my feet, propped them up on the coffee table, and covering me with a blanket, handed me the TV remote. "No, now you just sit here and find something to watch while I take care of things, ok?" He kissed me on the cheek and retreated to the kitchen. I smiled as I watched him take a pan from the cupboard and fill it with water.

Placing it on the stove, he then began to search for the macaroni and cheese. After searching three cupboards, he called out to me.

"Dana?" he said.

"Yes, Mitch, what is it?" I answered, knowing what he was going to say. I decided to turn on the TV and pretend I hadn't been watching him the whole time.

"Where is the macaroni and cheese?"

"In the cabinet right above the stove, sweetie." I still didn't look at him.

Mitch moved to that location. "Found it, thanks." He called back. "Finding anything good on TV?" he asked.

"No, not really, I think I'll just skip it." I said to him.

I turned off the TV and turned to watch Mitch still intent on making lunch for me. He was studying the back of the box, biting his lip. He checked to see if the water was boiling yet, and seeing that it was, he poured the macaroni noodles into the pan. He stirred them with a wooden spoon, then picked up the box again. I could hear him quietly reading the instructions to himself out loud, and I smiled.

"Margarine, ok, that would be in the refrigerator." He said to himself. He opened the refrigerator door and began moving things around. With his hand still on the door, he stood up.

"Uh, sweetheart?" he called out again.

"Yes?" I replied.

"Do you have any margarine? I can't seem to find it."

"Try the bottom shelf, behind the jar of applesauce." I instructed.

"Ah, yes, there it is!" He replied cheerfully.

"And Mitch?" I said to him.

"What dear?" he replied, this time turning toward me, spoon in hand.

"You'll need the colander to drain the noodles. It's behind the pots and pans."

Mitch smiled. "What? You think I couldn't find it myself?" We both laughed.

"Lunch is served, my love!" Mitch called out a few minutes later. He placed two bowls of macaroni and cheese on the table, and held out my chair for me.

"Why, thank you sir." I teased. "It looks wonderful."

Mitch poured us each a glass of milk, handed me a fork and sat down. He took a bite, then toyed with his fork. "You know," he began. "I could get used to this."

My heart skipped a beat. "Get used to what?" I asked.

"This. Us. Just being together like this. It's really nice, Dana."

"I think so, too." I said, smiling at him.

Our eyes connected for a moment and I noticed the way he was looking at me, familiar, yet still, very different. He smiled at me again, then turned his attention back to his lunch.

We finished our lunch and I helped Mitch clear the table, but he insisted on doing the dishes. "This is my deal, I'll clean up." He said firmly, yet lovingly. "You go on and get yourself ready. Dress warmly."

A few minutes later I returned, all dressed and ready to go. Mitch had his back against the sink, his arms folded, and one foot crossed over the other. I thought just the way he was standing there that he looked adorable.

"Well, it seems I've forgotten to ask you something." He said.

"Ask me what?" I said, pulling my hair back into a ponytail.

"Would you like to join me and my family for our annual Christmas Eve get together?" His eyes were eager with anticipation. "I'm sorry I didn't say anything sooner, sweetheart, but I just assumed you were going to. Guess I shouldn't do that, huh?"

I smiled at him. "It's ok, Mitch." I said softly. "But, I mean, are you sure? Maybe I should just let you have some time alone with your family. I haven't really let you do that since we started dating."

Mitch looked at me curiously. "What do you mean "let me"? I am going to be 26 years old, tomorrow in fact, and I make my own decisions. If I didn't want you there, I wouldn't take you." Mitch's voice sounded a little irritated.

"I didn't mean to upset you." I replied. "I just meant that, well, maybe you don't want me tagging along all the time."

Mitch sighed and walked toward me, stopping right in front of me. "Dana, look at me." Mitch said firmly. I lifted my eyes to meet his.

"I wish you would get it through that pretty little head of yours that there is nothing I enjoy more than being with you. If I could have you permanently attached to me somehow, I'd pay any surgeon in the world big bucks to do it." He looked at me, his jaw set. "Now, will you be joining me willingly, or do I have to drag you there?"

"I'd love to go, Mitch!" I replied. "I love you!"

He sighed and reached out to hug me. "I love you, too!"

We decided to enjoy the weather a little more, so we walked the seven blocks or so to the skating rink in the middle of the city. There were several people there, some of them couples, some families with children, and a few who seemed to be all on their own. We tied on our skates, and Mitch took me by the hand, leading me onto the ice. I felt a little unsteady at first, but everything quickly came back to me.

Mitch was a very good skater and even let go of me a few times to show off his skills. I would smile and applaud him, and he'd bow as if he were performing for me. What a clown, I thought. He didn't seem to mind who else was watching, and I concluded that he enjoyed being the center of attention more than he let on.

"Is there anything you can't do?" I asked him as he joined hands with me once again.

He twisted his jaw in thought and bit his lip. "A few things," he answered. "Like cook, for instance." He chuckled.

"Now, I think you did a fine job with that macaroni and cheese." I protested. "It takes a special kind of man to do that." I teased.

"Hey, that's nothing!" Mitch leaned toward me, as if sharing a secret. "You should try my peanut butter and jelly sandwiches sometime!"

I laughed. Just then, a very attractive young woman skated by, and glancing at Mitch, she smiled. He smiled back, and fixed his gaze on her. I shot him an icy stare. He looked at me and deciding to have some fun, he stopped, let go of my hand and folded his arms across his chest, pretending to look the girl over even more. Then he glanced over at me again, and smirked.

"Would you excuse me, please?" He pretended to start skating off after her.

"Mitchell Jacob Tarrington! Come back here! You stop that right now!" I yelled.

Mitch turned around and was laughing hysterically at the little joke he had just pulled. He put his arms around me. "I was just teasing, baby, honestly I was." He rocked me back and forth in his arms. "You are a jealous little thing, aren't you?"

"And tell me why I shouldn't be? Just look at you, Mitchell. You're gorgeous. You could have any woman you want!"

"I've got the woman I want, Dana. In my eyes, there is no one that even comes close to you!" he replied cheerfully. "In fact, I feel sorry for that girl, actually."

I looked puzzled. "Why?"

He kissed me. "Because she knows she isn't as beautiful as you are!"

"You are such a kiss up, you know that?" I asked, looking up at him.

"No, I just don't want the silent treatment again!" he teased. "But, Dana, it's true. You are the best looking girl around."

He let go of me and kissing me on the cheek, he showed off some more. I smiled at him in amazement, feeling like a million dollars.

Our time together, as always, ended much too soon, and we headed back to my apartment. Mitch escorted me up to my door and rubbed his hands together, as if to warm them.

"Want to come back in for a little while and warm up?" I asked.

Mitch smiled. "I'd like to, but I better get myself home and change for work. I don't want to be late. Besides, I didn't drive over today—I walked—so it'll take me a little longer."

"Alright, then." I said, unlocking the door. "Can I come down to the bistro later and say hello?"

Mitch put his arms around me. "Sure, that would be nice, sweetheart." He replied.

I had an idea. "Wait a minute, don't leave just yet." I hurried away from the door and Mitch stood there, watching me curiously. I took a plastic storage bag from the drawer, and rushed over to the coffee table, filling it up with cookies. Closing the bag, I handed it to Mitch.

He grinned. "For me?" he asked.

"I thought you might get hungry on your way home." I smiled.

"Thanks, you really do know how to take care of me." He kissed me on the cheek.

"Like I said, that's my job." I smiled and waved as I watched my man walk away.

Later that evening, I once again went to Gartano's, but much to my surprise, I didn't see Mitch. Kayla caught my look, and approached me.

"Yes, he's here, just doing some paperwork in the back room, that's all. Don't go getting into a frenzy." Then she added, "You can go back there, if you want."

I was going to take her up on it, then thought twice. "No, that's ok, Kayla. I don't want to distract him. I'll just wait here for a few minutes until he's finished."

"Ok, but I will go let him know you're here, anyway." Kayla smiled, pouring me a cup of hot coffee.

"Now, please, Kayla, tell him to take his time, ok?" I made her promise.

Kayla replaced the coffee pot and hurried to the manager's office. The door was open, and she found Mitch sitting at the desk, leaning back in his chair, obviously lost in thought. When he saw her standing in the doorway, he sat upright again.

"Hi Kayla." He said. "Something you need?"

"Didn't mean to interrupt your thoughts." She started. "I just wanted to let you know your girl is here!" She smiled. Then she remembered what Dana had told her. "And she said to tell you just take your time with whatever you have to do. She'll wait for you."

Mitch smiled and sighed. "Kayla, could you come in for a minute and close the door?"

Kayla looked confused, but did as she was asked. "You aren't gonna fire me or anything like that are you?" She smiled, trying to break the ice.

Mitch chuckled. "No, Kayla, I would never do that. You're the best employee I have." He stood up and motioned Kayla to the couch, and once she was seated, he sat down beside her. He dropped his eyes, and bit his lip. Kayla, like Dana, knew that was one of his Mitchisms, and she smiled.

"What do you want to tell me, Mitch? Go on out with it, now, this is Kayla here." She patted his hand.

"Kayla, I wanted to tell you this because, well, you're very special to Dana, and you're special to me, too." He began. "Dana has no idea, none whatsoever, but tomorrow we're going to my parents' house and, after dinner, I plan to ask her to marry me."

Kayla's face lit up with surprise. She laughed excitedly. "Well, how about that?" she said. "You'll make her the happiest girl on this earth, not that she isn't already!"

Mitch smiled at Kayla. "Kayla, I just don't know what to feel. I mean, I'm really happy, and I'm excited, and at the same time, I'm scared to death."

Kayla looked at Mitch sweetly. "You don't have anything to be scared about, Mitch. She loves you. She'll say yes."

Mitch stood up and placed his hands in his pockets. "I'm not so worried about that, Kayla." He said. "When I decided to buy out Jimmy's share of this place, I did it because I already knew that I wanted to be able to take care of Dana. I knew I couldn't do it just on what I was making then, and buying Gartano's would mean, well, more financial security for us. Going over those books just now made me realize that nothing is a sure thing. What will I do if this place starts to falter? What will I do if I don't keep it going?"

Kayla patted the seat next to her and Mitch sat down again. "Child, you're letting your worries take away from what should be the most exciting time of your life. Don't you go thinking that anything bad is going to happen. We're not put on this earth for worrying, we're put on this earth for enjoying." She patted Mitch's hand once again. "Now, listen, Jimmy wouldn't have even offered anything to you if he didn't think you could handle it. You are a fantastic manager, and you have the smarts and the drive to do anything you put your mind to.

This place isn't going anywhere, not as long as Mitch Tarrington is in charge!"

She noticed that Mitch seemed to be letting her words sink in. "Thanks, Kayla, you've made me feel a lot better." Standing up, Mitch shook his head and walked toward Kayla. Extending his arms, he invited her into a friendly hug, and she accepted.

"Now, then, go on out there and see Dana. And put a smile on, you don't want her to suspect anything, now, do you?"

"Nope, definitely not." Mitch replied. He straightened his tie, adjusted his glasses and hurried off to join Dana.

I smiled as I saw Mitch coming toward my table, and his face was shining, as usual.

"Hello again!" He smiled, leaning down to kiss me. Pulling his watch from his pocket, he looked at the time. "Gee, it's almost 9:00. Why so late getting here?"

"I just decided to tidy up a little at home first, that's all." I said.

Mitch turned a chair around from the table next to us and straddled it, facing me. "So, about tomorrow, here's the deal." He started.

I placed my chin on my hand and leaned my elbow on the table, giving Mitch my full attention.

He continued. "Christmas Eve is like, our big event. There's a four o'clock service we go to, and then to Mom and Dad's for dinner. We usually hang out there pretty late, opening presents and all. Mom always insists, too, that we throw in a birthday cake for me."

I giggled sarcastically. "Oh, and I'll just bet that breaks your heart!"

Mitch chuckled. "Ok, I admit, I like the attention. Gives me a chance to tease my brother and sisters about just how young I still am!"

"Really?" I teased. "I was thinking you're getting to be quite an old man!"

Mitch stood up and replaced the chair. "I still have some life left in me, little Miss Dana." He touched the tip of my nose with his finger. "Now, unfortunately, I'd better go back and help with all these customers. I can't believe how busy we are tonight!"

Kayla brought me a big slice of apple pie and I ate it slowly, watching all the action going on around me. I couldn't remember ever seeing the bistro this busy before, and I smiled at how happy all this must be making Mitch. And tired, too, I thought. But if I knew anything, I knew Mitch was just the person to handle it.

Mitch started to float around from table to table, talking to the customers, and doing his best to put a personal touch on things. When he finally ended up at my table, he smiled playfully at me, his eyes shining.

"Well, good evening, miss." He said, politely. "Dining alone tonight?"

I smiled, and decided to play along. "Yes, I am. My boyfriend had to work this evening and couldn't join me."

"Oh, my that's too bad. But..." He took my hand. "Do you think he would mind much if I joined you? You're much too pretty to be sitting here alone."

I pulled my hand back, pretending to be offended. "Oh, my sir, just what kind of girl do you think I am?"

Mitch snickered, a huge smile on his face, his dimple showing. Picking up my fork, he took about half of what was remaining of my pie and put it in his mouth. Then he answered, "The kind that shares her dessert with strangers." He tousled my hair and gaited off.

Finally, the end of the evening came and it was time to go home. Jimmy and the crew called out to Mitch as he was putting on his coat.

"Not so fast there, Mitch." Jimmy said. "Since we won't see you for a few days, we have something we'd like to give you."

Mitch walked back toward the counter where Jimmy had placed a large box. I came to stand beside him and watched as he took the envelope from the top of the box and opened it. Inside was a Christmas card, signed by the entire crew.

"That's nice, thanks guys." Mitch said softly.

"Open the gift, Mitch." One of the cooks said.

Mitch smiled and this time, he didn't take his time unwrapping it. He ripped off the paper, and lifted the lid off the box. Suddenly, his face filled with emotion. Inside the box was another envelope and a plaque. He picked up the envelope curiously and opened it. As he took the papers from within, he unfolded them carefully, and his hands shook a little. "Oh, wow." He said quietly. He lifted his eyes and looked at Jimmy. Jimmy smiled back.

"What is it honey?" I asked curiously.

Mitch was too choked up to say anything, so he just handed the papers to me and I read them aloud for everyone. I noticed him remove his glasses and wipe a tear from both eyes.

"Well, if I understand it correctly," I said, "this one is the official deed of ownership for Gartano's. It has Mitch's signature at the bottom. And this one," I continued, pulling out the next paper, "looks like a reestablishment deed. It says, 'Let it be known that on this 22nd day of December, 1987, Gartano's Italian Bistro was reestablished within city limits and from this day forward shall do business under the ownership of Mitchell J. Tarrington, III'."

Everyone applauded, and Mitch and Jimmy hugged, patting each other on the back. Then I hugged Mitch and kissed him. "I'm so proud of you, honey." I said.

"So, come on now," Kayla said. "Let's all see what else is in there!"

Everyone chuckled and Mitch, his hands still shaking, lifted a large plaque from the box. It was a beautiful, shiny gold, inscribed in bold black letters, and he held it up for everyone to see. He read it to himself, and then smiling proudly, read it aloud.

"Gartano's Italian Bistro, Established 1987, Mitchell J. Tarrington, III, Proprietor."

Again, everyone cheered and applauded. Jimmy spoke up.

"We have a place all picked out for that, where everyone will see it." Jimmy said. "When you come back after the holiday, it'll be right over there, next to the door."

Mitch's face once again filled with emotion, and I could see the pride shining in his eyes. "Thank you, everyone," Mitch said, his voice cracking. "This, and all of you, mean a lot to me."

A few minutes later we arrived at my apartment, and we stood by the door, holding each other tightly.

"What an incredible day this was." He said. "I have a lot of good people in my life, Dana, and a lot of good things, too. I'm truly blessed."

I smiled. "You are, Mitch."

"But, none of it would mean a thing if I didn't have you." His kiss was full of love and tenderness, and as he walked away, I realized that I never wanted to be without him. And, I had a feeling, he felt the same way.

The next morning I woke up thinking about Mitch and all that had happened the night before. I smiled and then remembered. Today was his birthday. I reached over for the phone on the nightstand and a sleepy voice answered on the other end.

"Hello?" Mitch said.

"Good morning, birthday boy!" I said cheerfully. "Did I wake you?"

"Well, kind of, uh, no not really." He replied. "I was awake, just not all the way up yet."

I pictured what Mitch must look like first thing in the morning, and I giggled, not thinking he would notice, but he did.

"Something funny?" he asked.

"I was just wondering what you look like first thing in the morning, that's all. I mean, you've seen me, but I was just wondering about you. I've never seen you just waking up, other than on my couch, that is."

I heard Mitch chuckle. He seemed to be fully awake now. "Well, sweetheart, we'll just have to try to do something about that, then, won't we?"

I giggled back at the thought. "I don't think so, mister." I said.

Mitch laughed. "Well, how about if I get some things done, and I will be over there in about, well, an hour or two. Ok?"

"Sure, that's fine." I replied.

Mitch sleepily rubbed his eyes and put on his glasses. There was still one thing he needed to do to make his plan complete for tonight. He picked up the phone and dialed his parents' number.

"Hi, Mom, what's going on?" Mitch said as cheerfully as he could.

"Just helping Alexander with a few things for dinner later. What's going on there, sweetie?" Olivia asked

Mitch sighed and tried to think of the best way to tell his mother what he wanted to say. "Mom, I need to talk to you about something, uh, well, pretty serious."

Olivia's heart sank. "Mitchell, what's wrong?" she said with concern. "Are you alright?"

Mitch suddenly realized he was worrying his mother, so he just came out with it. "I'm alright, Mom. I just wanted to tell you that, well, tonight, after dinner, I want to ask Dana to marry me!"

It took a minute for the words to sink in, but then Olivia smiled excitedly, and Mitch could hear it in the tone of her voice. "Mitch, that's wonderful!" Then the motherly concern crept back in. "Are you sure about this, son?"

"Mom, you know me. You know how I feel about Dana, how I've felt ever since I first saw her. I'm in love with her and I want to make her my wife." Mitch paused. "That is, if she'll have me."

Olivia laughed, but in a loving way. "Mitch, honey, I know you love her. Just one look at you tells the world that news. And I don't see any reason why she wouldn't "have" you. Dana loves you, too."

The butterflies were creeping back up on Mitch again, and he tried to fight the thought, but he just couldn't. "Mom, do you think that it's too soon? I mean, do you think Dana will think we aren't ready?"

Olivia could here the fear in her young son's voice, and she answered him soothingly. "Mitchell, when you truly love someone, time doesn't matter. I've told you that. Your father proposed to me just two weeks after we met, and two weeks later, we were married. It hasn't always been an easy road, I won't tell you that it has. But we knew then, and we know now, the love is real, and we've made it. You and Dana have a real love also, Mitch. You'll make it, too. I know you will."

Mitch smiled. "I sure hope so, Mom."

"Don't worry, honey, I know you have a lot of jitters right now, and when you face her tonight, you'll have them again. But let me tell you this. When you look into her eyes, you'll know for sure if what you're doing is right. And Mitch, you're a smart man. You don't do things you aren't sure about. You never have. If this is what's in your heart, then follow it, and don't question it."

Olivia's words sank deep into Mitch's heart, and once again, as always, she had placed his mind at ease.

"Now Mom, just one more thing." Mitch said. "I need to have you help me with my plan. I want to totally surprise her, and this is what I want to do."

Mitch gave his mother all the details of what he wanted to accomplish, and getting her okay that she would help carry them out, he told her goodbye and hung up the phone.

Pulling on his sweats, he made his way to the kitchen, put on a pot of coffee, and decided to shower and shave. As he was walking back through the living room, he spotted his guitar in the corner and had an idea. He had never told Dana he held that talent as well. Ever since that first Sunday in church, she had only heard him sing with the congregation. But tonight, after he proposed, he would sing just for her.

He picked up the guitar and glided his thumb across the strings, turned the tuning keys a few times, and finally, it sounded fine to him. He thought about what song he might sing for her. He wanted something appropriate. Getting up, he walked to his stereo, opened the cabinet, and studied the music collection he had there. He picked one out and placing the record on the turntable, he listened through it a few times. Then he listened again and tried to mimic the tune on his guitar. After a few minutes he had it, and began to hum softly to himself the song he would sing to the woman he loved.

Placing his guitar back in its place, he went about his business and an hour or so later, he couldn't wait any longer, so he left for Dana's. He had to be careful today, not to say or do anything that would make her suspicious. He felt his nerves starting to return, and figured the best way to fight them was to just take one hour at a time, and try to block it out until the time came.

In what seemed like no more than an instant, he found himself once again at Dana's door. He knocked and she opened it to him, a huge smile on her face.

"Happy Birthday, Mitch!" I said, putting my arms around his neck and giving him a quick kiss.

"Thanks!" He smiled brightly. His eyes noticed a small package lying on the table, next to a card. His childlike curiosity made me smile. "Is that for me?" he asked.

"Yes, it is, why don't you open it?" I said, leading him to the table.

"This is cool!" Mitch said playfully. "Today I get birthday gifts, and tonight I get Christmas gifts."

"Greedy, aren't we?" I said teasingly.

Mitch hung up his coat and sat down at the table. Picking up the card, he hastily pulled it out of the envelope and read it. He smiled. Then his expression softened as he read what I had written.

"Mitch, I never thought it was possible to fall in love with someone so quickly and yet so completely. You have made my life complete. I will always love you. Dana."

He looked up at me and smiled sweetly. Reaching out, he pulled me onto his lap and kissed me. "I love you." He said. Then he drew me to him and kissed me again, this time with more purpose. "Dana, I really do love you." Mitch sighed deeply. Then, as if he were trying to cool himself off, he slowly pulled away from me and smiled.

"I love you too, honey." I replied. Then, Mitch turned and picked up the gift still lying on the table. He tore off the paper and opened the box.

"Hey, this is pretty neat!" Mitch exclaimed, inspecting the pocket knife I had gotten him. "And I don't have one, either. Thank you, sweetheart!" he said, kissing me again.

I put my arms around his neck and faced him. "I have something else for you, too!" I stood up and opening the refrigerator, retrieved a small cake I had baked for him the day before, when I was making the cookies. I had simply iced it and decorated it with some candy sprinkles, writing "Happy Birthday Mitch" in blue.

"Oh, thank you, baby, that's sweet!" he said, hugging me.

I placed a candle on top and lit it for him. "I'm not going to sing for you, because I can't." I giggled. "So, you just make a wish and blow out the candle."

Mitch placed his arm around my waist and closed his eyes tightly. He opened them, and smiled at me before blowing out the candle.

"What did you wish for?" I asked, taking two plates from the cupboard.

Mitch smiled lovingly. "If I tell you, it won't come true." He replied.

I pointed my finger at him and said, "No secrets, remember?"

Mitch protested. "That doesn't apply to birthday wishes." He said. "Didn't anyone ever tell you those are sacred?"

"Oh, alright then, *don't* tell me." I said, acting irritated. Mitch smiled as I handed him a piece of cake.

After having seconds of the cake, Mitch stood up and led me into the living room, sitting down next to me on the couch. He placed his arm around me.

"So, are you excited about Christmas Eve?" he asked. "I am, it's always a lot of fun."

I sighed. "I am, I guess." I replied.

Mitch moved back and looked at me. "Now, come on, Dana, don't tell me you're nervous. You've been with my family lots of times."

"No, Mitch, it's just that, it's been a long time since I was really with, well, a family, on Christmas. For the last four years, it was just me and Eddie. That's all."

Mitch's heart ached for Dana. He couldn't imagine what it would be like not to be surrounded by his family at Christmastime, or any other time, for that matter. He was glad that Dana would never have to experience that loneliness again. He hugged her tightly and closed his eyes.

"Well, that was then, and this is now!" Mitch exclaimed. He stood up and pulled me to my feet. "Since it is *my* birthday, I get to pick what we do this afternoon before we head out, ok?"

"Ok, what would you like to do?" I asked.

"Well, first, I want to take my favorite girl down to Charley's for a big, fat cheeseburger, with all the trimmings. Then, we'll walk back through the park and by that time, we'll need to get ready to go." Then he stopped in thought. "When I drop you back off here to get ready for tonight, be sure you pack a bag with some extra clothes. And make sure they're warm, ok? Oh, don't forget boots."

"What for?" I asked.

Mitch chuckled. "Just trust me, ok?"

"Ok," I answered.

Mitch and I walked, hand in hand, engaged in lighthearted conversation. For some reason, I looked up at him and noticed, for the first time, just how tall he was compared to me. He noticed my look and inquired.

"What are you looking at me like that for?" He asked.

I squeezed his hand. "I was just thinking. I never noticed before, but just how tall are you, anyway?"

Mitch laughed at my question. "Oh, about 6'2"." he replied.

"Really?" I said, sounding surprised. "Where do you get that from? I mean, your dad doesn't seem to be quite that tall."

Mitch glanced over at me. "No, I think Dad is around five-eleven or so, but Chris and I both top six feet. In fact, I think I've actually got about an inch or so advantage, but he weighs more than I do, so I tell him that balances it out." He chuckled. "Our Grandpa Tarrington was a tall man, I'd say even taller than me. But, of course, everyone is tall when you're a little kid."

I smiled up at him. "Well, I didn't inherit any tall genes, as you can well see. I like to think of myself as vertically challenged."

Mitch laughed. "I think you're just the right size." He replied, putting his arm around me.

We finally reached Charley's and as we had expected, the place was bursting with last minute Christmas shoppers, stopping in for a quick bite to eat. Much to our surprise, however, we only had to wait a few minutes for a booth. Once seated, we ordered a soda and Mitch moved closer to me to inspect the menu.

"Now, listen." I said firmly. "You may have asked me to come here, but it's your birthday, so I'm buying." Mitch started to protest, and I put up my hand. "End of conversation."

Mitch leaned over and started to nibble my neck. "I just love it when you take charge." He said, in his sexiest voice.

I giggled. "Mitchell, people are watching." I said.

Mitch continued his little game. "I don't care." He said, nibbling my ear.

I giggled again and gently pushed him away. "Stop it, please." I said firmly, but softly.

Mitch smirked and moved away. He started to move toward me again, an impish grin on his face, but I moved back and he put his hands up, as if he were being arrested, laughing playfully. I just shook my head at him.

"Mitchell, you're....." I started.

"Terrible. I know." He teased. Then raising his eyebrows, he added, "But I know you love it!"

After only a few minutes our lunch arrived, but for some reason, Mitch seemed more interested in me than in eating. I thought about the way he had kissed me back at my apartment, when I had been sitting on his lap. I wasn't sure why, but it seemed like he was holding something in, and I didn't know what it was. I decided for now to let it go.

After lunch, we strolled through the park, just admiring the snow on the trees and enjoying each other's company. The air was crisp and clear, and I loved the weather. Just ahead we noticed a mother and father playing in the snow with their small children. They finished their play and the parents put their arms around each other, watching as the children ran off. I looked up at Mitch and I noticed a look on his face I had never seen before. He was really studying these people for some reason, and I just wondered if it reminded him of his own family. Then he put his arm around my shoulders.

"Dana, do you want to have kids?"

I looked up at him, totally surprised at what he had just said. "What are you asking me, Mitch?"

Mitch laughed at the misunderstanding. "No, sweetheart, I wasn't asking if you want to have kids, I was asking if it's something you ever thought about, you know, uh, someday."

I laughed and breathed a sigh of relief. "I was a little surprised there for a minute that you'd be asking me that!" I replied. "But, yes, I guess I've thought about it, and I would like children someday."

"Is that why you became a teacher, because you like kids?" He asked, prompting me to sit down on a park bench next to him.

I thought about the question for a minute. "Yeah, I guess so." I replied. "I've always enjoyed watching them learn and grow. There's such wonder in their faces when they discover something new. It's almost like rediscovering things yourself."

Mitch was studying Dana's face, and his heart warmed at the thoughts he was having. He looked back toward the couple he had been watching a few minutes before, and now they were walking with their children, still holding hands themselves, each with a child on the other hand. He could picture himself and Dana that way years down the road, and it made him smile.

I looked at my watch. "Oh, Mitch, we'd better get going. It's almost 2:30 and we need to get ready!"

"Ok, let's get going then." Mitch stood up and extended his hand to me. "You know what?" He asked, looking down at me.

"What?" I replied.

He wanted to tell her that he thought she'd make a great mother someday, but thought she might not understand, so he decided to lock that inside his own heart.

"I love you!" He said.

"I love you, too, Mitch, very much."

Mitch dropped me off at my apartment and went home to change. I showered and got dressed, then sat down on the couch and picked up a magazine, but I quickly placed it back down. My thoughts were on Mitch and our time together today. I was curious about some of the things he had said, and the way that he seemed almost distracted at times. I had caught him looking at me several times, but in a deeper, more meaningful way than he ever had before. I was trying to answer the riddle when he knocked on my door.

"Hello, handsome!" I said as I opened the door. Although he didn't usually wear a jacket to church, he had one on today, and it made him look all that more incredible to me. He must have noticed me checking him out, because he stepped inside and did a sweep of his hand across himself.

"Approve of the attire?" he asked.

"Yes, very much!" I replied, looking him up and down. Then I stood back for him to inspect me. "And what about me?" I asked.

Mitch's eyes slowly scanned me from top to bottom, and back again. "Beautiful, as always." He replied.

I reached for my coat. "Well, we had better get going. Could you help me put all these gifts in the car?" I pointed to the five large shopping bags filled with gifts for Mitch's family. He smiled.

"Sweetheart, what'd you do, buy out the mall?" he chuckled. Then he said playfully, "Are all these for me?"

"There you go, being greedy again!" I teased. "No, silly, they're for your family. But, if you're good, there might be one or two in there for you, too."

Mitch smiled and taking the coat out of my hands, he bent down and kissed me. "I can be good." He said, softly. "*Really* good." He pulled me to him and kissed me again. I playfully pushed him away, and reached for my coat.

"Mitchell, what's up with you today?" I asked.

"What did I do, Dana, I was just kissing you!" He said innocently. He looked like a little boy who was being scolded.

"Oh, honey, I'm not upset with you, you're just really full of yourself today, that's all!" I rubbed his arm reassuringly.

"Well, I'm sorry." He said quietly. "I don't want you to get mad at me, especially not today."

There, I thought, he did it again. Why did he emphasize today? Dana, you're imagining things, I told myself. He's just excited about it being his birthday, and Christmas Eve, and seeing his family. It's nothing more.

I helped Mitch grab a few of the bags and then put them back down again, remembering something else I needed to get. Mitch looked at me in disbelief.

"Wait, you don't expect me to carry all this stuff, do you?" he said, his hands full.

"No, I just forgot something, that's all!" I quickly scrambled into the kitchen.

Mitch's mouth dropped open and he stared at me. "What else could there possibly be?" he exclaimed.

I shot him a glance, and opening the refrigerator, I removed a large container full of Christmas cookies. Mitch smiled.

"I know you said your mom does a lot of baking, but I wanted to take something, too." I told him. "Is that ok?"

"Sure, baby, that's fine." He replied sweetly. "With my family, believe me, they won't go to waste!"

Somehow we managed to get everything downstairs and to Mitch's car. David helped grab a few of the bags when we got to the door so we wouldn't have to set anything on the snowy ground. As Mitch started to open the trunk of his car, he got a funny look on his face, and turned to me.

Remembering the guitar case in the trunk, and how he didn't want Dana to see it, Mitch thought fast. "You know, my trunk is pretty full already. Maybe we should try to get some of this in the back seat." He said.

I looked at him and shrugged. "Ok, but can't a few of these go back there? They may not all fit inside the car."

Mitch bit his lip. "Tell you what. I'll take these few from David and see if I can squeeze them in. You put the rest in the back seat, ok? You can set the cookies on the floor."

"Well, ok, Mitch, I suppose that'll work." I replied.

I looked at him again and I could see him close his eyes and breathe a sigh of relief. Wondering what that was about, I went about my business and waited for Mitch to get into the car.

"Ok, I think I got it all in there without doing any major damage." He smiled as he fastened his seatbelt. He clapped his hands and rubbed them together. "Let's go do this, huh?" he said excitedly.

I smiled at him. "You're really liking all this, aren't you, Mitch?" I asked him.

He grabbed my hand. "What's not to like?" he replied. "It's my birthday, and Christmas Eve, and I have my favorite person in the whole world right beside me. What could be any better than this?"

With that comment, Mitch's thoughts drifted to what was to come. The only thing that could make all this better, he thought to himself, was if Dana said yes to his proposal. He was excited, but the closer things were getting to that time, the more butterflies he was starting to feel. One hour at a time, Mitch, he told himself. Just take one hour at a time.

6

As we pulled up to the church, I could see some of Mitch's family just going inside. "There's Chris and Trudy," I told him, "but where are the kids?"

Mitch smiled. "If I know them, with Grandma and Grandpa, already inside." He said.

I smiled. Jake and Olivia held a very special affection for their grandchildren. It brought back memories of my own Grammy and how much she loved me.

Chris saw us and waved, and telling Trudy to go inside, he waited for us by the door. He shook Mitch's hand as we approached. "Happy Birthday, little brother." He said to Mitch. Then he smiled. "Can't you two ever get here on time? You're practically late every Sunday!" he teased.

Mitch pointed at me, and putting his hand up as if he were trying to tell a secret, he leaned toward Chris. "Her fault. She was being extra slow today!"

I gave Mitch a confused look. Chris put his arm around his brother's shoulders and just smiled. The two of them exchanged a look, as if sending a message to each other in secret code, and Mitch raised his eyebrows. I wondered what it was all about, but then, figured I probably didn't really want to know. They laughed and with Mitch taking my hand, we went inside.

Chris had already joined Trudy in the pew, so I moved in next to her, with Mitch sitting next to me, then Olivia and Jake. Suddenly, Chris leaned forward and it seemed he and Mitch were carrying on some sort of secret conversation above my head. I turned to Chris and he nodded, then noticed I was looking at him and sat back again. I then turned to Mitch, and he bit his lip, then just smiled at me, stretched and brought his arm down on the pew behind me. He rubbed my shoulder, and turned his attention toward the pastor, who had just come to the front of the church.

The pastor began. "Welcome everyone, on this beautiful Sunday afternoon. We're all here today to celebrate the true meaning of Christmas. We are going to do things a little differently today, so I'd like to begin by reading some scripture for you from the book of Luke."

Mitch took his arm from around my shoulder and leaned toward Olivia, whispering in her ear. Then he folded his hands in his lap and turned his attention toward the front again.

As I sat there listening, I couldn't help but think back to when I was a little girl, and how I loved to go to church at Christmastime. Although I was young when they died, I still had very fond memories of my parents sitting on either side of me in the pew, and how Daddy would always hold the hymnal down where I could see it to sing along. Then I remembered how Grammy got me involved in youth activities as I grew older, and how much of an influence that all had on me. At Christmastime, one of Grammy's favorite things to do was to read the Christmas story to me just before we opened our gifts. I smiled at the memories, and I wondered just what kind of wonderful memories were being made in the Tarrington family. Mitch must have noticed my expression, because he leaned toward me with concern.

"Something wrong, Dana?" he asked quietly.

"No, I was just reminiscing." I replied.

He looked at me curiously, yet lovingly. "About what?"

"About how my family used to go to church on Christmas." Then the smile faded from my face. "I guess I'm just missing them today, but I'm alright."

Mitch took my hand and gave it a squeeze. Then he turned toward Olivia, said something else to her, and then turned back to me.

"I'll be right back." He stood up and again, I saw him look at Chris, and they both smiled. He squeezed out of the pew past his parents, but before I could try to see where he was going, Olivia turned to me.

"You look very pretty today, Dana." She said quietly. "That's a lovely pin you have on."

I looked down at the pin I was wearing. It was a gold snowflake, adorned with small rhinestones. Although it wasn't new, it still had a beautiful shine and sparkle to it. I touched it lightly, affectionately.

"Thank you," I said softly. "It used to belong to my grandmother. I wear it every Christmas."

Olivia smiled and patted my hand. "That's nice, dear. It's good to have special things in your life like that."

I looked up again trying to see where Mitch had gone off to, but seeming to notice, Trudy tapped me on the arm and pointed to Chris, as if to tell me he had something he wanted to say to me.

"Did Mitch tell you today's his birthday?" He asked me.

Trudy gave him a funny look and leaned toward him, but I couldn't hear what she said. "Is that the best you could come up with?" She asked. Chris shrugged.

I looked at him curiously, wondering why he would think Mitch hadn't told me. "Yes, he did." I answered, nodding.

Chris smiled and leaned back in his seat, and I turned toward the front of the church again, trying to pick back up on what the pastor was saying. I could see someone standing just off to his side and slightly behind him, but a Christmas tree on the altar was blocking the person from my full view. The pastor picked up a microphone out of a stand, and checked to see if it was on. Why is he doing that, I wondered. He was wearing a wireless microphone already. I got my answer right at that moment.

"As many of you may know," the pastor began, "there's a fine young man in our congregation that has been blessed with a very special gift. Many of us have come to look forward to our holiday service even more because we know, undoubtedly, that every year he will be sharing that gift with us. It gives me great pleasure once again to present to you, for a very special song, Mitch Tarrington."

Mitch stepped forward, his face somewhat expressionless, and took the microphone from the pastor's hand. He nodded toward a boy at the front of the church, sitting next to a cassette player. The boy pushed the button, and the music began.

I couldn't believe it! And then it hit me. So, that's what he was up to, I thought. That's why he and Chris were acting so strangely and why they all started talking to me when Mitch left the pew. They were distracting me so I couldn't see Mitch walk to the front of the church. My eyes were fixed on him and the minute he opened his mouth, I was captivated. The song was "O Holy Night" and Mitch's voice took my breath away. I knew he could sing—I had heard him sing with the congregation every Sunday. But I had never heard him sing on his own. I watched him standing there, both hands wrapped around the microphone, his eyes closed, lost in the music. He hit every note perfectly and with such expression. Olivia and Chris both looked at me, but I couldn't take my eyes off Mitch. When I make it to Heaven, I thought, the choir won't be a big surprise. I've already heard an angel sing.

Everyone applauded as Mitch finished his song, and slowly opening his eyes, he smiled and looked right at me. Then he turned toward the pastor and handing him the microphone, left the platform and walked back to the pew.

"Wonderful job, son." Jake said, patting Mitch on the back as he stood to let him pass.

"Yes, honey, that was beautiful, as always." Olivia added.

Mitch paused before he sat back down and smiled at me. I was still awestruck and couldn't say a word to him. Sitting back down, he took my hand.

"Surprised?" he said, whispering to me.

"Mitch, you sound like an absolute angel!" I said to him.

Mitch smiled at me again. "You and I both know *that's* not true!" he chuckled softly. I squeezed his hand and together we enjoyed the rest of the service.

After church was over, Mitch and I got back in the car, but when he put his hand up to start it, I took hold of it. Turning toward me, I was sure he could see the wonder shining in my eyes, and he smiled a little.

"What?" Mitch asked.

I squeezed his hand tighter. "Mitch, that was the most wonderful gift that you could ever possibly give me. Thank you."

He smiled. "Every year the pastor asks me to do a special song for the service on the holiday, so I do. I feel it's kind of my way of giving back for all the blessings in my life." Then he squeezed my hand back. "Were you surprised?"

"Oh, was I ever!" I said excitedly. "And by the way," I went on, "that was quite a little plan you formulated with your mom and Chris. Having them distract me while you went to the front of the church."

Mitch laughed and kissed Dana on the cheek before starting the car. If you think that's good, just wait to see what I have up my sleeve for later, he thought to himself.

As they drove to his parents' house, Mitch began to think of what was to come, and once again, the butterflies started. As much as he tried to control them, they kept getting stronger. He had the plan all worked out, and he trusted Chris and the others to do their parts, but what if he messed up his? What if he got in front of her and the words wouldn't come? Then he had another thought. What was he going to say to her? How would he say it? He thought about his dad, Chris, Jim and Paul. They were all married. Was it this nerve wracking for them when they proposed? He didn't have an answer to that question, or to any of the other ones, for that matter. Feeling a little warm, he cracked the window a little and loosened his tie. Taking a deep breath, he told himself again that it would be alright. One hour at a time.

I looked over at Mitch and was instantly concerned. "Honey, are you ok? You look a little pale. Do you feel sick?"

Mitch tried to muster up a smile. "I'm ok." He said weakly. "It just seems a little hot in here, that's all."

I reached over and turned down the heat in the car. "Maybe you should try to slip off your jacket. Want me to help?"

Mitch took another deep breath. "That might not be a bad idea, Dana." He replied.

He took one hand off the wheel and one arm out of the jacket. I helped him do the same with the other one, and laid the jacket across my lap.

"Better now?" I asked.

"Yes, thank you." He answered. Not wanting Dana to worry, he tried to start a conversation. He couldn't let her start to suspect anything. "So, are you having a good day so far?" he asked.

"The best!" I replied. "It's been so much fun, just being with you today!"

"Well, I'm glad to hear that!" He replied cheerfully. "I like being with you, too."

About that time, we turned into the driveway of the Tarrington Estate, and a few minutes later, Mitch was parking us in front of the house. Just then, he remembered the guitar in the trunk again.

"Tell you what, baby, why don't you grab the things from in here, and I'll get the things from the trunk? I see Chris is here, I'll get him to help me."

"Ok, honey, I can handle that!" I said matter-of-factly.

Alexander met me at the door, and helped take some of the packages, and Olivia took the rest. With two free hands, I returned to the car, thinking I could help Mitch unload the trunk. By this time, Chris was there, and when Mitch saw me approach, he pushed the trunk closed. The two men exchanged looks, and Mitch started toward me.

"Dana!" he said, his voice cracking. "Uh, I thought you were taking things in the house."

I looked at him suspiciously. He was really acting strangely. Chris was leaning against the car, his hand on the trunk as if he were trying to keep it closed.

"I did already." I said. "I was just coming back to see if I could help you."

Mitch shot a glance at Chris, and Chris shrugged.

"Uh, well, thanks, but Chris can help me. You go on back in the house where it's warm." He took my arm and started to lead me toward the door, but I stopped and turned around.

I looked from Mitch to Chris and back again. "Mitchell, are you trying to hide something from me?" I asked.

Mitch turned slowly to look at Chris, and again, Chris shrugged. Mitch looked at me with a nervous smile. "Of course not, dear. What, uh, what would make you think that?"

Chris decided it was time to bail his brother out, but first he was going to have a little fun. "Oh, come on now, little brother, tell her the truth."

Mitch's look was a cross between shock, surprise and pure confusion. "What?"

Chris smiled and pointed to the trunk. "Why don't you just tell her that her Christmas gift's in there?"

I saw Mitch discreetly give his brother the thumb's up, and he turned back to me, smiling. "Now you know. I don't want you to see your gift." He took me by the arm again and turning me back toward the house, he said, "Go back in and I'll join you there in a minute."

I looked at him strangely, not sure I believed him, but I decided to obey just the same. "Well, ok, I'll go see if your mom can use any help." I stopped and looked back again as I was opening up the door. Chris was still leaning on the trunk, and Mitch was waving to me, a funny grin covering his face. As I closed the door, Mitch put his head down, shook it and started to laugh.

He turned to Chris. "*WHY* did you let me suffer like that?" he grinned, walking back to the car. "I thought brothers were supposed to help each other out."

Chris patted him on the back, as Mitch reopened the trunk. "Hey, I'm doing my share today, don't forget."

Mitch started to pick up the guitar and then turned to Chris. "You know, I just can't figure myself out, Chris."

"How do you mean?" Chris asked.

"Well, all day long I've been doing pretty well. I mean, I haven't been too nervous, and I really don't think Dana suspects anything. But, on the way here, I got to thinking about all this, and I got all hot and dizzy-like. Dana even asked me if I was feeling sick!"

Chris smiled knowingly. "And what did you tell her?"

"I just told her I was too warm, that's all. I took off my jacket and even rolled down the window a little, but it didn't help. I wasn't even sure I could get out of the car!" Mitch stood up and turned to put his back against the car. "Chris, I don't honestly know if I can go through with this!"

Chris moved closer to his brother and laid his hand on his arm. "You can do it, Mitch, and you'll be just fine, believe me. I was terrified when I asked Trudy to marry me, and we had been talking about it already for six months before that!" He gave Mitch's arm a little squeeze. "It's normal, little brother, trust me. You're just nervous. It's a big step. But the good part is, if you do it the right way, you only have to do it once." Chris could see Mitch managing a little smile, and he looked up at him. "Now, tell me, how're you feeling now?"

Mitch chuckled. "Like I'm going to throw up!"

Chris laughed. "Come on, give me that guitar and I'll sneak it in the back way. If I see Dana, I'll just throw it in a snow bank or something and go back for it later."

Mitch knew his brother was trying to make him feel better, and thankfully, it was working. "I paid $500 for that guitar, buster, and if I find it in a snow bank, you are in some deep trouble!"

Chris lovingly hit Mitch on the arm with his fist, then took off around the house with the guitar.

Mitch gathered the rest of the gifts and carried them into the house where Alexander met him at the door to take some of them. He saw Chris and motioned for him to take some, too, just in case they ran into Dana. When everything was tucked away safely, Mitch gave Alexander his coat and went off to find his girl.

"Oh, there you are, Mitch, I was wondering if you were coming in." Olivia greeted her son with a kiss on the cheek.

"Yeah, Mitch, it did take a long time for you two to unload that trunk." I said suspiciously.

"Well, there was a lot in there." He answered, taking the lid off the container of cookies I had placed on the table. "Chris and I were talking, too." He found a chocolate chip, looked at me and put the entire cookie into his mouth. I rolled my eyes at him and he smiled.

Olivia turned back toward Mitch. "I'm sorry, Mitchell, I didn't even wish you a happy birthday, did I?" Mitch pretended to pout like a wounded child, making her laugh. "Well, happy birthday, dear."

"Thanks—where's my gift?" Mitch teased, acting like he was looking around the room for it.

"Mitchell!" I said, laughing at him. "You're...."

"I know, I'm terrible. You keep telling me that. I'm really not that bad, am I, Mom?" he asked, picking up another cookie.

Olivia turned to me. "Dana, honey, I could tell you stories about this boy that would curl your hair!" She laughed and Mitch shot her a shocked glance.

I was having fun teasing Mitch. "Oh, would you tell me some of those? I'm all ears!" I laughed.

Mitch searched out a third cookie and once again, placed the entire thing into his mouth. "I don't have to take this abuse." He stated. "I'm going to join the others in the family room. You two can just stay here and swap stories!" He smirked and pretended to be upset as he left the room. I'm sure he could hear our laughter as he walked away.

"Hey Mitch, happy birthday!" Jake called out, extending his hand to his youngest child.

"Thanks, Dad." Mitch replied.

"So, son, how's it feel to be, what is it now, 26?" Jake inquired.

Mitch smiled. "Not a lot different than being 25." Then Mitch noticed the rest of the family, who seemed to all be congregated in one corner of the room. "Hey, everyone!" he waved.

"Hi, Mitch, happy birthday!" they all said, almost in unison.

"Thanks." Mitch turned back to his father and placed his hands in his pockets. "So, Dad, anything new?"

Jake extended a hand, motioning Mitch to sit down, and he took the chair across from him. "I was just about to ask you that very question, Mitchell. I hear you have some big plans for later this evening."

Mitch began to bite his lip nervously. "Yeah, I do, I guess." He nodded. "Yeah, some pretty big plans."

Jake studied Mitch's face. His thoughts suddenly took him back to a scene about seven years earlier, when they had sat face to face in his office at Tarrington Industries. He had offered Mitch a job, a future, and Mitch shot him down. Stubborn boy, he'd thought, he'll never be able to make it on his own the way he thinks. He'll be back in a month begging for a job and money. He has no idea what the real world is all about. Trying to teach him a lesson, he took back Mitch's trust until he turned 25. Now, looking at him, Jake realized it was Mitch who had taught him the lesson. He was young, but smart, sensitive, but tough. He was doing just fine, and Jake had no doubt it would stay that way.

He turned his attention back to his conversation with Mitch. "So, are you sure you're ready to do this, son? It's a life changing thing."

Mitch stood up, and thrust his hands in his pockets, obviously annoyed by his father's question. "Why does everyone keep asking me that? Why doesn't anyone think I'm doing the right thing here?"

Jake stood up and took hold of his son's arm. "Mitchell, sit back down," He said, calmly. Mitch clenched his jaw stubbornly, and did as his father instructed. Jake started again. "Son, it's not that any of us think this is the wrong thing to do. We're all very happy for you, believe me. It's just that we also love you, Mitch, and well, I think we need the reassurance, for our own benefit."

Mitch sighed, his expression softening. "Dad, Dana is the best thing that's ever happened to me. I feel complete when I'm with her. I can't do anything without her on my mind, and I miss her when she isn't with me. Heck, she's only in the next room, and I miss her right now! I love her, Dad, I'm sure of that. Truly, I am."

Jake smiled at his son. "I believe you, Mitchell. But, I have to say this, and please, listen." Jake looked right into Mitch's eyes. "I can remember you being in love with another girl once, too, son, and you thought she was the one for you. This has all happened very quickly, Mitch. You need to make me understand how this is different."

Mitch knew his dad was thinking about Jessica. He had toyed with the thought of proposing to her one summer, about four years ago. Much to his dismay at the time, he took his parents' advice and waited. Now looking back, he knew they had been right. He set his jaw and looked back at his father.

"The difference is, Dad, that I'm in love with Dana. Actually *in love* with her. I think, with Jessica, I was in love with the *idea* of being married, but I wasn't actually ready for all that marriage encompassed. Now I am ready, to be a husband, and eventually, a father." Mitch smiled. "Dad, you and Mom were right in talking me out of marrying Jessica. It would have been a mistake. I found out that she only wanted me because she thought I had money, not for me. That's the biggest difference, between then and now. Dana wants me for *me*, not anything else."

Jake had heard all he needed to hear. He stood up and reached out for his son, and they hugged tightly. Jake pulled him back to arms length and looked him squarely in the eyes. "Mitch, I've never told you this, but I'm very proud of you. I'll admit, when you turned down the job at Tarrington, I was angry. And as your father, I wanted to look out for you. I thought I could buy you happiness, son. But, you've proven to me that money really isn't the key to that. You're a wonderful man, son, and you're going to be a good husband for Dana."

Mitch smiled lovingly at his father, and felt a bond he hadn't felt in a long time. "Dad, can I say one thing?"

"Of course, son. Anything." Jake replied.

"Got anything for nerves?"

Jake laughed and patted his son on the back. "You'll be just fine, Mitchell, just fine."

I walked into the family room and Mitch smiled at me. "I really didn't forget about you, Dana." He said walking toward me. "Just catching up on things with Dad." He reached out with his hand and I took it, willingly.

"I just came to tell everyone that dinner is ready now. We can go eat, and I don't know about you, but I'm starving!"

Mitch squeezed my hand. "How can you be hungry after that huge lunch we had today?"

"Mitch, that was at least six hours ago! You mean you aren't hungry?" I looked at him again, remembering the way he'd looked in the car. I felt his forehead to see if he was fevered. "Are you coming down with something? You don't feel warm at all."

Mitch sighed and started to lead me into the dining room. "I'm fine, Dr. Dana. Let's go and have some dinner, ok?" Noticing that everyone else was out of the room, he put his arms around me and pulled me close. "I missed you when you were away, you know that?" He asked softly.

"Are you that attached to me?" I asked, looking into his shining eyes.

"More than you know, sweetheart. And I missed something else, too." Mitch said lovingly.

"What's that?" I asked him, smiling.

"This." And with that, Mitch bent down and gave me a long and wonderful kiss.

We entered the dining room, and Mitch pulled out my chair for me. I sat down and after Jake said grace, I wasn't shy about digging into the meal. Olivia and Alexander had prepared a wonderful feast of ham, mashed potatoes, stuffing and candied yams, along with about a dozen other things. Mitch was barely eating anything, and I looked at him once again with concern.

"Mitch, are you sure you aren't getting sick?" I asked again.

"Dana, please, I'm fine." He said, a little annoyance in his voice. "I'm just not very hungry, that's all." Not wanting to worry me, he added, "I think I just ate too many cookies when we got here."

"Well, ok, then, if you're sure you're alright...."

Mitch bit his lip, but then sighed and tried to soften his tone. "I told you I was, dear, now just enjoy your dinner, ok, and quit worrying about me."

I was a little surprised at how he reacted, but I thought perhaps he was just not wanting to worry me by admitting he didn't feel well. He managed to eat a small portion of ham, stuffing and potatoes, and about half of his salad. I decided that I would be happy with that, knowing at least that he'd gotten something on his stomach.

The adults were just finishing up their meals when a barrage of excited children came storming back into the room.

"When can we open our gifts?" Alexis asked excitedly. I noticed she looked just like Chris, but with Trudy's eyes.

Jake stood up and placed his napkin on his plate. "Well, my little buttercup, if everyone else is ready, we can do it now! But," he paused, "you have to ask everyone else."

Shyness evidently wasn't one of Alexis' personality traits. "Well, can we everyone?"

All the adults looked at each other, then smiled and nodded as the children cheered and eagerly ran to take their places around the Christmas tree.

Mitch once again sat down on the piano bench, placing me in the chair next to him. I noticed that he seemed to be preoccupied again, wringing his hands nervously in his lap. I leaned toward him and he put up his hand, as if to tell me not to ask again.

"I said I'm fine, let it go, please." He whispered to me. Thinking he'd hurt my feelings, he reached out and took me by the hand, giving it a squeeze. Then he smiled at me.

Chris played the role of Santa, calling out names and handing out gifts. The children were excitedly ripping open packages, and the room quickly became littered with wrapping paper. Alexander appeared with a plastic bag, cleaning up the mess and smiling all the while. Before long, he, too, was opening gifts with the rest of the family. I smiled at how they treated him as one of their own.

Soon I was surrounded by more gifts with my name on them than I had ever seen before. Feeling a little overwhelmed, yet excited, I turned to Mitch, who much to my delight, was not having any trouble opening his.

"Something wrong, baby?" He asked. "Why aren't you opening anything?"

"I've just never gotten this many gifts before, that's all!" I replied.

"Well, get used to it," Mitch smiled, "these women love to shop!"

I shrugged and decided to join in the fun, too. I opened what seemed like countless boxes full of beautiful sweaters, perfume, bath lotions and even a new handbag. The best gift, of course, was the necklace Mitch gave me.

"Honey, I love it, thank you!" I said, smiling up at him. "Will you help me put it on?" I asked.

He seemed pleased that he had made a good choice on his own. "Sure!" He said, taking the necklace from me. I noticed his hands were shaking, but I didn't say anything. After three or four tries, I could tell he was getting frustrated, not being able to fasten it.

"It's ok, honey, I think I can get it myself." I said, taking it from him.

"I'm sorry, it's just that....well, the clasp is really tiny, and my fingers aren't." He smiled.

I put on the necklace myself, picking it up off my sweater to admire it. I looked over at Mitch, and he smiled at me, but he was biting his lip and wiping his palms on his trousers. He looked up at Chris and Chris rolled his eyes in the direction of the foyer. Mitch stood up and turned to me.

"I'll be right back, ok?" He headed out of the room, and I saw him disappear up the stairs.

Trudy sent the children off into another room to play, and everyone began to engage in cheerful conversation. The clamor was interrupted by Chris, who seemed to be reaching for something under the Christmas tree. He came back up, a small box in his hands.

"Gee, it looks like Santa's slacking on the job today!" he smiled. "I seem to have forgotten something. It looks like it's for you, Dana."

Just then, Mitch walked back into the room. He looked nervous, but he was smiling, and I noticed he'd changed clothes and was now dressed in the same outfit he'd been wearing the first night I saw him at Gartano's. He was holding a single red rose in his hands.

"I'll take that one for you, Santa." He said, reaching out for the box. Chris smiled and gave him a reassuring nod. Then he took his place beside Trudy, and Mitch came to stand in front of me.

I looked up at him, not fully understanding what was going on. His eyes were shining with a love and affection I had never seen before. Handing me the rose, he bit his lip nervously and took a deep breath before he began to speak. His expression changed and he looked like he was scared to death.

"Well," he began, "I've never done this before, so I hope I don't mess up, but here goes. Dana, since the first time I laid eyes on you, I've loved you. And with each passing day, I grow to love you more and more. You're a part of everything I do and everything I am." Mitch paused, and took another deep breath. "I know, Dana, that all this has happened really fast, but like I told you before, time doesn't matter." He paused again and bit his lip. I smiled at him. "I know you're probably wondering why I've been acting so strangely today, well, why we all have." He turned to take a look at his family, and then turned back to me. He took my hand. "It's because, well, about two weeks ago, I realized that I never wanted to be without you by my side."

I was staring at Mitch now, my heart pounding. He was speaking right to me, completely, as if we were the only two people on earth at that moment. He let go of my hand, and with his hands still shaking, he took the lid from the box he was holding and removed a smaller box. Then he took my hand again and bent down before me on one knee.

"Dana, I know I can't offer you much, but what I can give you is all my love." He looked deep into my eyes, and suddenly, I felt myself trying to catch my breath at the way he was looking at me. He opened the box to reveal a beautiful diamond ring, and taking the ring from the box with trembling hands, held it before me. "Dana, I love you more than life itself. Will you marry me?"

I looked at the ring and then back at Mitch. Suddenly, everything made sense. The way he had been talking lately, the way he had been looking at me, the way he had been acting so nervous and uptight today. I knew in my heart, that I, too, had loved him for what seemed like a lifetime. And at that moment, I knew that I never wanted to be without him. Mitch had become such a part of me that life without him no longer made sense. I wanted nothing more than to be his wife. I looked at him and smiled. The love in his eyes mesmerized me and I couldn't speak.

"Dana," he said softly, taking a deep breath. I looked at him and he still looked terrified, but his face was glowing with love. "I'm dying here, sweetheart. Will you please answer me?" I heard everyone else chuckle softly.

I smiled at him, my face glowing. "Yes, Mitch, I will. Nothing would make me happier."

Mitch exhaled and the brightest smile I've ever seen spread across his face. His eyes were shining as he took the ring and placed it on my finger. Then, he did something else he had never done in front of his family before. Without taking his eyes off me, he took off his glasses, leaned toward me and kissed me with more passion than he ever had. And I knew, at that moment, that this was real, and right.

Pulling away from me, Mitch still had his eyes closed. "I want to do this right." He said. He put his glasses back on, and then slowly opened his eyes and smiled. "I wanted it to be special, the first time I saw my..... fiancé."

He stood up, his face beaming, as his family all applauded and offered congratulations. Mitch put up his hand. "Wait, everyone, there's one more thing I have to do."

I watched in curiosity as Mitch walked behind the tree and withdrew his guitar. He came back and pulling the bench out to face me, he sat down and placed the strap around his neck. I just shook my head at him.

"Don't tell me you know how to play that, too!" I said. Mitch raised his eyebrows at me impishly and smiled. Everyone chuckled.

"There are a lot of things you don't know about me, my love." He said. "But, guess what?" He said playfully, pointing to my ring. "You're stuck now!"

"Not until I say I do!" I teased back. Everyone laughed again.

Mitch looked back at me, still beaming. "Dana, today I know you heard me sing at church, solo, for the first time. But, at church, I was singing for everyone. Now, I want to sing just for you."

My heart skipped a beat. He never ceased to amaze me, and somehow, I knew he never would.

Mitch continued. "Although the song I picked isn't original, it says exactly what I want to say to you. I hope you like it."

Mitch began to play, and I was captured, as if I were hearing him again for the very first time. His voice was soft and angelic, and like the piano, he played the guitar beautifully. He was singing to me, just to me, and the fact that his entire family filled the room just didn't matter to either of us. Mitch once again was lost in his music, and I suddenly realized that, although he might not admit it, music was his passion. As he finished the song, he opened his eyes and smiled lovingly at me. He took off the guitar and I stood up, this time initiating the kiss. Everyone applauded again.

"Ok, you two," Trudy teased. "You act like you enjoy that or something!"

"Yeah, just wait 'til you're married ten years. It'll lose its appeal then!" Chris teased and gave Trudy a playful look.

"Oh yeah, Chris," she teased back, patting her unborn child. "It's obvious that you no longer like to kiss me!"

Everyone laughed and at that moment, Alexander appeared with a tray full of champagne glasses. Smiling at his son and future daughter-in-law, Jake took a glass, and instructed Alexander to pass them around the room. When everyone had a glass, he raised his in a toast.

"I would like to propose a toast to our son and soon to be, daughter-in-law. First of all, Mitchell, when you came here that night a few months ago and poured out your heart to us, I was sure that it was just a boy with a crush. Now, I look at you, and I know what your mother, God love her, knew then. You're a man in love. And Dana," Jake paused and smiled lovingly, "I can clearly see why my son adores you, and that you share those same feelings for him. You're a wonderful young woman, and I'll be proud to have you as part of my family. To both of you, I wish much love and happiness forever!" He raised his glass, and everyone joined in the toast. Mitch hugged me to himself, still smiling brightly.

Suddenly, Mitch and I were surrounded by his family, each hugging and congratulating us, and admiring my ring. It was a gorgeous diamond solitaire, cut in a marquise shape, the band near the diamond cut in an open teardrop shape on both sides. At the top of each teardrop were two strips of gold which connected to the diamond, pulling the entire thing together. I guessed it to be at least a carat. I was breathless each time I looked at it.

"So, Dana, when's the big day? Have you thought about a date?" Julia asked.

"Give them some time, Jul, they just got engaged ten minutes ago!" Paul said.

Mitch answered the question for me. "As soon as possible, I hope." He replied.

I looked at him. "Honey, although I've never done it before, I do believe it takes some time to plan a wedding."

Mitch smiled and turned back to Julia, pointing to me and smirking. "Like I said, whenever she wants!"

Paul and Julia laughed. "Good boy, you learn quickly!" Paul teased.

Mitch pulled out his watch and looked at it. His face grew excited and he turned to his family. "Ok, gang, let's go have some fun. Is anyone up for it?"

The Tarrington children looked at each other, knowing what the tradition was that their young brother was talking about. The annual after-dinner sled riding event.

"Let's do it!" Chris and Paul said.

"I just need to change first." Mitch told them. "Dana, I put your things in my parents' room. I'll take the first spare room and meet you back here."

Everyone else had gone off to get ready, and Jake and Olivia were helping with the children. I finally had a chance to talk to Mitch alone.

"Mitchell?" I started.

"Is something wrong, baby?" He asked, putting his arm around me.

"You were terrified, weren't you?" I smiled at him.

Mitch dropped his eyes. "Beyond belief, Dana. I could barely speak."

I pulled him into my arms. "Why, honey, it's just me. Were you afraid I might say no?"

Mitch didn't answer. He bit his lip and nodded. I pulled him closer to me. "But I didn't, now did I?"

He brought his eyes back up to meet mine for an instant, and shook his head, still not speaking.

"I love you, Mitchell Jacob Tarrington the third. And I will forever. I promise." I gazed into his eyes, and he smiled at me.

"You're incredible!" he sighed. "Now, come on, let's go get our snow gear on and have some fun!"

He took me by the hand and led me up the stairs. "Now, where did you say my clothes were?" I asked.

"In my parents' room. I'll show you."

Mitch led me down the hallway to where he had placed my change of clothes on top of the dresser. Turning to me, he took me into his arms and began to kiss me again, slowly and sweetly. With each kiss, I could feel him holding me tighter and tighter. Suddenly, Mitch became aware of where we were and pulled away.

"Honey, we better change and get outside, before they start missing us, ok?" Mitch sighed, and let me go, pulling the door closed behind him.

A few minutes later, we were joining the others at the top of a huge, snow covered hill. The children were gliding down merrily, laughing and shouting, their parents playing right along. I looked at Mitch and smiled. Now I understood what he saw today in the park, when he was watching that family there. He saw us in that family, years down the road, and now I could, too, looking at the Tarrington crew.

All of a sudden, Chris ran up to Mitch and shot him another one of those secret code kind of looks. Mitch turned to me with the excitement and mischief of a child. "Dana, baby, you go join the girls, and have fun. Chris and I have a job to do!"

I laughed at the childlike way he took off down the hill after his brother, and as the two of them constructed a wall of snow. Then, like two busy little worker bees, they soon had a pile of snowballs laying beside them. They slapped a high five and, arming themselves, lay in wait for the first victim. I decided it wasn't going to be me.

I joined Julia and Angelina at the top of the hill.

"Can you believe it? Just look at them!" Angelina laughed. "They never tire of it. Same thing every year!"

"Yeah," Julia said. "They get us every time we go down. Not the kids, not Paul and Jim, or Dad, just us!"

I laughed happily. "Oh, you know how men are. They're really just big overgrown boys. Hey, I know!" I said, being ornery myself. "Let's load a few snowballs on our sleds and when we get to the bottom, we'll sneak up on them and attack. They'll never know what hit them!"

The girls loved the plan, and soon the three of us, armed with our own icy arsenal, were gliding our way down the hill. Just as expected, as we approached the snowy wall, we were bombarded by snowballs from Mitch and Chris. Once at the bottom, we dismounted our sleds and ran toward them, throwing with all we had. They ducked and dodged our snowballs, but we still were able to make some direct hits. We hugged each other and headed back up the hill.

Meanwhile, Chris and Mitch were replacing their ammunition. "Can you believe they did that?" Chris asked. "They never fight back!"

"Yeah, well, I can tell you that was Dana's doing." Mitch laughed. "She's a little devil!"

Chris turned to him, an impish grin covering his own face. "I'll bet she is!" he replied.

Mitch looked at him curiously. "What do you mean?" he asked.

Chris looked at his brother. "Come on, little brother, you two were practically undressing each other in the family room. Wow, she really knows how to kiss! And I'll bet she's good at other things, too."

Mitch dropped the snowball he was holding, and walked closer to his brother. "What did you say?"

Chris looked at him, not quite understanding that Mitch was getting upset. In Chris's mind, it was all innocent conversation. "Mitchell, it's just us here now, buddy. You can tell me. I mean, just look at her. She's hot. I don't know how you can control yourself."

Mitch was standing right in front of Chris now, and he was starting to clench his fists at his sides. "Because I RESPECT her, Christopher!" he said sternly.

Chris laughed. "Mitch, why are you getting mad? It's ok. You're 26, I'm 33, we're all consenting adults. Nothing to be ashamed of."

Mitch took a deep breath. "You have no IDEA what you're talking about, Christopher. I've never touched her."

Chris looked at his brother in disbelief. "What are you telling me, Mitch? That you've never been with her? Come on, I can hardly believe that."

Mitch's eyes were full of anger, his voice getting louder and sterner. "I told you, Chris, I've never touched her. In fact, I've never touched any......."

Chris stepped back. His expression was one of disbelief and surprise. "Wait a minute, Mitchell. Are you saying you're still a virgin?"

Mitch dropped his eyes. "That's what I'm saying, Chris. And so is Dana."

Chris looked at Mitch and shook his head, starting to laugh again. "You are so naïve, little brother." Chris said. "The way she kissed you in there, Mitch, the way she looked at you..... there's no way she's that innocent." Chris paused. "You know, Mitch, maybe it's not her that isn't letting it happen. Maybe it's you. Maybe you're too afraid to let her teach you how to be a man."

I looked down the hill just in time to see Mitch draw back his fist and connect Chris squarely on the right jaw. "Mitchell!" I called out. Mitch had knocked Chris down and was standing over him, his fists still clenched. Hearing me say his name, he turned to look at me. Just when he did, Chris jumped up and hit him in the side of the face, knocking off his glasses. Mitch picked up his glasses and put them back on. He was glaring at Chris.

Chris stepped closer. "That was some blow for such a little boy." He said. "Now, come on, let's stop this before it gets carried away."

"No, Chris, I haven't even started with you yet!" Mitch said.

Mitch ran toward Chris with everything he had, knocking him down again, and the two were throwing punches left and right. Julia had run into the house to get Jake, and he was standing next to me now, watching his two sons. Trudy, who had been resting inside, came to join him.

"Aren't you going to do something, Dad?" Angelina asked

He put his hand up to Angelina, and started down the hill.

Chris was on the ground again, Mitch once again standing over him. "Come on, Chris, get up, I DARE you, get up!" He yelled.

"You don't want to do this, Mitch, trust me. You'll get hurt." Chris said, glaring at him.

Mitch had one fist drawn and was motioning Chris up with the other hand. "Try me, I'm not afraid of you!"

Just then, Jake was almost to them. "Mitchell, Christopher, STOP this instant!"

Mitch put his hand up to his father. "Stay out of it, Dad. This is between me and Chris."

Jake stopped in his tracks. By this time, Olivia was by his side. I stood still in my place at the top of the hill, with Julia and Angelina. I couldn't move.

Jim and Paul noticed the spectacle. "What's going on?" Jim asked.

I pointed down the hill. "I don't know. All I saw was Mitch hit him, and now this!" Then I turned to him in desperation. "Jake isn't stopping them, Jim. Please do something."

Mitch was still waiting for Chris to get up. "Come on, Christopher. I'm ready. Or," he paused, bringing his fist back more. "aren't you man enough?"

With that Chris got up and Mitch swung again, but this time, Chris ducked the shot. He connected with Mitch, and again, his glasses came off. Not stopping to pick them up, he went at Chris with a head butt into the stomach. Chris stumbled backwards, and Mitch straddled him now on the ground, holding him down, his fist drawn, his jaw tight.

Olivia pleaded with Jake. "Why aren't you stopping them?" she asked. "They're going to kill one another!"

Jake stepped forward again and Mitch once again told him to stay away. "I mean it, Dad, I don't want you coming over here. I have to do this. Please let me!"

Just as Mitch was about to connect to Chris again, Jake grabbed his hand. "Mitchell, enough!"

He beckoned for Paul and Jim, who were now at the bottom of the hill as well. Paul grabbed up Mitch, and held his arms tightly as he was still trying to take blows at Chris. Jim helped Chris to his feet. Chris indicated that he was alright, and Jim let go, but stayed close beside him. Paul, still holding on, picked up Mitch's glasses and handed them to him. Putting them back on, he started toward Chris again. Paul grabbed his arm, and twisted it behind his back. "Cool it, Mitch, calm down now." Paul said.

A minute or so later, Mitch told Paul to let him go. "I won't hit him anymore." He said. Paul wasn't so sure, but he let Mitch go anyway. Mitch looked squarely into his brother's eyes. "How dare you, you dirty son of a....." He shook Paul's arm off and started up the hill toward the house. I could see clearly that he was hurt, and he was limping. I started after him.

"Mitch, honey, what happened?" I asked, picking up my pace to catch him. I placed my hand on his arm.

Mitch wheeled around to face me, shaking off my hand. His eyes were still filled with rage. "Not now, Dana, leave me alone!"

"Mitch, please...."

"I said, leave me alone!" Mitch yelled, his voice both angry and hurt. I stopped where I was and watched him go into the house, slamming the door loudly behind him.

Chris and the other men were beside me now, as well as Trudy, who seemed to be trying to nurse her injured husband. I started off after Mitch again, but Olivia came after me and grabbed my arm.

"It's going to be ok, Dana." She said soothingly. "Let him be alone."

"But he's hurt, Olivia. Please, let me go to him." Olivia hugged me as I started to cry. "I don't know what happened. One minute everyone was having fun, and the next minute they were fighting."

"I don't know what happened, either, Dana, but I believe Mitch's pride was hurt more than anything. Let him work it out first."

Jake turned to his family. "Ok, everyone, let's go back in, but through the side into the dining room. We'll have some coffee." He could see the concern in everyone's eyes. "He'll be alright, just give him some time."

"Come on, Dana dear." Olivia chided, her hand still around my shoulders. "Let's go in and let everything calm down." Looking back toward the house once more, I reluctantly went with her.

Mitch was sitting alone in the front room of the house, his head in his hands. His wounds were beginning to hurt now, but the physical pain was nothing compared to the pain and anger he was feeling inside. He thought about the things Chris had said, and really tried to analyze why they had upset him so much. He told himself that it was because Chris had insulted Dana, and he couldn't let anyone get away with that. If his own father would have done it, he probably would have reacted the same way. But then, another thought crossed his mind. Perhaps the real reason it upset him was that he wasn't sure he didn't believe what Chris had said. At least the last part of it.

He thought about Dana, and all that had happened that day. Chris was definitely right about one thing, and that Dana's kiss tonight was passionate, much more so than anything they had shared in the past. He thought about earlier in the day at Dana's apartment, when he had pulled her onto his lap and began to kiss her, and about being with her when they had gone upstairs earlier to change for sledding. Dana hadn't resisted him either time. It was he that had stopped the action in both cases. Perhaps he had been lying to himself, letting himself believe that it was Dana who wasn't ready. Maybe he was sending her the signals somehow that he was the one who wanted to wait. And he wondered if perhaps he wasn't being for her all that she really wanted him to be.

Mitch stood up, and had to steady himself for a minute by grabbing onto the back of the chair. His head was starting to hurt, and he could tell his eye was swelling where Chris had hit him. He tried to take a step, but his left knee almost gave out. He steadied himself again and started slowly limping to the dining room where everyone had gathered once more. Then he stopped. He wasn't ready to face anyone just yet. He had ruined their celebration. He had ruined Dana's celebration. He sat back down. How could he make this up to her? He wasn't sure but he would figure it out.

Meanwhile, the others were trying to get on with the day. However, it was obvious that everyone's thoughts were consumed with Mitch.

"I should go and try to talk to him." I said, getting up from the table. Jake put his hand on my arm.

"I know you're concerned, Dana, but let him be." He smiled. "He'll come around in a few minutes, don't worry. Sit back down and drink your tea."

"But when he looked at me outside, Jake, his face was all cut up. His eye looked like it was turning black and blue already. And I noticed he was limping."

Jake turned to Jim to ask for his help. He had finished medical school a year earlier, and was now a licensed doctor.

"Jim, would you go and take a look at him? Make sure he's ok." He looked at Chris. "Appears he may have gotten the worst of things between them."

Jim nodded and went on his way. A few minutes later, he reappeared in the dining room after examining Mitch.

"How is he Jim?" I asked with concern.

"Hurting," Jim replied, but then he smiled. "His pride more than anything, I think. Physically, he has some minor wounds, nothing too serious." Jim turned to Chris. "You really did a number on that eye, fella. He has a cut there, too. Looks like you might have caught him with your wedding band."

Chris turned to me. "Dana, I'm sorry. I said some things down there today that I shouldn't have, and well, I upset Mitch. I never meant for this to happen. I feel responsible for ruining your special day, and I hope that you can forgive me."

I stood up and smiled at Chris. "Thank you, Chris, I appreciate your apology. And my day is far from ruined. I'm just thinking maybe Mitch needs to hear what you just told me."

Trudy spoke up, looking at her husband firmly. "I think he does, too, Chris, and I think you also owe him an apology." It was obvious that Chris had filled Trudy in on the details of the fight, even though everyone else was still in the dark.

Chris nodded to me, and stood up. "I'll go tell him, then," he said, and left the room.

Mitch was sitting on the couch, his foot propped up on the coffee table and an ice bag on his eye. He put the ice bag down and put his glasses back on to look at Chris.

"Still angry with me, little brother?" Chris asked.

Mitch shrugged and shook his head. "Should I be?"

Chris sat down across from him. "Look, Mitchell, I know I crossed the line out there today. I had no right to do that. You should know by now I have a big mouth, and I'm too stupid to know when to close it."

Mitch put his foot down slowly on the floor and sat more upright. He sighed deeply, looking at his brother.

"It's alright, Chris." He said softly. "I shouldn't have let my temper get the best of me." Then he smiled weakly, noticing a bruise and a rather large cut on Chris's cheek. "Man, did I do that?" He asked, pointing to it.

Chris put his hand up to his cheek and chuckled. "Yeah, you did. What, are you proud of yourself?" He teased.

Mitch's face sobered and he dropped his eyes. "No, I'm not." He said. "Dana probably thinks I'm a real idiot."

Chris stood up, and then kneeled down in front of his brother. "Dana wants to know why you're still sitting in here, feeling sorry for yourself. She loves you, and she's waiting for you to come and celebrate with her. We're all waiting."

Mitch looked up and managed a small smile. Chris helped him to his feet.

"Well, is all forgiven then? Are we ok?" Chris asked.

"Yeah, I guess so." Mitch replied.

"Good." Chris said. "But just one thing."

"What's that?" Mitch asked.

"If you two decide to get married before the next family get together, be sure you take your ring off before you come over!" Chris chuckled, lightly touching Mitch's eye.

Mitch looked at him. "Once it's on, it's never coming off." He smiled. "By the way Chris, thanks."

Chris looked at Mitch with confusion. "For what?"

"For, well, helping me today."

Chris assumed that Mitch was talking about his part in the proposal. He had no idea that Mitch was thinking that he'd opened his eyes about Dana.

"Not a problem, buddy. Now, let's go celebrate your birthday before they eat the cake without us!"

The two walked into the dining room together, Mitch just a few steps behind. He was still limping, but seemed to be doing a little bit better than before.

"There you are!" Julia exclaimed, looking at Mitch. "We were wondering if you were going to stay in there all night."

Mitch was biting his lip. "Sorry, I just had some things to sort out. And I'm sorry if I ruined your day everyone." Mitch looked at me and his eyes were still sad and distant.

Jake decided to try to bring a smile to his young son's face.

"Brought back memories for me." He laughed. "It's been a long time since I've seen you two fight like that!"

"Yeah, well, I've grown a little since then, Dad." Mitch said, and he started to smile.

Chris looked at him. "Well, that might be true, but you'll always be the baby to us!" He punched Mitch lightly on the arm.

"Ouch, don't do that. Everything hurts right now." Mitch said softly, and everyone laughed.

"Well, now, Mitchell, which do you want first, the cake or the gifts?" Julia asked.

I stood up and walked over to Mitch. He started to put his arm around me, and seemed to hesitate, as if he weren't sure I would want him to. I placed my arm around his waist, and pulling him toward me I said, "If I know Mr. Greedy here, he wants the gifts!" He smiled down at me and the old familiar sparkle was starting to return to his eyes.

Mitch's mood seemed to lighten as he opened all his gifts and with pride, he showed off the pocket knife I had gotten him. His mother brought out a wonderful cake for him, and placed a single candle in the center. Looking at me, as he had when I gave him my cake earlier, he closed his eyes and making a wish, blew it out.

Shortly after our little celebration, Mitch decided we should start home, and he and Chris loaded the car with the gifts we had received. Everyone was still gathered in the family room when they came back in from outside. Mitch smiled and raised his hand to get everyone's attention.

"Everybody, I know this was a kind of crazy day, but I want to let you know that I'm glad you were all a part of it. Before we go, though, there's one more thing I want to share with you." He reached into the inside pocket of his coat and pulled out the papers Jimmy had given him the night before. "A few weeks ago, I made two big decisions. The first, and best, of course, was to ask Dana to marry me." He put his arm around me. "The second one, actually based on the first, was to secure my future, our future." He held up the papers for all to see. "You're looking at the new owner of Gartano's!"

Everyone looked at each other with surprise and again, the room was filled with everyone's congratulations. Many hugs and kisses later, we were finally on our way home. A few minutes into our drive,

Mitch reached over for my hand. "Dana, I'm sorry I ruined your day. I shouldn't have let Chris get to me like that."

I leaned over and hugged his arm. "Honey, you didn't ruin anything. I was so worried about you. I've never seen you that angry before. What did he do to get you so upset that you thought you had to hit him?"

Mitch placed his hand back on the wheel. "Dana, I'd really rather not talk about it, ok?"

I sat back and turned toward the window. "Mitch, I thought you said no secrets. Why won't you tell me? I want to know."

Mitch sighed and collected his thoughts before he spoke. "I know what I said, Dana. But this time, I think it's better left unsaid. Besides, it's over. I'd rather just forget it." Then he managed a smile. "At least, until I look in the mirror the next time and see what he did to my face."

Mitch looked at Dana. She was so amazing. Here he had been a total idiot, fighting with his brother like a child, and all she could do was be concerned about him. She was so beautiful, he thought. So unbelievably beautiful. He wanted to make up to her for the way he had acted. And he suddenly thought he knew just what to do.

7

As we came back into the city, Mitch didn't turn toward my apartment like he normally would. I turned toward him.

"Mitch, where are we going?" I asked.

"I was just thinking two things. One, that I don't want to take you home just yet, and two, that you've never seen my apartment. I always come to yours, so I thought you might like to see how a bachelor, oops, I mean a betrothed man, lives."

I didn't see the harm in that, especially if it meant getting to spend more time with Mitch. "Ok!" I said cheerfully. "I'm up for it!"

We pulled up in front of Mitch's building and got out. His doorman, Pete, greeted us warmly. Then, taking a closer look, he questioned Mitch.

"Mr. Tarrington, are you ok?" He asked.

Mitch smiled, leading me through the open door. "I'm fine, thanks. Just had a little accident today, that's all."

He took me by the hand, leading me up the three flights of stairs to his apartment. Letting go for just an instant, he put the key in the lock and opened the door. Reaching around the corner to turn on a light, he let me go in ahead of him and he closed the door.

"Well, this is it!" He exclaimed, taking off his coat and helping me off with mine. "Not much, but I call it home."

"No, Mitch, it's really nice." I said.

"Thanks, but to be honest, Julia and Ang helped me decorate. They said it needed a feminine touch." Mitch turned to face me again, and his look was serious, as if he were once again lost in a thought. He was looking deep into my eyes now, and I felt like he could see into my very soul. He smiled at me and took my hand once again, breaking the moment.

"Would you like the grand tour?" He asked, lightheartedly.

"Lead on!" I said.

"Ok, well, obviously this is the living room, the balcony is out there, and here's the kitchen and dining area." He stopped in front of a bookcase. "As you can see, I enjoy reading, and over there," he pointed to his entertainment center, "is my very diverse music collection, which I already told you about. I have a little Christmas tree there that my mom gave me, and..." he paused, leading me into the hallway, "here is my closet where I keep, well, stuff." He was acting silly and making me laugh.

"Here's the bathroom, very important to know that, just in case," he smiled, "but this is the most important room of all." He said, still holding tightly to my hand. "This is my bedroom."

Mitch turned me to him now, and his face was glowing. There was only the light from the hallway shining into the room, but I wasn't having any trouble seeing him. He was looking deep into my eyes, his face full of love, his eyes shining with emotion. Slowly putting his arms around me, he kissed me slowly and softly. He pulled away for just an instant, brushing me lightly once again with his lips on mine.

"Dana, I love you, I love you more than anything." He whispered.

"I love you, too, Mitch." I said, softly.

Mitch bent down to kiss me again, this time pulling me closer to him still, holding me tighter, his hands flat against my back. I wasn't resisting him, until I felt his hands start to drop below my waist. I pulled away from him gently, yet still holding him in my arms.

"Mitch, what are you doing?" I asked.

He bent down again, this time planting soft kisses on my cheek, moving onto my neck. "Kiss me," he said softly, moving to meet my lips. I felt him slowly reach up to his tie and loosen it, then pull it off completely, dropping it to the floor. His kisses were now more passionate than ever before and he was pressing me tighter against him. He reached up again and his fingers fumbled to undo a few buttons on his shirt. Suddenly, I realized what he might be getting at.

"Mitch, I...." Before I could speak, he was kissing me again. I turned away, so that I could finish what I had started to say. "Mitch, I don't think we should do this."

I heard him sigh deeply, but he wasn't letting up. "Why not? It's my birthday. You're what I want. Think of this as my gift."

I almost laughed at the lame line he'd just given me, but I contained myself. He had lifted my sweater, and his hands were on the small of my back, moving slowly upward. I managed to pull them down, and put my sweater back into place.

"Don't fight it, sweetheart, it's alright." Mitch said softly, his breath coming quicker. "It's just you and me. I love you Dana. Let me show you how much."

It was getting harder for me to resist him, but I knew it was the right thing to do. "Mitchell, please don't do this." I pleaded once more. "I can't, I mean...."

Mitch was about to kiss me again, but he stopped and opened his eyes to look at me, still not letting me go. "Dana, why can't you? Why can't you just give in to what we're both feeling here?" Then his eyes filled with concern. "Don't you love me, Dana?"

My heart sank at that moment as I heard his words. I bent my head down and placed it against his chest. "Of course I love you, Mitch." I replied.

He pulled my head back up and kissed me again. I could feel him undoing the rest of the buttons on his shirt. "Then prove it to me, Dana. Show me you love me."

His words hit me as if I had been slapped in the face. Prove my love to him? Did he doubt my word? I pushed him away and tried to slip out the door past him, but he caught my arm, and gently pulled me back. He sighed heavily and looked deep into my eyes. "What's wrong, Dana? Why are you fighting this?"

I looked at him, hoping he would understand my words. "Mitchell, I made a promise to someone that I can't break. That I won't break."

Mitch slid his hands down my arms and was now holding both my hands. He looked at me curiously. "What kind of promise, Dana? And to whom?"

"To my grandmother, Mitch. I promised her I wouldn't do anything until I got married. Besides, it isn't right."

Mitch looked at me, as if not fully understanding. "Dana, what do you mean, until you get married? You mean you and Eddie never, that you never......"

I dropped my eyes and shook my head. "No, Mitch, I never have." Then I saw the way he was looking at me. "I'm sorry if that disappoints you."

"Why would that disappoint me?" He said, surprised. Then his face got serious. "Wait a minute, Dana. You think I'm experienced at this?"

I wasn't sure how to answer. Everything he had been doing seemed to point to the fact that he was. I decided to answer in the way that I believed. "You seem like you are."

Mitch laughed, and then pulled me to him once again. "Dana, I have a confession. I've never done this, either. This would be, well, my first time. At least, I'd like it to be."

I looked at Mitch and his eyes were filling with passion once again, as he leaned down to kiss me. I knew I couldn't let this go any further. I pushed him away.

"Mitchell, I'm *not* going to do this. I made a promise I intend to keep........" He cut me off mid-sentence.

"To someone who is *gone* now, Dana. Tell me, how will she ever know? Is one of us going to *tell* her? A little impossible, don't you think?" I could hear the frustration now in Mitch's voice. He looked up and exhaled loudly.

I couldn't believe how selfish he seemed at that moment. I gave him an icy stare. "I'll know, Mitchell, and that's all that matters."

Mitch took a step closer to me now. "No, Dana, all that matters is that we love each other. I really want to be with you, now."

I put up my hand, and he stopped. I tried to soften my voice as much as possible. "I want our first time together to be special, Mitch. Our time will come and when it does, it will be that much better because we waited. Trust me."

"How do you know that, Dana? Don't you believe we love each other enough right now to make it special?"

I was starting to grow tired of his begging. "Mitch, our love has nothing to do with this. I'm not giving in, and that's final!"

Mitch's face was starting to take on a look of not only frustration, but of anger. "For Heaven's sake, Dana, our love has *everything* to do with this! This is what people who love each other do. Especially people who are getting married." The words he said next tore me in two. "I give you a ring, and this is the thanks I get for it? Absolutely nothing!"

Mitch turned around and with his head down, he walked out of the room. I followed, and he was standing with both hands on the back of the couch, still looking down.

"Mitch, is that what you think? Do you think that just because you gave me a ring that I owe you something? Is that why you gave it to me, just so you could get what you want?" He didn't answer, and I'm sure he knew he had upset me.

"One would think that you could at least show a little more gratitude."

I couldn't believe what I was hearing. I was angry now and wasn't holding back. "Is that how you see me now, Mitchell? Do you think I've become your little plaything just because I took your ring? If so, you are dreadfully wrong!"

Mitch looked up at me, biting his lip again, but this time, it wasn't because of his nerves. He was angry as well. "Then, tell me, Dana, just why *did* you take it? It obviously wasn't because you wanted to actually marry *me*, now was it? Let's think about this." His tone was growing more irritated and his voice was getting louder. "I'm the namesake and a beneficiary of one of the richest men in the state, I drive an expensive, very sporty car, I own a restaurant, *and* I can manage to put a $2,000 engagement ring on your finger. Gee, Dana, it isn't that hard to see just why you said yes to me, now is it?"

Mitch's words cut me deeply, and I couldn't have hurt more at that moment than if he had actually hit me physically. I stared at him in disbelief. Did he really think that way, that I only wanted him for his money? I started to speak, but what he said next was the last thing I could take.

He put his head down again, chuckled to himself, and then lifted his eyes to me. They were cold, and his face was expressionless. "I can't believe I let myself fall for you, Dana Walker. I can't believe I actually thought you were different. I thought I'd left Jessica far behind, but you're just like her, Dana. All you want is my money, just like she did."

I could feel the tears starting to fall, and my heart felt as though it had been ripped right from my chest. I grabbed my coat and slowly opened the door. Pausing, I turned to look at Mitch once again. "I'm sorry you feel that way, Mitchell." I said, trying to keep my voice from cracking. "But I guess its better I found that out now."

Mitch bit his lip and turned away from me. "Yeah, I guess it is."

With that, I turned and closing the door behind me, headed for home.

Mitch closed his eyes tightly at the sound of the door closing behind Dana. He was feeling a rush of emotions right then that he didn't understand. He was hurt that Dana had rejected him the way that she had. Obviously, Chris had been wrong about her. She'd acted as if she didn't want him at all. Perhaps it had all been a little game with her, and she had played him well. In spite of those feelings, he longed for her. He longed for her kiss, her touch, everything about her. He loved her with his entire being, with each and every thing that he had. He thought back to the way she had looked at him earlier that evening when he had proposed to her, the love shining in her eyes, the way she had kissed him. He thought about her smile and the way she made him feel when they were together. Right at that moment, he didn't know what to believe was true.

He sat down in the chair, and looked at the clock. Almost 10:45 pm. His mind was racing and he felt as if his heart was going to explode. He thought about the hurt on Dana's face as he'd made his accusations. He thought about the tears streaming down her cheeks, and how the shine was no longer in her eyes as she looked at him before closing the door. He felt a tear running down his own face at that moment. He had done the one thing he had promised her he would never do. He had hurt her, and it was tearing him apart. He knew there was no sense going after her. It was over.

I ran almost the entire way home, the cold winter wind causing the tears to sting my face. I wished I could just keep running until the pain left me, but I didn't think that would ever happen. It was too deep, too strong. The love I felt for Mitch consumed me. He was the very air that I breathed. Something told me I couldn't let that go. I needed to try to talk to him, to help him believe the truth. I thought about what had happened this evening, and the way he must have felt when I told him no. He couldn't understand why a promise made long ago would mean so much to me. All he could see was that it was keeping us apart, and he thought that meant I didn't want him. It was very much the opposite. He had no idea just how much it took for me to pull away from him, to not let my passion take control of me as well. I looked down at my ring, and I knew what that meant. I turned around and headed back to Mitch's apartment. I had to try to make this right.

The silence was too much for Mitch to bear any longer. He needed to get out and try to get this off his mind. Re-buttoning his shirt, he got his coat and decided he would head down to Gartano's. They wouldn't be closing until 11:30, as the crew had decided to stay open a little later this Christmas Eve. Work always seemed to take his mind off his problems, and he was sure to find something to do down there.

The air was cold, and he tightened his coat around him. His knee was starting to hurt again, but he told himself to toughen up and continued on his way. Once he arrived, he decided to slip in through the delivery entrance so as not to draw attention to himself. He would let Jimmy know he was there, and then slip into the office and find something to occupy his mind.

I arrived back at Mitch's apartment and hesitated before I knocked on the door. What if he didn't want to see me? That was a chance I had to take. I knocked and he didn't answer, so I knocked again, this time louder. "Mitch?" I called. Still no answer. I turned away slowly and headed back home, deciding I would try to call once I got there.

Mitch caught Jimmy's attention and called him over. He didn't want anyone else to know he was there.

"God almighty, Mitch, what happened to you?" Jimmy asked, inspecting Mitch's face.

"It's a long story, Jimmy, and one that I'd rather not share right now. I really just want to hang out here for a little while, ok?"

Jimmy nodded, understanding that Mitch must have something he needed to sort out himself. "That's fine, Mitch, you just stay as long as you need to."

"Hey Jimmy? I really don't want anyone to know I'm here, ok? I just want to stay in the office tonight."

Jimmy nodded and walked away.

Mitch sat down at the desk and tried to do some paperwork, but he couldn't concentrate. His mind kept going back to Dana. Why wasn't this working, he thought. Work always took his mind off whatever his troubles were. But not tonight, the night he needed it the most.

I arrived back home and picked up the phone, carefully dialing Mitch's number. It rang once, then again, and still a third time. Finally, I heard his voice on the answering machine. I knew it wasn't him in person, but my heart melted just the same.

"Hey, this is Mitch. Leave me a message and I'll get back to you."

I hung up the phone. He wasn't going to answer, so leaving a message probably wouldn't matter, anyway.

Mitch was sitting silently in the office, still trying to focus on the paperwork, when Kayla appeared at the door.

"Why, hello there, Mitch!" She said. "What are you doing here? You aren't supposed to be working on your birthday!"

Mitch didn't want to be rude, but he also didn't want her to see the evidence of his earlier battle either, so he opened a drawer and pretended to be searching for something.

"Hi Kayla," he said, not looking up, trying not to sound distressed. "Just wanted to check in, that's all."

Kayla had entered the office now and was standing next to the desk. "So, now, how's that new little fiancé of yours?" She inquired.

"Not sure." He answered.

Kayla was too perceptive for Mitch. She knew that something wasn't right. "Mitch, what happened?" She asked.

Mitch slowly looked up at Kayla, and a look of shock came over her face. "Good lands of mercy, boy, what happened to you?"

Mitch knew he couldn't hide anything from Kayla. "Chris and I had a fight this afternoon, about Dana."

Kayla took a seat on the couch. "Does she know?"

"About the fight, yes. *What* it was about, no." Mitch answered. "I didn't tell her."

Kayla got up and closed the door. "I'm thinking there's a lot more going on here, Mr. Mitchell. Tell old Kayla all about it."

"Kayla, this is one time I really don't want to do that." Mitch answered. "I really need to handle this on my own, ok?"

Kayla could see that he meant what he said. "I can respect that, Mitch. I won't ask any more questions." She got up and walked to the door. "But if you change your mind, I'll be here." Kayla went back into the bistro.

I picked up the phone and tried Mitch's number again. As before, his answering machine picked up. I hung up, realizing it was no use. He was avoiding me. Suddenly, it rang, startling me.

"Dana, honey, this is Kayla."

"Hi Kayla, what's going on?" I tried to sound convincing, but again, I knew Kayla knew me too well.

"Sweetie, I don't know what's going on between you and Mitch, and I won't ask. But I wanted to let you know that he's down here at the bistro, and he seems pretty upset."

I breathed a sigh of relief just knowing where he was. "Kayla, I thought he might be avoiding me. I went to his place and when he didn't answer the door, I came home and tried to call. I got his machine."

Kayla sighed. "Well, like I said, it's none of my business, but maybe you should come down here and talk to him."

I decided that I needed to do just that. "Ok, Kayla I will, but please, don't tell him you talked to me. Or that I'm coming down, ok?"

"I won't say a word, promise."

I dried my eyes and decided to fix my makeup before I went to Gartano's.

Mitch was sitting alone once again, trying to collect his thoughts, when Jimmy came back to the office. "Hey, Mitch, there's a young lady here who says she knows you. You want me to send her away?"

Mitch stood up. His heart leaped. He thought it might be Dana, and Jimmy just wasn't telling him. "No, no Jimmy, that's ok, I'll see her."

He heard Jimmy tell the girl where to go, and a minute later, Mitch got the surprise of his life. The girl wasn't Dana at all. It was Jessica Radcliff, his ex-girlfriend.

"Mitch!" She exclaimed, giving him a hug. Then she looked at him. "Are you ok?"

Mitch didn't know what to say. It had been three years since he had seen her, and she was the last person he expected to see tonight.

"Jessica, what are you doing here?" he asked, not answering her question.

She smiled and walked into the office. "I was in town for the holiday, and my sister told me you own this place now. So, I thought I'd come down and surprise you."

Surprise, Mitch thought, was too light a term. Shock was more like it.

Mitch still wasn't sure what to say, so after a moment of silence, Jessica spoke again.

"I know it's a little late and all, but my family was over earlier and they just went home, so this is the first free moment I had. I thought maybe you and I could go out for a drink or something."

Mitch looked down. "I don't think so. I mean, I really don't drink, remember?"

Jessica smiled. "Still a good boy, huh? Yes, I remember." Then she sat down on the corner of his desk and crossed her legs. "I must say, though, Mitch, even with that black eye, you are still the most handsome man I've ever seen!"

Mitch couldn't help but look at her at that moment. She was just how he remembered her, tall, curvy, and with the most piercing blue eyes of anyone he knew. She had a nice smile, and always dressed in a way that made men admire her. A few years ago, he wouldn't have been able to take his eyes off her. But for some reason, today, she held no appeal for him. His heart belonged to Dana, even if she didn't want to take it.

"It was nice of you to stop by, Jess, but I'm really kind of busy right now, and we'll be closing soon." Mitch said, trying to get rid of her.

"Now, Mitch, I came all the way down here just to see you. The least you could do is give me a few minutes to catch up."

Mitch sighed, deciding that most likely the only way to get her to leave was going to be to let her stay for a few minutes. He invited her to sit down on the couch, and she did, motioning him to come and sit beside her. Reluctantly, he took a seat next to her, and tried to formulate a plan. Maybe if he led the conversation, he could end it more quickly, so he began to speak.

"I assume you graduated and all, with, uh, what was it, a nursing degree?" Mitch tried to fake his interest.

"Yes, I'm a registered nurse now. I really enjoy it." She put her hand on Mitch's face. "Looks like you could use a nurse right about now!"

Mitch tried to pull away, but Jessica didn't remove her hand. "I just had an accident earlier today, that's all. I had it checked out already." Mitch told her.

Jessica removed her hand and dropped it onto his leg. "So, what have you been up to, besides buying restaurants?"

Mitch started to stand up, but Jessica put her hand on his arm as if to hold him down. He wanted to tell her about Dana, and tell her to go away, but he didn't. His heart was telling him to, but his head was playing tricks on him. Dana didn't want him, or so he thought. It was apparent this girl did.

"Nothing else, really. Just the same old boring stuff. You know me."

Jessica moved closer and her voice softened. "Well, I did, and I would like to again."

Mitch looked at her in disbelief. "What happened to that guy you met in college, what was his name?"

Jessica laughed. "Oh, you mean Jeff? It didn't work out between us. He wanted a commitment, and I'm just not ready to settle down yet. We split about four months ago." She put her hand on Mitch's. "I must be honest, Mitch. I came down here tonight, well, hoping that you and I might be able to pick up where we left off."

Mitch stared at her. Here she was, a woman on the rebound, his for the taking. She was not making any qualms about letting him know that. He thought about Dana again. He knew that he loved her, but what he didn't know anymore was whether or not she loved him.

I got to Gartano's and Kayla met me at the door. "Dana, let me ask you first, girl, are you two ok?"

I looked at her sadly. "I don't know, Kayla. We had a major fight. Things were said, and I don't know where I stand anymore." I swallowed hard, trying not to cry. "I hope I can make it right with him."

Kayla touched my arm. "You want me to go tell him you're here? He's back in the office."

"No, that's ok." I answered. "I'll just go myself."

Mitch decided that he couldn't let this happen. No matter how Dana might feel, his love for her was just too strong. "Look, Jessica, there's something I have to tell you."

Jessica shook her head and moved closer to Mitch. "Don't talk, Mitch." She said. Then she kissed him. Trying to push her away, Mitch placed his hand on Jessica's arm.

I stopped, dead in my tracks, my heart dropping to my knees at the scene before me. I had come here to tell Mitch I loved him, to make things right, but it became apparent to me right then that he had already moved on.

Mitch suddenly became aware that someone was watching, and he turned white as a sheet when he looked up and saw me, my face full of dismay, standing in the doorway.

"Dana!" Mitch said with surprise.

"Mitch," I started, feeling the tears starting to come rolling down my cheeks. "What's going......" I put my hands up as Mitch got up from the couch and started toward me. "Forget it, I don't want to know!" As I turned and ran toward the front door of Gartano's, I heard Mitch call my name, but he didn't follow.

Mitch stopped in the doorway of the office, slamming his hands on either side of the doorjamb. He closed his eyes and clenched his jaw, looking up into the air.

"Who was that, Mitch?" he heard Jessica ask.

Mitch turned around, his eyes still closed and his jaw tight. "That was my fiancé." Mitch replied.

"Mitch, you didn't tell me you were engaged....." Jessica started.

Mitch opened his eyes and glared at her. "I was trying to, but you were too busy coming on to me."

Jessica stood up, and started to walk toward Mitch. "Well, she must not be taking good care of you, Mitchell Tarrington, because you didn't seem to mind much."

Mitch felt himself clench his fists. "Get out, Jessica, now, and don't come back."

Jessica grabbed her coat and stormed past Mitch. He picked up a glass off his desk and threw it as hard as he could at the wall, breaking it into a million pieces. Kayla and Jimmy heard the noise and ran back to him.

"Mitch, what's going on?" Kayla asked. "Did you see Dana?" Then she saw the shattered glass. "Mitch, come on, calm down. What is going on?"

Mitch stood with his hands on his desk, his head down. "Please leave me alone. Just leave me alone."

Jimmy nodded to Kayla and led her back into the bistro to finish closing up.

I somehow made it home, and into my apartment. I threw myself onto the couch and sobbed into the pillows. First Eddie had betrayed me and now Mitch. How could he do this to me? I didn't know who the girl was, but it appeared as if he knew her well. Very well. My heart was aching in a way I had never felt before, and hoped never to feel again. Mitch had made it perfectly clear where we stood. In one day, I had gained and lost everything I was living for. I cried myself to sleep, somehow knowing that I would never see him again.

Mitch couldn't believe what was happening. Dana had come to the bistro to find him, probably hoping to work things out. Instead, she found him with someone else. It was all innocent, he knew, but he was certain of the way it must have appeared to her. Twice in one day he had hurt her more than he felt he could ever make up for. Now he was sure she was gone forever.

The pain Mitch felt was more than he could bear, and he couldn't imagine anything being able to take it away. Then, as if some outside force had control of him at that moment, he looked up and noticed the storage room across from the office. The door was standing open, and he could easily see the shelves where they stored the wine for the restaurant. He put on his coat, and walking across the hallway, he picked up a bottle and placed it in his coat. He thought twice and picked up two more. Then he headed toward the door, not looking at anyone.

"Kayla, tell Jimmy to mark three Chablis off the inventory." And with that he was out the door.

Mitch fumbled up the stairs and into his apartment, closing the door behind him but for some reason neglecting to lock it. He took a glass from the cupboard and walked to the coffee table, placing all three bottles of wine down there. He took off his coat, and sat down on the couch.

Mitch opened the first bottle and with trembling hands, poured some into his glass. He had only drunk wine at his parents' house on holidays, and even then, had rarely finished a full glass. But tonight he knew that the only way to make the pain bearable was to become numb to it. And that was just what he planned to do.

Sighing deeply, he swallowed the first glass quickly, without stopping. He could feel it going down. He didn't especially like the taste of it, but he thought he could tolerate it. He would tolerate it, all of it, until it was gone.

Pouring another glass, Mitch sat back and closed his eyes, replaying the scene in his mind. His poor sweet Dana, how she must have felt, seeing him there with Jessica. Jessica. Why had she come back, anyway? He thought about that. She said she had heard that he'd bought Gartano's. That made sense. Money. All she cared about was money. All Dana had cared about was him. He knew that now, but he also knew that was gone forever.

He poured down the second glass of wine, then a third. It was getting easier. But the pain was still there, so he had to keep going. Leaning forward to pick up the bottle again, he noticed the chain of his watch falling out of his pocket. Placing his glass on the table, he took out the watch and placed it in his hands. His mind went back to the day Dana had given it to him, and how touched he was by her thoughtfulness. He remembered the love in her eyes as he'd kissed her that night. He couldn't fight the pain any longer, and he could feel the tears starting to come. He laid the watch on the table, picked up his glass again, filled it and poured it down.

Before long, Mitch had finished the first bottle of wine and a good portion of the second. He wasn't feeling much now, but every time he closed his eyes he saw Dana, so he kept pouring glass after glass. He thought he heard the phone ring, but he wasn't sure, so he didn't answer it. He didn't care who it was, because he knew it wouldn't be her.

Mitch heard someone knock on his door. He didn't move. He didn't want to see anyone right now. He wanted to be alone, just to keep drinking and drinking until Dana's memory was gone. The caller knocked again, and still, Mitch didn't get up from the couch. He closed his eyes once more until he heard them walk away.

The second bottle almost gone, Mitch could barely see enough to start opening the third, but somehow he managed. He poured another drink. His hands were shaking, and he wasn't getting it all in the glass now, but he was still getting enough. He couldn't tell anymore what it tasted like, and again, it didn't matter.

Across town, Chris was awakened by the phone. He looked at the clock, and wondered who would be calling him at almost one in the morning. He answered, and a somewhat, but not closely, familiar voice was on the other line.

"Chris, this is Jimmy Gartano, Mitch's partner at the bistro. I'm calling because I'm concerned about Mitch."

Chris sat bolt upright in bed. "What do you mean, Jimmy, what's wrong?"

"He came into the bistro earlier, and he looked like he'd been beaten up."

"Oh, that. That was my doing. Long story, but we actually got into a fist to cuff yesterday. Thank you for your concern, but he's fine."

"No, Chris, wait, that's not all." Jimmy continued. "He was acting very strangely when he came in here, and he was alone. Dana came in a little later, but she ran out crying. When Mitch left, he took three bottles of wine with him. I know he's not a drinking man, and it worried me. I tried to call and I also went over there, but he didn't answer. That's when I thought I should call you."

Chris was trying to make sense of what Jimmy was saying. "So, he wouldn't tell you what happened?"

"No, just told me and Kayla he wanted to be left alone. I've never seen him this upset about anything."

"Ok, Jimmy, I'll go over there and check on him. Thanks for letting me know."

Chris hung up the phone, and jumped up to get dressed. "Chris, what's wrong?" Trudy asked, turning on the lamp.

"That was Jimmy Gartano. Said Mitch came in there tonight and was pretty upset, something about Dana running out in tears, and then Mitch left with three bottles of wine."

"You don't suppose he was going to get drunk, do you Chris?"

"I don't know but I'm going to go to his place and find out. Call Paul and Jim and have them meet me there."

"Ok, honey. Should I call Dana?" Trudy asked.

Chris thought for a moment. "No, not until I find out what's going on."

Chris got to Mitch's apartment about the same time as the others and filled them in on what Jimmy had told him. They ran up the stairs and pounded on the door.

"Mitchell, it's Chris!" He called out. "Open up, buddy!"

Mitch was still managing somehow to down the wine. He had finished two bottles completely and was just starting the third. Chris called out again. Mitch didn't want to see his brother. He didn't want to see anyone but Dana. But he knew that wasn't going to happen.

Paul tried the door and much to their surprise, they found it unlocked and went in. Chris put up his hands to keep the others back, and he walked up to Mitch.

"Mitchell, what are you doing?" He tried to take the glass from Mitch's hand, but Mitch pulled away and drank it down.

"Go away, Chris, I want to be by myself ....right now." Mitch was clutching the watch once again, and a tear fell down his cheek.

Jim walked over to him, Paul right behind. Jim started to pick up the rest of the wine, and Mitch grabbed his hand. "Don't touch it, leave it right there." He said, firmly.

Jim looked at the other two. "No, Mitch, come on, let me have it. You've had enough." He slowly picked up the bottle and handed it to Paul, who took the rest and poured it down the sink.

Paul and Chris sat down on either side of Mitch, Jim on the coffee table facing him. Jim reached out and took off his glasses. He pulled down his eyelids and taking his chin in his hand, moved his head from side to side, still looking into his eyes. He put his glasses back on him and sighed deeply.

"Stop it, Jim, I don't need a doctor. What I need is what you just poured out."

Chris looked at Jim. "He seems pretty wasted. I'm surprised he's as coherent as he still is with as much as he's drank."

Jim looked back at him. "Actually, he was probably not feeling much after about three or four glasses, being that he's not used to this. But, it's not unusual. It'll probably just hit him all at once. Besides, he could be fighting the effects if he's really upset."

"You know, I'm sitting right here. I know you're talking about me." Mitch said.

Jim folded his hands and looked at Mitch. "Mitchell, do you want to tell us why you felt it necessary to do this? Did something happen between you and Dana?"

The pain Mitch thought had become numb was still there, burning in his heart. He looked at Jim, then at Chris and Paul, before dropping his eyes.

Chris put his hand on his brother's arm. "Come on, buddy, tell us about it, ok?"

"I only wanted to show her I loved her, that's all. I got mad and I said things I shouldn't have said. Then, at the bistro, she saw us....I didn't do anything with Jessica, I didn't Chris, I didn't do anything. I love Dana, please tell her I love her."

Jim realized that the alcohol was starting to take over. He reached out to check Mitch's pulse, nodding to the others that he seemed to be ok. "Mitch, how are you feeling? Do you feel sick at all?"

"I made her cry, I didn't mean to hurt her. I love her so much. Please tell her I love her, just her. Please tell her."

Jim placed his hand on Mitch's leg reassuringly. "She knows that, Mitch. You can tell her, ok?"

Mitch shook his head, the tears flowing like a river down both cheeks. "No, I can't. I hurt her. She doesn't love me anymore."

Jim didn't know what to say. His heart was aching for Mitch. He seemed to be hurting so deeply. Whatever had happened after they left the gathering at Jake and Olivia's must have been more than Mitch felt he could handle on his own.

"Let's try to get him into bed, guys." He said, standing up. "He'll be more comfortable there."

Jim and Chris got on either side of Mitch, and Paul walked behind, helping him get to the bedroom. Mitch wasn't resisting them now, his fight was gone, and was trying his best to walk, but between the liquor and his wounded knee, it just wasn't going very well. Suddenly, Mitch looked at Chris, his face very pale.

"Christopher, I...I don't feel so good....right now."

Chris looked at Mitch and then at the others. "Mitch, what's wrong? What do you mean?"

"Well, I kinda have to go to the bathroom," he said, and then Mitch placed his hand on his stomach. "And I mean I really...don't feel...so good, either."

The three knew that Mitch meant he was going to be sick, so they got him into the bathroom just in time. Everything being taken care of, they helped him back up, and got him into his bedroom. Without even undressing him, they put him into bed.

Chris looked down lovingly and touched his younger brother on the top of the head. "It's ok, Mitchell, everything is going to be ok. You sleep now. You need to rest."

Mitch struggled to sit up. "I can't sleep, Chris. I don't want to sleep. What I need is another drink." He said as he tried to get up.

Paul and Jim took him by the arms. Jim gently took off his glasses and laid them on the nightstand.

"Well," Mitch said. "Why did you do that? Now I can't see anything."

Jim couldn't help but smile a little. "Mitch, you don't need to see anything. You need to sleep. You are staying right here."

Mitch was starting to cry again. "But....it hurts....so much. I want another drink!"

Chris sat down on the edge of the bed. "You aren't getting anything else to drink, Mitch. You've already had a lot more than what you need."

Mitch's tone grew angry. "How do you know what I need? You don't know how I feel!"

Chris had to bite his lip to hold back his own tears. He had never seen Mitch like this before, and it was killing him. "No, Mitch, you're right. I don't know how you feel, but I do know that alcohol isn't the answer. I want you to settle down now and just rest. We'll be right here."

Mitch wiped his eyes and tried to look at Chris, but he was nothing but a blur. "I really hurt her, Chris. I never wanted to hurt her. I love her." And with those words, Mitch passed out.

Chris looked at Jim. "Is he going to be ok? Should we take him to the hospital or something?"

"He is pretty wasted, no doubt, but getting sick that time probably helped get some of it out of him."

"Well," Chris said, "actually about three times. That's what took us so long in there."

"Even better." Jim said. "You guys go on out, and I'll take a look at him."

After checking him over, and concluding that he didn't feel Mitch was in any danger, he joined the others back in the living room. "He's pretty drunk, as if we didn't know that already. But, I think once he sleeps this off, he'll be fine."

"He's not going to feel very well when he wakes up, either." Paul said. "Been down that road a couple of times myself."

"Yeah, I called it freshman year in college." Chris said. "Looking back now, I don't know why I did that."

The three of them took turns sitting in the room with Mitch, in case he got sick or woke up. Mitch seemed restless after a while, and kept saying Dana's name. Chris decided it was time to let her know what was happening.

He looked in Mitch's address book. Knowing how organized Mitch usually was, he assumed her number would be written there, even though he probably now knew it by heart. Dana's heart skipped a beat when she heard the phone, and it startled her out of her dreams of Mitch.

"Hello?" I said sleepily.

"Dana, it's Chris. I'm at Mitch's and I need you to come over here right away."

I didn't know what to think. "Chris, what's wrong? Is Mitch ok, did something happen to him?"

"Just come over, Dana, be careful, but hurry. I'll explain when you get here."

Even though Mitch only lived about ten blocks from me, it was late so I took a cab over to be safe, and once at his building, I ran up the stairs. Not bothering to knock, I went in. Jim and Chris were sitting in the living room and Chris came to me as I walked in. I was trembling, my heart pounding wildly. "Chris, what's going on? Is Mitch ok?"

Chris took my hand and led me over to the couch. "Dana, I don't know what happened after you left my parents', but whatever it was, Mitch decided that it was bad enough that he needed to get drunk."

I couldn't believe what Chris was saying. "What do you mean, drunk, Chris? Mitch doesn't even drink!"

"Well, I know that, but Jimmy called and said something about an incident at Gartano's, Mitch leaving with three bottles of wine, and not being able to reach him, so we came over here to see what was going on. By the time we got here, he pretty much had two bottles down and the third ready and waiting."

I looked at Chris as if his words weren't real, as if I were having a bad dream. I hoped I was and would soon wake up. I stood staring at Chris in disbelief, then looked at the others, as if hoping one of them would tell me it was a joke. No one said a word.

"Dana," Chris started, "I know my little brother well, and he doesn't do anything without a reason." Chris paused and looked at me deeper, as if searching for an answer. "I'm guessing whatever happened was something that caused him a lot of pain, pain that he felt he just couldn't deal with any other way."

I looked away from Chris to the ceiling and began to cry. A rerun of the evening's events was being played in my mind. I could feel the pain coming back and I tried to fight it but I couldn't. Jim sat down across from me on the coffee table, and both men took me by the hand.

"Dana, it's alright," Jim said softly, looking at me sympathetically. "Mitch is pretty messed up right now, but one thing he keeps saying is that he hurt you. How did Mitch hurt you?"

I choked back the tears and tried to speak. "We had a terrible fight. He accused me of not loving him, of only wanting to marry him for his money. He said a lot of cruel things to me. He was very angry with me, and I was hurt and angry myself, so I left."

Chris sighed deeply. "Dana, I don't believe Mitch would go to this extreme just over an argument. He has more sense than that."

I took another deep breath. "That's not the end of it, Chris." I continued. "I came back thinking we could try to work it out, but Mitch didn't answer when I knocked. So, I went home and called, but still nothing. Then, Kayla called and said that he was at the bistro, and he seemed upset. But when I went there to talk to him, I found him in the office......kissing another woman!"

The two men looked at each other in disbelief. "Dana, are you sure of what you saw? That doesn't sound like something Mitch would ever do." Jim said.

I looked at him squarely in the eyes. "Well, getting drunk isn't something Mitch would ever do, either, Jim, and he's done that, hasn't he?" I paused and rubbed my forehead, trying to collect my thoughts. "When he didn't get what he wanted from me, he found someone who would give it to him. Maybe the wine was just a part of his evening with her."

Chris turned back to me. "Get what from you Dana? Did you and Mitch...... did he try to......"

I looked at him. "Yes, Chris, he did try and no, we didn't, but he wanted to. Believe me, he wanted to. He kept saying he loved me and wanted to "prove" it. I told him no, that I wanted to wait until we were married and that was what started the whole argument. I can't believe Mitch would resort to this, just because I wouldn't sleep with him."

Just then, a thought crossed Jim's mind. "Dana, did Mitch know you saw him with this other woman?"

I nodded. "Yes, he saw me. He looked directly at me. As I was leaving the bistro, I heard him call after me, but I didn't turn around, and he didn't follow."

Jim looked at Chris and he nodded, as if it was finally all making sense. "Dana, Mitch didn't get drunk because you wouldn't sleep with him, or because he wanted to sleep with someone else." Chris said. "He got drunk because he thought he'd lost you. He couldn't stand the pain of losing the woman that he loves."

I looked at both of them just then, and they were both looking as if they had figured out the biggest secret in the world. But I wasn't so sure I believed it myself. I dropped my eyes from theirs. "You're wrong, both of you are wrong." I looked down at my ring at that moment. "He may have loved me once, but not anymore. If he does, why would he have been there, kissing her?"

Chris remembered something Mitch had said as they had been trying to talk to him. "He didn't do anything, Dana. Trust me, he didn't do anything wrong."

I glared at Chris. "What, have you suddenly gained psychic powers or something, Chris? How do you know that? How can you say that when you weren't even there?"

Chris sighed heavily and taking my hand again, he looked directly into my eyes. "Because of something Mitch said earlier. He said nothing happened with Jessica, that he didn't do anything wrong. I thought it was just the liquor talking, that he meant he didn't do anything when he and Jessica were *dating*, that maybe he was mixed up. Now it makes sense to me. Evidently, the girl who was there tonight was Jessica. I don't know why she'd be there, but it doesn't matter. He said he didn't do anything with her, and he meant tonight, Dana." Chris stood up, reaching for me, and I stood up next to him. He turned me to face him. "The one thing my little brother is not, is a liar. If he said he didn't do anything, he's telling the truth. And he also said, more than once, that he loves you and *only* you. He's telling the truth about that, and I believe him, Dana. You should, too."

I looked at the men and shook my head. "How can I? For crying out loud, Chris, he was with another woman. He cheated on me, just like Eddie!"

Chris took my hand once more. "No, Dana, he didn't. Trust me, he didn't." Then he took my face and turned it so our eyes met. "Dana, I know that a part of you is comparing this to the pain you felt in the past. But you can't punish one man for the crimes of another. Mitch loves you, and only you." I could feel the tears rolling down my cheeks as Chris spoke to me once again. "I know a lot has happened tonight, but it's nothing that can't be fixed. Do you want to fix it, Dana?"

I let the words Chris had said sink into my heart, and I nodded. "I just don't know how."

Jim stood up next to Chris, and each one gave me a hug. Then Chris spoke again. "All you have to do is love him Dana, make sure he knows that you do. You are the most important thing in the world to Mitch. Make sure he knows you feel the same about him."

I nodded again. "I will."

Chris and Jim led me to the bedroom where Mitch was sleeping. I could quickly see he wasn't resting well, and even though asleep, I could see the sadness on his face. Paul had been nodding off in a corner chair, and he got up when I entered the room.

"Hey, Dana." He said softly, giving me a peck on the cheek.

"How is he, is he going to be ok?" I asked, my voice full of concern.

Paul smiled reassuringly. "He won't feel much like doing anything later, I can bet. He drank about two bottles, by *himself*, and that's a lot. He's guaranteed to have one whopper of a headache, and he may even get sick a time or two more. But, this too shall pass, and he'll be just fine in the end, I promise."

"Can I go to him, Paul? Is it ok?" I hesitated.

Paul patted my arm. "He's not dying, Dana, he's just drunk. And besides, he's been asking for you."

I looked at Paul. "Asking for me?"

"Yes, ever since we got here, he keeps asking us to tell you he loves you. Go let him tell you himself."

Jim put his hand on my shoulder. "If you can help it, Dana, it's probably best not to wake him up. Just let him sleep this off, and then he'll be coherent enough to talk to you in the morning. If you need us, we'll be just outside, ok?"

I nodded and the three of them left the room. Walking slowly over to Mitch, and bending down, I softly kissed his cheek. I began to run my fingers through his hair, remembering how I had done the same thing the day he'd fallen asleep on my couch. Mitch seemed to be trying to say something, even though he was still sound asleep, and his face looked troubled. His eyelashes were still wet with tears, and gently, I wiped them away. I kissed him again on the forehead.

"Hush, now, sweetie, I'm here. Everything's going to be ok." Not wanting to leave him, I crawled up onto the bed next to him, and put my arms around him, laying my head on his chest. Soon, I too was fast asleep, next to the man I loved more than anything.

A few minutes later, Chris slipped back in. "Dana? Is everything....." Chris smiled at the scene before him. Quietly, he pulled the blanket off the chair that Paul had been using and covered Dana. He exited the room, closing the door behind him.

"Dana?" The sound of Mitch's voice awoke me. I opened my eyes, realizing it was morning and that I had slept through the night next to him.

I lifted my head from his chest and smiled. "Good morning, handsome."

Mitch had a puzzled look on his face. "How long have you been here? And how..." He grabbed his head, and groaned, as if it were hurting. "How did I get in here?"

I smiled, realizing that he probably didn't remember much of anything from the night before. "I've been here all night. And the guys put you to bed."

Mitch still looked confused. Then he got a funny look on his face, and stared at me. "Dana, why are you in my bed with me? Did we.... uh, I mean, did you and I......"

I smiled brightly at him, deciding to make light of the situation. "Well, technically, we *did* sleep together, but no, sweetheart, we didn't do anything."

Mitch reached for his glasses, his hands trembling, and placed them back on. He managed a weak smile and reached out to touch my face. "It really is you," He said softly. "I thought I was dreaming."

I smiled at him. "No, I'm really here." Mitch's eyes were full of sadness and what I guessed to be fear.

"Are you going to leave again?" he asked.

I hugged him tightly, trying to keep my tears from coming. "No, honey, no, I won't ever leave you, I promise." I looked into his eyes. "I love you too much to ever do that."

Mitch held me tightly to him, pressing his face into my hair. "I was so afraid.....so afraid that I would never see you again, Dana. That I would never hold you or touch you or kiss you again. I couldn't stand it, Dana, I just couldn't stand the thought of that." Even though I wasn't looking at him, I could hear in his voice that he was crying.

I sat up a little and touched his face, wiping away the tears. "You don't have to be afraid anymore, Mitchell. I'm not going anywhere. It's ok now." I kissed him softly and I could see him smile. "How are you feeling?" I asked.

"My head really hurts, Dana. I've never had a headache like this before."

I smiled. "Well, sweetie, I think this is what they call a hangover."

Mitch sat up a little more and I propped the pillow behind him. His face suddenly grew very pale. "Oh, no, please, no." He said.

I sat up and looked at him. "What, honey, what is it?"

Mitch pointed to the trash can sitting by his dresser. I leapt up and grabbed it, just in time.

I retrieved a cool washcloth and some mouthwash, per Mitch's request, put a fresh bag in the trashcan, and returned to Mitch. Jim and Chris were sitting with him now, and Jim was giving him a quick check-over.

"Hey guys," I said. "Where's Paul?"

Chris chuckled. "Let's just say this really is a bachelor pad. Not a thing around here worth eating, and nothing to cook, for sure. We sent him out for some donuts."

Mitch closed his eyes and took a deep breath. "Please don't mention food around me, ok?" We all chuckled. "I feel absolutely horrible." Mitch groaned. "I could never be a wino. How do people actually enjoy this?"

Jim laughed. "Well, I think winos are winos because they have acquired the ability to hold their liquor. I don't think you have anything to worry about." Mitch managed a smirk.

I looked at Mitch and noticed that the rim of his glasses was bent. I reached over and took them off. "Honey, did you know you're glasses are bent?"

"Blame that on Chris." He said wryly, giving his brother a look. Chris smiled back.

"Ok, Mitch, I want you to look right at my finger and follow it with your eyes, ok?" Jim instructed.

"Well, I would do that if I could *see* your finger, Jim," Mitch said sarcastically. "Dana took my glasses."

Noticing Mitch's attitude returning, almost in unison, the two men said, "He's fine!" and laughing, started walking toward the door. Nodding, I jumped up and starting walking with them.

"Hey," Mitch exclaimed, "where's everyone going?"

"You don't need us anymore." I said, glancing back over my shoulder.

"Wait," he said. "There is one more thing I need you guys to help me do." Mitch said, attempting to sit on the edge of the bed.

"What's that?" Jim asked.

"I'm not so sure I can stand up on my own, and, well, I could really use some help getting to the bathroom. I really gotta go!" Jim and Chris chuckled.

I smiled. "I think I'll let you guys deal with that."

Mitch was still a bit unsteady on his feet, but by the time he reemerged, he seemed to be doing a little better. He was walking slowly, but on his own. He flopped back down on the bed.

I sat back down beside him. "Mitch, would you like anything? Some hot tea maybe? It might help settle your stomach a little."

Mitch smiled and took my hand. "My sweet Dana, always taking care of me, aren't you?" Then he nodded. "I guess it wouldn't hurt to give it a try."

I left the room and went out into the kitchen to make him a cup of tea. Chris decided he would go and check on his brother once again. "Hey, little brother, feeling any better?" He sat down next to Mitch, and patted him on the hand.

"Other than the fact that I think I'm about to die, I feel pretty good." Mitch smirked.

Chris laughed. "Yeah, I know, buddy, I've been there. It's not fun." Chris turned to face his brother and looked at him squarely in the eyes. "Mitch, you really had me scared when I got here."

Mitch put his hand on Chris's arm, as if to reassure him, but his face was serious.

"No, Chris, I was the one who was scared. I thought I'd lost her forever."

Chris smiled. "I know, but she's back now and you need to make it right with her. She's special, Mitchell, don't let her get away again." Mitch bit his lip and just nodded.

"And," Chris added, standing up, "the next time you feel that down, you call me, and I'll be there for you, ok? Don't ever feel like you have to turn to a bottle to take the pain away."

"Chris, thanks. I......"

Chris smiled knowingly. "Yeah, Mitch, me too."

8

I brought a cup of tea for Mitch and put it down on the nightstand. "I was going to bring a donut, too, but I didn't think you would want it just yet."

Mitch smiled. "Right about that. You could have one though. I wouldn't mind."

I smiled. "I already had mine in the kitchen, well, I actually had two." I confessed.

Mitch was smiling at me, just staring at my face. He pulled me down to him again, and closed his eyes, breathing in deeply. "Dana, I am so very sorry. I don't think I will ever be able to tell you just how sorry I am."

I brought my hand up and put it on his mouth. "It's forgotten, Mitch. Don't say anymore."

Mitch gently took my hand away. "No, Dana, let me say what I have to say, alright?

I nodded and Mitch continued. "Dana, I should have never let things get to the point they did last night. I should never have tried to force myself on you, especially after you told me how you felt. I was being selfish and inconsiderate. I know I said a lot of things that hurt you, baby, and I will forever hate myself for making you cry. You don't know how that cut through me."

I looked into his eyes, still sad but yet full of love. I didn't speak, I just wanted to let him know I was there, listening to him.

"More than that, Dana, is that I hate myself for the scene at the bistro. I do want you to know that nothing happened, absolutely nothing. Please believe that. I didn't know Jessica was going to show up, and I definitely didn't want her there. I tried to make her leave, but she wouldn't go."

I didn't want Mitch to get upset, but I had to ask the question that was prying on my mind. "Mitchell, if nothing happened, then why were you kissing her?"

He sighed deeply and dropped his head. He closed his eyes, then opened them again and looked at me, placing a hand on each shoulder so I was facing him.

"I didn't kiss her, Dana, she kissed me. I didn't plan it and I didn't expect it. It just happened. I was trying to push her away, and that's when you showed up." Mitch sighed again. "I can only imagine what it looked like to you but I swear, upon my life and everything I am, nothing happened."

"When I saw you there with her, Mitch, I thought maybe you had found someone who would give you what I wouldn't. It tore me apart."

Mitch bit his lip again, and his face was sympathetic. "Dana, I won't lie to you and tell you that I couldn't have had her. She was willing, and she was right there for the taking. I looked at her, Dana, and she was just how I remembered her, but there was nothing there. Not even a spark, nothing. I'm not out for cheap thrills, Dana. When I make love for the first time, I want it to be based on true love. You are the *only* woman that can give me that." Mitch looked at me again, a very serious look upon his face. "Dana, I don't know if I can ever make up for the things I said and for what I put you through. All I could think about last night was that I had promised never to hurt you, and I broke that promise. That pain, coupled with the feeling that I'd lost you forever, was too much for me to bear."

"And that's why you got drunk?" I asked.

Mitch nodded. "Stupid thing to do, I know, but I just can't stand the thought of ever living without you, not even for a moment. I love you more than anything on this earth, and I promise, I will never, ever hurt you like that again."

"I believe you, Mitch, and I love you, too."

"One last thing." Mitch started. "I will never make you do anything you aren't comfortable with, or ready, to do. You have my word." Then he smiled at me, looking me up and down. "I can't say that I won't try, because, you are just so...darn... sexy, but I will never make you. Ok?"

"Ok." I answered. "But, can I say just one thing?"

"Absolutely." He said smiling.

"I know sometimes it's going to be hard to fight the passion we share, and it's even ok to let it sweep us off our feet at times. But, until we're married, we have to know just how far we can go, and when to stop. Mitch, my wanting to wait doesn't mean I don't love you, or that I don't find you desirable, because I do. More than you know. And believe it or not, sometimes it's just as hard for me to resist as it is for you. But, I want our first time together to be special, and I know that waiting will make it all that much sweeter."

Mitch smiled at me lovingly. "I respect that, love. And you have my word that I will do my best to control myself." Then he looked at me again, raising his eyebrows. "But you are just so darn sexy!"

Suddenly, something struck me and I giggled, looking at him from top to bottom.

"What's so funny?" Mitch said, chuckling himself.

"I was just looking at you and thinking that this is what I have to look forward to seeing every morning for the rest of my life!"

Mitch laughed. "Now, wait a minute! Here I just told you how sexy you are and what do I get? I get made fun of." Then he reached out for me, still smiling. "I know, sweetheart, I gotta look pretty bad right now, huh? Well, when I get a little more steady on my feet, I will gladly shower and shave for you. But, for now, I'm afraid this is what you get."

I leaned over and kissed his cheek. "It's alright, I'll take it." He grabbed my hand. "Does your head still hurt? I know Jim gave you some aspirin earlier." I asked.

He nodded. "Yes, it still does. Dana, how could I have been so stupid to do this to myself?"

"I don't know, Mitch." I answered. "I don't think people really stop to consider the consequences of their actions when they're in certain frames of mind." Mitch had closed his eyes again. "Sweetie, do you want to sleep?" I asked softly. "I can go out into the living room and leave you alone."

He shook his head. "No, please stay."

"Ok, Mitch, I'll stay right here with you. I won't go anywhere." I promised.

The guys popped back in. "I think it's safe for us to go home now, folks." Jim said. "If you need anything, don't hesitate to call, ok?"

Mitch opened his eyes and smiled. "Hey, thanks, guys, I owe you one. Big time."

The three of them smiled. "Don't think twice about it," Jim said. "That's what it means to be family."

I walked the guys out and returned to Mitch, who was now curled up under the covers, hugging the pillow next to him. I wondered why he was doing that, but figured it was probably just another Mitchism. Crawling up beside him again, I just sat there, watching him. Once certain that he was asleep, I slipped off the bed and decided to be inquisitive. I wanted to see more of what Mitchell Tarrington was all about. I felt a little guilty at first, but it wasn't really snooping, I told myself. I was just acquainting myself with my future husband's territory.

I started at Mitch's closet. Pretty organized for a guy, I thought. Everything hung up neatly, shoes all lined up in the bottom. My gosh, I thought. He even has his shirts lined up according to type and color. All blue dress shirts, then white, then plaid. Next his polo shirts, tee shirts, sweatshirts, etc. He would flip if he saw my closet, I thought. Guess I'd have to work on that.

I moved from the closet to his dresser. First drawer. Should I be doing this, I thought. I looked at Mitch, still sleeping like a baby. Like a thief in the night, I returned to my work. I opened the drawer. Socks. Pretty boring, so I moved on. Next drawer was summer shorts, then sweats. Wait, I missed one, and there was only one thing I hadn't found yet. I opened the drawer slowly. Just as I suspected. Mitch's underwear. Oh, interesting, I thought, boxers. So he's a boxer man. I slowly took a pair out of the drawer, and I couldn't help but try to picture him in them. Adorable, no doubt. Just then, the sound of laughter startled me from my vision, and I turned to see Mitch, sitting up in bed, watching me and laughing with all he had.

"Find something interesting?" he said, trying to catch his breath.

I threw the boxers back in the drawer and slammed it shut. "No, I was, uh, just, I mean....."

Mitch was smiling at me and still laughing. "You were snooping in my drawers is what you were doing."

"I was not, Mitchell Tarrington!" I said stubbornly. "I was, uh, dusting!" I wiped my hand across his dresser and pretended to blow off the dust.

Mitch was giving me his playful look and his eyes were shining again. I was glad to see he was coming around. Still laughing, he said, "I don't think you need my underwear for that, do you?"

I could feel the blush rising in my cheeks and I looked down. "I told you I was dusting. They were lying on the floor and I was, uh, putting them back." I slowly looked up at Mitch, grinning at me from ear to ear. I could tell he wasn't buying a thing I was saying.

"Now, come on, Dana," he coaxed. "I don't usually keep my underwear lying around on the floor. I know you were wondering what I look like in those, now weren't you?"

I could tell I was blushing again, and I looked away. "Mitch, stop it!" I said sternly.

Mitch was still smiling. He patted the bed next to him. "Come on over here, now. Come on."

"No, I think I would like a cup of tea. I think I'll go get myself one." I started toward the door.

"Dana, I'm still too woozy to get up and come after you. Now, listen to me and come here." Mitch was using his soft but authoritative voice. I didn't look at him but took my place on the side of the bed. I thought I'd try to change the subject.

"It's Christmas, Mitch! I just remembered. Merry Christmas, honey!" I chimed.

Mitch smirked at me. "It's not working, my love. Tell me what you were doing, and tell me the *truth* this time." He was trying to sound disciplinary.

I pretended to pout, and then I thought, I'll just tell him what I told myself. "I was just acquainting myself with my future husband's territory." I said, matter-of-factly.

He chuckled. "Well, I guess that's ok, as long as you weren't snooping." He reached up and tousled my hair. "But, you didn't make it to the most important drawer in the room."

I looked at him curiously. "Which one would that be?"

He reached over and patted the nightstand. I looked at him and smiled.

"Oh, go on, might as well. You've seen everything else I own anyway!"

I eagerly pulled open the drawer. Inside was a candy bar wrapper, the instruction manual for his stereo system, a few receipts, and a bookmark. Nothing too exciting. I looked at Mitch. He was smirking again. Then I pulled out a copy of the sports magazine swimsuit issue. I looked at him with a glare, and he just raised his eyebrows impishly.

"Mitchell Tarrington, what are you doing with this?" I asked firmly.

He raised his eyebrows again. "Then one might ask why you have a Chippendale calendar on the back of the closet door in your hallway." Then he smiled. "I acquaint myself with things, too, you know." He folded his arms and smirked again. I stuck my tongue out at him.

"My sweet Dana," he said, "you are really something else." Then he smiled. "I wonder what my mother would say if I told her my fiancé saw my underwear?"

I giggled. "Probably the same thing she'd say if you told her we slept in the same bed all night!"

We both laughed. "Well, Dana, I think it's time to get out of this bed again."

I looked at him with concern. "Why, honey, are you sick again?

"Not yet, but I did drink two full bottles and, well....."

"Oh, gotcha." I smiled and helped Mitch to his feet. "Let me walk with you, just in case you start feeling unsteady again."

"Ok, sweetheart, I can take it from here." Mitch said, stepping inside the bathroom and letting go of me. "Don't go anywhere." He closed the door and I turned around to iook at a picture on the wall. It was of two young boys, their arms around each others' shoulders, one holding a baseball, the other a mitt. I smiled. I had always wondered what it would have been like to grow up with a houseful of siblings. Mitch had been given that privilege. Just then, he came out of the bathroom.

"That's me and Chris, I was about 8, he was 15." Mitch said. "He's the one that taught me how to throw a ball."

"That's nice, Mitch." I said. "I wish I would have had a brother or a sister."

Mitch put his back to the wall to steady himself, and then pulled me to him. "You do now, sweetheart. You have a family now." I knew he meant his family. And I smiled.

Mitch decided he didn't want to lie down anymore, so we went into the living room and sat down together on the couch. It was starting to snow, and we sat in the silence for a short time watching it fall through the window. He was the first to speak.

"Hey, baby, I know you've been here for a while, and I was thinking you might want to go home and freshen up a little. If you do, it's ok. I'm doing ok now, except for a bit of a headache."

"But I don't want to leave you, Mitch. I just want to be here with you." I said.

He laid his head on mine. "I know, and I want to be with you, too. Want me to go with you?"

I looked up at him. "I don't think you should, Mitch. I mean, you've had a pretty rough night, and you aren't feeling well."

"Dana, I have a hangover. Whether I stay here, or whether I venture to your place, I'm still going to feel the same. I think the worst is over.

My stomach has finally settled down, thank goodness. Besides, I should try to move around and work the rest of this out of me."

"No, honey, I don't think you should walk that far, not today." I protested.

"Who said anything about walking?" Mitch said with surprise. "I have a car, remember?"

I turned around and shot him a shocked look. "Mitchell Tarrington, you are *not* driving that car in your condition."

Mitch laughed. "Dana, I'm sober now. I think that's the correct condition to drive in, last time I checked. Besides, again, you assume I'm talking about myself driving."

My eyes opened wide. "You mean *me*? You want me to drive?"

He smiled. "Sure. You know how, don't you?"

"Of course, I know how. It's just been a while, that's all. I never got a car when I moved here because, well, I just couldn't afford it, actually. But I drove Eddie's sometimes."

"Well, future Mrs. Mitchell Tarrington, that is all about to change. I don't want you taking the bus or a taxi everywhere you go from now on. I am going to have a key made for you first thing tomorrow, and whenever you need to go somewhere that you don't want, or can't, walk to, you are going to take the car. Got it?" He was being authoritative again.

I tried to protest. "Mitch, I can't, I ...."

He leaned up and put his hand over my mouth, as I had done to him earlier. "Why not, Dana? We're going to be married. I want to share everything I have with you. Besides, you take care of me, now let me take care of you."

I was still trying to protest. "That is a very expensive car, Mitchell. What if I have an accident?"

Mitch pondered the thought for a moment. "Well, that would be very unfortunate and I would be upset, but you are forgetting one important element. It's only a car, and I'm a rich man. I can just buy another one!" He laughed.

"Oh, you!" I said, hitting him with a pillow. He threw it back at me.

"Now, my love, if you'll excuse me for just a few minutes, I'm going to go attempt a shower, and shave, if I can get my hands to steady enough." Mitch slowly got up, but when he turned around to start down the hallway, he stopped and put his hand on the back of the couch.

"Mitch, what's wrong? Are you ok?" I asked, standing up.

"Just fine, sweetheart. I just lost my footing a little, that's all. Got up too fast."

I took hold of his arm. "Then sit back down. What if you get into the shower and fall, or something?"

Mitch rubbed my hand which was still resting on his arm. "Tell you what. If it'll make you feel better, I'll take a bath instead. Then neither of us will have to worry about me falling. I just really need to get out of these clothes."

"Ok, but if you need me to help you, I'll be right here." I said, sitting back down.

"I've been bathing for years by myself, Dana. I think I can handle it....unless you *want* to help." Mitch smirked.

"Mitchell, that's *not* what I meant and you know it! Now GO! I'll be waiting right here."

Mitch leaned down and kissed my cheek. "No, you won't." He said, smiling. "You'll be acquainting yourself with more of my possessions." He laughed as the pillow I threw hit him in the back.

I had decided to prove Mitch wrong by staying put on the couch, but there were just too many things to catch my attention. The first thing I noticed was a weight bench sitting in the corner of the room. That brat, I thought. He never told me he lifted weights. But, that would explain the muscular arms and chest. He did seem to be pretty physically fit. I wandered over to his entertainment center to study his music collection. He was right, very diverse. Then I took a look on his bookshelf. Everything from war epics to science fiction and westerns. At least he liked variety, I thought, and that was fine, as long as it was books and music, not women.

I paused to look at a collection of pictures Mitch had hanging on his wall in a collage frame. His sister Julia in her wedding gown, all his nieces and nephews, one of his parents at Christmas. A little boy with what appeared to be his grandfather, eating an ice cream cone. I wondered if that was Mitch and his grandpa. There was another of him and Chris next to Mitch's car, taken obviously not that long ago. More of his sisters, and one of his family together. I thought about my own family. Today was Christmas day, and I couldn't be with them, I couldn't even call them. They would never know I was engaged, they would never meet Mitch, they wouldn't be able to come to my wedding. Some things just didn't seem fair, I thought. He has all these wonderful people to share his life with. All I have is him.

"I'm back. Did you miss me?" I turned to see Mitch, all cleaned up, shaven, and looking as handsome as ever in khakis and a sweater.

I just looked at him. My whole world was standing right in front of me, right now. I couldn't help the tear that ran down my face. Mitch walked over to me, and put his arms around me. He bent down to look into my eyes.

"Didn't miss me that much did you?" He said, trying to get me to smile. "I was only gone for ten minutes." He rubbed my back. "Why the tears, sweetheart?"

I put my head against his chest, and held him tightly. "I was just looking at all your pictures, Mitch." I said softly. "You're so lucky to have all these people in your life."

Mitch bent down to look at me again. "And now, all these people are in your life, too. I told you, sweetheart, you aren't alone anymore. You don't need to be sad." Mitch kissed me and wiped away my tears with his sleeve. "Besides, it's Christmas. And I have something for you." Reaching into his pocket, he pulled out a small box. He handed it to me, and kissed my forehead. "Well, go ahead and open it."

I looked up at him and smiled, then eagerly unwrapped the box. Inside was a beautiful delicate gold ring, with two hearts on top. Inside one heart was my birthstone, and inside the other was his. "Oh, Mitch, it's beautiful!" I exclaimed, and hugged him tightly.

"Look inside." He said, taking the ring out of the box and handing it to me. I slowly turned the ring so that I could see, and inside the band he had inscribed "Mitch & Dana, 10-4-87." The day he first saw me.

"I love it Mitch, thank you!" I kissed him softly. "But I thought my necklace was my Christmas gift."

He smiled lovingly. "Can't a guy buy his fiancé two Christmas gifts? Why don't you put it on and see if it fits?" I slipped the ring on my right hand, and, just like my engagement ring, it fit perfectly. "Now," Mitch said, "wherever you look, you'll be reminded of me."

A thought crossed my mind. "Honey, I love my ring, and I love you for getting it for me. It's so thoughtful. But, I feel badly because I don't have anything to give you today."

Mitch pulled me to him and kissed me with all the strength he had. "Dana, you did give me the best gift I could ever hope for today. You."

Mitch helped me on with my coat and putting on his own, we headed out to his car. Once we got to where it was parked, he handed me the keys.

"Are you sure about this?" I asked again.

"Yes, Dana, I'm sure. Go on and get in now, it's cold out here." I unlocked the doors and we both got in.

"Ok, here goes. Promise you won't be too frightened of my driving. It has been a while." I started the car and Mitch grabbed my hand, deciding he was going to have fun with this.

"Dana, just how long has it been since you've driven?"

I tried to pull the information up from my memory. "I think about six or seven months. Why?" Mitch took my face in his hands and kissed me passionately, warming me from head to toe. "Wow, honey, what was *that* for?" I asked.

Mitch laughed playfully. "I thought I'd better kiss you, just in case I don't make it out of this car alive!"

"That is NOT funny Mitchell!" I said, putting the car in gear and starting to back up.

Mitch wasn't done with his little game. "Easy now, sweetheart, ok, now press down the brake, good, now put the car in drive, you know, where the D is."

I was getting annoyed. "Mitchell, stop it." He was really enjoying himself, and I knew he had to be feeling better. We pulled out onto the street, and I stopped at the light.

"Now, honey, when the light turns green, that means you can go. Just press on the accelerator. That's the one by your right foot."

I glanced over at him with an icy glare. "Mitchell, I'm nervous enough as it is driving this car without you annoying me with your little game. Please stop it!"

Mitch laughed. "I was only having fun, sweetheart, I'm sorry. You're doing just fine, don't be nervous." He pretended to hang on for dear life.

"Mitchell........"

"Ok, ok, I'm sorry, but you're just so much fun to tease." He laughed.

A few minutes later we pulled up in front of my apartment and I parked the car. Mitch and I got out, and I placed the keys back in his hand. "Never again, Mitchell Tarrington, never again!" I said sternly.

"Dana, come on. I was only having a little fun. Baby, don't be mad at me." Mitch had placed himself right in front of me, and was pretending to pout. I tried to go around him, but each way I moved, he would move also, blocking me from getting past. He was snickering all the while.

I lightly smacked him on the arm. He had broken me, and I was laughing, too. "You are so impossible! Why do I put up with you?"

Mitch bent down to my eye level. "Because I'm cute!" he said, batting his eyelashes.

Hand in hand we walked through the door David held open for us, wishing him a Merry Christmas as we did. Mitch started up the stairs, but I pulled him in a different direction. "Today, we take the elevator.

I don't want to risk you getting unsteady on me again and falling down the stairs."

Mitch tried to protest. "Dana, I'm fine now, really, just a little headache, that's all. I can......"

"I said no, Mitch, now press the button for the elevator."

"Yes, dear," he said, sighing deeply.

The elevator was empty as we stepped on and when the door closed, Mitch pulled me to him and started kissing me. "Maybe we should take the elevator all the time." He said.

"Maybe we should." I said, initiating the next kiss. Just at that moment the door opened, and an elderly couple, waiting to get on, caught us in our embrace. I looked at Mitch, and he looked down, smirking and turning red at the same time. The couple looked at each other and smiled. We hurried off the elevator hand in hand and rounding the corner, began to laugh.

"Did you see that look on the lady's face?" I asked Mitch.

"Yeah, but her husband's look was better. Maybe we gave them an idea of what to do in an empty elevator!" he laughed.

Still chuckling, I unlocked my door and we stepped inside, hung up our coats and went to sit on the couch. I looked at Mitch, and there just seemed to suddenly be something different about him. It was as if I were seeing him again for the first time. As I had laid on that couch the night before, I had cried, my heart broken, thinking I would never see him again. Now, here he was, and everything was right with the world once more.

"So, are you going to go freshen up now? I'll hang out here and see what's on TV or something." Mitch said. Then the way I was looking at him must have caught his attention. "Dana, why are you looking at me that way?"

I couldn't help all the love I was feeling for him at that moment. I leaned toward him and pushed him gently back on the couch. "Kiss me, Mitch. Please, kiss me." I said.

Mitch looked at me, his eyes shining with both wonder and love. He didn't hesitate to obey the command he was given. It was me this time who was lost in the passion.

"Honey," I said softly, between kisses, "remember what I said earlier, about waiting?" I was kissing his cheeks and working down to his neck.

"Uh huh." Mitch said.

"Well," I said, breathing deeply, still kissing him. "I want to take it back." Mitch moved closer to me, letting me set the mood. Suddenly, he sat up, pulling away from me.

"What, honey, what's the matter?" I said, looking at him strangely.

"No, no, oh, no Dana, we have to stop. We can't go through with this, we both know that."

"But, Mitch, I thought..........."

He took my hand. "Dana, I gave you my word that I would respect your wishes, and I know what those wishes *really* are. Besides, you made a special promise to someone, remember? I know you would regret it if that promise got broken, now wouldn't you?"

I looked at him and sighed. I knew he was right. "Thank you, Mitch. You're right."

He pulled me to him again. "I love you too much to let you do that when I know how you really feel. But, it doesn't mean we can't push the envelope a little, does it?"

"No, it doesn't mean that at all." I said. And we spent the next thirty minutes doing just that.

I finally decided it was time to take a shower and change clothes, so kissing Mitch once more, I retreated off to take care of things.

Mitch lay back on the couch and closed his eyes. He was thinking again about everything that had happened the night before, and still trying to piece it all together. When Dana left his apartment, he didn't try to go after her. First mistake, he thought. But he was so hurt and angry that his ego wouldn't allow him to do it. He also didn't think she would talk to him. The look in her eyes as she walked out the door told him there was no chance of anything with her again. Then the incident at Gartano's. Again, why didn't he go after her? Probably the same reasons, he thought. He cursed himself again for everything that he had done. He had no right to hurt her that way, to yell at her or say the things to her that he had said. None of it had been true, but he hadn't known that then. His foolish pride had taken over and he had let it get the best of him. Right then and there he made a vow to himself that he would never hurt her like that again. And especially, that he would never again let her go.

Turning to one side and opening his eyes, he saw the pictures of Dana's family on the top of her bookcase. He wondered what she must have felt like, growing up without any brothers or sisters. He thought about the pain she must have felt when she lost her parents as a little girl, and again when her grandmother passed away. He thought about his own parents and how it would hurt not having them around. Then he thought about Chris, and Jim and Paul, and how they had sacrificed sleep and Christmas morning with their own families to take care of him. He smiled. He had a lot of good people in his life, Dana was right about that. And now, he had her, too. He felt like the luckiest man alive.

He heard Dana starting to emerge from her shower, so he reached for the remote and turned on the TV. He didn't want her to start asking questions, knowing he had been preoccupied with his thoughts and feelings. Some things are better kept to yourself, he thought. Flipping through a few channels, he found a football game and figured she would easily believe he had been watching that the entire time.

"Ok, here I am, all fresh and clean." I said, coming around to the front of the couch. Mitch started to sit up to give me a seat.

"No, I know you're probably still a little tired. Here." Lifting his feet, I sat down and laid them back down in my lap. He smiled as I rubbed his leg . "Do you think you might want to try eating something yet? I can make something for you."

Mitch shook his head. "No, thanks, sweetheart. Surprisingly enough, I'm not hungry."

Then he looked at the clock on the wall and noticed that it was a little past noon. "But you must be, so go ahead and get something for yourself. Don't worry about me."

"Ok, I think I will have a cup of hot soup, maybe. Are you sure I can't get anything for you?" I asked again, getting up from the couch and replacing Mitch's feet where I had been sitting.

"Yeah, baby, I'm sure. Thanks." Mitch was actually starting to get interested in the game he was watching.

I headed into the kitchen and a few minutes later, returned with a cup of soup, some crackers and a glass of soda. Mitch sat up this time to give me a seat. As I opened the package of crackers, I noticed him watching me intently. I smiled, handing him the first one.

"Would you like one?" I asked.

"Sure, thanks," he said, leaning back again, munching the cracker. I took a few more out and put them in my soup, breaking them up with my spoon. Mitch extended a hand.

"Can I have another one, please?" He asked. "Oh, make it two." I handed the entire package to him and he smiled, sitting back again and looking content.

I picked up my cup of soup and took a bite. It was nice and warm, and I hadn't realized how hungry I was until just then. The next thing I knew, Mitch had his arm around me, and was leaning close, staring into my lunch.

"That really does look kind of good," he said, still studying it intently.

I started to put it back on the coffee table. "Would you like me to make you some?" I asked him.

"Oh, no, I'm really not hungry," He said. Then he pointed to my cup. "Maybe just a bite of yours."

I handed him the cup and he took a bite. "That is good," he concluded, taking yet another bite. He had the spoon in his mouth on the third bite, when he noticed me watching him, arms folded across my chest. He stopped, looked at me, and put the spoon slowly back in the cup. He had a little smirk on his face, and he was looking at me over the top of his glasses.

"I'm not getting that back, am I?" I asked. He smiled at me.

I sighed. "Ok, I'll go make another one for myself, Mr. "I'm not hungry." I gave him a loving little push.

"Hey, sweetheart?" Mitch called after me.

I turned to see what he wanted. "Yes, dear?"

"We may need some more crackers, too. And a soda, please." I smiled, shaking my head and preceded to make my lunch. He really was impossible. But I could live with that.

After lunch, I proceeded to curl up next to Mitch, who was still watching football. I sighed heavily. "Honey?" I started.

"Ah, man, why'd you drop the ball? A two year old could have made that play!" he said disgustedly at the TV. Then he jumped up excitedly. "Yeah, touchdown! About time you guys got moving!"

I shook my head. "Mitchell, honey, they can't hear you." I said.

The game went to a commercial, and Mitch took a sip of his soda, leaning back again. "What, honey, did you say something?"

I just looked at him. "Oh, no, nothing dear. Just continue talking to the TV."

He looked at me oddly. "What?"

"Nothing, Mitchell, nothing." I smiled as the game came back on. "Honey, do you think we should start thinking about planning the wedding?"

"Yeah!" Mitch exclaimed again. I looked at him, his eyes fixed on the TV, and realized he was talking to it again, not me. "I'm going to call Kayla." I said getting up from the couch.

"Hey, Dana, could you get me another soda, please, since you're up? Thanks."

"Of course, dear, whatever you want." I said under my breath. I refilled his cup and set it back on the coffee table. He was still talking to the TV and yelling at the players, so I slipped away unnoticed.

Closing the bedroom door behind me, I sat down on the bed and taking the phone from the nightstand, I dialed Kayla's number.

"Merry Christmas!" I said cheerfully as I heard Kayla's voice.

"Well, Merry Christmas to you, too, girl." Kayla replied. "I was just about to call you. I've tried a few times and was getting worried. I wasn't sure if I should call Mitch or not."

"I'm sorry, Kayla, it was a really rough night. I just got back a little while ago and I didn't even check to see if I had any messages."

"Oh, it's ok, I understand." Kayla said. "So, is everything alright now, with you and Mitch? And how is he? Jimmy and I were really worried about him, the way he left Gartano's." Then she paused. "He didn't do anything stupid, I hope."

"To answer your questions, yes, everything is fine with us. In fact, he's here now, watching the football game." I laughed. "Kayla, he's so wrapped up in it that he didn't even notice when I left the room. Just asked me to get him another soda, without even looking at me."

Kayla chuckled. "Uh, huh, honey I know that one. You should see Joseph when he's watching sports. It's like the rest of the world doesn't even exist. And the sad part is, Riley is getting to be the same way!"

I laughed back. "Must be a guy thing, huh?"

"Sure enough, I think it is." Kayla agreed. "So, you didn't answer my other questions."

"Oh, right. Mitch is much better now. And, yes, he did do something stupid, Kayla. You know those bottles of wine he took from the bistro?"

"Don't tell me he got himself drunk, now, Dana? Mitch isn't a drinking man."

"Well, he was last night, or at least he tried to be. He had two gone and probably would have downed the third if Chris and his brothers-in-law hadn't stopped him."

I heard Kayla sigh deeply. "That just isn't like Mitch," she said. "He must have really been hurting last night. He thought he lost his girl, that's why he did that, I'll bet."

"That would be why." I continued. I filled her in on everything that had happened, right up to him giving me the ring this morning, and the inscription inside.

"Now, you see, Dana, he is something special. Not a lot of men would think to do something like that." Then a thought crossed Kayla's mind. "Anything else happen this weekend?" She asked. She didn't want to come right out and ask about the proposal, in case it hadn't happened for some reason.

"Yes," I said slowly. "We got engaged yesterday evening!"

Kayla laughed excitedly. "Well, now, congratulations honey! That's wonderful news. Have you set a date yet?"

"No, not yet." I replied. "But I've been thinking about it." Then I smiled. "Kayla, I have to ask you something."

Her voice sounded concerned. "Sure, Dana, what is it?"

"Kayla, ever since I met you, you've been there for me through everything. Losing Eddie, getting Mitch, everything. In fact, if it hadn't been for you, I would never have met him. So, Kayla, I was wondering, will you be my matron of honor?"

Kayla laughed wholeheartedly. "Why, honey, nothing would make me happier!" she replied.

"And....." I continued. "Do you think Joseph would give me away? He has been kinda like a father to me, and well, it would really make me happy if he would."

Kayla still sounded very excited. "Well, I think he would be honored to do that, Dana. But, I think he might like it if you asked him yourself."

I smiled. "Ok, I'll do that then. Kayla, you should have seen Mitch when he proposed to me. He was so nervous I thought he was going to pass out."

She laughed. "I'll bet he felt like it, too. Tell me all about it, I can't wait to hear." I filled Kayla in on all the details, from Chris forgetting the ring, to Mitch singing to me.

"How romantic, Dana! I wish I could've been there to see that!"

"Me, too, Kayla, but you'll get to see the wedding, and that's even better!" I put my hand up to look at my engagement ring. "And Kayla, oh my, I can't wait to show you my ring. It is absolutely gorgeous!" Then I laughed. "I think I just figured something out. Remember how he wanted me to make him cookies the other day ? I'll bet that's the day the little sneak went to buy my ring!"

"Now, could be!" Then Kayla's voice changed. "Dana, I have a confession."

"What's that?" I said, placing my hand behind my head.

"Mitch told me he was going to propose. I already knew."

"No way! He told you? He is such a devil!" Just then, Mitch came in smiling. He walked over to the bed and taking the hand from behind my head, he pressed my arm down against the bed and straddling me, began to kiss my neck.

"So, I'm a devil, huh?" He asked playfully.

"Oh, oh, I think you got yourself some trouble, girl!" Kayla laughed.

"Mitchell, stop it!" I said. He was tickling me, and having a good time with it. I could hear Kayla laughing as well.

"I think I'll let you go now, Dana. I'll talk to you later." She said, a smile in her voice.

"Yeah, I better go. Mr. Tarrington here is harassing me!"

I hung up the phone and Mitch pinned down my other arm. He looked into my eyes, the mischief shining in his. "So, not only am I a devil, but I harass you, too, huh?" He started to nibble my neck again, but he was tickling me at the same time.

"Mitch, stop!" I laughed, trying to push away his hands as hard as I could.

"Forget it, sweetheart, I'm just too strong for you." He said, resisting my efforts, smiling all the while. "Remember, I work out." He changed to his best villain voice. "You are my prisoner. You cannot escape!"

We were both laughing now, out of breath from our little play battle. Finally, Mitch put his arms around me and rolled me over to my side to face him. He kissed me on the tip of the nose. "Talking to Kayla?" He asked.

"Yeah, I always call her on Christmas, just to say hello." I said.

Mitch smiled. "You just thought you'd call and tell her each and every detail about the last two days, is what you thought, dear." He kissed my forehead. "I know all about girls when they get on the phone. Remember, I have two sisters."

I scooted closer to Mitch and rubbed his back. "So, did your team win the game? Or didn't your armchair coaching help?" I teased.

He gave me a funny look. "Oh, you mean the way I was getting into it? Honey, that's how guys watch sports. You have to feel the game, you can't just watch the game."

"Oh, ok, well, I guess since I'm a woman, I wouldn't understand that, huh?"

"I don't know, maybe you would. It's just that guys and girls, well, they're different, that's all."

I giggled. "Gee, Mitch, and to think it only took you twenty six years to figure that out. You're such a smart man!"

He gave me a soft kiss. "Well, if we weren't different, it wouldn't be so much fun for me to do that, would it?"

"No," I sighed, "probably not." I reached up and pushed a few strands of his hair back with my fingers, then brought my hand down over the side of his face, and took his hand in mine. "Since you were so intent on your game and didn't hear me the first time, I guess I'll ask you again. Do you think we should start planning the wedding?"

Now it was Mitch who was playing with my hair. "Oh, I don't know. How soon do you want to get married? Do you want to do it right away, or would you rather have a longer engagement, being that the courtship was short?"

I pondered the question, and decided I wasn't sure how to answer. "I don't know, what do you want to do?" I asked.

"I asked you first." He said.

I looked at him, and could tell he wasn't going to make this decision. "Well, I've always heard that it takes time to plan a wedding. But I've never done it before, so I really don't know."

Mitch cocked his head, a half smile on his face and he was looking right into my eyes. He let go of my hand, and put both arms around me tightly again. "If I know you, Dana Walker, you've been dreaming about your wedding day since you were a little girl. You already have a vision of what you want it to be, am I right?" I nodded. "Well, then, I want your vision to become a reality. So, however long you think that will take, then fine. It won't be easy to be patient, but I'll wait." He kissed me again, smiling.

I rolled over onto my back again and Mitch propped himself on his elbow to look at me. Closing my eyes, I pulled that vision from deep within my memory. He was right. I did know exactly what I wanted it to be. And I had a feeling, together we could make it happen. Opening my eyes, I turned and propped myself up to face him.

"Ok," I said decisively, "then let's take our time and make the day special, ok?"

Mitch smiled. "Sweetheart, it's going to be special no matter when it happens." Then he saw the second thoughts creeping back into my eyes, and decided to nip them in the bud. "But, I think that's a good idea. Let's take our time, ok?"

"Ok, but just one more thing. We have to at least pick a date."

Mitch dropped his head and sighed. "Dana, we haven't even been engaged twenty four hours yet. Do we have to do that right now?"

I sat up. "If we don't know what day we want to get married, then how will we be able to plan for it?"

Mitch sat up as well. "Good point." He said. "What time of year do you want to get married? Do you like spring, maybe be a June bride, what?"

I flopped back on the bed again. "I don't know!" I whined. "Why is this so hard?"

Mitch chuckled. "It's not hard, sweetheart, you're just *making* it hard." He took my hand. "How about this? Let's think of a date that is special, one that holds a meaning for both of us."

We smiled at each other knowingly. "October 4!" We said together and sealed it with a kiss.

"You seem to be feeling better. I'm glad." I said to Mitch, sliding off the bed.

"I really am, now. I think that soup you made me helped a lot." He smirked, hopping off on the other side.

I smirked back. "You mean the soup I made *me*, don't you?"

Back in the living room, Mitch sat down in the chair, pulling me onto his lap. I snuggled up to him, and could hear his heart beating softly. "So, October 4th. I think that'll be a good day. Easy for me to remember our anniversary, too."

I lovingly poked his chest with my finger. "Yeah, you better remember our anniversary, buddy, or you'll be in big trouble."

"I'm sure of that!" he laughed.

I looked outside the window and in the distance I saw the playful antics of two happy children, busily making a snowman. They had caught Mitch's attention, too, and we just sat silently for a few minutes watching them. Mitch suddenly sat up and looked at me with a twinkle in his eyes.

"Come on, Dana, put your coat on." He said, prompting me to my feet. "We're going outside, too."

"For what?" I asked.

Mitch pointed at the children. "We're going to build a snowman!"

"But you don't have any snow gear with you, honey. You'll get soaked."

Mitch thought for a minute. "Ok, we'll just build a little snowman. On the balcony."

I smiled at him and he took me by the hand, leading me out onto the balcony. Eagerly, he began rolling snowballs for the different snowman parts, and I filled in the edges as he stacked them together. Just watching his childlike antics made my heart grow warm. Finally, it came time to add the other parts. We joined hands again, and stood looking at the little snowman creation we had made, deciding what finishing touches we needed.

"Now," Mitch said. "He needs arms, and a face. Do you have anything we can use?"

"I have a jar of buttons in the closet. That can be his eyes and mouth, and I'll get a carrot for his nose. But I don't know about arms."

"How about straws? Do you have any?" he asked.

"You know, I think I might have some hidden away in the kitchen drawer. I'll go look."

I hurried back inside and, finding what I needed, joined Mitch back on the balcony. I broke the carrot in half to make it the right size, and, laughing, stuck one half in the snowman and the other half in Mitch's mouth. He shrugged and began to munch on it. Mitch placed a straw on either side of the snowman for arms, and taking off his glove to get a better grip, he placed buttons for the eyes. I made the mouth, and our snowman was complete, except for one thing.

"Mitch, bend down here." I instructed.

"What for?" he asked.

"Please, just do it. You're too tall for me to reach very well without hurting you."

"I don't know what you want to do, but ok." Mitch bent down and I took the scarf off his neck.

"He needs this," I said, wrapping it around the snowman twice. "There, now he won't get cold!" I giggled.

"No, but I will. That's the warmest scarf I own." Mitch whined.

"Mitchell, don't be such a baby. I'll buy you another one tomorrow." I promised. He pretended to pout, and then broke into a wide smile. He put his arm around me and together we admired our work. "I think we make a great team, don't you?" I asked.

"Absolutely!" Mitch said. "What should we name him?"

I cocked my head to the side and looked at the snowman thoughtfully. "George." I said, decisively.

Mitch laughed. "George. Why George?"

"I don't know, he just looks like a George to me." I replied, still studying the snowman. "Why, do you have something better in mind?"

"Well," Mitch said, making a circle around the snowman. "I was thinking he looked more like a Waldo."

I laughed. "Waldo? Waldo the Snowman? Oh, honey is that the best you could do?"

Mitch folded his arms and mocked my voice, trying to sound like a girl. "Oh, honey is that the best you could do?" Then he stuck his tongue out at me and smirked.

"I have an idea, then. Let's flip a coin. Whoever wins the toss gets to name the snowman. Agreed?" I looked at Mitch and he was still smirking at me, but he was already searching his pocket for a coin.

"Ok, call it." He instructed as he flipped the coin into the air. I had called heads, and heads won.

"Ha ha!" I teased. "His name is George."

Mitch smiled at me. "Oh, alright, but I still think we should call him Waldo." He put his arm around me and was about to kiss me when we heard the phone ring.

"I'd better get that!" I said, opening the door to go back in. I glanced back to see Mitch throw up his arms, and then walk inside.

"Hello? Oh, hey, Chris, Merry Christmas to you, too!" I said. I looked at Mitch. He was wiping the steam from his glasses and grumbling something about hating it under his breath. I smiled. He proceeded to hang up his coat, and then kissing me on the top of the head as he passed by, put water in the teapot and placed it on the stove. He went to the cupboard and took out two cups, laid them on the counter, and found the sugar bowl as well. I marveled at the way he had become so comfortable with being here.

"Oh, Mitch? No, he's just fine. He's actually right here, taking over my kitchen." He smirked at me. "No, no, he isn't cooking, just making some tea, I think. We just came in from outside." I turned to see Mitch standing with his back against the sink, eavesdropping. Would you like to talk to him? Ok, see ya." I handed the phone to Mitch, then decided to go and sit on the couch once again, letting him have his conversation with his brother.

"Hi Chris, what's up?" Mitch asked.

"Just calling to check up on my little brother." Chris replied. "Feeling better now?"

"Oh, yeah, a lot better. I'm pretty much back to normal again. This morning, I felt like I'd been hit by a freight train!"

Chris laughed. "Yeah, buddy, you were pretty wasted last night. You weren't looking so hot when we got there."

Mitch's face grew serious. "Chris, thanks for being there for me. You don't know how much that means to me."

"Hey, you're my little brother. I'm supposed to help you. Just don't do it again, huh?" Chris said.

"Don't worry, I don't plan on it." Mitch replied. Just then the teapot whistled, and Mitch cradled the phone on his shoulder to take it off the stove. He preceded to make two cups of tea.

Chris continued. "Well, I also called to see if you and Dana have any plans for dinner tonight? Trudy is making a nice roast chicken, and we thought you might like to join us, unless you want to be alone today."

Mitch smiled. "Tell you what? Let me talk it over with the little future Mrs. and I'll call you back, ok?"

"Alright, sounds good. Catch ya later." Chris answered. "Oh, wait, hey Mitch?"

"Yeah, I'm still here. What?" Mitch answered.

"I just talked to Mom. She was wondering why you hadn't called to wish her a Merry Christmas yet."

Mitch gritted his teeth. "Oh, man, I completely forgot." He said.

"No sweat, I figured as much, so I covered you. Told her you were just spending some time with Dana, you know, the young and in love stuff."

Mitch laughed. "Oh, gee, that sounds real convincing." He said to Chris.

"Well," Chris said, "you are young and you are in love, aren't you?"

Mitch smiled. "Absolutely! Thanks, Christopher, I'll get back to ya on the other, ok? Bye"

Mitch picked the phone back up and began dialing. "Hello, hi Mom, it's me. Merry Christmas." I heard him say. I didn't listen to whatever else he said. I was thinking about how nice it must be to be able to do that, to call your mom on Christmas. I was glad he could.

Mitch hung up, and brought my cup of tea to me and sat down. "Hey, baby, how would you like to have dinner with Chris and Trudy tonight? Unless, you had something else in mind." He looked at me longingly.

"No, that actually sounds fine, if you think you're up for it." I replied, not catching his little joke.

Mitch leaned close to me and whispered in my ear. "I am, baby, I am."

I looked at him, still not getting it. He laughed. "Never mind, Dana, never mind."

9

We finished our tea, and after Mitch gave them a quick call, we decided we would head to Chris and Trudy's. "I really don't feel right not taking something." I said to Mitch.

As we were heading out, I told him to wait and I grabbed a plastic storage bag full of cookies from the refrigerator.

Mitch smiled. "Dana, just how many cookies did you make the other day?" He took the bag and began to open it. "And where were these hiding? I didn't see them earlier."

"I know you didn't see them, Mitchell, that was the plan. I knew if you saw them, we wouldn't have them for tonight." I took the bag back from him, but not before he was able to snatch a cookie. "Come on, you, let's go." I took him by the hand and we headed out.

Mitch decided he was feeling well enough to drive, and that was fine with me, as I wasn't up to going through his teasing again. He was being very talkative and his mood was very happy and lighthearted. It made me happy, too, that he was feeling so much better.

"So, sweetheart, now we have the date set for the wedding. Have you thought about bridesmaids and all that yet?"

"Oh, I didn't tell you, did I?" I said excitedly. "I asked Kayla to be my matron of honor and I'm going to ask Joseph to give me away, being that my dad is gone and all."

Mitch gave me a sad smile, and squeezed my hand. "That's nice, baby. I'm sure he'll love doing that for you."

"And I was thinking, do you think Trudy and Julia and Angelina will be the rest of my party? Oh, and my friend, Carrie, from work's husband is a photographer. He could take the pictures for us. But what about flowers? Do you know anyone who does flowers?"

Mitch laughed. "I ask one question and I open a can of worms," he said. "And no, I don't know anyone who does flowers, not that I can think of right off hand."

"So, who do you want to have in the wedding? For you, I mean?" I asked.

"Well, I plan to ask Chris to be my best man. I mean, he is my only brother, and he has really been there for me." He smiled sweetly. "And, well, probably Jim and Paul. What do you think about Megan for the flower girl? That would be fun for her to be in her favorite uncle's wedding."

"I think it would be more fun for you, actually." I quipped.

"Yeah, you're probably right. She's a special little girl, for sure." Then Mitch looked at me. "Hey, I just thought, you'll have one extra attendant than me. You'll have four and I'll only have three."

I gave the situation some consideration. "That's easy." I replied. "Just let Joseph stand in after he walks me down the aisle."

"Good idea." Mitch agreed. "Now, let's see. We have the date, and the attendants. What about the reception?"

"Gosh, I don't know, honey. We could do it at the bistro, but it doesn't really give us anyplace for dancing, and it's a tad too small, don't you think?"

"Yes, definitely. My dad used to belong to a country club. Maybe we can get that at a discount or something."

I sat back, suddenly overwhelmed by everything we were discussing. It was easy to say we were going to do this and going to do that, but I wasn't sure about how to actually pull it all together. I really wished my mom and my Grammy could be here to help me with all this, to see my wedding day. I knew in my heart that they would adore Mitch as much as I did. Grammy liked Eddie, but she always told me not to lose my heart to him. I never knew what she meant at the time. She said it again when I decided to move out here with him, and still, I never knew what she meant. I did now, though. And I also understood why she had me make her the promise about staying celibate until my wedding night. I really believed that she knew somehow that Eddie would leave me. I missed her so much.

"You're awfully quiet all of a sudden, sweetheart. Something wrong?" Mitch asked, taking my hand.

"No, just thinking." I said, turning toward the window. Mitch looked at me and I knew he was trying to read me. He already knew me so well, it amazed me.

"Don't worry, baby, it'll all come together. Just you wait and see. I'll be right there with you, all the way." He pulled me over to lean against him, and kissed my cheek.

"I just wish my mom and my Grammy were here, that's all. They would really love you, Mitch, I know they would."

Mitch took his hand off the wheel and put it around me. "And they would see how much I love their little girl." He said, kissing me again. "Dana, I can't even imagine what it must be like, not to have your parents or anyone like that in your life. But, I hope you'll eventually start feeling like you have a place where you belong now, with my family." He rubbed my shoulder. "Is there anything I can do to help with that?"

I sighed deeply and sat up. "No, Mitch, it isn't that I don't feel comfortable around your family. I adore all of them, really I do, and I feel like they like me, too." I turned to the window again. "But, it just isn't the same. I know you don't understand that, and I don't know if I can ever make you understand, but it isn't."

Mitch reached out and touched my cheek. "You're right, Dana, I probably won't ever know exactly how you feel. I just hate to see you sad, that's all."

We were silent for the next few minutes, and finally pulled up to Chris and Trudy's house. It was a large brick home with black shutters, and pillars on the porch, but not half the size of Jake and Olivia's, set in a very well off neighborhood. It was landscaped beautifully, from what I could tell with the snow, and I guessed it was probably very pretty in the summertime. Landscaping lights lined the walkway, and a lamppost lit the front lawn. Mitch turned off the car, but didn't get out right away.

He turned toward me. "Come here, Dana, let me hold you for a minute, ok?" I fell into his arms and he held me tightly. "I don't want you to be sad. It hurts me so much to see you sad about anything. I know you miss your family, and I want to take that pain away, but I don't know how. I just don't know how."

I looked up at him. "Just don't ever let me go, ok? Then I'll be happy."

Mitch hugged me with all he had in him. "I promise you, Dana, that I will always be here for you."

Chris and Trudy were waiting at the door when we got out of the car. "Merry Christmas, you two!" Trudy said, hugging us both. "Come in out of the cold."

We stepped inside and immediately three screaming children came charging toward us, right past me and hitting Mitch mid-thigh, practically knocking him over.

"Hi Uncle Mitch, come and see what we got." Mitch had one child on each hand tugging and the other pushing on his legs. I could see by the look on his face that he was loving it.

"Whoa, munchkins, slow down, I just got here!" He laughed. "And don't you think you should say hello to Dana, too? Or did she just turn invisible?" He pretended not to be able to see me, and the kids giggled.

Michael, the youngest one, around five or six I guessed, giggled and pointed at me. "She's not invisible, she's right there!" We laughed at him.

"Hi Dana!" They all said in unison.

"Hi kids, Merry Christmas!" I said, holding up the bag of cookies. "Can they have one, Mom?"

"Sure, but just one." Trudy smiled.

I bent down, and opened the bag to them. They all chose a cookie and even told me thank you. I was impressed.

Chris prompted them to go and play, and took our coats, hanging them on a beautiful brass coat rack in the foyer. Just this part of the house itself was breathtaking. A crystal chandelier hung high above us, and the stairs going up were open at the top, enabling you to overlook the foyer from that point. There were a couple of potted trees, and a hall table with assorted pictures and books. Even though a little on the fancy side, it was still cozy and inviting. I was guessing that the residents made it that way more than anything else.

"Mitchell, I'm going to steal your fiancé for a little while, ok? I could use some help in the kitchen." Trudy said.

Mitch looked from Trudy to me, and nodded. "Ok, but don't keep her too long. I'll get lonely." He smiled and kissed me. "Have fun, sweetheart." He said.

"What do you mean lonely? What am I, a potted plant?" Chris laughed and pushed his brother playfully.

The two men walked into the living room and I followed Trudy into the kitchen. Another impressive room, I thought. Big and spacious, more cabinets than I had ever seen, done in natural oak.

"Trudy, your house is gorgeous!" I exclaimed.

"Thanks, Dana, but you know, sometimes I think it's bigger than what we need."

I was surprised to hear her say that. "Really? Why would you think that?"

"Now don't get me wrong, I do love it and all. But it did take some getting used to at first. I came from a small house in a small neighborhood in a small town. Then, I entered Tarrington Country. Nothing is small there. But, it's ok when you consider that the main thing they're big on is love."

I smiled. "Yes, I can believe that." I said.

Trudy pulled out a chair and motioned for me to sit, also. "You know, Dana," she began. "I was scared to death the first time I met Jake and Olivia. Absolutely petrified. I felt small and meaningless and I just didn't fit in their big fancy world. I even considered breaking up with Chris, because I was afraid that his family wouldn't think I was good enough for him. But, you know what? I couldn't have been more wrong about anything in my life! The Tarrington's may have money, but the one thing they don't do is flaunt it. Sure, they have a big house and nice things. That's ok, who doesn't want that? But they aren't snobs, everyone is welcome in their home, and I've seen them bend over backwards to help people. They all stick together and they're very close. There's a great deal of love in this family, and that's what really matters."

I understood what Trudy was trying to do, and I appreciated it. "Thanks, Trudy, and you're right. They're all such wonderful people."

She got up and brought a salad back to the table. "Would you mind putting in the carrots for me? I'm a little carrot shy. Tried to put them in earlier and cut my finger." She held up a bandaged finger for me to see.

"No problem, I'm glad to help!" I said.

"While you do that, I'll set the table, and we can talk some more, ok?"

"Sure," I said. Trudy seemed to be a very happy person, who took life as it came. I felt good being around her, and not at all uncomfortable talking to her.

"So, have you two set a date yet?" She asked cheerfully.

"Yes, actually, we have. October 4th, the day we met." Then I corrected myself. "Well, actually, the first day Mitch saw me at Gartano's."

Trudy smiled. "Oh, Dana, that's so sweet." She exclaimed. "You know, Chris and I were at his parents that night when Mitch came over. I'm telling you, we could *all* see you really did something to him." She smiled. "Even if he didn't know it at the time, we all knew. He was in love with you." I let the words Trudy said sink in. Then she went on. "You know, it's plain to see that Mitch adores you, Dana. None of us have ever seen the guy so happy! Heck, we all knew you before we actually *knew* you because Mitch never stopped talking about you, from the very first night!"

"Well, there really isn't much to talk about." I said.

"Nonsense! You're a fabulous person, Dana, and we're all very happy to have you joining our family. Shoot, we consider you part of the family already!" She gave me a little hug. "I know you'll take good care of Mitch, and he'll take good care of you. You two are right for each other."

Chris came into the room just then. "Are we ready to eat, darling? If so, I'll try to tear Mitch away from the video games. Kids haven't had a turn since he got here!" He chuckled.

"This I have to see!" I said, smiling at Trudy. She followed close behind. Quietly, we entered the room where Mitch and the kids were. He was sitting on the floor, propped against a beanbag chair, doing his best to beat "Space Invaders". Kyle was coaching him.

"Come on, Uncle Mitch, you have to move the rocket the other way!" he said. "Here, let me show you."

"Nah, now I'll get it. Just hang on." Mitch said, pulling the controller away from Kyle.

Trudy whispered in my ear. "They're like big kids. But that makes them easier to train."

We both laughed. "Ok, kids, time to eat now." Trudy said. Her three got up and scrambled in to wash up for dinner. Mine stayed put.

I walked over to him and he looked up at me. "Wait, I just have to kill this one.....ah, man, he got me! See what you did?"

I crossed my arms, pretending to be annoyed. "What I did? I'm not the one playing the game!"

I held out my hand to him and reluctantly, he put down the controller and stood up. As I led him into the dining room, he turned around, although still walking forward, and pointed to the game system. "Can we get one of those?" he asked.

"Only if you learn to play nicer with the other children, *and* you eat all your dinner!" I replied.

I helped Trudy put the food on the table, as Mitch and Chris poured drinks, chatting about the football game that had been on earlier that day. I filed away another mental note. Mitch liked sports. Ok, common guy trait. I supposed I would have to find something else to do on Sunday afternoons. Or, get interested myself, I thought. Nah, shopping is much more fun, I smiled to myself.

After Trudy said grace, we all enjoyed a wonderful meal of roasted chicken, potatoes, green beans, salad, bread and what I soon learned to be one of Mitch's favorite things, applesauce. The conversation was lighthearted and lively, and I soon found myself feeling very comfortable here. Once the kids finished and were excused, Chris turned the conversation to us.

"So, Mitchell, how's it feel to be engaged? Has the whole thing had time to sink in yet?" Chris asked.

Mitch looked at me. "Yeah, it has, and so far, it feels pretty great. Didn't feel so wonderful last night, but today, it does."

Chris smiled. "Yeah, I know little brother. But let me tell you a secret. That won't be the last argument you two have. Trust me."

Trudy agreed. "No, people disagree, that's normal. You just have to remember, though, that one, you love each other and two, that there isn't anything you can't work out as long as you do."

Mitch and I smiled at each other. I think we learned that lesson, I thought.

Mitch looked at Chris. "Well, I know the way I handled it was wrong, and believe me, I won't do that again. But, that was not just because we argued. It was because," Mitch paused and looked me right in the eyes, very lovingly, "I thought I had lost the best thing in my life."

Chris and Trudy smiled at each other. They had never seen two people so much in love.

Trudy stood up and looked at Mitch. "Mitch, when Chris told me you two were coming over tonight, I made you something special."

Mitch looked at her curiously as she went to the refrigerator and pulled out a homemade cherry cheesecake.

"Hey, cool! Thanks Trudy. How'd you know that's my favorite dessert?" Mitch asked.

"Mitch, I've known you for, oh, about twelve years now. I've seen how you romance one of these every time someone serves it." She smiled and turned to me. "Dana, this is another way to make up if you have an argument. Just make him a cheesecake. Works every time." She pointed to Chris.

Chris put his arm around Trudy as she was cutting the dessert, and looked right at Mitch. "Of course, I like the other ways of making up much better......"

Trudy shot Chris a glance. "Christopher, you're terrible!" We all laughed.

Mitch leaned over to Chris and pointed to me. "Is that another one of those girl things? Or a Tarrington family trait, because she tells me that all the time, too!" Chris shrugged.

I turned to Mitch. "I thought chocolate chip cookies were your favorite." I said.

He took me by the hand. "No, what I *said*, dear, was that chocolate chip are my favorite *cookies*. Cheesecake is my favorite *dessert*. There is a difference."

"Ok, Mitchell, whatever you say." I answered. We enjoyed our cheesecake and coffee, and after, the guys went off again and I stayed behind to help Trudy clean up.

"Dana, I'm so happy for you and Mitch. And that proposal yesterday? Oh, it was just so romantic."

"Yes, I'll give him one thing, and that is that he is definitely romantic." Then I looked at Trudy inquisitively. "Do you think that will change much after we get married?"

Trudy looked as if she were pondering that question. "Well, you know, it does just a little bit. Only because they feel more secure after you get married. And they get caught up in the day to day like you do. But, one thing about Tarrington men is, they *are* very romantic. Chris still brings me flowers once in a while, and he tries to do all sorts of little things for me that he knows I like. For instance, I like to write poetry, just for fun. I had all these little spiral bound notebooks laying all over the place. So, one day, he came home with a gift for me. It wasn't even a special occasion. When I opened it, it was a beautiful journal, and a pen and pencil set."

"That's really sweet, Trudy." I said.

"Another thing about Tarrington men, Dana, is that the all hands sometimes. There are times I let Chris get away with smiled and patted her stomach, "and times I don't. A good th though, they respect their women. Jake taught them that well."

"Yes, I think he did." I replied.

Trudy smiled and placed her hand on my shoulder. "Dana, Mitch i a good guy. But, he's also human. There will be times when he'll make you so mad you'll wonder what you ever saw in him, and other times when you can't get enough. And, chances are, he'll feel the same about you. You two haven't been together that long, I know, but I don't have any doubts that you'll make it for the long haul."

I smiled at Trudy, as I finished drying the last glass and she put it away. "Think we should go see what those guys of ours are up to?" I asked.

"Sure, let's go" Trudy hung up the dishtowel.

"Wait, Trudy, first there's something I need to ask you." I said.

"Sure, Dana, what is it?" Trudy answered.

"Mitch and I were talking about the wedding on the way over here, about who we wanted to have as our bridal party. Well, I was wondering if you would be one of my attendants? It would really make me happy."

Trudy's eyes lit up. "I would love to be in your wedding, Dana! Thank you for asking!" and she gave me a hug.

"Good, one down, three to go!" I laughed. "I'm going to ask Julia and Angelina, too." I said.

Trudy smiled. "They'll be thrilled, Dana. And I just know Kayla has to be the matron of honor."

I smiled at the thought of the way Kayla reacted when I asked her. "Yes, she's already agreed to that. And Joseph is giving me away. They took me under their wing when I came here, and, well, they're kind of like parents to me, since my own are gone."

Trudy's eyes softened as she saw the sadness in my eyes. "Dana, I'm so sorry. I do know how you feel, though. My mother passed away about two years ago, and I still miss her."

I nodded. "I don't think that ever goes away, does it?" Trudy shook her head. "Mitch just doesn't understand that, either. He just tells me he doesn't want me to be sad."

Trudy put her hand on my shoulder once again. "That's because he loves you so much, Dana, and he wants to be able to save you from anything negative that life throws your way. And it bothers him that he can't. You just have to let him deal with that. He won't understand how you feel until he experiences that loss himself, which I hope isn't

. Chris is the same way." She hugged me again.
· too much, you can come and talk to me, ok?"

eans a lot." I hugged her back. "Now, let's
.ington men are up to!"
.e corner of the family room, I almost ran right

wondering if you two were going to stay out there all night."
..id, putting his arms around me.

"Did you miss her that much, Mitch?" Trudy teased.

"Absolutely!" he said smiling. "See Trudy, when she's not with me I can't do this," he tickled me. "or this," he said, pulling me close into a hug, "or....this." Mitch bent down slowly, looked deep into my eyes, and delivered a very passionate kiss.

Chris broke the moment with his laughter. "Very impressive, little brother, but save it for the honeymoon!"

Mitch shot a glance at his brother. "But, you know what they say, practice makes perfect!" he said playfully and started to kiss me again.

"Mitch, later honey, ok?" I said, placing my hand on his chest. He sighed and smirked at me, taking my hand and leading me over to the couch.

"Certainly aren't shy, are we Mitchell?" Chris smiled.

Mitch blushed. He looked adorable.

"So, Christopher, got a question for you." Mitch started. Trudy and I looked at each other knowingly and smiled. "How would you like to be my best man in the wedding?"

Chris's face softened and he almost looked like he could cry. "I'd be honored, Mitch." He said.

"Great!" Mitch said. "So, now we just have to ask the girls and Jim and Paul, and we'll be set, right sweetheart?" I nodded.

"So, I'm assuming you've set the date, also?" Chris asked.

"Yeah, October 4th, the anniversary of the first day Dana came into Gartano's". Mitch smiled again.

"Smart move, Mitchell. Won't forget the anniversary that way!" Chris laughed.

I laughed, too. "That's the same thing he said."

Just then, Alexis came into the room, carrying a Barbie doll. "Mommy, I can't get this dress to fit my doll. Will you help me?"

I smiled at her. "I used to have a lot of these when I was little," I said. "Can I help?"

"Ok," Alexis said, handing me the doll. "Would you like to come and play with me? Santa brought me a new doll house, and a camper that you can put them in."

I looked at Mitch and he smiled lovingly. "Go ahead, sweetheart. I'll hang out here" Then he spotted the video games again. "Or, maybe I'll take Chris on in *Space Invaders.*"

Chris chuckled. "You really think you can take me, huh? When will you learn? That black eye you're sporting is proof that you can't!"

"Well, I may have a black eye, thanks to you," Mitch smirked, "but I can still beat you at this game."

The two brothers got up and went to place themselves in front of the TV once more, teasing each other and laughing all the while. I joined Alexis while Trudy watched the men play.

"This is quite the setup you have here, Lex," I said, admiring her dolls and accessories.

"I didn't have all these things when I was little. But I did have a lot of dolls."

"You did?" She asked. "Did you have a favorite one?"

"Yes, I did. She wasn't a Barbie doll, though. She was just a regular doll and her name was Susie. She was very pretty, and she had long hair and pretty brown eyes, just like you do."

Alexis smiled, and handed me a doll to dress, then sat down across from me. "Dana, you and Uncle Mitch are getting married, aren't you?"

I smiled at her, still trying to manipulate the dress onto the doll I was holding. "Yes, we are."

"So that'll mean you'll be my Aunt Dana then, right?" she inquired.

"Yes, Alexis, I'll be your Aunt Dana. And you know what? I'm going to like that very much, because I don't have any nieces or nephews right now."

"You don't?" she said with childlike curiosity. "Why not?"

"Well, Lex, I don't have any brothers or sisters like your mommy and daddy do. I'm an only child."

"Oh," she said. Then she smiled. "Well, when you get married, Daddy and Mommy and Aunt Julia, and Aunt Angelina will be your brother and sisters."

Trudy caught the end of the conversation and she smiled at me. Just then, Michael and Kyle came to disrupt their sister's activity. Michael decided it was his turn to quiz me.

"Dana, do you love my Uncle Mitch?" He asked.

"Yes I do, Michael." I replied, thinking that would satisfy his curiosity.

"Well, how much do you love him? A whole lot or just a little bit?" He continued to ask.

I leaned over and touched the tip of his nose with my finger. "A whole lot!" I said. Out of the corner of my eye, I noticed that this conversation had caught the attention of Mitch and Chris, and they were both watching to see how I would handle it.

"Do you kiss him?" Michael asked, folding his arms like he was interrogating me.

I stopped to think about this. "Yes, Michael, I kiss your Uncle Mitch, and you know what? Sometimes, he even kisses me." I answered. I could hear the guys snickering behind me, and I was working hard to keep a straight face myself. Mitch had quietly come to sit behind me, placing his arms around me and resting his chin on my head. At my answer, Michael made a grimacing face.

"You *kiss* her, Uncle Mitch?"

Mitch smirked. "I sure do, Mike. Just like this." About the time Mitch began to kiss me, Michael yelled, "Yuck!" and ran away. Mitch was laughing hysterically, and turned to Chris.

"I certainly hope, for his sake, that he outgrows that attitude!" Mitch said.

"Mitch, you really *are* terrible." I said, still laughing. "You probably scarred the poor child for life!"

"Nah, he's a Tarrington man. He'll be fine with the ladies!" Mitch was acting all high and mighty. Chris nodded in agreement and the two of them gave each other a high five.

Chris walked over to Trudy, who seemed to be lost in a magazine article. "What's so interesting?" He asked, looking over her shoulder.

"Oh, it's just a little quiz they have in here." She replied.

"Really? Those are interesting sometimes." I stated. "What's that one about?"

"Well, it's kind of a compatibility quiz, you know, to see how compatible you are with your partner." She answered, looking at Chris.

"No, Trudy, don't give me that look. I am not taking any quizzes!" He said, moving around to sit in a chair next to the couch.

"Come on, Chris, it'll be fun!" Trudy coaxed. "You've taken them with me before."

"Yeah, and the last one landed me on the couch for the night!" he replied.

"Alright then, spoil sport." She said, giving him a look. Then she turned to Mitch and me. "How about you two? Want to give it a try?"

Mitch looked at Chris, who was shaking his head and pretending to cut his throat out of Trudy's eyeshot.

"Well, Mitchell, want to see how compatible we are?" I asked.

"Dana, I already know we're compatible. I wouldn't be marrying you if we weren't." he replied, placing his arm on the couch behind me.

I looked at Trudy. "Ok, Trudy, if he won't, I will. Go ahead with the questions."

"Great, ok, let's see. Question number one. If you could change one physical feature about Mitch, what would it be?"

Mitch was smirking and looking at me, waiting to see how I would answer. "Gee, I wouldn't change anything." I answered. "I think he's adorable the way he is."

"Oh, no, that's a cop out, Dana." Mitch answered. "You have to answer the question. I'm glad you think I'm "adorable" as you say, but there has to be one thing about me that you'd change. What is it?"

He had put me on the spot, and I could see the others were waiting, too, so I just decided to throw something out. "Ok, I'd change his ears."

"My ears?" Mitch said. "What's wrong with my ears?"

"Nothing, it's just, well, they don't seem to be in proportion to the rest of your face."

"What, are they too big, too small, what?" Mitch was really giving me the look now.

"Mitch, honey, you wanted me to answer the question and I did." I turned to Trudy. "Ok, Trudy, what's the next question?"

Trudy smiled at Mitch. "Mitch, what would you change about Dana?"

"Wait," I said, "he doesn't want to take the quiz, remember?" I looked at Mitch, who was grinning from ear to ear.

"Oh, now I think I just might enjoy this after all." He smirked. Then, Mitch looked me up and down and back again. "Let's see, hmm, ok, I've got it. She needs to work out more. Maybe I'll get her lifting with me, tone up those arms a little, give her some strength."

I was glaring at him now, my arms tightly folded across my chest. "I'm flabby, ok, Mitchell, I'm flabby." I was saying, almost under my breath.

"I just answered the question, sweetheart." He replied smugly. "Trudy, question two."

Trudy looked at Chris, who also had his arms folded, an I-told-you-not-to-do-this look on his face.

"Oh, here's a good one." Trudy began. "Is your partner better at starting arguments, or better at making up? Mitch, you go first."

"Starting them, definitely starting them." He answered, a little too quickly for me.

Still glaring at Mitch, I answered Trudy before she even asked. "He's pretty good at starting them, too." Mitch gave me an innocent look.

"Third question. Is your partner organized, or disorganized?"

Mitch started to answer, but I interrupted. "It's my turn, you answered first last time." I said. Mitch gave Chris a look and folded his hands obediently in his lap.

"This man is too organized." I said. "You should see his closet—he *categorizes* his shirts, for crying out loud!"

Chris found that humorous. "Mitch, buddy, you really need to find a hobby." He laughed.

"Hey, there's nothing wrong with keeping things neat. At least I can find everything in my place." Mitch replied.

"Is that why you had a pair of underwear lying on the floor that I had to put away for you?" I asked. I knew it really hadn't been on the floor, but I was still trying to cover up my little scavenger hunt.

"What?" Mitch said. "Come on, Dana, I was watching you. You took those out of my drawer, trying to imagine me in them. I don't have anything lying on the floor."

"Did, too, Mitchell." I said.

"I did not, Dana, you're not telling the truth. I was watching you, for Pete's sake . You took them out of my drawer!"

Chris and Trudy were taking in the whole thing, Chris finding it very funny. "Hey Dana, boxers or briefs?" he asked.

"Boxers, not that it's any of your business!" Mitch shot back at him.

"Ok, ok, and I'm not even going to ask why she was looking for those, anyway!" Chris laughed again.

"Good move, Einstein." Trudy said to him.

"You were right, Trudy, this quiz *is* kinda fun." Chris said, watching Mitch and Dana go at it.

"Ok, let's move on." Trudy said with authority. "Mitch, what is the one thing that attracted you most to Dana?"

Mitch smiled brightly now and his eyes lit up. "Just how beautiful she looked, the way her eyes seemed to show such emotion. It got to me."

"That's so sweet, Mitch." Trudy said. "How about you, Dana?"

I smiled sweetly back at Mitch. "That had to be his smile. The first time he flashed me that dimple, I was hooked." Chris was sitting back in the chair now, smiling too.

"Next question is for Dana. "Dana, what is one thing that Mitch does that really annoys you?"

"Well, let me think." I started. "Oh, wait, I know. He's an outrageous flirt, and I don't mean with me."

"Dana, I don't flirt." Mitch said, defending himself. "I only have eyes for you."

"Yeah," I laughed, looking at Trudy and pointing to him. "*and* the checkout girl at Jacy's and the girl at the skating rink, and ....should I go on?" Chris was laughing again.

"Dana,.....oh what's the use?" Mitch crossed his arms.

"Ok, Mitch, what about you?"

"The one thing that annoys me about her is that she can't make a decision. I ask her what she wants to do. She says "anything is fine, dear." I ask her where she would like to go to eat or what she's hungry for. "Anything is fine, dear," is what I get. I ask her if she wants to do something, and she says, "if you do." Drives me insane!"

I looked at Mitch now. Was he really serious? Did he really see me that way?

"Ok, Mitchell, I'll make a decision right now. I want to quit taking this quiz." I folded my arms again.

"No, no, Dana, we started it, we finish it. You're the one who wanted to do this in the first place. And, besides, I finish what I start." Mitch folded his arms as well.

"Fine then." I replied. "What's the next question?"

"Ok, last one." Trudy said. "If you could take a trip to one of these three places, which one would you go to? Paris, the Bahamas, or Hawaii?"

"As for me, I've always wanted to go to Paris. I just think it's such a romantic city. But, I'm not really much into French food, so I think Hawaii would be nice." I replied.

Mitch nodded in agreement. "I think Hawaii would be neat. I'd love to just walk along the beach and maybe do some snorkeling. I've heard that's really awesome."

"Ok, then, let's add this up and see how compatible you are." Trudy said, scribbling on the magazine.

Chris stood up. "While you're doing that, I think I'll get those cookies Dana brought. Anyone for a cup of coffee or tea?"

"Sure, I'll take a cup of tea. Want some help?" Mitch asked.

"No, thanks, I can get it. You better stick around and get your score. Might change your life!" Chris laughed and kissed Trudy on top of the head as he passed by her chair.

"Well, guys, congratulations. It says here you're compatible. Nothing we didn't already know." She smiled.

"See, honey, I told you we were compatible. How about a hug?" Mitch asked.

"Gee, Mitchell, I'm not sure I have the strength to wrap my flabby arms around you." I said smugly.

Mitch smiled at me. "Now, come on, sweetheart, stop that." He said, hugging me.

Chris returned with the cookies and four cups of tea. The cookies attracted the children and they came swooping in like vultures.

"Hold it, HOLD IT!" Chris said with authority. "I didn't hear one of you ask if you could have a cookie, now did I?"

All three of them stopped and pulled their hands back. "Daddy, can we have a cookie?" Kyle asked.

"Yes, but just one. And don't get crumbs everywhere, ok?" Chris smiled as his children gingerly took a cookie and ran away. "Those three keep us going, don't they, sweetheart?" he asked Trudy.

"Yes, and soon it'll be four of them," she answered.

"So, when's the baby due?" I asked Trudy.

"Only about, what Chris, four weeks to go?" He nodded.

"Yeah, then it's up all night, no sleep, diapers and bottles again." He took a cookie and sat down. "But," he smiled at Trudy, "it's all worth it."

Mitch smiled at me. I wondered what he was thinking about, and I had a feeling I knew.

It was close to 11 pm, so we decided to call it a night and let Chris and Trudy get the kids off to bed. Saying our goodbyes to everyone, we were off once again. Mitch and I were silent for most of the drive home, but just as we got back into the city, he broke the silence.

"So, Dana, what's wrong with my ears?" he said, pretending to sound annoyed.

"Mitchell, nothing is wrong with your ears. They're perfect, really." I replied.

"Then why did you say they weren't in proportion with the rest of me?" he asked.

"Well, why did you say I was flabby and needed to work out?" I shot back.

"I never said you were flabby, those were your words. And I only said that to answer the stupid question." He retorted.

"Well, that's the same thing I did. I had to say something." I replied.

By now we were parked in front of my building and Mitch had turned off the car. He took my hand. "Look, Dana, that was just a stupid quiz someone made up to sell magazines. It doesn't mean anything, you know."

"Yeah, I know. I was just hoping those things you said weren't really how you feel about me." I replied.

"No, Dana, they weren't. I love absolutely everything about you. To me, you're perfect." He said.

"Mitch, we both know no one is perfect. I'm sure you really don't love everything about me. There has to be something you would change if you could."

Mitch sighed and leaned over to me. "Sweetheart, I love you. I think you're wonderful. I want to spend my life with you. There is *nothing* I would change, ok?" Then he started to smile. "No, wait, there is one thing."

"What?" I asked.

"I really wish you would believe me when I tell you these things, and stop worrying so much."

"I'm sorry." I said.

"Oh, come here, it's ok. I forgive you." Mitch gave me a hug and a kiss. "Now, you know what I just remembered? All of our Christmas gifts are still in the trunk of the car. We never took them out last night." He got out and popped the trunk, and I helped him with my gifts. Underneath the pile was his guitar case. He smiled.

"It's not really good to leave this out in the cold." He said, picking it up. "I'd better take it in and let it warm up a bit."

We made it into my apartment, and I instructed him to take my gifts into my bedroom and place them on the bed. When he didn't come back right away, I decided to go see what was keeping him.

I walked into the bedroom and Mitch was standing against my dresser, a smirk on his face, holding something behind his back.

"Mitch, what are you up to?" I asked. "And what's behind your back?"

He smiled impishly, pulling out one of my sheer summer nightgowns. "I'd love to see you in this." He said. "I'll bet you look really sexy."

I ran at him. "Give me that!" I said, trying to take it from him. Mitch threw it on the bed, and I ran to pick it up before he had the chance. "What else did you see?" I asked him curiously. He just stood there and smiled. I walked past him and replaced the nightgown in its drawer. "Now, get out of here, nosy boy!" I said, pointing to the door.

"I was just acquainting myself with my future wife's territory!" he said.

Relaxing on the couch, I laid my head on his shoulder and began to watch the snow softly falling outside the window. "George looks cold." I said, referring to our snowman.

"No, he isn't cold." Mitch replied. "He has my scarf to keep him warm." Then he leaned back and pulled me down next to him. "And I have you."

Mitch had taken his guitar out of the case to warm up, and I suddenly noticed it sitting in the corner. "Honey, why didn't you tell me you could play the guitar?" I asked.

"Hmm, I don't know. Guess I didn't think it was that big a deal." He answered.

"You're so talented, Mitch. You can sing, you play piano and guitar, why haven't you ever pursued it professionally?" I looked up at him.

"Now, don't give me too much credit, love." Mitch said. "I'm not the only one in the family that has talent. Julia played violin for a while, Mom plays piano a little, and believe it or not, Chris isn't a bad singer, either, when he tries. He just doesn't have the vocal range that I do."

"Really? That's pretty cool." I replied. "So, any other musical talents I don't know about?"

Mitch chuckled. "I was starting to take up the drums in college, but I didn't go that far with it. Too many other things going on at that time."

I turned myself so that I could lay my head on his chest, and I began making circles on his sweater with my finger. "Mitch, would you sing for me?" I asked.

He smiled. "You really want me to?"

"Yes, I do." I said softly.

Mitch got his guitar and came back to sit next to me. "Any requests?" He asked playfully.

"You should know the answer to that one." I said.

Mitch smiled at me and looking deep into my eyes, he sang once again the song that he had sung to me after he proposed. My heart melted and I was taken away by the sweet sound of his voice. It was the perfect end to a perfect day.

He took off his guitar and, laying it on the chair, embraced me with a wonderful, soft loving kiss. Then he looked at me and smiled.

"Well, unfortunately, I'd better get going. I don't want to leave, but I have to work tomorrow." He had his forehead against mine. "But, before I do, just one thing."

"What, sweetie?" I asked.

"I never thanked you for the way you took care of me last night. I hurt you so badly, and yet, you were still there for me. How did I ever live without you before?"

"It was nothing," I replied. "If the roles were reversed, I know you'd do the same for me."

Mitch smiled. "Absolutely!"

10

The next morning I woke early, showered and dressed, and decided to surprise Mitch with breakfast, remembering from the day before that his cupboards weren't well stocked. There was a great little deli only two blocks from his place, so I planned to stop there for a couple of ham and cheese bagels on the way.

It was a bright sunny morning, and much to my surprise, not as cold as I had anticipated. I stopped off at the deli for the sandwiches, and tucked them inside my coat to keep them warm. A few minutes later, I was standing at Mitch's door.

I knocked lightly and waited. Nothing. I knocked again, this time a little louder. Finally I heard him unlocking the door. Mitch was in his sweatpants, pulling on a t-shirt and putting on his glasses at the same time. I could tell he hadn't been up long.

"Wow, hey sweetheart!" He said, giving me a kiss. "I wasn't expecting you this early in the morning."

"Well, I thought I would surprise you with some breakfast." I said, pulling the bag from within my coat.

"That's really sweet, thanks." He said, opening the bag. "What do we have?"

"Ham and cheese bagels, from Cutman's Deli. The best around!"

Mitch poured both of us a cup of coffee, and pulled out a chair for me to sit down. Then he joined me.

"Did you sleep well?" I asked.

"Sure did, how about you?" he asked, taking a bite.

"I don't remember anything after I turned off the light." I said. "But I do know I missed not having you next to me." I said, remembering how I had curled up with him the night before.

"I know, me too." He said. Then his eyes lit up. "Dana, how about if I go into work early today? Then, tonight I'll take you out, wherever you want to go. How does that sound?"

"I think I like that idea." I said. "But where did you have in mind?"

Mitch looked at me, still eating his bagel. "I said where *you* want to go, so you decide and then you can tell me later."

"Well, ok, I'll think about it and let you know." I answered. "Honey, do you want me to go so you can get ready for work?"

Mitch looked at the clock. "No, it's only nine, still too early to head in just yet. I was going to do a little lifting, if you want to watch. I mean, not that it's that exciting or anything, but get used to it. It's kind of my morning routine."

"I do have to learn those things, don't I?" I said, smiling at him. "Show me what you've got, muscle man!" I followed Mitch to his weight bench, and he laid back, taking hold of the weight. He lifted it off the rest, and then put it back.

"Gee, that was impressive." I said, teasing him.

He smirked at me. "I just decided I wanted to take off my t-shirt. Gives me a little more freedom to move." Mitch sat up and took off his shirt, and I had to fan myself to cool down. He was totally buffed! Mitch must have noticed the way I was drooling because he looked up at me and smiled, with a little laugh.

"See something you like, sweetheart?" he asked. I couldn't speak. I just nodded.

Mitch sat up and hugged me to him. "Then come and get it." He said, kissing me. He started to let go, but I pulled him back for a much longer version of kiss number one. "Dana, you're making it very hard to be good." He said, an impish grin on his face as he kissed me a third time.

I looked at him again. "So are you, Mitchell, so are you."

He smiled and letting me go, pointed to the couch. "You better sit over there, or I'll never get to do this." He said.

I watched as he lifted the weights, bringing them down to his chest and back up again, making it look effortless. Judging by the way he looked and the ease of his motions, I guessed he had been doing this for quite a while. After countless repetitions, Mitch moved the weights to the lower portion of his bench, and taking a few of them off, he positioned himself and began to lift them with his legs. After a few minutes, he sat up.

"Baby, could you hand me that towel on the back of the chair?" I was still checking this man out. And to think I get to wake up next to him every morning, I told myself.

"Dana, honey, my towel please?" I thought I heard Mitch say something.

Finally realizing I wasn't moving, he retrieved his own towel and wiping himself down a little, he replaced his t-shirt and came to sit next to me, laughing. "You look like a little girl who just saw her favorite movie star!" he said.

"I think I did!" I replied, turning to look at him.

He smiled. "Nope, just plain old me!"

I looked at him and leaned in for the big kiss. "Mitch, you are *anything* but plain!" I kissed him, pushing him back on the couch. I could feel his arms slowly come around me.

"Dana, love, I really should go shower and shave, ok? If you hold your thought, though we can continue when I get back."

"Why?" I said.

Mitch looked at me strangely. "Why what? Why shower or why continue?"

"Shower," I said, moving in again.

Mitch managed to wiggle free. "Because I'm sweaty and I need to." He replied.

I sighed and moved away so Mitch could stand up. Then he turned and leaned down over the back of the couch. "If taking my shirt off gets that reaction out of you, I won't ever wear one from now on." He laughed and walked away.

I fell back onto the couch, smiling. I had to be the luckiest girl on the planet, I thought. I had this incredibly handsome man who was thoughtful, romantic, hardworking and dedicated only to me, and a body like a God to boot. *And* to top it all off, he had asked *me* to marry him. Many women had told me that the perfect man didn't exist. They were wrong, I thought. They just didn't know where to look.

A few minutes later, Mitch returned, fully dressed, his tie hanging loosely around his neck. He walked up to the mirror hanging above his entertainment center, and quickly maneuvered the tie into a perfect half Windsor knot. Turning around, he smiled and came back to the couch, very slyly placing his arm around me. "Now, where were we before I left?" he asked.

"I'm not in the mood anymore." I teased. "You put your shirt on."

Mitch laughed and moved in anyway. A few minutes later, he pulled his watch from his pocket. "Still a little time with my girl." He said. He sat back and I snuggled up beside him. "Dana, can you believe everything that has happened in just two months?" he asked.

"It almost seems unreal, doesn't it? But, it has been wonderful." I said.

"Yeah, and you know what? The best is still to come." Mitch replied. We just sat for a few minutes letting that thought hold us. Then Mitch changed the subject.

"The kids were great last night, weren't they, Dana?" he asked.

"Yes, they're really sweet." I agreed.

"You know, sweetheart, I was looking at them and watching them last night, and it made me wonder what it'll be like when I'm a father."

"I don't know, Mitch. I think that's a ways off, but I know one thing. I think you'll be a great dad."

Mitch looked at me smiling. "Really? What makes you say that?" he inquired.

"Well, two things." I said, turning to face him. "One, you just seem to have a way with the kids. They adore you. And two, you're just a big kid yourself!"

He smiled. "I just like to have fun, that's all. What's life if you can't have fun?"

I sat with Mitch for a while, just enjoying being near him. It was a comfortable sort of silence, the kind you can only share with someone that understands you, someone that you truly connect with. I knew Mitch and I shared those things. And again, I felt like the luckiest girl alive.

"Dana, here." Mitch reached into his pocket and took out his keys. He removed the one for his car and handed it to me. "I want you to take this and I want you to have one made for yourself. And," he added, "I want you to take the car to do it."

"No, Mitch, I'm not taking the car. I'm too nervous. That's your car and I won't do it."

Mitch placed the key in my hand and folded it up. "Baby, don't argue with me, please. I want you to do this, ok? I told you that yesterday. Besides, I look at it as our car, not my car. I want to share everything I have with you."

I knew there was no changing his mind. "Ok, Mitch, I will. But I'm not going anywhere else in that car, I mean it."

He kissed my cheek. "I know what it's like to be behind the wheel of that car, Dana. You'll love it. Just wait until this summer, and we can put the top down. What a rush!" He smiled at me. "Take it wherever you want and have a good time, ok? Just make sure you get it washed, waxed, gassed up, and home by six!" He laughed.

"You are so bad!" I said, laughing back.

Mitch pulled me forward and stood up, helping me up also. "Well, my love, the time has come to depart, and I must do so." Mitch helped me with my coat, and put his own on.

"Come on, I'll walk you to the car." Once outside, Mitch put his arms around me. "Now, you be safe, ok, and have fun today." He said. "What have you got planned, anyway?"

"I'm not sure, but I was thinking, since Kayla isn't working until later, maybe I'd see if she wants to go looking for a wedding dress."

He smiled. "Pick something beautiful, beautiful!" he said kissing me. "I'll see you later." He started to walk toward Gartano's.

I got into the car, locked the doors and put on my seatbelt. It felt really different, but Mitch was right. It felt good. I started the car and pulled onto the street. I could see Mitch a little ways ahead, so I pulled up beside him and honked the horn.

"Hey handsome, how about a ride?" I called out to him.

He stopped and smiled. "Well, I don't usually accept rides from strangers, but you're too pretty to resist!" I unlocked the door and Mitch climbed in. I drove him the few blocks to Gartano's and pulled up in front. "Thanks for the ride, can I call you later?" he teased.

"Well, ok, but if you see my fiancé, don't tell him. He's a very jealous man!" I gave Mitch a kiss and sent him on his way.

Mitch pulled a key from his pocket and unlocked the door to Gartano's. He still couldn't believe that the place was his. It was a good feeling to know that he would never have to worry about how he was going to take care of Dana.

A few of the cooks were already there, starting to prepare things. Mitch greeted them and retreated to the office, then he sat down at his desk and leaned back. It felt different there today, a lot different than it had the last time he had been there. But, it was a better kind of different. He wasn't feeling miserable today, wondering where Dana was, and thinking he would never see her again. He knew she was out with Kayla, having fun, and that soon he would be holding her in his arms once more. How could one man be so lucky, he thought to himself. If anyone had told him three months ago he would be this happy, he would have thought them crazy. But not now.

I turned the corner and headed for Kayla's. This was going to be fun, I thought. Just like when I was in high school, and I used to take Grammy's car to pick up my two best friends and go shopping. Kate Miller and Renee Harwick. Gosh, I hadn't thought about them in a while. We were like the three musketeers back then, and I lost touch with them both over the last few years. Sad how things happen like that, I thought. But then, I thought about Kayla and how wonderful she was, and the friends I made here. She would be so excited to see my ring and Mitch's car and just everything. Just then, my eye caught a cassette tape hanging out of the radio. I reached for it. *Foreigner*. Ok, I could handle that. I pushed it back in and turned on the radio. The boy likes to jam, I thought, considering how high the volume was, but I left it there. Cool car, cool music, and a beautiful sunny day. What more could I want?

I turned the stereo down a little as I pulled up in front of Kayla's house, and parked the car. Tucking the key safely in the pocket of my jeans, I hurried up to Kayla's door. Joanna answered.

"Hi Dana!" She said, giving me a hug. "Mama's in the kitchen." Joanna was a beautiful young girl, about six months shy of 13. She was sweet and innocent, and when we had first met, she took an instant liking to me, and me to her.

Kayla was finishing up some dishes and smiled brightly when I entered the room. "Why, land's alive, I wasn't expecting you this morning! What a good surprise!" Kayla came and gave me a hug. Then she took my hand, still beaming, to inspect my engagement ring. "Ooo, wee, girl, that boy must *really* love you! It's gorgeous!"

"Thanks," I said, smiling myself. "Look at what else he got me." I showed her the birthstone ring and my necklace.

"He's gonna be one to spoil you, no doubt!" she said. "But that's alright, you let him do it."

I noticed a pot of coffee and pointing to it, Kayla nodded. I took a cup from the cupboard and filled it, then went back to the table. "Well, what are you doing today? Feel up to going shopping for a little while?"

Kayla nodded. "You know I'm always up for that," she replied. "What'd you have in mind?"

"Mitch let me have his car today........" Kayla's excitement cut me off midstream.

"He did what? Wow, that man really *is* spoiling you! I've seen that car!" she said

"He insisted. Wants me to have a key made so I can take it anytime I need to. He said he worries about me taking the bus, even though I've been doing it since I moved out here," I said.

"Well, now, honey, he wants to take care of you. He doesn't want anything happening to his girl." She smiled.

"I know," I replied smiling. "He is quite the protector." I thought back to the way he'd insisted I take the car.

Just then, Joseph came into the room. "I thought I heard someone out here!" he said. "How are you today, Dana?" he said cheerfully. Joseph was a big man, but as kind and gentle as they come. He was much like Kayla, always happy, and there was no doubt how much he cared for his family.

"Good morning, Joseph!" I said back. "I came to steal your wife for a little while. You know, for some 'girl' time."

Joseph looked at Kayla. "Well, I suppose that'd be ok. She's been working hard. She could probably use some time off, huh?" He was standing behind her chair now, rubbing her shoulder.

"You got that right, honey!" Kayla replied.

"Well, alright then, let's go!" I told Kayla, standing up. Then I turned to Joseph. "First, though, Joseph, there's something I need to ask you."

Joseph's face grew serious. "Alright, what is it, Dana?" he said.

"Well, I'm sure Kayla already told you Mitch and I are engaged now." I started. Joseph nodded. "Since my own dad is gone, I need someone special to walk me down the aisle and give me away. Will you do that for me, Joseph?" I asked.

Joseph smiled, and I could almost see a tear in his eye. "You want me to give you away?" he asked. I nodded. "I would be proud to do that, Dana. Real proud."

I smiled. "Ok, then it's settled!" I turned to Kayla. "Come on, the bridal shops are calling my name!"

Once in the car, Kayla started the conversation. "You know, Dana, you have a lot of things to do in the next year or so."

"I know, Kayla, I was thinking about it all the other night, and I actually started feeling overwhelmed then! But, I know Mitch will be a big help." I replied.

"What planet you from, sweetie?" Kayla quipped at me. "Ain't no man alive who helps the girl with all the plans. You're gonna be on your own for most of it."

I looked at her curiously. "Why do you say that, Kayla? This is Mitch's wedding, too, and he has a say in things. Besides, Mitch helps me with everything."

"Now, Dana, he might help you a little here and there, but trust me girl, the time will come when you ask him what he wants or what he thinks and you know what his answer will be? 'Anything you want, dear'."

I laughed. "Well, we'll see about that!" I said to her.

Going from bridal shop to bridal shop, I was already starting to feel overwhelmed. Each salesclerk gave me a different story about how I should plan, the order I should plan in, and what exactly I should plan for. I was also beginning to believe I would never find a dress I was happy with, or even more, that I could afford. I was about ready to give up when we walked into shop number six.

"Kayla, look!" I exclaimed.

Hanging on the wall was the most breathtaking gown I had seen. It was a very traditional style, with a high lace collar and long sleeves that I guessed would hit in the middle of my hand. It also had a chapel length train, which again, was nothing but lace.

"It's just what I've been looking for!" I said, taking the dress down from the hook. I handed it to Kayla. "I can't look at the price, Kayla. If it's more than I can afford, I don't want to know."

Kayla smiled and slowly looked at the price tag. "Well, Dana, I think you may have yourself a dress!"

We were squealing with excitement like two little children when the salesclerk approached us. She was an older lady, and she smiled sweetly at our antics.

"So, I see you've found something you're happy with." She said, taking the gown from me.

"Oh, you don't know the half of it!" I replied. "May I try it on?" We followed the clerk to the fitting room, and Kayla helped me get into the gown. When I turned to face the mirror, I couldn't believe I was actually looking at myself. The dress looked as if it were made for me!

"Dana, honey, you look like a fairy princess in that dress! Mitch won't be able to breathe when he sees you in that!" Kayla exclaimed.

"That's just the effect I'm going for," I replied cheerily. "Then I'll have to give him mouth to mouth resuscitation!" Kayla laughed.

The salesclerk rejoined us and pinned the dress for the few alterations it needed. After changing into my own clothes, I took the dress to her to hold for me. Then Kayla helped me pick a veil and headpiece, as well as a full hoop to wear under the dress. I was walking on air.

"I'm so happy you found something you liked." The clerk said. "Now, just let me get the information I need to hold these things for you, and a deposit." I gave the clerk everything she needed and we were on our way.

"Oh, Kayla, isn't that gown to die for?" I asked.

"You know it, girl! She said.

"Gosh, Kayla, I never thought I would find anything! I was beginning to think I'd have to get married in my jeans and sweatshirt! How would that look to my groom?"

Kayla laughed. "Somehow I don't think Mitch would mind at all!"

Meanwhile at the bistro, Mitch had everything put in order and decided to go ahead and open the doors for the lunch crowd. He was pleased to see the number of patrons who came streaming in, and he felt more than ready to handle them. He had Phyllis and Katie on hand to serve, and when Jimmy came in later to take over, Kayla would be there. Smooth sailing, he thought.

Mitch was busily checking orders and giving directions when he thought he heard someone call his name.

"Hey, Mitch, is that you?" Mitch turned around to see three of his old college buddies walking into the bistro.

"Newbie? Shep? Ty? Oh, man, I don't believe it!" Mitch walked over to the guys and they all exchanged handshakes. "What the heck are you guys doing here?" He directed the guys to a table and they all sat down.

"Well," Ty started, "we went to your parents' house first, to surprise you , but your mom said you didn't live there anymore. So, she told us we could probably find you here."

Mitch smiled. "No, I'm all grown up now. Haven't lived at home in, oh, three years or so. Got a place just about three blocks from here."

"So, like, you work here or something? What are you, a cook? Fancy one, if you wear a tie to do it!" Shep asked Mitch.

Mitch smiled and pointed to the plaque on the wall just over his shoulder. "One better, guy." He said. "I own the place."

The three men looked at each other in amazement and started to laugh. "No way!" Shep said. "You can't be serious." Newbie got up to read the plaque.

"He's not lying, dudes. Right here- "Mitchell J. Tarrington, III, Owner and Proprietor!"

"Well, congratulations, Mitch, you finally did something with your life!" They all laughed and teased. Then Shep spoke up. "Daddy's money finally paid off, huh?"

Mitch tried not to get upset by the comment. After all, it was innocent, he thought. "No, actually, I don't take money from my father. I did this all on my own."

"Hey, man, I was only kidding." Shep said, feeling a little guilty. "I think it's really cool that you could do something like this. Wish I could."

"No problem, it's ok. Yeah, it is pretty cool knowing you have something that's really yours." At that moment, he also thought of Dana, and smiled. "So, what are you guys doing here? Zach and Ash with you, too?"

"They'll be getting here later on today," Ty said. "And as for why we're here, we're pulling a few gigs this weekend, and we need a front man to fill in. Thought you might like to relive some good times." Ty patted Mitch on the shoulder.

Mitch exhaled deeply and sat back in his chair. "Man, I just don't know. It's been a long time, and, well, my life has changed. I don't know if I can."

The guys exchanged looks and then turned back to Mitch. "Look, dude, it's only for a weekend. Two spots, one on Saturday, one on Sunday. The headliner at Studio 14. Big gig, man, big. We could make it off this one." Ty leaned back in his chair and studied Mitch's face. "You're the best front man we ever had, Mitch. We need you for this."

"What happened to Kyle? Did he go out on you?" Mitch asked.

The guys nodded. "About a month ago. He said he didn't have it in him anymore, and we've been looking, but so far, the well is dry." Ty said.

Mitch couldn't believe what he was hearing. A chance to play with the band again! He thought back to college and how much fun it had been doing the gigs, just hanging out, hoping for a shot at stardom that never came. It had been a young boy's dream back then, but now he was a man, a man with responsibilities. He owned a restaurant. He had a fiancé. He couldn't go back. Or could he?

"I don't even have my electric guitar anymore, guys. Went acoustic a year back." Mitch said, thinking it might discourage them.

"No problem, guy, we got you covered. Shep has an extra one. We'll tune it up to fit you." Ty wasn't backing down.

Meanwhile, Kayla and I stopped off to make my car key and I bought Mitch a scarf, as promised, to replace the one I gave our snowman. She looked at the time.

"Well, Dana, I've had fun, but I better get home and get ready for work." She said.

"Ok, would you like a ride? I was going to see Mitch anyway." I asked.

"No, you go on sweetie and see your boy. I'm having Joseph do some errands for me later. He can drop me off."

A few minutes later Kayla was safely back home and I was on my way to Gartano's. Pulling up in front, I tucked my car key into my purse and put Mitch's in my pocket to give back to him. I grabbed the bag containing his new scarf and headed inside. Slipping inside, I looked around for Mitch, but I didn't notice that he was sitting down, or with friends, and they were still working on him. But then, suddenly, I was the one getting noticed.

"Yeah, come on Mitch, the band needs you. Just for the weekend, and you can fly after that if you.....whoa, check out this!" Newbie turned toward me and pointed.

"Wow, what a babe!" Shep agreed.

Mitch had been lost in his thoughts, but turned to see what the fuss was about. He saw me and smiled.

Ty leaned in to the others. "Doesn't look like she has a date. Maybe I should talk to her, huh? I'd like to get some time with her!"

"You?" Newbie laughed. "That's a woman and what she needs is a *man!* That would be me."

Mitch was having fun watching his friends drool over me. He decided to play a little trick on them. "Get a life, you guys," he laughed. Nobody's taking control here until I get a shot. And believe me, she won't know what hit her."

The other three men roared with laughter. "You never went up to a girl in your life, Mitch. What makes you think you even have a chance with a hot chick like her?" Shep asked.

Mitch smirked and pulled out his wallet. "Ok, put your money where your mouth is. Ten bucks says I get her to talk to me."

"Big deal." Newbie said. "I'll bet $20 that you can't get her to the table."

"Ok, dude, you're on." Mitch said standing up. He pushed in his chair, then turned around. Opening his wallet again, he laid a $50 bill on the table. "I bet this that I can go one better and get her to kiss me. Are we on?"

The three looked at each other. "Can't pass on that one. I'm a sure winner!" Newbie laughed and threw his money on the table.

"Watch a master in action." Mitch said as he walked up to me.

"Hi honey, I wondered where you were." I said leaning over to kiss him.

He pulled away, and I didn't know why. Then he got a little closer and whispered, "Don't ask any questions, just play along, ok?" I didn't have a clue what he was talking about, but I nodded anyway.

Mitch walked a little closer to where the guys were sitting so they would hear more of our conversation.

"Hi," he said to me, smiling.

"Hi." I said back.

"I don't usually do this, but well, I noticed you when you walked in, and you looked like someone I might like to get to know better." I could tell he was up to something, but I still didn't know just what. Meanwhile, the guys were taking this all in, not believing that he was actually talking to me.

"That sounds nice," I replied. "Can we sit down somewhere?"

"I have a table over here, if you don't mind joining some of my friends, too." He began to lead me toward the table. Leaning toward me again, he whispered, "You're doing great, just keep it going. Oh, hide your ring." I put my hand in my coat pocket.

"Check it out, she's actually coming over here with him!" Shep said. Ty threw $20 on the table and shook his head.

We were now standing by the table and Mitch was still smiling, enjoying his little prank. "I'd like you to meet my friends. This is Todd Sheppard, we call him Shep, Aaron Newsonberg, or Newbie, and Ty Sanders." They all said hi and shook my hand.

"You know, I didn't catch your name." Mitch smiled at me.

"Uh, Dana. Dana Walker." I replied.

Mitch was beginning to lay it on thick. "Dana, I'm usually not this forward, but there's just something about you." He had slipped his arms around me, and the guys' mouths all dropped open. "Can I ask you a question?"

"Sure," I said, looking into his eyes.

"Do you believe in love at first sight?" Mitch asked.

"Absolutely!" I replied, smiling at using his line. Mitch took off his glasses, and, laying them on the table, delivered a very long and passionate kiss.

"Dude, are you nuts?" Newbie jumped up. "You don't even *know* this girl!"

Mitch started laughing hysterically. "And what's wrong with that?" He asked.

I decided to get in on whatever this game was, too. "You know what, that was some kiss. But I can't do it again until I know who you are."

"Mitchell Tarrington, the third." Mitch pulled me to him and kissed me again. He let go with one hand, motioning the guys to throw their money on the table, which they all did.

I turned to him and smiled. "You aren't really going to take their money, are you Mitchell?" I asked.

Mitch was still laughing. "No, sweetheart, I'm not." Then he turned to the guys. "Guys, I'd like you to meet my fiancé, Dana Walker."

Ty stood up. "Wait, dude, did you say your fiancé?" Mitch nodded. "You pulled one on us, man, that was cruel."

"And do you think I was actually going to let any of you losers put the moves on my girl?" Then Mitch turned to me and pointing to each of the guys, he put them on the spot. "Sweetheart, Shep here thinks you're a babe, Ty wants to spend time with you, and Newbie here thinks you need a man." He started laughing again.

"Sorry, guys, but you're a few months too late. I'm quite happy with the man I spend time with right here." I smiled at Mitch.

Everyone was laughing now. "So, congratulations!" Newbie said. "When's the big day?"

"October 4, next year." Mitch answered. "The anniversary of the first day I saw Dana, right over there."

"You mean, you've only known each other, like, two months?" Ty asked.

Mitch beamed. "Yep, I work fast."

Shep smiled. "Looks like our Mitch has grown up after all!"

"Guys, could you excuse me for a few minutes?" Mitch asked, standing up. "I'll have Phyllis get your orders and it's on me. I can do that. I own the place!" The guys laughed and Mitch smiled.

I followed him away from the table. "Honey, please explain all that to me." I asked.

Mitch smiled. "Well, these guys are old buddies of mine from college. Seems they have a gig in town at Studio 14 this weekend, and they want me to front for them."

I was clueless. "I'm not following you, Mitch. Could you speak English, please?"

"Never mind, I'll explain later." Mitch suddenly noticed the bag in my hands and became curious. "What's in the bag?" he asked.

"Oh, I bought you a new scarf, just like I promised." I said, pulling it out of the bag.

Mitch grabbed it and stuck it back in. "Thanks sweetheart, I'll look at it later." He said, glancing at the guys.

"Ok." I said, looking at him strangely. "Can you have something to eat? I was going to maybe get some pizza or something."

"Uh, no, I better not. I haven't been doing very much work since I got here. I don't want to look like I'm slacking or anything." He smiled and kissed my forehead. "You sit down and I'll tell the girls to fix you up, ok?"

"Sure." I replied. Mitch seemed to be acting a little strange, but I just thought he was preoccupied with work.

Phyllis brought me a couple of slices of pizza and a soda, and I sat alone watching Mitch work, and his friends at their table. They seemed to be enjoying themselves, I thought. Since Mitch had said they were all college buddies, I guessed they were probably all right around his age. Shep was tall, maybe about as tall as Mitch, with sandy blond hair and blue eyes. He was rather nice looking, actually, but in need of a shave. Newbie was of medium build, probably about 5'10" or so I guessed, with dark hair and eyes. I could easily see by his mannerisms that he was the wild one of the bunch, sporting old jeans and a t-shirt. Ty seemed to be a little more conservative, like Mitch, in an oxford and tight jeans, also rather nice looking, with dark hair and hazel eyes, as well as a little mustache.

I thought about what Mitch had possibly been trying to say to me earlier. A gig in town at Studio 14. Ok, I thought, they must be musicians. And they wanted Mitch to front for them. Front what? Money? A place to stay? Then it hit me. The front man in the band. They wanted Mitch to play with them!

Mitch was making rounds at some tables now, so I motioned for him, and he came over placing one hand on the table, the other on the back of my chair. "Yeah, sweetheart, what is it? Something wrong?" he asked.

"Mitch, your friends are musicians, aren't they?" I asked him.

"Yes." He answered shortly.

"And the front man is the lead singer in the band?"

"Yes."

"And they're playing at Studio 14 this weekend, and they want you to play with them?"

"Right again."

"Why didn't you ever tell me you were in a band?" I looked up at him now, and he was looking a little guilty.

Mitch took a chair from the neighboring table, turned it around and straddled it. He took my hand. "Ok, I'll tell you. Remember when I told you that I worked two jobs in college? Well, this was one of them. We would do gigs, uh, shows and get paid to do it. Not a lot, but it helped. I dropped the band about the same time Jessica dropped me three years ago. It was a good time, and the guys, well, they're goofy but they're great just the same. I just couldn't see myself doing that for the rest of my life, so I moved on."

I looked at him with wonder. "So, is that when you started taking up the drums?"

Mitch nodded. "Newbie's a fantastic drummer. Very talented. Taught me all I know, which really isn't much. I was mostly lead guitar and vocals. They can all sing, too, especially Ty, but again, I had the range no one else could match." I could see a twinkle in Mitch's eyes as he was reminiscing.

"Do you miss it, Mitch?" I asked him, rubbing the top of his hand with my thumb.

"I don't know, Dana. I sold my electric guitar last year and bought the acoustic, the one I have now. I enjoy playing that a lot. I haven't really thought about the band in a while, just the guys time and again, and how it's sad the way you lose touch with people."

Funny, I thought. That's exactly what I'd been thinking about earlier, in Mitch's car. I doubted I would ever get a chance to rekindle my friendships. I didn't want Mitch to lose the chance to rekindle his.

"I think you should do it, Mitch. I think you should let yourself reconnect with your friends, before you lose them forever." I squeezed his hand.

Mitch looked into my eyes, and I was sure he was thinking about what I had just said. "But this weekend will be New Year's Eve, and I want to spend that with you. Besides, I have a responsibility now, Dana, and this is it." He motioned around the room. "I have to grow up sometime, and now's the time."

I leaned in closer and looked directly into his eyes. "Mitchell, aren't you the one who told me, just this morning, what's life if you can't have fun? It'll be fun for you to relive something you enjoyed. It's only for the weekend, not forever." I softened my voice. "I know you'll regret it if you don't, and I also know that deep down, you really want to."

Mitch was beginning to bite his lip, and he kept looking at the table full of his friends. Then he looked at me. "But, it'll be our first New Year's Eve together, sweetheart."

"But it won't be our last, Mitch. Do it. I'll come and watch."

Mitch nodded and got up from the table. He started to head toward his friends, but then stopped and turned around. He bent down by my chair and took both my hands. "How did I get so lucky?" he said, and gave me a kiss.

I watched as he walked over to the table to tell his friends he would join them. There were a lot of high fives, handshakes and happy faces. Then he turned around to me and smiled. I smiled, too.

Mitch went back to work, and I decided I should probably leave so he wouldn't be distracted. His friends were just getting up from their table, and they approached me.

"Hey, Dana," Ty started, "about those comments we made, well, we didn't know about you and Mitch."

"Yeah, we just see a pretty girl and get stupid. That's all. But, I can assure you, nothing disrespectful." Newbie added.

I smiled. "It's ok, guys, I know all about how young single guys can be. Trust me." I pointed to Mitch and they all laughed. "But, I'm really flattered, actually, that you would find me so, well, attractive."

"That's because you are!" Mitch said. He had sneaked up behind me, and had his arms around me now. "Gee, I'm losing my whole gang all at once. What's up with that?"

"Well, dude, we need to go get some sheets and stuff together for the gig. Can we get with you later on to go over some stuff?" Shep asked.

Mitch smiled at me. "Can't tonight, guys, I have a date. But I'm here late tomorrow, so how about before that?" Mitch grabbed a napkin and scribbled down his address and phone number. "Give me a call. We can jam out at my parents' place, like we used to."

"Cool," said Shep, taking the number. "We'll call you in the morning. See ya then, man, and I'll bring the guitar."

After they had gone, I turned to Mitch. He gave me a kiss, sending me on my way as well. "I'll come back and pick you up, ok? Around 6 or so?" I told him.

"Ok, sweetheart." He smiled. "I love you."

"I love you, too."

Around six, as promised, I pulled up to Gartano's and popped inside to pick up Mitch. Jimmy and Kayla were there now, so I said hello to both of them and scooted back to the office. Mitch was on the phone, so I slipped in and leaned over the back of his chair, slipping my arms around his chest. He smiled up at me, and placed his free hand on mine.

"Yeah, well, I don't know about that." I heard him say. "I'm quick to pick it all up, you know that, but the bridge on that one is a little strange." He was speaking a foreign language again. I stood up and began to massage his shoulders. He twisted his back a little as if he were enjoying it.

"Oh, same as always. Just my yearly solo in church, and an occasional song or two here and there. Nothing like this since I split with you guys."

Ok, I thought, he must be talking to one of his friends about the band. I wondered how long it would take me to understand everything he was saying. Or if I ever would.

"I want one in there, too, kind of a special request. No, now's not a good time to discuss that, get me? Yeah, exactly! Well, I gotta run, so give me a call in the morning. We can do a quick run through then. Cool. See ya!"

Mitch hung up the phone, and stood up, turning around to me. "Hey , baby, that was Ty. Just going over a few things."

"I noticed. Sounded pretty serious." I replied.

"No, just the set for Saturday." He picked up his coat off the rack and we headed out the door, but not before I slipped his new scarf around his neck. Once in the car, he turned to me. "So, where did you decide you want to go?"

"How about a nice juicy steak at The Mark, and then, oh, I don't know, we could go back to my place?" I proposed.

Mitch looked at me slyly. "Your place, huh? I like the sound of that. What did you have in mind when we get there, pretty lady?"

"Certainly not what you're thinking, I'm sure." I replied.

Mitch smiled. "Can't blame a guy for trying, can you?" He reached over and put his hand on my leg.

"Mitchell, behave yourself." I said firmly.

He snickered. "What, I'm not doing anything."

I took hold of his hand. "So, are you excited about doing this gig?" I asked, trying to sound like I knew what I was talking about.

Mitch nodded. "Yeah, you know, I think I am. The guys and I used to have a great time together. It'll be cool to see if we can still work like we did then."

I smiled. "Well, Mitch, why wouldn't you? You certainly have the talent, and these guys are in practice. I'm sure you'll be fine." I rubbed his arm for reassurance.

Mitch's face grew serious. "Dana, thanks."

"For what, honey?" I inquired.

"For encouraging me. For believing in me. I really do love you, you know that?"

"Yes, I do know that. And I love you, too. I will always be here for you."

We pulled into The Mark, and a few minutes later were sitting at a cozy corner booth. The lights were dim, and each table was adorned with a gas lit lamp and a single red rose, adding to the romantic atmosphere. Mitch scooted in close to me, and we shared the menu. I decided on a strip steak, Mitch on a t-bone, and we put our order in.

"So, did you and Kayla have fun today?" Mitch asked.

"Tons!" I said. "And I didn't tell you, I found a wedding gown!"

"Hey, that's great sweetheart. Is it what you were looking for?"

"It's perfect!" I replied excitedly.

Mitch seemed like he was waiting for me to say more. "So, tell me about it." He said.

I looked at him like he had just landed from Mars. "I can't tell you about it, Mitch. That would be bad luck. You'll just have to wait to see it for yourself."

"What do you mean bad luck? Will I like, self destruct if I know what your gown is like before I see you in it?" he teased.

"Stop it, Mitchell, and eat your salad." I scolded.

He folded his arms. "And what if I don't want to?" he asked playfully.

"Well, then watch me eat mine and sit there hungry." I answered smugly.

Mitch smirked at me and began to eat. "So, Dana, if I do this gig, that means Jimmy has the place most of the weekend. Think he'll be up for that?"

"Mitch, the bistro isn't open past seven on New Year's Eve anyway, and it's closed on Sunday. What are you worried about?" I asked.

"Yeah, I guess I wasn't thinking." Mitch answered between bites. "Hey, I was just wondering, who will you sit with at this thing? I don't want you there alone in that crowd of people."

I put down my fork, wiped my mouth with my napkin, and looked straight at him. "Mitchell Tarrington, are you trying to find a way to get out of this? And if so, why? What are you worried about?"

Mitch had finished his salad and pushed the plate away. He sat back and sighed, as if in deep thought, before he answered. "I'm not sure, Dana. I mean, it seems like it's been forever since I did this kind of thing. What if I totally mess this up for the guys?"

I had finished also, and I rubbed his back reassuringly. "You won't mess anything up Mitch. That's why you practice. And if you make a mistake, who'll know it but you?"

"The guys will know, Dana. This could be a big gig for them. I don't want to interfere with that."

I decided to play into Mitch's pity party. "All right, then, Mitch. When we get home, you call Ty or Shep or whoever and tell them you aren't going to do it. Maybe they'll get lucky and stumble across another multitalented individual before Saturday."

I took a drink of water and sat back. I could understand him being nervous a little. Anyone would be, I thought. But it wasn't like Mitch to want to quit anything. I wondered if perhaps his real fear was that he would find he missed the band more than he wanted to admit.

Our steaks arrived and Mitch and I began to eat in silence. His face was basically expressionless, but I could still see that he was mulling over his possibilities. I knew in my heart that he wouldn't back down, that he would find letting down his friends would be much worse than taking the risk of making a mistake in a song. Finally, he turned to me, as if seeking my approval.

"So, you think I should do it?" he asked.

I decided I was still going to let this be his decision. "Only if you want to, Mitch."

He nodded. "I really think I do, Dana." He smiled, and decided to change the subject.

"So, what other great finds did you stumble upon today with Kayla?"

"I got my veil and some other things to go with the dress. And your scarf." I added.

"Yeah, it is really nice. Thanks." He smiled.

I thought about the way he'd reacted when I showed it to him at the bistro, so I thought I would be a brat and ask. "If you like it so much, why didn't you want to look at it when I first gave it to you? Afraid your friends might see that your girlfriend is trying to take care of you?" I sat back and waited for his answer.

"Fiancé, and no, not at all." He quickly replied. "I like being taken care of, actually."

"That's good, because I like taking care of you." I smiled at him. "So, that having been said, when do you plan to get those glasses fixed? They're still bent."

"Oh, I can fix that myself." Mitch took off his glasses, and preceded to try bending the frames back in place. He was holding them in such a way that I could tell he was having difficulty even seeing what he was doing.

"Mitch, honey, you and I both know you can't see what you're doing. Put them back on. We'll just head over to the mall—there's an eyeglass place there that can fix them up for you."

Mitch sighed and obeyed. "You know, this assertiveness thing isn't so cute anymore." He said, looking at me out of the corner of his eye, smirking. He picked up the small menu sitting on the end of the table. "Want some dessert? I'll split something with you."

"Anything chocolate." I replied.

We picked out a hot fudge brownie topped with vanilla ice cream. A few minutes later it arrived, and Mitch dug right in. I had one bite to his three, and finally decided it wasn't worth the battle, so I put down my spoon.

"Why aren't you eating any of this?" he asked. "Don't you like it?"

"Oh, no, it's fine, sweetie," I replied. "I'm just enjoying watching you enjoy it."

Mitch put his head down, and then his spoon. "I'm sorry, I'm being selfish, huh? You finish the rest. I guess I'm just hungry because I didn't get a chance to eat any lunch."

I picked up a bite of the dessert on the spoon and started to eat it, but I glanced over at Mitch, who was watching me with big puppy dog eyes. I offered the bite to him, and he took it with a smile.

"You better get some before it's all gone." I said. Mitch smiled and willingly dug back in.

A short while later we arrived at the mall, had Mitch's glasses repaired, and decided just to do some window shopping. As we were approaching the jewelry store, I had a thought. "Honey, let's go in and look at wedding bands. We're going to need those, you know."

"Why?" Mitch asked. "You don't think I'm actually going through with this, do you?" He was trying not to smile, but his eyes were shining. I smacked him hard on the arm.

"Hey, that hurt!" he said with a half snicker. "Now I *know* I'm not going through with this, if you're that abusive." I pulled back to smack him again, but he grabbed my hand and then hugged me. "Come on, baby, I was just kidding. I love you." Still rubbing his arm, he took my hand and we went into the jewelry store. The salesclerk smiled as she recognized him.

"Hello, Mr. Tarrington, isn't it?" she said. "And this must be the lucky girl."

"Yes, this is my fiancé, Dana." Mitch said.

"Congratulations," she said to me. "What can I help you with today?"

"We'd like to take a look at wedding bands." I said.

The clerk led us to the display case containing the wedding bands. "I'll leave you alone for a few minutes to browse, and then I'll be back to see if I can show you anything." She said. We thanked her and she walked away.

"Gosh, I never realized it was this complicated." Mitch said, looking at the multitude of rings before him.

"It's not complicated, Mitch," I replied. "You just pick something you like, and I buy it for you."

"And then I suppose you'll think I have to buy you something, too, then, huh?" He was being really ornery this evening.

"If you don't be quiet, I'm going to smack you again." I said sternly, yet playfully.

Mitch kissed me on top of the head. We studied the rings for a few minutes and picking a few we liked, the salesclerk came back over to us. "So, what can I show you?" She asked.

"I really like the one there, third from the end in the back, and I think he wants to see the matching band." I told her.

The clerk withdrew a beautiful two tone band adorned with channel set diamonds, about ten that I could count. The man's ring was a brushed silver style with a small channel cut on top hosting one small diamond. I put the band on with my ring and inspected it.

"I don't know, honey, the engagement ring just looks so much bigger. It doesn't go well together, do you think?" I turned to Mitch and he just shrugged.

"I like this one." He said, inspecting his ring.

"It is nice, but let me see what I can find first, ok?" Again, he shrugged and handed it back to the clerk.

I picked out a wrap next, and put it on with my ring. "This one's pretty, don't you think so, honey?"

"Yeah, sure." Mitch said, without a lot of enthusiasm.

I gave it back to the clerk, and tried on a few more, each time asking for Mitch's opinion, and each time, not getting much of anything.

Finally, I tried one that I thought would be perfect. It was a beautiful gold band with beget diamonds that offset my engagement ring like they were made for each other. Together, the whole package was stunning.

"It's perfect, honey, don't you think?" I asked.

This time Mitch actually looked at the ring. "It's very pretty, Dana."

"Ok, now to find you a ring." I said, handing mine back to the clerk. She set it under the counter for safekeeping.

"I like the one I already looked at." Mitch said, matter-of-factly.

"But, honey, it doesn't match the one I picked." I retorted.

"Does it have to?" he asked back.

"Well, I think it's supposed to." I answered.

"Why does it have to match? I like it." He argued. I could tell he was getting agitated, and so was I.

The clerk was very perceptive. "I'll give you a little time to talk things over. Let me know when you're ready." She smiled and walked away.

I turned to Mitch. "Mitchell, the wedding bands are supposed to match. That's just how it's done." I started.

He had a look of disbelief on his face. "Why? Is that the way people can tell we belong to each other? Heaven forbid our bands don't match.

Why, we may just get confused and end up with other people." He was being very smug.

His attitude had finally gotten to me. "Stop, Mitchell." I said sternly. "Why can't you just cooperate?"

"What do you mean, cooperate?" He snapped. "Don't you mean, why don't I give up all rights to having my own opinion and let you control me?"

"I don't try to control you, Mitch. You're just stubborn, that's all."

Mitch had a stunned look on his face. "Me. I'm stubborn. There's a mirror right over there, Miss Dana. You'd better go look into it."

I glared at him. How could he be so pigheaded, I thought. Must be the overabundance of testosterone, I concluded.

"Ok, Mitch, you win. You can get your ring, and I'll pick something to match yours. How's that?" I motioned for the sales clerk to come back over.

"There is no way that is going to happen, Dana." Mitch said firmly. "For one, I'm not staying in this store for another minute, let alone another hour. For another, if you get anything other than what you already picked, I'll have to hear about it for the rest of my life."

"Did you decide?" The clerk asked as she approached us again.

"I think I would like to….." I started, but Mitch cut me off.

"She's going to take the one she picked, and I would like a plain gold band. Just a plain gold band, that's all."

The clerk handed Mitch a gold wedding band, and he tried it on. "Perfect. If you'll just ring all this up, we'll be on our way."

"Don't you want to know the price of the ladies band?" she asked.

"No, that's ok. It doesn't matter. I'll take it." Mitch was biting his lip and breathing deeply.

"Wait, I'm paying for his." I told her.

He pulled out his credit card and handed it to the clerk. "You can just put it all on there, please."

She smiled and a minute later, returned with the slip for Mitch to sign. He scribbled his name, put his card back in his wallet and took the bag. "Thank you for your help." He said, and turned to walk out of the store. I smiled at the clerk and followed. Mitch tucked the bag in the inside pocket of his coat and was not saying a word to me.

"Mitchell, why are you mad at me?" I asked. "What did I do?"

Mitch just looked at me, still biting his lip, and still, didn't say anything.

"Mitchell, I asked you a question. Would you please answer me?" I tried again.

"Maybe, right now, I don't feel like talking." He said. "I feel like sitting down." Mitch parked himself on a bench and folded his arms.

I sat down next to him. "Mitchell, I really wish you would tell me why you're mad. I mean, you didn't have to make such a fuss over the rings, did you?"

Mitch had a confused look on his face and he turned to look at me. "Me make a fuss? You were the one who was so caught up in, oh, everything has to match, why would you want anything else? Dana, sometimes I would like to have an opinion that matters."

"Who said it didn't? And why are you escalating this whole thing into an argument, Mitchell?" I was getting irritated, too.

He sighed. "First of all, it's Mitch, please. My name is Mitch. Second, because it doesn't matter if the rings match, Dana. What the ring looks like doesn't matter, it's what it symbolizes that matters. Once you put that ring on me, Dana, it's never coming off. And whether I have a fancy ring with sixty diamonds or a plain gold band or a ring from a gumball machine, it will still mean the same thing. That I am Dana Tarrington's husband." He sighed again deeply.

"Your name is Mitchell, not Mitch. Mitch is a nickname." I said softly.

"Well, that isn't my fault. I didn't name myself." Mitch said, pouting.

I reached out for his hand. "You're right, honey, I'm sorry." I said. "That was supposed to be a happy experience, not an argument." He sighed again. "Can I see the bag for a minute, please?" I asked.

Mitch took the bag out and handed it to me, and I took out his ring, then handed mine back to him. "Here, put this back in your pocket and wait here." I got up quickly before he had a chance to stop me.

"Dana, where are you going?" he called after me.

"Just stay there." I instructed.

I returned to the jewelry store and exchanged Mitch's ring for the one he had originally looked at. Charging it to my card, I happily left the store. Mitch was still waiting on the bench, but he was not looking as upset as he had been when I left. I handed him the ring box. "Here, put it with mine." I said to him.

"Dana, what did you just do?" he asked, opening the box to reveal his ring.

"You were right, honey. It doesn't matter if they match. But what does matter to me is that the one you are wearing is the one you want."

He turned to me and closed the box. "You didn't have to do that, you know."

"I know," I answered. "But I wanted to."

He smiled and placing the ring safely away, took my hand. "You know, I don't think we should come to this mall anymore." He said.

"Why not?" I questioned.

"Well, because every time we do, we get into an argument!" he smiled at me.

"I'm sorry I was being so controlling, Mitch. I don't ever want to be that way with you." I laid my head on his shoulder.

"It's ok, sweetheart. You know how to keep me in line. That's good, I need that sometimes. And I'm sorry I was being stubborn." he kissed my cheek. "Oh, and if you want to call me Mitchell, that's fine with me."

11

The mall was just about to close for the evening, so we decided to head back toward home. Once in my apartment, Mitch parked himself in the chair and pulled me down on his lap.

"There's George." He said, pointing to our snowman outside the window. "Know what he's thinking?"

"No, what?" I asked.

"He sees us and he wishes he had a little snow girl to go with him." Mitch put me on my feet and before I knew it, he was standing on the balcony, constructing another little snow person. He opened the door, and called out for me.

"I need the finishing touches," he said.

I smiled and retrieved two straws, some buttons, a piece of carrot, and a scarf. Within a few more minutes, the snow girl was created.

Mitch stepped back inside and was shivering from the cold. Rubbing his hands together, he sat back down and put me back into position as well.

"Now, I get to name her, since you named George." He said. He looked at her for a minute or two. "Beverly." He concluded.

"George and Beverly. Ok, I guess that sounds alright." I said. "Oh, look, honey, they're even holding hands." Mitch had positioned the straw so it was touching the one sticking out of George.

Mitch held me tightly. "You're nice and warm." He said. He picked up the TV remote. "Want to see what's on?" he asked.

"Ok." I replied, snuggling up to him. I could hear his heart beating softly, and it was comforting. Mitch kissed me lightly and brushed my hair back away from my face gently. Then he turned his attention back to the TV. I couldn't help but wonder if this was what it was going to be like every night we were together. I didn't know for sure, but I hoped it would.

I didn't remember falling asleep, but Mitch gently shook me awake around midnight.

"Dana, baby, come on, wake up." He said softly. "I have to go home now."

I opened my eyes for just a second, then closed them again and repositioned myself on his lap.

"Sweetheart, I would really love to stay right here, but if I don't go soon, I'll be falling asleep myself." I still didn't move. "Ok, just a few more minutes." He said, kissing my cheek. The next thing I knew, it was seven in the morning. We had slept there all night!

"Mitch, honey, wake up. Please!" I said, excitedly.

Mitch opened his eyes and sat up a little. "Wha....oh, oh! We didn't." He said, looking at me.

"We must have fallen asleep together last night, and didn't wake until now." I said.

I stood up and pulled Mitch to his feet. He seemed to be a little wobbly at first, mainly because I had been sitting on his legs all night. "What are people going to think when they see you leaving here, this early in the morning, Mitch?"

He smiled. "Who cares? Let them think what they will. We know we didn't do anything wrong." He kissed me. "Besides, who said I was ready to leave yet? You go get cleaned up, I'll make us some coffee." He said.

"I love you, Mitch Tarrington." I said.

"I love you, too, Dana Walker. Now go." He scooted me toward the hallway.

Fifteen minutes later, I had showered and changed, and was ready to greet Mitch again. I was surprised to see not only a fresh pot of coffee, but two omelets waiting for me.

"Hey, sweetheart." He said, greeting me. "I made breakfast. I just hope I did it right."

I gave him a hug. "Looks perfect. But if I die, my insurance policy is in the box on the top shelf of my closet." I smiled at him and giggled.

"Very funny." He said back. "Let's give this a try, shall we? You take the first bite. I'm too afraid." He laughed.

"I thought you were supposed to be my protector," I said, "but ok, here goes." He had actually done a good job. "Honey, this is wonderful. Really!"

He smiled proudly. "I'm a quick learner and I had a good teacher." He said.

"Don't you have to get with the band this morning, honey?" I asked. "What if they call and you aren't there?"

Mitch laughed. "Baby, they won't be up before ten. Don't worry about it. Besides, I have all day."

We finished our breakfast and Mitch helped me clean up the dishes. Then he took me by the hand and led me back to the couch.

"Dana, I have an idea. I don't know if you'll agree or not, but hear me out." His face was serious, but I could hear the excitement in his voice. "This whole situation, I mean, us sleeping here together last night, says something to me, sweetheart. Not only are we comfortable with each other, but well, it makes it obvious to me that we really don't like being away from one another."

I looked at him curiously. "Mitch, what are you getting at?" I asked.

"I don't want to wait a whole year to get married, Dana. I hate every moment I'm not with you. Let's move the date up, and get married sooner. What do you say?" His eyes were shining and I could tell he was trying to find his answer by looking into mine.

I suddenly felt dizzy. "Mitch, I don't know. There's still so much to do, so much to plan."

The smile faded from his face, but he managed to bring a small one back anyway. "Yeah, you're right. It was just a thought. I can wait. Besides, if we do it any other time, I may forget our anniversary."

I smiled and put my arms around him. "Mitchell, you didn't let me finish. We still have so much to do, yes, but we already have the rings, and my gown, and we know who is going to be in the wedding. I don't think it will be much trouble to plan the rest, by, say, May or June."

Mitch's face lit up like a radiant star. "Really, you mean it?" I nodded. "I sure do love you, Dana. I love you so very much!"

"I love you, too, Mitch." I replied.

Mitch leaned over and kissed me. "I want to give you enough time, so get your calendar and let's pick a date, ok?"

I retrieved my calendar from the kitchen and brought it back to Mitch. Then I had a thought. I opened the calendar to June, and sure enough, the date I had on my mind was a Saturday. Fate was smiling on me, I thought. I looked at Mitch.

"June 10, Mitch, it has to be June 10." I said, putting my finger on the date.

"Why? What's so special about June 10?" he asked.

My voice softened. "June 10 was Grammy's birthday." I said. "It would mean a lot to me, Mitch, I mean, since I can't have her there with me."

Mitch looked at me lovingly, and pulled me close. He took the pen from my hand and made a big heart on June 10. "Then that's when it has to be." He smiled at me.

"Will you be able to remember that?" I asked, making circles on his chest with my finger.

"Sweetheart, our wedding day is something I will never be able to forget!" And with that, Mitch kissed me again, and I could feel all his love.

"Mitch, we have to announce our engagement. We haven't done that yet, you know!" I told him.

"Announce it to whom? Everyone already knows about it." Mitch said.

"No, when couples get engaged they put an announcement in the newspaper so everyone will know." I explained.

"So, I need to take out an ad in the newspaper telling people I'm engaged to be married." Mitch let the idea sink in. Then he looked at me. "Will I be told I'm not cooperating if I tell you I don't understand why this is necessary?"

I leaned up to face him. "No, but it is something we should do."

Mitch sighed. "Ok, let's do it. I wouldn't want any bad luck to come upon us if we don't."

I got up and collected a pad of paper from the kitchen. Then I returned to Mitch. "Let's see, what should it say?"

"How about Mitch and Dana are engaged?" Mitch smirked.

"Mitch, be serious." I scolded. Then I started to write. "Dana P. Walker, daughter of the late Sgt. and Mrs. Patrick Walker, announces her engagement to Mitchell J. Tarrington, III, son of Mr. and Mrs. Mitchell J. Tarrington, Jr. Miss Walker is a kindergarten teacher at Lincoln Elementary and Mr. Tarrington is owner and proprietor of Gartano's Italian Bistro. The wedding date is set for June 10, 1988."

Mitch read it over. "Why are you announcing your engagement to me? Don't I get to announce my engagement to you, too?"

I looked at Mitch, rolled my eyes and sighed. "Ok, how about 'Dana P. Walker, daughter of the late Sgt. and Mrs. Patrick Walker and Mitchell J. Tarrington, III, son of Mr. and Mrs. Mitchell J. Tarrington, Jr., announce their engagement'. Blah, blah and all the rest. Is that better?"

"Yes, thank you. Now, what do you do? Send that into the newspaper or something?" Mitch asked. He was lightly brushing back my hair with his fingers.

"Yes, and we need to send a picture, too." Then I remembered. "Honey, we don't have any pictures together. We'll have to get engagement pictures taken."

Mitch sat up. "Dana, engagement pictures? Is all this really necessary?" he asked. "Sweetheart, why don't we just let Chris take a nice picture of us and we'll send that in, ok? He's a decent photographer."

"Because, Mitch, we need to have them done at a studio. That way, we'll always have them." I said knowingly.

"But...." Mitch stopped and looked at me. Then he smiled. "Ok, even though I don't understand why, I'll do it for you." He kissed me and stood up. Walking to the kitchen, he poured himself a glass of milk, then came back and sat down. "One thing though. We have to wait until my face doesn't look like I've been run over by a semi." He was referring to the cuts and black eye he'd received from Chris.

"Well, ok, maybe by next week everything will be back to normal. It's already starting to heal." I agreed. "Oh, you know what else? We need to make the guest list, too, honey and go to pick out invitations. I'll start on that today, while you're with your friends."

Mitch smiled and shook his head at me. "For crying out loud, Dana, we've only been engaged for two days, the wedding is six months away—do you have to do all this today?"

"Well, we have to start sometime Mitchell," I replied. "I don't want to be calling caterers as I'm walking down the aisle!"

Mitch finished his milk and stood up. "Ok, sweetheart, you do what you feel you need to, but I don't want you getting stressed out over this, ok? I mean it. If you don't think six months is enough time......"

I stood up and followed him into the kitchen where he placed his glass in the sink. "It will be plenty of time, Mitch, but only if you're willing to help me."

He smiled and put his arms around me. "Of course I'll help you, love. You know I will. But now, I need to get home and wait for the guys." He gave me a kiss, and grabbed his coat. "Tell you what, sweetheart. You take the car today and do whatever you need to do. I'll catch a ride with the guys. I can walk home from here."

"No, Mitch, I had the car all day yesterday. It's your car, you need it, you take it." I argued.

Mitch folded his arms and looked at me, his head cocked to one side and a boyish grin on his face. "Dana Walker, why are you so difficult? I said take the car. I will be fine. Besides, I expect to see you, oh, around one or so for lunch. You'll have a hard time getting there without transportation." He reached out for me. "Now, bring yourself over here and kiss me goodbye so I can get going." I walked over and gave Mitch a kiss, leaving lipstick on him. I wiped it off with my finger.

"Hey, you wiped off my kiss. Now you have to give me another one." Mitch said. So I did. "Be careful today, sweetheart and have fun. I'll see you later." Mitch turned and walked out the door.

"I love you, Mitch." I called after him.

He turned around and smiled. "I love you, too."

It was cold and a little blustery, so Mitch tightened his coat around him and headed home. Today he was extra glad for the scarf Dana had gotten him, and he brought it up to cover his face a little. He was feeling good about things, about the decision to move up the wedding, and the decision to play with the band. Dana was so good for him, he thought. He just hoped he could be the same for her.

He finally reached his apartment, and welcomed the warmth. Hanging up his coat, he noticed that he had a phone message. Who would have called, he thought? Maybe Dana. He pressed the button.

"Hey, Trip, it's Ty. It's around 8, and we're ready to jam. Don't know where you are, but call when you get in. See ya."

Mitch smiled. Trip. He'd forgotten that nickname. Ty and Shep had started it when he told them he was actually Mitch Tarrington, the third. Shep had called him a "triple Tarrington", which quickly got shortened to Trip. Kind of crazy now, he thought, but ok just the same.

Mitch was just about to call Ty when he heard a knock on his door. He put down the phone and opened the door to see all his band mates.

"My gosh, what are you guys doing here?" Mitch said with surprise. "How did you know where I lived?"

"You gave us the address yesterday, remember?" Ty said. "Besides, you didn't answer when we called, so we just thought we'd come over and harass you."

The guys all piled into the apartment, and Mitch greeted Zach and Ash, whom he hadn't seen the day before. Shep, being the most forward of the group, decided to ask the prize winning question. "So, where were you at eight o'clock this morning? Well, actually 7:30 is the first time we called, but didn't leave a message."

"I was out, and that's all you need to know." Mitch said, sitting down on the chair.

Shep looked him over. "Come on, Trip. You haven't shaved, but no big deal, and aren't those the same clothes you had on yesterday?"

Mitch was smirking. "What's your point, Shep? You aren't going to shut up until I tell you, are you?"

Shep grinned and shook his head. "I think I know, but I want to hear it from the man. Do tell, Mitch, do tell."

Mitch sighed. "I was with Dana. Happy now?"

Shep smiled. "You call on your lady at seven in the morning?" Then an even bigger grin hit his face. "Or maybe, you were already there?"

Mitch closed his eyes, and let out a deep breath. "Yes, Shep I was already there. I slept at Dana's last night. No big deal."

All the guys began exchanging high fives and smiles, laughing and teasing Mitch.

"Well, well, Mr. Tarrington got a little action. No wonder he looks all worn out." Newbie said.

Mitch put up his hand. "Now, hold on a minute, guys, it's not what you're thinking. I only slept with Dana, oh man, I mean slept *at* Dana's and that's all. Nothing else."

Ty looked at Mitch. "Nothing else, huh?"

"Guys, ok, this is a sensitive subject, but I want to set the record straight. Dana and I don't have that kind of relationship."

Shep looked at him with disbelief. "You're engaged to one of the hottest women on the planet, and you *don't* have *that* kind of relationship."

Mitch stood up and leaned on the back of the chair. "Yes, I'm engaged to a very sexy woman, I agree on that. But Dana and I made an agreement that we would wait until we got married, and if that makes you think any less of me, then that's your problem. I hate to disappoint you, but last night we fell asleep watching TV and didn't wake up until this morning. That's it. End of story." Mitch's tone told the guys he wasn't lying to them.

"Hey, Mitch, we're sorry. You know how dumb we can be. It's all cool." He said, patting Mitch on the shoulder.

"Yeah, I'm sorry too, man." Shep said. "I respect you. It's cool."

Mitch smiled. "Well, I didn't want you guys thinking things that aren't true. I told you more for Dana's reputation than mine." Then he pointed to his black eye. "In fact, defending her reputation with my brother is exactly how I got this."

Zach spoke up. "Hey, I hate to break up the little love fest here, but I think we need to get some rehearsing done" He turned to Mitch. "Can you shower and change in like, five minutes?"

"Give me ten, and I'm with you. You guys just hang out and make yourselves at home." he replied.

Mitch cleaned up and returned to find the guys doing just as he had told them to. Ash was on the weight bench, trying his best to lift the weight off the stand. Mitch laughed and walked over to him.

"Move out of the way, loser. Let me show you how a real man does things." Ash got up and Mitch took off his sweatshirt, handing it to him. "Here, you'll need this to mop up your tears of shame in a minute."

"Yeah, well I'm sure those are all on there just for show. You probably never use this thing!" Ash teased back.

The guys gathered around Mitch as he laid back on the bench. Taking a deep breath, he lifted the weight off the stand, then put it right back. They all laughed.

"Mighty Mitch, that's what we should call him from now on," Ty said.

"Hey, yeah, Mighty Mitch. Mighty Mouse is more like it!" Shep laughed, and so did the others.

"Mighty Mouse? Watch what you say, there, guy." Mitch placed his hand on the weights again, and this time not only lifted them off the stand, but brought them down to his chest. He did it four more times for effect, then sat up, grinning impishly. "You were saying?"

"Crud, man, when did you learn to do that?" Zach asked.

"I didn't inherit this upper body, believe me. Just something I took up a few years back." Mitch said. Ash handed him back his sweatshirt, and he stood up, pulling it back on. "Ok, I gave Dana the car today, so which one of you other losers is giving me a ride to rehearsal?"

Ash smiled. "You're with me, man. I'm afraid if I don't you'll beat the life out of me!"

Wanting to get started on the plans, I decided to make a few phone calls before I had to go to meet Mitch. Pulling out the phone book, I looked up photography studios. I could set up a date for the engagement pictures, and maybe pop downtown to see about invitations.

After calling about five or six studios and doing price and package comparisons, I was getting a little frazzled. This is worse than dress shopping, I thought. But it had to get done, so I dialed yet another number. The sales lady seemed very helpful and the price was reasonable, so I decided to book an appointment. Booking the date for a week away, I figured that would give Mitch enough time to get back to normal.

I looked at the clock. Eleven-ten. If I moved fast I would still have time to check out a few bridal shops for invitations. I grabbed my coat and started to head out the door when the phone rang.

"Hello?" I answered.

"Hi, beautiful!" I heard Mitch's sexy voice say. My heart skipped a beat.

"Hi, honey. What are you calling for? I thought you were rehearsing." I said.

"Well, we're taking a little break. We haven't really gotten too deep into it yet. I just wanted to hear your voice, that's all. I miss you." Mitch said.

That is so sweet, I thought. He only left two hours ago and already he misses me.

"I miss you too, Mitch. Oh, guess what? I set up the appointment for our pictures. Next Friday at 11, at Harrison's. Is that ok with you?"

I could tell Mitch was smiling, even though I couldn't see him. "That's fine, sweetheart. How soon are you coming out?"

"I was going to run downtown for a little while first, to check out invitations. Unless you'd rather I wait until you can go, too."

"No, no, that's fine, you go ahead. Whatever you pick will be fine with me." He answered. "Well, I better go, the guys want to start up again. I just hope I don't lose my voice. I'm not used to this anymore."

"I hope not, too. I'll see you soon. I love you."

"I love you, too. Bye."

Ok, that was nice, but now it was 11:20. I would really have to hurry to get to Jake and Olivia's by one. I got to the car as quickly as I could and started downtown. I stopped first at a bridal shop that Kayla and I hadn't gotten to the day before.

"Hi, I'm looking for wedding invitations," I told the clerk. She led me to a table with five very large books on it chock full of every type of invitation style known to man. I looked at her in disbelief. She just smiled.

"You can take a look through these and if you see something you like, I can give you samples to take home so you can share them with your fiancé."

"That would be fine, thanks." I said, and began to browse through the first book. White, ivory, cream, matte, glossy, plain, colored. I was getting tired, and after a while, they all began to look the same. By the third book, I had pulled only two out that really caught my eye. I reached for book number four and began to leaf through it. I found a few more. It was now close to noon, and I knew I didn't have time to continue, so, I showed the clerk what I had found. She gave me samples, and I went on my way.

As I drove to Jake and Olivia's, I glanced over at the bag containing the invitation samples. This might not be so bad, I thought. I could just show my findings to Mitch and let him help me pick. Then, that would be one less thing to worry about.

I pulled up in front of the house, and walked up to the door. Ringing the doorbell, I waited patiently for Alexander to answer. Nothing. I rang again. Still, nothing. Where was everyone, I thought. I tried again, and this time, Alexander came to the door.

"I'm sorry if you were waiting, miss," he said. "I'm having a little difficulty hearing things at certain points in the house."

I smiled as he took my coat. "Can you tell me where Mitch is?" I asked him.

"Just follow the noise." He answered. I smiled.

I slipped through the family room, following the sound just as Alexander had instructed. Suddenly, I heard everything grow quiet, except for Mitch's voice.

"You're supposed to come in on four, guys, not six. Newbie, count four and that's your cue in." I heard him say.

"Four and we come in. Got it." Newbie answered.

I heard them start to play again, and then suddenly everything stopped once more. This time, they were all laughing. I slipped quietly through the door unnoticed. Mitch was turned around facing them all, his face glowing.

"Tell me four and you do six. Good job, Trip." Newbie said, still laughing.

"Ok, let's try this *one* more time. I'll count it on the mic. Zach, lead in a little stronger, ok?" Mitch sounded so professional. I was impressed. I sat down on the floor with my back against the wall. I still wasn't being noticed, so I decided I would just try to blend in.

Mitch got back into position. "Ok, one, two, three, four." He counted. Silence.

He dropped his head, laughing and turned around again. "Uh, guys, aren't you supposed to be actually playing those instruments?" They were having a good time teasing him.

Then Mitch started playing and again, as I had in the past, my mouth dropped. He looked like he'd been born with that guitar in his hands. Newbie came in on the drums and the others followed. It sounded fantastic. Mitch started to sing, and I was totally lost in the moment. I knew the tune, and kind of hummed along. Mitch looked like a true rocker, and more than that, he looked so sexy at that moment. Now I know what groupies feel like, I thought.

They finished the song, and Mitch turned to them again. "Yes, that's it! Finally, we did it. Let's hit it again, one more time." They did the song again, perfectly. I decided to make my presence known, so I applauded. Ty pointed to me, and caught Mitch's attention. He smiled.

"Hey, baby!" Mitch said, trying to catch his breath. "Come here."

I walked up to him and he put his arm around me, giving me a kiss on the cheek. "Hey, Ash, Zach, this is Dana Walker, my fiancé. Dana, Ashton Marshall and Zachary Daniels."

Both men came down and shook my hand. "Nice to meet you, Dana," Zach said. He was tall and muscular, maybe just a little taller than Mitch, with dark hair and eyes.

"Hey, Dana, how's it going?" Ash said. I noticed he had a great smile, and was dressed very preppy, sporting an earring. His blond hair touched his shoulders, but was neat, and he had a little mustache.

"Well, what do you think?" Mitch asked.

"You guys are terrific! Can I be your first groupie?" I asked. I laughed as four of the guys walked up and surrounded me.

"Oh, no, as front man, I get the first one." Mitch said, reaching out for my hand. "You can have the leftovers." A few pretended to pout, and the others laughed.

"Well, don't let me get in the way. I'll go so you can keep rehearsing." I said.

Mitch took my hand and led me to the back of the room, then found a chair and placed me in it. "You park your pretty little self right here. We need a critic." Then he bent down close to me. "And don't ever think you're in the way. I love having you here." He smiled and walked back up to the front.

"Hey Mitch, wanna try the last tune in the set? We want to see that range of yours in action." Ty asked.

"Let me see the sheet." He said. "I know the tune, I just need the first few notes." Newbie handed him a sheet of music, and he looked at it, then played a few notes on his guitar. He laid the sheet down, and instructed them to start.

Look out, Hollywood, I thought. Here comes Mitch Tarrington! Were they *really* this good, or was I biased? I guess we'd find out after a few songs this weekend. The crowd would tell us all we needed to know.

They ran through three or four more songs, and Mitch called a break. "Hey guys, let's go get that pizza. I just saw the guy leaving, and I'm starved!" They all agreed and started out to the dining room. I caught Mitch by the arm and stopped him for a moment alone.

"Mitchell, you're fabulous!" I said. "You guys need to really consider going professional."

He smiled. "I'm glad to hear you think we have the talent," he said. "But it's just a lot of fun, that's all." I decided not to push it with him. If he was happy, I was happy.

"Oh, honey, I got some invitations for you to look at. You can help me pick one, ok?" I said eagerly.

We started to walk to join the others for pizza. "You can pick it, sweetheart. I trust your judgment," Mitch replied.

"But I want it to be something you like, too, Mitch." I told him.

"Dana, love, it really doesn't matter to me. You just pick it out, ok?" By this time, we were in the dining room. "Did you save anything for us?" Mitch asked the guys. Without speaking, Newbie opened up a box and pointed. Mitch pulled out a chair for me, and sat down, grabbing two pieces of pizza, handing one to me.

"So, Dana, how'd you get stuck with this guy?" Ash asked teasingly. "Did you feel sorry for him or something?"

I smiled. "Actually, he found me first." I answered.

"Really, Mitch, and you were able to convince her you really aren't that bad after all, huh?" Ash asked.

"It was the whipped cream and the couch in the managers office at Gartano's that did the convincing, I think." Mitch was smirking.

All the guys stopped eating and looked at Mitch. So did I.

"Mitchell Tarrington, unless you want this ring back, you'd better explain." I said, smiling at him.

He laughed. "Good, saves me $2,000," he said. I smacked him on the arm.

"Man, you're so mean to me!" he laughed, rubbing his arm.

"Hey, Trip, I think you got one there that's going to keep you in line." Shep laughed.

"Explain, Mitchell!" I said again.

Mitch laughed and told the guys the story of the whipped cream fight at Gartano's, and they all thought it was hilarious.

"And you know, it's been the time of my life." He said, leaning over to kiss me.

"So, when's the big day again? Didn't you say October?" Newbie asked.

"Actually, we moved it up as of this morning. It's going to be........."
he looked at me. "What day did we say again, sweetheart?"

"June 10th." I answered. I concluded right then that I would never
see an anniversary gift.

Everyone seemed to have their fill of the pizza so Mitch suggested
they run through a few more numbers before he had to leave for work.
I took him aside once more.

"Mitch, I was thinking about flowers. I know that I really like roses
and carnations. But do you think we should go with real ones, or should
we do silk, so we can keep them after? And how do you feel about pink
and blue as our wedding colors?"

"That's fine, Dana. Whatever you want." Mitch was heading back
to the guys.

"Mitch, wait. I was thinking we could invite everyone to the club
Saturday night, and we can ask them about being in the wedding. What
do you think?"

Mitch sighed. "Dana, I probably won't get much of a break away
from anything Saturday, but you can ask them, ok? He kissed my
forehead. "I really better get back to the guys. Are you coming?"

I shook my head. "No, I think I'll go see how your mom is doing.
Do you know where she is?"

"I think she's in the front room, or maybe the kitchen. I don't know.
I'll see you later."

Then he turned around, with a small smile. "Don't go anywhere
without me, ok?"

"Ok." I said, and with that, Mitch disappeared.

I walked over and sat down in the chair next to the piano bench.
I remembered the night Mitch had proposed to me. It was only four
days ago, but he already seemed to have lost his excitement. Kayla had
warned me that he wouldn't want to help with the plans. I thought
Mitch was different, though. He always had an opinion. He was always
willing to help. Not this time.

I could hear the band starting to rehearse again, and decided to go
find Olivia. But I didn't have to because she found me.

"Hi Dana, how are you dear?" she asked.

"Fine, thanks." I replied. "Just waiting for Mitch to get done
rehearsing. He has to work later."

"Oh, well, that will give us a chance to chat, then." Olivia said. "So,
did you and Mitch have a nice Christmas together?" she asked.

I nodded. "Yes, we did. He got me this beautiful ring." I took it off
and handed it to her. She smiled.

"It's lovely, dear. Mitchell really does think a lot of you." She said, handing it back.

"Did he tell you that we went to Chris and Trudy's for dinner? It was really nice. Their kids are so cute. And they really seem to love their Uncle Mitch." I was trying to make conversation.

"They are adorable, and you're right. Mitch always has had a way with children." She agreed. "So, how are the wedding plans going? Have you started anything yet?"

"Oh, yes, I've been busy." I said. "I asked Kayla to be my matron of honor, and her husband, Joseph, is going to give me away, since my own father is gone. And Mitch asked Chris to be his best man, and Trudy is going to be an attendant. We still need to ask the others, though."

"Well, it sounds like you have everything under control." She said.

"I'm trying, but there just seems to be so much to do!" I replied.

"I know, Dana, but just take your time. And let Mitch help you. He will."

If she only knew, I thought.

Just then, Mitch and the others emerged from the rehearsal, in a whirlwind of laughter and conversation. They still seemed to be speaking their own language, and they walked right past Olivia and I to the front door.

"Great jam today, guys. Tomorrow I'm working lunch shift, so tomorrow night around 6 we can go again. Meet ya here? Or better yet, file into the bistro before and I'll let you sponge another meal."

"Hey, Trip, that's cool. Count us in." Shep said. And with that, they were gone.

Mitch came into the family room and fell onto the couch beside me. "That was so fun, but I'm wiped out. I really could use a nap before work." Then he turned to his mom.

"So Mom, did Dana tell you? We changed our wedding date."

Olivia smiled. "You did? I'll bet you decided October was too far away, didn't you?"

Mitch grinned and put his arm around me. "Yeah, something like that. We decided on June... June something or another."

"June 10th, Olivia. It would have been my grandmother's birthday."

"A June bride! That's great, kids." She said.

"And did Mitch tell you? I found a gown yesterday, and we bought our wedding bands last night. I also scheduled our engagement pictures and got a few invitation samples today." I was getting exhausted just talking about it.

"It sounds like you two have been very busy the last few days." She said.

Mitch smiled. "Well, I hate to rush off, but I really need to rest before work. I have a feeling it's going to be a late night." We got our coats and were on our way, saying goodbye to Olivia.

Mitch smiled as we drove down the road from the house. "Thanks for talking me into regrouping with the band, sweetheart. It was a blast today."

"You're welcome." I said. "Mitch, are you excited that we're engaged?" I decided to ask.

Mitch somehow knew this would be an in-depth discussion, so he pulled the car over out of sight of the house and put it in park. "Where did that question come from?" he asked. "Of course I'm excited, in fact, I'm ecstatic. Don't you remember, I'm the one who initiated the whole thing?"

I found a string on my coat and began to play with it, so as not to look at Mitch. "Then why don't you want to help with any of the wedding plans?" I asked softly.

Mitch sat silent for a minute and rubbed his eye beneath his glasses. "I want to help, sweetheart. What makes you think I don't?"

"Every time I ask you to help me make a decision about something, you tell me to decide. I ask you about the invitations, and the flowers, and our wedding colors, or anything else and you tell me you don't care. Or, that we can discuss it later. Or you ask why it's necessary. Mitch, you can't even remember that our wedding date is June 10th! You keep telling everyone it's June something or another. Last time I checked my calendar, there was no such date." I could feel the tears starting to come. "It's your wedding, too, you know."

I could tell Mitch was looking at me, but not saying anything. He reached up and wiped my tears with his hand. "Please don't cry, Dana. I don't like it when you cry." He said softly.

"I just didn't know there were going to be so many choices. I can't do it all on my own. There's just so much to do."

"Dana, didn't I tell you not to let yourself get overwhelmed? I know there seems to be a lot to do, but we have time to do it, sweetheart. You don't have to do everything today, or even this week. Honey, we've only been engaged three days."

"But we can't put everything off until the last minute, either, Mitch." I sniffled.

Mitch reached out and pulled me to him. "No, we can't. But here's what we can do. Are you listening?" I nodded. "We'll sit down and make a list of all the things we still need to do. Then, next to each thing, we can put a date that it needs to be completed by. We'll only concentrate on a few things at a time, and that way, we won't get overwhelmed. How does that sound?"

I nodded again. Mitch's voice softened. "I'm sorry if it seems like I don't care. I really do, sweetheart. But it means more to me to see you happy with the choices that are made than satisfying myself. I promise I'll try to be more involved, ok?"

I nodded again, and Mitch wiped my face again with his hand. "Now, come on, no more tears, ok? We'll make that list as soon as we get home. Alright?"

"But I thought you were sleepy," I said.

"That's ok, I'll be fine. This is much more important to me." Mitch hugged me to him. "I want my best girl to be happy." Mitch gave me a kiss on the cheek, and put the car back in gear. "So, tell me all about what you did today. I want to know."

I had to smile. He really was wonderful, and I knew he would try to be interested in everything, even if he really wasn't. I concluded that maybe all the details were more for the bride, anyway. Men just don't care about fru fru, but women live for it.

"Well, first I set up the appointment for our pictures, a week from Friday. I figured your eye would be better by then. And I went looking for invitations, and I have a few here for you to look at to help me choose. They had five books full of them! I didn't realize how many styles there actually were." I rattled to him.

"That is a lot." He replied, smiling. "I probably would've just given up and said forget it." Then Mitch changed the subject. "Did I tell you that Ash is married? Has a couple of little kids, too, I think. He got married senior year, about a month before we graduated. Believe it or not, they eloped."

"That's neat." I said. "Maybe he can give you some insight on what married life will really be like."

Mitch reached over and took my hand. "I already know. It can't be anything less than wonderful, with you as my wife." He smiled at me.

"Ok, what are you sucking up for?" I asked.

He laughed. "Can't a guy even say something nice without being accused of wanting something?"

"Maybe." I replied.

We decided to go to Mitch's place for a while, and once inside the apartment, he hung up our coats and grabbed a piece of paper and a pen. He led me to the couch and sat down, leaning back so as to position me just under his left arm. Then he began to write.

"Things to do for our wedding. Number one." Then he stopped and looked at me, handing me the piece of paper. "Sweetheart, I'm sorry, but I don't have a clue. I've never planned a wedding before, in fact, I've really never even *thought* about planning a wedding before."

"Ok, well, let's think about it. What goes into a wedding? You need attendants, a cake, food, guests, a church, a reception hall, music, a minister, flowers, a gift registry, rings, which we already have, a gown, which we already have, a tuxedo......"

"Which I already have." Mitch interrupted.

"You own a tuxedo?" I asked.

He smiled. "Sweetheart, you're forgetting. I'm a rich kid, remember? It's part of the basic wardrobe. In fact, all of us have one, me, Chris, Jim and Paul."

"Well, that should be easy, then. We'll just need to get them the ties and cummerbunds to match the bridesmaids' dresses. What color is yours?"

"Mine is all black. Or do you want me to be in white? If so, I can rent a tux, no big deal." He said "What do you want, sweetheart?"

I gave him a half cocked look. "Mitch, don't do this. Do you want to be in white, or do you want to wear what you already have? And I want to know what *you* want, not what you think I want."

He smiled. "I prefer the black.

"Good, so do I. Then that's settled." I was starting to jot down notes. "What else?"

Mitch snuggled up close to me. "How about the most important part, the honeymoon?"

I turned to him. "The honeymoon! I almost forgot about that!" I said.

Mitch started to kiss my neck playfully, chuckling. "Not me." He said.

"Where do you want to go?" I asked.

He smirked impishly. "Oh, I don't know, right here is fine, or over there, or in the bedroom, or even your place would work........"

I giggled. "Stop it, Mitch. You're so bad. Tell me where you would like to go, and be serious."

He laughed. "I was being serious!"

I gave him "the look" and he just smiled, his eyes shining. "Ok, sweetheart, I think Hawaii would be great."

I looked at him with both excitement and shock. "Hawaii? Are you serious?" I said.

Mitch smiled. "Absolutely! I'd love to take you to Hawaii. How does that sound to you?"

I could barely hold in the excitement. "That sounds so awesome! Are you sure? I mean, Hawaii is a big trip, and, well, probably a lot of money."

"Well, I have some money saved, and don't most people give you money for your wedding anyway? We can put that with it, and wah la, we're there."

I squealed with excitement and actually knocked Mitch backward jumping on him to give him a hug and kiss. "Are we really going to Hawaii for our honeymoon?"

He was laughing. "Absolutely, especially if you promise to react to everything this way!" I jumped on him again, this time planting quick and playful little kisses all over his face. He was laughing but didn't seem to mind very much.

"Hey, baby, you're missing where those kisses are really supposed to be!" Mitch said, putting a finger on his mouth. So, I gave him exactly what he asked for. And he returned the favor.

Mitch looked at me, his eyes shining. His face was glowing and that dimple. I loved that little dimple in his cheek. "Well?" he asked.

"Well what?" I asked back

"Aren't you going to call Kayla and tell her? You do with everything else that happens."

I started to get up, but then hesitated and smiled at him with my best puppy dog eyes.

"Oh, go on!" he laughed.

I raced to the phone and dialed Kayla's number. A minute later I was lost in merry, excited conversation giving her the big news. I looked at Mitch, and he was smiling at me, his eyes full of love. He picked up the remote and, turning on the TV, began flipping through the channels.

Finishing up with Kayla, I called out to Mitch. "Honey, I'm getting something to drink. Would you like anything?" I waited for his answer, but nothing. Maybe he didn't hear me, I thought. "Mitch, do you want anything to drink?" Still nothing.

I walked back over to the couch, and there he was, sleeping like a baby. He must have been tired from all the excitement today, I thought. I remembered the blanket on the chair in the bedroom. I went to retrieve it, then came back and covered him up. I bent down and giving him a kiss, curled up in the chair and found a show on TV to watch. I had been sitting there about an hour or so, when Mitch began to stir.

"Dana, are you still here?" He asked, not quite yet opening his eyes.

"I'm right here, Mitch." I said. He reached out his hand for me, and I went over to the couch. He scooted over and pulled me down next to him.

"I guess I fell asleep, huh?" he said, putting his arm around me.

"Well, you had a big day today. You probably needed that nap." I said.

"Yeah, well, now I have to get up and get ready for work. I wish I didn't." he said.

I flipped over to face him. "Why, don't you like your job?" I asked.

Mitch sighed. "No, it's not that. I like it, but I don't want to leave here. I want to stay with you."

"I want you to stay with me, too, but we both know that you have to go." I kissed him.

"You are so right, my love. Late night tonight, early day tomorrow. But I'm all yours tomorrow night." He smiled and kissed me back.

"Wait, honey, didn't you ask the guys to come and rehearse again tomorrow night?" I reminded him.

He got a disappointed look on his face. "Yes, I sure did." Then his look brightened. "But you can come with me. Ok?"

"Count me in." I said. "I'll be there. Now, you better move yourself off that couch and go get ready for work."

"Will you wait for me? I mean, while I get ready?" he asked.

"I'll be right here, promise."

And as he walked away, he called back, "And feel free to 'acquaint' yourself with anything else you would like!"

A few minutes later, Mitch reappeared all spiffed up and ready for work. I stood up as he adjusted his tie in the mirror, and slipped my arms around him from behind.

"Hey, handsome, remember me?" I asked. "I'm the girl who gave you a ride to work the other day."

Mitch turned around and put his arms around me, and I put mine around his neck. "I sure do, beautiful."

"Well, I was thinking, maybe, I would like to have dinner with you a little later on, if you're interested. But we have to be sneaky about it, so my fiancé doesn't find out." I was tracing my finger along the side of his face, and he was smiling.

"Gee, I think I might like that. But, let's get our plan together. How about I meet you at Gartano's, say, around 6:30. I'll order a couple of burgers from Charley's and have them delivered to the back door, then we'll sneak into the office and no one will ever know."

"I like your plan, big guy. How about a kiss to seal the deal?" I smiled up at him.

"I think I can accommodate you." And bending down just a little, he delivered a wonderful kiss.

"I don't want to leave, Dana. Don't make me go, please." Mitch pleaded playfully. "It's so cold outside, but oh, so warm in here." He started to kiss me again.

"Mitchell, you better go. You'll be late." I said.

"Ok, then. I'll go, but it's under protest, I'll have you know." He took his coat off the rack and put it on.

"You can stick around here if you want and just come down to meet me at 6:30, or take the car and go home. It's up to you." He opened the door, and sighed. "I love you, Dana. I'll see you in a little while."

I gave him a kiss, and ushered him out the door. "I love you, too, Mitchell. See you soon."

Mitch walked to work, thinking all the while about Dana. Nothing new, he thought. She consumed everything he did. But today, she had asked for his help and it made him feel a little different somehow. Special. He had thought he would make her happy by letting her make the majority of the plans for the wedding. But she didn't want it that way. It was going to make her happier to have him involved. So he would have to do his best to make sure he was.

Then he thought about the band. He hadn't realized until today just how much he missed it. It was a rush to feel the music, to play and give your all to something that others could enjoy. And the guys. They were a bunch of cut-ups, no doubt, but every one of them were good guys who would stick by you no matter what. He wondered why he had ever lost touch with them in the first place. Then he smiled. Dana. Dana had made sure that he didn't take the chance of losing touch with them forever. He couldn't imagine how he had done without her in his life for so long. And he couldn't wait until the day that they sealed the covenant that would ensure her being in his life forever.

Then there was Gartano's. He had been the owner for a week and already he felt such a sense of responsibility, not to mention pride. Just looking around at the cars in the area told him business was booming as usual. He hoped that wouldn't change. He didn't know what he would do if it did. The biggest responsibility he had now was taking care of Dana. And he was going to make sure that he did just that.

The next few hours went by quickly and before he knew it, Mitch's watch was telling him it was six o'clock. Dana would be coming down to meet him in just a half an hour. He retreated to the office and made the phone call to Charley's, ordering the burgers he had promised. He smiled at the thought that he already knew what she liked. He felt like he knew her so well, and yet, there were still so many things about her that were a mystery to him. He looked forward to discovering each and every one of them.

I decided to take the car the three blocks to Gartano's. I didn't mind the cold, but I knew Mitch had had a long day already, and he would be tired when it came time to leave tonight. I could bring him home and take the car back to my place, I thought. Then I smiled. I couldn't believe he was actually letting me have free rein with his car. He was already protecting me, I thought. I felt good knowing that I had someone in my life who was going to do that. And I wanted to take care of him as well.

I slipped through the front door of the bistro, greeted Kayla, and headed to the office where she told me Mitch was waiting. He was actually sitting on the couch, looking very cute, and when he saw me, his face lit up. He walked over to me, and pulling me inside the office, he closed the door and pressed me up against it.

"Your fiancé didn't see you come in, did he?" He teased in his sexiest voice.

"I don't think so," I replied.

"Good, because I wouldn't want him to see me do this." He leaned down and kissed me with all he had in him. By the time he pulled away, I was breathless. His eyes were shining.

"Well, sir, I'm thinking I may have to tell him about us," I said. "because I think I've fallen in love with you."

"Be easy on him. Big guys fall harder." He smiled.

"Oh, I will, I promise." I said, and I kissed him again.

Mitch had pulled a chair up to the opposite side of his desk, and he ushered me to sit down, where our dinner was waiting. He had poured our sodas into two wine glasses, and he had a candle burning on the end of the desk, for effect. I smiled.

"So you're planning to wine and dine me, huh?" I asked.

He laughed. "Well, dine, yes. Wine, no, definitely not!" he said.

I laughed. "No, I don't think I want you to do that, either." I said. "Place is busy tonight, huh?"

"Yeah, it seems like we get busier and busier each night. The girls are running themselves ragged. I was actually thinking I may have to hire another waitress or two, maybe even a cook. Jimmy agrees. Said he can't remember when this place was booming so much."

I looked at him. "Mitch, why don't you let me help? That way, you'll only have to hire one more waitress. And you won't have to pay me, I'll just work for the tips, and that will give us extra money for the wedding." I said. I must have taken him by surprise, because he choked on the French fry he was eating.

"I can't do that, Dana. I mean, I don't want you doing this day after day. It's hard work." He was sitting back in his chair now, looking directly at me. "Besides, you already have a full time job. You'll wear yourself out. You won't have any free time for yourself, or for me, or to make those wedding plans." He was being the protector again.

"Ok, then, Mitch, if you don't want me here that much, I understand. I wouldn't want to be a distraction to you." I decided to play hard ball with him, and I knew I could hit a home run with the right strategy.

Mitch put everything down and sighed. "Dana, don't start that. You know that's not what I meant. I love having you here. I just don't think it's a good idea, that's all." He reached out for my hand. "I'm just trying to look out for you, sweetheart."

Ok, I thought. I'll drop it for a little while and try again later. I decided to change the subject, and try a different approach.

"You know, Mitch, we never did look at those invitations. But, I think I've narrowed it down to two that I really like. I'll probably pick one of those."

Mitch looked at me. "Now, wait a minute, love. Weren't you the one crying earlier that you wanted me to help you with all this? You aren't choosing anything until I have a look myself."

I smiled. "But, Mitch, honey, when will you have time? You'll be here more if you have to hire someone. I mean, you'll have interviews and all that to worry about."

He smirked at me and folded his arms. I had forgotten he could play ball, too, and was quite good at it. "Nice try, Dana. Won't work. The answer is still no."

"I don't know what you're talking about." I said, shoving three fries into my mouth.

"I think you do. I'm not going to let you work here, Dana. That's final. The subject is closed." Mitch finished his last fry and his soda. "Now, is there anything else you'd like to talk about, before I have to go back to work?"

"How about the fact that you are just stubborn?" I snapped.

He smirked. "You know, sweetheart, my mother always said the same thing about me. And my father. I never believed them. But, now you're saying it as well, so it must be true." He smiled. "But, I'm still lovable, aren't I?"

"I guess so." I said smugly.

Mitch got up and came over to me, bending down by my chair. "You go ahead and pout if you want to. When you're done and ready for some dessert, come and find me." He kissed my cheek and left the office.

Oh, he makes me so mad sometimes, I thought. First of all, where did he get off telling me he wasn't going to *let* me work here? Was he my father now or something? And second, he knows my idea was good. It would help us both in the long run. There just had to be a way I could pull this off. And I thought I knew what I could do.

I cleared away the empty food containers, and sat down at Mitch's desk. Searching through the drawers, I found a blank application and began to fill it out. If he was going to conduct interviews for this position, then I was going to be a formal applicant.

About ten minutes later, I had finished everything and was reading it back over for detail. Mitch came back to look for me.

"Are you still back here pouting?" he asked.

"I wasn't pouting. I was busy." I replied

"Busy with what?" He asked. I handed him my application. He started to laugh. "An application? Come on, Dana, what do you think you're doing?"

"Well, if you won't just hire me on your own, then I'm going to apply formally and go through the process." I said firmly.

Mitch walked over to the desk, still reading my paper and laughing. "Excuse me, but that's where I sit." He said to me. I stood up, and he closed the door. "Ok, you want me to interview you, I will." He said. "But it'll be a real interview, I'm warning you. Just like I would do with anyone else."

"That's fine, I'm ready." I replied.

He stood up and extended his hand to me. "Hello, Miss Walker, I'm Mitch Tarrington." I shook his hand. "Won't you please have a seat?"

"Nice to meet you, Mr. Tarrington, and thank you." I said. He was trying to be so serious, I was having a hard time keeping a straight face.

"So, Miss Walker, it says here that you are interested in a waitressing position, is that correct?"

"Yes it is."

"Do you have any prior experience, either in the food industry, or in waiting tables?" He put down my application, folded his hands and sat back, waiting for my response.

"Yes, actually, I do. I worked as a waitress during college, at a little café near the campus. I really enjoyed it." I replied.

He smirked, but fought to keep his composure. "Great. And tell me, what do you like best about this type of work?"

"Well, I just enjoy being around people, and being able to serve their needs. It makes me happy to see them enjoying themselves."

Mitch nodded. "Let me outline a few things for you, Miss Walker. First, we're a very busy establishment. We do our best to make sure all employees get a break during their scheduled working time, but depending on the amount of patrons we have, you may not get to take as long of a break as you'd like, or take it at the time you'd like. You would be expected to know the items on the menu thoroughly, and be able to describe any of the dishes to a patron should they ask. We do serve alcohol, so you will need to be 21 or older, and I expect all employees to be dressed neatly in uniform and on time each day. Your hours would vary, and there may be times when we ask you to come in early or stay later than your scheduled shift. Do you have any questions or concerns about anything I just said?" He was looking official again.

"No, I don't think I do." I replied.

"Good. Let's see, oh, yes. Do you have reliable transportation to and from work each day?" He was starting to smile.

"Yes, my fiancé allows me to use his car, and should it not be available, I live within walking distance, so getting here shouldn't be a problem."

Mitch picked up my paper again and pretended to be looking it over. "Sounds like your fiancé is a pretty good guy." He said, not looking up at me.

"Oh, he is—when he wants to be." I answered. Mitch looked at me over the top of his glasses.

"I see you're a kindergarten teacher. Tell me a little bit about that." He sat back again.

What's there to tell, I thought. I'm a teacher. I teach. But, he wanted to play so I would play, too.

"Well, I've been in that position a little over a year, and I really enjoy it. The children are wonderful and it's very rewarding." There, smarty pants, try to ask me another one, I thought.

"I'm assuming that's a full time position. Will it interfere with you being able to work with us?" Was he ever going to stop asking questions, I thought.

"No, it shouldn't. I can come here right after school, if necessary, and you can schedule me anytime on weekends. I can also work holidays if needed, and I'm also available anytime there's a break from school."

Mitch nodded, sat back, and with a huge smile asked the mother of all questions. "So, Miss Walker, tell me why I should hire you."

I took a deep breath. I always hated this question, but I was ready with my answer. "I feel you should hire me because I am hardworking, punctual, trustworthy and dedicated. I have experience in this field, and I know I could be an asset to your team."

I folded my hands in my lap and smiled sweetly at Mitch.

He was smirking at me again, biting his lip and rocking in his chair. "Miss Walker, I must tell you one other thing. The pay for this position isn't much, but what I can't offer you in pay, I can make up for in fringe benefits." His eyes were shining with mischief.

"I think I will be satisfied with that." I said.

Mitch sat looking at me again. "Well, Miss Walker, I would say you are a good candidate for the position, however, I don't like to make snap decisions. I think it's best to take your time with things. I plan to be interviewing within the next few days, and I will be calling back the top candidates after that." He stood up and opened the door. That brat, I thought. He put me through all this for nothing? Ok, I was still playing.

I got up and again Mitch extended a hand to me. "It was very nice meeting you, Miss Walker, and I'll be getting back to you with my decision."

"Thank you for your time, Mr. Tarrington." And I started to walk out. I could hear Mitch behind me starting to laugh.

He popped his head out the door. "Where are you going?" he asked.

I turned around. "The interview is over. I'm leaving." I replied, starting to turn around again.

Mitch stepped out and grabbed my hand. "Get back here, you!" he said.

He closed the door, and once again, I found myself with my back against the wall. Literally.

"You really are impossible, you know that? I can't believe you sat there and let me interview you. But, I must say, I'm impressed with how well you did."

"Why? Did you think I would bomb? No way, buddy!" I said.

"No, I just didn't think you would actually take it so seriously." His face softened. "Does it really mean that much to you, to help me here?"

"It does, Mitch, it really does. I know I can do it."

Mitch sighed deeply. "If I say no, I'll live to regret it, I'm sure. And if I say yes, I may still live to regret it, because if anything happens to you, I'll feel guilty. See where you've put me?"

I slipped my hands around his neck. "I'll be fine. Please give me a chance to do this for you."

Mitch bit his lip and looked into my eyes. "Ok, I'll give you a chance. But," he put his finger up to make the point. "if you start getting burnt out, you're done. Alright?"

I nodded. "Alright." I said. "Now, when can I start?"

Mitch smiled and slid his hands around my waist. "Wouldn't you like to review the benefits package first?"

I giggled. "I'm sorry, Mr. Tarrington, but I have a strict policy about doing this sort of thing with coworkers."

He laughed and kissed me anyway.

12

Mitch handed me an apron, and pulling the other girls, and Jimmy, aside, he told them about the interview and that I would be their new coworker. He also told them that I would be working strictly for tips, but that they shouldn't show favoritism toward me because of that, as far as giving me extra tables and such. They all agreed that giving me a chance was the right thing to do, and that they would help me however they could.

For the rest of the night, I helped serve the customers and do whatever else was needed of me. By the time we closed at ten o'clock, I was exhausted. We got everything finished up, and sent the crew on their way. Mitch turned off the lights in the office and got our coats off the rack.

"I brought the car, so I could give you a ride home." I said. "But if you'd rather give me a ride, that's fine, too."

"Let me take you home. That way, you won't have to drive back later. I know you're tired." Mitch said.

"No, I'm fine, really." I knew he didn't believe me. "Ok, I am a little tired. But I'll get used to it."

Mitch opened the door, and we stepped out, locking it behind us. The wind had turned brutally cold, and we were both glad to get inside the car. He turned it on and let it heat up for a minute or two. "Sweetheart, I'm really proud of you. You did fantastic tonight."

"Thanks," I said. "It really was fun. And I think I did pretty good in tips, too."

Once inside the apartment, shoes went one direction and coats another, and once again, we were curled up on the chair, looking at George and Beverly Snowman outside the window. Snow was beginning to fall, and we could see the wind blowing it around in the glow of the streetlights.

"Well, where are those invitations?" Mitch asked. "I'd like to see them."

I got up and retrieved the bag for him, and he began to shuffle through them. He picked out two and laid them on the coffee table.

"These are the two I like. How about you?" he asked.

I looked at his choices. He had actually picked one that I had picked as one of my favorites.

"This one." I said pointing to it. "It was one of my top choices, too."

Mitch picked it up and looked at it closer. It was white in color, with two hearts on the front that connected together, one containing the groom's name and one with the bride's. The hearts were outlined in pink, and there were little pink and blue flowers on the bottom. Simple, yet pretty.

"Only one problem." Mitch said jokingly. "We aren't Charles and Joann."

"You're such a goof!" I said, taking the invitation from him. I got up and retrieved the list we had started earlier in the day from my purse, and I brought it back to him. "Ok, we just picked the invitations, so we can cross that off." I said. Then I looked at him and the way I did must have startled him, because he leaned forward and took hold of my arm.

"Dana, what's wrong?" He said.

"I was just thinking, we have to make out a guest list, Mitch." I sighed.

"You about gave me a heart attack, girl. Why did you look like something was wrong?" he asked.

"I have no clue who I'm even going to invite. I don't know anybody." I said. "Everyone will be sitting on your side of the church, and there won't be anyone on mine."

Mitch got up and sat down beside me on the couch. "Sweetheart, why does that bother you so much? I'm sure you know more people than you think you do." He put his arm around me. "Besides, why do we have to have my side and your side? If it'll make you feel better, we'll just put people wherever. Then no one but us will know the difference."

"I guess we could do that. Do you think anyone will mind?" I asked.

"Baby, who cares? It isn't their wedding, it's ours. We can do what we want." He was rubbing my arm reassuringly. "Now, let's get some paper here and jot down a few names, ok? I'll help you."

I started with the obvious. Kayla and her family, but she and Joseph were part of the bridal party. So, they really didn't count.

"I don't know anyone else, Mitch." I said, sadly. "You go ahead and make your list, ok?"

Mitch smiled. "How about the teachers at your school? And the principal. Aren't you friends with them?"

"Well, yeah, I guess," I replied.

"Ok, give me names. First and last, if you can." He started writing as I told him. "Now, look, Dana, there are at least fifteen or more right there, if you count their husbands and wives, or whatever." Mitch put the end of the pen in his mouth, and thought for a moment. "Sweetheart, do you have any old college friends that you would like to ask, or maybe friends from back home in Iowa?"

I had to think long and hard. "Mitch, I really didn't keep in touch with any of them. I mean, when I moved here, my life was all about Eddie, and nothing else. I wish it had been different, though."

"Dana, look," Mitch put down the pen and paper. "You gave me a wonderful gift when you encouraged me to get back with the band. It may only be for a weekend, but we've all rekindled a bond that I don't plan to let grow cold again. This is your chance to do the same, with some of your friends."

"I'm not sure I would even know where to begin to find them, Mitch." I said to him.

"Tell you what. Let's just write down names for now, and we'll worry about the rest later." He smiled.

"Well, when I was young, my two best friends were Kate and Renee. My college roommate was Gina, uh, Gina Templeton, and then there was Britney Clooney and Alicia Chavez."

Mitch jotted down the names and smiled. "Ok, do you have any aunts or uncles or cousins, anyone that still lives in Iowa?" he asked.

"Not that I know of, anyway. I know my mom didn't have any brothers or sisters. And I think my dad had one brother, but he was older and I believe he died in Korea. He wasn't married. I told you, Mitch, I'm all alone, except for you." Mitch pulled me to him and held me close. "Mitch, would you mind too much if we finished this later?" I asked. I was starting to feel sad again, and wanted to get my mind on something else.

Mitch must have known what I was thinking. "Oh, uh, sure sweetheart. We have plenty of time." Then he kissed my cheek and whispered softly. "I'm sorry if I made you sad, Dana. I didn't mean to."

"No, honey, you didn't. I'm just getting a little tired, that's all." I answered.

"Then I should go and let you get some rest, ok? It's been a long day, for both of us." Mitch stood up, but I grabbed hold of his hand.

"I don't want you to go yet. Please stay a little longer, ok?" I looked up at him.

He smiled. "Ok, but if I get too sleepy, I'm going to go. Ok?"

"Yeah, ok." I said, snuggling up to him once more. "I love you, Mitch." I whispered.

"I know, and I love you too, sweetheart." Mitch kissed me softly.

A few minutes later, Mitch looked at Dana. She was fast asleep. She was so beautiful, she looked just like an angel lying there. Carefully, he stood up and laid her head on a pillow. He took her favorite blanket from the basket she kept it in, and covered her up.

"Good night, my love. Pleasant dreams." He whispered softly, kissing her on the cheek. He locked the doorknob and quietly sneaked out.

The next few days were busy, filled with Mitch's band rehearsals, and both of us working at the bistro. I was picking up things quickly, and Mitch finally realized that he had made the right choice by letting me work there. Finally, before we knew it, New Year's Eve was upon us.

I got dressed quickly, ate a bowl of cereal, and called Mitch. He was going to swing by and pick me up for work, then the guys were meeting him there to go to the club for one last rehearsal. Shep and Zach had gone over early to check everything out, and the others were meeting them there to set up the equipment. When Mitch got there, they would run through the set at least once before the doors of the club opened.

Mitch got to my apartment right around ten. "Hello, handsome." I said, opening the door for him.

"Good morning, beautiful." He replied, kissing me. "Ready for another day?"

"I think so. I'm just excited about tonight. It's going to be so cool!" I said excitedly.

"Well, yeah, glad one of us thinks so. Dana, do you know how long it's been since I did a live performance? Three years, Dana, three years. What if I get stage fright and forget all the words?"

I smiled at him. "Honey, stage fright is definitely *not* one of your problems. You love being the center of attention. It seems to come naturally for you."

"Is that a nice way of saying I'm somewhat of a showoff?" He asked.

"Might be." I replied. "You quit worrying. You guys are great, and everyone is going to love you."

"If they don't, will you still love me?" He pretended to pout.

"Always and forever!" I said.

We made our way to Gartano's and got things ready to open for lunch. The daily routine had become second nature to me, and I actually enjoyed helping Mitch make sure everything was taken care of. Just before we were ready to open, Mitch ushered me into the office, and closed the door. He sat down at his desk and pulled me onto his lap.

"Mitch, honey, this is all well and good, but we have a restaurant to open. People are waiting outside in the cold." I said.

He laughed. "Let them be cold for a minute longer. I have something I need to show you."

Mitch opened the desk drawer and pulled out a small brown envelope. "What's this?" I asked.

"Open it and see." He said excitedly.

Inside was a travel brochure, two round trip airline tickets and hotel reservations for the Hyatt Regency Waikiki. He had booked our honeymoon!

"Mitch, when did you do this?" I squealed excitedly.

"Let's just say, I have connections. All it took were a few phone calls. You don't think I work all the time when I come back here, do you?" He was grinning like the cat that had just swallowed the mouse.

Giving him a repeat performance of the day he told me he would take me there, I almost knocked him over with my hugs and kisses.

He laughed. "Gee, baby, I really do wish you wouldn't keep your emotions so bottled up. It's not healthy."

I hugged the envelope to myself. "Can I show the girls? Please?" I asked.

"Later, sweetheart, ok? We really should go open up the doors now. Here, let me have that and I'll tuck it away safely."

Reluctantly, I handed Mitch back the envelope and he locked it in the desk, placing the key into his pocket. "Now, one last kiss and we need to get going." Three long kisses later, we were headed for the door.

Busy, as usual, we went through the next two hours hustling and bustling around until it was time to go. I could tell Mitch was getting excited, and every once in a while I would catch him singing to himself softly, rehearsing the words to the songs he would do at the club tonight. He excitedly wished everyone a Happy New Year, then told the entire restaurant they needed to be at Studio 14, 8 pm to watch *his* band, Ace, rock in the New Year. I finally got him out the door and into the car.

"You are going to explode, Mitchell Tarrington!" I laughed. "You just need to settle down so you aren't exhausted before you even get there."

"Well, we're only doing partials in the club rehearsal, except for two. We'll do those completely. So, anyway, plenty of water, dress light, and take a break in the middle. I'll be just fine." He was talking a mile a minute.

"Honey, what time do you have to be there?" I asked.

"Around 2:30. Why?"

"Are the guys already there, or are you meeting them?" I asked.

"The plan is for them to come piling over to my place around 2:00 or so. By that time, I will have left you so you can get ready, then six wonderful men will be coming back and escorting you to dinner around five, and then to the club. My family will join you there later, and they have instructions of where to find you." He smiled.

"Gee, you've got it all worked out, don't you?" I said.

"Yep. I just hope I don't lose my voice. I'm not used to this anymore." He replied.

We were inside the apartment and Mitch walked over to the thermostat on the wall. "It's warm in here, Dana, don't you think?" He asked, turning it down a little.

"No, not really, but I think you're just all wound up." I smiled.

Mitch stretched out on my couch. "Well, then come and unwind me." He said mischievously. I smiled at him and climbed up next to him. He put his arms around me and just held me there for the longest time. "You know, sweetheart, nothing beats this." He said.

"Nothing beats what?" I asked.

"Just being here with you, holding you, having you near." He was rubbing my back and I was enjoying it. The next thing I knew, Mitch and I were kissing and cuddling, and just being together.

"You know, this really isn't winding me down.   If anything, it's winding me up." He smiled.

"Do you mind?" I asked him softly.

"No, not at all," he answered, continuing to kiss me.

"Mitch, I hate to break this up, but it's 1:30 and I don't want you to be late meeting the guys, ok?" I got up off the couch and helped him up.

"Yeah, you're right."   Putting on his coat, he walked to the door. "We'll be here by five, so I'll see you then, ok?"

"Ok, honey, I'll be ready.   Promise.   I love you."

With a kiss goodbye, he was gone.

Mitch wasn't the only one who was excited about this whole thing. I had been watching most of their rehearsals this past week, and I knew they were good, even if they didn't want to admit that themselves. They were all very talented musicians individually, and most of them had decent vocals as well.   Along with the musical and vocal talents Mitch possessed, they were a sensation when they were put all together.   They just seemed to click in a special way.   I knew that they would be nothing less than wonderful.

I knew I still had plenty of time to get ready, but I wanted to make sure I looked extra special for tonight.   Retreating to my closet, I pulled out my secret weapon, my little black dress.   It hit me just above the knee in length, and was very fitted, but not too tight that it was uncomfortable.   The sleeves were long, but sheer, and it was cut in a V at the top.   The necklace Mitch got me looked great with it, but I decided to frame it with one a little longer, as well as a bracelet.   I would wear sheer black hose and my black heels with the little bow on the back.   I had a feeling he was going to love it.

Grabbing all of my manicure essentials, I plopped down in front of the TV to do my nails.   A deep red, and I would wear the same shade in lipstick, I thought.   Just as I was getting ready to apply the first coat of polish the phone rang.

"Hello?" I said.

"Hi beautiful!" Mitch said cheerfully.

"Didn't you just leave here?" I asked.

"Well, yeah, but does that mean I can't call you?" he said.

"No, I like it when you call me.   What's up?"   I was actually wondering why he did call me.

"Nothing.   Just killing time until the guys get here." He laughed. "Dana, I've done this a million times.   Why am I so nervous today?"

I smiled.   I could just see him sitting there, biting his lip and wiping his sweaty palm on the leg of his pants.   "I don't know, honey.   Maybe because tonight there will be a lot of people there that you know. In college you probably played mostly to a bunch of strangers, I would imagine."

"You know, that might be it. I mean, Dana, my *parents* are coming, for crying out loud. I can't imagine my mother coming to a dance club! I can just see her storming the stage when she hears some of those, what she would call, 'suggestive' lyrics."

I laughed. "Mitchell, stop worrying, will you please? Your mother knows it's all just music. She won't think a thing about it, I'll bet. Besides, honey, your mother does have four children, and you are 26 years old. I'm sure she understands what it's all about. And she knows you do, too."

"Ok, I'm going to make myself a nice cup of tea, and sit down and watch some senseless show on TV for the next 15 minutes. By then the guys should be here." I heard him sigh deeply. "I can't wait to see you, baby. Remember, five o'clock."

"Yes, Mitch, I remember." I smiled. "Honey, remember this, ok? If you feel yourself getting nervous up there tonight, look at me. I'll give you a sign that you are doing just fine. I love you, and I believe in you, Mitch."

He sighed again. "Thanks. That means a lot. Well, they should be getting here soon. I love you, Dana."

"I love you, too, sweetie. I'll see you soon."

Mitch took the teapot off the stove and poured it over the teabag in the cup. He took some honey from the refrigerator and mixed it into the tea, taking a nice long sip. That should sooth the vocal cords, he thought. But he hoped more that it would calm his nerves.

Right around two, he heard a knock on his door, and Newbie's voice calling out to him. "Hey, Trip, it's show time!" He laughed and opened the door for his friends.

After they were all gathered in the apartment, Mitch got their attention. "Guys, I have just one question. Are any of you as nervous as I am right now?"

They all looked at each other, and of course, they all said no.

"Great," Mitch said. "I'm the main man here, and the only one who may faint on stage. I haven't been this nervous since I proposed to Dana."

Ash smiled and patted his friend on the back. "Just wait 'til you're standing at the altar. Talk about nerves. Or, when she goes into labor with your first kid. Cindy was actually telling *me* to breathe!" Everyone laughed.

"Your just a little out of practice, dude." Newbie reassured. It'll all come back to you, trust me. We are gonna rock the place!"

"Then, let's go do it!" Mitch said.

The manager of Studio 14 was waiting for the guys as they arrived.

"Hey, Rob!" Shep called out.

"Hi, guys," he said, unlocking the door and holding it open for them. Once they were all inside, he relocked the door, and turned to Mitch.

"You must be the front man I've been hearing about. These guys are telling me you have a lot of talent." He said extending his hand to Mitch. "Rob Winslow, I'm the manager here."

"Mitch Tarrington." Mitch said, shaking his hand. "I don't know about that talent thing, but I do my best."

"Well, let me take you to the stage and run through a few things with you. Then you can rehearse as long as you like." Rob gave Mitch the ins and outs of the studio, and left them to their rehearsal.

Mitch turned to the guys. "Well, let's see what we can give them, shall we?"

The band ran through the set, and Mitch was impressed with the way everything sounded. About 4:30, he called out to everyone.

"Ok, guys, the time is now 4:30 and we have a hot date in one half hour. Let's call it a wrap, and cool down a little." He was smiling in anticipation.

Mitch gathered the guys for a quick briefing. "Ok, in my car I have a corsage and five red roses. Before we go in, each of you take one and hand it to Dana as you walk into her apartment. I'll follow you and give her the corsage last. But, one thing."

"And that is?" Shep asked.

"I don't know what she's wearing tonight, she wouldn't tell me. So, if she looks really hot, you guys will have to leave." Mitch smiled.

Just before five, the much anticipated knock came at the door. "Your dates are here, Miss Walker." I heard Newbie say.

Straightening my dress and taking one last peek in the mirror, I opened the door. The five guys were all standing in front, each one holding a red rose. Mitch was in the back, not really looking at me. But the wolf whistles and wow's got his attention.

"Hey, guys, are those all for me?" Each one came in, handed me a rose, and gave me a little peck on the cheek. I just stood there smiling.

Mitch just stood there staring at me, his eyes shining. He was holding a beautiful wrist corsage with red carnations and sweetheart roses. I could see his eyes move up and down me, and I looked at him.

"Dana, you look amazing!" he said.

"Thank you. Is that for me?" I asked.

"Oh, yeah." Mitch said, stepping inside, but still not taking his eyes off me.

The other guys were watching him in amusement. "So, Trip, you gonna give it to her, or just stand there and hold it?" Shep asked. The others laughed as Mitch smiled and fastened the corsage on me.

Mitch slipped his arms around me. "Wow" is all he could say, until he realized he was being watched. "Uh, guys, how about a little privacy here?" He said.

They all started talking at once, making comments about warming up the car, and waiting outside. Within ten seconds, Zach closed the door and we were alone.

"Hey, handsome." I said softly to Mitch.

"Dana, you are so beautiful." He said, and he leaned down to kiss me, very passionately.

"Let's skip dinner, what do you say? I just want to stay here and neck." He said, which was where he was now planting his kisses.

"I would love that, honey, but what about your friends?" I asked between planting kisses on him.

"They can go without us." He said.

I put my head against his chest. "That wouldn't be very nice." I replied. "Besides, it might be hard to sing if you have chapped lips, you know."

He smiled. "You always have to make sense, don't you? But, just one more, ok?"

"Well, ok, but only because you asked nicely." I said, kissing him again.

Mitch helped me on with my coat and escorted me out the door. "I'm not sure I can trust all these guys around you tonight." He said, smiling.

"Well, I think Ash is safe, since he's married." I replied.

"Yeah, I guess, but even married men look, Dana, or so I've heard." He said.

"I know one soon to be married man who better not, or he will be in big trouble!" I said, poking his arm with my finger playfully.

"I only have eyes for you, my love." Mitch smiled back. "Besides, I don't look now. Why would I do it when I'm married?"

I shot him a look. "Oh, please, Mitchell. What about the girl in Jacy's, and the girl at the skating rink, and.........."

"Dana, I refuse to discuss this subject with you." he said.

"Because you know I'm right!" I was waiting for him to open the car door for me.

Ty caught the last half of our conversation, and he was chuckling to himself.

He turned to Mitch. "Buddy, I'd help you out here, but Cindy and I have this same argument all the time. And I still haven't learned how to get out of it myself!"

Mitch opened the door for me and I got in, but not before I heard him say, "She is so insecure. I can't even look in the direction of another female without her getting upset."

The other guys started out to the restaurant, and Mitch turned to me before starting the car. He started to say something, but I cut him off.

"So, you think I'm insecure? Look at you, Mitch. You are absolutely gorgeous. What woman wouldn't want to be with you? Shoot, I'll probably have to fight them off tonight!"

"Sweetheart, they may want to be with me, but I only want to be with you. And besides, take a look at yourself. One guy makes a move tonight and he's toast." He reached for my hand. "I'm a loyal man, Dana. I have what I want right here. You don't have to worry about anything, ever. I promise."

"I know, I trust you, Mitch." I said, rubbing the back of his hand.

"Well, you don't act like it sometimes." He replied, starting the car.

"I trust you, I just don't trust other women. I know how they can be when they want something."

"Yeah, maybe, but wouldn't I have to be a party to that, too? It will never happen." He smiled and looked at me again. "Lady, I am proud to be the one with you."

"That's good to know." I said, smiling. "I'm pretty happy being with you, too."

We decided on The Mark again for dinner, and the guys were already there waiting. "Hopefully, you did make a reservation, Mitch," Ash said. "This place is packed."

"Oh, ye of little faith." He smirked. "Of course I have a reservation." Mitch walked up to the hostess. "I have a reservation for 5:30. Mitchell Tarrington, the third."

"Yes, Mr. Tarrington, for seven guests. Your table will be ready in just a moment."

"Thank you," Mitch said. Then he turned to Ash. "All set."

"Decided to be formal tonight, huh, 'Mitchell Tarrington, the third'." I teased.

"Sure, it's my name, might as well use it." he smiled back at me.

A few minutes later, I was sitting at a table surrounded by six men. I felt like all the eyes in the place were upon me. The server came to our table, and stood next to Mitch and I.

"Good evening, everyone, I'm Janine and I'll be taking care of you tonight." She smiled. Then she looked at me. "Wow, I'm lucky to get one guy to take me out, and here you are with six, and all quite handsome at that."

I laughed. "Well, I just couldn't decide who I really wanted to be with tonight, so I brought them all." Everyone laughed.

"What a lucky girl!" Janine smiled.

I laughed and put my arm around Mitch. "No, actually this one belongs to me. The others just tagged along." I noticed out of the corner of my eye that Newbie was really checking out Janine, and I smiled.

Janine took our drink and appetizer order and disappeared. Mitch put his arm around me and smiled. "So, guys, what are you all doing around, say, June...." He hesitated, and looked at me. "June 10th?" They all kind of looked at one another. "Well, we need a band for our wedding. What do you all say to that? It pays well, and we'll even feed you." Mitch looked from one to another. They all looked shocked.

"That sounds cool to me, Trip!" Shep happily said. The others agreed. "But, only on one condition. You let us do it as our gift to you and Dana. No comp."

Mitch's face softened. "Guys, I can't do that. I mean, you deserve to be paid for your time. I wouldn't feel right."

Ash looked at Mitch. "So, call it a date for exposure. We won't do it unless you let us do it for free."

Mitch looked at me. "What do you think, sweetheart?" he asked.

"I think that would be really sweet, guys. But, you'll have to find someone else to front for you that night. He's going to be a little busy." They all smiled. Then Mitch looked at me with a pretend pout. "Oh, ok, maybe one or two songs."

Our appetizers and drinks came, and we all enjoyed the food and each other. I was really beginning to feel at ease with all the guys, and I loved the way they all talked and joked amongst each other. I was happy that Mitch had them back in his life again, and by the way he looked, I could tell he was, too.

By the time our food came, the topic of conversation had turned to Ash and his family, and he looked at us, smiling.

"You two planning on having kids?" he asked.

I looked at Mitch. "Well, I think so, but not for a few years. We want to have time to get to know each other more first."

"That's a smart idea." Ash agreed. "Cindy and I waited about two years before Jenny was born, and we just had Jonathan seven months ago. You think you know each other before you get married, but nobody really does. It's good to have that adjustment time together."

"That's what I've heard." Mitch said. "Plus, being that Dana and I have only been together for a short time, it'll be good for us."

I nodded in agreement. "Yeah, I have to decide if I want to keep him around or not before I have a baby with him." I teased.

Mitch smirked at me. "I'll get you for that one later." He said playfully.

After enjoying a wonderful dinner, we all decided it was time to head to the club. Once we arrived, Mitch escorted me to the table I would be sitting at for the night.

"After this whole ordeal is over, I'll come and get you, ok? I'll be able to see you the whole time I'm up there." He pointed to the stage.

"Mitch, you're going to be fantastic, you know that don't you?" I asked him.

"I really hope so, Dana." He looked around at the crowd starting to file in. "The family should all be getting here soon. I put all of you right up here in a little cluster of sorts. But, I wanted you right in the center. Maybe I shouldn't have done that, though."

"Why not?" I asked.

He pulled me very close to him. "Because every time I look at you, I have difficulty breathing. And that isn't a good thing for a vocalist."

"Well, maybe I could give you a little mouth to mouth, you know, just in case." I said, kissing him.

"I think that will help, but we had better make sure." Mitch started to kiss me again.

We weren't aware that Mitch's family had quietly come up behind us. "I swear, is that *all* you two ever do?" Chris asked, teasingly. Mitch continued his kiss, putting up a finger to tell his brother he'd answer in a minute. I think he made the kiss last a little longer, just for show.

Mitch pulled away and looked at Chris. "For now." And he smiled impishly. Chris laughed.

"Hi everyone," Mitch said, greeting his family. "I've seated you all right around here. Keep Dana where she is, so I can see her from up there, ok?"

"Is that a good idea, Mitchell?" Julia asked. "We wouldn't want you falling off the stage or anything."

"Oh, it's ok, Jul," Angelina laughed. "We have a doctor in the family." She pointed to Jim.

Mitch rolled his eyes and ignored his sisters' playful teasing. "We're the headliners tonight, so they have another group that's going to be out for an hour or so. We'll be on about nine'ish and play through midnight." Mitch turned to me. "Now, I have to go and wait backstage. Promise me that you'll stay with my family, ok? There're a lot of people here tonight. I don't want anything happening to you."

"Honey, I'll be fine. You just go up there and have a great time." I gave him a hug.

"How about a kiss for luck?" He asked.

"Ok, but just one. You need to get moving." I gave him a kiss and another hug.

Everyone else moved in for a group hug, too. Mitch was laughing.

"Guys, I know this family is close, but let's not go overboard," he said.

"Good luck, little brother, knock 'em dead," Chris said. Everyone else gave him their well wishes, too.

He turned back to me. "Remember, stay here. I love you."

"Ok, and I love you, too. Now go." I gave him a gentle little shove and he turned around and smiled at me.

Kayla and Joseph came in right about then. "Hi, Dana, hi everybody!" Kayla greeted and she gave me a hug.

"Kayla, I am so excited! You are going to be so amazed." I told her.

"I can't wait to see this myself," she said.

Julia sat down next to me. "You know, Dana, I have never, in my whole life, seen Mitchell this happy. He really adores you, you know."

I smiled. "I adore him, too. He's really something special."

Angelina smiled and pointed. "Your something special is coming back." We turned to see Mitch returning to the table.

"I almost forgot." He said. "Julia, Paul, Jim, Angelina, it would make Dana and I very happy if you would all agree to be attendants in our wedding. Chris is going to be my best man, and Trudy is going to be in it as well." He put his arm around me, and was smiling brightly.

"I, for one, would be honored." Angelina said.

"We would, too." Julia said.

Everyone was looking at Jim. "Of course, I will. Wouldn't miss it."

Mitch and I smiled at each other. "That's great, everyone, thanks." Then he turned to me. "How about one more kiss for luck? I need all I can get!" I stood up and gave him a nice loving kiss.

"Oh, gee, Mitch, would you just go already? You're making the rest of us guys look bad." Chris teased. Mitch waved and was gone again.

I turned back to the group. "You know, these guys are really, really good. I've been listening to them rehearsing this week. I'm telling you, I was totally impressed."

"Oh, we know Mitch is talented." Olivia said. "He always had a natural affinity for music."

"You should have seen him when he was a little kid. He was always wanting to put shows on for us." Julia said. "Then Mom made the mistake of giving him piano lessons, and he played all the time." She laughed at the memory. "The standing joke was, if you want to find Mitch, go look at the piano."

"That's great, though. When did he learn to play guitar?" I asked.

"I think that was high school," Chris replied. "He came home one day and announced that he wanted a guitar. So, Mom and Dad got him one, and he actually taught himself. But, of course, he didn't want an acoustic. He wanted an electric, with the amp and the whole nine yards. Drove us crazy until he *did* learn to play it!"

"I loved what he did for you when he proposed," Angelina said. "That was so romantic."

"It certainly was! And the thing is," I said excitedly, "he never told me he could play guitar, only piano. And he never sang for me before that, either." I smiled. "He does have a beautiful voice, too."

The club lights dimmed and Rob, the manager, appeared on stage. "Good evening, everyone!" The crowd applauded. "Welcome to Studio 14's rocking New Years Eve bash!" More applause. "I'm Manager Rob Winslow, and tonight we have some fantastic entertainment coming your way. First, Paradise will take the stage, and to help us ring in the New Year, we have a fantastically talented band of young men who call themselves Ace. So let's get this party started with Paradise!" More applause.

The band began to play, and although they were good, we were all eagerly waiting for Ace. We continued to try to carry on a conversation over the music, which was difficult, and we all agreed that this group just didn't have the crowd. We would see what Ace could do.

Paradise finished playing around 8:45, so we had a fifteen minute break in between acts.

"I can't wait for you all to see this." I said. "I'm telling you, they are so good."

Trudy smiled. "But you wouldn't be a little prejudice, now would you?" she asked.

I laughed. "Ok, maybe just a little. But you know, I heard they have this lead singer that is just to die for." I was bursting with nervous energy.

About five minutes before nine, Rob came back on the stage again. "Are you all having a good time?" Everyone applauded. "Well, the night is still young, and the best is yet to come. Let's keep this party going with Ace!"

The lights came up over the stage and they started to rock. The girls and I were suddenly all clustered in front of the table, singing and dancing and screaming at our main man. He noticed us and smiled.

Even Kayla was getting into it. Then he noticed everyone else. There was no one in the place sitting down. And his smile got even bigger.

At the end of the third song, Mitch breathlessly took the microphone. "How's everybody doing tonight? He said cheerfully. "Having a good time?" The crowd was going insane. "Well, let's keep it going then, what do you say?" Again, they were all cheering.

Mitch was starting to catch his breath, but he was still pumped, I could tell. "Ok, let's go!" He was pulling up his guitar again and readjusting as he talked. Just then, Shep and Ty came running up to him.

"Hey, Trip hold it, hold it." Shep said.

Everyone quieted down to see what was going on. Ty put his arm around Mitch's shoulders, and Mitch was just looking at him, a stunned and curious look on his face.

"What are they doing?" Trudy asked.

"I'm not sure." Chris said.

Ty stepped up to the microphone with Mitch. "We've been doing this song all week in rehearsal, and well, it's been sounding pretty good, to us that is. But our front man here keeps telling poor Newbie up there on the drums that he's missing beats. So, we got together this morning, and made an executive decision." Mitch started to smile.

"What are you doing?" he asked Ty. Ty just smiled.

Shep took over. "We decided that if he thinks he can do better, we're going to let him." Everyone was cheering and applauding. "You've seen this guy's talent tonight on leads and guitar, but what you don't know is that he has another hidden talent or two." Shep turned around and motioned for Newbie, who brought his drumsticks, handed them to Mitch and proceeded to undo his guitar strap. Mitch knew now what they were doing, and he was smiling and shaking his head.

"Oh, no, no no" he said.

Shep stepped back up to the microphone again. "Taking over on lead guitar, let's hear it for Aaron 'Newbie' Newsonberg!" Everyone cheered. "And, on drums, our multitalented front man, Mitch 'Trip' Tarrington!" Shep and Ty had Mitch by the arms leading him to the drum set. He was laughing and still protesting.

He pointed to the drums and the crowd went ballistic. "I have to adjust a few things here." He said bringing the stool higher and the mic up. He looked at Newbie and said into the mic, "Man, like what are you, fifteen inches shorter than me?" Everyone laughed.

Mitch finally sat down and pulled the mic to him. "Well, I have a confession, and that is that I really haven't touched a set of sticks in like, three years. But, I'm willing to try if no one cares how bad I mess this up. How about it?" Everyone cheered.

I was waiting, holding my breath. Mitch told me he started taking up the drums but never really pursued it. I was so afraid for him at that moment. I turned to Chris.

"Can he do this, Chris?" I asked.

"Watch him." Was all he said, and he was smiling.

"Ok here goes." And they broke into the song. Being that the majority of the song was percussion, Mitch really got to strut his stuff. He definitely could play and the guys knew it.

"You better catch me, because I'm going to faint!" I said. Chris laughed.

Even Olivia and Jake started to clap. You could see the pride in their faces as they watched their son having the time of his life.

"Well, what do you know about that?" Joseph said smiling. He and Kayla were enjoying this, too.

The song ended, and Mitch stood up. Everyone was on their feet cheering and clapping, whistling and screaming. Mitch handed the sticks back to Newbie and put him in a headlock, rubbing his head with his knuckles. Then he gave high fives to Ty and Shep.

Mitch picked up a stool from the stage hand, and Zach handed him his acoustic guitar. He pulled the microphone down, and everyone got quiet again, and some sat down.

"I have a little story to share with you all, and I'll probably get in trouble for this later, but here goes anyway." Everyone chuckled. "About two months ago, my life changed forever when I first laid eyes on the woman who had a lot to do with me being here tonight. If not for her love and encouragement, I wouldn't be sitting here in front of you right now. But the best part is, on Christmas Eve, she said yes when I asked her to become my wife." Everyone cheered. He smiled at me. "Dana, this is for you."

Everyone cheered, and he began to play, a melody soft and sweet. He didn't take his eyes off me the entire time he sang. I started to cry. Kayla and Julia were on either side of me, and gave me a hug.

"I can't believe him." I said. Jake and Olivia were smiling at their son.

"Dana, you are so lucky." Angelina said. Jim gave her a look. "Oh, go on, you." She said to him.

Mitch smiled at me. "She didn't have a clue that was coming!" He said to the crowd. "But now that I made her cry," Everyone went "ahhhhh", "I'd better go dance with her!"

He strapped on a headset microphone and came down the front stairs of the stage, right up to me. He moved the mic away from his face for just a moment.

"Hello, beautiful." He said, smiling at me.

"Hello, handsome." I said back. Then Mitch cued the band and moved his microphone back up to his mouth. He took me by the hand and led me a little ways onto the floor, and the light came down upon us. I was never so embarrassed in my life, and he was smiling with all he had in him. He started to sing, and his dance moves would have made Patrick Swayze look like a beginner.

"Hey Dana, I told you he could dance!" I heard Julia yell out to me.

But I didn't pay attention because I was so lost in Mitch, and I was dancing with him now, too. He finished the song and gave me a hug. Moving the mic again he whispered, "I love you, baby." He moved the mic back. "Let's keep it rocking!" He smiled impishly.

Again, he was dancing with me. But this time he got closer to me, and stole a kiss, as if no one was watching. At the end of the song, he ran back onto the stage.

The group broke into two more songs, sounding like they had been making music all their lives. There was not a doubt in anyone's mind that these guys had what it takes to make it big. And Mitch was truly a showman.

After the next song, Mitch stepped up again. "We're gonna take a little break, but before we go, I'd like to take a minute to introduce you to the guys that make Ace what it is." Everyone was still cheering.

"We'll start over here to my left, helping me out with lead guitar is the very talented, and ladies, very available, Zach Daniels! Behind me here, is the big prankster of the group, on drums and vocals, also available ladies, Aaron "Newbie" Newsonberg!" The crowd was cheering as he introduced each one. "Next, we have on keyboards and vocals, my good friend, Ty Sanders! Helping out on keyboards, percussion and just about anything brass, the very talented, and very married, Ash Marshall! Last but not least, on bass guitar, Todd "Shep" Sheppard!"

Shep stepped over to Mitch. "And not to be left out is a guy that has more talent than anyone I have ever known. On lead vocals, lead guitar, drums, ok well, sometimes," Everyone laughed. "and he can also play keyboards, but we won't do that to him tonight, our very own Mitchell 'Trip' Tarrington the third!"

I looked around. There was not one person sitting down, not one person who's eyes weren't on Mitch at that moment. I could see so much pride and excitement in his face. He stood there taking it all in for a few moments, then thanked everyone and saying they'd be back in about fifteen minutes, the guys all exited the stage.

Everyone in the club was buzzing around now, and Mitch's family and I were excitedly commenting on the band's performance thus far. Suddenly, I heard someone calling out to me from behind.

Mitch was standing on the edge of the stage, and when I looked at him, he smiled and reached out his hand, and my heart melted. I climbed the stairs to the stage, and taking Mitch by the hand, he led me backstage.

He picked me up and spun me around, giving me a kiss at the same time. "I feel so great, Dana! This is all so great!" He put me down and slid his arms around me. "And I have you to thank for it."

"It's nothing," I replied. Then I laughed. "You told me that you couldn't play drums very well. Mitch, you were fantastic!" I said excitedly. "And, oh, by the way, just where *did* you learn to dance like that?"

He smiled impishly. "Impressed, huh? Well, honey, I have moves that would make you blush." He laughed.

"Mitch, you are terrible! Why are you so bad?" I laughed.

"Because I can be, and because I like to watch how you react to me." His face was glowing. "So, is everyone having fun, my family I mean? And what about Kayla and Joseph?"

"I think they're loving it, Mitch. You should see the look on your mom's and dad's faces. They are really proud of you."

"Well, you could be confusing pride with shock, Dana. My parents aren't really much into the modern music scene, you know."

"No, honey, trust me, they're liking this show. Your mom was even dancing a little bit." I smiled.

Mitch's expression softened. "I just want you to know, Dana, that I couldn't have done this without you. I would never have had the confidence to get up there and perform the way I am tonight. But I look down at you there, and it inspires me to do even more."

I smiled at him. "I'm just glad to see you so happy, Mitch." I said.

"Hey, Trip, it's almost show time. Hour and a half and counting. You have, like, two more minutes for all the mushy stuff." Zach was smiling at him.

"Yeah, ok, I'll be there." Mitch replied. Then he turned back to me. "You better get back out there and get your seat. Soon it will be midnight, and we'll be done shortly after. Then I'll come and get you, ok?"

"Ok. Mitch?" I started.

"Yeah, sweetheart?" he replied.

"Can I have your autograph?" I teased.

Mitch smiled. "Well, I don't have a pen. Will a kiss do?"

"I think I can accept that." And I did.

Ace took the stage once more, playing with all they had. Finally, it was about one minute until midnight. Mitch stepped up to the microphone.

"Ok, everyone, it's almost time. Guys, grab your girls, girls grab your guys, and if you don't have one or the other, well, just grab anyone." Everyone laughed. "And I need to cover myself, too, so, Dana, come on up here, sweetheart." He came back to the stairs and reached out for me. As I walked onto the stage, people were applauding and I even heard a few whistles. Mitch smiled and put his arm around me. "Sorry, guys, this one belongs to me." I smiled at him, and his eyes were shining.

It was ten seconds to midnight. "Ok, ten, nine, eight...." Everyone was counting with him. "three, two, one, Happy New Year!" The place was going wild and everyone was kissing and hugging everyone else. Mitch turned to me.

"Happy New Year, Dana. Six months, nine days and counting. I love you."

"Happy New Year. I love you, too."

For a moment in time, there was no one there but us, lost in each other's love. That is, until Ty tapped Mitch on the shoulder. He pointed to the crowd, and suddenly we realized that our kiss was the main attraction now, not the band.

Mitch and I pulled apart, and he was chuckling softly, his eyes shining and a blush coming upon his face. I looked at him and started laughing, burying my face in his chest.

Ty pointed to me. "The future Mrs. Mitch Tarrington, folks." He said. Everyone cheered.

I walked back down the stairs to my seat, still blushing. When I got to the table, everyone started laughing.

"That boy needs to learn to control himself!" Chris teased.

"No, you need to learn to be more like him!" Trudy teased back.

"What, you want me to kiss you, is that it?" He got up and planted one on Trudy. She laughed.

"Now, honey, see, that's how we prevent this." She patted her stomach.

"No, honey, I think that's how we *start* that." Chris replied, still laughing. Everyone else laughed, too.

Julia smiled. "I think it's neat that they aren't afraid to show how much they're in love." She looked at Paul. "He would never think of kissing me in public like that."

Paul got a look on his face, a mixture of a smile and shock. "Hey, didn't I just kiss you at midnight, and we're in public, aren't we?" Julia waved him off with a smile.

The band was playing again, and kept going until around half past twelve. Finally, it was time to wrap up the show.

Mitch grabbed the microphone, sporting a huge smile. "We want to thank all of you for letting us play for you tonight, and a big thanks to Rob for giving us this opportunity. We had a blast! Be safe driving home. We're Ace, and good night!" The guys all gathered in a line at the front of the stage, and placing their arms around each others shoulders, they did a group bow. The crowd was going crazy.

"Well, that's it!" Jim said. "Is Mitch coming out here?" He asked me.

"Yeah, he told me to have everyone just wait right here." I started to bounce with excitement. "But I've never been one to listen. You all stay here. I'm going to go get him!"

The band had exited the stage and I slipped around to the backstage door, only to be stopped by a security guard. "Do you have a pass, miss?" he asked.

I looked at him curiously. "No, but my fiancé is the lead in the band. I'd really like to go see him." I was afraid at first he thought I might be making up my story. Then he smiled.

"Oh, yeah, I remember now. That was some kiss you two exchanged." I blushed. "Go on ahead."

He opened the door and let me go through. But what I saw amazed me. If he stopped me, how did these other, oh, ten or fifteen women get in here? I didn't care, as long as I got to Mitch before they did.

A few of the guys were talking to a girl or two, and they smiled at me as I walked by. But I wasn't seeing Mitch anywhere. Finally, I saw him standing against a wall, surrounded by at least four girls, and the biggest smile on his face I had ever seen.

I stopped myself. Ok, Dana, you can handle this. Your guy was good out there tonight. He's handsome, he's charming, he's sexy. If you see that, they see that. I looked down at my ring, reminding myself that it meant something. I wasn't going to be jealous this time, I said. I was just going to calmly walk up to him and say hello. That is, until I saw two of them put their arms around his waist, and one leaned her head on his arm. A third was lining up for the picture. Ok, now this is war, I thought. I was not losing my man to some cheap little groupie sexpot.

"Excuse me!" I said pushing my way through.

"Hey, sister, wait your turn." One of them said.

"Just trying to get to my fiancé!" I replied, placing a lot of emphasis on the last word.

"Hey, sweetheart," Mitch said. Then he turned to the ladies. "Nice talking to you, ladies. I'm glad you had a good time."

He moved away from them toward me, but he stopped when he saw the icy glare of death I was giving him.

"I know that look. I don't like that look." He said, keeping about two feet away from me.

"Your family is waiting for you, Mitchell." I said sternly.

He stepped closer to me. "Let them wait." He said. "You need to calm down."

"Why? I'm perfectly fine. Looks like you are, too. So, let's go." I started to walk away.

"Dana, stop." Mitch commanded. "They only wanted a picture. I guess they think I'm like, a celebrity or something."

"Well, a picture is one thing. Letting them hang all over you to get it is another." I had folded my arms.

Mitch smiled at me. "If I live to be a very old man, I will never figure out why you're like this, Dana. Now, stop it and come over here." I walked closer to Mitch and sat down in a chair. "Now, then, tell me what I was supposed to do? Tell them they couldn't have their picture?"

"Tell them they couldn't put their hands all over you, for starters. And not look like you were enjoying it so much." I said.

Mitch sighed. "Dana, if you want to get all upset over this, I can't stop you. I also can't stop you from thinking you have to be afraid I'm going to dump you for someone else. I can't make you believe that I really do love you, and I can't make you believe that I was standing there wishing they would hurry up so I could come to find you. I wasn't exactly enjoying it, but what kind of reputation would it give the band if I was rude to the people who come to see us? It's all up to you what you want to think or feel. So, you can either stay here and act like this, or you can come with me and have some fun. Now, which is it going to be?"

"You know what they're going to do with that picture, Mitch? They'll probably take it home and put it in their bedrooms and fantasize about being with you. That's what they'll do."

"Then let them do it, Dana. Who cares? A fantasy is all it will ever be. You have the proof of that on your finger, sweetheart. That is my promise to you that I will always be faithful. I really wish I didn't have to keep repeating myself." He leaned down to me.

"I have an idea. How about if I prove to you that you have nothing to worry about? Tomorrow night, when we start the last number, I'll have Max, that's the security guard, put you backstage. That way, when I'm all done, you'll be the first person I see. Ok?"

I looked up at Mitch, and his face was soft and sweet. He was trying to make this right. "Ok, Mitch." I said and I stood up to hug him. "I'm sorry. I just don't have a lot of trust for women like that."

He hugged me tightly. "It's ok, but you need to know you can trust me. I almost lost you once, Dana. I'm not stupid enough to risk doing that again. I could never live with myself." He kissed me. "Now, we have people waiting. Let's gather up these guys and head out, ok?" I nodded, and he took my hand. "Hey, guys, let's go meet our critics, shall we?"

"Wait" I said, holding up my hand. "First, I want to tell these five very talented and good looking men how proud I am of all of them. And......" I looked at Mitch with a smirk, "I want a hug from each of you!"

They all agreed to that, and I hugged each one of them, telling them all how fantastic they were. I turned back to Mitch. "See, two can play this game." I smiled.

"Yeah, but only one is doing it on purpose." He smirked back.

13

We all filed out to the tables where Mitch's family were sitting, and as we approached, they all stood up and applauded. All the guys looked like they were eating up the attention.

Chris stood up and walked over to Mitch, as did his parents. "You were great, little brother!" he said, and he gave him a hug.

"You are quite the showman, Mitchell. I'm really proud of you, sweetie." Olivia said.

Now Mitch was standing face to face with his father. Jake was looking at his son, the pride showing in his face. "Well, Mitchell, you have a lot of talent. More than I gave you credit for. I'm really proud of you, son. You did a great job tonight." He reached out for Mitch's hand, but then pulled him into a hug instead.

"Thanks, Dad. That means a lot." Mitch said. And I knew that Jake's comments meant more to him than anyone else's.

"Well, let me introduce everyone. I know some of you haven't met." He said turning to the guys. "This is Shep, Ty, Newbie, Ash and Zach. Guys, you know my parents, and Dana, of course, and I'm sure you may remember Chris. But, these are my sisters, Julia and Angelina, and their husbands, Paul and Jim. And these are our very close friends Kayla and Joseph Turner." Everyone exchanged greetings and handshakes. Then he turned back to his family. "So, you all had a good time?"

"The best!" Angelina said. "I didn't know you had it in you. I mean, all of you were fantastic, but Mitchell, wow, you have talent guy!"

"Thanks, Ang. It was a lot of fun, I gotta admit." Mitch was beaming.

"Mitch, boy, you sure do know how to move. Why, you were making me hot under the collar when you were dancing with her!" Kayla said, smiling. Mitch blushed.

Jim turned to Ty. "So, how far in advance did you plan that little stunt with the drums? That was pretty slick."

Ty and Shep laughed. "Actually, after rehearsal yesterday, we got to talking. We knew Mitch could drum, but he'd never admit it. So, anyway, we decided to play a little trick on him, you know, to get him to showcase his talents a little bit." Ty said.

After a few more minutes, everyone else decided to head for home. We hung out with the guys for a while longer, talking and laughing and enjoying each other's company. Finally, it was time to go. After saying our goodbyes, Mitch and I got into his car and started the drive home.

Mitch looked at me and smiled. "So, are you over being mad at me?" he asked.

"I wasn't mad at you, Mitch. I just didn't like all those girls hanging all over you, that's all." I said back.

"Well, now it's just you and me, love." He said. "So, did you make any New Year's resolutions?"

"Not really. Just that I hope I don't gain any weight and not be able to fit into my wedding gown." I replied.

Mitch laughed. "I don't think you have anything to worry about."

We pulled up to my apartment building and Mitch came around and opened my door for me. He took me by the hand and we went up to my apartment.

"You have to be really tired." I said to him.

"I'm starting to feel it a little, but man, Dana, what a rush! I don't remember it being that much fun." He replied excitedly.

"It wasn't hard to tell that you were enjoying yourself." I said. "You really know how to play the crowd, too, Mitch. Everyone was in your control."

Mitch smiled. "I was just having a good time, that's all." He said. "And you know, sweetheart, you aren't a bad dancer yourself."

"Thanks. I do love to dance, but I don't get the chance that much. I mostly turn on my stereo and dance around here while I'm doing things."

Mitch gave me a look, then stood up and walking over to my stereo, he looked through my collection and took out an album. Placing it on the turntable, he reached out for me.

"The one thing I didn't get to do with you tonight is slow dance. Would you dance with me, Dana?" he asked.

I smiled. "I'd like that." I said. Mitch held me tight and together we swayed gently to the music. He really was a good dancer, and I found it easy to follow his lead. The song ended and he reached over to switch off the stereo with one hand, still holding me with the other.

"Dana, I know you're going to think I'm crazy, but there's something I need to ask you." Mitch said looking into my eyes.

"Sure, what did you want to ask?" I replied.

"Dana, will you marry me?" He said softly.

I looked at him curiously. "Honey, I think I already said yes to this one." I said.

Mitch slid his hands down my arms and took hold of both my hands. "No, Dana, I mean now. I want to get married now. It's getting harder and harder for me to be away from you, even for a little while. When I first saw you tonight, I didn't want to leave this room. I wanted to stay here with you forever." He smiled. "Sweetheart, I know we just decided a few days ago to move the date up once already, but I was thinking there isn't anything stopping us from doing it again. We could have the wedding around Valentine's Day. What do you say?"

My heart was beating so fast I thought it was going to jump right out of my chest. I didn't have to think very long to give my answer.

"Let's do it Mitch. Let's get married." I said to him.

"Yes!" Mitch said excitedly, and he picked me up and spun me around. He put me down and looked at me again, his eyes shining. "Will that give you enough time to plan everything? I, mean, I'll help you."

"If you help me, we can do it. Let's pick out the date right now." I grabbed the calendar once more. "February 18, Mitch. That's the day. *And* this time, we aren't changing it!" I laughed.

Mitch and I talked well into the wee hours of the morning, and around three, he decided that he really should go home.

"Soon, we won't have to do this anymore." He said, kissing me.

"I know. Won't that be great?" I said.

Mitch kissed me again and grabbing his coat, opened the door. "Dana, I know I won't sleep tonight. I'm too wired now." He smiled.

"I know, me too, but try. It's been a really exciting day for you, and you'll need your energy for the show tomorrow night, oh, I mean, later today."

"Ok, sweetheart, sleep well. I'll see you soon. I love you." Mitch said as he walked out the door.

"Me, too, see you soon." I closed the door and locked it. I got ready for bed, and slipping under the covers, I looked over at the empty spot next to me. Soon, I would have my husband there that I could cuddle up with each and every night. I grabbed the pillow and turning it lengthwise, I hugged it close to me, imaging I was holding Mitch. It was then that I realized what he had been doing when I had seen him hugging his pillow. And I smiled, falling into a blissful sleep.

I slept soundly, and by the time I awoke, it was almost ten o'clock. I thought I heard a soft knock on the door, so I grabbed my robe, pulled my hair into a ponytail, and went to see who it was.

"Hey beautiful, it's me. Open up." Mitch said softly.

I unlocked the door and opened it. He was standing there with a bouquet of flowers and a very big smile.

"Good morning, beautiful." He said stepping inside and handing me the flowers. He kissed my cheek.

"Honey, these are so pretty, thank you." I said. I took a vase down from my shelf and put the flowers in it with some water, setting them in the middle of my table. I turned around to see Mitch snickering at me.

"Ok, Mitchell, the last time you surprised me like this in the morning, you laughed at me. You're laughing at me now. Are you going to laugh at me every morning like this?"

He smiled. "Sweetheart, I'm sorry, I'm not laughing at you. I'm just thinking how cute you look. Pajamas with feet, huh?"

"I like them. They're nice and warm." I said.

"You aren't planning to take those on the honeymoon, are you?" He asked, walking up to me.

"I don't know. I might." I replied.

He peeked inside my robe. "Do they have a zipper? Ok, we're good." He smiled and chuckled to himself.

"Mitchell!" I said to him, and pushed him playfully.

Mitch laughed. "Go on and get dressed, baby. I want to take you out for breakfast."

"I'm up for that." I said. "Give me fifteen minutes."

Mitch took out his watch. "I'll see you around eleven." He laughed.

I smirked at him and went in to get ready. Exactly fifteen minutes later, I reemerged and we were heading out the door.

"So, what made you decide to do this?" I asked.

"I don't know. I just got up this morning and thought it might be fun. I know a place that has some fantastic pancakes. They'll even put whipped cream on them, if you want. I know how you like whipped cream." He snickered.

"I am hungry." I replied.

"Well, then I thought we could spend some time with the wedding plans. My mom called this morning and said everyone is going to be out there around 2 or so, for a kind of late lunch, so if you want, we can go and let them all know we moved everything up. After that, the guys are meeting us for dinner at six, just a quick burger or something, and after that, to the club for the show."

I looked at Mitch. Mr. Organization had the entire day all planned out.

"Sounds like we have a lot to do, doesn't it?" I said.

Mitch thought a minute. "Yeah, you know, it really does, doesn't it? Tell you what. Let's call Mom, ask her to move it all to four. I'll get the guys over there and we can announce everything at once. That will give us more time alone, and we can head to the club from there."

"You are so brilliant, my dear." I told him.

We got to the restaurant and got a little table in the corner. It was cozy, and the atmosphere was inviting. We both ordered pancakes with bacon, Mitch got coffee and I hot chocolate. He smiled when I told the waitress to put extra whipped cream in it.

"I'm going to go give my mom a call, and have her call the guys, ok? You wait here, I won't be long." He gave me a quick peck on the cheek as he left the table. By the time he got back, our food had arrived.

"Wow, this looks great." He said. "Everything is set. Three o'clock at my parents."

"What did you tell her?" I asked.

"I just told her that we had some things to get done and we couldn't be there by two. She was ok with it, except that she said three would be better. So, I told her ok." He took a bite of his pancakes. "This is good." He said.

"I agree." I said. "And lots of whipped cream on the hot chocolate." Mitch smiled.

It didn't take us long to finish eating, and we headed back toward home. Mitch was in a particularly good mood, and he was being very talkative.

"What are the wedding colors going to be? Did you decide?" he asked.

"I thought pink and blue. What do you think?" I replied.

"Whose wearing the pink?"

"Well, I thought Julia, Trudy and Angelina. Then the guys could wear the matching ties and cummerbunds. I thought we went over this already, honey."

"Uh, teacher, I must have been absent that day. I don't remember ever agreeing to pink." Mitch said.

I looked at him. "Honey, it will be so pretty. Trust me."

Mitch smiled. "Dana, I don't think any of the guys care much about looking 'pretty'. How about all blue?"

I sighed. "Ok, how about we put three of them in blue, and only Kayla and Chris in pink?"

Mitch chuckled. "Somehow, dear, I can't picture my brother in pink anything."

I threw up my hands. "For crying out loud, Mitchell, it's only a stupid tie and cummerbund. I'm not asking them to wear pink suits."

Mitch looked at me. "You don't have to get upset about it, sweetheart. You did ask for my opinion, didn't you? Or is this another one of those cases where I'm supposed to just agree with you?"

I sighed again. "No, Mitch, your opinion counts. If you don't want pink, we won't do pink. It will be all blue. Let's move on."

Mitch looked at me with a smirk. "No, now, if you want pink, we can work it out."

"I'm not discussing this anymore, Mitchell. We have decided on all blue." I folded my arms.

"No, dear, you decided on all blue. I'm willing to compromise." Mitch was having a good time with this.

"Ok, then, here's the compromise. We put everyone in green!" I was getting annoyed with him.

Mitch smiled and couldn't help a little snicker of mischievousness. "Green is a nice color, baby, but what shade of green?"

"Just please be quiet, Mitchell, before I scream." I said in a huff. I turned toward the window as we drove the rest of the way home.

Mitch was still laughing as we pulled up to my apartment building. He came around and opened my door, and tried to take my hand, but

I wouldn't let him. I walked silently up the three flights of stairs as Mitch snickered, continuing to find my anger humorous. Once inside, we took off our coats and I went to sit down on the couch.

Mitch came and sat down beside me. "Dana, why are you getting so upset about everything? I was only having fun." Then he added, "But I'm really not into the pink very much."

"I just want you to help me, Mitchell, not tease me all the time, ok? Do you think you could do that?" I asked.

Mitch smiled. "I'm sorry, sweetheart. You're just so much fun to tease. You're so cute when you get mad, and the way you fold your arms, like you are right now."

"It isn't meant to be an endearing trait, Mitchell." I snipped back.

"Can I give an option?" he asked.

"I guess so." I replied.

"Ok, since it's kind of a Valentine's wedding, why not some shade of red?" He was trying, I had to give him that much.

"Red with the black might be pretty, or even a burgundy, if we make it a little lighter shade, instead of dark." I agreed.

"Good, then we have our colors, agreed?" he asked, picking up the pad of paper we had been making our list on.

"Yes, agreed." I replied. "Now, what?"

"Caterers, but we can't call anyone on the holiday, so how about we work on the guest list again?" He suggested.

"Well, my list is done, so now it's up to you." I said.

Mitch picked up the list with my ten or fifteen names on it. "You know, sweetie, we have a lot of mutual friends."

"Like who?" I asked.

"Well, let's jot them down.   First, we have Jimmy and Susan Gartano, and pretty much everyone else at the bistro, so that would be........" Mitch wrote down everyone's name. "Ok, then there's all the guys in Ace, and of course, Ash's wife, Cindy. We should probably let them bring dates, too, if they can get one." He chuckled. Before I knew it, we had close to seventy five or eighty names on the list.

"Now, we can talk to Mom later on today to see if she can give me addresses and all that for my aunts and uncles and cousins, and whatnot."

"Mitch, what about our reservations for Hawaii? Are you going to be able to change the dates?" I asked him.

"I did ask about that, believe it or not. The travel lady said we could, and that all I would have to do is call. I'll make a note right now to do that, ok? He jotted it down on the paper.

"What about the cake?" I said. "What kind of cake do you want?"

Mitch smiled. "Probably the sweet kind with lots of icing that you can eat." I smacked him lightly on the arm. He laughed.

"We're supposed to put the top layer of the cake away in the freezer, and then we bring it out on our first anniversary and eat it. So, it has to be something we both like a lot." I informed him.

"My guess would be chocolate." Mitch said, decisively.

"Perfect, and we'll do, oh, a marble for the rest. How's that?"

"Fine, that sounds good." Mitch put down the piece of paper, and leaned back on the couch, taking me with him. "See, sweetheart, it's all coming together. We're going to be just fine."

I laid my head on his shoulder. "Mitch, is there anything that you are really looking forward to when we're married?"

He looked at me. "Sure, lots of things."

"Like what in particular?" I asked.

Mitch sighed. "Well, like just being together all the time, being able to go to bed and wake up next to you, sharing my joys and sorrows with you, and, well, other things too." He smiled.

"Is there anything you're afraid of?" I asked.

He thought about the question for a moment. "That's a tough question, Dana. I think my biggest fear is of something happening to cause me to lose you. Or not be able to take care of you. I don't know how I would ever handle either one of those things." I thought about that for a moment. Then Mitch spoke again. "How about you? What are you looking forward to, and what are you afraid of?"

"Well," I started, "I'm looking forward to all the things you are. And I'm looking forward to having a family someday, and us growing old together. Just knowing I have someone to love me."

Mitch smiled. "I'll always love you, Dana, I promise." Then he started to stroke my hair. "Is there anything you're afraid of?"

"I'm afraid of losing you, of not being the kind of wife you're expecting me to be. Of not making you happy." I said.

Mitch's eyes were sympathetic and loving. "Dana, you won't ever lose me. I told you that. And as far as expectations, sweetheart, I have none. The only thing I expect is that you keep the vows we make, and I know you'll do that. You make me happier than I've ever been in my life, and that can never change."

I smiled at him, his eyes full of love. "I'm glad." I said.

I looked out at the balcony with our two little snow people. They were still holding hands. I somehow knew that, even fifty years from now, Mitch and I would be, too.

Just then, Mitch noticed some children having a snowball fight outside. They were laughing and frolicking and just enjoying being children. He smiled.

"Dana, I know we both agree that we want children. But have you ever thought about when, or how many?"

"I don't know. Those are things we'll have to decide together." I replied.

"I agree. But, I've thought about it. I want at least three, maybe more. But I want to wait a few years. I want us to have time to just be us for a while, to get to know each other as a married couple first." Mitch said.

I thought about what he was saying, and I agreed. "I want to wait awhile, too, Mitch, for the same reasons you do. As far as how many, I always thought three was a good number, too."

We sat and watched the kids playing for a little while, then Mitch picked up the list again. "Let's see, now, where were we? Oh, what about a place to have the reception?"

"Didn't you say something about your parents and some country club?" I asked.

"Yeah, we can ask them, I guess, but I don't want my mom going all fancy snazzy on me. Not really my thing." Mitch said.

"I know, honey, but it is our wedding. It's the only day we will really get to be that way." I replied.

Mitch smiled. "You know, sweetheart, that's true. Besides, it'll be decorated a little bit, as far as centerpieces and that, so we can just add anything that we want."

"Hey, and I'm sure they have a caterer there, in fact, they may not want us to use anyone else. Two birds with one stone, so to speak." I concluded.

Mitch was busily jotting things down. Then he looked at me. "You know what? I'm getting a little hungry."

I smiled. "Mitch, how could you possibly be hungry after that breakfast you ate? It was only two and a half hours ago."

He stood up. "Dana, I'm a guy. There are two things that I always am, and one of them is hungry." He had his devilish little grin on his face.

I stood up and gave him a loving little shove toward the kitchen. "Well, if you can control one, you can control the other. But, come on, I'll get something for you anyway."

I made two cups of soup and handed one to Mitch. "See, this time you have your own, so you won't eat mine." He smiled.

We carried the soup to the coffee table, along with some crackers, and Mitch went back to retrieve two glasses of milk. He returned, set them on the table, and sat down. "We're going to need flowers, aren't we? And I know this might upset you, but I'm going to let you handle that on your own."

"Why? Don't you like flowers?" I asked him.

"Sure, I like flowers. But, that's more of a girl thing. I'm not planning to carry a bouquet down the aisle." He said, taking a bite of soup.

I sighed. "Gee, now that you've shattered my illusions," I teased, "I guess I can handle that part."

He smirked at me. Then a smile crossed his face. "Hey, I get to have a bachelor party, don't I?" He was looking at me for a reaction. I decided not to give him one.

"That's fine, honey, as long as you don't drink too much. I really don't want to have to deal with that hangover thing again." I smiled sweetly.

Mitch looked at me. "If I drank at all, love, it would probably amount to about half a beer, which would be hard for me since I don't even like beer, but I have had it before, believe it or not." I started to ask when, and he must have read my mind. "In college."

I still decided to shake him up by not reacting. "Well, that's still fine dear." Then I threw in the finishing touch. "Maybe you boys can all go to a strip club somewhere and get your fill. I know how much you like to flirt. You'll have plenty of opportunity there. And don't worry, I won't mind at all. I mean, after all, we won't be married yet, and I *do* trust you."

Mitch was giving me his most stunned look, and starting to laugh. "Dana, you can't be serious. You would actually let me go to a strip club?"

I smiled at him and took a drink of my milk. "Sure, honey, why not? I mean, guys like those sorts of things, don't they? Just start saving your dollars now. You'll need them for the ladies." Then I looked right at him. "I've heard if you let them know it's your bachelor party, one of the ladies will even dance just for you. I know you'd enjoy that."

Mitch was staring at me in disbelief. He pinched himself. "No, ok, I'm not dreaming, I'm fully awake and coherent, so that can only mean one thing. What did you do with the real Dana?"

I smirked. "I'm right here, Mitchell. Why?"

He was still staring at me. "Because the Dana I know would threaten me with sure and immediate death if I even drove past a strip club, let alone actually walk into one. The Dana I know doesn't even want me to look at other women, let alone have one do a striptease for me."

I smiled at him again. "Well, maybe I've changed, sweetie. Maybe I've realized the error of my thinking."

"And maybe I've lost all concept of reality in the last 24 hours, too!" Then he smiled, catching on to my little joke. "Dana, that wasn't nice."

"What wasn't nice?" I asked, snickering.

"Getting my hopes all up for nothing." He was starting to laugh.

"Oh, and you would actually go to one of those places, huh, Mitchell?" I asked.

He put his arms around me. "Of course not, sweetheart. Why would I spend my money to watch a woman undress when I can come home once we're married and watch you do it for free?" His eyes were shining.

"Oh, is that how you think it's going to be? Mitch wants, Dana performs?" I teased.

"Hmmm, uh huh, pretty much." He was smiling mischievously.

"Well, you better change that way of thinking, mister, or you are going to spend a lot of lonely nights on the couch." I laughed and placed my finger on his chest.

"Is that so?" He was laughing now, too. "I paid for the bed, so I'll make you sleep on the couch. How do you like that?"

"You wouldn't." I said.

"Watch me." He shot back. I grabbed his hands and was trying to push him backwards in a little play battle, but he pulled me down instead. Then he started to kiss me.

"You know, you are really something else." He said, between kisses.

"Had you going, didn't I?" I said back, playfully.

Mitch kissed me again. "No, actually, you have me going right now."

I smiled. "Mitch, do you think we will still love kissing each other this much, oh, ten years from now?"

He looked at me. "I think we'll enjoy it even more, sweetheart. At least I will."

I had to ask what was on my mind. "Well, do you think we will still ever just stop at kissing?"

He smiled and pushed back my hair from my face. "I think that there will be times when all we want to do is kiss and be close, and times when we want more than that. But just know that I will always do my best to make you happy. Whatever you want is what I want, too."

I gave him a gentle hug. "Do you really mean that Mitch?"

He smiled impishly. "I'm a guy, Dana, of course I don't mean it!" And he laughed, kissing me again.

"Mitchell Tarrington, you're terrible!" I laughed back.

Mitch started to brush back my hair again. "So, I know someone who has a birthday in a few days. Anything special you'd like to have?"

I gave it some thought. "I really can't think of anything off the top of my head." I replied.

He smiled. "Well, you think about it and let me know, ok? And I'm taking that day off, too, so we can spend the whole day together, if you want."

"That's a good enough present for me," I said, looking at the clock. "Honey, we better get going. It's almost 2:30 already."

Mitch sat up. "Don't change right now, ok? Just take whatever you are going to wear and we'll change at my parent's before we head to the club. That way, you'll be more comfortable. My clothes are in the car, too."

"Ok, let me go get what I need then. I'll be right back." I headed off to my closet, picking a nice pantsuit and blouse. I stuffed everything into a little travel bag, along with my heels and my evening bag from the night before. Then I returned to Mitch who was waiting with his coat on.

Mitch took the bag from me. "Why is it that I have jeans and a shirt laying on the backseat of my car, and you have half your closet all neatly packed into a suitcase?"

"That is hardly half my closet, Mitchell. Besides I want to look nice for you." I replied

Mitch handed me my coat. "You always look nice to me." He said.

About twenty minutes later we found ourselves pulling into the long drive leading up to the Tarrington Estate. Mitch stopped about a third of the way to the house, and put the car in park.

"Don't even tell me she did what I think she did." He said.

I had no clue what he was talking about. "Did what?" I asked.

He pointed to the multitude of cars parked in front of the house. "Dana, there are at least twenty cars or more up there. My family doesn't even own that many vehicles."

I looked at him curiously. "So, who do they all belong to?" I asked.

Mitch was biting his lip. "My *extended* family. Evidently, my mother feels it's necessary for her son to formally announce his engagement. She did it to Chris, and she did it to the girls, and now she's doing it to me. She calls it a 'surprise' engagement party. I would think she would know me well enough to know I'm not into it."

"Why, Mitch? What's the big deal?" I asked.

He turned to look at me, half a smile on his face. "The gesture is nice, don't get me wrong. But," He chuckled. "some of these people are just insane, Dana. And critical. Oh, man, can they be critical."

I remembered back to the day I first met Mitch's immediate family, and those familiar jitters started to return. "Just how critical are they, Mitchell? I mean, am I ok to meet them like this?" I looked down at my khakis and sweater.

Mitch smiled and took my hand. "No, sweetheart, you're fine. You look great. I didn't mean to make you self conscious. What I mean is," Mitch sighed. "Well, just let me fill you in a little, so you'll be prepared, ok?"

"Ok, but you better stay by me this time. No letting anyone whisk me off into another part of the house." I instructed.

Mitch laughed. "You have my word, love. Now, let's see. First, is Aunt Beatrice, my dad's older sister. She never calls me anything but Mitchell Jacob. Why she feels it necessary to insert the middle name is beyond me. She likes to play twenty questions, too. Then there's Aunt Elaina, my mom's sister. To this day, she pinches my cheek. I absolutely hate it!"

I laughed at the thought of that. "She actually does that? Maybe it's that adorable little dimple that she loves." I reached out and pinched his cheek myself.

"Not funny, dear." He said, smirking. "Now, Uncle Neil, my dad's younger brother, is Mr. Corporate. He can't seem to get enough of trying to find something I've failed at since I didn't go into the family business. And he will compare me to Chris in that area until the day they bury him. My Uncle Anthony, well, he's ok. He actually sticks up for me when he can against the others. Aunt Katherine is my mom's other sister. She will be shocked and appalled when she finds out I played the club last night in a rock band, and even more so when she finds out we've only known each other two months. She also hates public displays of affection. Julia kissed Paul one time in front of her, and she told her that she needed to save it for the bedroom."

I sighed. "Sounds like an interesting bunch of people." I said.

"Oh, wait, there's more. Aunt Beatrice is married to Uncle Anthony, and that's an odd mix. Aunt Elaina's husband is gone, and Uncle Neil is married to Aunt Louise, and she seems to think that I'm still growing for some reason. She always tells me how 'big' I've gotten since she last saw me." I was laughing. "Aunt Katherine never got married, and I think it's because any guy who ever went out with her was henpecked to death before he had a chance to propose."

"Is that everything I need to know?" I asked.

"Well, just be prepared for any type of surprise, but don't worry. They may be eccentric, but they're basically harmless. And deep down, I know they all mean well." Mitch turned to me. "Don't you worry about a thing, sweetheart. We'll be out of here by six and on the way to the club. Ok?"

"Sure. Let's go." I said.

We pulled up to the house and Mitch gave me a kiss. "Just relax, baby, it'll all be over soon. You look wonderful." He came around and opened the door for me, and we walked up to the house. I grabbed his arm just before he reached for the doorknob.

"Are you sure I look ok? I mean, if I would have known about this, I would have dressed a little more. Maybe I should slip upstairs and put on my suit." I said.

Mitch smiled at me and put his arm around me. "You look wonderful. Besides, you'd blow the surprise if you looked too prepared. Now, just relax and come on."

I grabbed Mitch's hand, and he opened the door. Alexander greeted us, followed by his parents.

"Hi, kids." Olivia said, giving each of us a kiss on the cheek. "I'm sure you noticed all the cars out front."

"Yeah, we did, as a matter of fact. Who else is here?" Mitch was trying to play along.

"Come in and see." Olivia said, leading us to the family room.

"Surprise!" Everyone yelled as we entered. Mitch and I exchanged a knowing look. Everyone's eyes were upon us and I think we both felt like running, but we didn't.

Olivia had placed fresh flowers on the piano, and there was a banner up high that said 'Congratulations Mitch and Dana'.

Uncle Neil spoke up first. "So, Mitchell, are you going to tell us who the pretty young lady is?"

Mitch smiled and put his arm around me. "Sure, Uncle Neil. Uh, everyone, this is my fiancé, Dana Walker. And thank you, this is a nice surprise."

"Nicely done." I whispered to Mitch.

"Ok, let's get this party started. And finished." He whispered back.

Uncle Neil approached us. "Dana, this is my dad's brother, Uncle Neil. Uncle Neil, Dana."

Uncle Neil took my hand and kissed it in a very chivalrous manner. "Very pleased to meet you, Dana." Then he turned to Mitch. "You certainly picked a pretty one, Mitchell."

"Thanks, Uncle Neil. I think so, too." Mitch said, smiling at me.

Everyone was buzzing around again, but the aunts and uncles were making their way to us. Next came Aunt Beatrice. "Mitchell Jacob, why I can't believe it. I can't believe you're getting married. And to such a sweet little thing. Why, she looks so much younger than you are."

"I'll be 23 in a few days," I said. "Not really that much younger."

She shook my hand. "Well, you don't look a day over 16. And so petite." I wasn't sure how to answer that, so I just smiled.

Mitch got a smirk on his face and tried not to smile. I assumed by his look that Aunt Cheek Pincher was approaching. I was right.

"Mitchell, look at you, still handsome as ever." Aunt Elaina said, pinching his cheek. "And Dana, you are just adorable. Olivia told us you were pretty, dear, but I never imagined just how much."

"Thank you." I said shyly.

"And I swear you've grown a foot since I last saw you, Mitchell." Aunt Louise said, coming up behind. "How tall are you now, child?"

"I'm about 6'2", Aunt Louise. And I don't think I'm going to go much beyond that." Mitch said.

"And to think you hooked up with such a little thing. Why, I pictured you with someone much taller, but she is just sweet." Aunt Louise shook my hand.

"She's perfect to me." He said back. Mitch turned to me. "Ok, only one more. Be ready, ok?"

I looked at him. "For what?" I asked.

Mitch moved so that he could put both arms around me, and he put my head on his chest. Then he bent down and delivered a long, sweet kiss. I smiled.

"Aunt Katherine, hi. It's good to see you." Mitch said.

"Hello, Mitchell. And nice to meet you, too, Dana," She said. "Mitchell, maybe if you let go of the girl, I could shake her hand."

Mitch smirked. "Oh, sorry, I just can't get enough of her." He kissed my cheek for effect, and I shook Aunt Katherine's hand. Aunt Katherine walked away, shaking her head. Mitch and I snickered.

"Mitch, you are so bad!" I said. "But that was fun."

"Just wait, sweetheart, the fun is just beginning." He said.

Jake and Olivia walked up to us. "So, son, isn't it nice to see everyone here today? They were all so excited when we told them about the engagement that they insisted on meeting Dana. So, I decided to just throw a little party for you two." Olivia said.

"It's really wonderful, Olivia, thank you. And everyone seems very nice." I said.

"And we did tell everyone to mark their calendars for June 10th, so they can attend the wedding." Olivia added.

Mitch looked at me, and then to his mother. "Well, Mom, only one problem. If they come on June 10th, there won't be any wedding going on, at least not ours."

Jake and Olivia got a puzzled look. "Is something wrong, son?" Jake asked.

"Oh, no, we just decided we don't want to wait. We want to get married right away, so the date is now February 18. And no changing it this time." He smiled at me.

"Well, we'd better let everyone know that, hadn't we, Mitchell?" Jake said. Then he put up his hand. "Everyone, we'd like your attention for just a moment. Mitchell and Dana have something they'd like to share with everyone." The room got quiet.

"Well," Mitch started. "Dana and I would like to thank you all again for coming here to help us celebrate our engagement. I guess Mom and Dad told you all that our wedding date was set for June 10. Well, as of last night, our date has been changed. Our wedding will be on February 18th, and we hope you can all join us."

"Third time's a charm, little brother." Chris said. "First October, then June and now February."

Aunt Katherine spoke up. "You mean, Mitchell, that you have changed the date already twice?"

"Yes, that's right, Aunt Katherine." Mitch replied.

The aunts and uncles were exchanging looks. Everyone started talking, and Aunt Elaina walked up to us. "Mitchell, I don't mean to be forward, dear, but is there any particular reason you keep moving the date?"

Mitch understood perfectly what she meant by that comment. "Unless Dana has been with someone other than me, the only reason is that we don't want to wait to get married."

"Now, don't be too anxious, Mitchell. Enjoy being single as long as you can." She advised.

"I did, Aunt Elaina, now I'm ready to be married." He replied. Mitch took me by the hand. "Will you excuse us just a moment, I need to talk to my mom."

"I'm hating this, Dana. One more stupid comment and I'm outta here." I could tell he meant it.

"Honey, it's just that they don't get to see you that often. They don't know anything about me, and they really don't know that much about you, either. Just take it tongue in cheek, and don't let it get to you. Ok?" I kissed his cheek. "Try to have fun."

"Hey, Mom, can I see you for a second?" Mitch called out to Olivia, who was talking to Julia.

"Anything wrong, sweetie?" She asked, trying to read his face.

"Well, only that Aunt Elaina thinks Dana is pregnant, and that I should enjoy being single a little longer. Aunt Katherine doesn't think I should hug her, and Aunt Louise thinks she's too short for me. Otherwise, Mom, everything is great." Mitch was biting his lip.

"Mitch, don't let them get to you. You know how they can be, and well, they don't mean anything by what they say." Olivia placed her hand on Mitch's arm. "They were all so excited on Christmas Day when I called them with the news. They wanted to meet her."

"And that's fine, Mom, but I don't need the critical statements." Mitch said, clearly irritated.

Olivia looked at me, and then at Mitch. "Listen, sweetie, we all love Dana very much, you know that. And we all know how much you two love each other. Let them see that, Mitchell. They just don't understand. They all come from the old school, son."

Mitch nodded. "And, by the way, where are the guys?" he asked.

"They'll be here, I called them, don't worry." Olivia said, smiling. "Now, go mingle and have a good time, ok?"

Mitch nodded again and Olivia smiled and walked away.

"Come on, Mitch. You told me I was in for some fun. Let's have some." I smiled and took his hand. "They really aren't that bad."

He shot me a look. "Let's go talk to Uncle Neil, so I can defend my honor. Haven't had the chance to do that in a while."

Mitch and I approached Uncle Neil. "Hey, Uncle Neil, how have you been?" Mitch asked. "It's been a long time since I've seen you."

"That it has, Mitch. Why, I could hardly believe when your dad called and said you were getting married. From what I hear, it was quite the proposal."

"Well, I was nervous as all get out, but I pulled it off." Mitch smiled.

"I can remember when I proposed to your Aunt Louise. I got down on my knee and was too nervous to stand back up." We laughed. Then Uncle Neil got into the big discussion. "So, Mitchell, what is it you're doing now? Working at a restaurant?"

Mitch smiled proudly. "Well, actually Uncle Neil, I don't just work there. I own it."

Uncle Neil got a stunned look on his face. "Really, now? You own a restaurant?"

"Yes, I sure do. Gartano's Italian Bistro, downtown. Bought it shortly after Dana and I met."

"So, is that a profitable sort of thing for you son? I mean, taking on a wife is a big financial responsibility, you know. I don't know how I could have done it without taking up your dad's offer to join him at Tarrington."

"I do fine, Uncle Neil. The bistro is very busy most of the time, and, well, I also have a nice savings stashed away. Dana works, too, as a teacher, so I think we won't have to worry."

Uncle Neil smiled. "You know, there's always a place for you at Tarrington. Does quite well by Christopher. I hear he and Trudy have a nice big home, and well, with three little ones and another on the way, they must be doing alright. He's a good worker, too, so business minded. Oh, but you always did have a mind of your own, Mitchell."

Mitch smiled. "I'm quite happy with my life, Uncle Neil. I have a good job, a comfortable place to live and a wonderful future wife. There's nothing else I could possibly have that would make me any happier." Then he added, "Chris is much more corporate minded than I am, and I'm proud to see how well he does. I'm happy for him. But as for me, I don't think I could survive a week in that environment. It's just not my kind of life."

Uncle Neil smiled. "Well, Mitchell, I guess you have to do what you feel comfortable with." Just then he was called away by Aunt Beatrice. "Excuse me." He said, walking away.

"You handled that very well, sweetie." I said.

Just then, the guys came rushing through the door. "Hey, Trip!" Shep called out.

"Hey, guys, I'm glad you're here." Mitch said, greeting them all. "Prepare yourselves to be amazed by the extended family of Mitchell Jacob Tarrington the third." They all laughed. Mitch got a mischievous look in his eyes. He held up his hand. "Everyone, could I get your attention for just a moment? I have some special friends I'd like to introduce to you." Everyone got quiet again. "These are my good friends, and also the members of my band, Ace." Mitch introduced them and everyone said hello.

Suddenly, Mitch and I found ourselves being swept into a circle of aunts. "Mitchell, Dana, we haven't had a chance to talk to you yet." Aunt Louise said.

"Translated: we haven't had a chance to dissect you and your fiancé yet." Mitch said. The guys laughed.

We walked into the midst of Mitch's aunts. "So, Mitchell Jacob, how did the two of you meet?" Aunt Beatrice asked.

I looked at Mitch and I could see the mischief forming on his face. I knew he was thinking of giving her the answer he had given his sister when she asked that same question. I nudged him lightly. "Behave, Mitch." I said.

Mitch bit his lip. "I met her at the bistro that I own, Aunt Beatrice." He said.

"You own a bistro?" she asked.

"Yes, I do. Gartano's downtown. I bought it about a month ago." Mitch answered.

"How wonderful, Mitchell." Aunt Louise chimed in. "So, do you two work together then?"

I decided to take this one. "Well, sort of. I just started helping Mitch out part time. I'm actually a kindergarten teacher by trade."

"I'm sorry, I'm not sure I understand. If you just started working there, but that's where you met, how did you actually meet?" Aunt Louise was confused.

Mitch smiled at me. I nudged him again. "No, see, Dana came in on October 4th, and when I saw her, I guess you could say it was love at first sight. It actually took us about a month to muster up the courage to talk to one another. And, as they say, the rest is history." He put his arm around me and gave me a little hug.

"So, then, you two haven't known each other very long." Aunt Elaina said.

"Just about two months or so. But Mitch always tells me time doesn't matter if you truly love someone. And I believe him." He smiled at me.

"Well, I guess that could be true. It seems to be the case with your parents, Mitchell Jacob." Aunt Beatrice said.

"Dana, are you from the area?" Aunt Katherine asked.

"Not originally. I was born and raised in Iowa. I moved here about four years ago." I replied.

"So, is your family still in Iowa?" she asked.

Mitch knew that was a tough question for me, and he rubbed my shoulder reassuringly. "No, ma'am, I don't have any family. My parents are gone and I was an only child."

They all took on a sympathetic look. "That must be very sad for you to not know anyone here, and be all alone." Aunt Louise added.

"But I'm not alone," I replied. "I have Mitch, and his family, and now, all of you, too. And I have good friends." Mitch smiled at me as if he were glad to hear me say that.

Aunt Katherine wanted another turn. "Where will you two be living after you get married?" she asked.

"Dana will be moving in with me. I have a nice apartment downtown. Just a few blocks from the bistro." Mitch said.

Then she turned to me. "So, that must mean you have your own place then? Are you two in the same building?"

I sighed. "No, I have an apartment about ten blocks from where Mitch lives. It's nice, but we decided that it would better for him to stay closer to work."

I could tell by Mitch's expression that he was getting tired of fielding questions, so I decided to go in for the save. "Honey, I think we better go check in with your friends for a minute. They're starting to look a little lost."

But Aunt Katherine wasn't ready to abandon ship just yet. "Mitchell, when you introduced your friends earlier, didn't you say they played in a band?"

Mitch smiled. "Well, actually, we all play in a band. I'm what they call the front man, or the leader, I guess you could say."

The aunts all exchanged looks. "So, what exactly do you do, Mitchell? I'm assuming it's rock and roll music, or is it that loud, noisy kind that all the young people are listening to today?"

I had to bite my own lip to keep from snickering. I knew Mitch was going to give this one his all.

"Well, Aunt Katherine, as the front man, I do all sorts of things. In my case, I have lead vocals, lead guitar, last night I did drums for one tune, I can also do keyboards if I feel the need to, in fact, I kind of head up the entire show. As for the music, yes, it's rock, some top 40, a little heavy metal. Working the club, most of it has to have a good beat that people can dance to, but I try to throw a few slow ones in there, too, just to give them the chance to, you know, get close to each other."

She looked at me as if wanting me to translate. "Oh, and you should see Mitch dance! He danced with me last night, and he made Patrick Swayze look bad. You know, the guy who played in *Dirty Dancing*." I had to bite my lip again.

Mitch finished it up. "That was before we kissed on stage wasn't it, baby?"

"I think so, because the kiss came at midnight, remember? We didn't realize everyone else was watching us?" I added.

We thought Aunt Katherine would faint.

"Well, it was good talking to you. We really need to circulate a little now." Mitch said, and he grabbed my hand to lead me away before they could ask anything else.

"Oh, Mitch, I didn't think we would ever escape!" I said.

"Me, either. Tell you what. Let's go check in with the guys, then we'll slip out for a few minutes. I need some alone time, how about you?" he said.

"Definitely." I sighed.

We found the guys doing one of the things they did best, and that was cruise the appetizer table.

"Hey, Trip, we thought you got lost or something." Shep said.

"No, just ripped to shreds by my aunts." He replied. "I think they know everything about us except what we ate for lunch today, and I'm surprised they didn't ask us that."

The guys laughed. "So, ready for tonight?" Ty asked.

"You know it! I was so pumped last night, guys, I felt like I was on the moon." Mitch was smiling.

"Man, you were red hot. The crowd was wild about you. See, man, we need you to front for us again. It's not the same without you." Ash told him.

Mitch smiled. "Hey, give yourselves credit. You were jammin' no doubt. I think Newbie had smoke coming off those drumsticks."

"What about you, 'I can't drum boy'? I had to replace a skin this morning!" Newbie laughed.

"Ok, guys, six bells and we're blowing this joint. We have a studio to rock tonight!" They all exchanged high fives. "We should be eating soon, but first I need a little air. I'll check back with you all in about five or ten. Why not go talk to Chris? He had a great time last night!"

"Cool, Trip, we'll go check him out. Later." Shep said, and with that they started off.

14

Mitch took me by the hand. "Come on, sweetheart, let's find someplace quiet and a little less crowded, ok? I'm getting claustrophobic."

Mitch led me upstairs and into a bedroom, closing the door behind us. "Mitchell, don't get any ideas." I told him.

He smiled. "Don't worry. I just thought this would be the quietest place to come. This used to be my room."

I should have guessed, as the color scheme was primarily blue. However, there were a few feminine touches, and I asked Mitch about them.

"Oh, well, Mom changed a few things after I moved out." He replied. "Come and sit down with me for a minute, ok?" He walked to the edge of the bed and sat down. I hesitated. "Sweetheart, come on. Come sit down next to me."

I walked over and sat down. Mitch put his arm around me and I laid my head on his shoulder.

"Dana, I'm sorry you had to go through that down there. They've even gotten more brutal than I remembered." He smiled. "But I must say, you handled yourself well."

"It's ok, honey. I know they're just trying to find out about us, that's all. It really isn't that big a deal." I told him.

Mitch laughed. "I wonder what Aunt Elaina would say if she knew I had you alone in my old bedroom."

I had to laugh as well. "I think she might just start planning the baby shower!"

Mitch chuckled. "Let's give her something to talk about, shall we? And be sure to leave lots of lipstick on my face, for effect."

"Mitch, you are...." I started.

"I know, terrible. But it's so much fun." He said softly, pulling me in for a kiss.

Mitch's kisses were soft and sweet, and I could feel his love with each one. He reached up and took down my hair, and brushing it off my shoulders, began to kiss me on the neck. I kissed his neck as well, and then I kissed his forehead and his cheek.

"Mitch, I love you." I whispered.

"I love you too, sweetheart. I really do." He was lingering longer with his kisses now, and he started to lay me back on the bed. He must have known what I was thinking.

"No, sweetheart, it's ok. I just want to hold you, that's all. I promise." Mitch said.

Suddenly we heard a light knock and the door opened. Both of us sat up suddenly, to see Chris standing in the doorway, smiling. Mitch blushed and I just smiled. We felt like a couple of love struck teenagers caught by a parent.

"Uh, sorry to interrupt, but Mom is looking for you two. She'd like to eat now, but not without the guests of honor." He smirked. "Should I tell her you'll be right down, or tell her you're busy?"

Mitch stood up. "We just needed to get out of that crowd for a little while. We just came up here to, uh, talk."

Chris smiled and wiped a smudge of lipstick from Mitch's cheek. "I see that, little brother." Mitch smiled and Chris patted him on the back. "It's ok, I won't tell Mom." Chris said in his best childlike voice.

"Thanks, Chris, I wouldn't want her to ground me or anything." Mitch smiled.

Chris started to walk away, but called back to his brother. "What? You never got in trouble a day in your life, Mitchell. Mom let you get away with murder."

"Obviously, that's not true." Mitch stated, going after Chris. "You're still here."

"Oh, you think you could take me? I've already proven you wrong on that one, but I'm willing to let you try again." He swung a playful punch Mitch's way, and Mitch ducked it.

"You were just lucky, that's all." Mitch said, doing the same back to his brother. Suddenly, Mitch realized I wasn't behind him. "Gee, I forgot Dana!" He said, doing a quick turn around.

"Those are the sorts of things that will get you in trouble." Chris called as he approached the stairs. "I'll let Mom know you'll be right there."

I was fixing my hair in the dresser mirror when Mitch came back for me.

"Where were you? I thought you were right behind me." Mitch said.

"Well, you could have waited on me." I said back.

"Sorry, love. Let's go get something to eat, and then we can start thinking about getting out of here, ok?" He reached out for me.

"Wait a minute, honey, I want to make sure I don't look too rumpled. I don't want any rumors started." I replied.

Mitch walked over to me. "Sweetheart, you know you don't have to worry about my family or the guys, and who cares what anyone else thinks? You worry too much, did I ever tell you that?"

I turned to look at him. "Yes, you have, and you have and you have."

Mitch put his arm around my shoulder, prompting me to exit the room. "And, I have a feeling it's not going to do me a bit of good, either." As we started down the stairs, I noticed Mitch get an impish little grin on his face. "Wanna have some more fun?" he said.

"Mitch, behave, ok? Whatever you are thinking of doing, don't." But somehow I knew he wasn't listening.

I watched as he pulled his shirttail out of his pants, and undid a few buttons.

"Mitchell, I'm warning you, behave yourself." I couldn't help but laugh, because I knew what he was up to.

As we entered the room, all eyes were upon us again. "Sorry to keep everyone waiting." Mitch said to the crowd.

Aunt Elaina walked up to him. "Mitchell, where were you? We were worried." We noticed her eyes move over him questioningly.

He got that look in his eyes. "Oh, not to worry, Aunt Elaina," he said as he re-buttoned his shirt. "Dana and I were, well, uh, just talking. Upstairs. Alone." He tucked his shirt back in, and adjusted his belt.

I looked over at Chris, Paul and Jim, who had all been standing within earshot of the two. They were all trying hard to keep from laughing. Aunt Elaina looked like she was going to faint. Olivia had been standing with them, and she just rolled her eyes at her son. Mitch smiled sweetly at her.

We were all ushered into the dining room to find a wonderful buffet, boasting everything imaginable. I couldn't believe Olivia and Alexander had prepared everything themselves. I was truly impressed, as well as touched, by the gesture.

We caught up with the band once again. "So, where were you two?" Zach asked.

Mitch smiled. "I'm not one to kiss and tell, Zach, but let's just say, I enjoyed it." Zach smiled and patted Mitch on the back.

"Hey, guys, we have a little change in plans that we need to tell you about," Mitch started. Dana and I decided to get married in February." He said proudly.

"And I promise, this is the *last* time we're changing the date." I added, throwing a look at Mitch.

"That's cool, Trip." Shep said. "Just let us know the day, time and place."

With full plates, we sat down in our pre-assigned seats, compliments of Olivia. She had us as the center of attention, as if we were at the head table at our wedding reception.

"Ok, we eat, we leave. I can't take anymore." Mitch whispered to me.

"Mitch, just relax. Make your mother happy, ok?" I whispered back.

"You're right, sweetheart. She did go to a lot of trouble for all this." He replied.

Olivia stood up. "Could I get your attention everyone?" The crowd quieted down. "I know that the aunts did get a chance to talk to Mitch and Dana a little bit earlier, but I'm sure that there are still a few things everyone would like to know. So, I'm going to ask them to fill us in on everything."

Mitch and I looked at each other. He motioned for his mom to come over to him, and she leaned down close. "Mom, fill them in on what? Help me out here."

"Just tell them your story, sweetie. They all want to know." Olivia smiled and started to stand up. Mitch grabbed her arm and she leaned back down.

"What story, Mom? I'm totally lost here." Mitch was starting to feel a little uncomfortable.

"Just tell them how you met, when you proposed, the wedding date, where, what time, etc. Tell them about Gartano's, too. That's great news for everyone."

Mitch sighed deeply and started to bite his lip. "It's ok, honey." I whispered. "Just pretend you're performing at the club."

He was still biting his lip and looked around at everyone who was there. Ok, he thought. I just love being put on the spot. But I can handle this. I can.

"Well, let's see." He began. "Dana and I met at Gartano's, the little Italian bistro that I own downtown. I proposed to her on Christmas Eve, and we plan to get married on February 18th. As for the time and all that, we're still working out the details, so we'll have to let you all know." He smiled. "I'm not sure if there's anything else I should be saying, because I'm not really good at this sort of thing. But, anyway, Dana and I are glad you all came today, and we hope to see you at our wedding." He sat back down and let out a deep sigh.

"Now, see, honey, you did just fine." I said, leaning close to him. He sighed again.

Everyone finished eating, and Mitch and I decided we should talk to everyone once more before we headed for the club, so we started visiting briefly with aunts and uncles, brothers and sisters and in-laws, and of course, the band. Finally, around 5:30 most of the guests had departed, and it was pretty much down to just Mitch's immediate family and the guys. We joined everyone in the family room, and Mitch sat down in his favorite spot on the piano bench.

"That was a very interesting experience." Mitch said, referring to the party.

"Your little performance was the best, Mitch." Paul said, laughing. "I thought your aunt was going to have a heart attack."

Mitch laughed. "Yeah, well, I gotta say, that was fun. Now I just have to think of something to do at the reception."

I gave him "the look". "Don't you dare, Mitch, or you'll be going on the honeymoon alone." I warned.

Mitch laughed and looking at the guys he said, "See what I have to put up with?" I smacked his arm. "I really wish you wouldn't do that." He said, rubbing his arm.

"That's right, Dana, keep him in line." Julia said. Then turning to Mitch she said, "You deserved that."

Mitch turned to me. "Well, I think we'd better go change so we can head to the club. Coming with me, love?"

"Sure." I replied. Mitch took my hand and we headed upstairs.

Just as I finished changing, I heard a light knock on the door. "Sweetheart, are you ready yet?" Mitch asked.

I opened the door. "Hello, handsome."

His eyes looked me up and down. "You get prettier every time I look at you."

I smiled. "We better go, Mitch, or we'll be late." I started to walk past him, but he didn't move. "Honey, you really need to move one way or the other."

He just stood there looking at me. "Dana, you were a real trooper today. Thank you."

"It was nothing. Your aunts and uncles really aren't that bad. Just really inquisitive." I smiled, and took his hand. "Now, come on, mister. We have to get going."

He sighed. "Yes, dear."

A few minutes later, we found ourselves in the car once more, heading to the club. I took Mitch by the hand, and leaned on his shoulder. "Mitch, you said I could wait backstage during the last song tonight. Can I still do that?" I asked.

Mitch smiled. "Sure, sweetheart, I'll make arrangements for you to do that. Don't worry." He said.

"Well, I just want to make sure I'm the first girl in line for you tonight. Not to mention the *only* girl." I shot back at him.

He glanced over at me. "Dana, let's not have this conversation again, ok? You have nothing to worry about."

"Uh, huh." I said, staring out the window.

Mitch looked at me and I could tell he wasn't convinced that I believed him.

"Sweetheart, did you hear what I said?" He asked again.

"Yes, Mitch, I heard you." I answered.

I decided it was time to change the subject. "Well, my vacation is over as of tomorrow. I get to go back to school on Tuesday." I said.

"Well, I thought about that, so we won't be going into the bistro tomorrow until around four or so. We can do some running around in the morning, if you want. Or, you can, and I can just kind of vegetate." Mitch said.

"If we play this right, we can get a lot done tomorrow, Mitch. Maybe I can go turn in the invitations, check on flowers and go back to the shop where my gown is and let them know I need it sooner. You can make a call to your mom about the country club, and ask about the catering, and you could also call Pastor Michaels about getting the church." Then another thought returned to me. "Honey, what about an organist?"

"Remember, Pastor's wife does that. I'll have him ask her, ok?" Mitch said.

"That's fine." I sighed. "Who ever thought there was so much to do for just one day?" I asked.

"That's why we're only doing it once, baby." Mitch replied, smiling.

We got to the club and we were surprised to see that everyone else was already there, waiting on us. They had secured our table in front of the stage, and were already talking and laughing, eagerly awaiting another performance by Ace. As we walked in, Rob, the manager, approached us. I said hello and proceeded to the table to let him talk to Mitch.

"Mr. Tarrington, how are you?" He greeted, extending his hand. "I just wanted to commend you on the fantastic job you did last night. I think that your band has been the biggest hit around here in a long time, and the amount of talent you personally possess astounds me."

"Thanks!" Mitch said, shaking his hand. "We had a great time, and we're looking forward to our finale tonight. Oh, by the way, please call me Mitch."

"Well, Mitch, that's something I wanted to talk over with you. I don't want tonight to be your last night here at Studio 14. The crowd loved you. In fact, I've had several people ask me if you were ever playing here again. I look for those people to come again tonight."

Mitch looked at him. "Do you mean you want us to come back?" he asked.

"Well, something like that. Actually, Mitch, what I had in mind was negotiating a deal with you to be a permanent part of the studio. Kind of like a house band of sorts. At least one show every weekend, maybe two. Not only would it provide some security and publicity for your group, but I don't see how it couldn't boost our standing as well. What do you say?"

Mitch was clearly stunned. He looked at Rob, then at me. "Rob, I don't know. I mean, we weren't planning anything like this, and well, I manage, well actually own, a restaurant, and I'm getting married next month." He took a deep breath. "I'm really honored, but I just don't know."

Rob smiled. "Mitch, I know you'll need some time to think it over, and talk to the other guys, too. So, here's my card and I'd like to hear from you by Wednesday, ok? That way, should you decide to stay on, we can get you on the marquis for the weekend."

Mitch started to bite his lip. "I just don't know, I mean I wasn't expecting this at all."

Rob laughed. "I know, it's a big step. That's why I want you to think about it for a few days. But, please, think about it. I'd hate to see all that talent not being used. And..." he smiled. "if it provides any influence, we occasionally have record producers and talent scouts stop in to check out our acts. I wouldn't be surprised at all if one of them signed Ace to a record deal."

Mitch smiled. "Wow, now I really don't know about that, but I will let you know, Rob. And thanks, I'm honored that you have faith in us."

"Now, have a great show tonight. And please, be sure to get back to me by Wednesday, alright?" Rob said as he walked away.

"Sure thing. I'll call you." Mitch said, staring at Rob's card.

Mitch turned around and was completely speechless. He walked over to the table and pointed at Rob, but didn't say anything.

"Mitch, is something wrong?" I asked. I stood up and pulled out a chair for him. "Honey, sit down. You look a little pale."

"Rob just asked us to become Studio 14's house band. He wants us to stay here permanently." Mitch said.

"Are you serious?" Jim said. "That's really awesome!"

"Are you going to do it, Mitch? You guys are great. You'd pack 'em in every weekend!" Angelina added.

Mitch sat down. "Man, I just don't know. I mean, I don't know if I can take this on with everything else."

"What everything else, Mitch?" I asked. "What is there besides Gartano's?"

He turned and looked right at me. "There's you, Dana. We're going to be married in about six weeks. When would I see you, between work and this?"

I reached out for his hand. "Mitch, you're doing those things now, and it hasn't prevented us from seeing each other. Actually, honey, if anything, we'll be together more when we get married. You can take me home, and you won't have to leave."

He smiled. "I just don't know. I mean, it's really exciting and all. I guess I just need time to think it over. Besides, I don't know what the guys will think. And, Dana, what about the honeymoon? How can I go to Hawaii if I have to be here on stage performing?"

Trudy put up her hand. "Wait a minute. You're going to Hawaii?" She turned to Chris. "Christopher, why didn't we go to Hawaii?"

"Hold on, now, dear, you wanted to go to the Pocono's remember? All your idea." Chris replied.

"Yes, but if you would have said, 'let's go to Hawaii, Trudy' I would have jumped on that idea." She said back.

Chris looked at Mitch. "You just can't seem to stop getting me in trouble, can you?" He laughed. So did everyone else.

I turned back to Mitch. "Mitchell, I think this is really something you need to discuss with the guys, and give some thought to. But, don't become so preoccupied with it that you let it influence your performance tonight." I smiled. "And as for the honeymoon, I think they can live without you for one weekend."

Mitch stood up. "Well," he smiled, "I'd better go see what the guys are up to, and let them in on all this." He gave me a kiss. "Last song, you be at the side door. Max will let you in. I love you."

Mitch walked backstage and found Shep and Ty engaged in conversation over the evening's set sheet. Ty greeted him.

"Hey, Trip, what's up?' He said. Then he noticed the serious look on Mitch's face, and his face turned serious as well. "Hey, man, is something wrong?"

Mitch smiled. "No, Ty, actually, everything is great. Well, it could be. We just all need to have a little meeting, right now."

Ty called for the rest of the guys and they all came over. "Hey, Trip, what's going on?" Ash said with concern.

"Well, when I came in tonight, Rob approached me. He said he was really impressed with our talent and how great a job we did last night." All the guys were buzzing. "Hang on, that's not all," Mitch continued. "He wants to negotiate with us to become the studio's permanent house band."

"Are you serious?" Zach asked. "You mean, like, play here all the time?"

"Yeah, that's what I mean. At least one show every weekend, maybe more. And, he said that there's a chance, *just* a chance, that a record producer could come in and hear us." The guys were all whooping and cheering, exchanging high fives and hugs.

"This might be our big break, dudes. I mean, we could be famous!" Newbie said excitedly.

"Yeah, and think of the money, not to mention the women!" Shep added.

Ty turned to Mitch. "So, Trip, when do we sign the contract?"

"He wants an answer by Wednesday so he can bill us next weekend if we accept." Mitch answered.

Shep seemed to be the only one who caught Mitch's words. "Hang on, Mitch, what do you mean, 'if' we accept? This is our big break, man. It's what we've been waiting for."

Mitch put his hands in his pockets and leaned back against the wall. "No, Shep, it's what *you* all have been waiting for. I'm not so sure about me."

The guys all exchanged looks. "Man, what are you talking about? We can't be Ace without you." Ty said.

"Yeah, dude, that's why we came back for you when we got this gig. You make this band rock." Zach answered.

Mitch looked up at Ash, hoping at least he might understand. "Look, guys, I love being a part of the band. I feel such a rush when I'm out there performing. But, I'm not in college anymore. I have a different life now, different responsibilities. I have my own business and soon, I'm going to have a wife. I just don't know how this will fit, or if it will fit at all."

Ash smiled knowingly. "You know, Mitch, I can relate. I thought that when I married Cindy that I should give this up, and that I was too grown up to play a boy's game anymore. But Cindy made me realize that it would be more wrong for me to do that. We all have dreams, man, and very few of us ever get to fulfill those dreams. I do that every time I step out on that stage. And I actually think it makes me a better husband and father, because of it. I'm doing something I love." Ash walked over and placed his hand on Mitch's shoulder. "I have another job, too, Trip. By trade, I'm a plumber. Yeah, not very glamorous, I know, but it feeds my family and pays the bills. But you know, my music gives me energy. It gives me passion, passion that I can put into the other things in my life."

Mitch looked at Ash, and he saw sincerity in his face that gave him the answer, the same answer that his own heart was screaming. A slow smile spread across his face.

"If it gets to be too much, I'm out, got it?" He was bombarded by the hugs and pats of his friends.

Meanwhile at the table, Mitch's family and I were also discussing this new turn of events.

"Wow, can you believe it?" Angelina started. "Mitch a permanent fixture in the club. How neat would that be?" She asked.

"Do you think he'll do it?" Julia asked.

"I don't know," I replied. "I mean, we're fine, and he loves doing this. You only have to look at him up there to know that. I know he's afraid, but I don't know why."

"I think I can answer that," Chris said. "Mitch is the kind of guy who doesn't like to fail. I mean, yeah, most people are like that, but Mitch takes it one step farther. He's been pretty good at most of the things he's ever done. The only thing he hasn't done yet, Dana, is be a husband, and someday, a father. He's afraid of failing in those areas somehow if he takes on too many other things."

I thought about what Chris was saying, and I stood up. "Well, I think it's time I took that fear out of him. I can't let him pass this up." I headed for the backstage door.

Max was standing guard, as usual. "Hi." I said. "Can I go back for a minute to talk to Mitch, please?"

Max smiled. "Oh, yeah, you're his fiancé. He told me to let you in. Go ahead." He opened the door and thanking him, I slipped inside.

The guys were all talking cheerfully, and I could see even Mitch's face was now holding a smile. Ty pointed to me and his smile grew even bigger.

"Hey, beautiful, to what do I owe this privilege?" He said, walking toward me.

"I need to talk to you, Mitch." I said, taking him by the hand and leading him a few steps away from the guys.

His face grew serious. "Something wrong?" he asked.

I smiled. "No, not really. I was just thinking about this proposal that Rob made to you earlier. Mitch, I think you should accept his offer."

I noticed Shep started to say something, but Mitch put up his hand, as if to silence him. "Why do you think that, Dana?" Mitch asked.

"Honey, I saw how much you loved being on that stage last night. You were having so much fun, there was no way you could hide that fact, not from me or anybody else. I know you're worried about being able to manage the bistro, the band, and well, me, but I know you can do it. You're strong, Mitch. You have a good head on your shoulders. I know if it gets to be too much, you'll handle it." I took his other hand so now I was holding both. "This is a once in a lifetime opportunity for you, honey, and I know deep in your heart, you want this. I don't want to be the thing that stops you from taking advantage of it."

Mitch took a deep breath, and let it out slowly. "So, you think I should stay with the band, huh?" he asked me. "And you'd be ok with it?"

I nodded. "I really do, and yes, I would."

He smiled. "Well, sweetheart, I have to be honest. Ash already helped me see the light on this one. But, hearing it from you makes it that much more right. I'm staying with the band."

I gave him a hug. "I'm glad to hear that, honey. It'll be great, you wait and see."

He smiled. "You know, I have a feeling that even if I hadn't already decided, I wouldn't have been able to tell you no. You have that influence over me. I'm not sure if that's good or bad."

I giggled. "I would have to say I think it's good. I'll get away with more."

Mitch laughed. "You really think so, huh? I'm not that easy."

I smiled. "We'll see."

Mitch leaned down and gave me a very soft kiss. "You better go back out there now. We only have a few minutes until we start." He smiled. "I'll be waiting for you after the last song."

"I have to do something first." I said, and I walked over to the guys. "Congratulations, guys. Group hug!" I was nearly knocked over by the guys. Mitch stood back and laughed.

After they all let go, I turned to Ash. "Thanks." I said. "I don't know what you said, but evidently, it was what he needed to hear."

Ash smiled. "Glad to help." And we exchanged another hug.

"Hey, lady, you're enjoying this hug thing a little too much. Let's go! Outta here!" Mitch teased, pointing to the door.

I started to walk right past him, but turned around and grabbed him into a big bear hug. "Good luck tonight, Mitch. I love you."

"I love you, too, sweetheart." He replied, giving me another kiss.

"We love you too, sweetheart." All the guys said in unison.

Mitch and I laughed. "She's *not* kissing any of you!" He said.

"Now look who's getting jealous." I teased. "I thought you were secure in our relationship." Mitch laughed and shook his head.

I rejoined Mitch's family at the table. Paul was the first to notice my smile. "Something good must have happened back there." He commented.

"Yes, he's going to do it! He's staying with the band!" I said, and all the girls squealed with excitement.

"So, we have a celebrity in the family now!" Trudy said.

"Yeah, and by the looks of how this place is filling up, I'd say the word has already gotten out." Chris added.

There was no opening act, so we waited patiently for Ace to take the stage. I was so excited just knowing that Mitch was going to get a chance to pursue something that he enjoyed. I hoped that he had the chance to do it for many years to come.

The house lights dimmed, and the girls gathered around me, like a bunch of teenagers at a big rock concert. We all joined hands and cringed with excitement. Rob took the stage.

"Good evening, everyone! Welcome to Studio 14! If you had a chance to be here last night, you had a chance to hear, for the first time, the band that will performing for you tonight." There were already people cheering and applauding. "If not, you're in for a great time. This young group of multitalented guys really know how to make this place rock. Let's give it up one more time for Ace!"

The girls and I screamed and were jumping up and down. We looked at each other and screamed, "We love you, Mitch!" as loud as we could, and started laughing. Mitch must have heard us, because he smiled at us and shook his head.

The songs were all in a different order, and we were having such a good time. But, more than that, we could clearly see that Mitch was in heaven. He was having so much fun he looked like he would just burst any second. As the next song ended, a very winded Mitch took the microphone.

"Hi, everyone! Are you having fun tonight?" Everyone applauded and cheered. "We're gonna keep this party going, but first, we have a little announcement. Rob, if you're around, we need you to hear this." Rob came up near the stage and waved his hand to get Mitch's attention. "Ok, there he is, good. Earlier tonight we got an offer to join Studio 14 as the permanent house band." Again, everyone cheered and applauded. "That would mean you'd have to put up with us at least once every week. So, if you think you can do that, we are ready to take Rob up on that offer. What do you say?" Not a person in the place was sitting down.

You could feel the energy as Rob walked up the stairs and shook hands with Mitch. A minute or two later, Rob exited the stage and the band began to play again. Around an hour later, Mitch once again took the microphone.

"I just want to take a minute to acknowledge a very special group of people sitting right here in the front. I think they are the first members of the unofficial Mitch Tarrington fan club. They've been screaming that they love me all night!" Everyone cheered. "Ok, I have to be honest, folks, they may be just a little biased. This is my family, and the love of my life, the soon-to-be Mrs. Dana Tarrington." He smiled right at me and I told him I loved him.

"See," He said. "She said it again." Everyone laughed. "Let's slow it down a little here, so you can all get close." They did a few slow songs and then got the tempo back up again. Finally, it was break time, and the guys left the stage.

"See ya later, Dana." Jim joked, pointing to the stage. Mitch was there waiting for me as he had the night before.

We went backstage and Mitch turned to me. "Oh, Dana, am I crazy or what?" he asked.

"Yes, but I love that about you, honey." I said.

"Why does this make me so happy? I mean, I thought these days were long gone, and now look at me. I'm acting like a college kid again!" Mitch was grinning from ear to ear.

"That's good!" I replied. "I'm not looking to marry someone who has one foot in the grave." I said.

Mitch pulled me into his arms. "Do you think you can put up with me?" He asked.

"I do that now." I replied, smiling. "What's going to be any different?"

Mitch's face softened. "Dana, this whole thing is going to mean a lot of commitment from me. I'm going to have to hold rehearsals, and come up with sets, and be here every weekend, at least once. That's going to be in between keeping up with everything at the bistro, and making sure I don't neglect you. Do you really think I can do this, sweetheart?"

"Mitch, I told you before, I believe in you. I know you can make it work. I'll help you, if I can. If it means teaching me how to do some of the behind-the-scenes things at the bistro, then I'll do that. If it means you having to be here and me having to be there to make it run smoothly, then I'll do that. If it means we spend a few evenings apart while you go and rehearse, that's ok. I'll be there waiting for you when you get home. As long as you're happy, that's all that matters to me."

Mitch looked at me, his eyes full of love. "I honestly don't know how such a big heart fits in such a tiny little body. But you're proof that it's possible."

"There's only one thing I'm going to ask." I said.

"Sure, sweetheart, anything." Mitch smiled. "Ask away."

"Can I have a special t-shirt made for you to wear if I can't be here when you come off stage?"

Mitch was smiling. "And just what would this shirt say?"

"How about, 'back off I'm married'?" I said, looking up at him.

He laughed. "What if it doesn't work?"

"Well, it's also going to be equipped with a little alarm that will go off at home should any of those little groupie girls come within fifty feet of you." I answered.

Mitch was laughing and smiling at me. "You jealous little thing. You'd really do something like that, wouldn't you?"

"Absolutely." I said. "Anything to keep you out of trouble."

Mitch looked at me. "Baby, I can assure you, there won't be any trouble to keep me out of. I'm all yours."

An hour later, the band started playing the last song, and Mitch gave me a little signal to head backstage. Max greeted me again, and opening the door, I stepped inside to wait in the wings for Mitch. Some other girls were already starting to gather, but one in particular caught my attention. She was tall and blond, but very natural looking, pretty but not in a fake way. The thing that made me notice her the most was that she wasn't alone. She was holding a baby, and standing next to her was a little girl, whom I guessed to be about two. She leaned down to the little girl and said something, and pointed out onto the stage. Just then, I heard Mitch say goodnight, and the band began to exit.

"Daddy!" the little girl screamed, and when Ash saw her, he bent down as she ran into his arms. Now it all made sense. It was his wife and children.

"Jenny, what are you doing here?" he said excitedly.

"Mommy brought me and baby Jon." She said to him, pointing to her mother and brother.

Ash's face lit up as he approached his wife, hugging and kissing her. Just then I felt Mitch's arms around me. "Look at them. That's really nice that she came up here and surprised him like that." He said.

"Yeah, it is. They really look happy together, don't they?" I said.

Mitch turned to me and smiled. "Yes, they do. But, I think we're just as happy, don't you?"

"Uh, huh. And do you notice anything?" I asked.

"Should I?" he asked curiously.

"Yes, dear. You and Ash are the only ones not getting attacked by all the women." I replied.

"That's fine with me, sweetheart, and I have a feeling it's ok with him, too." Mitch took my hand. "Let's go say hello, ok?"

We walked over to Ash and he smiled. "Cindy, you remember Mitch Tarrington, don't you?"

She smiled. "Of course, I remember Mitch. Good to see you again! That's quite the show you put on out there. Ash was telling me when we talked last night how awesome you did, and I just had to come and see for myself."

Ash looked at her. "So, you came here to see Mitch, not me, huh?" he teased.

"Ashton, stop it." She laughed.

Mitch looked at Ash. "Oh, she does that to you, too, huh? Uses the full given name when she gets mad?"

Ash smiled. "All the time. But, it's when she inserts the middle name that I know I'm really in for it. And, when she adds the last name, the couch and I have a date for the night!"

Mitch laughed. "Yeah, I only got that once so far."

Cindy and I looked at each other, and smiled. "Ashton, you'd better stop the conversation right there." She said, sounding playfully firm.

"That goes double for you, Mitchell." I added. We all laughed.

"I'm sorry," Mitch said. "Cindy, this is my fiancé, Dana."

I shook her hand. "Congratulations, you two. Dana, you're even prettier in person than Ash told me you were." I blushed.

"And this is Jenny, my daughter, and my son, Jonathan." Ash said proudly, introducing his children. "Jenny, can you say hi to Mr. Tarrington and Miss Walker?"

Jenny tried to say Tarrington, but it didn't come out very well. Mitch laughed.

"Tell you what, Jenny. If it's ok with Mom and Dad, how about you call us Mitch and Dana? Those names are a little easier to say." She looked at Ash and he nodded. Then she whispered something in Ash's ear, and he smiled. "You tell him, Jen." He said.

She smiled and reached out for Mitch, and he took her into his arms.

"Something you want to tell me, Jenny?" he asked.

"Can I give you a kiss, right there?" she asked, touching Mitch's cheek.

He smiled. "Sure, I might just like that." She leaned over and lightly pecked Mitch's cheek. Everyone laughed. Mitch turned to me. "I don't think this one poses much of a threat, sweetheart." He said.

"She likes to kiss." Ash said. "It's ok now, but I don't know about ten years down the road." He smiled.

Just then, Ash noticed Newbie holding hands with a girl, and they seemed to be enjoying each other's company. The girl looked a little familiar, but I wasn't sure from where.

"Hey, Mitch, isn't that the girl that waited on us at the restaurant last night?" Ash asked, discreetly pointing to her.

Mitch studied her for a minute. "You know, I think you might be right. Well, well, Newbie must have struck a chord with her."

"That's nice." I said. "Maybe they'll end up like us, Mitch." I said. He smiled.

"Tell you what. I'm going to go check in with my fan club out there, you can fill Cindy in on what's happening around here, and then, I think we need to sit down with Rob for a few." Mitch patted Ash on the shoulder.

"Sure, thing, Trip, see ya in a few." Ash said.

I took Mitch's hand. "I think Jenny likes you, Mitch." I said.

He smiled. "She is pretty cute, isn't she?" Then he looked at me. "Do you think our kids will be that cute?"

"If they look like their daddy, they will." I replied.

He looked at me again. "I was thinking just the opposite." He said, smiling.

As we approached the table, the girls started to giggle. All of a sudden, they yelled out "We love you, Mitch!" and started to laugh. Mitch smiled.

"Don't ask me to sign autographs." He said. "You know, I could hear you guys over everyone else here. I always said you had big mouths, and you never believed me."

"Mitch, we all are so excited for you!" Angelina said, giving her brother a hug.

"Yeah, it's so cool, Mitch. Guess we know where we'll be every weekend!" Trudy said. She turned to Chris. "I think we're gonna need a night away from the kids."

Chris nodded. "I couldn't agree more. And they love being with Alexander. He's actually getting quite good at the video games."

Mitch laughed. "Alexander plays the video games? No way!"

"He does and he's good, I'm telling you." Chris said.

Mitch turned a chair around from the neighboring table and straddled it. "So, you all think this is a wise idea, I mean, taking on this permanent gig thing?"

"Definitely!" Paul agreed. "Mitch, you need a chance to show off what you can do. You've been blessed with these talents, buddy, you should use them."

"I couldn't agree more." Jim added. "I think it would be wrong not to do it."

"Well, I'm just going to have to really work out a schedule that fits everything in. I don't know how hard that will be, but I'll find out." Mitch said.

I looked him right in the eye. "You're always telling me to quit worrying about everything. Now, I'm telling you. It's going to be fine, Mitchell. If you keep trying to find excuses not to do this, I'm really going to be upset."

Chris cleared his throat and sat back, giving Mitch a look that said he knew I meant business. Mitch smiled.

"Listen, Miss Assertiveness, I'm not trying to make excuses. I just want to make sure I don't slack anywhere, that's all. I have a lot of responsibilities." He stated.

"And you'll take care of them all, Mitchell. I know you will. Stop worrying about it." I said.

Just then Rob approached our table. He greeted everyone and then turned to Mitch. "Mitch, can I have just a few minutes of your time, with the band, if possible? I'd like to go over a few things with all of you."

"Sure, no problem." Mitch replied. "Let me just go get them." He stood up.

"Stay here, Mitch, I'll go." I told him, and scooted off before he had a chance to say no.

I slipped backstage to find the guys all talking together, all the women gone except Cindy and Newbie's girl, Janine.

"Guys, Rob is ready to talk to you all now. Mitch is waiting out there with him." I told them.

"Cool, future Mrs. Trip." Shep said to me, smiling. "Let's go do this, guys!" he said, summoning the others to follow him.

As we rejoined Mitch and Rob, the others decided they were going to leave, so we said our goodbyes and turned back to the situation at hand.

I joined the girls at a nearby table, and we got lost in our own little conversation about the guys, and the band, and this opportunity. Meanwhile, the band was engaged in their own conversation with Rob.

Rob began to negotiate the terms of the contract, and finally got around to the compensation. "I was thinking, how about I start you out at, oh, let's say, $350 each per show, for the band members, and Mitch, $500 for fronting. Does that sound fair?"

The guys were all smiling and nodding, except Mitch. "No, I'm sorry Rob, but I don't think that's fair." He said.

Rob got a funny look. "What, Mitch, you need more?"

Mitch smiled. "No, no, I just don't want to get paid more than the rest of the guys, that's all."

"But you front, Mitch. Most of the responsibility is on you, man. You deserve it." Ash said.

"Look, guys, that may or may not be true, but I see us as one unit here. I get paid the same, or I don't front." Mitch was firm.

Rob sighed. "Ok, Mitch, if that is truly how you feel, then you will also get $350 per show. Does that sound alright?" Mitch nodded. "Well, then what questions or concerns do you have?"

"Well, Mitch is getting married on February 18 and we're playing his wedding. So, we can't be here then." Zach said.

Rob smiled. "I'm glad you brought that up. I was going to ask about that, and I assume, Mitch, there's a honeymoon planned?"

Mitch nodded. "We're spending a week or so in Hawaii. But the band can still play without me, if they want to."

"We can discuss that in a few weeks." Rob said. "Let me ask you. How do you want to be billed? As 'Mitch Tarrington and Ace', or just 'Ace'?"

"Just Ace." Mitch said. "Like I said, we're all together in this. I may be the front, but I don't want any special treatment."

Rob smiled. "You know, Mitch, I like that in you. I like team players." Rob opened a folder that was laying on the table. "I have the contract here, so all I need are a few signatures, if you're ready to do this."

Mitch looked at the guys. "What do you think, guys? Do you want to discuss this, or have questions or anything?" Everyone shook their heads. "Ok, Rob, I think we're ready. Oh, wait." He said. "I do need to talk to them for just one second."

Rob stood up. "Sure thing. I'll be right over here when you're ready." He left the table.

"Hey, what's the problem, Trip?" Newbie asked.

"Guys, I just thought of something. I'm the only one who lives here. What do you all plan to do about rehearsals and doing a gig every weekend?" Mitch asked.

"We're one step ahead of you, Trip." Newbie said. "Zach, Ty and I are talking about moving closer. We've got nothing to tie us down."

"And Cindy and I only live about 45 minutes out, so the drive isn't a big deal for me." Ash said. "So, chill, big buddy, we're here to stay!"

Mitch smiled. "You guys amaze me." He motioned for Rob. "Ok, let's do this!"

Rob brought the contract back over. "We'll start with our front man, here. I'm assuming Mitch is short for Mitchell, right? So, it's Mitchell Tarrington. Middle initial?"

"Actually, you may need two lines for my handle." Mitch laughed. "You're right about the first, it is Mitchell, middle initial is J and I'm actually the third."

"Ok, Mitchell J. Tarrington, the third." Rob smiled. "And these other guys?" All the guys gave their full names and Rob jotted them down. Then he handed the contract to Mitch. "Front man, you're the first to sign." Mitch smiled brightly and signed his name, passing the sheet to the others. Finally it was all said and done. They all stood up and shook hands with Rob. Mitch looked at me and smiled.

"Oh, this is so great!" Ty said. "Can you believe it?"

"Pinch me, I'm dreaming!" Shep replied.

The girls and I walked back over to our guys and took our places beside them. Mitch smiled at me, and then looked at Ash and Newbie. "Well, guys, shall we really make this official and seal the deal?" Ash nodded, but Newbie just looked at Janine.

"Well?" he asked her.

She smiled at him. "I think I can handle that." She replied. And we all gave our guys a kiss.

15

"We need to celebrate!" Mitch said. "How about a pizza or two or three? My place!"

They all agreed and Mitch made the call for the pizzas. "Should be there by the time we are," he said.

We spent the next few hours enjoying the company of our friends, talking and laughing and celebrating this exciting new twist to our lives. As our time together came to an end, the guys set up a rehearsal for Tuesday evening, and they were all on their way. Mitch closed the door and turned to me.

"Alone at last!" he said. "But first, I probably need to take a quick shower. Ok?"

"Ok, but hurry back." I smiled.

I tidied up the pizza boxes and such, and was getting comfortable when Mitch got back.

"Miss me?" he asked, moving in for a kiss.

"Always." I answered.

Mitch seemed to be in an overly amorous mood tonight, and he was putting the moves on me any way he could. His kisses were full of passion, and he was holding me so tightly I felt as if I might be a part of him. He pulled away to look at me.

"Dana, I really don't know if I'll survive another six weeks." He said, moving in to kiss me again. I felt his hands moving slowly down my back, then drop to my waist. He stopped their descent and pulled away from me slowly. Kissing me again lightly, he stood up.

"I think I need something cold to drink." He said, putting his finger under the collar of his shirt, as if to loosen it. He smiled. "Don't go anywhere." He instructed.

I smiled. "Feeling a little warm, honey?" I asked.

"Uh, yeah. Just a little." He said, clearing his throat.

A minute later, Mitch came back with a glass of water, and placed it on the coffee table. He sat back down and looked at me. "Oh, girl, if you only knew what you do to me." He said, putting his arm around me.

"Well, you do the same thing to me, mister." I said.

He smiled. "That's good to know."

I put my head on his chest. "Mitch, can I ask you something?" I said.

He brushed back my hair with his hand. "Sure, sweetheart."

"Well, are you nervous about, well, being with me? I mean, like on our wedding night?"

He smiled. "Sure, a little. But I think more than anything I'm looking forward to being able to be yours completely." He kissed me lightly on the forehead. "Why? Are you nervous?"

"Yes, I am, Mitch. Very nervous." I answered.

He gave me a hug. "Don't be, sweetheart. I promise I'll do everything I can to make you feel comfortable. I love you, Dana. I'll be new at this, too, you know. We'll learn together, ok?"

I smiled. "I love you, Mitch."

"I love you, too, sweetheart. Everything will be fine, I promise. I'll make sure of it." Mitch said lovingly.

He took his watch out and looked at the time. "Are you ready for me to take you home now? It's almost twelve thirty."

"No, but I know you have to be pretty tired. It's been a long day." I said.

"It has, you're right. But how about if I take you home, and I give you a few more minutes there? How does that sound?" He asked, standing up and stretching.

"I think I like that idea." I said.

We arrived at my apartment and Mitch came inside, placing his coat on the chair and sitting down on the couch. He leaned back, and summoned me to sit down next to him. He smiled.

"So, honey, you never told me about the contract at the club. What did you guys work out?" I asked with interest.

"Well, basically, it's one show a weekend, we choose which day, we make up the set, and we can use their sound and lights. We can take time away, as long as we let Rob know, and we get paid pretty well, too. Three-fifty a show. More if it's a holiday."

I looked at Mitch with surprise. "Wow, sweetie, that's great. That will really be good for us."

He smiled. "Yeah, I figured either a car payment or almost the rent. It will help us out a lot, Dana. You know, I am looking forward to it. I really do have a good time with those guys."

"I know you do, honey. I'm so happy for you." Then I laughed. "Why, I've even decided that I am going to be the president of your official fan club."

He laughed. "That's fine with me." He said. He stood up and helped me to my feet as well. "I'd better go, love." He said, slipping his arms around me. "Tomorrow's another day and we need to get some rest. What time would you like to get started in the morning?"

I thought for a minute. "Why not be here around, oh, 9:15? I'll fix us some breakfast and then we can go from there, ok?"

He smiled. "Sounds like a good plan." He gave me a kiss and opened the door. "Good night, beautiful. Sleep well."

"Good night, Mitch. I love you." I said, and he smiled and waved as I closed the door.

Just before 9:15 the next morning, I heard a light knock on the door. I smiled and opened it to see my handsome fiancé's smile.

"Good morning, beautiful." He said, giving me a kiss and stepping inside. He inhaled deeply. "I'm guessing by the smell, we're having pancakes, and maybe, bacon?"

"You guessed right." I said. "Are you hungry?"

He smiled. "Remember, I told you that's one of the two things I always am."

"And the one I'm most willing to satisfy, at least for now." I smiled back.

I put everything on the table and we sat down together. Mitch just kept looking at me.

"What?" I said, looking back at him.

"Nothing." He said, smiling, but still looking at me.

"Mitchell, you're making me self conscious. Why are you looking at me?" I asked.

"Because I want to." He said.

I put down my fork. "Then, I'll stare at you too." I said, and he laughed.

"I was just looking at your eyes. They are so pretty." He said.

"They're brown, Mitch. Brown and pretty don't fall into the same category."

"No, you're wrong. You have very pretty brown eyes." He smiled sweetly.

"Well, you have pretty blue eyes. Very pretty blue eyes." I said.

Mitch and I just gazed at each other for a moment, but our moment was broken by the ringing of the phone.

"Hello?" I said. "Oh, hi Kayla. I was just thinking about calling you." I said.

Mitch got a funny look on his face, but continued to eat his breakfast.

"I have so much to tell you, Kayla!" I said. "First, you'll never guess what happened last night. Rob, the manager of the club, asked Mitch and the guys to be the permanent house band! Yeah, isn't that cool? He signed the contract last night. Uh, huh. Every weekend. Well, just one show, so he'll still be able to manage both."

Mitch was just munching away, watching my animation as I talked to Kayla. He reached for the last piece of bacon, and I playfully slapped his hand, snatching it away from him. I took a bite, then fed him the rest.

"No, actually, he's here right now. We're going to go do some wedding stuff before we come in today. Yeah, I made him breakfast. The poor man would starve if it weren't for me." I smiled at Mitch. "We will have to go and look for dresses sometime soon. Did I tell you? We decided on red. I know, me too, but Mitch said he couldn't see any of the guys in pink. Yeah, I know. Well, ok, I guess I'll see you later. Bye!" I hung up the phone and Mitch started laughing at me.

"What are you finding so funny, Mitchell?" I asked.

"It's strange, no, actually, it's scary, but I completely understood that conversation." He said. "I also picked up on the fact that I'm getting blamed for changing this color thing. Maybe we should talk about this." He said, taking a drink of milk.

"No one is blaming you for anything." I said. "We made the decision, and we're sticking to it."

Mitch got up and started to clear his plate from the table. "Yes, love, *we* made the decision, but *you* aren't happy with it, are you?"

I took my last bite, and stood up with my plate. "I just had my heart set on pink and blue, that's all. But red will be ok, I guess."

Mitch sighed. "Hand me the phone, please."

"Who are you calling?" I asked.

"Dana, baby, just hand me the phone." He said, reaching for it once more. I handed it to him and he dialed.

"Hi, Grace, is Chris available? This is Mitch. Thanks." He smirked at me. "Hey, Chris, sorry to bother you at work, but Dana and I are trying to have a discussion about our wedding colors." He chuckled. "Exactly, how did you know? Anyway, we decided since all the guys already have black tuxedoes and the wedding is close to Valentine's Day, we'd go with some sort of red. Yeah, I thought so, too." Mitch smirked at me again. "But, my lovely fiancé really has her heart set on pink and blue." Mitch laughed. "You would. I know, that's what I told her, but would you be willing to buck up for one day? I'd owe you big, you know how it is. Yeah, right. You sure? Excellent. No, we're going out for a while first. She'll be happy to hear that. Thanks Chris, see ya." He hung up the phone and turned to me. "Ok, sweetheart, it's done. Chris has agreed to wear pink, much to his dismay, but he said he'd do it for you."

I couldn't hold in my excitement. "You mean we can have pink and blue?" I said.

Mitch nodded. "If that's what will make you happy, I guess it's ok with me."

I hit Mitch with a hug, actually causing him to have to step backwards. He laughed. "You know, you're already spoiled."

"I don't mind." I said playfully.

"Well, I guess I don't either, as long as you're happy, love." He kissed the top of my head. "Let's get all this cleaned up and get going, ok? What's the agenda?"

I handed him back the phone. "First, you need to call Pastor Michaels and ask him about the church, and the organist. Then, we can take the invitation in and have them start printing them. We're going to need to send them out in the next few weeks, you know."

"Really, that soon?" Mitch asked.

"Yes, Mitch, you have to give people time to respond. So, after you call Pastor, call your mom and ask her if she can get names and addresses for you, ok?" I continued to clear the dishes, and rinse and stack them.

"Anything else, Miss Bossy?" Mitch teased.

I sighed and kissed his cheek. "I'm sorry, honey, but there is just so much we need to get done, that's all."

"And it will all get done, Dana, trust me." He said, dialing the phone. "Pastor Michaels, Mitch Tarrington. Fine, thanks. Dana and I have decided to move our wedding date up, and I wanted to see if you and the church are available for February 18? You are? Fantastic. Yes, that's right. Oh, would your wife be available to play for us during the ceremony? Great. Oh, that I don't know. Let me ask her." He put the phone against his chest and turned to me. "Sweetheart, what time are we getting married?"

"Well, it's bad luck to get married on the hour, so how about, say 2:30? Is that ok with you?" I asked.

He smiled. "Pastor, a 2:30 ceremony. Yes. Ok, I'll let her know and we can make arrangements for that on Sunday. Ok, thanks. Bye." He smiled. "Church is booked, love. But one thing. Sometime before our wedding, he wants us to have what he called a pre-marital conference with him."

I looked at Mitch. "Why?" I asked.

"I guess it's standard procedure. No big deal" Mitch said.

He took the phone and dialed again. "Hey Mom, how are you? I'm fine. No, actually she's right here. She made me breakfast. Pancakes, and bacon. Yeah, she sure does, but I need that, you know. Look, Mom, we're going to the printer for the invitations, and we figure we'll need to start getting them out in a few weeks. Could you throw together a list of names and addresses for me? Yeah, that's right. As soon as you can, if it's not too much trouble. Oh, and Mom, do you think Dad could check into the club for the reception? We don't really know of anyplace else to have it. Oh, that would be great. What's that? No, but don't they do that there, too? If you could, and let me know? Probably, I don't know, around six or so. Ok, thanks Mom. Love you too. I will. Bye."

"Mom's going to have Dad ask about the club and the catering, and she said she'll have the list to us by Sunday." Mitch smiled and put the phone back on the cradle. "Oh, and she said hello."

"Good. Now see, we haven't even left home yet and already we have four things accomplished." I said.

Mitch came over to help me finish up with the dishes. He took the towel I had draped over my shoulder and started to dry the plate I handed to him. "You know, sweetheart, even this is nice. Just being with you like this." He smiled.

"It is, Mitch. I think it's great how comfortable we are with each other." I said.

He reached out and rubbed my back with his hand. "Yeah, me too."

We finished up the dishes, got our list and the invitation, and a few minutes later arrived downtown at the printer. I led Mitch over to the table with the five books full of invitations I had looked at the day I came in by myself. He laughed.

"I don't even want you to start going through those again, Dana. You'll inevitably find something else you like and second guess your decision. Let's just stick with what we have." He said, leading me away from the table.

"Mitchell, are you saying I'm indecisive?" I asked.

"Absolutely." Mitch said confidently.

"Well, I didn't have any problems saying yes to you, now did I?" I retorted.

He smiled. "That's because you can't say no to a sure thing."

I laughed. "No, that's because I can't say no to a diamond ring," I teased.

"Oh, now I know the truth," he chuckled.

The clerk approached us and we gave her the invitation, telling her we needed them printed as soon as possible.

"Wonderful, we can do that for you." She said. "I'll just need the two of you to fill out this information sheet so we can be sure everything is printed correctly." She handed it to Mitch. "Please print it as clearly as possible and be sure to fill in all the information."

Mitch handed the form to me. "She said print clearly. I'm incapable of doing that."

I smiled. "Ok, come here and help me at least."

We sat down at the table and started to fill out the form. "Mitch, on the front of the invitation, do you want it to say Mitchell and Dana or Mitch and Dana?"

He started to answer, but then hesitated. "Is this a trick question?" he asked.

"What do you mean?" I answered.

"Well, if I say Mitchell, you'll say it's too formal. If I say Mitch, you'll say something like 'but your name is Mitchell'." He smiled. "So, why don't you just decide?"

I sighed. "Mitch, it's not a trick question. Would you prefer one over the other, or does it matter?"

He smiled. "Doesn't matter."

"Why did I know you were going to say that?" I replied. "Ok, on the front, we'll go with Mitch and Dana. On the inside, we'll have our full names listed anyway."

I continued to fill out the form and then read what I had written to Mitch. "Now, listen. On the front it will say Mitch and Dana. On the inside, it's going to say, 'The honor of your presence is requested to celebrate the marriage of Miss Dana Patrice Walker to Mr. Mitchell Jacob Tarrington , III on Saturday, the 18th of February, 1988, 2:30 pm', church, blah blah blah."

"Sounds pretty formal." He said, taking the sheet from me for inspection.

"It's supposed to be, silly, it's a wedding." I replied.

"So, hiking boots with the tux would be out of the question?" He smirked.

"Mitchell, stop it, would you? I swear, I can't take you anywhere." I got up and started back to the salesclerk with the completed form.

"How many invitations will you be needing?" She asked.

"Gosh, I don't know." I turned to Mitch. "Honey, what do you think?"

"Gee, I'm not sure either. I do have a large family, though. Oh, let's start out with 150. If we need more, can we get them later?" He asked.

"Certainly. We can put a rush on any extras you might need at the last minute." The clerk answered and she took the sheet, marking down what we had just told her.

"I'm assuming we need to pay for these, so here's my card." Mitch reached for his wallet and I grabbed his arm.

"No, Mitchell, I'm paying for the invitations." I said.

He smiled. "Listen, sweetheart. Ultimately, in the end, I will be paying for everything. The bills will all come to our mailbox, I will sit down with the checkbook, and I will write out the payments. So, just let me give the nice lady my card and we can move on."

"But I want to pay for them myself, Mitch. I have a paycheck, too, you know." I replied.

Mitch handed the salesclerk his card and nodded for her to go ahead with the transaction. Then he turned to me. "So, is that how you want it to be? You control your money and I control mine? I had thought once we got married it would all just be our money. But, that's fine."

The lady handed Mitch the slip to sign, which he did, and she gave him a receipt. He thanked her and put his card and the receipt into his wallet.

"Mitchell, of course I want everything to be shared. But I can pay for these before the wedding, honey. I want to do something." I was getting upset.

Mitch put his arm around me and gave me a kiss. "You did do something. You agreed to marry me. Now, where are we going next?" He asked, opening the door for me.

I stepped out onto the sidewalk. "Mitchell, why are you so stubborn?" I asked him.

He laughed. "I don't know. Maybe you should ask my mother that question. She always said I got the stubbornness for all four of the kids. Personally, I always thought it was Chris."

Back in the car, Mitch turned to me once more. "Didn't you say your friend's husband was a photographer? Are you going to ask her about that?"

I sighed. "You know, I forgot that she told me he wasn't doing it anymore. He got a promotion on his other job, so he doesn't have the time."

"Hmm. Guess that means we need to find someone else, huh?" Mitch stated. "Hey, who's doing the engagement pictures? Maybe we should just have them do it all."

"We could do that, I guess. They're pretty reasonable. We can just talk to them on Friday when we go for our appointment." I replied.

"Ok, done." Mitch said. "How about we go see about flowers, and then stop by the tux shop for the ties and that?" He smiled at me. "Pink and blue. Are you still sure about that?"

I nodded shyly. "I really like those colors."

He smirked. "Well, alright then. Let's go."

It didn't take us long to pick out the flowers for the wedding as Mitch was agreeable to the carnations and sweetheart roses, in white, pink and blue. He would wear a single pink rose, and my bouquet would have pink roses, but the girls would carry only carnations. Each of the guys would wear a white carnation. We also ordered the altar bouquets, the ribbons for the pews and the runner for the aisle. Mitch was right. It was all getting done.

The next stop was the tuxedo shop. Mitch was still hesitant about the pink, but seemed more receptive when I showed him how well it would all come together. After taking care of business, we were ready to go again.

"How about we check into cakes? I said. "We could stop at the bakery where I got your cake for the party at the bistro. I really liked that, didn't you?" I asked.

"Sure, it was great. We can do that, if you want." Mitch answered.

As we drove the few blocks to the bakery, I looked over at Mitch and couldn't help but smile. He was being so cooperative about all this, and so willing to help. I was almost starting to believe that he was beginning to enjoy all this. He noticed me looking at him, and he smiled.

"Something on your mind, sweetheart?" He asked.

"No, not really. I'm just thinking how much I appreciate your help with all this, honey. I know I couldn't do it all on my own."

He took my hand. "I'm glad to help."

Once inside the bakery, the clerk sat us down at a table with a large book containing pictures of different types and styles of wedding cakes. Mitch and I just looked at each other.

"Let's get this over with." He said, opening the book. Flipping through the pages a few times, we finally narrowed it down to four choices.

"How are we ever going to decide, Mitch?" I said.

"I don't know. I never realized choosing a cake could be this involved." He replied. Then he smiled, as if he had just come up with the best idea of his life. "Let's narrow this down to pros and cons. For instance, we're going to need a cake large enough for at least 300 people. So," He turned the page to one of the pictures. "that eliminates this one. It's too small."

"And, we want it to be delicate, but not to the point where if someone bumps the table it goes flying onto the floor." I eliminated the second cake.

"Now, it's down to just these two." Mitch said, pointing at the pictures. "Which one do you like?"

I pointed to one of the pictures. "I really like this one, because of the little fountain thing." I said.

Mitch smiled. "That was my first choice, too. Really."

I looked at him with a half smile. "Mitch, are you just saying that because I picked it, or do you really like it for your first choice?"

He sighed. "Dana, baby, it's a cake. All I'm going to do is smash a piece of it into your pretty little face. I don't care what it looks like." Then he smiled. "But, yes, if I must choose, I honestly like this one best."

"Ok, then it's settled. We'll get this one." Then I turned to him, realizing what he had said. "What do you mean, smash a piece of it into my face? Is that your plan?"

Mitch just smiled. "I'll try to be gentle." He said coyly.

We ordered the cake and left the bakery with a great sense of accomplishment. "Mitch, do you have clothes to take on the honeymoon?" I asked.

He smiled impishly and placed his hand on my leg. "I didn't think I was going to need any." He said.

I pushed his hand away playfully. "Well, think again, buddy." I replied.

Mitch sighed. "Well, if you're going to insist upon it, I guess I could use a few things. Is this your way of saying you want to go shopping?" he asked.

"You are so perceptive." I replied, hugging his arm.

"Where? The mall?" He asked, turning the car in that direction.

"Ok, that sounds good." I answered.

We drove to the mall and Mitch parked the car, but instead of getting out, he turned to me. "Dana, while we're here, I want you to show me at least three things you want for your birthday. I don't care how much they cost, or what they are. But I need some ideas, ok?" Mitch didn't tell me that he already had his own idea, anyway.

"You don't have to get me anything, honey, really." I said.

Mitch gave me just enough of a smile to show his dimple. "Dana, I know better. If you don't have a gift to unwrap, you'll be disappointed. Now, let's go in here and see what we can find. Ok?" Coming around to open my door for me, he put his arm around me and we hurried into the mall to escape the cold.

Once inside, he rubbed his hands together to warm them up and wiped the steam from his glasses. "How about a nice cup of hot chocolate?" He asked. "I'm freezing."

"With lots of whipped cream." I smiled.

We bought the hot chocolate and sat down on a bench in the mall for a few moments, just to enjoy it and each other. The mall was a lot less crowded than it had been a few weeks ago when we came, and now all the pretty sights and sounds of Christmas were gone. All the stores were boasting clearance signs and I couldn't believe many of them were already starting to display spring and summer merchandise.

"I know this sounds crazy, but I don't think we'll have any problems finding warm weather clothes. Just look at all these windows." I commented.

"And to think we're sitting here trying to get warm. I just feel so cold today. But this hot chocolate feels really good." Mitch replied. He put his arm around me, changing the subject. "Do you think you'll enjoy Hawaii, sweetheart?"

"Everything except the plane ride there." I said.

Mitch looked at me curiously. "Don't you like to fly?" he asked.

I got a sheepish look on my face. "I've never done it before, not commercially anyway." I answered.

Mitch smiled. "It's no big deal. Smoother than riding in a car, and actually, statistically, it's safer, too. Just take a book or two to read and you'll be fine."

"Is it scary, I mean, when you take off and when you land?" I asked.

Mitch kissed me. "Not really. When you take off, it feels a little like someone is pushing you backwards in your seat, and when you land, sometimes the altitude change makes it hard to hear. But it all clears up again once you're on the ground. "

I looked at Mitch. "If I get scared, will you hold onto me?" I asked.

He smiled and kissed my cheek. "Absolutely." He answered. Then he looked at me curiously. "Dana, you said your dad was a pilot. Didn't he ever take you up?"

I sighed. "Only a few times. He didn't have his own plane until I was around eleven or so, and it was different for me than this will be, Mitch. That was a little plane and Daddy was the one at the wheel. I trusted him. But, you have to remember, that plane is what took my mom and Daddy away from me, Mitchell. I had just turned twelve, and I haven't flown since then. That's why I'm a little nervous about it."

"I'll be with you, sweetheart. It'll be fine, ok?" He said reassuringly.

"I know." I replied softly.

We finished our hot chocolate and hand in hand, started our trek through the mall. I noticed a few cute outfits in a store window, and managed to pull Mitch in to take a look at them. Finding my sizes, I announced that I was going to try things on.

"You wait here and I'll model for you." I said.

"Too bad this isn't the lingerie store." He said, smirking. The clerk heard what he said and smiled. Mitch smiled back and shrugged.

"Mitchell, behave yourself, or at least try." I said, hurrying off into the fitting room.

Mitch parked himself in a chair just outside the entrance to the fitting room, and I found him there a minute later, waiting patiently. My first outfit was just a simple pair of denim shorts and a polo shirt, but he smiled as if he were looking at Miss America.

"I like it." He said, decisively. "You should get that one."

"Ok, let me try the others first, and then I'll decide." I told him, disappearing once more.

The next outfit was a little sundress with spaghetti straps, in a bright blue trimmed in white. Again, it got Mitch's approval. The third outfit was a khaki colored skirt, which hit just above the knee, topped with a red sleeveless tank. Again, Mitch approved.

Finally, I reappeared in my own clothing to find him still patiently waiting for me. He was such a good shopping companion, I thought. "Ok, honey, now help me decide which one to get."

He looked at me with shock. "You mean we have to wait for Dana to make a decision? Not happening." He took all three outfits from my arms and proceeded to the checkout stand. "Mitch is making this decision. You get all three. Happy Birthday."

I stood there, shocked, and watched as he paid for my clothes and then returned to hand me the bag. "Ok, that's done. Where to now?" He asked, taking my hand once again and leading me out of the store.

"I thought I was the assertive one in this relationship." I commented.

"Not today." He said, his eyes shining. He smiled. "Sweetheart, let's get something straight. I know that in your heart you loved all of those outfits. I thought you looked fabulous in all those outfits. Why make the process any more difficult by trying to decide on just one? Besides, I needed to get you a gift anyway. You just helped me pick it out."

I gave him a kiss. "Thank you, honey, that was very sweet."

"So, what else did you have in mind?" He asked.

"I could use a new swimsuit." I said. "I may be able to find one, too. I know that Jacy's is already putting them out." Then I paused. "Wait, I can't take you in there." I said.

Mitch laughed. "Still don't trust me, huh? How about I promise to stay with you?" He said.

"Well, ok." I answered playfully. "I really would like to find something."

We entered Jacy's and headed for the ladies department, and just as I had suspected, they already had a large selection of swimsuits on display. As I started to browse, I noticed Mitch didn't seem to mind being in this department very much, either.

"Hey, Dana, how about this one? I like it." He was holding up a skimpy little two piece that didn't look like it held enough material to cover up his niece, Megan, let alone me.

"I'm sure you do, Mitchell, but no." I said.

"Too conservative, huh?" He said with a smirk.

"You better just stay by me, dear. I'll find my own, thank you." I said.

Mitch continued to make his suggestions, and continued to get shot down on each occasion. Finally, I found a few suits to try on and parked him next to the fitting room.

"Sweetheart, why are all the ones you picked one piece?" he asked.

"Because that's what I feel comfortable in, Mitch. I'm really not much into showing the world what I own, which really isn't much, and definitely isn't enough to fill any of those other things up." I answered.

Mitch looked at me. "Don't sell yourself short, sweetheart. You're beautiful, and I'd love to see what you look like in one of those." He pointed to a two piece suit hanging close by.

"I guess you'll just have to use your imagination." I said. "Now, I'm going to go try these on." I gave him a kiss as he sighed and folded his hands in his lap. "I'll be right back."

A few minutes and a few suits later, I emerged from the fitting room. Discouraged with my luck, I plopped the suits back on the rack and summoned for Mitch to follow. He stood up.

"You didn't model for me." He said.

"That's because they were all wrong." I said. "I hate shopping for a swimsuit. It's too depressing."

Mitch put his arm around me. "Why do you say that?"

"It just is. Nothing goes with this body. Maybe I should just buy a wetsuit." I sighed.

Mitch laughed. "You're beautiful, Dana. Don't worry, baby, you'll find something. Maybe you can come out with Kayla or the girls and they can help you."

I smiled at the thought. We could all compare body fat, get depressed together, and drown our sorrows in hot fudge sundaes. Sounded like a plan to me.

"Let's shop for Mitchell now." I said, taking him by the hand. "Can I help you pick out a few things?" I asked.

"Well, ok, but nothing pink." He warned.

I found a nice medium green polo with a little alligator on it and showed it to Mitch. He smiled.

"Definitely a rich kid's shirt." He said. "Very preppy."

"Well, rich kid, I know for certain that you have a red one in your closet just like it. I like this green. It'll look nice with your skin tone. And, I like preppy." I told him. Mitch found his size and handed it to me.

"Dana, just for the record, I don't make a habit of matching my clothing to my skin tone, or my hair or my eyes. I just pick out what I like and buy it." He said, matter-of-factly.

"Well, that's why you need me." I replied. "I can make you more fashion conscious."

He laughed. "Not really my goal in life, but ok, if you really want to. Besides, what's wrong with how I dress now?"

"Nothing, sweetie. I just think you could add a little more color here and there, that's all." I rubbed his back with my hand. "I think you're very handsome."

Mitch picked out a few pairs of shorts and a couple of t-shirts, and I picked out another casual shirt for him, and a pair of khaki's. He smiled.

"Ok, let's go pay for all this and get some lunch. I'm getting hungry." He said.

"Honey, aren't you going to try anything on? What if it doesn't fit?" I asked.

He smiled. "I got the sizes I need. It'll all fit, trust me." He replied.

"Must be nice." I grumbled.

Mitch paid for all his items, we left the store and went back into the mall. "Well, that took care of the paycheck from the gig this past weekend." He smiled.

"I didn't tell you to buy my outfits, Mitch. I would have been perfectly happy with just one of them." I replied, feeling a little guilty that he had spent all his money on me.

He laughed. "Oh, no, baby, I didn't mean it that way. I've got plenty of money to cover everything. I just meant that, well, clothes are not cheap anymore, that's all." He kissed me on top of the head. "I love buying you things, so get used to it."

"Ok." I said playfully.

Mitch laughed. "Gee, that took a lot of convincing," he said happily. He put his arm around my shoulder. "So, what are you hungry for, my love?"

"From the way I looked in those swimsuits, I'd better opt for a salad." I replied halfheartedly.

Mitch smiled, a sympathetic kind of smile. "My sweet Dana." He said, kissing me. "You are so beautiful. I love you just the way you are."

"Are you sure?" I asked.

He gave me a funny look. "Absolutely!" he replied.

"Ok, then, I'll take a cheeseburger!" I said, smiling.

Mitch laughed. "You got it." He said.

Mitch smiled as I took a huge bite out of my cheeseburger. "I don't get it, sweetheart. You are such a little thing, but you have a huge appetite. What's your secret?"

"Camouflage it with the clothing." I replied. "And be lucky enough to have a high metabolism."

Mitch laughed. "Darling, you don't have an ounce of fat anywhere on that body, I'm sure."

"Maybe not fat, but a little extra fluff in a few places." I replied.

"Fluff, huh?" Mitch chuckled. "I highly doubt that, too."

"Mitchell, do you honestly believe I'm that perfect, or is this a vision of grandeur you've created about me?" I said, eating a fry.

"To me, you are perfect in every way." Mitch replied. He took out his watch to look at the time. "Are you ready to go home for a while and relax before work?" he asked. "I'm getting a little tired myself."

"I think that sounds pretty wonderful." I said.

Once back in the car and heading for home, Mitch looked at me and smiled.

"We got a lot accomplished today, didn't we?" He asked.

"We did. Thanks for being so helpful, honey. I'm glad we did this together." I told him.

Mitch reached out for me, and I leaned on his shoulder as he put his arm around me. "I told you I'd help, didn't I? I'm a man of my word, Dana."

Back home, Mitch sat down in the chair and pulled a blanket over himself. "Gosh, I just can't get warm today." He said. "Dana, come here and keep me warm, sweetheart."

I went to the chair and he lifted the blanket, pulling me underneath with him. Then he placed the blanket back around us and put his arms around me. "Hey, you know what? This is nice."

"I agree." I said, trying to snuggle even closer.

Noticing a pad of paper lying on the coffee table, Mitch leaned forward as much as he could and just managed to pick it up. Inspecting it more closely, he smiled.

"What's this?" He asked.

I blushed a little as I took the pad from his hands. Scribbled all over the page was my future name, written every way conceivable. "I was just practicing," I said. "You know, it's going to be a lot of work to write Mrs. Mitchell J. Tarrington, the third. It's an awfully long name."

"Yeah, I know, but like I told you before, blame my mother for that one." He said, smugly.

I looked at Mitch. "But, you aren't the firstborn son, Chris is. Why didn't he get the name?"

"Chris was supposed to be the Mitchell in the family, but my mom's dad passed on just before he was born, so he was named after my Grandpa Ciserelli, Christopher Anthony. Then, when I came along, I got stuck with the family curse." Mitch answered.

"So, your mother's Italian, huh?" I said.

Mitch smiled. "Yes, she is. One hundred percent. Grandma and Grandpa Ciserelli came here right from Italy."

"That's pretty cool." I said. "Now I know the basis for your temper." I teased. Mitch smirked.

The next few days flew by, and finally, January 4th arrived. I was stirred awake by a knock on the door, and when I opened it, I saw Mitch standing there, his face glowing as he began to sing *Happy Birthday*. I smiled.

"Good morning, beautiful." He said as he finished. "I thought I'd come by and surprise you."

"Good morning, handsome. That was sweet, thank you." I said, kissing him.

"Would you like some breakfast? I can make you something." He asked.

"Well, I only have time for something quick, but ok. I need to go jump in the shower and get dressed for work." I told him. "Since I plan to leave early today, I told them I'd come in early."

"I'll have it ready when you get back." Mitch said, sending me off.

A few minutes later, I was showered and dressed. I came back to find Mitch waiting for me with two bowls of oatmeal, toast and coffee.

"This is nice, someone else doing the cooking for a change." I said.

Mitch pulled out the chair for me and then joined me for our little breakfast. He smiled at me sweetly. "How does it feel to be 23?" he asked me.

"Gee, not much different from 22." I said, smiling. I spread some jelly on my toast. "I should get home around 12:30 or so, ok? Then we can spend the rest of the day together." I told him happily. "You can just stay here, if you want, instead of going home."

"I think I might just do that," he replied. "By the way, I want to take you out tonight. I thought maybe dinner and dancing. What do you think?" He was smiling so brightly I wanted to just melt when I looked in his eyes.

"That sounds fantastic, sweetie." I finished up my breakfast and started to do the dishes quickly. Mitch picked me up and moved me out of the way.

I laughed. "What are you doing, Mitchell Tarrington?" I asked.

"You go to work, I'll take care of this. You're going to be late." He said kissing me, and handing me my coat. "In fact, take the car. I won't be needing it the next few hours. I'd rather you not take the bus anymore."

"Mitchell, you are......." I started.

"Terrible, I know." He smiled and kissed me again. "Now go!"

As soon as he was sure she was gone, he grabbed the phone and called Jim.

"Hey, Jim, it's Mitch. I need to ask a little favor. Today's Dana's birthday, and I have something in mind, but I need a ride downtown.

Can you swing by her place and pick me up on your way in to work? She took my car today."

"Sure, buddy, no problem. How about I be there around nine or so?" Jim asked.

"Perfect, I'll be waiting." Mitch replied.

To kill time, Mitch tidied up Dana's apartment for her, then called and made dinner reservations for them at Chandler's, a fancy little restaurant across town. Everything accomplished, he settled down in the chair with the newspaper to wait for Jim.

Promptly at nine, he heard the knock at the door, announcing Jim's arrival. "Now, tell me, what's this little fiasco you've gotten me into?" Jim asked as he stepped inside.

Mitch proceeded to tell Jim his plan, and then they headed out. A few minutes later, Jim was dropping Mitch off at Murdock Motors, in search of Dana's gift. It didn't take him long to find what he wanted, and he went to hook up with a salesman.

"Good morning, sir. Tom Perkins." The salesman said, extending his hand.

Mitch shook his hand. "Mitch Tarrington, nice to meet you. I found something over here in the showroom I'm really interested in."

"Sure, Mr. Tarrington, let's have a look." Tom said.

Mitch led Tom to a brand new Iroc Z-28 Camaro t-top, candy apple red with gray interior, and loaded with all the bells and whistles. He smiled brightly as he walked around it again, inspecting it closely. Just like he'd been able to picture the ring on her finger, he could picture Dana in this car.

"So, you like the sporty cars, huh, Mr. Tarrington?" Tom asked. "This one's a real beauty."

"Yes, but actually, I already have a car. Today's my fiancé's birthday, and I'm buying it for her." Mitch said, opening the door to sit inside. "Oh, and please, call me Mitch."

"Your fiancé's a lucky girl, Mitch. Not many guys would buy a car for their girl's birthday." Tom said.

"Well, probably not, but I actually think I'm the lucky one." Mitch smiled as he got out and closed the door. "So, can we work something out here?" he asked Tom.

"I'm sure we can, let's step into my office." Tom said.

After a few minutes of negotiating, Mitch and Tom came to an agreeable deal. "Well, Mitch, it looks like you have yourself a great car for your fiancé." Tom said. "So, when's the big day?"

"February 18." Mitch answered. "Now, I need to drive this off the lot like, right now. Is that possible?"

"Sure, Mitch, we just need to make sure she's all cleaned up for you and once your financing goes through, you can take her right out."

Mitch smiled and pulled out his checkbook. "That shouldn't take long, because I'm not financing." He said.

Tom gave him a stunned look. "You aren't going to finance. What method of payment do you plan to use?"

"Well, if you'll take my check, I can give you about ten forms of identification, and you can feel free to call my bank to verify funds. I want to buy it outright." Mitch smiled.

"We can do that for you, Mitch, not a problem at all. Let's just get all the paperwork done, I'll take that check for you and you can be on your way. Allow me to get this into cleanup first, and I'll be right back."

A few minutes later a dealership employee pulled the car out of the showroom, and Tom reappeared. "Now, since she isn't here, I'm going to assume we'll put everything in your name. That'll be fine."

Mitch gave Tom all the information he asked for, and signed his name where he was told. About five papers later, Mitch was the proud owner of a new car. Tom stood up and shook Mitch's hand. "Great doing business with you, and good luck on your marriage."

"Thanks." Mitch said.

Tom showed Mitch where to wait for the car. He bought himself a soda from the machine and sat down to peruse through a magazine until the car was ready. Finally, right about eleven o'clock, he was driving away in Dana's car. He felt on top of the world. She would be so surprised, he thought. And she really deserved this. She did so much for him, and now it was time he did something for her.

Around 11:30, he pulled into the parking lot of her school, and chuckled. He loved to surprise her, and this would be so much fun, he thought. Mitch spotted his car, and parked Dana's just in front of it. Taking out his keys, he moved his car out of the way, then jumped back in hers and parked it where his had been. Locking the doors, he laughed as he returned to his car and headed for home as quickly as he could.

16

Right as expected, around 12:10, the phone rang. He snickered to himself mischievously as he picked it up.

"Hello?" he said.

"Mitch, can you find a way to come down here, please. Right away." I could barely keep my voice from shaking.

"Sweetheart, what's wrong? Is everything ok?" Mitch said, doing his best to sound genuinely concerned.

"Honey, I don't know how to tell you this, but I think someone stole your car." I was sure he could tell I was about to cry.

Mitch was feeling a little guilty to put her through this, but it was all part of the plan. "It's ok, sweetheart, don't worry. I'll get someone to give me a ride down there right away, ok? Don't panic, I'll be right there, baby. I love you."

"Ok, I love you too." I said.

Right on cue, Jim showed up at the door. "Ready, you sneaky little devil?" he asked.

"Jim, this is, oh, so beautiful!" Mitch said. "I may die at my true love's hand tonight, but it'll all be worth it." He grabbed his coat and prepared to make his entrance.

Pulling up to the school, Jim turned to Mitch. "I'm not sure if I should stick around to watch this or not, buddy. She may just outright kill you." Jim said.

"Nah, come in with me. She'll want to know how I got down here, and besides, I may end up needing a doctor!" The two laughed.

I was waiting for Mitch in the office, shaking like a leaf, when he came in. He walked over and took me in his arms. "I thought you'd never get here." I said, my voice filled with despair.

"Baby, what happened?" He said, biting his lip, trying to keep from smiling.

"I went out to get in the car, Mitch, and it's not there. I thought that maybe I'd just forgotten where I'd parked, but I walked all over the parking lot and it isn't there." A tear started to fall down my cheek, and Mitch kissed my forehead.

"Now, don't cry Dana, let's go check things out, ok? Come on." He took me by the hand and held open the door for me. Jim followed.

"Did you call the police?" Mitch asked.

"No, not yet. Scott thought you should be here first." I said.

"Show me where you parked." Mitch instructed, and I walked him to where I had left the car that morning.

"I parked right there, Mitch, and now your car isn't there." I said.

Mitch smiled. "Sure it is, honey, it's right there."

I looked at him as if he were having hallucinations. "Mitchell, that is not your car. Your car isn't here."

He smiled at me again. "Dana, sweetheart, darling, it's right there." He pointed to the same car again.

I looked him right in the eyes. "Mitchell Tarrington, don't do this to me. I'm upset enough as it is. That is not your car."

"You're right, Dana. It isn't my car." He pulled a key from his pocket and held it out to me. "It's *your* car."

I looked at him in total shock. Mitch's eyes were shining and his face was bright. "Happy Birthday, sweetheart." He said, handing me the key.

I looked at Mitch, then at the car and back to Mitch. "What are you telling me, Mitchell?

"I'm telling you, Happy Birthday, Dana. Go look at your new car." Mitch said, pointing to it again.

"Oh my gosh, Mitch, you bought me a CAR!" I literally jumped into his arms, knocking him backwards into Jim, who kept both of us from falling. Both men were laughing hysterically, until I virtually wrapped myself around Mitch and kissed him with all I had in me. By now, some of the other teachers, aides, and Scott, the principal, had gathered to watch it all take place. Little did I know that Mitch had tipped Scott off, too, so the police wouldn't be called. Jim tapped Mitch on the shoulder.

"Hey buddy, you're drawing a crowd." He said.

Mitch still kept me in his embrace, kissing me passionately. He wasn't about to give up this moment for anyone.

Finally he put me down, and everyone applauded, with me dragging Mitch by the hand to my car. He opened the door for me and I sat down in the driver's seat, and ran my hands along the steering wheel. I couldn't believe that he had actually bought a car for me. I looked up at him and smiled.

"Now, there is one other thing, Dana. I ordered personalized license plates. Unfortunately, they won't be here for a few weeks, but since the temps run out in thirty days, I'll have to put them on when they come. I know they won't really apply for a few weeks after that, but I don't have a choice."

"What do they say?" I asked curiously.

"Mrs. MT 3." Mitch replied smiling.

"Clever!" I said. "I can't wait to see them!"

Mitch looked at me lovingly. "Want to drive me home, beautiful?" he asked.

"Anything." I said. I waved goodbye to my friends, as Mitch slipped into the passenger seat. I turned to him and smiled. "Mitchell Jacob Tarrington, you are the most wonderful man alive. Do you realize that?" I asked him.

"Well, I don't know about all that, but I was starting to miss my 'Stang." He said, teasingly. Then he looked at me and smiled. "I don't suppose you're interested in taking this to show Kayla, are you?" he asked.

"Yes, yes yes!" I said. Then I looked at him. "I'm almost afraid to drive it, Mitch. It's so incredible. I've never had my own car before."

"You do now, sweetheart. Now, how about if we go to Kayla's, and then I'll take you out to lunch, ok?" he asked.

"Let's go!" I said, starting the car. Just the sound of the motor made me feel powerful. Mitch looked at me.

"You know, when I saw this car, I knew it was perfect for you, and I was right." He said.

"It really is awesome, Mitch." Then I had a thought. "Mitch, where is your car? You didn't sell it to get me this one, did you?"

He smiled. "No love, my car is safe at home. I told you, I bought this one for you. It's yours, Dana, free and clear."

We were stopped at a light, and I turned completely toward him. "Mitchell, I know I shouldn't look a gift horse in the mouth, but this is a very expensive car. How did you afford to buy it outright?"

Mitch bit his lip and smiled. "Well, Dana, I'm a rich kid, remember?" He said.

"But Mitch, I thought you told me that you used all your trust money, except for a little bit in a savings account." I said.

"Well, I guess it won't hurt to tell you, love." Mitch started. "Besides my trust fund, there was one other tie to the Tarrington fortune that I had, and that was stock in the company. My parents gave each of us a few shares when we turned eighteen. I really got to thinking about it, Dana, and I thought that would be a great way for us to make it when we got married, you know, kind of a nest egg, just in case. But, then I realized, Dana, that I wanted to take care of you, of us, not live off my profits from my dad's company." He paused. "So, I decided to sell my stock in Tarrington Industries. I got around fifty grand, enough for a car and enough for a wedding and a honeymoon."

"Mitchell, why is it so important for you to do everything on your own? What have you got against your father and his money?" I asked.

"Absolutely nothing, Dana. But that's just the point. As long as it comes from Tarrington Industries, it's Dad's money, not mine. I want to be the one who takes care of you, who pays the bills and buys the groceries, and takes you out on Saturday night. I want to be the one to buy you things you desire, and eventually, take care of our kids and someday, send them off to college. Me, Dana, not money that comes from how well my father does in his work. My money, from how well I do in my work."

I reached over and took his hand as we pulled up to Kayla's house. "Mitchell, I can't say that I fully understand that, but I do respect it. I know it means a lot to you to make it on your own. But, honey, I want to take care of you, too. You have to let me help, Mitch. I can work, and I know I'll never make as much money at what I do as you do, but I still want to help."

He smiled. "Go get Kayla, I know you're anxious." He said, seeming to ignore what I had said to him.

I smiled and jumped out of the car, practically running up to the door. "Hey Kayla, come out here!" I yelled as I knocked on the door.

Kayla answered it. "Dana, honey, what is it?" she asked, concerned.

I grabbed her by the hand, practically dragging her into the driveway. Mitch was standing with his back against the car, taking in the whole scene with a smile.

"Look what Mitch got me for my birthday!" I squealed, pointing to the car and jumping up and down.

"Yes, please come and look before she goes into shock!" Mitch told her.

"Good Lord of Mercy!" Kayla squealed back, grabbing my hands. "Dana, honey, that's a CAR!"

"Gee, Kayla, that's the same thing Dana said when she saw it. It's great to know the two of you are on the same wavelength." Mitch was smiling.

"Oh, Mitch, stop it!" I said. "And stop leaning on my car. You're going to get it dirty." I told him.

He cleared his throat, and smirking, put both hands up and slowly moved away from the car.

"Come on, Kayla, let's go for a ride!" I told her. "I'll make it real warm in there and you won't need a coat."

"Oh, my, Dana, it's so wonderful. You sure are a lucky girl!" Kayla said.

"And it has EVERYTHING, Kayla! Wait until you see! And the radio. Oh, man, I can really jam now!" I said, pulling her to the car.

I started to open the door and climb in, Kayla doing the same on the other side. Mitch was just standing back with his arms folded, realizing we had virtually forgotten he was even there.

Mitch pointed to the house. "I'm just going to......go......inside and see where.......Joseph is." He said, still being ignored.

As Kayla and I pulled out of the driveway, I turned to see Mitch walking into the house, a big smile on his face.

"Kayla, can you believe this guy?" I said. "Just when I think I know all there is to know, he pulls something like this. You won't believe what he did to me, though." I told her about how Mitch made me think his car had gotten stolen. She laughed.

"He's a sly one, that boy." Kayla said. "He's gonna be a good husband, Dana. He takes care of his girl."

"And I want to take care of him, too." I replied. Then a thought occurred to me. "Kayla, I told him today that I want to help with things, you know, financially after we get married, and he pretty much ignored me. I'm not going to let him take responsibility for everything."

Kayla smiled. "That's a good thing, Dana, but you have to try to understand how Mitch operates. It's a big thing for him to take care of you. It gives him a sense of accomplishment, not in a bad way, but in a way that makes him know that he's showing his love for you."

"Then shouldn't I do the same for him?" I asked her.

"It's like I told you before, Dana. Men just look at things differently than women do. To him, taking care of him means that you'll be there when he gets home, have a hot meal ready for him, and well, satisfy his needs when he asks."

I shot her a glance. "And just how often do I have to do that?" I asked.

She laughed. "As often as the two of you decide."

"Oh, my, I think I may be in trouble!" I chuckled.

We had made a big circle around town, and were pulling back into Kayla's driveway. Joseph came filing out the door, Mitch close behind. Kayla turned to me.

"Look here now, Dana. Mitch is a strong willed man. You need to sit him down and talk to him if you feel the way you do. I think he just might understand if you sweet talk him enough." She smiled. "Now, let's come on and let Joseph see this fancy car. Anyhow, I have your present in the house, so we can go in there out of the cold."

Mitch was beside the car and he opened the door for me. "Have fun, sweetheart?" he asked.

"I may just sleep in this car tonight!" I told him.

He smiled. "You might get a little cold, considering it is only about thirty degrees out here."

Mitch showed the car to Joseph while Kayla and I went inside. Laying on her kitchen table were two boxes. She motioned for me to sit down and slid them both my way.

"Happy Birthday, Dana. Go on and open them."

"Kayla, you shouldn't have done this. You're too much." I told her, opening the card first.

It was a beautiful card with a gorgeous bouquet of flowers on the front, and the words, "Happy Birthday to My Dear Friend." On the inside was a touching verse, and Kayla had written me a little note. It said, "Dana, Thank you for showing me the meaning of true friendship. I am so happy that you and Mitch finally got together. I always knew in my heart that's where you should be. I hope you have a wonderful birthday full of surprises, and many more. Love, Kayla."

I looked up at her and smiled. "Thanks, Kayla." I said.

I picked up the first gift and ripped off the paper. Opening the box, I stood back in awe. Kayla had made me a beautiful quilt and had stitched "Mitch and Dana" right in the center, inside a heart. I felt a tear fall down my cheek.

"Kayla, it's beautiful. How long did it take you to make this?"

She smiled. "Truth is, I started it the first night Mitch smiled at you. I knew, Dana. I just waited to put your names on it. I was going to give it to you for your wedding, but I just couldn't wait." She laughed. "You might just want to snuggle under it before that."

I unwrapped the next package to find a lovely sweater and blazer that she had picked out for me. I stood up and gave her a hug. "Thank you Kayla, I love everything!" I told her.

Just then, Mitch and Joseph came back in. I motioned for Mitch to come to the table, and opening the box, I showed him the quilt Kayla had made for us.

"That's beautiful, sweetheart." He said. "Look, it even has our names on it."

"I know, she said we can snuggle under it if we want to." I smiled at him.

Mitch rubbed my back with his hand. "I like that idea." He said.

"That's some sharp car you got there, Dana." Joseph said. "Kayla never got me a car for my birthday." He teased.

"Next birthday." Kayla teased back.

"You both heard her. If I don't get my car, I'm gonna be mad." He laughed.

We said goodbye to Kayla and Joseph, and headed out to get some lunch. As we got to the car, I handed Mitch the keys. "Want a turn?" I asked him.

"Why, are you tired of it already?" he asked.

"No way! I was just being polite, but if you don't want to......." I snatched the keys back from him and hopped into the car.

Mitch laughed. "You never gave me a chance to answer!" he said. "So, where would you like to go for lunch?" Mitch asked, getting into the car.

"You know, I could go for some pizza . How about Gartano's?" I asked.

"That sounds fine with me." Then he smiled and took my hand. "I'll get off cheap that way, too!"

A few minutes later, we pulled up in front of the bistro, and Mitch told me to wait while he came around and opened my door for me. We walked inside, and it just seemed so comfortable, so warm and familiar. I had really grown to feel that this place was a part of who I was.

"Hey, Mitch!" Joe called out as Mitch entered. I sat down at a table as Mitch went to talk to him.

"Hey, Joe, how's it going?" Mitch asked.

"I was just going to ask you that," he replied. "Out with your special girl today, I see?"

"Yeah, Joe, you're right. She's really special. In fact, today's her birthday." Mitch said.

"Well, that's nice. Doing anything special?" Joe asked.

He smiled at me, and turned so I couldn't see his face. "She doesn't know it, but I planned a surprise party for her tonight at my parents' house with my family. She thinks I'm taking her out for dinner and dancing." Mitch said cheerfully.

"I bet she'll like that Mitch." Joe smiled. "You treat her real good. She's a sweet little thing." He patted Mitch on the back.

A few minutes later, Mitch rejoined me at the table. "Sorry to keep you waiting, lovely lady." He said, handing me a menu. "Order whatever you'd like. I'm personal friends with the owner of the place. Quite a nice guy, if I do say so myself."

"Yes, and I hear he's very modest, too." I smiled.

We decided on a sausage and pepperoni pizza, two sodas, and a piece of apple pie for dessert. I could tell Mitch was a little antsy as we were waiting and he was looking around as if he wanted to be in on the action instead of just observing it.

"Honey, is something bothering you? You seem a little distracted." I asked him.

"Oh, no, sweetheart. Actually, I still can't believe this is my place. Dana, I sit and think sometimes about all the good things that have happened to me in just the past three months, and it blows me away." He smiled. "First, there's you, and Gartano's, now the band, and us getting married. Sometimes I'm afraid I'm actually dreaming, and I'm gonna wake up one morning to find none of it was real."

I reached out for his hand. "I know what you mean, Mitch, but believe me, it's all real. That's the best part."

"And soon we can be together all the time." He smiled.

"I can hardly wait, Mitch." I told him. Then I had a thought cross my mind. "Honey, I've often heard that people can get along fine when they're dating, but when they get married and they actually live under the same roof, that they fight all the time. Do you think we're going to be like that?"

Mitch took a drink of his soda. "You know, I don't doubt we'll fight sometimes. Heck, we do that now." He smiled. "But I think we're going to be just fine. It's just going to mean some compromise on both our parts, that's all."

I summoned Katie for a refill on our sodas. "Mitch, there's something I need to ask you." I started. Mitch looked intent on listening to what I had to say. "Earlier, when I said that I wanted to help with the financial end of things after we get married, you kind of ignored me. Don't you want me to help you, Mitch?"

Mitch's face got a serious look, and he bit his lip, as if he were trying to put the right words together. "Dana, try to understand something." He started. "One of the reasons I'm marrying you is that I want to be the one who takes care of you for the rest of my life. I want to go to work everyday so you can have the things you want and need. Giving to you and providing for you makes me happy." He paused. "You working, too, is definitely going to help us, sweetheart, don't get me wrong. I just don't want myself to get so caught up in it that I start slacking in what I need to do. There may come a time, Dana, when you can't work, or that you choose not to, and I want you to know that's fine with me. I just want to know that if and when that time comes, I've done my part to make sure everything is still alright."

We finished the pizza and Katie brought out our apple pie. "I understand, Mitch, and it makes me feel wonderful that you want to do that for me. But I need you to understand something, too. Our marriage is going to be a partnership. It's just as important for me to take care of you as it is for you to take care of me."

Mitch smiled at me with love in his eyes. "You do take care of me, Dana. You're great at it, and I love it. Really. But you're wrong about one thing. We're not going to be partners just after we get married. We're partners right now."

I reached out for Mitch's hand and gave it a gentle squeeze. "Do you realize just how much I love you, Mitchell Tarrington?" I asked.

"I think I do, but you just may need to keep reminding me." He smiled.

"Hey, Mitch, it's still pretty early in the day. Want to go ice skating or something?" I asked.

"Sure, that sound's like a good time." He said. "It's your day, love. Whatever you want to do."

Then I remembered I was still dressed up from school. "Oh, darn, we can't do that. Not in these clothes, anyway." I said.

"Then tell you what? Why don't you go home and change, then we'll go?" Mitch suggested. "We have all day."

We headed back to my apartment, and went inside. "Mitchell, did you clean my apartment this morning?" I said, noticing right away his handiwork.

"Just a little. No big deal." He replied.

"Honey, it is a big deal. That's so sweet of you." I said, giving him a hug.

"Well, I was going to bake you a cake, but we both know how that would have turned out. So, I decided cleaning would be safe." He smiled. "By the way, there's something over here on the table for you." I walked over to the table, and Mitch handed me an envelope with my name on it. I opened it and inside was a beautiful card with a picture of a couple walking along the beach.

"It reminded me of us on the beach in Hawaii." Mitch said.

I opened it and read the verse. It was loving and romantic, just like Mitch. He had written me a little note inside, just like Kayla had.

"Dana, The last three months have been the most incredible time in my life. You have shown me so many things, but mainly, what true love really means. I feel like the luckiest man alive and I can't wait until you are Mrs. Mitch Tarrington. Thank you for everything you've given me, and I hope that you will give me the chance to prove to you each day what you mean to me. With all my love forever, Mitch. PS Happy Anniversary."

I looked up at him and he smiled. "It is our anniversary, too, you know. Not only of the first day I saw you, but the day we started going out."

"You know, you're right." I told him. "Happy anniversary, sweetie." I stood up and gave him a gentle kiss.

"Ready to go ice skating now?" He asked.

"Sure, but only if I can drive." I told him.

We got to the rink, rented our skates and of course, Mitch had to show me once again how good a skater he was. Then he came and put his arm around me, smiling. "Hey, I wonder if my friend will be here this time." He said, looking to see how I would react.

"Maybe she will be, Mitchell. Then she can watch and see what it looks like for you to get clocked in the jaw by a girl ten inches shorter than you."

He laughed. "You really wouldn't hit me, now would you, sweetheart?"

I glanced back at him. "Totally depends on the situation at hand."

"I'll make a mental note of that." He stated. Then he turned to me. "Want to learn a neat little trick?" he asked.

"Like what kind of neat little trick?" I asked cautiously.

"It's pretty simple, actually. All you do is this." Mitch proceeded to do some sort of little jump and spin on his skates, and then come back to me.

"Oh, yes, that looks really simple." I said sarcastically. "What, like, do you know Scott Hamilton personally or something and he taught you that?"

Mitch laughed. "No, actually, Angelina taught me that when I was about twelve. Took me a little time, but I caught on, and I never forgot."

"I think I'll just let you be the showoff in the family." I said, taking his hand. "I'd much rather just hold your hand and skate next to you."

Mitch pretended to yawn. "Sure, Dana, let's be safe, huh?" He teased.

"Sorry I'm too boring for you, Mitch." I said.

Mitch stopped and came around to stand in front of me. "Don't start, Dana. I never said you were boring. Can't you take a little joke?"

"Apparently not." I said. "Sorry."

Mitch smiled. "You make me crazy sometimes, girl, you really do." He kissed me on top of the head. "But that's ok. I'll keep you."

I smiled at him. "That's good to know." I said.

We skated and talked for about an hour or more, then decided we both wanted to get in out of the cold. Back in the car, Mitch undid his coat and pulled the watch from his pocket. "It's almost 4:30, Dana, we need to get ready to go to dinner. Just drop me by my car, then I'll go home and come back for you, ok?"

"How about if I drop you at your car, but when you come back, you just leave it at my building?" I asked. "I love my car, Mitch, and I really want to take it tonight. Can we, please?"

He laughed. "I've created a monster. Ok, we can take your car, but I get to drive, ok? I've decided I want my turn." He said.

I pretended to ponder the question. "Well, if you promise not to wreck it, then I guess it'll be ok." I told him.

"Gee, sweetheart, wrecking the car isn't among my priorities for the evening. So, I think you're safe."

A few minutes later I pulled up in front of my building. "You go ahead up, baby and get ready. Our reservations are for 5:30 so we don't have a lot of time, ok?" Mitch leaned over and kissed me.

"Wait, honey, where are we going? I need to know what I should wear." I said.

"Anything you want will be fine. We're going to Chandler's. Ever been there?" he asked.

"No, but I've heard it's a pretty fancy place. And expensive." I said.

He smiled. "It's fine, love. You just look pretty, ok? Not that you don't always look pretty, anyway." He kissed me again. "Scoot on up now, and I'll be back soon. I love you."

Mitch got out of the car, and waved to me, then turned to get into his car. I walked upstairs feeling on top of the world. I still couldn't believe he had actually bought me a car for my birthday. Most boyfriends got their girls jewelry or clothes. But I had the best man in the world.

Once inside my apartment, I took a quick shower and throwing on my robe, I decided to look for something to wear. Chandler's was a bit on the fancy side, and I assumed Mitch would be in a jacket and tie, so I opted for a very fitted red dress that I would couple with a black bag and heels. I decided to wear my hair up, and let a few strands come down just to frame my face. At 5:00, I heard Mitch knock on the door. Drat, I thought, I wasn't quite ready for him to see me. He knocked again. I didn't want him to get uptight, so I went to the door.

"Honey, is that you?" I asked.

"Who else would it be?" He answered.

"Well, I'm not quite ready yet. I need about five more minutes." I said.

I heard Mitch sigh. "Dana, that's fine. But do you expect me to stay out in the hallway and wait? I'd much rather come inside."

I gave the question serious consideration. "Tell you what. I'll unlock the door, but you have to count to twenty before you open it, ok?" I told him.

He sighed again. "Dana, this is stupid. Just open the door and let me come in, would you please?"

"You have to promise, Mitch. I'm not ready for you to see me yet." I said.

"Fine, Dana, whatever. Just unlock the door." I could hear the agitation beginning to fill his voice.

"Promise me first." I said.

"Ok, Dana, I promise. Geesh!" He said.

I unlocked the door, then hightailed it back into the bedroom as fast as I could, slamming the door behind me. About ten seconds later, I heard Mitch come in and close the door behind him.

"You didn't count to twenty!" I yelled out to him.

"I count fast." He yelled back. "Please hurry, Dana, we're going to be late."

I finished my makeup, put on my shoes, and threw a few essentials into my black bag. A minute later, I emerged from the bedroom. Mitch was standing with his back toward me, hands in his pockets, looking at the pictures on my wall. He turned around slowly, and his eyes ran over me once, twice, then again. I did the same, as he was dressed in a black suit with a white shirt and a red tie designed with tiny blue diamonds. He was breathtaking.

"Wow, that was definitely worth the wait." He said, walking over to me. "You look incredible, as always."

"Thank you, and I must say, you aren't too bad yourself." I told him, smiling brightly.

"I have an idea." He said. "Let's skip dinner, and go right for dessert. What do you say?" He leaned down to kiss me.

"That sounds very tempting." I said, kissing him back.

Mitch gave me a hug. "But, if we do that, I won't be able to show you off. So, I guess we better go, and we can take up where we left off later."

Mitch helped me on with my coat and I handed him the keys to my car. "This is only because I trust you." I teased.

Mitch stopped in his tracks. "Repeat that last comment." He said, playfully.

"What? I said I trust you." I repeated.

"That's good to know." He said.

About ten minutes later, we were inside Chandler's. Mitch took my coat and checked it for me, then approached the maitre d'. "I have reservations for 5:30, under Mitchell Tarrington the third."

"That would be for two, correct sir?" The maitre d' asked.

"That's right. And I also had a special request as well. Did you get that?" Mitch asked.

"Oh, yes, sir, we did take care of that for you. Not a problem. Right this way."

Mitch extended his arm to me in a very formal fashion, and I took it, feeling like the Queen of England. I just knew as we walked in that all the other women had to be jealous that they were just with ordinary men, and I was with Mitchell Tarrington.

Just as I had expected, Chandler's was high class all the way. The entire dining room was dimly lit, the lamps giving off a romantic glow. Each table was adorned with a deep wine colored tablecloth, the napkins slightly lighter in color, the chairs of cherry wood with seat cushions in a paisley design of the same colors. As we approached our table, Mitch held out the chair for me. Laying on the table in my spot was a single red rose, and there was a bottle chilling next to the table. The maitre d' handed us each a menu, and was off.

"Mitchell, this is so beautiful. Did you send this rose for me?" I asked, picking it up and taking in its sweet aroma.

"Of course." Then he picked up the bottle. "And I thought this might be appropriate." It was actually a bottle of sparkling grape juice. I smiled.

"What, no wine?" I laughed, and Mitch grimaced playfully. "Nice touch." I said. "How about we try some of that?" I asked.

"Sure," Mitch said, starting to open the bottle. He poured some into my wine glass, then took some for himself. Holding up his glass, he smiled. "A toast, to my beautiful future bride. Happy Birthday, Dana."

"Thank you, Mitch." I said, lightly touching his glass with mine and taking a sip. "That's pretty good, isn't it?" I said.

Mitch was staring at me, his face somewhat expressionless, but his eyes full of love. "Absolutely." He answered.

We studied the menu for a few minutes and I looked up at Mitch. He must have read the look on my face, because he reached across the table and took my hand.

"Dana, don't look at the prices. Just order whatever sounds good to you, ok? I mean it." He said, smiling. "I've got it covered." I started to protest, but Mitch held up his hand. "If you don't, I'll order for you." He said firmly.

I sighed and began to look back over the menu. There were many good choices and I narrowed it down to a few, but I still wasn't sure about the price thing. I decided I would be sneaky by letting Mitch order first, then just order the same thing for myself. I closed my menu and smiled at him.

"Did you decide on something, sweetheart?" Mitch asked, still browsing.

"Yes, actually, I did." I said, taking a drink.

"Oh, well, I can't decide, so I'll just get what you're having. I trust your judgment." Mitch smirked at me, adjusted his glasses, and put his menu down.

I glanced at him. He took a drink and then sat back. "So, what is it we're going to be eating tonight?" He asked smugly.

I picked the menu back up. "You know, I was just thinking maybe I would take another look." I said.

Mitch chuckled. "That's what I thought." He smiled at me. "Sweetheart, please, just get what you want. If I couldn't afford to bring you here, I wouldn't have. Besides, you're starting to make me feel badly."

I looked at him. "Why?"

"Because, Dana, I want you to enjoy your dinner, not analyze whether or not I'll have to take out a loan to pay for it."

I sighed. "Ok, sweetie, I'm sorry. It's just, well, I'm not used to all this." I said.

"Well, Dana, get used to it, because I plan to spoil you." He smiled.

I finally decided on a filet mignon and Mitch on some sort of veal. The names of everything were so fancy, I couldn't even begin to pronounce them, let alone know what they were. Steaks are usually pretty safe, I thought.

"So, Mitch, where are we going dancing tonight?" I asked. "I'm really excited about it."

"I thought I'd take you to a special club that I know about. I'm sure you're going to like it, and I hear the band is awesome." He said.

The maitre d' approached our table. "Mr. Tarrington, you have a call. You can take it right out here in the foyer. Follow me."

"Gee, wonder who that could be." He said, standing up. "Excuse me a minute, love. I'll be right back."

"Ok, Mitch." I said, as he walked away. Strange, I thought. Who knew he was bringing me here?

A few minutes later, just as our dinner salads arrived, Mitch returned. "It was my mom." He said. "She said that she needs me to stop over before we go out. She didn't really say why, just that it was kind of important."

I gave him a funny look. "Mitchell, how did your mom even know we were here?" I asked him.

Mitch looked at me as if I had asked the million dollar question. "Oh, I, uh, talked to her this morning and I told her." He said, taking a bite of his salad. "You know, I'm really hungry. That pizza just didn't stay with me very long."

"Yeah, ok." I said. Something about this whole thing seemed odd, but I decided not to let him know I felt that way.

"Now, you do know I'll be working pretty much all day tomorrow, right? And rehearsal tomorrow night. I have you working at the bistro just from 4-6, so you can come to rehearsal with me, or you and the girls can go dress shopping or whatever." He took another bite. "By the way, when is this picture thing on Friday?"

"It's at eleven. I'm taking an early lunch from work. I can just meet you there." I told him.

"What do you want me to wear? Something like what I have on, or just a shirt and tie, or something more casual?" He asked.

"What do you want to wear, Mitch?" I asked, deciding to let him decide.

He smiled. "Sweetheart, I know better than to answer that on my own. You know what you're wearing, and I know that you *also* know what you want *me* to wear. So, tell me, or I just may show up in my underwear."

I laughed. "That could be interesting, but if you do that, I'd be forced to wear my pajamas, you know, the ones with the feet. Or, we could both wear our pajamas and make it really special."

He smiled. "Considering I don't own any pajamas, that really would be interesting if they shot the pictures in what I sleep in."

I put down my fork and looked at him. "I know I'm going to regret asking this, Mitch, but just what do you normally sleep in?"

Mitch looked up at me over the top of his glasses, an impish grin slowly spreading across his face. He didn't have to give me an answer, because I already knew it. I must have blushed, because he laughed. "That's right dear." He said.

"You're joking, aren't you, Mitchell?" I asked. He shook his head.

I slowly lowered my head, and Mitch laughed again. "Does that bother you, sweetheart? It shouldn't, after all, I will be your husband, you know."

"It's fine, Mitch, really. Let's change the subject, ok?" I said.

He smiled. "Sometimes I do wear my boxers, too. If it makes you feel any better."

"That's great, Mitchell. Now, let's change the subject." I said.

Mitch reached out for my hand. "You are going to be so much fun." He said, chuckling.

Our meals arrived and they were delicious beyond belief. After we were sufficiently stuffed, Mitch asked the waiter for the check. "I thought we could get dessert later, if that's ok with you." He said.

"No, I'm stuffed. I couldn't eat another bite right now anyway." I said.

Mitch paid the check, picked up my coat, and we headed out. It was a beautiful evening, the sky full of light from the moon, and too many stars to count. It was crisp, but not windy, so the night air was actually tolerable. As Mitch reached for the door handle to let me into the car, I stopped him. I slipped my arms around him and gave him a big kiss.

"Wow, what was that for?" he asked.

"Because you are about the best man in the world." I said.

"Ok, I'll buy that." He said, chuckling.

"No, Mitchell, I mean it. This has already been an incredible day, and it's not even over yet." I said.

"No it isn't, and I'd love to stand here with you like this, but sweetheart, I'm really cold." He said.

He put me into the car and raced around to the other side, jumping in himself. He started the car and after a minute or two, put the heater on full force.

"Honey, are you feeling ok? I don't want you to get sick. Maybe we should stop off and get your coat." I told him.

"I'm fine, Dana, I just caught a chill, that's all. I'm already starting to warm up." He said reassuringly. "Now, let's stop out at Mom and Dad's and then we can go dancing."

The drive to the Tarrington's was pleasant, and Mitch seemed to be in an especially happy mood. I looked up at the night sky through the window of the car, and the closer we got to his parents' house, the more stars there seemed to be.

We pulled into the long driveway, and I could see another car parked near the house. "Oh, honey, it looks like Chris and Trudy may be here, too." I said.

"Yeah, I see that." Mitch replied. He was thinking that he hoped the others had hidden their cars around the back. He was relieved to see they weren't there as he got closer. As Mitch came around and opened the door for me, I paused to look up at the sky.

"Millions of them, aren't there?" He commented.

"Yeah, isn't it pretty?" I said. "So romantic."

Mitch smiled. "I get the hint." He said, and he leaned over to kiss me. But as he pulled away, I pulled him back again, and brought him to me even tighter, kissing him again.

"We should go in, sweetheart." Mitch said softly.

"Not yet." I said back, pulling him to me again. This time, he didn't resist, and he started to kiss my neck.

"Dana, I don't think we should do this right now." He said. "They're going to start wondering where we are."

"I'm sure they can figure it out. They were young once." I commented, pulling him to me again. Mitch returned my kiss more passionately now, and he was starting to breathe more rapidly. He began to kiss my neck, and he whispered in my ear.

"Sweetheart, we really need to stop or I may get carried away." He said.

I pulled away from him. "I know the feeling." I said. "Let's go inside." I smiled.

Mitch put his arm around me and pulled me to him, kissing my forehead. "I love you, Dana."

We stepped inside, and Mitch took off his glasses to wipe away the steam. Alexander greeted us and took my coat, as Chris walked up to us with a smile.

"Took you a while to come in. Anything wrong?" he said, looking at Mitch.

Mitch replaced his glasses, smiling. "No, we were just admiring the stars." He said.

Chris reached out as he had before, and wiped a smudge of lipstick off Mitch's cheek. "Those stars can be something else, can't they?" He smiled knowingly at his little brother.

"Yes, they sure can." Mitch said. Then he cleared his throat. "So, where's Mom and Dad? Mom said she needed me to stop over for some reason."

Chris proceeded down the hallway. "I think they're in the dining room. We were just getting ready to have a little snack."

Mitch smiled at me, and took me by the hand. "Come on, love, let's go see what she wanted, ok?"

The dining room doors were closed, which I thought to be somewhat unusual, and Chris opened them, and stepped aside.

"Surprise!" Mitch's entire family was gathered in the dining room, which was decorated with streamers and balloons, and a giant homemade banner that said "Happy Birthday, Dana."

I looked up at Mitch. "Mitchell Jacob Tarrington, I don't believe you. You are so....."

"Terrible!" Mitch and Chris said at the same time, laughing. Mitch turned to me and smiled. "Happy Birthday, sweetheart. I hope you like your little surprise." He said.

"Happy Birthday, Dana." Chris said, giving me a kiss on the cheek. "By the way, you look very pretty tonight." He added.

"Thanks, Chris." I said. "Gee, I didn't expect this at all." I said to everyone.

"Well, that fiancé of yours arranged it all." Olivia said, smiling.

"Yeah, the little sneak. Two surprises in one day. I'm afraid to go home tonight." Everyone laughed.

"Two surprises, Dana?" Paul asked. "What was the first one?"

Mitch smiled. "It may be a little dark now to see it clearly, but it's parked out front." Mitch pointed in that direction.

"You mean he bought you a car?" Trudy asked.

"He did, and it is so incredible! Why don't you come and see?" I said.

Everyone jumped up at the same time and it was like a stampede to get to the door. Trudy turned to Chris. "You never bought me a car, Christopher. Must be nice to be spoiled like that."

Chris threw up his hands, and then proceeded to bring one down, smacking Mitch on the shoulder. "Do you live to get me in trouble, little brother, or is it purely coincidental?"

"That hurt, Chris." Mitch said, rubbing his shoulder. "I didn't do anything wrong. You did."

"What?" Chris said, surprised at Mitch's comment. "I'm not the one who keeps bragging about all the money he's spending on his girl. You are."

Mitch stopped and turned to Chris. "Who's bragging? And besides, Chris, it's my money. I can do with it what I want. If I want to buy something for Dana, and it'll make her happy, I'm going to do it. I don't think I need to seek your permission first."

"Well, the night you announced you were going to Hawaii, do you know how long I had to hear about that?" he said.

"That's not my problem." Mitch said. "Stop being so cheap and take Trudy to Hawaii. Buy her a car. Do whatever, but don't blame me for your problems."

"The only problem I have, Mitchell, is your boastful attitude." Chris said.

"What's wrong, Chris? Are you feeling guilty and trying to blame me?" Mitch said. "Or," he laughed, "did Trudy get mad and cut you off and you're upset about that?"

"That's it, Mitchell, you little showoff. How about we step outside with this, and we'll see how you can show off then?" Chris challenged.

"That works for me." Mitch said, taking off his jacket and tie. He was rolling up his sleeves and following Chris toward the door when Jake stepped in.

"Where are you two going?" Jake asked his sons.

"Outside, Dad. For a little fresh air." Chris answered. "Mitchell has something he wants to show me, don't you Mitch?"

"Yeah, how to shut your big mouth." Mitch answered.

"Hold it right there. Come here, both of you." Jake ordered. The two stopped and turned around.

"I don't know what this is about, but I want it settled here and now. You are not about to ruin this night for Dana, understand?" Jake said firmly. Chris and Mitch just looked at each other with set jaws and angry eyes.

Mitch spoke first. "I don't brag about anything, Chris. Dana needed a car, I bought her one. She wanted to go to Hawaii, I'm taking her. She wants a big wedding, with all the trim, I'm giving her one. If you have a problem with that, I'm sorry. And if your wife gets upset because I give Dana more than you give her, maybe you should listen to her, because maybe, Christopher, just maybe, she's trying to tell you something you need to hear."

Jake stood back and listened to what Mitch had said. Then he waited for Chris to react.

"Mitchell, I just want to know one thing. Where are you getting all this money? I know your trust is gone, and I know Dad isn't giving it to you, so where is it coming from?" Chris asked, coming very close to Mitch.

Mitch bit his lip and looked at his father. He wasn't sure if he should say anything or if he did, how his father would react about him selling his Tarrington stock. He looked back at Chris. "That's my business, Chris." He said. "But just know it isn't from any dishonest means."

Jake looked at his two sons. "If you need to discuss this further, go off somewhere and do it. But I mean discuss, with your mouths, not your fists." He said firmly. "Right now, I want you to shake hands and Mitchell, put your jacket and tie back on. I don't want Dana to suspect anything."

Chris reluctantly extended his hand to Mitch, but instead, Mitch turned, and picking up his jacket and tie, he walked into the front room. Chris dropped his hand and walked back into the dining room. Jake followed his youngest son.

Mitch was standing before a large mirror on the wall, retying his tie. He pulled the knot up, then unrolled his sleeves, buttoned them and put his jacket back on. Everyone was coming back in from the cold, chattering noisily and happily about the new car.

Olivia and I stopped in the doorway when we noticed the two men. "Is everything ok, Jake?" Olivia asked, looking from her husband to her son.

"Fine, dear, but I would like to talk to Mitchell for just a minute or two. Why don't you go into the dining room, and let Dana start opening her gifts?" Jake suggested.

I looked at Mitch. "Go ahead, sweetheart. I'll be there in a minute." He said.

I nodded and Olivia placed her hand on my shoulder, leading me down the hall. But as I glanced back, I noticed a sad look in Mitch's eyes.

"Mitch, tell me what's going on." Jake said.

Mitch was still looking into the mirror. "There's nothing to tell, Dad. Chris got all hot and heavy because Trudy said he never bought her a car. I think he's just feeling guilty and needed someone to blame. Conveniently enough for him, that always seems to be me."

Jake touched Mitch on the arm and motioned for him to sit down. Mitch obeyed.

"Son, you know that's not what I meant. Chris had a point. That car was not cheap. A trip to Hawaii, and a wedding for three hundred guests is not cheap. Buying a restaurant, and a car for yourself, and a $500 guitar. Not to mention the ring you put on Dana's finger. Mitchell, where are you getting all this money?"

Mitch bit his lip nervously. "Well, Dad, Chris is right. I did use my trust money for my car, for the guitar, to pay the down payment on Gartano's and to buy Dana's ring. I still have a little nest egg left for us, too. The other things, well, I bought with the money I got when I sold my stock in the company."

Jake folded his hands and sat silently looking at his son. How did he raise a child that was so strong willed, so independent? Then he looked up and saw his own reflection in the mirror across from him, and he knew the answer. Mitch was just like he had been at that age. He remembered his own father asking him why he didn't want any financial help from him, and he remembered the feeling he had inside when Tarrington Industries became a reality. He had accomplished it all on his own, merely by his own sweat and blood. He knew how much more that made it mean to him. He looked at Mitch now, and he understood exactly why he had done what he had, seven years ago and today.

"Mitchell, that could have been a good means of income for you and Dana. It could have come in handy in case......" Mitch cut him off.

"In case what, Dad? In case I fail?" Mitch said, angrily. "I don't plan to fail, Dad, not at the restaurant and not as a musician. I don't set myself up to fail."

Jake looked at his young son. "No one does, Mitchell. But don't be naïve, son. Things happen. Anything could happen, and then what would you do?"

"Dad, the one thing I want to do is take care of Dana on my own. I want to build a life with her based on the results of what I do, not the results of how well Tarrington Industries does. I sold the stock, Dad, because as long as I had it, and was gaining from it, I wouldn't have felt like I was doing what I needed to do. You might not understand that, but it's just how I feel. It's how I've always felt. That's why it was so important for me NOT to work for you. I wanted to prove to myself that I had what it takes to make it without relying on your money, like I always had. That's why I spent the trust, too. And look at me, Dad." Mitch stood up and extended his arms, as if to invite his father to actually look at him. "I made it."

Jake stood up and stepped closer to Mitch. "Mitchell, I'm not upset with you. In fact, I understand. Seven years ago, I understood. I was angry, Mitchell, but I understood. I wasn't angry because you refused to take a job with me. I was angry because when I looked at you, Mitch, I saw myself, just like I do right now. I didn't want to see you struggle the way I did, and I don't want to see you and Dana struggle that way, either, son."

"But Dad, look what that struggle got you. It made you everything you are today. Why don't you just let me find out for myself?" Mitch stepped closer to his father. "I don't plan to fall, Dad, but if I should happen to, I need to know that you'll be there to help me get back up again. I know I have Dana, but I need to know I have you, too."

Jake reached out for Mitch and pulled him into his arms. "I will always be here for you son. I love you and I'm proud of the man you've become. If you ever need me, I'm right here."

Jake pulled away from his son, but still held his hands on his arms. Mitch smiled. "Thanks, Dad, I love you, too."

Jake put his arm around Mitch's shoulder, and tousled his hair like he used to do when he was a little boy. "I think we have a party to go to now, don't you?"

Mitch nodded. "And what a party it's going to be!" He answered.

17

We were all gathered in the dining room when Mitch and Jake entered. Jake still had his arm around Mitch, and they looked happy. I smiled at Mitch, and patting his dad on the shoulder, he walked over to me.

"Mitch, is everything ok?" I asked. "You didn't look happy when we came in earlier."

He smiled. "Everything's fine, Dana. Dad and I were just talking, that's all. I'll tell you about it later, ok?"

"Ok" I said. "I've started opening my gifts. Come and see all the things I got!" I said excitedly, pulling his hand. I led him to the spot where I had been sitting, and there was a pile of gifts, sweaters, tops, gloves and a jacket. He smiled.

"Just like Christmas again, isn't it?" he said.

"Yes, and I still have these left to open!" I said, pointing to three more.

He sat down next to me. "Well, open them." He instructed.

Julia had gotten me a pretty sundress to wear in Hawaii, Angelina a pair of earrings, and Trudy got me a cookbook.

"I'm sure you already know how to cook, but I also know Mitch likes to eat, so maybe you can try some new things." She said.

"I like that, thanks." I said.

"Shall we have cake now?" Olivia asked.

"Not quite yet, Mom. I'd rather go into the other room first, for a little while, ok?" Mitch said.

"Sure, Mitchell, that's fine dear. Let's go everyone." Olivia said, leading the way. Everyone was following her into the family room, but no one seemed to be stopping to sit down. I stopped Mitch and he put his hands in his pockets and turned to me.

"What is it, sweetheart?" he asked.

"Where is everyone going?" I asked him.

"Why don't we go find out?" he responded, coaxing me along.

We walked through the family room and I noticed everyone seemed to be migrating toward the rec room. Then I noticed why. Through the open doors I could see that virtually all the furniture that had been in there had been moved either out of the way or completely out of the room. I also noticed all the instruments were set up for the band, as if they were planning a rehearsal. Mitch took me by the hand and led me into the middle of the room.

"Welcome to the Tarrington Dance Club." He said playfully. "Tonight, we are featuring a fantastic band which hales all the way from Philadelphia, PA. Let's give it up for Ace."

Mitch's family broke into applause, and the side door to the room opened. In came the guys, who had evidently been waiting there the whole time. They all smiled at me and took their places at their instruments. Mitch kissed me and trotted up to the front.

"Thank you, everyone. We have a very special occasion we're celebrating tonight, so we're going to give you a very special concert." Mitch pulled out his headset microphone and put it on. "It's gonna get loud in here but let's have some fun, shall we?"

He cued the guys and they started playing. Mitch walked up to me and took me by the hand.

"I told you I was taking you dancing and I am. Just on my terms, that's all." He took off his jacket, loosened his tie, and started dancing with me. Everyone else was dancing too, and the kids even rushed in to join us, followed closely by Alexander, who stood at the back smiling. The guys finished the first song and we applauded.

"Now, I *am* going to dance with you, Dana. But, well, I have to admit, I really did need a rehearsal tonight. So, we're going to run through Saturday's set with you all."

As always, he was fantastic and hit each note perfectly. He seemed to be having the time of his life, dancing and singing for me. I was, too. I remembered the few birthday parties I'd had as child, but they were never anything like this.

Jake and Olivia were watching their son with pride and affection. "That boy is something else." Jake told her.

"He certainly is, Jake. He reminds me so much of you when you were young. We never danced like that, but you could cut a pretty good rug yourself at one time." She replied.

"What do you mean, at one time? I still can." He said, taking Olivia by the hand. He was dancing what looked to be a jitterbug with her. Mitch got a huge smile on his face, and we all stepped aside to watch them take the floor. Mitch kissed my cheek, and ran back to the front to give a full performance. They finished the song and everyone applauded Jake and Olivia.

"That was awesome, Dad!" Julia said.

"Yeah, who would have known you could dance?" Chris said. "You're really good!"

Jake smiled and looked at Mitch. "Where do you think he gets his talent from?" he said.

Mitch smiled back at his dad. "Let's do a slow one, guys. Set list, number 5."

Mitch walked back out to me. "Before we do this, though, I have to say something. I've never written anything before, so I don't know how this will turn out, but I wrote this for you, Dana. I know you'll understand it, even if no one else does." He cued the guys and they began to play.

Mitch took me in his arms and he sang softly and sweetly, and as I heard the words, my mind drifted back to the night I first saw him, and the way he had looked into my eyes.

"From Day One, I knew there was something about you, you captured my thoughts, my heart, my soul. From Day One, I knew I'd never make it without you, and girl, I won't ever let you go." Mitch sang, and as the music ended, he looked into my eyes with such love that I felt like I could see his very soul. Then he kissed me and smiled.

"I love you Mitch." I said.

"Yeah, I love you too." He said back.

He turned back toward the guys. "Let's wrap this up!" He said, and they started playing again. This time, Mitch took up his guitar and played along. A few songs later, we were all applauding and screaming. Julia, Angelina, Trudy and I looked at each other. We gathered at the front of the room and in unison yelled, "We love you Mitch," just as we had the night at the club. Mitch laughed.

"Ok, guys, how about some birthday cake?" He asked everyone. "Oh, but first........"

He cued the guys into *Happy Birthday* and everyone sang to me. I didn't know whether to laugh or to cry, but I decided to stand there and just smile. I hadn't even noticed that Olivia and Alexander had snuck out and came back in with a huge birthday cake, decorated in pink and blue flowers, with the words, "Happy 23rd Birthday, Dana" written on top.

Mitch came and put his arm around me, and now the emotion was getting to me. I felt a tear drip down my face. He smiled and wiped it away.

"I hope that's a happy tear." He said.

I looked at him. "It is. Thank you for the best birthday I've ever had." I said. Then I turned to his family. "Thank you for all of this. It really means a lot to me." Alexander lit the candle and I looked at Mitch. Then closing my eyes, I made my wish and blew it out.

"Gonna tell me what you wished for?" Mitch asked.

"Don't you know? Birthday wishes are sacred." I told him, and he smiled.

We spent a few more hours with the family and after Mitch loaded my car with my gifts, he announced that we should be going. I was saying goodbyes and talking to the girls about dresses and things, when I saw Chris walk up to him, and again he extended his hand.

"Are you ready to shake it this time, little brother, or are you still upset with me?" Chris asked.

Mitch was biting his lip. "Just don't go blaming me for what happens in your marriage, Chris. I'm not responsible for those things."

Chris nodded. "You were right, Mitch. I've just gotten so caught up in the day to day that I forget about what really matters sometimes. Thanks for helping me see that."

Mitch put his hand in Chris's and they shook. Chris smiled. "You're always ready for a fight, though, aren't you, Mitchell?"

Mitch smiled. "Only because I know I could take you." He said.

Thanking everyone again, Mitch and I walked out the door, the band close behind. I turned to all of them.

"Guys, once again you are going to knock the place down this weekend. It amazes me that you can get things so perfectly just on the first try." I said to them.

Mitch laughed. "Oh, my dear, that set was not perfect, trust me." He turned to the guys. "Tomorrow, one o'clock for a quick run through. Then, Friday at four. Got it?"

"Yeah, Trip, we got it. Tomorrow at four, Friday at two." Shep joked.

"Get out of here, you losers!" Mitch laughed. "See you all tomorrow."

Mitch put me into the car, and got in, starting it up. He waited for the guys to go, then pulled the car out and started down the drive.

"I can't believe all the things you pulled off today, Mitch." I told him. "This was an absolutely amazing day."

"I just wanted your birthday to be special, just like you are." Mitch said, smiling.

"I've never had a better birthday." I told him. "I'll never be able to top it for you." I said.

"Listen, Dana, we'll be married by then. I'm sure I'll be able to think of a few ways you can top it." He smiled.

I smacked his arm. "I swear, you are so bad." I told him, laughing as he tried to rub his arm and drive at the same time.

Once we got back to my apartment, Mitch carried everything in for me and piled it in the bedroom. "Well, love, I really should get going. It's pretty late and we both have an early day tomorrow." He said, giving me a gentle hug.

"I wish you didn't have to go. I like having you here with me." I said.

"Soon, sweetheart. Soon, we'll be together all the time. Won't that be nice?" he said.

"Yes, it will be." I answered. "Mitch?"

"Yeah, Dana?"

"Thank you again for everything. I can't ever remember a better day." I said.

"You're welcome, love. I'm glad you enjoyed it." Mitch gave me another hug and a kiss. "Happy Birthday." He said softly, opening the door. "Pleasant dreams, sweetheart. I love you."

"I love you too, Mitch. Sweet dreams." I said as I kissed him again and slowly closed the door.

Mitch and I spent the next few days busily working and taking the time we could in between to make wedding preparations. Our engagement pictures were done, and Mitch decided to wear the outfit he wore the night he proposed. "It's my lucky outfit." He told me with a smile.

Saturday afternoon, we were working at Gartano's and having a particularly busy day. Mitch seemed to be extremely stressed, and I just wrote it off as a combination of the busyness of the day, and the fact that he had a show that night at the club. I decided it best just to do my work and try to stay out of his way as much as I could.

Finally, about three o'clock, I went into the stock room to get a few bottles of wine off the rack that we needed up front. Though try as I could, I just couldn't reach the last bottle that I needed. Steadying myself as much as possible, I stepped onto the bottom shelf of the rack. The rack swayed for a minute and I put one foot back on the floor, holding it there until the rack was level again. Slowly, I placed the foot back onto the rack, and then brought it up to the second shelf. Stretching as far as I could, I got a hold of the bottle. At that instant, I felt two hands around my waist, pulling me off the rack.

"For crying out loud, Dana, just what do you think you're doing? You could kill yourself!" Mitch said, putting me on the ground.

"I couldn't reach it, Mitchell. I had to get it somehow." I replied.

Mitch had an angry look on his face. "Why didn't you just ask me? Or did you suddenly forget I'm something like, ten inches taller than you are?"

"You were busy. I didn't want to bother you." I said softly.

"I'm not that busy, Dana. Don't do this again, understand? I don't need you falling and getting hurt." Mitch said firmly.

I sighed. "Stop treating me like a baby, Mitchell. I do it all the time. I'm not going to fall."

Mitch took me by the arms and looked right into my eyes. "Dana Walker. I said don't do it again. Is that clear?" Mitch took the keys from his pocket. "No, you know what? I'll just lock the door, and if you need something, you'll have to come and get me."

"I'm sorry, Mitch. But you are overreacting." I said smugly.

Mitch took me by the hand and led me out into the hallway. "Those racks aren't made for you to be climbing on, Dana. You don't weigh much, but they still won't support you." He put his hand on the doorknob. "Now, is there anything else you need from in here?"

"No." I said.

"Ok, then, I'm locking the door." Mitch pulled the door shut and turned the key, then put them back in his pocket. "Now, come on, we only have about another hour or so." Mitch turned to walk away, then noticed I wasn't following. He turned back around. "Dana, let's go. We have customers. If you haven't noticed, we're just a little busy today."

I sighed loudly and started out after him. He stopped and turned around again to face me.

"Dana, I love you and I don't want you to risk getting hurt. Do you understand?" he said firmly but softly.

"Yes, Mitch, I understand." I said.

"Good, now let's move so we can get out of here on time, ok?" Mitch turned and walked back into the bistro, this time with me following.

Mitch went to make rounds on the floor, which is what we called it when he talked to the customers. I continued to do my work, and around four o'clock, I hung up my apron in the office. Mitch followed me in and closed the door behind us.

"Dana, sit down, I want to talk to you for a minute." Mitch said, pointing to the couch. I sat down and he came to sit beside me. He took my hand and looked into my eyes.

"Look, sweetheart, I'm sorry I got so upset earlier. I just don't want to see anything happen to you, that's all. I could just picture that rack falling over with you, and it scared me."

"I'm sorry, Mitch, I didn't mean to scare you. I should have asked for your help, but you've been so tense today, and we were so busy, I didn't want to bother you." I put my other hand on top of his. "Why are you so uptight, Mitch? Is something wrong?"

He signed. "I've just been thinking about us playing tonight. We're the house band now, Dana. That means we have to do everything just right. If we don't, it not only ruins our rep, but also the club's. That's a big responsibility, Dana. A big one."

I made a circle on the top of his hand with my finger. "Mitch, you guys are great. You're great. I don't think you should be worrying about it." I told him.

"Well, that's easier said than done, Dana. You know me. Mr. Perfectionist." He smiled.

"Mitchell, no one is perfect, not me, not you, no one. If we were, think of how boring the world would be. No one will even know if you make a mistake. Heck, I thought you guys were great in rehearsal the other night, and you told me you made all kinds of mistakes. Only a trained ear could pick up on it, sweetie."

He smiled. "Yeah, you're probably right. But, right now, this trained ear is very hungry and needs to be fed. Wanna join me?" He asked.

"What did you have in mind?" I asked.

He smiled. "Truthfully, I was going to go home for a TV dinner and let you go home and change. But, I'd much rather be with you. So, let's go get something, shall we?"

"I have a better idea. Do you have anything at home worth actually cooking, or is it truly the bachelor pad of the century?" I asked him.

"Does soup, bologna, macaroni and cheese, and maybe some peanut butter count? Oh, and I think I may have some potato chips, somewhere." Mitch added.

I shook my head. "You go home, Mitchell, and you shower and change. Then you come to my place, and I'll have dinner waiting. Ok?"

He smiled. "Sure you want to go through all that trouble? We can just go get something."

"No, I'll drop you off at home, you change, then jump in your car and come over. We can head to the club after we eat." I said, handing him his coat.

"Yes, dear. I keep forgetting that you are so assertive." He sighed.

"Well, get used to it." I said.

After dropping Mitch off at home, I hurried to my own place and started dinner. I figured he was probably getting a little tired of Italian food, so I opted for a chicken and rice dish my Grammy used to make for me. It was quick and simple, and tasted good, and I thought Mitch would like it. I prepared some green beans and made some homemade drop biscuits from a dry mix I had, then popped into the shower while everything was baking.

Just as I was getting out of the shower, Mitch knocked on the door. Why does he do that, I thought. I was really needing to talk to him about the timing issue. I dried off quickly and grabbed my robe, wrapping it tightly around me. I ran out to the door. "Just a second, sweetie." I called.

"Dana, not again." He said.

I opened the door, and Mitch's face lit up as he stepped inside. He reached out to hug me but I backed away.

"Dana, why can't I give you a hug?" He said, smiling and looking me up and down.

"Because you can't. Not yet." I said.

Mitch stepped closer to me. "Why not?" he said.

"Because you know I just got out of the shower, Mitchell, and you also know that I don't have anything on under this robe. And until I do have something on, you aren't coming near me." I said, taking a step backward.

Mitch smiled and raised his eyebrows. "And what if I do?" he said, stepping closer to me still.

"I'll run from you!" I said.

"What if I can run faster and I catch you?" He said, taking another step in my direction.

"Won't happen." I said. And with that I did turn to run, Mitch right behind me. I slammed the bedroom door and locked it, and I could hear the sound of his laughter on the other side.

"Mitchell," I said.

"I know," he said, trying to catch his breath. "I'm terrible." He was still laughing, and it made me smile.

I got dressed quickly and found Mitch in the kitchen, setting the table for me.

"Thanks, honey." I said, as I walked up to him.

"Can I give you a hug now?" he asked.

"I suppose so, now that I'm fully dressed." I said, giving him a hug and a little kiss.

"You were dressed before." He said. "You're much too modest." He smiled.

"Yes, and it's going to stay that way." I said.

I pulled everything out of the oven, filled our plates and we sat down. Mitch looked at me and smiled. "I guess I don't ever have to worry about starving to death." He said. "I could really never pick up on this cooking thing. Every time I've ever attempted to cook, they've had to call in the fire department."

I laughed. "It's not that bad, is it?" I asked.

Mitch chuckled. "Almost. In fact, one time I baked cupcakes. They were so hard that we actually used one of them for a hockey puck."

I looked at him and laughed. "Mitchell, you are such a goof." I said.

He was smiling. "No, baby, I'm not lying. Ask my brother and sisters. Chris thought it would be neat to try it out, so we went out on the pond behind the house and we did. My cupcake was our hockey puck. Until Julia hit it into the snow and we couldn't find it."

We were both laughing hard, and I could actually picture poor Mitch's cupcake being scooted around on the ice. "Don't worry, Mitch, I'll be happy to do all the cooking."

"Well, that's good, because I don't think we'd be too healthy if we ate mine. But, I can clean and do laundry and iron." He smiled.

"I really hate to do laundry, and I avoid ironing whenever possible." I told him. "It's just so time consuming."

"Don't worry, we'll balance everything out." He said.

Mitch had a second helping of everything, and seemed to be enjoying it. After we finished eating, he announced that it was time for us to go.

"Why don't you go ahead without me and I'll do the dishes and come in a little while?" I suggested. "I have this thing about leaving things undone."

Mitch looked around the kitchen and then at the clock. "Can we knock them out in, oh, ten minutes or less?" he said.

"Ok, let's do it." I said. With Mitch helping, we were done in about seven minutes.

"Now can we go?" He asked.

"I think it's safe now." I smiled.

We made it to the club with time to spare, and Mitch and I went to the table that had become our spot there. A few minutes later, Angelina and Julia came in, with Paul close behind. Mitch looked at Angelina.

"Hey, Ang, where's Jim? Isn't he coming?" Mitch asked. "And what about Chris and Trudy?"

Angelina smiled. "Well, we tried to call you at Dana's but you had already left. Trudy went into labor. They're all at the hospital."

Mitch smiled. "Hey, that's cool. I could be an uncle again before the night's over!" Then his face grew serious. "Was she doing ok? No problems, I mean?"

Angelina smiled at her brother's concern. "Just fine, last I heard. Chris called Jim and asked if he would ride with them. Mom went over to watch the kids. She said Chris was a basket case."

"You would think that after three already, that it wouldn't be such a big deal to him." Paul said.

"I don't know." Mitch said. "I think I'd be nervous, too. Just the whole idea of it is enough to make you nervous."

I smiled. "So, does that mean I'll have to request sedation for you when we have kids?" I asked him.

"Nah, I think I can handle it. But it may not be a bad idea to have them standing by, just in case." He added.

I laughed. "I can just see us in our Lamaze classes. I'll be teaching Mitch how to breathe!" I said, the girls agreeing with me.

Mitch stood up. "If you girls are just going to pick on me, I'm leaving." He said, but with a big smile.

"You do that, Mitchell, and then we can talk about you some more!" Julia teased.

The crowd was starting to file in, and it was easy to see that the house was going to be packed yet again. I looked up at the stage. Everything in its place, as usual. Newbie and Ty were taping down the set sheets near each instrument, and Zach was making sure everything was secured. Mitch came out on the stage and walked up to Ty.

"Hey, we need to change this." He told him, holding a song sheet, and pointing to something. Although he was not close to me, I was still able to make out the words, even though I didn't know what he was talking about.

"Change it to what? Why?" Ty asked him.

"We need to bring it down a key or something. I can't hit the note." Mitch said.

Ty gave him a funny look. "Mitch, that's E flat. Since when can't you hit E flat?"

"Since today, I guess. I have to really strain to get there. I can take a deep breath and bring it out, but it doesn't come easy." He said.

"Ok, let's try it in D and see if that helps. But I don't know if the rest of it will sound right, Trip." Ty argued. "Besides, you hit it fine in rehearsal. Throat giving you problems?" He asked.

"I don't think so, I just can't hit it for some reason." Mitch said.

"Hey, Trip, don't sweat it. We can do a quick check on the D, and if it doesn't feel right, I can back you. No one will know if you miss it, trust me." Ty told him.

I could see by the look on Mitch's face that Ty's answer wasn't good enough. "Forget it, Ty, just leave it alone. I'll hit it. Don't worry." He said, turning to walk away.

Ty started to speak, but Mitch interrupted. "Didn't I say leave it, Ty? It's all cool. I'll bring it out." And with that, he started to walk off stage again, then seemed to think twice and turned back around.

"Hey, Zach, on the third song, I want the riff. So, you take backup at that part, and let me have it, ok?" Mitch said, sounding rather authoritative.

Zach acted as if he didn't know how to respond to Mitch. "It sounded great all week, man, why change a sure thing?"

I saw Mitch take a deep breath. "Look, Zach, let's not make this hard, ok? I think it would tie in better if I do the riff and you back me up. So, be sure we have it straight so we don't fumble, ok?"

Zach looked at Newbie and Ty, who were both staring at Mitch in disbelief. "Ok, I'll make a note." He told Mitch.

"What about me, Trip?" Newbie spoke up. "Any changes for me..... boss?" Newbie sounded annoyed.

"No, why? And why did you call me 'boss'?" Mitch asked.

"Hey man, you just seem a little, well, bossy right now, that's all." Newbie said.

"I just don't want us sounding like a junior high garage band tonight." Mitch responded.

The guys looked at each other again. Ash overheard the last part of the conversation and stepped up to Mitch.

"What's the problem, Mitch?" he asked. "Is that how you think we've been sounding all week, like a bunch of kids?"

Mitch looked at his friends. "Did I say that? Of course I don't, I just want to make sure we're at our best tonight. No screw ups."

"We always are at our best, man." Ash took hold of Mitch's arm and pulled him aside. "What's up, dude? You seem really uptight."

"I'm fine, I just want this to go smoothly. Now, let's clear the stage before we get mobbed by a bunch of screaming little girls." He said, walking away.

Zach, Newbie and Ty just looked at one another, and then preceded to follow Mitch off the stage. I started up the stairs and called after Ash.

"What's up, Dana?" he asked.

"Ash, what was that all about?" I asked him.

Ash looked in the direction of where the guys were and then back to me. "Seems our front man thinks we need to make some changes tonight. We're sounding too much like a garage band to him."

I sighed. "I don't know what's up with him. He's been like this all day today. All he would tell me is that he thinks if you guys do anything wrong, even miss one little note, it will blow this whole deal for you."

"Ah, yes, the pressures that go with being Mitch the Perfect." He said, seeming somewhat annoyed. "You know, all of us know that about him, but he never tries to overpower us with it. Always seemed like he put the pressure on himself, not everyone else. This is different for him. He's usually a pretty nice guy, Dana, but today he's acting like an ......"

I cut off Ash's statement. "I'll go see if I can have a talk with him. If he goes on in this mood, he will blow it."

Ash looked at me with concern. "Dana, don't take this the wrong way, but please don't make him mad."

"I'll do my best. I think I'm learning how to handle him." I said.

I slipped backstage, and Mitch was standing alone, his back against the wall, seemingly lost in thought. I walked up to him and touched his arm.

"Dana, we go on in thirty minutes. What are you doing back here?" He asked.

"I want to talk to you, Mitch. It's important." I said.

Mitch turned toward me and put his hands in his pockets. "Ok, love, I'm listening. What's on your mind?" He said.

"Mitchell, I noticed the way you were talking to the guys out there a few minutes ago. You weren't very nice to them." I said.

"Dana, I made a few changes in the set. That's all. Did you want me to kiss each of them after and tell them I loved them?" His attitude was beginning to show.

"No, but you do need to respect them. You guys are a team, Mitchell. You work together. You told me that the rehearsals were great this week, that Ace never sounded better. What changed?" I planted myself firmly in front of him.

"The fact that we are now a big deal around here, Dana. I've been really thinking about that." He said.

"Yes, and I think you've given it too much thought. You are so afraid of making a mistake, of doing something wrong, that you are going to analyze every move these guys make tonight. You are going to make them so tense, Mitchell, that they will mess up. And so will you."

Mitch sighed. "So, my little expert, what do you suggest? That I let Zach take a riff he had to practice, like, eight straight times because he kept missing the end note? That I keep a song in a key I can't hit, possibly straining my voice and messing up the other ten songs in the set?"

"What I suggest, Mitchell Tarrington, is that you cool down, stop worrying, and apologize to your band. Then, change everything back the way it was during rehearsal and do it like you have been. If you keep changing everything, they aren't going to know what to do." I looked him right in the eye. "But the main thing I suggest is that you lose that attitude."

I started to walk away, but Mitch caught my arm and turned me around. "Fine, Dana, I'll do it your way. But if I screw this up, it will be on your shoulders. Not mine." Mitch called the guys into a huddle.

"Look, guys, I'm just really tense about all this tonight. Let's keep everything like we rehearsed, no changes. Let's make it work, ok?"

"Hey, man, we got your back. We're on it for you, Trip." Shep said.

"Yeah, Trip, we won't let you down. It's gonna rock." Newbie threw in.

Ash looked at him and smiled. "Mitch, just be cool. It's just another gig. Look at it like that."

Mitch looked at his band mates, then at me. "Guys, look, I don't know why I'm feeling like this tonight. I guess I just realized, we're the main act around here now. I want them to know they made the right choice."

"They did, Mitchell, they couldn't have gotten anyone better if they tried." I told him. "Now, take a few deep breaths, say a prayer, and give it your all."

Mitch smiled at me and gave me a hug. "Anything for you, love. I'm sorry."

"It's ok, I forgive you." I said. "But I'm not really the one you should be saying that to, Mitch."

Mitch looked at his friends, and they were all smiling at him. "Guys, I....."

"Keep it, Trip, it's all cool. No hard feelings." Newbie said.

Ty extended his hand to Mitch, who shook it and then pulled his friend into a hug. "You're the man, Mitch, don't forget that." Ty said. Mitch smiled.

"I'm going back out, Mitchell. Good luck!" I said, giving him a kiss for luck.

I smiled as I heard Mitch say, in his best British accent, "Let's rock and roll!"

The house lights dimmed and as the crowd settled to a buzz, Rob walked up on stage and the spotlight hit him. "Good evening, Studio 14, are you ready to party?" Everyone cheered. "Those of you who joined us last weekend got your first taste of our band, and those who didn't, well, get ready to rock. Studio 14 is proud to welcome, as our new house band, Ace!"

As Rob exited the stage, the lights came up and Mitch and the guys started into the first song. Mitch looked much more relaxed and he was seeming to just let the music take him. He was hitting all the notes perfectly, the guys not missing a beat and the energy they were bringing into the club was electrifying. More and more people had begun to stream into the club, and soon it was standing room only. I looked up at Mitch, catching his eye for just a moment, and he smiled at me. He wound down the first song, and started right into the second, giving it even more energy than the first. When Zach started into the guitar riff, Mitch stopped playing himself, ran over and put his arm around Zach's neck, pointing to him and prompting cheering from the crowd. Zach smiled brightly, knowing he had his front man's approval.

At the end of the second song, Mitch was breathing hard, but was far from ready to give it up. The third song was just as much fun for him, and he stood close to Ty on the harmony. Ty smiled at him, and put his head close to Mitch's as they sang together. The camaraderie they were sharing made me feel good inside. I knew it was Mitch's way of making up for they way he had acted earlier. And they were accepting it.

As the song ended, Mitch made his way back to the front of the stage. "Hello, Studio 14!" he called out to the cheering crowd. Everyone began to quiet down a little as Mitch continued to speak. "Man, I've never seen so many people in my life! We appreciate you coming out to hear us play tonight. We hope you enjoy the show!"

The band went into another tune and then another, and it was clear to see the crowd was enjoying themselves. Everyone was dancing, some with each other, others just standing by their tables, but not many people weren't on their feet. Julia, Angelina, Paul and I were dancing, too, and every once in a while the girls and I would call out to Mitch that we loved him, just for effect. He would usually notice us and smile.

Mitch strapped on the headset microphone and I wondered what he was up to. He came and sat down on the end of the stage, and beckoned for me to come over to him, so I did. I was amazed to see two security guards standing close by the stage, and Mitch motioned to them that it was ok to let me through. I got to him and he grabbed my hand and hopped down. The spotlight once again was on us, and I blushed.

"Those of you who were here last week probably remember this pretty lady, and most likely remember that kiss she delivered on the stage up there," Newbie did a little thing on the drums, and made us all laugh. "but if you don't, I'd like to introduce my fiancé, Dana Walker." Everyone applauded. "Dana just had a birthday a few days ago, and it gave me a chance to try out a song which I actually wrote for her. I'd like to share it with you tonight. It's called 'Day One'."

Mitch put his arm around me and began to sing with all the emotion he had in him at that moment. My heart melted and I felt as if the entire crowd had disappeared around us. Just as he was about to finish, he looked at me, then closed his eyes, and took a very deep breath, bringing the last note from deep within. But he didn't miss it, like he thought he would. He hit it straight on, his voice ringing like an angel.

The crowd went wild as Mitch gave me a hug and a kiss. "I love you, Dana." He said, moving the microphone away. "Thank you for helping me come to my senses."

"I love you too, Mitch. That was sensational." I told him and he smiled.

Then he let me go, ran back on the stage, and rocked the place again. A few songs later, the band took a break, and I was about to head backstage when I heard a familiar voice behind me. I turned to see Eddie, smiling at me.

"Dana, you look lovely tonight." He said, giving me a once over which actually made me a little uncomfortable.

"Thanks. What are you doing here, Eddie? I thought we already said our goodbyes." I inquired.

Eddie smiled. "Well, actually, Dana, I have a confession. I was here last weekend and I saw you then, but I couldn't get up the nerve to approach you. Since then, I've been thinking about things. I was watching you with your boyfriend......"

"Fiancé." I corrected. "Mitch is my fiancé, not my boyfriend."

"Ok, fiancé, and I realized, Dana, that I made a big mistake in letting you go. I realized that Kathleen isn't the one I really want to be with. I want to be with you, Dana. I realized that I was the one who should have placed the ring on your finger, not some other guy. Just now, when he sang that song to you, I thought to myself that if there was any chance left with you, I had to make my move now."

I couldn't believe what I was hearing. I stared at Eddie, my mind racing with questions. Why was he doing this? Why, after being gone from my life for four months, was he trying so desperately to come back in?

"Eddie, why are you doing this? Why all of a sudden are you trying to come between Mitch and I? Did Kathleen dump you, so you think you can patch it all up with me? You always did have a problem with being alone, Eddie. Well, now I guess you're going to have to get used to it." I said.

Eddie's face grew serious. "Look, Dana, all I'm trying to say is that I realized the mistake I made. I know you're engaged, but you aren't married yet. We have five years of history together, Dana. We moved out here to be together. I screwed that up four months ago, and I regret it. There's still time to make it right, and I want that chance." He looked down as if collecting his thoughts, then back at me again. "Dana, this whole engagement thing, it happened so fast. I know you think you're in love with this guy, but there's no way. I know you, Dana. This is just a rebound thing, it's not going to last."

Little did I know that Mitch had been sitting on the edge of the stage, listening to the entire conversation. He approached us now, his face very solemn and serious. He took his place beside me but didn't say anything.

Eddie looked at Mitch, as if not sure what to say. The two men stared at each other, and I broke the silence. I needed to get this settled once and for all.

"Mitch, this is Eddie Williams. You may remember him from Gartano's a few months back. Eddie, this is my fiancé, Mitch Tarrington." Eddie extended his hand and reluctantly, Mitch shook it.

"So, you're the guy who seems to have stolen my Dana's heart." Eddie said to Mitch.

"And you're the guy who broke it." Mitch retorted.

"Touché." Eddie replied. "Look, pal, I'm not here to make trouble. I'm here to talk to Dana. Would you give me a minute to do that?"

I could see Mitch clenching his fist, and I said a silent prayer that he wouldn't do anything stupid. He looked at Eddie, and bit his lip. "No, I won't do that Eddie. It should be clear to you where Dana stands on things. There's no need for you to talk to her, or be anywhere near her, for that matter."

Eddie looked at Mitch, then to me and back to Mitch. "I know you two are engaged, but this past week I realized I made a mistake in ever letting her go. I know in my heart that Dana still loves me. I'm the only man she's ever loved. Why don't you step aside and give her the chance to be happy?"

I was starting to actually feel faint at the words coming from Eddie's mouth. I always knew he was arrogant, but this was his best performance yet. Was he insane? I looked at Mitch, who was still biting his lip and seeming to be trying to sort all this out, too. He looked at me, his eyes starting to show not only anger, but fear. Was he actually afraid that what Eddie was saying could be true? I took his hand and gave it a loving squeeze. "Mitch, honey, could you give me just one minute alone with Eddie? There's something I need to say to him." Mitch looked at me, the fear even stronger in his eyes. I smiled at him reassuringly. "It's alright, I just want to settle this. Ok?"

Mitch took a deep breath and nodded, and went to sit on the stairs of the stage. He placed his hands in his lap, wringing them and biting his lip nervously. I looked at him and smiled again, but he just looked at me. I turned back to Eddie.

"Look, Eddie, I don't know why you're doing this. But you're wrong. I'm not in love with you anymore. I'm in love with Mitch, very much in love with him. I know to you and maybe to the rest of the world, you can't understand how that could happen in such a short time. Sometimes, I don't understand it myself, but it did. I've never been happier, Eddie. What we had was special, and I will always cherish those times. But those times, and you, are in my past. The past is over, and all I want now is my future, my future as Mrs. Mitch Tarrington." I looked right into Eddie's eyes. "I'm sorry, Eddie, but there is nothing left for you and I. You need to move on with your life, and let me move on with mine. I hope you find what you're looking for, but please leave me alone. I know that there's always a chance we'll see each other again sometime, but I want you to know, I have no feelings for you, and that isn't going to change. Mitch is my life now. Let me have my life."

Eddie looked at Mitch, then to me. "I guess I was wrong to come here tonight, Dana. I thought things would turn out differently, or at least I had hoped they would." He looked at Mitch again. "So, you really are in love with this guy, it's not just a rebound thing like I thought, is it?"

"Eddie, you should know that's not how I work. I really am in love with him. I can't ever imagine my life without him in it." I said.

Eddie smiled. "I'm sorry, Dana, I guess I made a fool of myself once again. But I had to try. I hope you understand that." He took my hand. "If this is what you truly want, then I wish you the best. And I won't bother you anymore." He must have read the question in my eyes. "Yes, Dana, I'll be fine. I guess I just needed to put closure to all this, one way or another."

"Well, now you have, Eddie. Goodbye." Eddie let go of my hand and walked away, not looking back.

I turned to look at Mitch. He was still sitting on the stairs, a sad and solemn look on his face. He looked lost and alone. I walked over to him, and he looked up at me.

"So, is everything ok?" He asked softly.

I reached out for his hand. "Yes, honey, it couldn't be better." I looked into his eyes. "Mitch, why do you look so sad?" I asked him

He bit his lip and looked at me. "I guess I was afraid. Afraid maybe he was right, Dana. All this, us, has happened so fast. He made me think about something I hadn't thought about before. I don't like that feeling, not at all."

I put my arms around him, holding him tightly. "Mitch, it's over between me and Eddie. He knows that now. You are the only person I love, the only person I want to be with. Now and always. Today, tomorrow and a hundred years from now, it will be Mitch and Dana. That's what I want."

"I'm glad to hear that, sweetheart." Mitch said. "That's what I want, too." He stood up and wrapped his arms around me. "I'm glad you straightened me out back there earlier. Things are going great tonight, aren't they?" He said.

"They sure are. You guys have it made, Mitch. Just look at all these people. They love you." Then I smiled up at him. "But not half as much as I do."

He smiled back at me. "Well, I guess it's time for me to get back to work. My public awaits. But first........" Mitch leaned down and gave me a long and wonderful kiss.

When I got back to the table, Janine was there. "Hi, Dana. These guys said that the band sounds great tonight. I haven't had a chance to see Aaron yet. I had to work later than I thought. He probably thinks I stood him up."

The band was coming back out and I pointed to Newbie. "There he is, Janine. I'll get Mitch's attention and he'll let him know you're here."

I walked closer to the stage and called out to Mitch, pointing to Janine. He smiled then turned to Newbie, pointing to her as well. Newbie's face lit up and he waved at his girl. She smiled and blew him a kiss, which he pretended to catch and place on his cheek. Mitch and I looked at each other and smiled.

About a half hour later, around eleven o'clock, Chris showed up, a huge smile on his face. All of us surrounded him, but none of us had to ask the question that was on all our minds.

"Diana Marie, seven pounds, five ounces, twenty one inches long. Not a whole lot of hair, but big beautiful eyes. Born around nine forty five. Both of them are fine." He was beaming.

I gave him a hug and a kiss on the cheek. "Congratulations, Chris, that's wonderful news." I said.

Julia and Angelina hugged their brother as well, and Paul shook his hand. Just then, Mitch noticed our scene. Even though he was right in the middle of a song, he told the guys to stop. He ran to the front of the stage and hopped down, motioning for Chris to come to him, which he did. The place grew silent, and you could have heard a pin drop for a few moments.

"So, tell me the news, Christopher." Mitch said to his brother.

Chris looked around, then at Mitch. "Mitchell, you're in the middle of something here. It can wait." He answered.

Mitch took his brother into a playful sort of headlock. "I said tell me, Chris. Tell me so I can get back to work."

Chris smiled and told Mitch the news about the baby. Mitch broke his headlock and gave his brother a hug. "Congratulations, Chris. That's gotta feel great." He said.

"It does, little brother, just wait." Chris said.

Mitch ran back up on the stage, a huge smile on his face. "Sorry about that folks, I'm sure you're probably wondering what's going on. I just got the news that I'm an uncle again!" The crowd applauded. "The proud dad is here, my brother, Chris Tarrington. This makes baby number four for him and his wife Trudy." Everyone cheered and Chris actually wiped a tear from his eye. Mitch smiled lovingly at his big brother. Cueing the band, they broke back into the rest of the song, then went on to do at least five more. Finally, around a half hour later, they said their goodnights and left the stage, the crowd going wild.

I grabbed Janine. "Unless you want your boyfriend to be bombarded by groupies, we'd better get you back there."

"I know how to fight." Janine laughed.

Max was waiting for us by the backstage door. "Hi, Dana, who's this?" He asked.

"Oh, this is Janine. She's ok, Max, she's dating Aaron Newsonberg, you know, Newbie, the drummer." I told him.

"No problem. I'll learn you all eventually." He said, opening the door for us.

The guys were all chattering and laughing, and you could feel the excitement they were generating. Newbie saw Janine and walked over to give her a hug and a kiss. Mitch had his back to me, talking to Ash and Shep, and I walked up behind him, putting my arms around him. He jumped as if I had startled him, and I laughed.

"You could give me a heart attack sneaking up on me like that, sweetheart." He said, turning around to face me with a smile.

"I don't think you're quite old enough to be worrying about that yet. Besides, I didn't sneak up on you. You just weren't paying attention." I told him.

"I guess you were right after all, Dana, these guys were terrific tonight." He said. "And I managed to keep my voice, too, much to my surprise."

"See, you were worried for nothing." I said.

The guys all huddled around for a few minutes, deciding that they deserved a celebration. They all looked at Mitch.

"You can come to my place, but the rest of it's up to you. I'm not buying this time!" he teased. I looked at him with a smile. "Ok, maybe I am. But let's get the gear packed up first, and I'm gonna go out real quick and ask the others to come, too. Be right back."

Mitch took my hand and we proceeded to where his family was waiting. He smiled brightly. "Hey, we're all going to my place for some pizza." He said with a smirk. "How about joining us?" he asked.

"Mom took the kids for the night, so I'm game." Chris said. "Besides, I could use a chance to unwind."

Julia and Paul looked at each other. "Count us in."

Then Mitch looked at Angelina. "Go call Mom, tell her to keep Meg. I'm sure she won't mind. Then catch Jim and see if he can meet us there." She smiled and headed off.

"Sweetheart, you go call for the pizzas. About a half hour or so. I'm gonna hurry up and help the guys pack up." He gave me a quick peck and trotted off.

A short while later all of us were gathered once again in Mitch's apartment. It felt good to be there with all his family and friends, just talking and laughing and enjoying each other's company. Ash turned to Chris.

"So, Chris, how's it feel to be a dad again?" he asked.

"Pretty good, actually. It just seems to get better each time it happens." Chris replied.

"Yeah, I know. It felt fantastic when Jenny was born, but yet I was still elated when Jon came along." He smiled at Chris. "So, are you two planning on having any more?"

Chris shook his head with determination. "No, we agreed that this is it. She's taking care of that before she comes home."

Ash smiled. "We did the same thing. One girl, one boy, that's enough."

Shep had been intently listening to this whole conversation. "So, Trip, when you gonna start the baby thing?"

Mitch laughed. "Well, Shep, first I think it would be nice if we got married. Then, well, I don't know, not for a couple of years, at least."

I nodded in agreement. "I'm ready to be a wife, but I don't think I'm ready to throw the title of mother in there quite yet." I said.

Mitch smiled. "I want her all to myself for a while." He said, giving me a hug.

Our little party lasted until the wee hours of the morning, and finally everyone was gone except Mitch and I. I helped him clean everything up and then we sat down together on the couch.

"What a night, Dana." Mitch exhaled deeply. "Can't say it wasn't fun, though."

"I know, it sure was. That is, after you got over your little fussing fit earlier." I stated.

Mitch turned and looked at me. "I don't have fits, Dana. I reserve that right for you."

"Oh, so just what are you saying Mitchell?" I asked, in a bit of shock.

He laughed. "It's so easy to get you going, isn't it?" He said. "I was only teasing. Don't get all mad at me now."

"I'm not mad at you, Mitch." I said. "You just tease me too much."

"That's because you're so much fun." He said, chuckling. "You know I love you, though, don't you?"

"I suppose so." Then I turned to him. "Honey, what do you think was up with Eddie? Why do you think he was trying to break us up?"

Mitch thought for a minute. "You know, I guess maybe he's not happy, so it bothered him to see you happy."

I pondered that thought for a minute. "Or, do you think he really did feel like he made a mistake in letting me go, as he put it?"

Mitch looked at me. "I don't know, I guess it's possible. But does it really matter? I mean, his loss is definitely my gain." Then he looked right into my eyes. "Unless you agree with him."

"Mitchell Tarrington, how could you say that?" I shot back. "You know I don't agree. I love you."

Mitch smiled. "I know. I guess I just wanted to hear it." He said.

"NOW who's being insecure?" I said, beginning to make circles on his sweater with my finger. "I think you're jealous, Mitch."

He laughed. "Jealousy is not part of my chemical makeup, love. I was just inquiring, that's all."

"Ok, then, I'll just say you're very inquisitive, how's that?"

"Much better." He laughed. Mitch yawned and stretched. "Come on, beautiful. I better get you home."

A few minutes later, we were standing inside my apartment. Mitch had his arms around me, rubbing my back with the palm of his hand. "I wish we were married now, Dana. This waiting is really getting to me. It's harder and harder to leave you every time I have to do it."

"I know, it's hard for me, too, Mitch. But it's only a few more weeks. Then we won't have to be apart anymore." I smiled. "Besides, basically, the only time we aren't together is when we're sleeping."

Mitch laughed. "But, honey, I WANT to sleep with you, really I do." He said with a big grin.

I shook my head. "Yes, Mitchell, I know you do, believe me. And in more ways than one, I'm sure." I said. Mitch smiled and raised his eyebrows impishly. I kissed him. "Now go home before you get yourself into trouble."

Mitch gave me another kiss and opened the door. "I'll be thinking about you." He said, a coy little grin lighting up his face.

"I'm sure you will. Goodnight, handsome." I said. I blew Mitch a kiss, and just like Newbie had done with Janine, he caught it and put it on his cheek. Then he turned and walked away.

18

The next few weeks flew by, and between work, rehearsals, shows at the club and all the other wedding plans, it seemed as if we were going non-stop. Mitch was doing well with managing everything and I wondered why he had ever been worried. Gartano's had become very comfortable for him, business was better than ever, and he seemed to love his times with the band. As the time went by and he fell into a routine, it seemed to make Mitch feel even better about things.

Almost everything was set for the wedding, and with only about a week or so to go, I was getting to the point where I was excited, yet just anxious to get it all over with. The girls and I picked out dresses for them to wear, beautiful chiffon and lace, Kayla's in a pastel blue, the other girls' in pastel pink. We decided to put Megan in a dress which seemed almost a miniature version of mine, accented by little pink and blue silk roses at the waist and cuffs. She looked adorable when we tried it on her, and she told her Uncle Mitch that she was going to marry him in her bride's dress, which made him laugh. We had been bombarded with RSVP's and were battening down the hatches for at least 250-300 guests.

The girls planned a bridal shower for me to take place that Saturday. They thought it might be easier to do it then, as Mitch planned to move my things into the apartment the following week and spend his last few days as a bachelor with his parents. I had a lot of furniture we wouldn't be needing, so I gave some things to those in Mitch's family who wanted them, and decided I would donate the rest to charity. The things I was bringing into our marriage were things I couldn't or just didn't want to part with, and Mitch agreed that it was important for us to "blend our lives" as he put it.

Early that Saturday morning, Mitch showed up around nine with a bouquet of flowers and two ham and cheese bagels from the deli. I smiled as I opened the door.

"Good morning, beautiful." He said, kissing me and stepping inside.

"Good morning, handsome." I replied, taking the things from his hands. "This is so sweet, honey, thank you." I said, kissing him again.

Mitch went to the cupboard and pulled out two cups, then proceeded to pour each of us a cup of coffee. He put the cups on the table, then handing me one of the bagels, he sat down. I joined him.

"Dana, I can hardly believe that next Saturday we'll be getting married. Can you?" He said excitedly.

"No, Mitch, I can't, but I do know I'm really excited." I told him. "So, sweetie, what are you going to do while I have my bridal shower today?" I asked him.

He looked at me with a funny expression. "I thought I was going to be a part of that, actually, sweetheart. I mean, aren't the gifts for me, too?"

I smiled. "Mitchell, they call it a bridal shower because it's for the bride. Guys aren't allowed, sorry."

He took a sip of coffee. "But I'm the groom. Don't I count for something?" he asked.

"Yes, but you can't come. Now, what are you going to do?" I asked.

Mitch thought for a moment. "Well, I had planned for the whole day off, but I guess I'll just go to work after all. I really need to do that, anyway. Then tonight we can just hang out, since I had the show last night, so that'll work."

I smiled. "Do what you must, but don't crash my shower, Mitchell, I'm warning you." I said firmly.

He laughed. "Would I do something like that, sweetheart?" He asked, looking innocent.

"Yes, you would, that's why I said it." I answered. "By the way, I want you here after work, or whatever you decide to do. I'm making dinner tonight, ok?"

"Ok, baby, I'll be here." Mitch looked around the apartment. "You know, love, what I should do is stay here and keep packing for you. You're never going to have everything ready to move by Tuesday at the rate you're going."

"Yes, I will, Mitch. In fact, we can spend all day tomorrow after church doing just that, if it will make you feel any better." I told him. "The shower starts at one, so I figure I should be done with everything around four or so. That will get me back here around five'ish and I can have dinner ready by six. How does that sound?"

"Fantastic!" Mitch said, clearing the table for me. He retreated to the chair in the living room and motioned for me to come over to him. He pulled me down on his lap and put his arms around me. Then he began to kiss me, softly and sweetly, each kiss being delivered a little more deliberately than the one before. I felt his hands move slowly onto my back, and pressing his palms against me, he pulled me closer to him. He pulled away from me a little to look into my eyes, and then kissed me again, lingering a little before he pulled away again. He smiled and his eyes danced with love. "Just one more week," he said softly, "and I won't have to let you go."

"I know, but today you do. However," I paused, "I don't think a few more minutes would hurt anything, do you?"

"Probably not." Mitch said, kissing me again. He pulled me closer and just held me there, taking in a deep breath and exhaling slowly. "You know, I still can't believe all this is happening, Dana. It just all seems too good to be true."

Just then the phone rang and I kissed Mitch again before I got up to answer it.

"Hello, oh, hi Chris. No, Mitch is right here. Hang on." Mitch got up and took the phone from me. I started to walk away, but he pulled me to him, and rested his chin on top of my head, kissing me there softly.

"Hey, Christopher, what's up?" He asked.

"Well, Mitchell, the guys and I were talking the other day, and well, we'd like to throw a little bachelor party for you, little brother. How does tonight sound?"

Mitch kissed me again and stood up straight. "A bachelor party, huh? Tonight? Uh, well, Dana's making me dinner after her shower, so I don't know. What exactly did you have in mind?"

Chris chuckled. "Well, buddy, just the guys, thinking a poker game, my place, pour back a few, and do the male bonding thing. Thought about taking you out, but why bother? We can do everything in that we'd do out."

Mitch looked at me as if he needed to get my permission, or approval, or both. "Dana, do you mind?" he asked. "Just going to Chris's for a game or two of poker, my traditional half a beer and talk about guy things."

I laughed. "Honey, I'm not your mother. As long as you don't do anything she or I wouldn't approve of, you're fine. We can still have dinner, then you go and have fun, ok?"

Chris was also laughing. "She says that, but I'll have to fill you in later on what she REALLY means." He told Mitch. "Hey, if you want, bring the band, too. The more the merrier. I've got Paul and Jim covered, and I'm calling Joseph right now. Be here around, oh, seven thirty, or eight."

"Cool, Chris, see you then. Bye." Mitch hung up the phone and looked at me. "Dana, are you sure you're ok with this?"

"With what, honey? You going out? Why wouldn't I be?" I asked. "I know you won't do anything you know I wouldn't approve of. I trust you completely, Mitchell. Besides, you'll be at Chris's. What kind of trouble could you possibly get into there?"

"Do you really mean that, that you trust me, I mean, or are you just trying to make me feel good?" he asked.

"Mitch, I mean that. I truly do trust you." I said.

The phone rang again and Mitch answered this time. "Hi, Jul, what's going on?"

"Hey, Mitchell. Just the person I wanted to talk to. We're going to play a little game at the shower today, and I want to ask you some questions, but I don't want Dana to hear the way you answer them. Then, I'm going to have you answer those same questions about her and ask her the answers. Kinda just some fun to see how well you know each other. Can you step into another room or something so she doesn't hear you?"

Mitch looked at me. "Yeah, I'll go in the bedroom. Hang on."

I looked at him curiously. "What's going on Mitch?"

"Julia has some questions she's going to ask me, and she said you can't hear the answers. It's for some sort of game you're going to play today. Hang up when I get in there, ok?"

I smiled. "Ok, go on."

A minute later, Mitch called out that he had the extension and I hung up the phone. As I straightened things up a little, I got to thinking about the whole idea of Mitch having a bachelor party. I had heard stories of things that had gone on at these so-called celebrations, and I wasn't very eager to think of my future husband taking part in those sorts of doings. But in my heart I knew Mitch, and I knew that he would never do anything that he knew would hurt me. I could honestly trust him to do just what he said he was going to do. Go to Chris's, have half a beer, talk about whatever it was guys talked about, and go home. I felt confident that it would be nothing more than a harmless evening of camaraderie for him, and I decided not to make a fuss about it.

Mitch emerged from the bedroom, laughing. "That should be interesting to see how well our answers match." He said. "Sounds like they have a good time planned for you, sweetheart."

"I'm looking forward to it." I said.

"Dana, if I lose all my money tonight playing poker, will you still love me, even if I'm poor?" he smiled.

"Well, I don't know, Mitch." I teased. "You know I was only marrying you because you're a rich kid."

"Yeah, well, I won't tell you the only reason I'm marrying you, then." He teased back.

I laughed. "I have a feeling both of us are in for a disappointment." I said.

Mitch pretended to pout. "Gee, I sure hope that isn't true." He said.

"Let's pack a few more boxes, shall we?" I suggested.

"Well, ok, I guess I could help you, if I really have to." Mitch said playfully.

I handed him the packing tape and a couple of flattened boxes, and beckoned him to follow me into the hallway. I opened my hall closet and sat down on the floor.

"Tape the boxes together, Mitch, and I'll start packing all this stuff." I told him.

Mitch opened the door as wide as it would go and looked inside, then at me. "Dana, if you take all this, plus what you've already packed, along with what still needs to be packed, I'm going to have to live someplace else."

"Come on, honey, I don't have that much." I told him. "Besides, this stuff will benefit both of us."

Mitch took out a curling iron. "Sweetheart, somehow I don't think I'll be using this." He commented.

"Well, you want me to look pretty, don't you?" I asked.

"Sure." Mitch said and threw it into the box.

We pulled out everything we could that I wouldn't be needing in the next few days and packed it in boxes. As I was pulling things out, I came across an old photo album. I tugged on Mitch's pant leg and got his attention.

"Look, honey, it's some old pictures. Want to have a look?" I asked him.

"Sure, I'll look with you." He said. "But let's take it out to the living room. A 6'2" guy doesn't fit very well on the floor of a hallway."

I reached up for him and he took my hand, helping me to my feet. Following me to the couch, he sat next to me and I opened the album. As soon as I opened it, I realized which album it was. It had belonged to my parents, and my Grammy gave it to me just before I moved here from Iowa. The first page had written at the top, "Patrick and Kimberly, August 17, 1963" and the pictures were of a young couple's wedding.

"Your mom and dad, huh?" Mitch asked. I nodded. "You look like your mother, sweetheart. She was very pretty."

"Yes, she was. And look how handsome my Daddy was in his uniform. They really loved each other, Mitch. Just like we do." I said.

Mitch put his arm around my shoulder and I snuggled as close as I could get to him. Turning the page, I smiled. "That's their first car, and their first house. See the tree there in the front?"

"Yeah, you mean that little stick of a thing?" Mitch asked.

"Well, that little stick grew big enough to give me apples when I was little." I said. "Daddy planted it right after he and Mom moved in. She told me that he was really proud of it."

I turned the page again, and there were a lot of pictures of the two of them doing different things, including some pictures of their first Christmas together, and Mom in her Easter dress. But she looked a little different than she had in the other pictures.

"Look, Mitch." I said smiling. "See that?" I pointed to my mom's stomach. "That's me in there." Mitch smiled as I turned the page to reveal my first baby pictures.

"Take a look at that." Mitch said, still smiling. "I wonder if that's what our little girl will look like?"

I looked at him. "What if we never have a little girl? What if we only have little boys?"

"Then maybe they will still look a little like that. You were really adorable." He said.

We sat for a while flipping through the pages, my mind going back to a place and time long ago. There were pictures of all of us on our summer vacation in Cape Cod when I was ten, some with my Grammy and one of my parents and I together, my mother standing with her arm around my dad who was pushing me on a swing. I touched the photo, as if I could feel my parents' presence through the paper. Mitch looked at me with love and sadness in his eyes.

"That's the last picture we took together, before my parents died." I said softly. "It's always been my favorite one."

Mitch pulled me to him and kissed me softly on top of the head. "It's wonderful, Dana. You looked like you were a happy family."

"We were, Mitch." I said. "I really wish they could be here to see us get married. I miss them all so much." I could feel the tears starting to come, and I wiped my eyes in an attempt to hold them in. I closed the album and ran my hand across it once more, and smiled.

Mitch took the album from me, and laying it on the coffee table, he put his arms around me in a tight, loving, protective kind of hug. "I know you do, Dana. But, remember what I told you before? If they are in your heart, then they will be here, sweetheart. They will always be a part of you." He kissed me softly on the cheek. "Please don't be sad anymore, ok?"

I smiled up at him and wiped my eyes. "I'll try." I said. I picked the book up and walking back to the box, I gently packed it away.

I looked at the clock which told me it was almost noon. "Mitch, are you hungry? I'll make something for you if you are." I asked.

"I'll just grab something at work, baby, that's ok." He said. "I should probably go and let you get ready for your little party."

I walked over to him, still feeling a little sentimental from looking at the pictures. I put my arms around him, and lay my head on his chest. "Please stay with me until I go, ok? I just want you to be here." I said.

He slowly brought his arms around me and held me close. "Ok, love, I'll stay." He said softly.

"Come and help me pick out something to wear, ok?" I told him, trying to get myself out of my mood.

He laughed. "You look great in anything, love. Just put something on."

"No, Mitch, I have a few ideas, but I want your opinion. Come in the bedroom with me, ok?"

He laughed impishly. "Now, that's an invitation I'm not going to refuse."

"Oh, you brat, come on." I laughed.

Mitch sat down on the edge of the bed as I pulled out different combinations. As I had anticipated, he told me he liked each one, not really helping much in the decision making process. Finally, I was becoming frustrated with his seeming lack of interest.

"Mitchell, I don't want you to say they're all fine. I want you to help me pick one. Which do you like the best?" I asked.

"Sweetheart, I honestly don't have a preference." He said. Then he saw the way I was looking at him, with my arms folded tightly across my chest. "Ok, I like the black skirt with the peach colored sweater."

I gave him an odd look. "But it's too cold today for a skirt. I'm going to wear the black pantsuit with the yellow blouse underneath. There, it's settled."

Mitch laughed. "Dana, why did you drag me in here for this if you weren't going to listen to me anyway?" he asked.

"Because I wanted your opinion, Mitchell." I said.

"But you didn't.......oh, forget it." He sighed, looking at me. He stood up with a smile. "I'll go out so you can change."

A few minutes later I was all dressed and ready to go. Mitch smiled approvingly at my outfit. "Nice choice I made, isn't it?" he teased.

We put on our coats and headed out the door. Mitch walked me to my car and opened the door for me. "You be careful, ok? Have a good time and I'll see you later." He said, giving me a kiss.

I had never been to the Tarrington estate without Mitch being with me, and I found myself to be a little nervous as I started out. I loved Mitch's family, that was for certain, and they had always made me feel welcome whenever I was around them. I didn't doubt that today would be any different in that respect, but there were going to be people there I had never met before, friends of the family and more extended relatives, and I couldn't help wishing Mitch was going to be there, too.

As I started up the driveway, I stopped for a moment to look over the whole estate, something that in my countless trips here before I had never really done. It was truly breathtaking. To my right I could see the rolling hills, filled with trees that were now snow covered, glistening in the sunlight. Closer was the stable, which Mitch told me was once the home to four horses. Since the children had grown and moved away, the horses were sold, but the stable was still in good condition, as well as the fence around it. Of course, to the left was the Tarrington's home, large and majestic at the top of the hill, a combination of light brown brick and white, green shutters accenting the front, and pillars on the front porch. There was so much room here that I could imagine all the fun Mitch and his siblings had growing up here.

I took a deep breath and drove the rest of the way to the house, parked the car, and walked up to the door. I rang the doorbell, and Alexander came to let me in.

"Good afternoon, Miss Walker." He greeted. "I'll take your coat."

"Hi Alexander, thank you." I said. Julia appeared out of nowhere, and gave me a hug.

"Hi Dana, that's a beautiful outfit. I love that yellow, it looks great on you." She said.

"Thanks," I replied, taking another deep breath. Julia smiled.

"You don't have to be nervous, Dana. No one will bite. It's just us."
She smiled.

"I'll try, but to be honest, I just realized that I've never been here
before without Mitch. And I tend to be a little shy around people I
don't know very well." I told her.

"Well, you know us, and soon you'll know everyone else, too.
Besides, there will come a time when you and Mitch won't be
permanently attached at the hip, so you have to get used to it." She said
sweetly. "Everyone's in the dining room, come with me."

I timidly followed Julia down the hall and into the dining room. It
was decorated with pink and blue streamers and balloons, and beautiful
carnations of the same colors on the main table. A large table had been
placed to one side, which was overflowing with gifts, and a table on the
other side held a large cake, a punch bowl, and some appetizers. Most
of the guests turned toward me as I walked in, and I stopped in the
doorway, suddenly feeling a little awkward. Olivia smiled and came
toward me, and gave me a hug.

"Hello, dear," she said smiling brightly. Then she leaned close to
my ear and whispered, "Don't be nervous, Dana. We're all here and
we'll stay with you."

I smiled as she put her arm around me and called out for everyone's
attention. Now all eyes were upon me, and I wished at that moment
that the floor would open up and swallow me. But I just stood my
ground and smiled.

"Everyone, our guest of honor has arrived. For those of you who
haven't had the pleasure, I'd like to introduce Mitchell's bride-to-be,
Dana Walker." Everyone applauded and I managed a timid, "Hello,
everyone." Olivia smiled and led me to a chair in the center of everyone.
Trudy and Angelina approached me, each offering another reassuring
hug. Then Kayla made her way through the crowd as well.

"I'm so glad you're here, Kayla. I need all the moral support I can
get!" I told her.

"Don't you worry, honey, Kayla's right here," she said lovingly.

I turned to Trudy. "Trudy, there are so many people here." I told
her. "Mitch didn't tell me he had this many relatives."

She smiled. "Well, the Tarrington clan does spread far and wide,"
she replied. "But some of these people are just friends of the family,
other's wives of Jake's business colleagues. Olivia's not one to exclude
anybody."

Angelina called everyone's attention and said we would be starting
a few shower games. They were the typical things like unscrambling

words related to a wedding, and doing a word search. Then Julia took center stage.

"Ok, everyone, just for fun, we're going to see how much Mitch and Dana really know about each other. Now, before we start, though, we'd like Dana to tell everyone how she and Mitch met, and a little bit about everything leading up to today."

Great, I thought. I'm just getting my sea legs and she's docking me already. I took a deep breath and stood up.

"Well, I'm not really good at speaking in front of a lot of people, so forgive me if I'm a little shaky." I started off, thinking it might not be a bad idea to cover myself, just in case. "The first time I saw Mitch was actually on October 4th, in Gartano's, which is a little Italian bistro he owns in town. My best friend Kayla tried and tried to get us together, but both of us were too stubborn to admit we had any attraction to each other. Finally, about a month later, fate took over and we started dating. On Christmas Eve, Mitch proposed to me and I said yes. Next Saturday, I'll be Mrs. Mitch Tarrington the third."

Everyone oohed and ahhed and then they clapped as I sat down. Julia stood up again.

"Ok, Dana, I called Mitch this morning and asked him to answer these questions for me. Then I asked him to tell me how he thought you'd respond to the same questions. First, I want to ask you the questions and I want you to answer them the way you think he did. Then, give me your answers and we'll see how he did."

This should be easy, I thought. I think I know Mitch pretty well.

"Dana, what is Mitch's favorite color?" Julia asked.

"That's an easy one. Mitch likes blue." I said. "And I like pink, blue and yellow."

"Correct! Ok, his favorite dessert." She said.

I smiled at Trudy. "Well, I used to think it was chocolate chip cookies, but I was corrected on Christmas Day, so it's cherry cheesecake. And mine would be chocolate cake."

Julia smiled. "He told me you'd say chocolate chip cookies, but you're right—cherry cheesecake! But Mitch said apple pie for you, sorry. Now, what is Mitch's favorite season of the year?"

Ok, not fair, I thought. He seemed to enjoy being outdoors and the cold didn't seem to affect him very much. I thought about the sledding, and the snowball fights, and building the snowman. He usually walked to work, so I took a stab in the dark.

"I've got to admit, I don't really know this one, but I would say winter. He seems to like being outdoors. And I think I like autumn."

Julia grimaced. "Ooo, no, first one wrong. Mitch said his favorite season is summer because he doesn't like to have to bundle up to go outside. And his glasses don't steam up when he comes indoors." Everyone chuckled. "By the way, he guessed right on that one for you."

So, I missed one, no big deal I thought. I waited for the next one to be fired my way.

"Let's get a little more personal. Tell me Mitch's waist size, his shoe size, his shirt size and," she smiled, "boxers or briefs!"

I blushed. "Ok, first let me tell you, I ONLY know this because I went snooping through his closet and his dresser one day. JUST to be nosy, nothing more." Everyone chuckled. I rattled through all his sizes, amazed that I actually remembered them all. Then I finished. "And Mitch is a boxer guy."

"Perfect, on your part that is. Mitch copped out on this one. All he said was, she's little." Julia said, and everyone clapped and giggled. "Boxers, huh?" She smiled, teasingly.

I had to defend my honor here. "I swear, I've never seen them on him, only in his dresser drawer." I said. Then, as everyone ooed and aahed again, I realized how that sounded and I blushed.

"Ok, Dana, I won't ask." Julia said, laughing. I put my head down on the table and buried my face in my hands. "It's ok, we know what you meant. We're just teasing." She said. "Next question. What is the one physical feature Mitch likes best about you?"

I smiled. "My eyes." I answered. "And I love his smile. That dimple really gets to me." I smiled just thinking about it.

"Right again! Ok, here's a tricky one. What's the one thing Mitch is looking forward to being able to do after you get married that he can't do now?"

I blushed again. "Do I have to answer that question?" I asked her. Everyone laughed.

"Yes, you have to answer it. But, if it helps, I told Mitch he had to give me an answer OTHER than that one." She smiled.

I was starting to relax now, and have fun with this. "Was it hard for him to come up with anything?" Everyone laughed again. "Ok, I know that he told me he's really looking forward to us being together all the time, and not having to leave at the end of the day. I'm looking forward to that, too."

"You are scoring great here, only one wrong so far. Ok, down to the last few. How many children does Mitch want to have?"

"Three and so do I." I replied, affirmatively.

"Actually, his first response was that he doesn't want to have any. He's going to let you do that." Everyone chuckled. "But, then, oh, oh, he said five." She said.

"Who's he having the other two with?" I asked teasingly, and again everyone chuckled. "Guess we need to talk some more, huh?"

"What is Mitch's biggest pet peeve about you?" she asked.

"Gosh, does he have one?" I said, laughing. "Ok, he claims I can't make a decision to save my life, so I'd say that's probably it. As for him, well, I'd say he's way too flirtatious."

"Good, almost. He did say you have trouble making a decision, but he said you would say that he worries too much about failing at things."

"Well, that's true, too. So, do I get partial credit for that one?" I asked, everyone chuckling.

"Well, alright." Julia teased. "Last question. How long after you started dating was it before Mitch realized that he was in love and wanted to marry you?"

I smiled. "Well, that's kind of a tricky one." I stated. "The way I understand it, Mitch actually fell in love the first time he saw me. But, we had been dating, oh, I'd say about a month or so before he decided to give me a ring." Then I looked at her. "As for me, I don't think I actually realized I was in love with him until the first night we actually talked, which was about a month after we first saw each other. I can't really say when I realized I wanted to marry him. I guess right around the time he proposed."

She smiled. "Here's how Mitch answered that question, and I thought it was so romantic that I have to read it to you. And I quote, 'The very first time I looked at Dana, I felt something, and at first, I didn't know exactly what it was, but each time I saw her after that, I realized more and more that I was in love with her. It didn't take me long after we actually started going out to know that I couldn't live without her, and I honestly don't know how I existed before she came along. The timing doesn't matter. All that matters is that we are where we are'."

Everyone applauded and I smiled sweetly. What a great guy I'm getting, I thought. How could I have gotten so lucky?

"Well, it seems like you two know each other pretty well, so I guess timing doesn't matter. But let me give you one piece of advice." Julia said. "I know everyone has their own secret to having a long and happy marriage. But the one thing I have always tried to do as far as Paul and I are concerned, is I try to look at him each day and find something new that I can fall in love with about him. Sometimes it isn't easy, but it keeps our relationship fresh. You and Mitch still have a lot of discovering to do, but try to do that anyway."

Angelina stood up. "Before we eat, we're going to go around and let everyone introduce themselves, because there are a lot of ladies here today that Dana doesn't know. But, we're going to make this a little more fun for Dana. Most of you have known Mitchell for a long time, so tell Dana one thing about him that you know, and one piece of advice you would give her as a new bride."

The introductions started, and I realized a third of the way through there was no way I would ever remember all these people, so I decided it wasn't even worth trying. I just nodded and smiled at each one, listening to what they all had to say. Most of them were saying things like Mitch was a nice boy, kind, sweet and loving. Things I already knew, anyway. The advice was typical, like treat each other well and don't go to bed angry, or make sure each time he leaves the house that you tell him you love him. But one lady caught me off guard, and made everyone laugh.

"My name is Josephine Penske and I'm an old friend of the family. Mitch and my daughter, Carla, used to play together quite often as small children, in fact, I actually feel safe to say that she was his first crush." Olivia smiled and nodded in agreement. "The summer before we moved out of the area, Mitch and Carla decided they wanted to spend an afternoon playing together, which was nothing unusual, so he came to our house. They went off to the playroom, but after a while they seemed to get particularly quiet. I went to check on them, and," she paused to laugh, "found both without a stitch of clothing on, playing doctor. And I must say, Mitch seemed to be giving her quite the examination! Even after I made them get dressed and come out into the room with me, he kept asking her if she needed another checkup." She paused. "So, Dana, my advice would be, if you want to keep Mitch happy, buy him a stethoscope."

Everyone roared with laughter, and I could just imagine the thought of little Mitch, giving this little girl the once over. Even then he was ornery, I thought.

"You know, somehow that doesn't surprise me at all." I told her.

Next was Kayla's turn. "My name is Kayla Turner, and I'm Dana's matron of honor, her best friend, and whatever else you might want to throw in there." She smiled. "I've only known Mitch a little longer than Dana has, but I've learned a lot about him in a short time. The one thing I know is that he's head over heels for this girl. In fact, I'm another one who knew it before he did." She turned to me. "Dana, my only advice is to remember that Mitch is just a man, made of flesh and blood, and he's not always gonna do all the things you want him to. He'll make mistakes, and he'll make you mad, and sometimes he may even make you cry. But underneath it all, never forget the love that the two of you share. That kind of love doesn't come along but once in a lifetime. Make it last."

I looked at Kayla with love. "Don't worry, I will." I said.

After the last few people had their turn, Olivia beckoned my bridal party and I to start the line for lunch. Once again, she outdid herself with a wonderful spread of quiches, salads, deli meats, desserts and all the trimmings. I had second thoughts about whether or not I would be able to eat any dinner, but decided I'd still make it for Mitch anyway.

As we ate, several of the ladies stopped by to chat with me, offering me congratulations, admiring my ring, and asking me questions like where we were going to live, or what made us decide on the date we had. I particularly enjoyed the expression most of them gave when, asked that question, I would simply respond by saying Mitch couldn't wait for me any longer. I decided they could take it any way they wanted, but in the end, it was the truth.

Lunch finished, Alexander quickly cleared things away so that I could have plenty of room to open my gifts. Angelina sat down next to me to write down who gave what so that I would be able to follow up with appropriate thank you notes. Julia handed me gifts, and I decided, to save time, I wouldn't read the cards, just the name. I began to open what seemed like an endless sea of gifts. I was appreciative of everything, even though I realized many people may not have realized that Mitch and I were actually merging our two apartments and had most of the things needed to "set up house." But I thought I would donate the old and use the new. It would be nice to have everything fresh for my new life as Mrs. Tarrington.

Just when I thought I was finally going to be done, Julia and Angelina handed me two more gifts. "Dana, we wanted to save the best for last." Julia said, handing me a box. I looked at her curiously, and ripped off the paper. I slowly lifted the corner of the box, then put it back down again.

"Oh, my," was all I could get out as I blushed. Everyone laughed, and were chiding me to show them what I had received. Shyly, I opened the box and held up a very sheer and sexy blue teddy, trimmed in lace, which left little, if anything, to the imagination. They all ooed and ahhed.

"Is that for her or for Mitch?" I heard Trudy say, laughing.

I noticed that the next one actually had Mitch's name on it. "Should I wait and let him open it?" I asked.

"Oh, no, that's ok. You can open it for him." Julia smiled.

"I'm half afraid to." I said, starting to slowly rip off the paper. I got down to the box, and looking up at them, I opened the lid. A pair of very sexy blue silk boxers. Of course the crowd insisted that I hold them up for everyone to see.

"Happy honeymoon!" The girls all said in unison.

"Thank you everyone for coming and for all the gifts. Everything was really wonderful." I said. The ladies all started buzzing around, some talking amongst themselves, others stopping by to inspect all the gifts on the table. I turned to Kayla, lifting the edge of the teddy box once more. "It's pretty, but I just can't see me wearing it." I told her softly.

"Shoot, why not, girl? Heaven knows you have the figure for it. Besides, Mitch will love it." She replied.

"Oh, I don't know. I'm far from bathing suit model material." I said.

"Go on, now, girl. You just wait. That boy will be all over you." She said.

Something told me I didn't have to doubt that in any way, shape or form. But I closed the box and gently pushed it aside, hoping no one would notice and want to see it again.

Around four o'clock most of the guests had gone, and the phone rang. Alexander called out to me. "Miss Walker, it's Mitchell on the telephone for you." He said, leading me to the phone in the den. "It will be a little more quiet in here for you." He said, smiling and closing the door as he left. I picked up the phone.

"Hello?" I said.

"Hi, beautiful. How's the party going?" he asked.

"Well, I think we're pretty much done. You should see all the things we got, Mitch. I think we may have to think about getting a bigger place," I said excitedly.

He laughed. "Do you want me to come out there and help you bring things home? We can just take everything to my place so we don't have to move it later. I've pretty much done all I'm going to do at the bistro, and I was headed out anyway."

"Sure, I can wait here for you. But we can't stay too long, or I won't have time to make dinner before you go to Chris's," I told him.

"Well, if we don't have time, I'll just take you out for something, and you can cook tomorrow, ok?"

"Ok, that sounds like a plan. I'll be waiting for you," I said.

"See you soon. I love you," Mitch said sweetly.

"I love you too, bye," I said hanging up the phone.

I returned to the dining room, and everyone was gone now except for Kayla and Mitch's family.

"Sorry, but I had to take a call from Mitch. He's coming to help me take all these things home," I said.

"That's good. Then he can get a chance to see all that you got," Olivia said.

"So, Dana," Angelina said, "what did you think about those last two gifts? Pretty sexy, huh?"

I could feel the blush rising in my cheeks again. "Uh, yeah, pretty sexy." I said back, managing a smile. I didn't have the heart to tell her that if I had my way, Mitch would never see me in that teddy. I just couldn't picture it happening. For some reason, the thought of sexy didn't make me feel very much that way.

A few minutes later, the happy sound of Mitch's voice echoed in the entry hall, and I quickly went to greet him. "Hi, honey!" I said, giving him a hug and a kiss.

"Hey, beautiful." He smiled. "Where's all this bounty you were telling me about?"

I took his hand. "In here." I said, leading the way to the dining room.

"Hi everyone." Mitch greeted as he walked into the room. Then he saw the table. "Man, you weren't kidding, were you?" He said. "Let me check all this out."

The others began cleaning things up and carrying leftover food into the kitchen, giving Mitch and I a chance to be somewhat alone. He was inspecting each gift, smiling in wonder at all the new things we had. Kayla walked in and noticing the lingerie boxes I had left on the table alone, she picked them up and placed them on the gift table, right in front of Mitch.

"Don't forget these, Dana." She said. "Probably the ones Mr. Mitchell will want to use the most." She smiled jokingly.

Mitch picked up one of the boxes. "What are these?" he asked, starting to open it up. I saw the edge of the teddy and snatched it from his hands.

"That's nothing." I said, closing the box back up and taking a step backwards.

Mitch smiled and held out his hand. "Come on, sweetheart, let me see."

"No, you can't see this one, but that one is for you." I told him, pointing to the other box.

He smiled and opened the lid. "Silk boxers, that's nice. Let me guess. Jul and Ang, right?"

"Yes, you're right." I said.

"And I would probably also be right to guess that the something in that box would go with these, except that the something would probably be for you to wear." He said, taking a step toward me, still holding out his hand.

"Never mind, Mitchell. Let's just get these things packed into the car, ok?" I said.

In one quick swoop, Mitch had me with one hand and grabbed the package with the other. "Well, well, what have we here, my love?" He said seductively, slowly lifting up the teddy for inspection. "Wow, that's really something else." He smiled at me. "How about a date, say next Sunday afternoon, after we get into Honolulu? You can model this for me."

I grabbed the teddy and the box from him and stuffed it back inside. "I'm not ever wearing that, Mitchell, so erase it from your mind right now." I told him.

Mitch looked at me, smirking just enough to show his dimple. "Come on, sweetheart, why would you say that? You'll be gorgeous in it, I'll bet. Besides, if I wear the boxers, you have to wear yours, too."

"No, I don't. Now can we please just get things moving here?" I said.

Mitch stepped closer to me and took my hands. "Dana, you're embarrassed. Tell me why."

I looked down at the floor. "I just don't like things like that, that's all. I don't feel comfortable with it." I looked at him. "Besides, why do I have to dress like some sleazy girl in one of your magazines to appeal to you? I don't look anything like that."

Mitch pulled me into a hug. "Is that it? You think I'll compare you to one of those girls in the pictures and I'll be disappointed, or that I have these grand expectations of what you look like undressed? Dana, I don't. Those are only pictures. You're real, and you're beautiful, and you are going to be the one with me. That's all I care about, and that's all I want. Trust me."

I hugged him tightly. "Ok, maybe I'll take it along, but no promises. And if I do, you have to promise not to laugh at me, like you did when you first saw me in my pajamas."

Mitch chuckled. "Oh, you silly little girl. I wasn't laughing at the way you looked, well, not really. I was laughing because I thought you looked so adorable. I would never laugh at you, love. Never."

Julia and Angelina came back into the room at that moment, Olivia and Kayla close behind. Mitch smiled and pointed to the boxes.

"Thanks for the gifts, girls. I must say, I'm impressed." He smiled impishly.

Julia smiled at him. "Somehow, I thought you would be, Mitchell." She said.

Mitch and I began to carry gifts, loading as much as we could into my car, then putting more things into his. There were only a few things we couldn't fit in, so Trudy agreed to take those home with her, and Mitch would take them to his place later when he left the poker game.

"So, honey, are the guys coming tonight, too?" I asked.

"No, it doesn't look like it. I tried to call them in between things this afternoon, but as it turns out, they all have other things going on." He said. "But, it's not all bad. Shep apparently organized a little Ace party on Wednesday. They want to take me out since they can't make it tonight. That is, if you're ok with it."

I smiled. "That's fine, sweetie. I don't mind. I can always stay home and unpack boxes. I'll be needing to do that, anyway." I said.

"Hey, Dana, why don't we have a girl's night out? Let us take you to dinner or something. How does that sound?" Trudy asked.

"I like the idea." Angelina added. Julia nodded in agreement. "Mom, you can come, too."

"Ok, I'd like that. Sounds like fun." She said.

"If the boss will let me have an evening off, I guess I could make it too." Kayla teased, and Mitch nodded.

"Then it's settled. We all go out Wednesday night!" I said.

Mitch and I said our goodbyes and I followed him back to his apartment, helping him unload everything. We finally had everything piled in the corner of his living room, and we both fell onto the couch.

"It's going to take forever to put all this away." I told him. "Do we even have room for everything?" Then I had another thought. "And we have to wash all the dishes and the pots and pans and all that."

Mitch took me by the hand and led me into the kitchen. "Obviously, my love, there is an appliance in my kitchen you never noticed. Probably because I never use it myself." Mitch pointed to an automatic dishwasher.

"Wow, too cool! That will definitely come in handy!" I said. I looked at the clock. "Mitch, we better get to my place if we have any hope of getting dinner in before you have to go to Chris's."

Mitch smiled at me. "You know what? Let's take a rain check on dinner for tomorrow, and order in some Chinese or something. I can help you start organizing all this. In fact, you can even stay here as long as you want. Here." Mitch reached into his pocket and took a key off his key ring. "I had this made for you, but kept forgetting about it. Now you have your own key to the place."

"I guess that makes it official, huh?" I said. "Maybe I will stay a while and try to organize things. Then I'll feel a little better knowing I have at least one thing out of the way."

Mitch got the phone book and ordered the food while I started to unpack gifts. There were so many things, dishes, pots and pans, linens, and even a microwave, which Mitch was happy about.

"Let's go ahead and sit that baby right here. I'm ready to retire this dinosaur." He said, referring to his old one that took up half a counter.

Just then, our food arrived, and Mitch paid the delivery boy, then brought everything in and poured us each a glass of soda. "So, I'm curious about that game, you know, the one with all the questions. How did we do?"

"Great, I only missed two. I didn't know summer was your favorite season, and, Mitchell, I thought we agreed on three kids. Where on earth did you come up with five?" I said, looking straight at him.

He chuckled. "I know, sweetheart. I just said that to be a brat. Three's perfect with me." He said, taking the egg rolls from me.

"Oh, and by the way, do you remember a girl by the name of Carla Penske?" I asked.

Mitch bit his lip and thought for a moment, then a smile came to his face. "I sure do. She used to live near us, and we spent a lot of time together, when we were just little kids." He replied.

"Did you have a crush on her?" I asked.

Mitch looked at me questioningly. "I guess maybe I did, but Dana, don't tell me you'd be jealous of someone I liked twenty years ago."

I laughed. "No, Mitch, I was just wondering. Her mom was there today and she seemed to think you did. In fact, so much so that the two of you played doctor?"

Mitch's face turned five shades of red. "Oh, my gosh, she actually remembered that? I think I was only about six or seven years old. My first taste of the female anatomy." He laughed.

I caught what he'd said. "First taste, Mitchell? And just when was your second?"

He stood up and opening the refrigerator, he stepped back and leaned down to my ear. "Next Saturday, with you." He kissed the top of my head, and sat back down, pouring another glass of soda. He reached across the table for one of the take out containers. "Stop hogging all the noodles, will you? I'm hungry too, ya know." He smiled at me.

Mitch and I finished dinner and after helping me unpack a few more things, he decided to head over to Chris's. "You stay here as long as you want, but be extra careful driving home, ok? I want a message on my machine when I come in that you're safe. Looks like it may be starting to snow pretty heavily."

I wrapped my arms around him and gave him a hug. "If the roads are slippery from the snow, please call me when you get there, ok? I'll worry if you don't."

Mitch gave me a few gentle kisses. "Ok, I'll call. Love you, sweetheart."

"I love you too. Have fun." I said, sending him off.

19

Mitch started his car to let it warm up, then began to brush the snow off the windows. It was coming down harder now, but he wasn't worried. Driving in the snow was something that had never bothered him. He was cautious, and tonight wouldn't be any different. He would take his time getting to Chris's and if it got too bad, he could always stay there for the night.

He climbed into his car and started off slowly. Not too bad, he thought, at least not at this point in the trip. He switched on the radio and turned it down low, focusing his attention on driving. But his thoughts, as always, quickly turned to Dana, and all the things that lie ahead in the week to come. Just six and half days, and he would be a husband. What an awesome responsibility, he thought, but not one that he wasn't ready, or willing, to take on. He thought about all the things marriage was going to encompass, and he smiled. He loved the thought of having someone he could totally be himself with, that he didn't have to be afraid of offending or losing just by simply being who he was. He was far from perfect, he knew that, but he also knew Dana didn't expect him to be. She loved him even with all his flaws, and there was something to be said for that. He knew that in years to come, even when they got to the point where there wasn't much mystery anymore, that they would still be good together. For at that point in their lives, they would take comfort in the familiarity of each other, of not having to live up to expectations or try to impress each other to win the other's affection. The affection would still be there. They could share each other's joys and triumphs, and comfort each other when times got tough. That's what it was really all about, he thought. That one person that you could always count on, no matter what. Even though he knew they would inevitably disagree sometimes, when it came down to it, he knew she would always stand beside him when he needed her the most. And that's why he loved her so much.

A few minutes later he found himself pulling up to Chris's. He smiled as he thought about his older brother, and how much he meant to him. Chris was another one he could always count on in his life, to be there when he really needed a shoulder to lean on. As all siblings do, they had their differences, but Chris looked out for Mitch, and Mitch appreciated that more than anything.

He walked up to the door, and rang the doorbell, pulling up the collar on his coat to keep out the cold. He buried his hands in his pockets and waited until Chris opened the door.

"Hey, little brother, welcome to, well, your bachelor party." He said, ushering Mitch into the house. He stood for a moment, looking out the front door at the snow that was rapidly falling. "It's really coming down, isn't it?" he said, closing the door behind him.

"Yeah, it really is. I hope everyone else can make it ok." Mitch said. "By the way, I guess it'll just be us tonight. All the Ace gang had other things going on that they couldn't get out of. They promised to make it up to me on Wednesday night, though, by taking me out then."

"Well, that's ok, come on in and have a seat. Can I get you something to drink maybe?" Chris asked.

"No, not yet. We just had dinner. I'll wait a little while, thanks." Mitch answered. "House is kinda quiet. Where is everyone?" He asked.

"Trudy took them all into the back. They're having their own little party. She made popcorn and they're going to watch videos until they go to bed. We've been banished to either the kitchen or the rec room downstairs. Either one is fine, they both have a refrigerator and snacks can travel." Chris laughed. Mitch smiled. "So, only a week, Mitchell. Are you getting nervous?" Chris asked.

Mitch sighed. "No, I don't think nervous is quite it." He answered. "I mean, I am a little, but I think I'm more excited and anxious to get the whole thing over with. It seems like it's been dragging out forever. I never could've waited a year, that's for sure."

Chris laughed. "I hear ya, little brother. You never were a patient one." He smiled. "So, are you two boarding the plane on Saturday for Hawaii, or did you get a room for the night and decide to head out on Sunday?"

"Wait, is this a trick question? If I tell you where we're staying, are you going to sabotage it or something?" Mitch asked, smirking at his brother.

"No, buddy, I honestly wouldn't do that. I know I'm rotten, but not that rotten. So, I'm assuming you got a room for the night?" Chris asked.

"Actually, I'm just taking her home and we'll head out from there on Sunday morning." Mitch looked at Chris and leaned forward in his chair. "I wanted our first night together to be as comfortable for her as possible, and well, I thought it'd be better if we were on familiar turf." He chuckled to himself. "You know, Chris, for some reason, she's scared to death. I don't know why, but she is."

Chris smiled and patted Mitch on the leg. "Think about it, Mitch, you can figure that out. She's young, she's innocent, and all she knows is probably what people have told her. She sees you as the man, the one who's supposed to take the lead and know how to handle it all. She probably figures you have expectations, or at least ideas, of how your first time together will be, and she doesn't want to disappoint you. She might also just be timid about the physical part of it, too, you know, not knowing really what to expect."

Mitch looked at him and sighed. "Funny thing is, Chris, I really don't have any expectations. In fact, I'm just as ignorant about all this as she is. That's what makes it even more awkward."

Chris looked at Mitch reassuringly. "Look, you don't need to really worry about a thing. It all kind of, well, just happens naturally. You'll know what to do, it'll just come to you. The main thing is, don't get too anxious, give her time to adjust to everything. Give yourself to her and let her take her time giving herself to you. Trust me, little brother, you'll be fine." Chris smiled at Mitch. "You know, I have to say one thing, and that is, I really respect you, Mitchell. I respect the fact that you had enough in you to wait until you knew you were really in love, until you chose the woman you wanted to spend your life with. That says a lot about your character, Mitch."

Mitch looked at Chris curiously. "What do you mean, Chris? You mean, Trudy wasn't your first?"

Chris shook his head. "No, she wasn't, Mitch. Tina Lawery, frat party, near the end of my freshman year. She was beautiful, and I thought we might have something. Or, at least I wanted to have something. But, you know, I knew it was a mistake an hour after it happened. It was only once, and I was never with anyone else until Trudy. It's been special with Trudy, because I really love her. But I regret that she wasn't the only one."

"Does she know?" Mitch asked.

"Yeah, she knows, and it bothered her at first, I think. But she soon came to realize that one time does not an expert make, and when we were finally together, for me, it was more like the first time than it had been with Tina. It meant something. The love's important, Mitch, no matter what guy tells you it isn't, it really is. You and Dana will be fine, little brother. Don't you worry." Chris smiled as the doorbell rang. "I think the rest of our party is here. Let's go let them in."

Mitch stood up. "Wait, Chris." He said, and Chris paused. "You didn't have to tell me all that, but I'm glad you did. Thanks."

Chris patted Mitch on the shoulder. "That's what it means to be the big brother." He said, smiling. "Someone has to look out for you."

Mitch and Chris went to the door to find Paul, Jim and Jake, with Joseph just pulling in behind them. Mitch smiled.

"Welcome, come on in," he said, standing back from the door.

"Hey, Mitch, hey Chris." Jim said. "It's really getting nasty out here."

"It sure is, but we all made it safe, that's the important part." Joseph said as he tapped the snow off his shoes.

"Hang your coats here, and let's go take this young man's money, what do you say?" Chris said, smiling at Mitch.

"I think I'll be the one going home with the padded wallet." Mitch replied. "It's been a while, but I used to be pretty good at the game."

"Let us be the judges of that." Paul said, patting Mitch on the shoulder.

Chris led the men to the rec room in the basement, thinking it would be more private for them, and that if they got loud, the family wouldn't be disturbed. Chris got all the refreshments in order, and then sat down to play cards. After the first few hands, it was clear to see that Mitch really did know the game. He smiled at the pile of chips and cash now in front of him, and looked at Chris.

"So, Christopher, who's taking who's money here?" He said snidely.

"You're just having a lucky streak, that's all. Don't start gloating just yet. The night is young." Chris answered.

"So, Mitch, only one week of the single life left. What are you going to do with it?" Paul asked.

Mitch laughed. "Actually, it won't be spent living it up, that's for sure. I'll be working until Thursday, we have our pre-marital counseling thing with Pastor Michaels, moving Dana, the rehearsal on Friday, and the band is taking me out Wednesday night. It's going to actually be a pretty busy week."

"Sounds like it." Paul replied.

Mitch dealt the next hand, and took a drink. "Well, guys, since all of you have been married, like, forever, what advice would you give me? I'm sure there's a lot of things I'm gonna need to know."

"My advice is stay single." Jim said, and they all laughed. "No, seriously, Mitch, always let her win the arguments. Even if you know she's wrong, let her win. Keeps the harmony, trust me."

"Yeah, that's for sure." Paul agreed. "If I let Julia win the argument, she's a lot more receptive to, well, other things."

Chris nodded in agreement. "That's another ticket, little brother. If a woman thinks she's right, and you don't let her believe *you* think she's right, she has the power to keep the fire cold, trust me."

Mitch smiled. "How about you, Joseph? Any expert advice?" he asked.

Joseph thought for a minute and smiled. "If you do something you know is gonna make her mad, make up to her before she has a chance to get mad. Buy her some flowers or some candy, or take her out someplace special. Then tell her about it. She'll be so wrapped up in the nice thing you did, she won't get so bent out of shape over the other. Works like a charm for Kayla."

"So, is it all about staying out of trouble?" Mitch asked.

"Definitely." Paul answered, and they all laughed again. "Stay on her good side as much as possible."

Jake was just sitting back, listening to the conversation. He smiled at his young bystanders, and thought to himself, they don't have a clue. After forty years, he felt he knew the secret and decided it was time to speak up and share the truth with his son.

"Mitchell, this advice is all well and good. But, do you want to know the secret of forty years?" Jake asked Mitch.

Mitch took another drink and picked up a card. "Sure, Dad, tell me," he said.

Jake looked right into his young son's eyes. "Honesty, Mitchell. Always be honest with her. Put her first, after God, in everything you do. Do little things that you know make her happy, like bring her flowers and candy, even when it's not a special occasion. Never let her doubt, not even for a second, how much she means to you. Show her that you respect her. Those are the things that will make your marriage worthwhile. Trust me, son."

Mitch sat silent for a minute, as if filing his father's words away in a special place. "Sounds like you know what you're talking about, Dad." He said.

Chris looked at his father and smiled lovingly. "He does, Mitchell."

A few more hands and a few more wins later, Mitch reached into his pocket for his watch. Nine thirty. It was at that moment that he realized he'd forgotten to call Dana and let her know he'd arrived safely. He stood up. "Well, time to make a pit stop." He said, starting toward the stairs.

"Mitch, there's a bathroom right over there." Chris said.

"Oh, yeah, right. Uh, well, I thought I'd see if there were any more potato chips, too. While I'm up there." He answered.

Chris smiled. "Cabinet to the right of the stove." Mitch nodded and started up the stairs. "And by the way," Chris called after him, "tell Dana we all said hello." Mitch could hear the sound of the guys' laughter behind him, and he smiled.

Mitch got to the kitchen and picked up the phone, dialing his home number. A few rings later, he heard a sweet familiar voice.

"Hello, beautiful." Mitch said sweetly.

"Hey, Mitch, you made it ok? I was starting to wonder." I said.

"I'm sorry, love, I just got caught up and didn't realize how late it was. But, yeah, I'm here and I'm fine. How're things going there?" he asked.

"Great. I just about have everything put away. I sorted through some things you had here, honey, so you'll have to tell me what you want to keep and what you don't." I told him.

"That's fine, my stuff was so mismatched I'm sure I don't need any of it anyway." Mitch answered. He looked outside at the snow that was still coming down. "You know, baby, I may just camp out here tonight on Chris's couch. The roads were starting to get a little slick on the way here, and it's still snowing. Why don't you just stay there tonight? I'll come early enough tomorrow that I can take you home before church, ok?"

I smiled at his concern. "Honey, don't worry, I'll be fine. I can make it ten blocks home, I think."

Mitch sighed. "Dana, you haven't driven in this much snow for a long time. You have a new car that you really aren't used to driving in this. Please humor me, love, and stay there. You can sleep in a pair of my sweats or something, and try out the bed." He smiled. "Don't get too used to having all of it to yourself, though."

"Alright, Mitchell, I'll stay here. I really wasn't cherishing the thought of going back out into the cold, anyway. You sure Chris will be ok with you staying there?" I asked.

"Not a problem. He's got the room. Besides, when he sees outside, he may make us all stay here, anyway. Kind of a bachelor slumber party, huh?"

I chuckled. "Sounds like fun." I said.

"Well, I'd better get back before they miss me. Don't want them dipping into my winnings, either." He said.

"I guess I'll see you in the morning, then. I love you, Mitch."

"I love you too, Dana. Sweet dreams." Mitch smiled as he hung up the phone, grabbed the bag of potato chips and retreated back downstairs.

Mitch rejoined the guys and opening the bag of chips, he poured them into the empty bowl on the table. "What's the game?" He asked.

"Baseball. Deal you in?" Jim asked.

"That's my sport." Mitch replied.

The guys continued to talk and laugh, swapping their best marriage stories for Mitch, who was having fun taking it all in. Jim relayed a story about Angelina that made them all laugh, and it reminded Mitch of the day in Jacy's Department Store, when he and Dana had been Christmas shopping.

"Well," Jim started. "It was my fifteen year class reunion, and a couple of old buddies of mine talked me into going. We're there, and we're having a good time, and I get up to get us a drink, when out of nowhere, this girl walks up to me. I didn't recognize her at first, because she looked a little different, but it turned out to be the girl I dated my sophomore year and part of my junior year. So, she's talking to me, you know, asking me what I've been up to and all that, and that's all fine and dandy. Except, Claire, that's her name, was always a really touchy feely sort of person. The kind that can't talk without a hand on you somewhere." The guys were all chuckling, putting the scene together in their minds. "Let me put this into perspective for a minute. I said she looked different. I mean better. I thought she was cute when we dated, of course, but she had really grown up into something pretty hot. I couldn't help my eyes wandering a little and of course, I'm sure I must have smiled too. And she's got her hand on my arm, looking right in my eyes. Ang is sitting at the table, taking in the whole scene. Of course I tell Claire I'm married, and she wants to see my wife, so I pointed to Angelina, and instead of just turning to look at her, Claire puts her arm around my shoulder and leans toward me." The guys were all listening intently to the story. "I try to move away, but she just turns back and slides her hand down my arm and keeps it there. By the time I finally break away from her and get back to the table, Ang is ready to spontaneously combust. She suddenly forgets anyone else is sitting at the table, and she tears into me like there's no tomorrow." The guys were all laughing hysterically. "She accuses me of coming to the reunion just so I could see Claire, like I knew she would be there or something. I finally convinced her that it was all innocent, and of course, I had to renounce any ounce of manhood I still had in me to get her to make up, including $200 for a little diamond pendant." The guys were all still laughing loudly.

"Why is it women are so jealous?" Mitch asked. "Dana's the same way. Drives me insane. She's always accusing me of flirting with other women."

"Well, do you Mitchell?" Jake asked. "You know, you are my son, but you are a handsome young man, and I'm sure the ladies notice."

"Well, they may notice me, but I really don't notice them. And if I do, it's only in passing. But try telling Dana that." Mitch took another drink. "For instance, we go Christmas shopping, and she tells me I need to get something personal for Mom, so I pick out that apron I got her. I go to pay for it, and the salesgirl just happens to be young and somewhat attractive. Not the type I'd ever go for, kinda fake, actually. But, anyhow, this girl starts talking to me, and I'm a nice guy, I don't like to be rude to people, so I make small talk while she's ringing me up." Chris and Joseph were both sitting back in their chairs, watching Mitch's animated way of telling the story. "Dana's right beside me the whole time, or so I think. I get done with the sale, and I turn around and she's gone. I'm thinking, ok, what happened, where did she go? Then I see her off to the side, so I smile and I wave, and she throws two bags at me and starts stomping off." The men start to chuckle, as does Mitch. "I'm talking to her, asking her what's wrong, and she won't tell me, and I'm trying to carry six bags worth of stuff and follow Miss Attitude out into the mall."

Joseph laughed. "She's a little spitfire, no doubt about that." He said.

"Yeah, well I finally figure out what's happening, and I try to reason with her. No dice. She tells me I was practically undressing this girl with my eyes. I'm thinking she's nuts, but I try to keep my cool. She wants to go home. So instead, I take her to Gartano's, thinking a little dinner, a little romance, she'll come around. Didn't happen." He looked at Joseph. "It actually took Kayla's coercing to get her to cool her jets on that one. Don't know what she said, but keep her handy, Joseph. I may need her again sometime." Mitch chuckled.

The men played and talked until the wee hours of the morning. Joseph, Jim and Paul decided to go home since they lived the closest, and Jake and Mitch decided to stay. The three promised to call when they got home, and Chris closed the door behind them.

"Well, one of you can take the guest room, the other can take the fold out in the den." Chris said. "I wish the others would have stayed, too, the roads look pretty bad."

"They'll be fine, Christopher." Jake said. "They all live within ten minutes. Besides, they said they'd call. Speaking of which, I'd better call your mother and let her know my plans." With that he went off to phone.

"Thanks for a great time, Chris." Mitch told him. "It was really cool of you to do this for me."

"No problem, little brother. I just wish you'd have let someone else win a hand or two." Chris said.

"Told you I was good." Mitch replied, smirking. "Besides, I didn't win all of them. I think I let someone else win one." He looked at the clock. Almost two. "Look, I'm pretty beat. Tell Dad I'll take the den. I'll be fine there."

"Cool, buddy. The bed should already be made up. I think Trudy did that this morning, in case anyone wanted to stay. There's an extra blanket in the closet if you want it, and the clock on the desk has an alarm."

"That works. Tell Dad goodnight for me, ok? I hate to end the party, but I told Dana I'd come home early and take her home to get dressed before church. I told her to stay at my place tonight. Didn't want her out on the roads." Mitch said.

"Probably a smart move." Chris answered. "Sleep well, Mitchell."

"You too." Mitch said, and he headed off for the den. Locking the door behind him, he got undressed and pulled out the bed, slipping under the covers. The phone rang three times, almost in succession, and he knew that the others had made it home safely, putting his mind at ease. He took off his glasses and laid them on the table next to him, and closed his eyes. He was thinking about Dana now, and could picture her tiny body all curled up sleeping, seemingly lost in his great big bed. He smiled at the thought of her wearing his sweats, and how big and baggy they would be on her. He couldn't believe how much he wished he could be right there next to her. Soon, he would be. But for now, he drifted off to sleep so he could be with her in his dreams.

On the other side of town, I awoke to the sound of the TV. I must have drifted off to sleep with it on, I thought. It took me a minute to remember that I was still at Mitch's. Getting up, I went to make sure the door was securely locked, then I turned off the light and went into the bedroom. I could just stay on the couch for the night, I thought, but soon I would be sharing this bed with Mitch, so I might as well get used to it. I washed up a little, and began my search for something to wear. Finding the shirt he had obviously worn to work that day left on the chair when he'd come home and changed, I picked it up and held it to me. It had the scent of his cologne on it, and made me think of him, so I slipped it on, rolling up the sleeves a few turns to uncover my hands. I climbed into bed and turned off the light, rolling over to hug the pillows I knew he slept on. Soon, I thought, I could roll over and hug him. I smiled as I fell asleep once more, thinking of Mitch.

The next morning the alarm went off early, and Mitch got up and dressed, straightened up the den, and went into the bathroom to wash his face and comb his hair. Much to his surprise, he found Chris sitting in the living room, with a cup of coffee and the newspaper.

"Good morning, little brother. Sleep well?" he asked.

"Sure, just fine." Mitch answered. "Got anymore coffee?" he asked.

Chris pointed to the kitchen, and Mitch disappeared, returning a minute later with a cup for himself, as well as a cinnamon roll.

"See you found those, too." Chris smiled. "Trudy made them yesterday. Pretty good, huh?"

"Yeah, not too bad. Dana's a great cook, too. Good thing, because I can't boil water." Mitch laughed.

Chris smiled. "I've learned a little, but I pretty much leave it up to Trudy. She enjoys it."

Mitch reached out and picked up part of the newspaper that Chris had laid down. He held it out at arms length, and then pulled it in close. Taking off his glasses, he rubbed his eyes, then put them back on. Chris noticed and asked him.

"Mitch, are you having trouble seeing that paper?" he asked.

"You know, it seems like my glasses aren't working this morning, for some reason. I mean, overall, I can still see pretty decently most of the time, but I'm thinking I may need a new prescription." Mitch replied.

"You can't see anything without them, can you?" Chris asked.

Mitch took them off and then put them back on, as if to prove his point. "Not really, only images. Everything's kind of a blur."

Chris thought back to the day Mitch proposed to Dana, and remembered he had taken them off when he kissed her, then put them back on before he looked at her again. "So, now that makes sense to me." Chris said.

Mitch looked at him curiously. "What makes sense?" he asked.

"The day you proposed to Dana, we all wondered why you took your glasses off before you kissed her, then put them back on before you opened your eyes. You wanted to be able to see her in a special way, like for the first time, didn't you?"

Mitch smiled at the memory. "That's why." He said, his face shining. "And speaking of Dana, I'd better get home and get her going so we don't miss church." He stood up and took his coffee cup back to the kitchen, then walked out to the foyer for his coat, Chris now behind him. "Thanks again, Chris, for everything." He shook Chris's hand and gave him a hug. "I'll see you at church."

"Anytime, little brother. Be careful out there." Chris smiled as he closed the door behind him.

A short while later, Mitch quietly unlocked the door to his apartment, stepped inside, and closed it behind him. The apartment appeared somewhat different than the night before, a small pile of empty boxes in one corner to be tossed out, and some things on the table Dana had taken out of his cupboards evidently to make room for the new things she had gotten at the shower. He smiled at the set of flowered canisters on the countertop, and the frilly dishtowel hanging from the handle on the oven door. He opened a few cabinets to see things neatly tucked away, all clean and sparkling, and wondered just how long it had taken her to do all this alone.

Noticing the blanket on the couch, he wondered if she had fallen asleep there and decided to leave upon waking, or if she was indeed still asleep in bed. He tossed his keys onto the table, and quietly walked in the direction of the bedroom. Pausing at his bookcase, he smiled at the delicate crystal frame she had placed on top, obviously another gift, containing their engagement picture. Picking it up, he couldn't help but notice just how beautiful she was and how happy they looked together. Placing it back, he softly crept into the bedroom and seeing her there, he smiled and whispered her name.

"Dana, sweetheart, I'm home." He said, liking the way that sounded.

I rolled over and slowly, sleepily opened my eyes to see Mitch sitting on the side of the bed next to me. He bent down and kissed me softly on the cheek. "Good morning, beautiful." He said. "Did you sleep well?"

"Uh huh." I answered, rubbing my eyes. "Did you?" I asked him.

"Yes, I did. But I was thinking about how much I would rather have been here with you." He smiled.

I sat up, and remembering I was only wearing Mitch's shirt, I made sure to keep the covers up around me. He smiled.

"I love your choice of nighttime attire." He said, looking at me. "Very sexy."

"Well, it's warm and comfortable, and it smells like your cologne." I said. "And, I didn't have to look far to find it," I said, pointing to the chair where he had left it the night before.

"It's fine, sweetheart." Mitch said. "So, it looks like you were a busy little bee last night. I like what you've done with the place."

"It took me a while, but it's one less thing to worry about." I replied. "I still need you to tell me what things you want to keep. I put everything on the table."

"I'll take a look later. Right now, we need to get Miss Dana home so we can make it to church. I'll drop you off then I'll come home and shower, and come back for you, ok?" he said.

"I have a much simpler idea." I said, taking his hand. "Why don't you shower and dress, and while you're doing that, I can get dressed and drive home, and you can come and get me when you're ready. I have my car here, you know, and I'm sure the roads are cleared by now."

"Always logical, aren't you?" He said. "First, how about if I do this." He scooted closer to me and putting his arm around me, he leaned down and gave me a kiss, and then another. Before long, my arms were wrapped around his neck and we were lost in the moment. Finally, Mitch pulled away and smiled at me.

"As much as I'd like to stay here, I think we better get going, or we'll be late." He said standing up. "Come on, I'll leave so you can get dressed." He bent down and gave me another kiss before he left the room. A few minutes later, Mitch lightly knocked on the door, and I told him to come in. I was making the bed, and he came over and helped me finish.

"Go on home now, and I'll be over in a little while to pick you up, ok? Come on, I'll walk you out." He took me by the hand and led me to the door, helping me on with my coat. Mitch gave me another soft kiss as he opened the door.

"You be careful, now, and I'll see you in a little while." He said, waving to me.

"Ok, see you soon." I said, as I waved and walked away.

I had to brush the snow off my car before I got in, and the snow came up over the tops of my short boots, but I managed to get it all taken care of and get home within ten minutes. I quickly showered and dressed, and waited for Mitch to arrive.

While I waited, I carefully packed a few more boxes, finishing up with the little things sitting around the room, then moving to the closet. I decided to pack the top shelf first, then whatever I wouldn't be needing in the bottom. Pulling over the chair, I climbed up on it, remembering what Mitch had told me about climbing that day at the bistro. He was so protective, I thought. How many times in the past had I done this? Hundreds. And how many times had I fallen? None. But in having that thought, I must have jinxed myself. As I reached into the far back corner of the shelf for a box, I felt the chair starting to tip. I tried to grab onto the shelf to steady myself, but it didn't work. The chair toppled over, taking me and the box I was reaching for and a few other things with it. The edge of the chair hit the nightstand, knocking over the lamp, sending it crashing to the floor as well. Just as everything hit the floor, Mitch knocked on the door. Hearing the commotion, he pounded louder and called out for me.

A little stunned, I got up and went to the door, realizing that somehow I had torn the sleeve of my blouse. I knew Mitch was going to ask questions, so I tried hard to think of a story, but was still having trouble coming up with it as I opened the door for him.

"Dana, what was that I just heard? It sounded like something falling." He said with concern.

I looked up at him sheepishly. "It was, Mitch, it was me."

Mitch glared at me, his expression of concern and anger. "Were you climbing again, Dana?" he asked. "Please tell me you weren't." Then he noticed the sleeve on my blouse. "Dana, just what were you doing? Are you hurt?" He took my arm and noticed a small scrape that I didn't even notice myself.

"I was just packing things from my closet, that's all. No big deal." I told him, walking back toward the bedroom.

Mitch followed close behind, and stopped dead when he saw the results of my fiasco on the bedroom floor. He walked over to me and grabbing my arms firmly but gently, swung me around to face him.

"Dana, what is it going to take for you to learn? I want you to take a look at all this. You are lucky a torn blouse and a little scrape are all you got. You could have hit your head on something, or broken a bone, or anything. I told you, don't climb. You knew I was coming over. Why couldn't you have waited until I got here to get the things you couldn't reach? I swear, Dana, you act like you don't know how to think sometimes." Mitch was clearly angry with me, which hurt my feelings. He let go of me, and going to my closet, he pulled out another blouse and handed it to me. "Go put this one on so we can go to church." He said firmly. Then he sighed deeply and turned toward me. "Are you sure you're ok?" he asked.

I nodded, a tear starting down my cheek, and I turned to go into the bathroom to change. Mitch walked up behind me and gently turned me toward him, taking me into his embrace. "I'm sorry I yelled at you, sweetheart. I just don't understand why you won't listen to me. I'm trying to keep you safe, Dana. I don't want you to get hurt." He kissed my forehead and wiped away my tears. "Would you like me to help you put something on that scrape?" he asked.

"No, it's ok." I said softly. "You know, I'm not as tall as you are, Mitch. I can't reach things up high. How else am I supposed to get to them, if you aren't here?"

Mitch sighed. "You really don't listen, do you?" he said, embracing me again. "You leave them until I am here. I don't want you climbing anymore, it's not safe."

"Like you've never done it yourself." I retorted.

"As a matter of fact, I haven't since I've grown up. I'm 6'2", Dana, I have no need to climb, ok? Now, go get yourself ready while I clean this all up for you." Mitch let go of me and started to pick things up, mumbling something under his breath about me being stubborn.

"So are you, Mitchell Tarrington." I shot back, heading toward the bathroom. Mitch paused and exhaled deeply, shaking his head, then returned to his work.

A few minutes later I returned to Mitch who was just finishing up with everything. He stood up and looked at me, his expression now much softer than earlier. "Are we ok now?" he asked.

"I don't know, you tell me." I answered.

He smiled. "I got everything down from the shelf so you have no need to even get up there anymore. Now, come here and give me a kiss, and let's get going, ok?" Mitch leaned down and kissed me softly. "How's that arm?" He asked.

"It's fine. Doesn't even hurt, really." I said. "We better go now, or we'll be late."

Mitch and I walked out and he helped me on with my coat, put his own on, and we walked out to the car in silence. He opened the door for me, then came around to get in on the other side.

"Dana, are you angry with me?" he asked. "I mean, for raising my voice earlier."

I sighed. "No, I'm not angry. You just hurt my feelings, that's all. But I'm over it."

He looked at me. "Are you? You don't act like it." He said.

"I am, now let's move on, ok?" I said.

Mitch shrugged. "Ok, sweetheart, I believe you." He smiled. "So, this time next week, we'll be on our way to Hawaii. Are you excited?"

"Yes, I am." I replied, the thought of it breaking my melancholy mood. "It's going to be so much fun. Walking on the beach, seeing the sights, and I hear you can even go to a real luau. That would be kinda neat, I think." Then I hugged his arm. "And, of course, they have some great stores there, ones they don't have here. We have to do a little shopping, at least."

Mitch smiled. "That blows my plans. I wasn't planning to leave the room," he said, laughing, and I smacked him on the arm. "I really wish you wouldn't do that. It hurts," he said.

"It's supposed to, Mitchell." I told him. He looked at me and snickered.

As usual, Mitch's family made it to the church before us, and we slipped in quietly just as the service was about to start. We had asked Pastor Michaels to make a general announcement to the congregation about our wedding the following Saturday, which we got there just in time to hear.

"I see the subjects of my next announcement just arrived. Don't sit down yet." He told us, and we looked at each other, obeying and a little embarrassed that we'd been caught sneaking in late. Pastor continued. "This coming Saturday at 2:30, I will have the pleasure of performing the wedding ceremony for this fine young couple, Dana Walker and Mitch Tarrington. They would like to welcome and invite everyone to join in that celebration with them." He smiled at us and teased, "And you have to be on time for that, kids." Everyone laughed, and Mitch and I sank into the pew.

The service was wonderful, and afterwards, we gathered as usual to chat a few minutes with Mitch's family. Pastor Michaels approached us.

"Mitch, Dana, I need to ask if we can make a slight change in plans." He said. "It seems there's a meeting I have tomorrow night that I had forgotten about and I know we were supposed to meet. Would you have some free time right now? I know it's short notice, but it shouldn't take more than an hour or so."

Mitch and I exchanged looks. "I guess that would be ok. We really didn't have anything definite planned." He said.

"Good. Well, what I'd like to do, Mitch, is take your lovely fiancé and talk to her for a few minutes, then I'll have her come for you. I'll talk to you alone, and then the two of you together. Ok?"

"Sure." Mitch said, letting go of my hand. "I'll just hang out here," he said, and I smiled as I walked away with Pastor Michaels.

He led me into his office, and closing the door, prompted me to sit down. "So, Dana, first, don't be nervous at all in meeting with me. This is just a standard thing I like to do with all my young couples before they get married," he said, taking his seat on the other side of the desk, and smiling at me. "I know you and Mitch have only known each other a short time, and I also know that everyone and their uncle has probably asked you this, but I feel compelled to ask you as well." He smiled sweetly. "Are you positive that you feel ready to be married to Mitch?"

I didn't hesitate with my answer. "Definitely, Pastor. I'm very much ready to get married. I'm positive."

Pastor smiled. "I thought so, but you know, I have to make sure of these things." He said. "Dana, I just want to talk to you a little bit, and ask you a few questions, ok?"

"Ok." I said timidly, not exactly sure what to expect.

Pastor and I talked for about fifteen minutes or so, then he sent me to get Mitch. I found him sitting in the back of the sanctuary alone, a hymnal in his hand, softly singing to himself. I smiled at how peaceful and lost in meditation he looked. He closed the book when he saw me and laid it down next to him.

"Just passing the time." He said. "Ready for me now?" he asked.

"Yes, and I think I'll take your seat here. It's very peaceful." I said.

"So, what should I expect?" he asked standing up.

"No big deal, just general stuff. Go on now, he's waiting." I told him.

Mitch didn't seem satisfied with my answer, but he trotted off anyway in the direction of the Pastor's office. I sat down and looked to the front of the church. The most beautiful sight in the entire place, I thought, was the huge wooden cross on the wall behind the pulpit. I stared at it for a few minutes, closing my eyes and saying a silent prayer that our marriage would be blessed. When I opened my eyes, I looked up to see Mitch standing next to me.

"Ok, tag team time." He said, reaching out for my hand. I took hold of it and walked with him back to Pastor Michaels' office.

We sat down across from him once again, and he smiled. "Well, I must say that it seems from what I've heard, and also from what I've seen over the past few months, that you two are very much in love, and more than ready to make the whole thing official. Is that a pretty accurate statement?" He asked.

"Absolutely!" Mitch smiled, and I had to smile, too, at the Mitchism.

"Well, let's talk about a few different things then, shall we?" Pastor led us into a discussion about what we were expecting from our marriage, and what we should expect, about our dreams and fears and anxieties, and also, about our wedding night. He was very pleased to hear we had been abstinent, and commended us for making that choice. After about an hour, he led us in a prayer and sent us on our way.

"That wasn't so bad, was it?" Mitch said once we were outside.

"No, I guess not. Just that it seems like there's so much we just don't know." I said.

Mitch smiled. "You know, love, I bet somewhere else in the world right now there's a couple just like us walking out of a church saying the exact same thing."

"You're probably right." I said. "Well, my future husband, are you ready to help me pack some more boxes? I'll make you lunch first."

"You have a deal." He smiled, kissing me. Out of the corner of my eye I caught Pastor Michaels standing in the doorway, smiling at us.

I made a couple of hot ham and cheese sandwiches, threw some potato chips on the side with two glasses of milk, and carried it into the bedroom where Mitch was busily packing the contents of my closet.

"Baby, you know I love you, but some of these shoes have to go. What do you need with all these shoes, anyway? I'll bet you only wear one or two pair of them." He said, grabbing his sandwich off the tray and taking a bite.

"I do so wear them all." I said, defensively. "I can't very well wear them all at the same time, now can I?"

He laughed. "Dana, I don't have enough room in my closet for all this stuff. Can't you at least take a look and see if there's anything here you can part with?"

I reached down and threw one pair of old tennis shoes to the side. "There, are you happy now?" I asked, taking a potato chip off his plate.

He rolled his eyes and sighing, put the other shoes into a box.

"Honey, wait, you can't pack everything. I'm going to need clothes for the next few days, you know."

Mitch sat down in the chair. "Take what you need and put it on the bed. Then we can pack everything else." He said, stuffing three potato chips into his mouth at once. I looked at him disgustedly. "What?" he said.

"Nothing." I replied. I went to my closet and soon had what I needed piled on the bed. "There, now you can put everything else in the boxes."

"Sweetheart, we need to talk about something. That something is, I've come to the conclusion that you are a packrat." He was starting to laugh. "We really need to get rid of some of this stuff, Dana. I can't begin to think where we're going to put it all."

"Well, Mitchell, I thought the whole idea was that your apartment is bigger than mine. So, that means more room, right?" I asked.

"Yes, but remember, I have all of my stuff there. We're merging two living spaces into one, love," he reminded.

"Then why don't you get rid of some of your things?" I asked.

"I have, Dana. What do you think all that stuff on my table was? It all went. I put it in a box and we'll donate it with what we aren't keeping or giving to someone from here." Mitch stuffed three more chips in his mouth and smiled at me.

"Fine, you want me to get rid of something that I just have laying around most of the time, I will." I picked up a box and laughing, put it over Mitch's head.

"Not funny." He said from under the box, smiling as he took it off. "Come on, now Dana, let's go through this stuff. I'll help you." Mitch took a marker and wrote the word "Donate" on the top and the sides. He placed it on the floor and threw the pair of shoes in it that I had placed aside earlier. "Now, help me continue putting things in there," he said.

I finished my sandwich and dug back into the box of clothes Mitch had already packed, much to his dismay. But, I soon found at least seven items that I could donate. I continued to search through, and added another two items, plus four pairs of shoes. Mitch seemed to be pleased.

"See, wasn't that easy?" he asked. "We can continue to do that as we pack the other things, too, ok? If you don't need it, don't use it or don't wear it, it goes. Deal?"

I sighed heavily. "Ok, but you have to let me go shopping so I can replace these things."

He laughed and shook his head. "Oh, no, little miss, no shopping. I can clearly see there is nothing you could possibly need."

"You're no fun, Mitchell Tarrington," I said smugly, sticking my tongue out at him.

"Is that so? Well, you'd better take that back, Dana Walker," he said, standing up and coming toward me.

"Never!" I shouted, and with that, Mitch grabbed me up in his arms and tossed me lightly into the middle of the bed, landing to straddle me and tickling me with all he had in him.

"You're going to wrinkle my clothes!" I managed to squeeze out amidst my laughter.

"I don't care. You were being mean to me, you deserve to be tickled," he said, laughing almost as hard as I was.

"I'm sorry, I'm sorry, just please stop, Mitchell," I pleaded.

He stopped tickling me and sat back lightly on my legs, taking both my hands and pushing my arms up to lay flat against the bed. Then he smiled at me, still catching his breath from the laughter, and kissed me softly. "I love you, Dana," he said, and pulled me up to him, kissing me more intently each time. He slipped his hands under the back of my sweater, and brought them up slowly, stopping at the middle of my back.

"Mitchell, what do you think you're going to do?" I asked him.

He sighed and let me go, looking at me with a somewhat guilty expression. "I'm sorry, love," he said. "I wasn't going to do anything, honest. But I did think about it."

"I know you did, that's why I asked," I said. "It's ok, I appreciate that you stopped yourself."

"Well, I have to tell you, it's getting harder and harder for me to do that," he admitted, standing up.

I stood up and put my arms around him. "I love you, Mitch," I said, hugging him. "Thank you for respecting me." I looked up at him. "You look tired, honey. Why don't you go out and curl up on the couch, and I'll finish up in here? I'm sure there's some sort of sport thing on TV that you could watch. I'm pretty much just down to my dresser anyway."

He yawned. "No, I'll stay here and help. I told you I would."

"Grab that tray and come with me, Mitchell." I told him, and he obeyed.

Mitch put the tray on the counter, and followed me to the couch. "Down." I instructed, and like a well trained animal, he did as he was told. I took off his shoes and covered him with the blanket. Handing him the remote control, I gave him a kiss on the cheek. "Find something to watch, and relax." I said firmly.

"Ok," he said.

I walked into the kitchen and got a drink of water, and as I walked back through, I noticed Mitch had taken off his glasses and laid them on the coffee table, as if preparing to go to sleep. I stood for a moment watching him shift through the channels, knowing he couldn't possibly be able to see anything he was looking at. Noticing my presence, he turned in my direction.

"Dana, I know you're there, I can't see you clearly, but I know you are. Is there something you want, sweetheart?" he asked.

"No, honey, you just rest. I'll be in the bedroom packing." I said, smiling.

A few minutes later, I crept back out into the living room. I peeked over the back of the couch and just as I had suspected, Mitch was sound asleep. I smiled at him and slipped back into the bedroom to continue packing. Grabbing a box, I opened my dresser drawer and began to stuff things inside. I tried to humor Mitch by finding things that I didn't need any longer, and was happily able to put some additional items in the donation box. I had all but one drawer packed when Mitch came in and sat down on the floor beside me.

"So, how's it going?" He asked, yawning.

"Fine, sleepy head. Did you have a nice nap?" I asked.

"It was wonderful. Thanks. I was up kind of late last night. We played cards until, like two or something like that," he replied.

"Oh, yeah, tell me about it. Did you have a good time? What did you talk about?" I inquired.

Mitch smiled. "Yes, I had a good time. We just talked about stuff," he answered.

I looked at him, still putting things into the box. "What kind of stuff?"

He kissed me on top of the head as he stood up to get the tape for the box. "Just stuff, Dana. Nothing you'd be the least bit interested in."

"Oh, I don't know, Mitch, try me." I said, leaning back on my hands and smiling at him. "Or, is it just that you don't want me to know what you talked about? Maybe some loose women or something along those lines?" I raised my eyebrows.

"Why, Dana Walker, how dare you insult my mother, my sisters and my sister-in-law that way. And I never thought you'd refer to yourself as loose." Mitch smiled.

"Mitchell, what are you talking about?" I said.

He sat back down beside me. "Sweetheart, the only women we talked about last night were Mom, Julia, Angelina, Trudy, you, and oh, yeah, Kayla," he said.

"I'll bet you were giving each other all the dirt about us, weren't you?" I asked, taking the tape from him and putting some on the box next to me.

"Listen, Dana, we just talked. We joked, we laughed, we had a good time. We did the male bonding thing. We drank beer, ate potato chips and played poker. That was all, ok? Stop worrying about it. I would never say anything bad about you." He put his arm around me. "Did I ever tell you that you're paranoid?" He asked softly.

"I'm not either. I just know how men are, that's all," I said smugly.

Mitch laughed. "Did you suddenly grow body parts I should know about, Dana? You don't know how men are. I'm sure we're nothing like you think."

"No, actually, you're probably worse," I said, standing up.

Mitch stood up beside me, laughing and shaking his head. "And like women are perfect."

"Not perfect, just closer to it than men." I shot back.

"Ok, if that's what you want to think, love," he said, smirking. "What's left to do here?" Mitch asked, stretching.

"Just one more drawer, and I'll pack that one myself. Things you don't need to see," I said.

He laughed. "What, your underwear? Baby, no big deal. Six more days and I'll see it all I want."

"You really think so, huh?" I said teasingly.

Mitch grabbed me into a hug. "Uh huh," he said with a smile. He gave me a quick kiss. "I feel like doing something. How would you like to go bowling? That's something we've never done together. It'll be fun."

I laughed. "Gosh, Mitch, I haven't bowled in years. I'm up for it, if you promise not to laugh at how lousy I do."

"I wouldn't laugh at you. Besides, I'm not that great myself." Then he smiled. "Hey, how do you feel about asking Chris and Trudy to join us? They haven't been out since the baby was born. I'm sure they could get a sitter."

"Sure, give them a call." I replied.

Mitch let me go and grabbed the phone off the nightstand. Two minutes later, we had a date with Chris and Trudy.

"Told them to be here around five, ok? Chris said he knows a place with open lanes all night." Mitch said, hanging up the phone. "Trudy seemed excited about getting a night away from the kids."

Mitch and I decided to relax a little while and watched an old movie until Chris and Trudy knocked on the door, right around five.

"Love what you've done with the place, Dana." Chris teased, looking around at the empty walls and stacks of boxes. Then he turned to Mitch. "Mitchell, I think you better just move all your things out. You won't have any room when she gets all her things in there."

"We've had that discussion." Mitch told him. "I think we may just have to ask my neighbors to move out, knock down the wall, and take both apartments."

"Mitchell, I don't have that much stuff. Besides, if you'll look in the bedroom, there are two boxes full of things to donate. You know, you could get rid of some of your things. Take that weight bench for instance. Takes up a whole corner of the living room." I said, smiling and waiting for his reaction.

Mitch and Chris looked at each other. "Good grief, girl, have you gone insane?" Mitch smiled. "I'd get rid of the couch before I'd get rid of my bench." He grabbed me into a tight hug. "How do you think I got this body you're so crazy about?"

Chris laughed. "Tough break for you, little brother. I was born with my great physique."

Trudy folded her arms and gave Chris the once over. "Must be hiding it from me, then." She said and we all laughed as Chris pretended to pout. She gave him a kiss. "It's ok, I still love you." She told him.

"Well, how about we head out? We brought the van so we can all ride together, if that's ok with you two. Mitch, you can sit up front with Chris since there's more room. Dana and I can sit in the back."

20

The bowling alley was noisy, but not overly crowded, and we quickly settled into our lane. Mitch smiled sweetly and leaned close to me. "I love you, sweetheart," he said, kissing my cheek.

"I love you two, honey," I said, returning the kiss.

Chris smiled at us. "Look, you two. Let's get something straight," he said, pretending to sound authoritative. "These public displays of affection have got to stop. Those of us who have been married for a while, well, it tends to make us a little uncomfortable. We've gotten past that 'can't get enough of each other stage' and have moved into the, 'oh, you're still here' stage. Makes us look bad."

Trudy laughed. "Yeah, makes you wonder how on earth we got four children, doesn't it, Christopher?"

"I didn't say we don't have those occasional moments where we regress, dear. Happens to the best of us." He smiled and kissed Trudy's cheek.

"Sorry, Chris, I promise I'll try harder." Mitch said, smiling. Then he turned to me. "I'm just weak, I guess."

Chris and Mitch decided they wanted to team up guys against girls, and Trudy and I were happy to oblige. After about three frames, it was clear that the girls had the advantage, much to the guys' dismay. I smiled at Mitch.

"So, honey, it looks like I may have finally found something I can beat you at." I said smugly.

Mitch stood up to take his turn. "The night is young, Dana darling. Don't go getting too confident just yet." Then he turned to Chris. "You hear this nonsense, Chris? She actually thinks they're going to win."

Chris nodded. "Foolish girl. So young and naïve." He laughed.

Mitch picked up his bowling ball and started into his approach. As if he had it planned, the ball went straight to the middle and all the pins fell down in a mighty crash. He made a fist and pulled it down toward him. "Yes!" He exclaimed, looking right at me. "Ha. Now who's better?" he said, smirking at me.

"Eat my dust, baby." I said, standing up to take my turn. I picked up my ball and put my full concentration on the arrows. Between the second and third, I told myself. Just reach out and grab the victory. Just as I was about to let go of the ball, my concentration was totally broken by the sound of Mitch's voice.

"Hey sweetheart, I'm liking the view from back here. Nice approach!" he said, chuckling.

I let go of the ball, and it went straight, alright. Straight into the gutter. I turned around to glare at Mitch, as he and Chris laughed hysterically and exchanged a high five.

"Mitchell, that was NOT funny at all!" I said. "In fact, that was rather mean. You made me miss my shot."

He smiled at me. "But I was complimenting you, sweetheart. I thought you liked it when I said nice things about you."

I looked at Trudy, who was shaking her head at Mitch. "Can you believe him?" I asked her. "Oh, I swear, what are men good for anyway?"

Mitch smiled and raised his eyebrows, he and Chris exchanging a knowing look, and the two of them laughed.

"Dana, remember, men are basically pigs. That's all, just pigs. Without us, they wouldn't be able to function," Trudy said, sticking her tongue out at Chris.

"Oh, really? Is that why I'm always hearing, 'Chris can you get this for me or Chris, can you make the baby a bottle, or Chris, would you mind stopping at the store on your way home or..........'" Chris was having fun mocking her.

"Ok, ok, point taken, just bowl, would you?" Trudy pulled her husband up by the hand and pushed him toward the lane as he continued to laugh at her.

Mitch got up and moved to sit beside me. "Sorry, baby, I was just having fun. Forgive me?" he said, giving me his best puppy dog eyes.

"I might think about it, if you'll get me a soda, and maybe some potato chips?" I said, giving him the puppy eyes right back.

"Fine, a soda and potato chips. How about for you guys?" He asked Chris and Trudy.

"Just a couple sodas, Mitch." Chris said.

It was Trudy's turn to bowl and getting a strike, she came back smiling. "Put an X in the box right there, Christopher." She said, pointing to the score sheet and smirking at Chris.

Mitch returned just then with the sodas and chips. "You're up Mitchell." Chris said. "Bowl another strike and you'll put us ahead."

Trudy and I exchanged glances, and I beckoned her close to me. "Remember what we do at the club when Mitch is about halfway through the set?" I asked her. She smiled and laughed.

"Let's do it!" She said.

Just as Mitch was about to throw the ball onto the lane, Trudy and I yelled, "We love you Mitch!" He dropped the ball and it rolled slowly down the lane, knocking down two pins. He spun around with a smirk and walked right toward me. Trudy and I were laughing so hard we had tears in our eyes.

Mitch stopped in front of me, folded his arms and looked down at me, Trudy and I still laughing. "Dana, that wasn't nice," he said, smirking.

"You know what they say about paybacks, Mitchell." I smiled.

Mitch bowled his next frame and picked up the spare. I was up and prepared to make up for my last turn. But first, I took out my insurance policy.

"Listen, Mitchell Jacob Tarrington, the third. If you so much as even *breathe* loudly when I get ready to throw that ball, you'll be sorry." I said to him, firmly, but smiling all the while.

"And just what do you plan to do to me, Dana Patrice Walker?" he said, mocking my use of his entire given name.

I smiled sweetly. "You don't want to be left standing at the altar on Saturday, now do you?" I asked.

Mitch blew me a kiss. "Good luck, sweetheart," he said, pointing to the lane.

"Gees, not even married and already whipped." Chris said, laughing.

I paused a moment before throwing the ball, waiting to see if Mitch was indeed going to be quiet, and he was. I rolled a perfect strike, doing a little dance all the way back to my seat. I gave Mitch a kiss.

"Hey, no contact with the opposing team," Trudy said.

"But he's so cute," I said, smiling at Mitch.

We bowled the rest of the game, and Trudy and I won by ten pins. We did a funny victory dance as the guys watched.

"Can you believe these two? You'd think they won the lottery or something." Mitch said.

"Ok, next game is couples. Trudy and I against you two. But, let's play for something to make it more interesting," Chris suggested.

"I know, whoever wins takes the other team out for coffee and dessert before we go home," Trudy said.

Mitch and I nodded in agreement. "Sounds good. Let's do it," I said.

Deciding to keep the same order, Mitch and I bowled, he throwing a strike and me an eight with a spare. Chris and Trudy weren't quite as fortunate, and after six frames, Mitch and I were up by five pins.

"Gee, sweetheart, what are you thinking you'd like for dessert? A piece of pie or maybe a hot fudge brownie sundae?" Mitch asked playfully.

"Oh, I don't know, honey, just about anything sounds good to me," I said, smiling.

Chris and Trudy exchanged looks while Mitch and I smiled at them.

The game ended and Mitch and I pulled it off by two pins. Mitch smiled at Chris.

"Let's bowl one more, then we'll go for that dessert. How about it?" He said.

"Ok, let's just bowl individually. We'll see who the best is out of all four of us." Chris replied.

We bowled our last game and Chris ended up beating all of us. As we piled back into the van, he decided to tease his brother.

"Well, well, Mitchell. Again I hail victorious over the younger Tarrington male. He can't fight and he can't bowl. Almost lost the last few hands of poker, too, but I guess you just got lucky there." He patted Mitch on the back.

"Hold on there, Chris," Mitch said. "You only beat me by three pins. And who said I couldn't fight? Knocked your behind on the ground a few times, if I remember it right. You couldn't take me if you tried, face it. And the poker thing? Pure skill, buddy. What I'm good at, I'm good at. I don't have to rely on luck, like some people." Mitch replied, the two men enjoying their friendly cajoling.

"Tell ya what? Wanna give me a shot right now? Plant one right here. See what happens." Chris pointed to his jaw, and playfully punched Mitch on the arm.

Mitch jabbed back at his brother playfully. "Don't tempt me, Christopher. You'll be sorry."

"Ok, you two, knock it off." Trudy smiled. "Let's go have that dessert."

Mitch and Chris smiled at each other and got into the van. "You're lucky you gave up when you did, Mitchell," Chris said, chuckling.

Chris and Trudy took us to a quaint little diner just a few blocks from the bowling alley, where we enjoyed pie, coffee and each other's company. About an hour and a half later, they were dropping us off back at my apartment.

"Hey guys, that was a lot of fun," I said. "Let's do it again soon, ok?"

"Sure thing." Trudy said. "It was nice to finally get out of the house for a little while."

We said our goodbyes and Chris and Trudy drove away, leaving Mitch and I standing in the cold.

"Coming inside?" I asked him.

"It's kinda late, sweetheart, and I do have to work all day tomorrow. Maybe I should just go home now," Mitch replied.

I wrapped my arms around his neck and kissed him softly, slowly moving my hands down his back and stepping closer to hold him tightly. "Suit yourself, then," I said, brushing his lips again lightly with a kiss.

He smiled. "Well, maybe just for a little while," he replied, taking me by the hand and leading me inside.

Once inside, Mitch didn't wait to take off his coat before he had me in his arms, kissing me softly and sweetly, moving from my lips to my cheek and then to my neck. I reached up and undid his coat for him and helped him slip it off, never completely breaking the embrace. He kissed me for what seemed like an eternity, then just pulled me close to him in a tight hug.

"Is it always going to be this wonderful, Dana?" he asked me.

"I hope so," I said. "We'll find out soon enough, won't we?"

He lifted his head and smiled at me lovingly. "Not soon enough for me." He replied.

Mitch rocked me back and forth in his arms gently. "So, what are you going to do with all your free time this week, love? Must be nice not to have to work at all."

I smiled. "It will be, but I would hardly say I'm going to have much free time. I have to pick up my dress, get the girls' dresses, confirm the caterer and the flowers and the photographer, plus move and unpack everything, and oh, we have to get the marriage license......."

"I know, love, Wednesday," Mitch said, smiling at me.

"And then there's packing for the honeymoon, and I still haven't found a bathing suit, and........"

"Whoa, there sweetheart. Don't go blowing a gasket on me, now, ok? I can help with some of those things," Mitch said.

"Tell me when you'll have time to help me, Mitch. You'll be working until Friday, plus helping me move, and the guys are taking you out on Wednesday. You won't have any free time to think let alone make phone calls." I said firmly.

"Why don't you ever listen to me? I said I can help and I will. I'll make time if I have to," he said. "Besides, I took the whole day off Tuesday to move you. I told Jimmy I'd check in by phone."

"Fine, I'll let you call the caterer and the photographer, how's that?" I asked him. "Oh, we have to get the ties and cummerbunds for the guys, too." I sighed. "Why is there so much to do? Why can't this be simple?"

Mitch kissed my cheek. "Because you're not letting it be simple. Just relax, it's all going to work out."

"Glad one of us thinks so." I told him.

Mitch kissed me again. "Oh, come on now, sweetheart. We only have five more days. I don't really want to have you going neurotic on me. Might dampen the honeymoon a little."

"Trust me, I wouldn't want to disappoint you there." I told him sarcastically.

"You won't, I'm sure." He smiled. "I'd better get going. It's going to be a long day tomorrow." He put his coat back on and gave me a kiss. "I'll call you in the morning, before I go to work, ok?" I opened the door and gave him another kiss, sending him on his way.

The busyness of Monday seemed like it would drive me insane, but somehow I managed to make it through the day and maintain my sanity as well. Just as promised, Mitch called me before work, and made me promise to take a break to meet him for lunch at noon, with Kayla and his sisters in tow. Of course, Megan had to come along as well, and she enjoyed seeing her uncle at work. Exhausted from a twelve hour work day, I insisted, much to his protest, that Mitch go straight home after work and sleep, with the promise that Tuesday would be a whole day together. He finally agreed, and I felt good knowing he would be well rested to help me move everything then. It also gave me the opportunity to bake him some chocolate chip cookies for Valentine's Day.

Bright and early Tuesday morning, just after my first cup of coffee, the much anticipated knock came at my door. I opened it to see eleven very handsome, strapping guys at my door, ready to help me move. Jim, Paul, Chris, Jake and Joseph had all managed to take the day off from work, as well as all the guys in the band, and of course, Mitch. I smiled brightly.

"This is every woman's dream, to open her door to all these men," I said, moving out of the way to let them pile in.

Mitch took up the rear and I smiled at the way he looked. He was dressed in jeans and an old sweatshirt, hiking boots and sporting a baseball cap. I hadn't seen him dressed this down before, but he looked adorable. Then again, he always looked adorable to me. He smiled when he saw me and gave me a kiss. In his hands were a dozen beautiful red roses, a huge box of chocolates and a card.

"Happy Valentine's Day, sweetheart. These are for you," he said, handing everything to me.

"Thank you, honey, this is so sweet." I said, taking the things from him. I took the cap from his head and put it back on, pulling it down further than he had it. As he adjusted it, I kissed him again. "New look for you. Cute. I like it," I said.

"Thanks, glad you approve," he smiled. "Now, how about we get this show moving?" he said. He turned to all the guys. "Ok, all the boxes go to my place, except the ones in the bedroom that say 'donate' on them. The dresser, and the bookcase go to my place, and the rest of the stuff goes to whoever said they wanted it. If no one claims it, we donate it. Any questions?"

"Yeah, when's our lunch break?" Zach asked and everyone laughed.

Mitch smiled. "I'm sure we can work something out," he said cheerfully.

I walked up to Mitch and slipped my arm around his waist. "I just love a man who takes charge," I said, and he smiled at me.

"I'll keep that in mind, baby," He said, mischievously. I smacked him on the arm.

Just then, Jake walked by, and Mitch pointed at me, tattling like a little boy. "Hey Dad, she hit me."

Jake smiled. "You probably deserved it, son," he said, matter-of-factly.

Mitch looked at him, smirking in disbelief, and I laughed.

As the guys started buzzing around here and there, I pulled Mitch aside. "I have something for you, too. Happy Valentine's Day," I said, handing him a card. "Your gift is out there in that container on the counter. It's up to you whether or not you want to share."

Mitch smiled and went to the counter, lifting one corner of the container very slowly. His grin grew even wider, and he took a few cookies out, placing a whole one in his mouth. "Cool, thanks, baby, these are great," he said, giving me a kiss. He placed another cookie in his mouth and opened his card. His face grew serious as he read it, and the note I had written inside for him. He smiled at me lovingly and gave me another kiss. "I love you, too, sweetheart. You're so sweet."

"Hey, Mitch, how about a hand here, little brother." Chris called out. Mitch kissed me again and walked away to help.

I placed the flowers in a vase and opened up the card Mitch had gotten me. The sentiment of the card itself was beautiful, but it was the simple words that he wrote himself that warmed my heart more than anything.

"Dana, There is no other woman in the world that I would rather spend eternity with. I am a one woman man and I graciously accept you to fill that spot in my heart. With all my love forever, Mitch."

I looked up at him and smiled, and he smiled back and winked at me.

I scurried around the apartment, looking for last minute little things that I may have forgotten, and noticed a cookie jar on top of my refrigerator that my grandmother had given me years earlier. In the hustle and bustle of things, apparently I had forgotten to pack it. It seemed like all the guys were busy carrying out boxes and things, and with Mitch nowhere to be seen, I decided to get it down myself. I scooted a chair over from the kitchen table and stood up on it, just about to reach for the jar when Ash came up beside me.

"You really shouldn't climb, Dana," he said. "I'll get that for you." He held the chair until I was down, and reached the jar down for me.

"Thanks, Ash." I said. "Don't tell Mitch, ok?" He smiled and nodded.

Mitch had walked in as I was stepping down, and walked over to me with a disgusted look.

"Too late, dear, Mitch already saw you," he said, his arms folded tightly across his chest. He picked up the chair I had been standing on and moved it back to the table. "You know, I'm going to take all the chairs out of the apartment and we'll sit on the floor if we have to, if that's what it's going to take to get you to stop that climbing." He sighed and turned to Ash. "Thanks, guy. She's already fallen once and almost pulled a shelving unit onto herself. I don't know why she won't listen."

Before I knew it, my apartment was just about empty and I was starting to feel a mixture of excitement and sadness. I had lived in this apartment since I moved from Iowa, and it had been the only home I had known for four years. But, now my new life was beginning, in my new home, and I knew in my heart that it would be better than anything I had ever known. I looked out onto the balcony, and saw what was still remaining of George and Beverly. Though their bodies had started to melt away, their little straw hands were still holding on to one another. Mitch noticed me and came to stand next to me.

"You aren't going to go all sentimental on me, are you?" He asked.

"I don't know, Mitch. I've been in this place for four years. There's a lot of memories here." I told him.

He put his arm around me and smiled sweetly. "I know, but there are a lot more memories just waiting to be made. Are you ready?" he asked.

"I think so," I said, taking him by the hand and leading him to the balcony. I opened up the door and stepping outside, I took the scarves from our little snow people, handing them to Mitch. He smiled.

"I suppose you want to save these?" he asked. I nodded. "Ok, I think we can find room for them somewhere," he replied, stuffing them into his coat pocket.

"I guess we better go home, hadn't we?" I said. "I have a lot of unpacking to do."

"Let me help Chris with these last few things, ok? You go on ahead if you want to, and I'll meet you there. I gave Dad a key, and they should already be over there taking things in," Mitch said.

I made one last round of the apartment, paused to look at George and Beverly once more, and left to go to my new home.

I pulled up in front of the apartment and had to smile at the way all the guys looked like busy ants scurrying back and forth, carrying boxes and things into the apartment. I made my way upstairs, and once inside, suddenly felt overwhelmed by all the piles surrounding me. Newbie smiled at me and put his hand on my shoulder.

"Looks like you got your work cut out for you, future Mrs. Trip." He said cheerfully.

"I think you may be right." I agreed. "After I get back from my night out with the girls tomorrow, Mitch will be with you guys, so I can knock some of it out then."

"We have a fun evening planned for him," Newbie said.

He had aroused my curiosity. "Where are you guys taking him?" I asked.

Newbie smiled. "Just out someplace for a few drinks, even though he really doesn't drink, and you know, the male bonding thing. No big deal."

"Oh, yes, the male bonding thing. Seems to play a big part in the pre-nuptial period of a man's life," I replied.

Ash overheard the last part of the conversation and smiled. "Yes, the pre-nuptial male bonding rituals date back to primeval times. Very important."

I saw Shep and Zach nearby, so I called them over into a little huddle. "Listen, guys, I need your help, but you can't breathe a word to Mitch, ok?" I told them.

"Sure, what's up?" Zach asked.

"I'm getting Mitch an electric guitar for a wedding gift, and I kinda have one picked out already, but I need one, or both, of you to come down to the shop with me and tell me if what I'm getting is the right thing. I don't know too much about all that." I admitted.

Zach and Shep smiled. "We can help you out with all that, no problem. Want to sneak out now? We can make up an excuse." Shep said.

"Great! I'll tell Mitch we're taking the things to donate. Then we can stop by the music shop and you can give me your advice." I smiled.

As we waited for Mitch to arrive, I unpacked a few of my boxes and proceeded to put things in the closet. I looked around the room. Mitch had moved his little study desk from the bedroom to the other corner of the living room, making room for my dresser. It didn't exactly match his oak bedroom set, but the wood tone was close enough that we agreed it would work until we decided to buy new furniture altogether. I was working busily when Mitch walked in.

"Hey, beautiful, how's it going?" he said, his cheeks rosy from the cold.

"Just fine. I decided to get these things put away. At least then I'll have one thing done." I said.

"Well, Chris and I brought the bookcase. I put it next to mine, but if you don't like it there, we can move it later. He's taking the bed and table to his house now, and on the way, we dropped off the donations." He sat down on the edge of the bed. "You are now officially moved, my love."

My heart sank. They had dropped off the donations. Great, I thought. Now how was I going to get Shep and Zach out of the house without Mitch suspecting something? I thought fast.

"Honey, why don't I go and pick up something for us to have for lunch? What do you think everyone would like?" I asked.

"We could just get pizza and have it delivered," he said.

Keep going Mitch, I thought. I'll never get this plan worked out.

"We could do that, but I noticed you have nothing in the house to drink. I need to go get some soda," I said.

"Ok, love, if that's what you want to do. I'll hang out here with the guys," he said.

"You know, Mitchell, maybe I could just pick the pizzas up, you know, while I'm out. Maybe someone could go with me to help." I smiled.

"Whatever, Dana, that's fine," he said. "Want me to go?"

"Uh, no, sweetie, you should probably stay here, and play host. Ok?" I said quickly.

"Ok." Mitch said suspiciously. "How about I call for the pizzas and you go get them? I need to call Jimmy anyway. I'll just get them from Gartano's, alright?"

"Sure, that's fine." I said, quickly hurrying to find Shep and Zach before Mitch threw another monkey wrench into my plan.

I called them over to me. "Mitch and Chris already dropped off the donations, so you are going to help me pick up pizzas and sodas, got it? We'll go now, since we have to stop off. By the time we get to the bistro, the pizzas will be ready, so it'll all work out."

"Cool, let's do it," Shep said.

Mitch appeared from the bedroom, a dumbfounded look on his face.

"Sweetheart, why'd you run out on me?" he asked. "I started to say something and next thing I knew you weren't there."

"Sorry," I said. "Shep and Zach are going to help me with the pizzas, ok?" I asked.

"Ok, love, that works. I'll give you some money for the soda, but tell Jimmy to put the pizza on my tab." He smiled. "Like I said, I can do that. I know the owner personally."

"Yeah, I hear he's pretty cute, too. Not to mention a very good kisser." I said, pulling Mitch down into a kiss. As I was kissing him, he reached into his pocket for his wallet. I pulled away and he opened it, giving me a twenty dollar bill.

"Gee, have to pay for those kisses now, huh, little brother?" Chris said as he walked in. "Or, are you just practicing the main move of married life? The wallet reach." He laughed.

"Something like that, I guess." Mitch replied, smiling.

I tucked the money into my purse, grabbed the guys and we were off. "I know men hate women drivers, so which one of you wants to be the chauffer?" I asked.

"I can drive, my car's right here anyway," Shep said, stepping up to a really hot red Beretta.

"Nice wheels, Shep," I said. "I'll tell you where we're going, ok?"

I directed Shep to the music store and the three of us went inside. I led the guys to a beautiful bright blue electric guitar with an amp. Shep smiled.

"You have excellent taste, Dana. This is top of the line." He said, picking up the guitar. He handed it to Zach, who also inspected it closely.

"Think they'll let us try it on for size?" he asked.

"We can find out," I said, walking up to the counter.

"Hi." I said to the clerk. "I'm interested in this guitar, and my friends were wondering if we could maybe try it out first?" I asked.

The man smiled. "Sure thing," he said, walking with me over to the guys. "Do either of you play?" he asked.

Shep and Zach just looked at each other. "Yeah, a little, I guess." I could see they were headed toward showing this guy what they had.

I looked at them as if to scold them both. "Yes, they both play. Actually, they're part of my fiancé's band. We're getting married Saturday, and I'd like the guitar for a wedding gift. They agreed to come and help me pick it out." Shep and Zach looked like they were disappointed that they wouldn't be pulling off their joke.

"Well," the man said as he plugged in the amp, "let's see what you can do."

Zach adjusted a few knobs on the amp, and strummed his thumb across the strings. "Nice feel," he said. Then he played part of the riff he had played during his set the week before. The salesman was clearly impressed.

"Not bad, dude, not bad at all. What band are you guys with?" he asked.

"We're part of Ace. I'm back up lead and he's bass," Zach answered.

"Hey, Ace, aren't they over at Studio 14? Club band now, aren't they? I heard you guys a few weeks back. You are pretty awesome, and that front man of yours is something else. Anything the dude can't do?" The salesman asked.

"Not much, and that's the one that belongs to me." I said proudly. "I'm the future Mrs. Mitch Tarrington."

"Congratulations." he said. "So, what do you think of the ax here? She's a real beauty and about the best you can get."

I looked at Shep and Zach, and they nodded approvingly. "It's a good one, Dana, and I think Mitch would love it," Shep said.

I looked at the salesman and nodded. "Consider it done. I'll take it." I told him. "If I could pay for it now, and pick it up tomorrow, that would be great. I can't risk him seeing it."

We settled the deal, and the salesman even agreed to come and see Mitch play it for the first time at the club after we returned. I turned to the guys as we were leaving the store.

"Thanks for your help, guys. I just picked it because it was blue, which is Mitch's favorite color. Outside that, I'm clueless." I said. "But, please, don't even hint to Mitch that you know anything about it. I'm going to hide it until I have a chance to give it to him Friday night after the rehearsal dinner."

"No problem, Dana, we won't say anything. Promise." Zach said. Shep nodded in agreement.

We went on to pick up some soda and then to Gartano's for the pizzas. Kayla greeted us as we walked in.

"Well, now, Dana, sowing our wild oats a little before the big day? And two mighty fine ones, I must say!" she hugged me and smiled playfully.

"Oh, now Kayla, don't tell Mitch. You know how jealous he gets!" I teased back. Then I turned to the guys. "Guys, you remember my friend Kayla. Kayla, I'm sure you remember Shep and Zach, from Ace."

"Of course, I do. How are you fellows doing?" Kayla asked.

"Just fine, thanks." Zach answered.

"We ordered some pizzas and the guys volunteered to help me pick them up. Actually, they helped me pick out Mitch's wedding gift. I got him an electric guitar." I said.

"Dana, he's gonna love that, honey!" Kayla smiled. "That boy loves his music almost as much as he loves you."

We picked up the pizzas and telling Kayla I would see her the next night, we headed back to the apartment where the rest of the crew was anxiously waiting.

"Hey, what took you so long, baby?" Mitch asked, taking the bag of soda from me.

"Uh, the pizzas weren't quite ready when we got there." Shep said, smiling at me.

"Well, I think everyone is pretty hungry, so guys, dig in." Mitch said, opening a box and taking out the first slice. The rest of the crowd followed his lead, taking their lunch and sitting wherever they could find room. Mitch sat down in the chair and I sat on the arm, until he pulled me down on his lap. I smiled and gave him a kiss.

"Only one problem with this arrangement. I can't reach my soda." He said, attempting to reach his glass sitting on the coffee table. I handed him mine and he took a drink, smiling. "Thank you. I was afraid I might die of thirst," he said.

"But now you have my germs, and girls have cooties you know." I told him.

"It's ok, I've had my cootie vaccine. Besides, if we don't have each other's germs by now, we never will," he replied.

"Thanks, everyone for taking the time to help us today. We really do appreciate it," I said.

"Now all we have to do is find someplace to put all this stuff," Mitch said, looking at me.

"So, Trip, ready for your bachelor's night out?" Newbie asked, stuffing in the last bite of pizza.

"Sure, where are we going to go?" Mitch asked.

Newbie and Shep exchanged looks. "Just out, no place special," Newbie said.

I looked at both of them, then at Mitch. "You'd better behave yourself with them, Mitchell Tarrington." I told him.

Mitch smiled. "You can trust me, Dana. You know that."

Zach laughed. "Yeah, Dana, you can trust him. We won't let him go home with any of the girls from the club," he said.

Ty chimed in. "We'll make sure he just observes from a distance," he smiled.

I laughed, thinking they were all trying to get a rise out of me, and I decided not to oblige them. "Looking is one thing, touching is another," I said.

About an hour later, all the boxes and things were safely inside the apartment, and the moving crew left. Mitch was instructed to be "ready and waiting" by seven o'clock sharp the next evening, and the guys bid their farewells. Mitch started to help me unpack things and put them away, and I was most grateful for the walk in closet. He had moved all of his belongings to one side, and mine more than took up the other. He laughed at the way his wardrobe looked measly in comparison to mine.

"Well, honey, guess we'll just have to take you shopping." I told him.

"That's not really my forte, love, but you'll be the first to know when I get into the mood. Ok?" he said.

"If you don't want to go, I'll just have to go without you and pick out things for you myself," I said smugly.

"I'm not sure how I feel about that. I'll get back to you," he said smiling.

The closet was in order and Mitch and I started on the dresser. He opened one of the boxes and smiled. "I found the one you packed." He said impishly in a sing-song kind of way. He started to pick up a pair of my panties and a bra.

"Mitchell, put those back and leave them alone! They're off limits to you!" I said, leaping over the box and landing on top of it.

Mitch was laughing hard. "Dana, did you not see my boxers? Let me just have a peak, it's only your underwear in a box. It's not like I'm asking you to undress for me."

"No, Mitchell, now please, close the box and move on to another one." I said.

Mitch was smiling at me and my little attempt at modesty. "Sweetheart, let me ask you a question. Are you going to hide those types of things from me forever? Most everyone wears underwear, Dana. No big deal. If I walked into a store, would I have to avoid the area where the women's underwear was on display?"

"The point is, Mitch, we aren't in a store. We're in your bedroom in your apartment, and it's *my* underwear." I told him, still laying across the box.

"No, Dana, you're wrong. We're in *our* bedroom in *our* apartment, and soon, it will be *our* underwear," he replied.

I laughed at what he had just said. "Oh, are you going to start wearing it too? Honey, that just scares me."

"Uh, it scares me too, and you know that isn't what I meant," he said, smirking at me. "But we are getting married. I don't know why you're so embarrassed by all this, Dana."

I climbed off the box, deciding I would try a different strategy. Maybe if I granted him permission, the urge wouldn't be there anymore. "Fine, Mitchell, if it means that much to you, knock yourself out. Take it all out. Try it on, even. I don't care, honestly I don't." I said to him, folding my arms and plopping down on the floor next to him.

Mitch looked at me with a sideways kind of grin. I expected him to say, forget it, but he didn't. "Well, I'm definitely not trying anything on, but I am going to look." And with that, he had the box open, taking things out one by one and inspecting each piece, as if he were conjuring up images in his mind. Every once in a while he would look at me and smile, and I could feel my face turning red. I decided he was having way too much fun with this whole thing, so I thought the best course of action was to exit while I still had an ounce of dignity left.

I stood up and started toward the door. "I'm going to go get a little snack," I said.

Mitch put down the bra he was holding and stood up next to me. "Ah, Dana, sweetheart, what's wrong? Did I upset you?" he asked, touching me lightly on the arm.

"No, Mitchell, I'm hungry, ok? Would you like something?" I asked.

Mitch looked back at the box, then at me. "Maybe something really cold to drink," he said smiling. Then he gave me a hug. "You are such a funny little girl, you know that?"

"Well, you shouldn't tease me so much. You aren't very nice to me sometimes," I added.

He gave me a kiss. "Come on, I'm always nice to you. I could have opened that box while everyone was here." He smiled impishly. "But I didn't. I waited until we were alone. That was nice of me, now wasn't it?"

I sighed. My inability to stay mad at him made me angry sometimes. "I suppose so." I picked the bra up that he had dropped and placed it back in the box. "Are you done eyeballing these things yet?" I asked.

"I'm hoping that's only the beginning, love." He said with a big smile.

It took us about two more hours to unpack everything and put it away, and Mitch and I sat down on the couch to observe. Some of my pictures were now intermingled with his on top of the bookcases, and I had some favorite knick knacks adorning the shelves in the living room. Here and there we could see touches of our two single lives merging to make one married life. I snuggled up close to him and lay my head on his chest. I could hear his heart beating softly, and I closed my eyes and smiled, breathing deeply to take in the scent of his cologne. Just being close to him felt so good and so right. I couldn't imagine life being any better.

Mitch took his hand and lightly brushed the hair back from my face. I opened my eyes and turned over on my back to look up at him, putting my head in his lap. He touched my cheek gently with his thumb and smiled back at me.

"You know, love, I was just thinking, I'm probably going to have to pull a long day tomorrow at the bistro. I'll have my lunch, but what if we have to wait a long time to get our marriage license? I wouldn't want to be away too long. I mean, Jimmy is already going to be essentially alone for over a week." He said thoughtfully.

"I understand, but we have to get a marriage license, Mitch. Can't do it without one." I answered.

Mitch pulled out his watch and looked at it. "Well, it's about three thirty now. We could go down there and do it today. What difference does it make what day we get it, as long as we get it?" he said.

The two of us cleaned up a little and grabbing our birth certificates, we headed to the city hall. We were glad we had made the decision to come then, as there was a wait of about thirty minutes. Finally, we were called to the desk, and I grabbed Mitch's hand happily as we walked up to the clerk. Of course, I noticed right away that the clerk waiting on us was very attractive and young, probably around Mitch's age. And I could see he noticed too, even though he was doing his best to pretend not to.

"Hello." She said sweetly. "What can I help you with today?"

"We need to get a marriage license." I replied, holding Mitch's hand even tighter.

"Oh, well, congratulations." She said, pulling a paper out of a file on her desk. "Let me ask you a few questions, then I'll need to see photo identification and your birth certificates." She turned to Mitch as she jotted a few things on a piece of paper. "We'll start with you. Please give me your full given name, first, middle and last, and if you have any title such as Jr., etc."

Mitch smiled and I noticed his eyes drop, but I tried to tell myself he was watching her write, not looking at anything else. "Mitchell Jacob Tarrington, the third." He said in response.

The clerk looked at him. "Where have I heard that name before?" She asked, making direct eye contact with Mitch. "Do you own a company or something in the area?"

He smiled brightly. "Well, yes and no. My father owns the medical products company. I own a little Italian bistro in town, Gartano's. Have you ever been there?" he asked.

"No, actually I can't say that I have. But now, I will definitely have to stop by sometime soon." She said sweetly.

"I'm also a musician, front man actually, in the band Ace. We play regularly down at Studio 14." He went on to tell her.

I was starting to feel a little warm. What was he doing, telling her his life story? I squeezed his hand tighter, and he wriggled it away from me, giving me a strange look and rubbing it with his other hand, as if I had hurt him. I smiled coyly.

"Yes, that's it. I was there a few weeks ago with some of my girlfriends. They love to go out and dance." She smiled. "You know, I do remember now. The band was great and you really have a lot of talent. I like to sing myself, and I love a guy with a great voice."

"That's great that you liked my fiancé's band." I said trying to refocus things. "Do you need information from me?" I asked, and Mitch shot me another look.

"Oh, yes, your name is?" she said.

"Dana Patrice Walker." I answered.

"And where will you be residing?" she asked.

Mitch opened his mouth, but I shot the answer back to her before he had a chance to say anything, adding the phone number as well. The clerk jotted everything on the paper with a smile. She looked up at Mitch again.

"When is the wedding?" she asked.

"Saturday afternoon at two thirty," he answered. "Just hope the weather holds out for us."

"I hear it's supposed to be nice on Saturday, a little chilly but sunny. That should be nice for you." She said again, smiling as she looked right at Mitch.

She asked for our birth certificates and copied down some information, then took our driver's licenses as well, and did the same. Handing them back, she smiled once again at Mitch. "If you can wait right here for just a moment, I'll be back in a jiffy with what you need." She got up and started to walk away, and again, I noticed Mitch trying hard not to notice the swing in her hips as she walked off. He turned to me and smiled.

"Nice girl, huh?" he said, only turning halfway toward me.

"Sure, I guess so," I answered. "Why don't you invite her over for dinner sometime? The two of you can discuss your singing talents."

Mitch gave me his disciplinary look. "Stop it, Dana," he said. "I was only being friendly."

"Well, learn to be rude." I told him.

Mitch shook his head and started to say something else, but the girl returned.

"Well, Mr. Tarrington, here's your marriage license. Be sure that you don't sign it until after the ceremony, and you will also need your minister to sign it as well as two witnesses. They can be anyone of your choosing, as long as they attend the actual ceremony from start to finish." The girl handed the envelope to Mitch, who tucked it into the inside pocket of his coat. "Have your minister send a copy to the state for public records filing, ok?"

"Sure thing." Mitch said, cheerfully.

"Oh, one more thing." The clerk said. "I'm assuming there's going to be a honeymoon?"

"Yes, we're going to Hawaii." Mitch told her.

"That sounds wonderful!" She said. "When you return, will you be playing at the club again?" she asked.

"We'll be back there two weeks from Saturday," he said.

"Great, I'd love to bring some of my other friends down there to hear you, too," she said. Then she turned, finally acknowledging me. "Good luck with your wedding."

"Thanks," I said, trying to actually sound grateful.

"Thanks." Mitch said, smiling at her. "Try not to work too hard, it looks like you're pretty busy."

"Oh, I won't," she answered.

I grabbed Mitch's hand and squeezed it tightly. Again, he tried to pull away, but I wouldn't let go.

"Dana, you're hurting my hand. Either give it to me completely, or lighten up on the death grip, would you?" he said.

I turned to him. "I can't believe you, Mitchell Tarrington. We come in to get a marriage license, for Pete's sake, and you sit there flirting with the clerk. You are so unreal."

Mitch stopped and looked at me. "Dana, what are you talking about? Why is it I'm not allowed to have a friendly conversation with a female without you saying I'm flirting?"

"Because, Mitchell, you do flirt. You do it all the time, and it really bothers me." I told him.

Mitch sighed heavily. "In my defense, I don't flirt, only with you. But, from your standpoint, I do, so tell me why it bothers you?" He said, and I could see he was trying not to lose his temper.

"It bothers me because, well, it just does." I said back, not really knowing how to formulate an answer for him.

"I can answer it Dana. It's called insecurity. For some reason known only to God and yourself, you think I'm not satisfied with you. You think that I'm looking for something I don't have in you. You think I'm going to see another pretty girl and run off with her. Well, for your information, none of those things are true. What you see as flirting, Dana, is only an attempt on my part not to be rude to people. I was taught to be a nice person, Dana, and I won't compromise my upbringing, or my values, just to play into your silly little game." He started to walk away. "You need to get past it, Dana, and realize that I'm in love with you and perfectly happy. If I weren't, why on earth would I even be here?" I looked at Mitch, who was looking right at me and starting to smile. He put his arm around me. "You silly little girl, I'm crazy about you. No one in this whole wide world will ever come close to making me feel the way you do. Will you please stop worrying about it?"

"I'll try." I said, attempting to smile back at him.

"Good, because you're stuck with me. And that's how I want it. Now, let's go home." Mitch took my hand once more and returned my death grip, but with more gentleness, and I smiled.

21

Back at the apartment, Mitch packed a few things that he could take to his parents' house to hold him over for a few days. Noticing that he didn't have a lot in his refrigerator, I turned to him. "Honey, I was going to make you a nice dinner for Valentine's Day, but I forgot about going to the store. I can go and get something now, if you don't mind me leaving you here alone for a little while." I told him.

Mitch smiled. "I already made something for dinner, love. Reservations. Go and change, nothing too fancy. Just let me grab something from my closet first and I'll jump into the shower, ok?"

"You are such a doll." I said, kissing him before I ran off to choose an outfit.

Mitch and I spent the evening dining at Chandler's, and then he took me home, rounding out our evening together with a special song and a lot of romance. When it was finally time to say goodnight, he looked at me with love in his eyes.

"The first of many happy Valentine's Days. I love you, my sweet Dana," he said.

"And I love you too, Mitch, more than you'll ever know." I said back.

Wednesday flew by, and I worked busily for most of the day unpacking boxes and putting things away. Mitch left work around four thirty so that we could spend some time together before our big prenuptial nights out. Around five thirty, the girls came by, ready to whisk me away. I looked at Mitch and he smiled.

"You have fun, but be careful, ok?" he said, giving me a kiss. "Don't do anything I wouldn't do." He said with his boyish grin.

"That leaves it wide open, Dana." Angelina said, and we all laughed.

The girls filed out and I told them to wait just a minute for me in the hall. I turned back to Mitch, who had his arms folded, back against the counter, knowing what was about to come his way.

"Mitch, I know that I can trust you, but can I ask one thing?" I said.

He smiled. "Go ahead."

"Four of these guys that you're going out with tonight are single. Three of them don't even have girlfriends, that I know of. Promise me that you won't go anywhere that you shouldn't."

Mitch looked at me lovingly. "Sweetheart, I don't think you need to worry. I'm not going to do anything wrong. I promise you, ok?"

I walked up to him and put my arms around his neck. "You are just so handsome, I don't want anyone stealing you away from me."

"It will never happen, love, I can guarantee it." He said. "Now, you better go. The girls are waiting. I'll see you tomorrow, ok?"

"Ok, you have fun and be careful too." I told him.

"I will." He replied, and he leaned down to kiss me again, but this time, I didn't pull away. For some reason, I just felt like I needed to hold on to him. I pulled him tightly into another kiss, and then another. He smiled at me sweetly.

"Some reason you don't want to let go of me tonight?" he asked.

"I just love you, that's all." I told him.

"I love you too, baby, but you have people waiting. Now scoot." He said, opening the door and giving me a little push. I looked back at him, and he smiled and waved before closing the door.

"So, where are we going?" I asked as I caught up with everyone.

"How about dinner, shopping and a movie? Or, if we don't feel like a movie, we'll just do whatever. Is that good with you?" Trudy asked.

"Sounds fabulous!" I replied happily. "I need a bathing suit and you guys can help me pick one out." I laughed. "One thing I learned already, never take Mitchell shopping for a bathing suit with you."

"Why is that?" Julia asked.

"I'll have to show you what he wanted me to buy. Let's just say, I'm not sure it would have fit Megan." I said, and they all laughed.

We piled into Trudy's van and started on our way. "You know, why are men such animals? I mean, all they want is to look at women's bodies. I swear, it's all they think about." Trudy said.

"Is Chris like that?" I asked.

"Oh, please. He's got to be the worst. Why do you think we have four children?" she laughed.

"Well, at least it's your body he wants to look at, Trudy. Mitch just likes to flirt with everyone else." I said.

"Mitch, a flirt, why that's just *so* hard to believe!" Julia laughed. "He's so inhibited."

We all laughed at that comment. "I have to tell you what happened when we went Christmas shopping a few months back. Mind you, we hadn't been dating very long, and Mitch asked if I wanted to help him pick out things for the family. So, we went to the mall, and decided we were going to Jacy's so he could get your mom that apron. Well, he picked it out and we took it to the checkout, and behind the counter was this flirty, sexy little Barbie doll, perfect in every way. Totally the opposite of me. Naturally, his eyes were all over her, and I'm not too sure they didn't have to call maintenance when he left to mop up the drool he left on the floor." The girls were all giggling. "Of course, Barbie thought she had her Ken all lined up and she was doing the eyelash thing and the fake giggle thing and the whole shebang. And he was buying it, hook, line, and sinker. Neither of them seemed to notice that I was still standing there. So, I moved away, and I was still watching, and I thought seriously about what kind of jail time I would do if I were to throw a pot or pan at him off the display." The girls were starting to laugh. "So, then he got done and when he finally spotted me, he smiled and waved like he was all innocent. Of course, I got upset, and he couldn't figure out why. When the brain finally reengaged and he was enlightened, he tried to tell me he wasn't looking at her at all, that he was just being friendly. Then, when I told him it makes me uneasy when he flirts, he told me I was being silly and I have no reason to feel that way. Look at the man. Any woman in the world would love to have him. I swear, I'll never figure him out."

The girls were all nodding in agreement, except Kayla. "You remember, Dana, I told you men see things differently than we do."

"Yeah, but Kayla, do you like it when Joseph flirts with other women?" Trudy asked.

Kayla smiled. "He doesn't do that, because he knows how hard this mama can come down on him!" We all laughed.

"You're right, Dana, even if Mitchell is my brother, he is awfully handsome. All our husbands are. They just don't understand that we get upset because we don't want to lose them." Angelina said.

"I know." I said. "And if I try to tell him that, he just says, don't worry about it. I try, but it's just not easy."

"Let me tell you girls about something that happened with me and Jim, at his high school reunion." Angelina started. "A few of his friends called and asked him to go, so I agreed, and it was really starting to be a nice time. All of a sudden, Jim decided he wanted another drink, so he got up and headed in that direction. Next thing I knew, I saw this very attractive girl standing next to him, and they were talking and smiling, and she had her hand on his arm. Of course, I saw his eyes go down and then up and then down and up again over this girl, and he was smiling like the cat with the mouse all the while." We were taking all of this in. "Then, I saw Jim point in my direction, and the girl put her arm around him and they looked at me, then she slid her hand down his arm very seductively and kept it there. Jim was doing nothing to try to get away from her. Finally, he decided that he was going to come back and sit down with me, but I let him have it. I finally understood why he wanted to go to this thing in the first place, because he knew his old flame would be there, and he figured he'd do a little comparison shopping, for old time's sake, I guess. Anyhow, it wasn't a pretty evening, but I did get this diamond pendant out of the deal. Guess he was feeling pretty guilty."

Olivia, being the oldest and longest married among us, decided to put in her two cents worth. "It's easy to be jealous when you see the one you love being friendly to another. But you really have to take a step back and realize, they may have every opportunity in the world to go astray. In the end, though, they always come home to you." She smiled. "You know, girls, it's alright to want to protect that relationship. But sometimes you need to step back and let that trust protect the relationship. Try it on for size. Only if it falters do you need to do something about it."

All of us were silent as we pulled into the restaurant, thinking about what Olivia had said. Once we settled inside at our table, Angelina reopened the conversation, only on a different topic.

"So, Dana, are you excited about Saturday? I'll bet you are," she said.

I looked at her and then at Kayla and Olivia, who would probably be the only ones to catch my statement. "Well, yes, about parts of it anyway." Kayla smiled knowingly at me.

"I remember when Paul and I got married. I think he was more nervous than I was." Julia relayed. "He could hardly get the ring on my finger."

Angelina laughed. "I know what you mean. When Jim was saying his vows, he looked terrified. I was just waiting for him to go running back down the aisle and forget the whole thing!"

"I'm really not too afraid of Mitch being nervous. He's so sentimental, I'm afraid he might cry." I said, smiling at the thought.

The girls all smiled. "You know, Dana," Olivia started. "I think out of all my children, Mitchell is the most like that, too. He's always been very sensitive and compassionate. But he's also very stubborn, and I really don't know if he'd let himself cry in front of all those people."

"Oh, you don't have to tell me he's stubborn." I retorted, chuckling. "I've known that almost from the first day." They all laughed.

I decided to ask these marital experts some advice. "So, girls, what are some things I need to do to keep my husband happy?" I said. Angelina and Trudy exchanged looks and giggled. "BESIDES the obvious." I said, with a giggle.

"Well," Kayla started. "One thing that works for me is, if something happens in the course of the day that I know will upset Joseph, I don't tell him about it until later in the night. By that time, he's all relaxed and settled in, and he doesn't have all the fight left in him, so most of the time he lets it pass without getting too upset."

"I know what works for Jim is to let him think he's right. Even when he isn't, if I admit defeat in an argument, it really pumps up the ego and keeps things at an even kilter." Angelina said, smiling.

We enjoyed a fabulous dinner, and shopping was more fun than I had experienced in a while. They were very understanding and sympathetic in the bathing suit department, and I was finally able to find something that made me feel comfortable. During the evening, the girls gave me lots of advice and we talked and laughed and bonded. I really was starting to feel more and more like I was part of the family, and I knew that, like Mitch had told me, I was not alone anymore.

At seven sharp, the members of Ace were standing inside the apartment. Mitch smiled brightly at his little circle of friends.

"Well, guys, one thing I have to say is, you're punctual." He said to them. "So, what's the game plan for tonight?"

"Ever heard of Caroway's?" Ty asked.

"No, can't say that I have. What is it, like, a club or something?" Mitch asked.

"Something like that." Ty answered. "I think you'll enjoy it. Grab your coat and we'll head out. Ash brought his van, so we can all ride together."

"Cool, just one thing first." Mitch said. He walked to one of the drawers in the kitchen and took out a pad of paper and a pen. Smiling, he wrote a little note to Dana, then drew a heart on the bottom as best he could and signed his name. He propped it up on the table where she would see it, and turned back to the guys. "Ok, let's go." He said, putting his coat on.

"Oh, aren't you just the sweet thing." Zach teased, giving Mitch a playful push. "Leaving your girl a love note."

"Well, at least I have a girl." Mitch teased back.

"Hey, I don't have *just* a girl, man, I have *GIRLS*. Plural. I'm far from ready to settle for just one." Zach replied.

Ash put his hand on Zach's shoulder. "You don't know what you're missing, dude. Married life isn't so bad."

"And dating one girl isn't so bad, either." Newbie chimed in with a smile.

The guys all headed toward Ash's van, and got in. "So, Newbie, you and Janine are like, the thing now. Pretty cool, huh?" Ash asked him.

"Yeah, I really like her. She's sweet. She's not fake like some of the other girls I've dated. In fact, I didn't tell you guys. I just got an apartment in her building. I'm moving here for good in a couple of weeks." He was smiling brightly.

"That's cool, Newbie. Say the word and I'll help you move." Mitch volunteered.

"Yeah, we will too, man. That's cool." Shep said, volunteering the others. But none of them seemed to mind.

The group pulled into Caroway's and the guys all piled out of the van to head inside. The atmosphere was pretty typical of most clubs, loud and smoky to an extent, and they seemed to do a good business. But two things set the place apart that Mitch noticed right away. One was the fact that the waitresses were all very scantily clad. The other was that they were the only women he saw. An uneasy feeling came over him at that moment.

"Guys, let me ask a question." Mitch started. "Just what type of club is this?"

"The best kind, Trip." Shep said with a smile, leading the six to a table near what appeared to be a stage. He summoned a waitress and ordered drinks for them all.

"Relax, guy, you're in for a treat."

Mitch turned to Ash, and beckoned him close. "Ash, tell me this isn't a strip club." He said. Ash just smiled. Mitch grabbed his collar and pulled him back in. "Dana will kill me if she finds out I came here."

"Chill, will you Mitch? It's all cool. Dana won't find out, unless you tell her. We won't let it out." He replied. "Besides, women know that when men have bachelor parties, it usually involves other women. Don't worry about it."

"Does Cindy know you're here?" Mitch asked him.

"Well, I told her we were taking you out to a club, and we are. So, actually, I didn't lie to her, now did I?" Then he smiled. "Besides, we did tell Dana the same thing yesterday afternoon. So, you won't be lying to her either."

Mitch thought about that logic as he looked at his friends. They were just trying to show him a good time, he thought, and after all, it wasn't like he was going to do anything. He would sit, have a drink, and that would be the end of it. Actually, he wasn't even drinking anything besides soda, so that was a plus in his favor, too. Besides, the guys probably brought him here more for themselves than for him anyway. And in essence, Dana did know they were going to a club. It wouldn't hurt anything if she never found out what kind.

A few minutes later the waitress arrived with their drinks. "So, you're all a handsome lot of guys. Here just to enjoy the show?" She asked.

"Well, actually, we're having a little pre-nuptial party for our buddy here." Zach spoke up, pointing to Mitch.

"Oh, a bachelor party. Well, that's a special occasion. We'll have to see what we can do to make it even more special." She said, as she smiled at Mitch. "Must say, your girl's pretty lucky. You are a handsome one."

Mitch didn't know what to say, and he could feel the blush rising in his cheeks. The waitress put her hand on Mitch's shoulder and got very close to him. "Enjoy the show, blue eyes. I'll be back in a little while to see if you need anything."

"Wow, she's pretty hot, hey Trip?" Ty asked him.

"She's ok, I guess, but remember, I already have a hot girl waiting for me at home." Mitch replied.

Ash leaned toward Mitch. "Hey, dude, nobody's asking you to sleep with her. But it doesn't hurt to look. You know, believe it or not, when a good looking guy is in sight, our ladies look, too. They just won't admit it. I mean, I've caught Cindy eyeing guys before. It doesn't mean she wants them, she's just, well, enjoying the scenery." He smiled. "I love Cindy, she's everything to me. But I'm here tonight to have a little hands off fun, then I'll go home and have my hands on fun with her. Get it?"

Mitch smiled. "Yeah, I get it. Just enjoying the scenery."

"Right, and I think the show's about to begin." Ash said, taking a drink and settling back in his chair.

In the blink of an eye, the crowd full of men were all drooling over six women on the stage, each very seductively removing the few clothes they were wearing. Mitch looked at his friends, and they were all intently watching the show, like a bunch of schoolboys sharing a girlie magazine they had stolen from their father's drawer. He smiled at them, and then turned to the stage himself. He thought about Dana, and how upset she would be if she found out he was here. Watching as the girls took more and more off, he was starting to feel a little guilty, both because he knew Dana wouldn't approve, and because he was finding that he was enjoying it a little more than he thought he should. He loved Dana more than anything, and to him, her beauty far surpassed anything these girls had to offer. And he knew in his heart that the last thing he wanted to do was upset her. How could he leave, though, he thought. Ash had driven here, so he was pretty much at the mercy of the guys. He could always take off his glasses, he thought, and then he wouldn't be able to see the girls. But he wouldn't be able to see anything else, either, and he didn't think any of his friends felt much like wearing his drink. So, the most logical thing to do, to him, was to pretend he was alright with it, so as not to let his friends down. After all, they had thought enough of him to take him out. In the end, what was it going to hurt anyway, especially if he never told Dana? He wasn't planning to talk to any of the girls, and he would never think of doing anything else with them, either. He decided that what he would do was keep the whole incident a secret, and never look back. He couldn't risk telling her and taking the chance of losing her again. He loved her too much to let that happen.

A few minutes later, the show ended, and the guys all were lost in chatter about what they had seen. Mitch sat somewhat silently, just listening to all of them, nodding and smiling when he felt it to be appropriate. He was starting to get lost in the camaraderie, when he felt someone tap him on the shoulder. Shep pointed, and Mitch turned around to see their waitress and another very attractive blonde standing next to her.

"Hi, blue eyes." The waitress said to Mitch. Then she turned to the other girl. "Gloria, this is.......oh, you know, what is your name?"

Mitch bit his lip nervously. "My name?" he asked. "Uh, Mitch. My name's Mitch," he replied.

Gloria smiled. "So, Mitch, is that short for Mitchell?" she asked. Mitch just nodded. "I like that name. It's nice," she said. "And Kandy was right, you do have beautiful blue eyes."

"Thanks." Mitch replied, looking at the guys as if he wasn't sure what else to say. They were all sitting back, taking in the scene, smiling at him.

"Well, I hear you're having your bachelor party tonight. So, I wanted to do something a little special for you, Mitch." She put her arm around his shoulder, and he could hear the guys chuckling softly. Mitch was turning five shades of red. Gloria smiled at him. "You're a little bit of a shy one, aren't you, Mitch? Well, save it for your girl, sweetheart, because tonight, we're going to celebrate the fact that you're still single."

Before Mitch knew what was happening, Gloria was engaged in a very sexy dance for him, running her finger down the side of his face and down his chest. She was right in front of him, and with each move she seemed to be drawing him in to her. Gloria smiled at him as she started to take off her top, and without realizing it, he smiled back. "You're adorable, Mitch." She said to him, and very seductively, stripped down to a g-string with ties on each side, sitting down on Mitch's lap. She then put her arms around his neck and gave him a little kiss on the cheek, then placing her hand on his face, she slid it very slowly and seductively down his cheek and down his chest, anchoring onto his leg as she stood up. The guys were all eyes, intently watching her every move. Ending her little sideshow, Gloria put her top back on and moved close to Mitch. "Congratulations," she said, in a very sexy voice, and walked away.

"Whoa, Trip, I want a bachelor party if that's what you get. Find me anyone, I'll get married tomorrow." Shep said excitedly.

"I'll get married right now." Ty said.

Mitch was still in shock from what had just happened. He was really starting to feel guilty about the whole ordeal, and he knew he needed to find a way to tell the guys. But, looking at them, his heart told him not to hurt their feelings. They saw it all as innocent male bonding, of sorts. "Guys, all I can say is, I'm going to get killed if Dana finds out about this."

They all laughed. "Trip, who's going to tell her? You didn't do anything anyway, man. You just watched a pretty girl dance." Shep said.

"Shep, you don't know Dana. She's extremely jealous, and I told her I wouldn't go to a strip club. And here I am."

Ty put his hand on Mitch's shoulder. "Hey, we just wanted to have some fun and show you a good time. We didn't mean to cause a scene, man."

Mitch smiled. "No, guys, I'm just weird that way, that's all. I guess I'm just getting nervous about things. I appreciate you all taking me out. I had a good time, really." Mitch felt that sparing their feelings was more important than anything he felt at that moment. He smiled. "I'll buy the next round, and I think I see a pool table back there. Who wants to lose a few bucks?"

"You're on, dude, lead the way." Ash said, and the six of them headed for the billiard room.

Around one in the morning, the guys dropped Mitch back at the apartment to pick up his car, and headed off. He stood in the cold of the night, and looked up to the third floor where their apartment was. He thought about Dana, and assumed that she was probably up there sleeping, lost in her dreams. He wanted to go upstairs and see her, but thought better of it, and got into his car. Thoughts of the guys crossed his mind as he drove toward his parents' house, and the evening they had shared together. He couldn't blame them, he thought. They cared about him, and in their hearts, they just wanted him to enjoy what they saw as his last few days of freedom. They didn't have a clue, he thought, except maybe for Ash. He didn't want to be free. And if marrying Dana was going to mean he would be "tied down" as they saw it, he wanted nothing more.

Mitch pulled up to his parents' house and taking his suitcase from the trunk, he crept quietly inside. Placing his suitcase down next to the door, he saw a light shining from the family room, and decided to go and see what it was.

"Mitchell, is that you?" he heard his father say.

"Yeah, hi Dad." Mitch said softly. "Why are you up so late?"

"Just doing a little reading, that's all." Jake replied, not wanting him to know he was really waiting for him. "Did you have a nice time with your friends?"

Mitch decided not to let on. "Sure, Dad. We just went to a club and played some pool. No big deal." He smiled. "Did Mom tell you if the girls had a good time tonight? How's Dana?"

"Yes, she said that everyone, including Dana, seemed to enjoy themselves. I guess they just took her out to dinner, and then went shopping and out for some dessert." Jake replied.

Mitch smiled at the thought of Dana, and suddenly, he realized that he missed her.

"Well, I think I'm going to get a shower and turn in. I have to work tomorrow. Good night, Dad." Mitch said.

"Good night, son." Jake replied.

Mitch picked up his suitcase by the door and softly walked up the stairs into his old room. Closing the door, he turned on the lamp on the nightstand and sat down on the side of the bed, taking in the old familiar things. He smiled as he remembered the day of the engagement party, when he had brought Dana up here, and chuckled softly to himself at the memory of Chris walking in on them kissing. In just three days she would be his wife, and he would be with her forever. His heart warmed just at the thought. He never dreamed it possible to care about another person so much. He wondered if she was alright in the apartment alone, and picked up the phone to call her, but decided once again that he didn't want to disturb her sleep. He unpacked his suitcase and slipped into the bathroom to shower before getting into bed.

A few minutes later Mitch came back into his room, set the alarm and pulled down the covers. Turning off the light and taking off his glasses, he closed his eyes and tried to sleep. Suddenly a multitude of things started racing through his mind, thoughts of not only that night, but the next few days, and they overwhelmed him. He knew then that sleep wasn't going to come easy and he decided to try going downstairs for something to drink. Maybe a glass of milk. That had always worked for him. He slipped on his sweats and quietly crept back down to the kitchen. Taking a glass from the cupboard, he poured himself some milk, and noticing a plate of cookies his mother had evidently made earlier that day, he took the plastic wrap off and decided to indulge himself. He sat down at the table with his snack, and once again, began to think about Dana.

"I see you found those cookies. Your mother made them just for you." Jake said, smiling as he saw his son in the kitchen.

"Yeah, they are pretty good." Mitch said, taking another off the plate. "I just couldn't sleep, so I thought a little snack might help."

Jake sat down and looked at his son. "Is something troubling you, Mitchell?" he asked.

Mitch sat back in his chair and sighed deeply. "I'm not sure, Dad." He replied. "I think maybe everything is just catching up to me, that's all."

Jake looked at him lovingly. "Mitch, it's normal to be nervous. This is a big time in your life, son. But don't let it get to you. Everything has a way of working itself out. You'll be just fine, trust me." Then he looked Mitch in the eye. "You aren't having second thoughts, are you, Mitchell? About getting married, I mean?"

Mitch shot his father a look of shock and disbelief. "Of course not, Dad. I want to marry Dana more than anything. Backing out of it has never crossed my mind, not even for an instant."

"Well, I'm glad to hear that. She's a wonderful girl and I know you'll be a fine husband to her," Jake said, patting Mitch on the arm reassuringly.

Mitch smiled. "I hope so, Dad, I mean, I want to be. I don't want anything more than for her to be happy."

"Mitchell, I'm going to tell you that she's not always going to be happy, son. Not with you, and not with being a wife. There are going to be times when she's going to be frustrated and angry and hurt and maybe even frightened and sometimes, it will be your fault, and sometimes it won't. There aren't any perfect marriages, Mitchell. You just have to do your best and let that be enough. Just remember during those times, though, that you love each other and that will hold everything together."

Mitch let his father's words sink in. "I just keep thinking that for all these years, I've taken care of just me. Now I'm going to have her to take care of, too. What if I can't do that? What if I mess that up?"

Jake looked at Mitch directly in the eyes. "If there's anyone in the world, Mitchell, that I have confidence in, it's you. You have always been the one to make things work, even when it seems like there isn't any hope. That's one of your many strengths. You may make some mistakes along the way, but learn from them, don't let them bring you down. There's not a doubt in my mind, son, that you'll be a good provider. Not one doubt."

Mitch smiled and he felt as if a weight had been lifted off his shoulders simply with Jake's words. "Thanks, Dad, I'm feeling better now about things. I think I'd better try to get some sleep."

Jake smiled at his young son. He understood the feelings that were racing through him. He had been that young man himself once, and like before, he was seeing more and more the similarities that he and Mitch shared. But looking at him now, he realized that Mitch had something he had never had. A father who was willing to allow him to lean on him, someone that would be there to help him over his rough spots. Although Jake had known his father loved him, they never shared that closeness. Jake had vowed when his own family began that he would always remain close to his children, that he would always let them know not only that they were loved, but that he valued each of them in their uniqueness. Seeing the man that Mitch had grown into made him proud, and he knew that he would be just fine.

Returning to his room, Mitch once again climbed under the covers and closed his eyes. But this time, he felt a comfortable calmness come over him, and before he knew it, he was sleeping peacefully.

Early the next morning, I sat with the newspaper nursing a cup of coffee, when I heard a key in the lock. I smiled, knowing that it could only be Mitch. He opened the door and smiled at me brightly.

"Hello, beautiful." He said, his face radiant. "I just couldn't go to work without seeing you." I stood up and Mitch came and put his arms around me tightly. "I missed you last night, love. Did you have a fun evening?"

"Oh, it was great!" I answered cheerfully. "First, we went out to dinner, and then we went shopping. I actually found a bathing suit, too."

"That's good, sweetheart. Are you going to model it for me?" He said, raising his eyebrows.

"No, you'll just have to wait until we get to Hawaii." I told him, and he pretended to pout. "Did you have fun with the guys? Where did you go?"

Mitch bit his lip, but smiled at me, looking me directly in the eyes. "Yeah, we had a good time, you know, just doing the guy thing."

I looked at him curiously, wondering if he had purposely avoided answering the second part of my question. "So, honey, where did you go?"

Again, Mitch looked me in the eyes and smiled. "They just took me to some little club, I'm not even sure of the name of it. It was your typical place, nothing special. The guys had a few drinks, and I actually just had soda, and we played some pool. No big deal, really."

"Was this place like, a dance club or something?" I asked.

Mitch smiled. "You could say that, I guess." Then he looked down at me. "Dana, why all the questions? Is there something specific you want to know?"

"I'm just curious, that's all." I answered.

Mitch chuckled and took my face in his hands, so that we were making direct eye contact, and he smiled. "Dana, I know what you're thinking, and you're wrong. No strip club, no naked women, no contact with anyone other than the waitress, and Shep was the one who talked to her. I was a good boy, Dana, just like I told you I would be. We played pool. That's it. Nothing more, I swear."

Mitch was surprised at how easily the lie had come, and it made him feel ill at ease. He had never lied to Dana before, and he didn't want to make a habit of starting to do it now. Looking into her eyes, his heart was almost telling him to confess the truth, but his fear of her reaction overpowered the urge to be honest. Somehow, he felt that this was one time he had to spare her feelings, so he tried to dismiss it and move on.

"I know I can trust you, honey. I guess I just needed to hear it." I told him.

"Well, you did, so let's move on, ok?" He said. "So, what are your plans today?"

"I'm actually taking Kayla with me to go and pick up my dress. So, from now on, you can't go in the closet, ok? Not until after Saturday, because I don't want you to see it." I said.

He smiled. "Not a problem, love. If I need anything, I'll let you get it for me, ok?"

"Deal." I said.

Mitch kissed me, then went to the refrigerator for a drink. But, much to his dismay, he didn't find much.

"That's the other thing I'll be doing today. Getting some food for this place." I told him.

He smiled. "Something else I'm not good at. But, here, take this and get what you need." Mitch handed me his credit card. "I've already called the company, you're on there, so just sign it as Dana Tarrington, ok?"

"It's ok, honey, I have money. I'm not planning to get much, anyway, since we won't be here next week. We can go shopping again when we get home." I explained.

He gave me a half cocked smile. "We? What's this we stuff? I'm leaving all that shopping stuff up to you, my dear. And, besides, you keep the money you have for other things. I'm the man here, I'm taking care of the groceries."

I gave him a look. "So, because you're 'the man' as you put it, I'm not allowed to contribute to buying anything around here? That's nonsense, Mitchell. I thought we were sharing the responsibilities."

Mitch sighed. "Look, maybe I didn't word it correctly, but I would rather have you just take the card for the groceries, and keep what you have for, well, how about the honeymoon? We're going to need to have some cash on hand for that, right?"

I knew he was only trying to make me feel better. "Ok, I'll do it. It'll give me a chance to practice writing my new name." I smiled.

Mitch looked at the clock. "I need to get moving, love, but you take that and if there's anything else we need for Saturday, go ahead and get it." He kissed me as he opened the door. "I love you, sweetheart. See you later?"

"Yeah, see you later. I love you too." I said.

I picked Kayla up around eleven, and we chatted as we drove to the bridal shop.

"So, Dana, only three more days, girl. Bet you can't wait!" she said.

"I am getting anxious. I can hardly believe it's all happening, Kayla. It really sank in last night, as I got into bed. I realized, that's where I live now. And in three days, I'm going to have Mitch living there with me, being with me during the day, going to bed with me at night and waking up with me in the morning. I just don't know what that's going to be like, but I know I can't wait to find out." I smiled at the thought of it all.

"I can tell you, Dana, it's a nice feeling. It's a good thing knowing you have that someone there you can count on," she replied.

"I just hope I can be everything for him that he wants me to be." I said with concern.

Kayla smiled. "Now, come on girl, you know that man lives for you. He doesn't expect you to be anything more than you are right now."

"I sure hope not, because if he does, he's going to be disappointed." I told her. Then I looked at her. "I'm really afraid he may be, anyway."

Kayla looked at me. "Dana, what are you talking about, disappointed? In what way?" I just gave her a look that didn't need explaining. "You mean on your wedding night, don't you? Why on earth are you worried about that?"

I sighed. "Kayla, isn't it obvious? Just the way he looks at me, the way he kisses me, the way he holds me. He's tried to put the moves on me a couple of times, and I'll tell you, he sure makes it hard to believe that he has never done anything himself. I don't have a clue, Kayla. I don't even know where to begin. I know he's got it all figured out in his mind, and he's looking for those fireworks. I don't know if I can give him that. I'm so frightened of the whole idea of it all, I don't honestly know if I can give him anything."

Kayla looked at me. "First of all, you don't have anything to be frightened about. It's not going to be some monster there with you, it's going to be Mitch. And he loves you. He knows you're nervous, but you know what? You're forgetting one thing. He's probably nervous, too. Dana, he's new to this, too. He isn't going to know if what you are doing is right or wrong, he has nothing to compare it to. As far as that all goes anyway, honey, it's all natural instinct. It comes to you. Whatever you do, he's still going to feel those fireworks, because he wants to be with you, whether or not you think you did anything special. And I have a feeling, when it's all said and done, you'll feel them, too. Just let your love take you, Dana. Don't focus on the act, focus on the love that you share, and give that to him."

I thought about what she said, and it did make sense. "Thanks, Kayla, I'll try. I just want him to be happy with me."

She smiled and touched my arm. "He will be, girl. Don't you worry about anything."

We arrived at the bridal shop, and retrieving my gown, the sales clerk directed me to a dressing room to try it on one last time. Kayla helped me with everything, and slowly, I turned to look in the mirror. I could hardly believe it was my own reflection staring back at me.

"Oh, Kayla, it's so beautiful. I can't believe it!" I said excitedly. I turned to her. "Do you think Mitch will like it?"

"Honey, that boy won't know what to do with himself when he sees you walking to him in this." She smiled brightly and gave me a hug.

"I sure hope you're right." I said to her.

"Now, do you have your something old, something new, something borrowed and something blue to wear on your wedding day?" Kayla asked.

I thought for a minute. "Well, my new will be my wedding ring, my garter's blue, but I don't have anything old or borrowed. That's what I need." I said.

Kayla smiled. "I thought you might say that." She answered. Reaching into her bag, she pulled out a small box and handed it to me. I opened it up to reveal a beautiful strand of pearls. I looked at her and smiled. "I wore those pearls in my own wedding many years ago, and I want my girl to wear them in hers."

"But Kayla, Joanna's your girl, not me." I said.

Kayla hugged me. "No, I have two girls as far as I'm concerned. It don't matter if I gave birth to them both or not. Joanna will wear them when her time comes. You'll wear them first."

"Thank you, Kayla, you know I love you dearly, don't you?" I said hugging her back.

"I sure do, sweet girl. I sure do." She replied.

Kayla and I packed the dress as carefully as possible in the trunk of my car, and headed to Gartano's for lunch. I just had to see Mitch and tell him about the pearls.

As we walked in, Katie was on for lunch, and she greeted us and found us a table. I didn't see Mitch, and assumed he must be in the office.

"I'm going to go see Mitch. I'll be back in a minute, ok?" I told her.

"I'll wait right here." She replied.

I said hello to Jimmy and the cooks, and slipped back to the office. Sure enough, Mitch was busily working at his desk, and I crept up behind him, leaning over the back of the chair and wrapping my arms around him.

"Hello, handsome." I whispered into his ear.

He turned the chair around and pulled me onto his lap. "Hey, beautiful, what are you doing here?" he asked, kissing me.

"Kayla and I just picked up my dress, and we came here for lunch." I said.

"Darn, and here I thought you were missing me," he said, smirking.

"Well, that too." I said, giving him another kiss. "Guess what?"

"What?" he said.

"Kayla is lending me the pearls she wore in her wedding to wear with my gown on Saturday. Isn't that sweet?"

"Yeah, it sure is, sweetheart. Are you having a good day so far?" he asked.

"It would be better if you would have lunch with us." I said, smiling.

Mitch took out his watch and looked at it. "Are you sure you want me to join you? I mean, I wouldn't want to spoil your girl time." He smiled.

I slid off his lap and held out my hand, helping him up. "Come on, silly boy, let's go eat something." Mitch rubbed his eyes. "You're tired, aren't you?" I asked him.

He nodded. "Yeah, I really am. I didn't get a lot of sleep last night and I only have, well, maybe nine more hours here," he said.

I looked at him with sadness and concern. "Honey, why don't you go home for an hour and get a nap? You can't function when you're that tired. You're going to get yourself sick."

He smiled. "I appreciate your concern, baby, but I can handle it. Really. I'll just drink a lot of caffeine and wire myself." He picked up his coffee cup from the desk. "In fact, I think I'll get some more right now. And some lunch." He took my hand and we went back out to join Kayla.

"Hi, Mitch, are you going to have lunch with us?" Kayla asked him.

"How can I refuse an offer from two such lovely ladies?" He replied, pulling up a chair for himself. Then he smiled at me. "Besides, she's buying." He laughed.

"Ok, I can do that." I replied. "I have your credit card, remember?" I laughed. "But, you know, I'm in pretty good with the owner. I think he might let us eat for free, what do you think?"

"Maybe, if you're really good." He smiled. Then he leaned very close to me and whispered softly, "And I'm sure you will be." I glared at him and he just smirked. I couldn't help but smile.

The three of us enjoyed our lunch together and lighthearted conversation. Soon, it was time to take Kayla home and let Mitch go back to work.

"Honey, please don't let yourself get too exhausted, ok? I don't want you to get sick, especially for the honeymoon." I said, holding onto his hand.

"Stop worrying about me, Dana, I'll be fine. I just got in late last night, that's all. I'm only working eight tomorrow, and then I'm off for almost two weeks. Besides, I just drank four cups of coffee, love. I'm good for at least another twelve hours." He smiled.

"I love you, Mitch." I said, giving him a soft kiss.

"I love you, too." He said, giving me another kiss. "I'll call you later, baby."

I took Kayla home and then went to the grocery store. I only got what I thought would really be needed to get through the next few days, figuring I didn't want to leave much in the refrigerator during the honeymoon. I used Mitch's card to pay, and I felt a little twinge of excitement as I signed the receipt Dana P. Tarrington. I looked at it for a minute, and realized, I would be signing everything like that in just a few days. I smiled.

The rest of the day flew by and around ten that night, I heard Mitch's key in the lock once more. I smiled as I got up to go to the door.

"Hey, sweetheart, I'm home," he said with a big smile.

"Hi, honey. I wasn't expecting you to actually come over."

"Why not? Didn't you want to see me?" he asked, the glow fading from his face.

"Of course, I always want to see you. I just know how exhausted you are, that's all. You really need to go and get some rest." I told him.

Mitch plopped onto the couch and laid back. "I swear, I didn't think this day would ever end. We were so busy, and I feel like I'll never get everything in order to go away for a week. I honestly don't know how Jimmy did it by himself for so many years."

I sat down on the coffee table across from Mitch. "Well, Mitchell, things were different back then. And you have to remember, you're still learning how to do everything. It'll get easier."

"I guess you're right." He said, yawning and stretching. He sat up and pulled me over onto the couch next to him. "I'd better do something so I don't fall asleep." He said, leaning over to kiss me. He pulled me close to him and continued to kiss me sweetly and softly, not with passion but with love. Finally, he looked at me.

"I think I should go, love." He said. "I don't want to, believe me, but I'm just so beat. You won't be upset, will you?"

I smiled at him. "Of course not, honey. But please call me when you get there so I don't worry, ok?"

With a promise and a kiss, I sent Mitch back out into the night. I took a shower myself and climbed into bed with a book. A few minutes later the phone rang.

"I'm here." Mitch said. "I wanted to let you know."

"Thanks, sweetie. You go on to sleep now. Sweet dreams, I love you." I replied.

"You too. Goodnight, love." He said sleepily, hanging up the phone.

Only two more days, I thought as I turned out the light and fell asleep.

22

Well rested and renewed, Mitch got through his eight hour day at the bistro, and bid the crew farewell. "I'll be a married man the next time I walk through that door." He told them. During his lunch break, he slipped downtown to the jewelry store and bought Dana her wedding gift, a pair of beautiful diamond stud earrings. He knew she would like them.

We spent our evening just enjoying each other, making all the last minute arrangements and picking up the gifts for our wedding party, pearl earrings for the girls, money clips for the guys, and little things for the kids that we thought they would like. I cooked dinner for Mitch, pork chops and stuffing, and once again, he was happy with my ability to keep him well fed. After parting ways and sleeping well,

Friday morning was finally upon us. I awoke around nine and picked up the phone to call Mitch.

"Hello, Tarrington residence." Alexander answered.

"Hi Alexander, it's Dana. Is Mitch up yet?" I asked.

"Yes, he's right here, actually. One moment." I heard him tell Mitch it was me.

"Good morning, beautiful. I was just going to call you," he said.

"Well, now you don't have to," I replied cheerfully. "Are you coming here, or am I coming there?" I asked.

"Let me ask you one question. Have you packed yet for the honeymoon?" Mitch inquired.

"Yes, Mr. Smarty-pants, I did it yesterday. Didn't think I'd have it done already, did you?" I said smugly.

"No, actually I didn't. But I haven't done that yet, so I guess I'll come there. But I, uh, have a little stop I need to make along the way, there's something I need to pick up. So, it'll be a little while yet, ok?" he said. "Unless you want to come and have breakfast with us."

I smiled. "Thanks, but I already ate. By the way, what are you picking up, Mitch?" I asked curiously.

"Just something I, uh, we're going to need," he said, looking at his parents who were sitting at the table.

"Ok, honey, well, I guess I'll see you soon. I love you."

"I love you, too. Bye." Mitch said as he hung up the phone.

He sat down at the table at the place his mother had set for him, and took a few pancakes and some bacon. "This is nice, Mom, thanks. Between you and Dana, I'll never be hungry," he said.

"You were being a little secretive on the phone just now, son. Did you forget to pick up Dana's wedding gift?" Olivia asked.

Mitch could feel himself starting to blush. "Well, not exactly, Mom, but I guess it would depend on how you look at it."

Jake caught on and put his head down, trying not to show his smile. He looked up briefly across the table at Olivia, as if sending her a message. A look of understanding suddenly came across her face, and she smiled at Mitch.

"I understand now, Mitch. I'm a little embarrassed," she said.

"You're embarrassed?" he said, standing up and starting out of the room. "I'm the one who has to go through the checkout at the store." He smiled at them both, and headed for the door.

Mitch made his stop, and completing the transaction as quickly as possible, stuffed his purchase in his coat pocket and headed for the apartment. He unlocked the door and stepped inside.

"Hi honey." I said, giving him a tight hug. I could feel something in his coat pocket, so I reached in and pulled out the bag. "What's this?" I asked.

Mitch said nothing, and just smiled at me, allowing me to open up the bag and see what he had just picked up at the drugstore. I closed the bag quickly and handed it back to him.

"Do something with these, Mitchell," I said.

He smirked and chuckled. "I plan to," he replied mischievously.

"No, I mean put them somewhere, would you please?" I said, and he started to laugh, seeming to enjoy my embarrassment. I was getting frustrated. "Mitchell Tarrington, you know what I mean. Just do it, would you?"

Mitch stepped closer to me and pulled me to him, laughing wholeheartedly. "You are such a funny girl, the way you set yourself up like that," he said, kissing my forehead. "I'll go put these in the nightstand."

Mitch returned a minute later and walked over to me once again, looking at the blush still in my cheeks. "It's ok, sweetheart, all taken care of." He smiled. "Now, how about we go and pack my things for Hawaii?" he suggested.

"Ok, but you can't go in the closet, Mitch. My dress and everything is in there, and you can't see it." I told him.

"Fine, I'll let you get my things from in there, and I'll just pack from my dresser, ok?" He said, taking me by the hand and leading me into the bedroom. Next to the dresser, he saw my two suitcases, plus my small carry on. "Dana, we're only going for a week. Why on earth are you taking so much?"

I looked at him questioningly. "I'm hardly taking anything, Mitchell. All I have are the things I'm really going to need. There's quite a bit I actually decided to leave behind." I told him.

"Look, we need to condense, ok? It will be a lot easier on both of us if we only take one bag, and a carryon. Can you manage that?" he asked.

I sat down on the side of the bed and let out a loud, deep sigh. "Why don't you just go to Hawaii, and I'll stay here, if it's going to be that much trouble," I said.

"Now, why would you say that?" he asked. "I wouldn't have any fun at all without you. I just don't see myself with the ability to carry four suitcases from the airport terminal to the rental car, love. I only have two hands, and I'm sure they're too heavy for you." Then Mitch had a thought. "Wait, in the back of the closet there is a really big suitcase that my mom gave me a long time ago. Go find it and bring it out, ok?"

Following my orders, I retrieved the suitcase and brought it out into the middle of the room. Mitch smiled. "There should be plenty of room in there for all your things. Then, I'll just take one bag and the carry on. How's that?"

"That'll be fine, except for the fact that now I have to unpack everything and repack it," I said.

"Gee, that should take all of two minutes." Mitch said sarcastically.

He opened up the suitcase for me and together, we unpacked my two and condensed them into one. Mitch then opened his own suitcase and had me running back and forth, retrieving items from his closet. I wasn't at all surprised at the way he neatly folded everything and tucked it all in, putting together outfits as he went along. I laughed.

"I swear, Mitch, the way you're doing that outfit thing, you should have been a girl." I told him.

"It makes it easier when I get there. I won't have to go looking for everything. There's nothing wrong, or feminine, I might add, about a man who likes to be organized." He told me.

Less than a half an hour later, we had everything packed and ready to go.

"We have nothing left to do now but go to rehearsal later." Mitch said. "Kind of a nice feeling, isn't it?"

"Yeah, I'll say. So, how should we spend the last day of our engagement?" I asked him.

"I don't know. Anything special you'd like to do?" he asked.

I thought about it for a few minutes. "Why don't we just cuddle up on the couch and be together for now?" I suggested.

"Sounds like my kind of activity," he said, taking me by the hand.

He plopped down on the couch, pulling me down beside him and began to kiss me. He was holding me close, just kissing me softly and lovingly. I began to kiss his cheeks, then his forehead, and his neck, and I could hear him starting to breath more rapidly. He pulled me closer to him, and started kissing me passionately, holding me as tightly as he could. I ran my hands across his chest and slowly wrapped them around his shoulders, still kissing him with all I had in me. He was planting his kisses on my neck now, and nibbling on my ear, as I returned the favor. His hands moved down my back slowly, and he stopped at my waist, almost as if he were attempting to draw me to him even more. As if an alarm suddenly went off, I pulled myself slowly away from him.

"Uh, honey, what just happened?" I asked him.

He looked at me, as if just waking up from a dream. "I don't know, but I think it might be called eager anticipation? At least on my part, anyway," he replied.

"You know, I don't think I was far behind," I said, smiling at him.

He smiled and brushed my hair back from my face. "Maybe we should find something else to do, before we do more than we should, huh?"

I sat up and taking his hand, pulled him up as well. "That might not be a bad idea. Want to go for a walk in the park? It's a pretty day out today. We can bundle up," I suggested.

"That sounds nice. I think I like that idea," he said.

We found hats, gloves and scarves and went out to brave the chilly February air. Mitch took my hand in his, and smiled at me, his cheeks becoming rosy from the cold, but his eyes shining as brightly as the sun. We were silent for a while, just enjoying the closeness we were sharing. We walked the few blocks to the park, and strolled the path hand in hand, marveling at the way the snow sparkled on the trees, and stretched out over the grass like a blanket of glitter. We came to the bench we had sat on the last time we were here, but it was too snow covered this time to sit, so Mitch stopped and took me into his arms.

"Remember that family that we saw the last time we were here?" he asked. "I was looking at them that day, Dana, thinking that I hoped that's how we would be someday. That we'd bring our kids here to play, and you and I would just stand back, like that couple did, watching them."

I smiled at the sentiment he was expressing. "You know, Mitch, that was the first day of our engagement. Now, here we are again, in that same spot, on the last day of our engagement."

He smiled sweetly at me, and leaned down to give me a kiss. "But you know what? It's not really an end, Dana, it's a beginning. Our beginning."

Mitch took my hand and we began to stroll once more through the winter wonderland. "Hey, sweetheart, look at that!" he said, softly but excitedly. He pointed just ahead of us on the path where a young deer was crossing, not seeming to notice we were there. We stood quietly where we were, watching, until the deer sensed our presence and ran away.

"Wow, that was really neat," I said, looking up at Mitch with a smile.

"Yeah, that was, love. You know, I don't think I've ever been that close to one before."

"I have, in fact, I've been close enough to almost reach out and touch them before," I said. "When I was little, my daddy would take me with him sometimes and we would go for walks in the woods by our house. There were all sorts of animals back in there, deer and chipmunks, squirrels, rabbits, and we even saw a raccoon or two from time to time. Daddy taught me how to be still and very quiet, and if you move slowly, sometimes you can get close. I think those walks are part of the reason why I love the outdoors so much."

Mitch smiled at me lovingly. "It might be, sweetheart. It sounds like a lot of fun."

"Oh, it was." I said, reliving the memories in my mind. "My Grammy had even more land than we did, and at the bottom of the hill behind the house there was a pond. I used to like to go there at dusk, with a flashlight, and look for bullfrogs. I'd hear them croaking and when you shined the light on them, they'd just sit there and look at you with these great big froggy eyes." I laughed. "I tried to catch them sometimes, but I wasn't very good at it. Most of the time they'd get away, and all I'd go home with were muddy jeans and shoes. But Grammy never got mad at me. She'd just smile and tell me to go and change. And the next day, I'd be right there again."

Mitch turned to look at me. His eyes were full of love and emotion, and he chuckled softly. "Somehow, I just can't picture this beautiful woman standing beside me in a pond chasing frogs."

"Maybe not, but I wasn't always a woman, either, Mitch. But you know what? If I knew where there was a pond, I'd do it even today, I think. I'm not afraid of a little dirt, or frogs, either." I smiled.

Mitch laughed. "I'll remember that when our son comes home with a frog in his pocket and you're screaming for me to get it out of the washing machine."

I smiled at that thought. "Did you have any pets growing up, Mitch?"

"I think we had a few dogs when I was really little, but I don't remember for sure, but my most special pet was my horse, Shady. I used to spend a lot of time in the stable with him, and I was even there the night he died. I gotta say, that was really a hard day in my life." He said, and I looked at him lovingly, seeing a twinge of emotion come over him at the memory. "Oh, and there was an old stray cat that wandered into the stables one time, and had a litter of kittens. Jul and Ang kept taking them into the house and Dad kept taking them out. He told them that he was afraid they were too wild to keep as pets, and that they had to stay outside. Eventually, they all ran away, and I remember the girls bugging Dad for a kitten. So, he finally got them one and we had it for a long time. I think I might have been eight or nine when it died. I made Dad have a funeral for it and everything. Snowball's buried out behind the house, just a foot or so south of the big oak."

"Do you think we could get a kitten, sweetie? I'd love to have one." I asked.

Mitch smiled. "I wouldn't mind that at all, baby, but our landlord would. No pets policy. But, someday, when we have our own house, you can get anything you want."

"How about an elephant? Can I get an elephant?" I asked, playfully.

"Ok, maybe not anything. I don't think we'd be able to keep an elephant." He smiled and kissed my cheek.

Heading back toward home, Mitch took us a roundabout way and we stopped at Cutman's Deli for lunch. It was warm and inviting inside, and we welcomed the chance to thaw out a little. I ordered a hot chocolate with lots of whipped cream, and Mitch took his spoon, stealing most of it from the top of the cup.

"To think that this tasty white fluff is responsible for us being here today," he said. "Who would think it possible?"

"Yeah," I giggled. "Kind of funny, isn't it?"

After lunch we bundled up once again, and faced the cold once more, hand in hand. Back at the apartment, we put away our cold weather gear and settled onto the couch to watch TV. Finding an old movie, we sat together under a blanket, cuddling up to get warm again. After a few minutes, both of us fell asleep.

A while later, Mitch woke up and shook me gently. "Dana, wake up sweetheart." He said softly. I opened my eyes and looked at him, and he smiled sweetly. "I guess we got a little too warm and comfortable."

"I didn't even realize I was tired," I told him. "Did you sleep, too?"

He nodded. "I guess I must have. I remember waking up, but that's it."

I looked at the clock. "What time do we need to be at the church, honey? It's four thirty now," I said.

"Well, Pastor Michaels said something about six o'clock, I think. We need to take the license, too, and he'll hang onto it until tomorrow. Oh, yeah, Mom and Dad are taking us all to Chandler's for dinner tonight, too, did I tell you?" He said.

"No, you didn't tell me. Now I don't know what I'm going to wear," I whined.

"Dana, just wear anything, ok? Don't make a major crisis out of this," he replied.

"Well, it wouldn't have been a crisis if you had told me earlier. I could have gone shopping or something." I said snidely.

"I swear, do you go shopping for a new outfit every time you have to go somewhere? I certainly hope not. I'll go broke!" Mitch said, looking at me.

"No, I don't, Mitchell, but now I do have to go and try to find something appropriate for not only church, but Chandler's as well. And you know, your sisters will all have very nice things on. I don't want to look like the little Raggedy Ann." I stomped off to the bedroom, Mitch in tow.

"Here you go again, making things complicated." Mitch exclaimed, throwing his hands in the air. "Just go to the closet, pick out a nice skirt and blouse, put them on, and we can go." He folded his arms and stood watching me leaf through all my things.

"I have to shower first, you know." I replied, not even looking at him.

"Then I suggest you go and do that. No, wait. I'll go and touch up my shave job and I'll shower and dress. Then, in that ten minutes, you can choose an outfit, alright?" He sighed deeply and taking his clothes from the chair where he laid them earlier, he retreated into the bathroom, slamming the door loudly as he muttered something about women under his breath.

I heard Mitch turn on the shower, still mumbling to himself. Men just don't get it, I thought. All he has to do is decide if he wants to wear black shoes or brown. I need to think about a top, a skirt, or a dress, which shoes, which bag, which jewelry. And, top it off with put my hair up or wear it down. Then, of course, coordinate the eye shadow. To think they feel they have it so rough. Give me a break, I said to myself.

Exactly ten minutes later, as if he had it all planned, Mitch emerged from the bathroom, clean shaven, showered and fully dressed, complete with tie and jacket. Noticing the bedroom door still open, he stepped back inside and sighed loudly at the sight of me, still leafing through my clothes.

"For crying out loud, Dana, just pick something, would you?" He pleaded.

"It's not that easy. Nothing's right." I replied disgustedly.

Mitch put on his best authoritative tone. "Listen, I'm giving you exactly two minutes to come out of that closet with something you plan to wear, or I'm going to come in there and pick something for you, wedding gown or no wedding gown. We need to get moving, it's now almost five o'clock."

I managed to pull out a basic black skirt, and I handed it to Mitch, who laid it down across the back of the chair. I pulled out two blouses, one a fuchsia, the other a soft blue. I held both of them out for inspection.

"The pink one, Dana. Go with the pink one." Mitch said, sounding irritated.

I hung the blue blouse back up and stepped out of the closet. Thinking twice, I turned back to get the blue one, but Mitch caught me gently by the arm.

"Dana, wear that one, please. It's very pretty. And we need to get moving." He said, handing me the skirt.

"At least give me the chance to get the things I need to go under all this." I told him, moving to my dresser. I opened my underwear drawer, as Mitch watched.

"Do you mind?" I said, my own attitude coming out. "You don't really need to stand here and watch me."

"I do if I have any hope of ever getting you to actually leave this room," he replied. "And if you recall, I've already seen those things when I helped you unpack."

Gathering all my things, I gave Mitch a look and stepped past him, slamming the bathroom door loudly, and muttering something about men under my breath.

About twenty minutes later, I heard a knock on the bathroom door. "Dana, are you still alive or did you drown in the shower?" Mitch asked.

"I'm still getting ready, Mitchell, and this outfit is all wrong." I told him through the door.

"I'm sure it's fine, sweetheart. Please hurry, ok? It's almost five thirty."

Being fully dressed, I opened the door to look at him. "This doesn't look right, Mitch. It's too plain." I whined, looking down at my outfit.

"No, Dana, it's not. It's very nice. Please, let's get going." Then he looked at me. "You haven't done your hair or makeup yet? Come on, Dana what HAVE you been doing in there?" He was clearly agitated.

"Why don't you go find something to do other than bother me?" I asked, getting irritated myself.

"Bother you? All I'm trying to do is get us out of here on time. I don't think a wedding rehearsal works very well without the bride and groom, dear." He said, taking off his glasses to rub his eyes.

I grabbed my makeup bag and began the female war paint ritual as my future husband stood, arms folded, watching me with a curious but aggravated look on his face. When I got to my eye shadow, he sighed deeply as I fumbled through three compacts before finding the shades I wanted to use. Finally, Grumpy spoke.

"Why do you feel it necessary to do all that? You don't need makeup, Dana. You're beautiful the way you are." He said, his tone not quite as nasty as before.

"I'm glad you think so, but it makes me feel better, ok?" I said, not quite ready to be sweet to him just yet.

Finishing my makeup, I looked at my hair and decided to wear it up since I would be keeping it down for the wedding. Mitch took his watch out and looked at the time, sighed again, and leaned up against the doorway, still watching me.

"Mitch, you're making me nervous. Please go away." I pleaded.

"No, I'm not going anywhere until you're with me. Dana, it's now five forty. It takes fifteen minutes to get to the church from here. Please, let's go now, ok? You look wonderful." Mitch was going into begging mode.

I was pinning the last few strands of hair up and bringing just a little down on my forehead. "I still need my shoes, and my jewelry." I said, again, not looking at him.

"For the love of......." Mitch said, throwing his hands up again. "I'm going to call Chris and tell him to let Pastor know we'll be late. This is crazy, Dana. Just crazy." He stomped off to the phone, and I stuck my tongue out at him.

Mitch picked up the phone, dialing Chris's number. "Hello?" Chris answered.

"Hey Chris, we've gone into crisis mode here. Could you let Pastor know we may be a little late?" Mitch asked.

"Sure, buddy, is everything ok?" Chris asked with concern.

"Well, it was until I told Dana we were going to Chandler's after the rehearsal. Twenty minutes to pick the outfit, which by the way, is now too plain, forty minutes to shower, dress, do the makeup and hair, and she still isn't ready. I'm about to go on overload!" Mitch told him.

Chris laughed. "Get used to it, little brother. I made Trudy pick her outfit this morning to avoid a similar situation. I don't know what the big deal is, but they think they have to try to outshine each other or something."

"She did make some sort of comment about not wanting to look like Raggedy Ann. Like she's capable of that, anyway." Mitch sighed. "Well, I'll let you get over there. I'm going to go see how close Miss Perfect is to completing her ensemble."

"Ok, see you there. Try to be patient, little brother, and be careful coming over, ok?" Chris said.

"I'm past the patience stage, man. See ya." Mitch hung up the phone as I came into the room.

"Ok, I have one last dilemma." I said. "I decided to wear a longer necklace with the one you gave me, you know, to frame it, but now I don't have any earrings to wear that look right. I wish you had told me about all this sooner." I sighed.

Mitch walked into the bedroom and I heard him opening up a drawer on his dresser. He reemerged and handed me a tiny box, smiling. "What's this?" I asked, looking at him.

"Your wedding gift." He replied. "I wasn't going to give it to you just yet, but under the circumstances, I think it's necessary. Go on, open it."

I looked at him again, then back to the box in my hands, and I opened it up to reveal a pair of brilliant diamond stud earrings. I smiled, and all the irritation toward him that had built up in the last few minutes suddenly faded away.

"Mitch, they're gorgeous!" I exclaimed. "Thank you so much, honey, I love them." I gave him a hug, and a kiss, then decided I wanted to make it linger a little longer, but Mitch pulled away gently.

"Save it, love, we really have to go, ok? Put those on quickly and I'll get your coat and the gifts for everyone." He smiled, and noticing I looked a little dejected, he gave me another quick kiss.

Much to Mitch's delight, we were finally in the car on the way to the church. I reached over for his hand, and he smiled brightly. "You know I love you, don't you?" he asked.

"Yes, I know that. And I love you too. But you irritate me sometimes," I said.

He shot a glance at me. "Well, you do well in returning the favor, love." He commented. "But that's ok." Then he looked at me, as if he could see my outfit through my coat. "You look very pretty, Dana."

"So do you, I mean, you look very handsome." I said, smiling at him.

We arrived at the church about five minutes after six. "See, we aren't that late." I said smugly.

"The point is, sweetheart, I don't like to be late at all. We should have been here at least fifteen minutes ago." Mitch said, opening his door to step out. He came around the car and opened my door for me.

"You aren't going to start griping at me again, are you?" I asked, getting out of the car.

Mitch put his arm around me. "No, love, I'm not. Let's go do this and try to have a good time with it, ok?"

We stepped inside the door of the church, and all eyes were upon us. Jim and Chris looked at their watches. Mitch smiled and pointed to me. "Her fault." Was all he said. I shot him an irritated glance and started down the aisle to the rest of the group.

"Sorry we're late everyone." I apologized.

"No problem, kids. We're just going to do a few runs through of what we'll be doing tomorrow, I'll give you all a few details and you can be on your way." Pastor Michaels said.

Megan suddenly spotted her uncle and ran up to him, hugging his leg. He smiled and picked her up, giving her a kiss on the cheek. She smiled brightly at him.

"Me and you are getting married Uccle Mish." She announced. "I have my pretty dress at home that Dana got for me."

Everyone laughed and Mitch looked at her lovingly. "No, Meggie, Uncle Mitch is going to marry Dana tomorrow. But you get to wear your pretty dress and walk with Michael. Then you can sit next to Grandma and Grandpa, ok?"

Her little face grew somber. "But I want to marry you. Dana can sit with Grandma and Grandpa." Everyone laughed again.

Mitch smiled at her again and gave her a hug. "Sweetheart, it doesn't work that way. You have to be all grown up to get married, and besides, you can't marry me because I'm your uncle. You have to wait and find another boy that you want to marry." He gave her a kiss on the cheek and put her down. "Tomorrow I'm going to marry Dana, and then she'll be your aunt. Won't you like that?"

Megan's face lit back up and she looked at Dana. "Ok," she said. "I'll sit with Grandma and Grandpa." She ran back to Jim, who picked her up and hugged her tightly.

"Glad we cleared all that up." Mitch said, chuckling softly, as did everyone else.

Pastor Michaels instructed us all as to where we would be standing and got the details of who was serving in what position. Then he told us all to actually pretend like we were having the ceremony, placing Joseph and I in the back hallway, Mitch and the guys at the front. Even though Ty couldn't be there for the rehearsal, Mitch let him know that he would be singing a few songs prior to the ceremony, and that he would take care of his music and everything when he got there. Pastor said that would be fine, and then his wife played the organ to start our pretend ceremony. First, Mitch's parents walked down the aisle, followed by Kayla and then by Julia, Trudy and Angelina. Finally, Michael and Megan walked down. Michael was not happy about having to hold her hand, but they did fine. Finally the organ cued Joseph and

I, and we were instructed to pause momentarily in the doorway, thus giving the congregation time to stand up. Mrs. Michaels didn't want to play the entire song, so Mitch, being the clown, hummed it for us as we walked down the aisle. As we got to the front, we stood for a moment as Pastor told us what he would say, Joseph giving me away, and then going to stand with the rest of the guys. Mitch and I would step onto the platform, facing each other and then stand with our hands joined to say our vows. Even though it was only a rehearsal, Mitch looked at me with love in his eyes, but he also looked a little nervous. But he smiled brightly. After Pastor gave us a brief overview of what to do, Mitch looked at him.

"Since we're practicing everything else, can I practice the kiss, too?" He asked, smiling. Everyone laughed.

Pastor smiled. "I suppose it wouldn't hurt." He said, and Mitch kissed me.

We ran through everything a few more times for effect, and it all seemed to come together perfectly. Pastor instructed everyone as to what time to arrive, where to go, and what to do. We told the guys that we were just meshing our guests, no bride or groom's side, and they smiled, agreeing that they thought it was a great idea. As we finished up and were about to leave, Pastor approached Mitch and I.

"Well, Mitch, Dana, tomorrow's the real deal. It's normal to be nervous, so don't let that bother you. The entire ceremony, start to finish, will only take about thirty minutes, ok?"

"That sounds great." Mitch replied. "The shorter the better."

We thanked Pastor and headed toward the back of the church where everyone was gathered. Paul smiled. "Well, are those butterflies creeping up on you yet?" he asked.

"No, not really." I replied, looking at Mitch for a response.

"If I sleep at all tonight, it will be a miracle." He admitted, squeezing my hand, and everyone smiled.

Jake patted him on the shoulder. "We all survived, son. You will, too." He smiled. "How about dinner? Is everyone hungry?" We all nodded in agreement. "Ok, then, we'll see you all at Chandler's."

As Mitch got into the car, I looked at him. "You're nervous, aren't you?" I asked.

He put the key in the ignition and smiled. "Nah, not really," he replied.

I smiled at him. "Then why did you tell Paul you didn't think you'd sleep well tonight, Mitchell?"

He dropped his eyes and smirked. "Ok, maybe I am, just a little. But, gee, Dana, I'm getting married in less than twenty four hours.

That's a big thing, sweetheart." Then he looked into my eyes and took my hand. "But you know what? I'm more excited than I am nervous."

"Me, too," I said. "At this time tomorrow night, I'm going to be Mrs. Tarrington. That's pretty cool."

"Absolutely!" Mitch said, smiling brightly.

We arrived at Chandler's and Mitch took my hand as we walked inside. After checking our coats, we joined the rest of his family, who had already been seated. They all smiled as Mitch pulled out my chair for me, then unbuttoned his jacket and sat down.

"This is really nice of you to do this for us, Mom and Dad. Thanks," Mitch said.

Olivia smiled. "It's our pleasure, Mitchell," she said. Then she turned to Jake. "Dear, isn't there something else you wanted to tell them?"

Jake smiled and looked at Mitch and me. "We wanted to do something a little special for you tomorrow, kids, so you're mother and I took the liberty of booking a limousine for your transportation. We hope you'll enjoy it."

Mitch smiled and I giggled excitedly. "A limo? How cool is that?" I exclaimed as everyone chuckled at me. "I've always wanted to ride in a limo. Have you ever been in one, Mitch?" I asked him. He just smiled at me, finding no need to answer. "Ok, so you have. But I haven't."

He smiled at me sweetly. "Just when they all got married. That will be fun. Thanks, Dad."

"No problem, I'm glad you're both happy. Now, everyone, please order whatever you'd like, and let's have a nice evening together, shall we?"

We all ordered, Mitch and I deciding to get what we had the last time we had gone there together. Just then, the waiter brought two bottles of champagne to the table, pouring us all a glass. Jake stood up for a toast.

"I'd like to propose a toast to Mitch and Dana. First, to my youngest child. I can remember as vividly as if it were yesterday the day that you came into this world, the best Christmas gift your mother and I have ever received. You were the hardest to let go, but you proved yourself worthy, son, and taught me a thing or two along the way. I'm so very proud of the man you've become." Mitch smiled. Then Jake turned to me. "And to you, Dana. I must admit, I thought my son was crazy when he came home and announced that he had fallen in love with a beautiful woman he had never even met. But, when I finally met you myself, I understood exactly how that was possible. I know that there is no one better for Mitchell than you are, and we have all grown to love you almost as much as he does. We are proud to have you as part of this family." I felt a tear come down my cheek, and Mitch lovingly wiped it away gently. "To both of you, much love and happiness always." Everyone toasted us and Mitch kissed me softly.

I thought the toasting was done, but much to my surprise, my fiancé refocused everyone's attention.

"I don't know exactly what to say to everyone that will appropriately express my feelings, but I'll try." I could see that deep love for his family once again consuming his very being, just by the look on his face. "I want to thank you all for the love and support you've given me over the past few months, and especially, for welcoming Dana into the family and accepting her the way you have. It would have been easy for you to dismiss my feelings as just a schoolboy's infatuation, but you didn't. You believed they were as real as I knew they were, and are. A lot of changes have come into my life recently, and I never could have faced any of them without all of you. I love you all so very much." He bit his lip to hold back his emotions. Then he swallowed hard and turned to me. "And to my beautiful, sweet Dana. You make my life complete. I don't know much about this husband stuff, but you know I'll give it everything I have, because nothing means more to me than you and your happiness. I love you with all my heart." We all toasted again, and I gave Mitch a tight hug. "I love you, too, so much." I whispered.

Our meals came, and we all dug in hungrily, no one shy about their appetites. Our conversation was happy and lighthearted, and we joked and laughed, strengthening the bond between us. I looked around the table at Mitch's family, and realized, they were now my family, too. It was a feeling like none I had felt in a long time.

All too soon our evening together ended, and Mitch and I were on our way back home. As we pulled into the parking lot, Mitch turned off the car and looked at me.

"I really hope you had a nice time tonight, in spite of the way it all started," he said.

"Yeah, I did." I replied. "It felt really good to have all your family there, Mitch. They really are a bunch of special people."

"You're right, they are. I don't know what I'd do without any of them."

We got out of the car and walked upstairs, and once inside the apartment, I smiled at Mitch. "Well, mister, I have a wedding gift for you, too. Would you like me to go and get it?"

"Really, you got something for me, too?" he asked excitedly. "Sure, go get it for me."

After unburying the guitar and amp from the back of the closet where I'd hidden them, I returned to where Mitch was waiting. He was sitting on the couch, so his back was to me as I approached.

"Ok, sweetie, here it is. I really hope you like it." I said.

Mitch stood up and a wide grin spread across his face when he saw the guitar. He reached out for it, inspecting it thoroughly. "Wow, Dana, this is awesome! You got me my own electric guitar!" He said excitedly. He ran his hands along it and turned it over, then back again, trying it on for size. He looked at me in amazement. "Sweetheart, this is one of the best you can get. How on earth did you ever know?"

I smiled. "Well, I had a little help from Shep and Zach. I got it when we went out to get the pizzas on Tuesday. All I really knew about it was that I liked it because it was blue, and that's your favorite color. They helped me with the rest of it."

Mitch put down the guitar and took me into his arms. "It's such a thoughtful gift, Dana, thank you. You are amazing." He said, kissing me. "Think the neighbors would mind if I tried it out?"

"Well, I don't know, but maybe if you don't play too long and keep it low." I said, smiling.

Mitch plugged in the amp and adjusted a few knobs, then strapped it on and began to play around with it a little. He smiled brightly as he expertly maneuvered the guitar, and when he was through, he laughed playfully and took a bow for me as I applauded him. He lifted the guitar again to look at it, then took it off, turned off the amp and came back to me.

"That is so great. Every time I have it on stage with me, I'll be thinking of you. Not that I don't do that, anyway." He said, holding me once again.

As if we were reading each other's thoughts, we both looked up at the clock. "Mitchell, it's almost eleven, honey. You have to leave before midnight. It's bad luck for you to see me on our wedding day before the ceremony." I told him.

"I know, love, but what about talking to you? I'm allowed to call in the morning, aren't I?" he asked.

"No, Mitch, you can't call me either. You can't have any contact with me until the wedding after you leave here tonight. You just have to go home and sleep, and look forward to that." I said, giving him a gentle hug.

"I'll go home, but I don't know about the sleeping part." He said, looking at me. "I think I may have a little trouble there tonight."

"Why? Are you nervous?" I asked.

"Yes, Dana, and excited and anxious and everything else. But, I'll be ok, don't worry. I'll be bright eyed and bushy tailed come tomorrow afternoon, promise." He smiled at me sweetly. "Now, remember, the car will pick you and Kayla up here. Joseph is going to drop her off before he comes to the church. Chris is picking me up and everyone else will get there on their own, ok? I'll give Chris a key on Sunday morning so he and Trudy can take care of your dress and my tux, and they can put all the gifts here so we can open them when we get back. It's all worked out."

"Sounds like it. I'll be ready." I promised. I pulled Mitch close and held him tightly, breathing deeply to take in his scent and his warmth. "I love you so much, Mitchell Tarrington." I said.

"And I love you, too, baby, I really, really do." With that, he gave me a kiss and smiled, putting on his coat and opening the door. "See you at the altar."

"I'll be there." I said, and blew him a kiss, which he caught and put on his lips. Smiling, he waved and was gone.

Closing and locking the door, I headed into the bedroom and went to the back of my closet to take out my gown. I took it out of the plastic bag protecting it and laid it over the chair, tracing the delicate details with my finger. The next time I saw Mitch, I thought, I would be wearing it, and I would be saying the words that would bond us together forever. I washed up and undressed, then feeling the need to be close to him, I searched for the shirt he had worn earlier and put it on. Like the one I had worn that time before, it had the scent of Mitch's cologne, and for some reason, just that was enough to make me feel secure. I pulled on a pair of sweatpants with it, and climbed into bed, thinking that I would try to rest and prepare myself for the day ahead. But, like Mitch, sleep wasn't going to come easy, so I took my book from the nightstand where I had placed it, and tried to read. I was seeing the words, but I couldn't concentrate. My mind was filled with too many things. I thought back just a few months earlier, to the night Mitch and I first met, and smiled at the memory of our silly little whipped cream battle. I remembered the way I felt inside as he smiled at me, and the way my heart skipped a beat the first time he kissed me. I thought about his proposal, and the awful fight between us later that night, but thrilled in the memory of our reunion the next day, and marveled at the way our love had only grown stronger since then. I put my book down and decided to lay down, turning off the light. I reached out and touched Mitch's pillows, and my heart warmed knowing that just twenty four hours from then, he would be lying beside me, my husband. I closed my eyes and soon, sweet slumber came to me, and I rested peacefully.

Mitch walked into the house to find his parents sitting in the front room talking. They both smiled as he walked in and sat down.

"Dana all home safe and sound?" Jake asked.

"Yep, she's all well and good." Mitch replied. "Knowing her, she's probably fast asleep by now."

Olivia smiled. "You should try to do the same, dear. Tomorrow's going to be a very long day for you."

Mitch sighed. "I know, but I really don't feel very sleepy right now. I think I may go into the family room and read for a while or something." He stood up, and turned back to his mother. "Hey Mom, any more of those cookies anywhere?" He asked smiling.

Olivia smiled back. "Yes, Mitchell, in the cupboard next to the refrigerator. Get yourself some milk, too. It'll help relax you," she said.

"Thanks, I will." Mitch replied, and headed off in that direction.

Snack in hand, Mitch walked into the family room and sat down in the chair next to his parents' bookcase. He scanned over the titles, but nothing appealed to him, so he just sat there and looked out the window. There was a bright moon shining and the reflection off the snow almost made it appear to be daytime. Mitch looked at the piano, then got up and took a seat on the bench, lightly fingering a few of the keys. Music was not only Mitch's outlet, but also a comfort to him. He began to play softly and the more he played, the more soothing it was to him. He sang softly to himself as he played, and he wished he could have Dana there to sing for her. He felt himself beginning to relax, but continued to play, and when he finished, he looked up to see his mother standing in the doorway, watching him. She smiled sweetly at her son, and he got up and walked over to her.

"Feeling a little better now, Mitchell?" she asked.

"Yeah, I think I'm ready to try to go get some sleep. I hope I didn't bother you, I mean, playing this late at night."

"Never, Mitch. God gave you a wonderful gift, and it makes me happy to know you enjoy using it. I love to hear you play and sing." She kissed him on the cheek. "You better go to bed now, honey. Tomorrow's going to be a wonderful day."

Mitch smiled and went up the stairs to his room, closing the door gently behind him. He undressed and crawled into bed, his thoughts still with Dana. He reached out beside him and imagined her there, knowing that soon she would be. He closed his eyes and drifted to sleep, his heart anticipating the day to come.

Early the next morning, I awoke around eight to the sound of my alarm. I smiled and stretched. My wedding day, I thought. I could hardly believe it had finally arrived. I jumped up quickly and trotted off to make a pot of coffee, then jumped in the shower and threw on some clothes. Kayla would be coming by around nine thirty, and we were meeting the other girls at the beauty shop to have our hair and nails done for the wedding. I ate some oatmeal and toast, drank a cup of coffee and decided to tidy up a little. I changed the sheets on the bed, and left the blankets pulled down just a little. Mitch had told me that he decided to spend the night at home, his logic being that we would be in a hotel for a week, and he wanted to make sure we got a good night's rest. But, he didn't know that I knew he really thought it would make me more comfortable with everything if he brought me to a familiar place for our first night together. I smiled at the sentiment, but realized that it really didn't matter where we were, I would probably still be nervous. Deciding not to think about it, I went about my business until Kayla arrived.

"Happy wedding day, girl!" she exclaimed, giving me a hug as she came through the door. "Excited?"

"Oh, Kayla, you just don't know!" I told her. "I can't believe it's finally here!"

Kayla had brought her things for the wedding, and she laid them on the couch. "Well, let's go get ourselves all prettied up, ok? Then we're gonna stop for some lunch on the way home, my treat, and we'll get you to that church on time."

I smiled as I put my coat on. "I wonder what Mitch is doing right now. I wish I could call him."

"Oh, no, don't you dare!" Kayla warned. "I don't want any bad luck on this marriage, uh, uh!"

I laughed. "Don't worry, Kayla, the next time I talk to him will be at the altar, trust me." Then a thought occurred to me. "Oh, Kayla, I'd better give you his ring while I'm thinking about it!" I ran into the bedroom and opening my dresser drawer, I brought out the box which held Mitch's wedding band. I handed it to Kayla, and she opened it up to see.

"Oh, that is beautiful, Dana!" she exclaimed. "Has he seen it?"

I laughed as I remembered our little fiasco the day we bought the rings. "Yes, he's seen it, in fact, he picked it out." I told her. And as we rode to the beauty shop, I relayed the whole story to her, and we laughed together and shared, as only best friends can do.

Mitch woke up around ten and sleepily rubbed his eyes, put on his glasses and stepped out of bed. He looked at the clock. Just four more hours, he thought, and he would be pledging his life to the woman he loved. He smiled, thinking of her and wondering what she was doing right now. He remembered her saying she was going for a "beauty appointment" as she put it, and he wondered just how she thought she could make herself any more beautiful than she already was. He took a shower, shaved, then threw on some clothes and went downstairs to greet the day.

"Good morning!" Mitch said to his parents as he walked into the kitchen.

"Good morning, son." Jake greeted back. "So, today's the big day. How are you feeling?"

Mitch smiled as he poured himself a cup of coffee. "Pretty calm right now, but I'm sure it won't last."

"Well, like I told you, Mitch, that's normal. You'll be just fine. Before you know it, this whole day will be nothing more than a memory." His father replied.

"Then I guess I have to do my best to make that memory a good one, don't I?" Mitch said.

"It will be, Mitchell, just relax." Jake told him.

Mitch managed to eat some cereal and toast, and decided to unwind a little by going for a walk. He bundled up and went outside, starting down the long driveway in front of the house. The day was sunny and bright, and the air was brisk but not all that uncomfortable. Mitch paused about a third of the way down the drive, leaning on the fence to look out over the land. He remembered as a child how he thought that the land never ended, and how he imagined what might lie beyond what his eyes could see. Now his vision was different, and he thought about being married, and what was going to lie beyond that afternoon. He was anxious to find out what this new world was going to be like.

He continued on down the road, pausing again to watch two squirrels scurrying up a tree, and a hawk flying high above. He never noticed before how tranquil and quiet it was here. He walked up the path leading to the stables, and remembered a time long ago when this place was often filled with the laughter of the Tarrington children, either playing in the loft or tending to the horses they kept here. He remembered Shady, the horse his father had brought home shortly after his tenth birthday, and how Chris and Julia had taught him how to ride and care for him. He remembered getting up early in the morning to run down to the stable to make sure Shady was fed, and how he would often just stand for what seemed like hours petting him and brushing him. Shady had been a big part of young Mitch's life. He remembered the summer Shady had gotten ill, and how the night he took a turn for the worst he had sneaked down to the stable to be with him. The next morning his father and Chris had awakened him there, to tell him

Shady had passed away in his sleep. Mitch was strong in front of them, but as soon as they left, he had climbed the loft and cried alone for a very long time.

His train of thought was broken by the sound of his brother's voice. "Hey, Mitchell, what are you doing, little brother?" Chris called out through the open window of his car.

Mitch smiled and waved, walking up to the car. "Just taking a walk, and well, reliving some old memories, that's all."

"Well, buddy, it's a little after twelve. Get in and I'll take you back up to the house. We need to get you ready to go make some new memories." Chris smiled as Mitch climbed into the car.

The two drove back up to the house and went inside. Olivia greeted them at the door.

"Look what I found, Mom." Chris teased. "Can I keep it?" He said, pointing to Mitch.

Olivia laughed playfully. "He's cute, Chris, but I think he'll eat too much."

"Gee, thanks Mom." Mitch said, pretending to sound disappointed. Then he turned to Chris. "And what do you mean, 'it'?"

Chris laughed. "Come on, little brother, let's grab a quick sandwich. I haven't had any lunch. Is that ok, Mom?" he asked.

"Of course, I'll even make it for you boys. Come with me," she prompted.

Chris gave his overcoat to Alexander, and Mitch stopped to look at his brother's attire.

"Well, now, Christopher, don't you look dapper?" He said, nodding approvingly. "And I must say, the pink is very becoming on you." He teased.

"Don't get used to it, Mitch. I'm only doing it for Dana." Chris said, matter-of-factly.

"Chris, you look so handsome." Olivia said as he entered the kitchen. "I do like the pink on you, too, honey."

Chris made a face as Mitch smiled at him playfully. "Don't say a word, Mitchell." Chris warned. Mitch laughed.

The two ate lunch quickly as Olivia went off to get ready herself. Jake was one step ahead, already in the shower. Finishing lunch, Mitch retreated upstairs to get dressed. Opening the closet in his room, he pulled out his tuxedo, and undressed, then proceeded to slip everything on. He was beginning to feel the nerves settling in, and his hands seemed to be a little shaky as he tried to button his shirt. Just as he reached the top, the button pulled off in his hand. Great, he thought. He hardly had time to sit and try to sew on a button, something else he really wasn't good at, either. He did the one thing he could think of doing.

"Mom!" Mitch yelled, opening up the door.

Luckily for him, Olivia wasn't like most women who took a long time to get ready. She was already downstairs, waiting with Chris and Jake. Hearing her son call for her, she went to the bottom of the stairs and called up to him.

"What's wrong, Mitch?" She asked.

"A button came off my shirt. Can you put it back on for me?" Mitch asked.

"Yes, dear, just bring it here, ok?" she told him.

Mitch sighed and took off the shirt, walking to meet his mom halfway on the stairs. "Please hurry." He pleaded.

"I will, you go and get your shoes on and wait, I'll bring this up in a minute, ok?" And with that she was off.

Mitch found his shoes and put them on, then sat on the side of the bed waiting for Olivia. Less than two minutes later, she reappeared with his shirt.

"Thanks." He said, taking it from her and starting to button it. She smiled and walked back downstairs.

Mitch opened the little box on the dresser that contained his cufflinks, or so he thought. Much to his dismay, they weren't there. He looked around on the dresser and on the floor, thinking they may have fallen out, but he couldn't find them.

"Mom!" Mitch yelled again. "I can't find my cufflinks. Can you help me?"

Olivia looked at Chris and Jake and sighed, smiling. "They never outgrow that, do they?" She said, starting to walk to the stairs once more.

"Mitchell, go to the little box on your father's dresser and take his extra pair. You don't have time to look for yours." She called up to him.

"Ok, thanks Mom." Mitch called back, and did as he was instructed.

Mitch returned to his room and inspected himself in the mirror. He only needed his tie, he thought, but looking closer, decided to touch up his shave job a little. First, the tie, though. He had known how to tie a bow tie for a long time, but the combination of lack of practice and his shaking hands was getting the best of him.

"Mom!" Mitch called out once more. "I can't seem to get this stupid tie."

Olivia sighed and started to the stairs once more, but Chris caught her arm, smiling. "Stay here, Mom, I'll go help him." He said, and went up to Mitch's room.

"What's the problem, Mitchell?" Chris asked walking in. "Come here, I'll do it for you."

Mitch walked up to Chris and handed him the tie, and Chris proceeded to tie it for him.

"You'd think I'd never tied one of these before. My fingers just won't work." Mitch told him.

"Calm down, Mitch. You're just getting nervous, that's all. It's going to be fine, and it'll all be over soon. Hang in there." Chris told him, straightening the tie and turning Mitch to face the mirror. "You look great," he added.

"Except for this five o'clock shadow, which I'm going to take care of right now." Mitch said, heading into the bathroom. Chris followed.

"Hang on, little brother. You'll cut yourself to shreds if you try to shave again right now. I'll get Dad's electric and you can touch up with that, ok? Wait here." Chris went off and a minute later, reappeared with what Mitch needed.

Mitch finished getting ready and stopped in front of the mirror for one final inspection. He turned to Chris and took a deep breath. "Well, let's go do this."

"Wait, buddy, just one more thing." Chris said. "Is there anything else you need?"

Mitch looked at him curiously. "Like what?" he asked.

Chris smiled. "Like maybe, well, something for later on tonight? If so, we can make a stop."

Mitch looked at him, and then smiled. "Oh, uh, no, I already took care of that, thanks," he said. "Most embarrassing thing I've ever done in my life."

Chris laughed and looked at his brother, his face full of love. "You know, you really are an innocent thing, aren't you? But, I'm really proud of you, little brother. You're gonna be ok." The two exchanged a hug. "Come on, let's go get you married."

Kayla put the last pin into my hair to hold on the veil, and straightened it, turning me around to face the full length mirror on the closet door. "You look so lovely, Dana, just like a fairy princess."

"I hope Mitch thinks so." I said, nervously straightening out the train on my dress. "Do you have his ring?"

"I sure do, now stop your worrying, would you?" she said. "Let me take one more look at you." Kayla walked around me, eyeing my gown up and down. "Perfect. Are you ready to go become Mrs. Tarrington?" she asked.

I smiled. "You bet! Let's go!" I exclaimed, taking my wrap from the back of the chair.

"Wait a minute, dear. Can I talk to you one minute?" she said.

"Sure, Kayla, what is it?" I asked her, sitting on the side of the bed.

Kayla looked at the way I had left the covers turned down a little and she smiled, coming to sit beside me. "I know that today a lot of changes are coming into your life, but just remember what I told you. Know that Mitch loves you, and let him know you love him. Everything else will take care of itself." She smiled and took my hand. "Which one of you is taking care of the responsibility?" she asked.

I had to think for a minute as to what she meant, then I finally caught on. "Oh, uh, he is, I mean, he did." I pointed to the nightstand.

"That's good." She replied. "Don't you worry about a thing, girl. I'm so proud of you. You're gonna have such a happy life." Kayla said, giving me a warm hug and a kiss on the cheek. "Now, we got a limo waiting, and a boy that wants to become a husband today!"

23

Kayla and I arrived at the church to find the other girls waiting for us in a big room in the back, just off the main entrance. I saw Chris's car and knew Mitch was already there, so I asked the girls for an update.

"So, have any of you seen Mitch?" I asked. "How's he doing?"

"I went to talk to Chris and Mitch when they first got here." Trudy said. "He's so nervous, Dana. He was just pacing back and forth and Chris said he had to do his tie for him! But he looks so handsome. Wait until you see him."

I smiled. "I'm nervous, but I'm starting to get really excited, too."

At that moment, the lady from the florist showed up, giving us all our bouquets. I held mine close up to me, breathing in deeply to take in the scent of the roses and carnations. She showed me a smaller version that they would leave at the club for the reception, and that would be the one I would throw later to all the single girls.

"I just pinned the flowers on the men, the groom last. He's a handsome one. You two make a lovely couple," she said.

I smiled. "Thank you, I'm glad to hear that."

The photographer came in just after she left, snapping some photos of the girls and me, as well as us with the kids. Then he went off to find Mitch and his groomsmen for the same thing. A few minutes later I began to hear music and someone singing.

"That must be Ty." I said to the girls. "He's doing a few songs before everything starts. How close are we now?" I asked.

Joseph must have heard me, as he appeared as if on cue. "Just about five minutes, so I think we all better get into position now."

The girls all gave me a kiss and a hug, and straightening my dress, I took Joseph's arm and went to join the others in the foyer. We would stand just out of sight until the girls were at the front, and then we would move to the doorway until all the guests were standing before walking up the aisle.

I heard Ty finish and the organ started. I began to shake.

"Joseph, I'm so nervous." I said to him.

"It's alright, girl, take a deep breath, ok?" He smiled at me. "Listen, I know I'm not really your daddy, but I want you to keep two things in mind. First of all, he is here, Dana, and your mama and grandma, too. They're watching all this right now. And I'm so proud that you asked me to stand in for him. Kayla and I love you a lot, Dana." He kissed me softly on the cheek and put down my veil. "Are you ready?" he asked, as we heard our cue.

I nodded and smiled at him. "More than ever."

Joseph and I were now standing in the doorway of the church, and I looked down the aisle at the altar, all decorated with flowers in pink and blue. I saw the girls all lined up on one side, the guys on the other, and what seemed like an endless sea of people in the pews. But suddenly, as Joseph began to walk me toward them all, everything seemed to fade away except the sight of my Mitch, standing there, watching me. His face was glowing in a way I had never seen before, and the closer I got to him, the more I could see the love shining in his eyes. I was awestruck at how handsome he was in his tuxedo, looking so proud and strong. Just seeing him there confirmed in my heart that what I was doing was more right than anything else in the world.

Mitch stood looking at Dana, and the sight of her made him catch his breath. She looked like an angel, all dressed in white, her face glowing as she walked toward the man she loved. Even behind her veil he could see her radiant beauty, her eyes sparkling like two diamonds in the sun. His heart was overflowing with the love he felt for her, and he knew in his heart that this was the day he had been waiting for all his life. As she stopped in front of him, he smiled at her, and she smiled back, and just that look told him she felt the same way.

"Dearly beloved, we are gathered here today in the sight of God and these witnesses, to join together Dana Patrice Walker and Mitchell Jacob Tarrington the third in holy matrimony. If anyone here present knows of a reason these two should not be joined together, may they speak now or forever hold their peace." The pastor said. Everyone was silent as he turned to Joseph. "Who gives this woman to be married to this man?"

Joseph looked at me, then at Pastor Michaels. "On behalf of her parents, her best friends do." Joseph placed me beside Mitch, and with another gentle hug, he took his place with the other men.

Mitch and I walked onto the platform, Kayla carefully straightening my dress behind me. Pastor Michaels continued.

"Let us begin today with some scripture from the book of Ruth, chapter one, verse sixteen and seventeen." As the pastor read the scripture, I looked at Mitch. He was biting his lip nervously, and I realized that he was doing it unconsciously and I smiled. I loved all those little Mitchisms, I loved everything about him.

After a brief prayer, the pastor softly instructed me to hand my flowers to Kayla, and then for Mitch and I to face each other. "Mitchell and Dana, with full and free consent to keep the marital covenant, and with thoughtful determination of the same, if you desire to enter into holy matrimony, please acknowledge the same by joining your right hands." Mitch and I joined hands, and looked into each others eyes.

"Mitchell, do you take this woman to be your wife, to cherish her with all your heart, to respect, honor and guard her love, in sickness and in health, for better or worse, for richer for poorer, and forsaking all others, remain faithful to her until death do you part? If so, answer I do."

Mitch looked deep into my eyes. "I do." He said softly.

"And Dana, do you take this man to be your husband, to cherish him with all your heart, to respect, honor and guard his love, in sickness and in health, for better or worse, for richer or poorer, and forsaking all others, remain faithful to him until death do you part? If so, answer I do."

I felt as if I were looking into Mitch's very soul. "I do." I answered.

"Mitchell, do you possess a token of your love and affection to give to your bride, a seal of this holy covenant you are taking?" The pastor asked.

"Yes, I do." Mitch answered. "A ring." He turned to take the ring from Chris, and he handed it to the pastor.

The pastor continued. "In all ages and among all people, the ring has been a symbol of that which is measureless, and is now a symbol of your measureless love and devotion. The circle has not a beginning or an end, and in keeping your vow, this ring will serve as the sign and seal of your commitment to Dana." He handed the ring back to Mitch.

"Mitchell, place the ring on Dana's finger and repeat after me. I, Mitchell, take thee, Dana, to be my wedded wife, to have and to hold from this day forward, sharing with you all my worldly goods, remaining loyal to you and loving you only, faithfully keeping the vows I have made, in the name of the Father, the Son and the Holy Spirit."

Mitch's hands were shaking, but he didn't look at the ring he was placing on me. Instead, he was still looking deep into my eyes, his face so full of emotion I could hardly breathe. As he repeated the words, he smiled lovingly at me, and my heart overflowed.

The pastor turned to me. "Dana, do you also possess a token of your love and affection to give to your groom, a seal of this holy covenant you are taking?"

"Yes, I do. A ring." I answered, taking Mitch's ring from Kayla. She smiled sweetly as she handed it to me.

"Dana, place the ring on Mitchell's finger and repeat after me." I looked into Mitch's eyes as I repeated the words the pastor was saying and I slid the ring on Mitch's hand, rubbing the top of his hand and the ring with my thumb. He smiled and looked down at it, then at me.

Pastor instructed us softly to step up to our unity candle. "You are entering into the holy estate of marriage, the blending of two individual lives, each with its own personality and interests. Your lighted candles are symbols of these individual lives. Marriage is an act of loving surrender, so now you will no longer go your separate ways, and as you bring the flames of your candles together, lighting the candle of a larger fuller life, your lives are now blended as one. Now each of you must blow out the candles of your individual lives, and cling to God's words that a man shall leave his father and mother and cleave unto his wife, and the two shall be as one." Mitch and I blew out our candles, and went back to stand facing each other once more.

Pastor smiled and said softly, "Almost done, kids. Hang in there." Mitch and I smiled at one another.

"Mitchell and Dana, by seeking to be married in the sight of God, you have expressed that you believe marriage is not just a legal institution, but it is a covenant, a bond of union sealed in Heaven. From this day on, you shall be not two but one, united and undivided. As you continue to increase in your love and faith, so too shall the blessings on your lives increase. Let us pray."

Mitch and I were holding each other by both hands now, and as the pastor prayed for us, I too, said my own prayer, asking that this special bond never be broken, that we would be given the strength and love to endure whatever life threw our way. The prayer ended and we looked up, the pastor smiling.

"For as much as Mitchell and Dana have consented to this union, and have witnessed the same before God, these family and friends, and have pledged their faith to each other, I now, by the power invested in me by the church and this state, pronounce that they are husband and wife. What God has joined let no man put asunder."

Mitch and I smiled brightly at each other. Then Mitch looked at the Pastor as if asking the one remaining question. Pastor smiled.

"Yes, Mitchell, you may now kiss your bride." We heard a faint chuckle through the congregation.

Mitch took a deep breath, and lifted my veil, but turned to Chris instead. He took off his glasses, and handed them to Chris, and Chris smiled at him. Then, Mitch turned back to me and softly, sweetly, and with all the love he had, kissed me, his new bride. Without opening his eyes, he reached out for his glasses, and putting them back on, he opened his eyes and looked at me, his face shining. I smiled at him as he offered his arm, and we turned to face the congregation.

"Ladies and gentleman," Pastor began, "I am proud to introduce to you, for the very first time, Mr. and Mrs. Mitchell Jacob Tarrington the third." Everyone applauded as Mitch and I walked down the aisle to the foyer of the church.

Mitch turned to me and smiled brightly. "I must say, Mrs. Tarrington, you are the most beautiful sight I have ever seen." He said, leaning down to kiss me.

"There'll be plenty of time for that stuff later, little brother." Chris said playfully, reaching out to shake Mitch's hand. He pulled him into a hug and gave him a pat on the back. Then he looked at me. "He's right, though, you are looking very pretty, sister-in-law." And he gave me a hug and a kiss on the cheek.

Trudy was next with her congratulations, followed by the rest of the family. Kayla grabbed me in a huge hug and smiled at me.

"You did it, girl! You're all married now!" she said. "You're not nervous any more, are you?" she asked.

I looked at Mitch and he was smiling at me. "Well, not like I was anyway." I answered and she smiled.

Joseph reached out to shake Mitch's hand, and gave him a hug as well. "You sure got yourself a special one there, Mitch," he said. "You better take good care of her, now, you hear?"

Mitch smiled and put his arm around me. "Don't worry, I'll definitely do that," he said.

Kayla gave him a hug and kiss as well. "Yes, that's right, I know you will, Mitch."

Olivia and Jake came to stand in front of us and they both smiled, Olivia wiping a tear from her eye.

"Come on, Mom, don't do that." Mitch said, his face full of compassion. "You're supposed to be happy."

She smiled and gave her youngest child a loving hug, rubbing his back with her hand. "I just can't get over that my baby is all grown up and starting a life of his own. You'll find out someday." She pulled away from him, and took both of his hands. "I am happy for you, Mitchell. You've given us a beautiful new daughter to love." She smiled and gave me a hug. "Welcome to the family, Dana. We love you very much."

"Thanks, Olivia, I love you too." I said back, returning her hug.

Jake reached out to shake Mitch's hand, and he placed his other hand on Mitch's shoulder. "Congratulations, Mitchell. Stay as happy as you are right now." He gave Mitch a hug.

"I'm sure it won't be too hard, Dad." He said, looking at me.

Jake leaned down and hugged me tightly. "That's my little boy you have there, you take good care of him, ok?" He said, choking back his emotions.

"I will, Jake, I promise."

I took Mitch by the hand as we were flooded by what seemed like an endless stream of friends and relatives, each offering a hug and their best wishes. Finally, it appeared as if everyone was gathered outside except Mitch and I.

"I think they're waiting for us, honey." I said to him. "Are you ready to get bombarded with birdseed?"

Mitch gave me a funny look. "Birdseed? I always thought it was rice that got thrown at weddings."

"Well, it used to be." I answered. "But I guess rice isn't good for the birds that clean up afterwards, so now they throw birdseed. Then the birds can eat it and it won't hurt them."

He looked at me with a half cocked smile. "Ok, then, but it's cold and I'm going to move fast. So, pick up your dress, lovely lady, and let's go."

Before Mitch opened the door he peaked out to see our limo waiting at the end of the sidewalk, and the chauffer standing at the door, waiting to open it. He grabbed my hand and we ran down the sidewalk, jumping inside the limo and laughing all the while. Once inside, Mitch pulled me to him.

"You know what the cool thing is about limos?" he asked me.

"No, but I have a feeling you're going to tell me, aren't you?" I replied.

"Well, one cool thing is, you can do this." He reached up to a little button. Pressing it, a dark window went up, separating us from the driver. "Everything is tinted, so we now have total privacy. We can see them, but they can't see us." He said, moving closer to me still. "And, there is plenty of room back here, especially when there are only two people." He smiled at me, then taking off his jacket, leaned over and kissed me slowly, his eyes shining, his hands starting to wander.

"Mitchell, what are you doing?" I asked him.

"Well, nothing just yet." He answered.

"Honey, not now. Later, ok?" I said to him.

Mitch sighed. "I was afraid you'd say that." He said, looking a little rejected.

I laughed and gave him a kiss. "You are so impatient, Mitchell Tarrington."

"But you are just too beautiful, Dana Tarrington." He smiled back, starting to kiss me again, but pulling away. "But, I'll be good."

We circled around and now were heading back toward the church. Mitch took my hand and looking at my rings, he smiled. Then he looked at his own, and smiled even more.

"Are you happy, sweetheart?" he asked.

"Ecstatic." I answered. "How about you?"

"Beyond words, love. This is the best day of my life, so far." He answered.

"Were you nervous?" I asked him.

He laughed. "Dana, didn't you see the way I was shaking when Chris handed me your ring? I thought I would either pass out, drop the ring, or not be able to say my vows. Or, possibly all three."

I laughed. "Yeah, I know what you mean. I had a little trouble keeping your ring straight enough to slide onto your finger."

"Well, you did a good job, sweetheart, and trust me, it's never coming off. Not ever." He smiled, and kissed me again.

We arrived back at the church and spent the next hour or more taking pictures, then Mitch and I met with Pastor Michaels, Chris and Jake at the back of the church to sign our marriage license. Mitch tucked it away safely inside his jacket.

"Remind me to take that out of there tonight, or Chris will have it dry cleaned with my tux." He told me.

"Gosh, not even married two hours and already he's telling me what to do." I teased.

It was finally time for us to leave for the reception, and everyone went their separate ways, Mitch and I finding ourselves inside the limo once more. Once we started on our way, Mitch cuddled up close to me again.

"Well, sweetheart, we have about a half hour ride to the club. What would you like to do to pass the time?" he said, giving me a crooked smile.

"Oh, I don't know, we could talk, I guess." I smiled back.

Mitch chuckled. "My second choice, but ok, let's talk." Mitch smiled. "Tomorrow, Chris is coming by around eight to pick us up for the airport. Our flight leaves at nine forty, so that should give us plenty of time." Mitch paused, giving me yet another little crooked smile. "You aren't going to take an hour to get ready this time, are you, not like last night?"

"I'll try, but last night you told me last minute, Mitchell. You didn't give me any time to prepare." I defended.

"Yes, dear." He replied, and then smirked. "See, I already know how to say it."

"Good boy." I teased, giving him a kiss. Then I looked at him and took his hand, rubbing my finger along his wedding band.

Mitch reached inside his jacket and pulled out the marriage license. Taking it from the envelope, he opened it up for closer inspection.

"I guess this makes it official, huh?" he said. "You know, I really need to talk to my mom about giving me such a long name. I could hardly fit it all on that line."

"Well, sweetie, you weren't alone this time. Look at your dad and Chris's signatures as well. You guys just don't do anything small, do you?" I said.

"No, that's for sure." Then he turned, and his face grew serious, and he was looking right into my eyes. "Dana, when I saw you standing in the doorway of the church today with Joseph, I could hardly breathe. You just looked so beautiful, and I felt just like I did the first time I ever looked at you. Only this time, I knew what I felt was love. Right then and there I thanked God for giving you to me. I'm so blessed, and I don't deserve to be. I know I haven't been the greatest at times, but I can promise you I'll do my best to be a good husband to you."

I almost felt like I was going to cry, just at his words and the way he was looking at me. "I know you will, and I promise I'll try to be a good wife, too." I smiled. "You know, when I saw you standing up there, I felt the same way. You are just so incredibly handsome, Mitch. And that dimple of yours makes me just feel like melting every time you smile."

"You mean this one?" he said, touching his cheek and smiling brightly.

"That would be the one." I said, and I kissed him softly.

Mitch decided he wasn't satisfied with just one kiss, and he began to kiss me more passionately, holding me closer and closer to him. He started to kiss my neck, and I could feel his hands beginning a journey of their own. I pulled away and smiled at him, taking his hand.

"Come on, Dana, I'm legal now." He said, chuckling softly. "See?" He held up his wedding band, as if I needed visual proof.

"Patience, honey, patience." I told him.

"Dana, I'm really about to lose my patience." He said, smiling. Then, he noticed that we were pulling into the parking lot of the country club and he shifted his position. "You got lucky this time, but later......." He was smirking at me, his eyes shining mischievously.

"You really are terrible, you know that?" I asked.

"That's what you keep telling me." He said back.

The chauffer opened the door for us, and we stepped out, Mitch taking me by the hand. "Come on, Mrs. Tarrington. Our guests are waiting."

Mitch opened the door for me, and I stepped inside, almost wanting to turn back around and run when I saw all the people who were suddenly looking at me. Mitch stepped in behind me and just smiled. Being the center of attention might be his thing, I thought, but it definitely wasn't mine.

"Honey, there are a ton of people here." I whispered to him.

"Just relax, baby, I'm right here. It'll be fun," he said.

Ty smiled at us as we stood there, just observing, not really sure what to do. Finally, the awkwardness was broken by his words. "Everyone, our guests of honor have arrived. I'm pleased to introduce Mr. and Mrs. Mitchell Tarrington the third." Everyone applauded and I gave Mitch my deer in the headlights look. He laughed.

"Dana, sweetheart, they won't attack, I promise. Let's go and mingle a little, ok?" He took me by the hand and began leading me into the sea of people. I hesitated for just a moment, until I saw Olivia approaching us.

"Hi kids!" Olivia greeted, giving us both a kiss on the cheek. "Did you enjoy your ride?"

Mitch just looked at me and rolled his eyes playfully, so I decided to answer. "It was really fun. I'd never been in a limo before." I told her.

"Mom, are you sure we actually KNOW all these people? I don't remember getting this many responses back." Mitch asked her, looking around.

"Of course we know all these people, Mitchell. Most of them are friends and relatives. Some are colleagues of your father's who wanted to wish you well."

Mitch sighed and gave her a displeased look. "Mom, I thought I asked you not to do that. I thought we agreed it would only be friends and family."

I had a feeling I knew where he was taking this discussion, and I didn't want an argument at my wedding reception. "Mitch, honey, it's ok. I'm sure that they are friends with your dad."

He looked at me and sighed again. "Well, I think we should try to get around a little before dinner, don't you sweetheart? I mean, we'll probably be pretty tied up in things after."

"That's probably not a bad idea, Mitchell." Olivia said to him. "I'll catch up with the two of you later." She turned and walked away.

"Mitch, what's the big deal if your dad invited some guests? It's not like we don't have the room or anything." I told him.

He looked at me. "I know, but it's just that I don't want him making our wedding reception into a business dinner for his colleagues. That's not the purpose of all this, Dana. It's suppose to be a time for us to celebrate our marriage, not for my dad to make business deals."

I brushed a strand of hair back from his forehead, and touched his cheek with my hand. "Sweetie, leave well enough alone, ok? Don't go getting upset. Think of it this way, Mitchell. Whether or not your dad is here making business deals, or he's here dancing his heart out to the band, he's still here. I don't have that luxury, Mitch. Be glad that you do."

Mitch looked at me, his face stern, but his eyes full of compassion. He pulled me to him, and gave me a hug. "You're right, Dana, thank you. I'm sorry."

"Now, come on and let's start mingling, or I may just run away!" I told him, taking his hand once more.

We made our rounds to as many tables as we could, Mitch introducing me to people I didn't know, and allowing me the chance to relax by chatting a little with those I did. We finally came to where his parents were standing, talking to a colleague of Jake's. Jake smiled warmly and approached Mitch, placing his hand on his shoulder. He pointed to a distinguished looking, gray haired gentleman sitting at the table next to a very rich looking, much younger woman that I guessed to be his daughter. They smiled a friendly smile at us.

"Eric, I'd like you to meet my youngest son, Mitch. Mitch, this is Eric Tallmadge, of Irving Manufacturing. We just signed a deal to do some packaging through his company." Mitch shook Eric's hand. "And this lovely lady is his wife, Vanessa."

Wife, I thought? She didn't look to be much older than Mitch. Talk about robbing the cradle!

Mitch shook her hand as well then turned to me, the one that his father had forgotten. "Nice to meet you both, and this is my wife, Dana." He said it with such pride that my heart skipped a beat.

I shook both their hands and put my arm around Mitch. Eric decided he wanted to start a little conversation.

"So, Mitch, your dad tells me that you own a restaurant in town. Gartano's is it?" he said.

"Yes, that's right. I took over just before Christmas." Mitch told him.

"I was telling Jake how impressive that is, for someone your age to be in business for yourself. You must have inherited your father's good business sense." Eric added.

Mitch bit his lip. "Yeah, I guess so," he replied.

Jake pointed to the band setup. "Mitchell is also a musician, Eric. In fact, his band is going to be playing for us later tonight. He's what they call the front man. Does all the lead guitar and vocals." He smiled and patted Mitch on the back. "He's a very talented young man." I looked at Jake and could see the pride shining in his eyes.

"My, Dana, you seem to have hooked a jack of all trades there." Eric said to me.

"Well, actually, he found me first. But I do feel pretty lucky." I said back.

After a few minutes, we heard Ty, our master of ceremonies for the evening, announcing loud and clear.

"At this time we'd like the wedding party to take their seats at the head table, Mitch and Dana, at the center. We'll begin serving dinner in about ten minutes or so."

We excused ourselves from Jake's friends, and started toward the table. I turned to Mitch. "See, Mitchell, your dad is so proud of you. You thought he was doing business, and he was bragging about you to his friend." I scolded.

Mitch bit his lip and looked at me. "Yeah, I noticed that too. Guess I shouldn't be so quick to judge, huh?"

"No, you shouldn't. He really loves you, Mitch. He probably brought all those people here tonight to show you off." I smiled. "Now, come on and let's sit down, so I can show you off."

"Oh, so I'm your little trophy, huh? Now I know why you married me. I make you look good, don't I?" He smirked.

"You wish!" I teased. "If anything, it's the other way around."

Mitch smiled at me. "Actually, sweetheart, that's true. You do make me look good. You make everything about me better." He said, giving me a kiss.

Our moment was interrupted by the greetings of Mitch's band mates. He smiled as they approached, all of them dressed and looking sharp in suits and ties. He held out his hand to them, as if to shake, but they walked right past him and came to me.

"Hey, little Mrs. Trip!" Shep greeted, giving me a hug and a kiss. "You look stunning." He said, giving me a once over.

"Dana, you are so pretty. Congratulations." Ash said, also giving me a hug and a kiss.

"Don't let Janine catch the bouquet." Newbie whispered as he did the same as the others. I laughed.

Zach smiled at me. "Trip's a lucky man." He said as he stepped back from his hug.

Ty was the last to approach. "You are a vision of beauty, Mrs. Tarrington." He said, kissing my hand and taking a chivalrous bow.

Mitch stood there, watching the whole scene. "Gee, guys, what, am I not in this, too?" He teased.

All the guys looked at each other playfully, then at the same time, they rushed into Mitch, hugging him tightly. "What's the matter, Trip, jealous? We can take care of that!" Newbie said. And then three of them kissed Mitch on the cheek as well. He was laughing so hard he was crying.

"You are all such losers!" He told them.

We took our place at the head table, and were soon surrounded by the rest of the wedding party. Kayla was sitting next to me, and she gave me a hug as I sat down. Everyone's attention then turned to Chris, who was now standing in the center of the room with a microphone and a glass of champagne.

"Everyone, on behalf of Mitch and Dana, I want to thank you all for coming here tonight to help us celebrate their wedding." Chris began. "I'd like to take just a moment to say a few words to my little brother and my new sister-in-law." Chris turned to face us. "I was just seven years old when this guy came into the world, and I must say, as a little boy, I wasn't much impressed." Everyone chuckled. "He was nothing more to me than a crying, drooling little mess that wouldn't leave me alone. Well, then I got older, and wiser, and I realized that he needed me, but what's more, I needed him. I never told you that part of the deal, Mitchell. It's been a journey full of laughter and tears, joys and sorrows, but you've always stuck by me no matter what. And I honestly don't know how I could make it without you. Today, little brother, you start a new journey, and it too, will have laughter and tears, joys and sorrows. But you have someone truly special to share it with, someone who will be there for you, too, no matter what. I heard about love at first sight, but I wasn't sure I believed it was true. Then I saw the two of you, and I realized that it's more than possible. And it's not a passing thing. What you two share is the best kind of love, a forever kind of love. The kind that can take whatever life throws it's way, and still endure. Mitchell, I have watched you grow into what I see today, and I am so proud that you are my brother. I love you, buddy, more than you know. And Dana, over the past few months, you've taken a special place in my heart as well, and I know in the days to come it will only grow stronger. I've never seen my brother so happy as he is when he's with you, and I know that you will be the best wife anyone could hope for. To both of you, I wish much love, and a lifetime of happiness." Everyone toasted us, and Mitch and I wiped away a tear. Chris came back to his seat and gave Mitch a tight hug. I smiled at the special relationship they shared. It must feel good to have that, I thought.

As Chris sat back down, the crowd started to clank on their glasses. Mitch looked at me and smiled.

"Time to show them what we can do, baby." He said, and he leaned over and kissed me. Everyone applauded, but they immediately started the clamor again. Mitch looked at me, a crooked smile coming over his face. "Guess that one wasn't good enough, huh?"

"Guess not." I replied, and this time, I kissed him, lingering a little longer. Again, we got the applause.

The 'clanking for kisses' continued every few minutes for about the next ten or fifteen, and it became a friendly battle of the sexes between us. First, Mitch would initiate the kiss, then I would, each trying to outdo the other, much to the delight of the crowd. Finally, the serving staff approached us and told us we could lead the buffet line. I smiled at Mitch.

"Golly, I'm glad for this. I was afraid I'd get chapped lips and not be able to eat anything." I said, taking his hand. As I picked up a plate and began to put on it whatever would fit, I turned to him. "I don't know about you, but I'm starving." I said.

"Didn't you eat lunch?" Mitch asked me.

"Sure, Kayla took me to Charley's, but that was seven hours ago. All I had was a burger and fries, and a milkshake. Oh, yeah, and some cheese fries."

Mitch laughed. "Dana, I'm still amazed by your appetite. I swear I don't know where you put it all."

"You don't do too shabby for yourself, there, lover boy." I shot back, pointing to his heaping plate.

"Well, all I had for lunch was a salami sandwich." He said in defense.

We sat back down and had no sooner begun to eat when the clanking for kisses started again. I gave Mitch a quick little kiss, but the crowd wasn't satisfied, and started clanking again. I sighed and gave him another one, lingering a little longer. They decided that was good enough to hold them over, for at least five or six bites.

Mitch looked at me, and I could see that look in his eyes. "Dana, I swear, if they keep it up......."

As if on cue, the clanking started again. Mitch stood up and turned toward everyone, giving his best smile. He took off his jacket, then his tie, and started to unbutton his shirt. He was now getting ooo's, ahh's and a few wolf whistles from the crowd. He reached out for me and pulled me to my feet, then took about three steps back from the table. He tapped Chris on the shoulder, handed him his glasses, and then dipped me into a very long and passionate kiss, working his way from my lips to my neck and back again. When he stood me back up, I was as red as a cherry. Mitch replaced his glasses as the crowd applauded loudly, he smiled and took a bow, then sat back down to his dinner. Chris gave him a high five over my head, and the two of them laughed.

"Mitchell Tarrington, I swear." I said to him, just shaking my head.

"Gotta give the people what they want, sweetheart." He said with a grin. It must have worked because we were able to finish our dinner in peace.

We watched Ty take his place back at the front of the room and pick up the microphone. "Now that everyone has had a chance to enjoy their dinner, and the little sideshow Mitch gave us," everyone laughed and Mitch stood up for another bow, "we're going to ask our newlyweds if they will come and cut their cake so we can all have some dessert."

"Mitchell, make yourself presentable again, will you? I don't want our children asking someday why Daddy was half undressed in his wedding pictures." I told him, starting to re-button his shirt.

Mitch smiled and handed Chris his tie. "You can do this for me since I don't have a mirror." Chris quickly had Mitch's tie back in order, and we walked around to the table where the cake was.

Mitch reached out and took a finger full of icing, ate half of it off, then gave me the other half. I smiled, and picking up the cake knife I stood close to him and he put his hand on top of mine as we cut through the cake. I took out the first piece and smirked at him, his eyes as full of mischief as mine. We each picked up a piece of cake and turned to each other.

"I don't like the way you're looking at me, Dana Tarrington." Mitch said, taking a step back as he started to laugh.

"Where are you going, sweetie? Come here and let me give you a bite of this." I said, stepping toward him.

"Ok, same time, we hold each others free hands, and we do it nicely, deal?" Mitch said.

Not responding, I reached out for Mitch's free hand and a minute later, both of us were wearing our cake as everyone laughed, including us.

"I thought we made a deal!" Mitch exclaimed as he wiped his face with a napkin, still laughing.

"I never agreed to anything." I replied, kissing the rest of the icing off his mouth.

We returned to our seats as the servers gave everyone a piece of cake and we fed each other bites nicely, kissing in between. Finally, it was time to start dancing, and Mitch smiled as Ty once again took front and center.

"Ladies and gentleman, before we start the bridal dance, I'd like to make a special announcement." Ty started. "Tonight we are going to play a very special song which was actually written by Mitch about a month or so ago especially for Dana. But, on the way here today, I realized that I could never do the vocal part as well as the one who originated it. So,........" Ty walked up to Mitch and handed him a headset. Smiling, Mitch put it on and positioned the microphone. "I decided to let him do it for his new bride. The song is called 'Day One' and now, here's our guests of honor, Mitch and Dana Tarrington."

Everyone applauded as the band began to play, and the lights went dim, except for where Mitch and I stood. He took me in his arms and began to dance slowly with me, holding me tightly as he sang our song once again. His voice was soft and sweet, as always, and I closed my eyes and drank in each word, each line, each note, as I knew he was doing the same. As the song ended, he stopped dancing and just stood gazing into my eyes as he sang the last line, then he whispered "I love you" and he kissed me. Everyone applauded and stood up, and Mitch smiled at me.

"A standing ovation, like that's never happened before." I teased, kissing him again.

Mitch took off his headset and handed it back to Ty, then returned to me. He called Joseph over and gave him my hand. "It's your turn now." He said. "Dance with my beautiful wife."

Joseph smiled. "I'd be honored." He said, taking me onto the floor.

I looked for Mitch to go and sit down, but instead, he walked up to the front where the band was, took a stool and placed it front and center. Then I watched as he walked slightly behind Newbie and picked up his acoustic guitar, which the guys had apparently smuggled in for him. He took a seat on the stool and positioning the microphone, smiled again.

"I may pay for this later, folks, because I kinda told her I wouldn't do this tonight." Everyone chuckled as he turned to me. "Sweetheart, I have one request. If you decide to punish me for this, please wait until tomorrow." Everyone laughed as Mitch began to play.

I looked up at Joseph. "What a brat." I said, shaking my head and smiling at Mitch.

Joseph smiled. "The music's in his blood, little girl. He has to let it out."

"I know, I'm not angry, how could I be? Just look at him, he's so at ease up there." I said.

Mitch sang sweetly as Joseph and I danced. He was as easy to follow as Mitch, and I laid my head on his shoulder. I knew he wasn't really my father, but I closed my eyes and in my mind Daddy was there, holding me in his arms and dancing with me. Joseph kissed me softly on top of the head, and I knew that if Daddy was watching, he would be glad that I had Joseph and Kayla here to watch over me. They had taken me under their wings four years ago, and I thought of them as if they were truly blood relatives. Our song ended and Joseph smiled at me, giving me a gentle hug.

"You go on now and be with your husband." He told me.

Mitch put down his guitar, and came to join me, cueing up the band to play the next song, as Ty introduced us once again.

"Now, we're going to ask our bridal party to join us, starting with our best man, Chris Tarrington, and his wife Trudy, and matron of honor Kayla Turner and her husband, Joseph."

The others joined us and began to dance near us, all smiling at each other.

"Next I'd like to ask Jim and Angelina Macklin to join the others, as well as Paul and Julia Stevens." Ty smiled. "Last, but not least, flower girl Megan Macklin and ring bearer Michael Tarrington." Mitch and I smiled as Megan took Michael's hand and pulled him out to dance. Michael looked at Chris.

"I don't want to dance, Daddy, not with her." He said, under protest.

"Mike, just this one, ok, buddy?" Chris told him. "Then you don't have to do it anymore."

Michael made a face. "Just this one, but I'm not kissing her."

Chris and Trudy laughed, and so did Mitch and I. "I really do hope he outgrows that." Mitch told Chris.

"Finally, I'd like to introduce the two people who ultimately made this day possible, the groom's parents, Jake and Olivia Tarrington."

Mitch smiled as he watched his father and mother dancing. He wondered if he really had inherited that talent from his father, because his father was quite the dancer.

Mitch pointed to the other kids who were gathered at the edge of the dance floor, and Ty smiled. "I'd also like to invite the others who helped at the wedding to come out onto the floor, Alexis and Kyle Tarrington, and Riley and Joanna Turner."

Everyone was on the floor now, and we looked around us at all the people that meant the most in our lives. I smiled up at Mitch.

"You know, Mitchell, you are a very lucky man, to have all these people in your life. And I'm lucky that I married you, so they can be a part of my life, too." I said.

"But you know what, Dana? As special as they all are, you mean more to me than any of them, and that's the truth," he said.

I gave him a kiss. "And you are the most important person in my life, too." I told him.

Our dance ended and Ty called us to attention once more. "Let's get Dana up here right now, and all you single girls can line up behind her out on the floor. Now, remember, tradition says that whoever catches the bouquet will be the next to marry." All the single girls were starting to flood the floor, and I was surprised at how many of them there actually were. "Now, all you single guys, these are the ones you have to choose from tonight." Everyone laughed.

I saw Janine, and she smiled at Newbie, who was smiling back, shaking his head. I laughed and looking at him, pretended to line myself up with her. He formed the words "Don't you dare," and I smiled.

"Ok, Dana, you ready? On three, one, two, three!" I tossed the bouquet behind my back, then turned to see who had caught it. It was Janine, and I lost it. Newbie was standing with his face in his hands, and Mitch walked up to him, taking him by the arm and leading him out to the floor. He took the microphone from Ty.

"Everyone, this is our drummer, Aaron Newsonberg, whom we lovingly refer to as Newbie, and can you tell? His girlfriend, Janine just caught the bouquet. Let's see if he can get lucky with the garter." Paul placed a chair in the middle of the floor and told me to sit.

All the single guys, including the band, were lining up at the back of the dance floor. Newbie ran back up to his set, and did a drum roll as Mitch reached for the garter. Then Mitch put his hand up and Newbie stopped. He turned to me with an impish grin.

"I'm gonna do this the right way." He smiled, and he put his hands behind his back and started pulling the garter down with his teeth as everyone cheered him on. He got it down to my ankle and pulled it off the rest of the way, smiling like the Cheshire cat. I just shook my head and smiled.

Mitch prompted Newbie back to the floor, and when he was in position, he threw the garter over his shoulder, seemingly right into Zach's hands. Newbie folded his hands as if in prayer, looked up and said thank you. We all laughed at him.

"Just one more special dance tonight, and that one is for Mitch and his mom, Olivia. Could we have you two out here, please?" Ty said, as the lights dimmed again.

I gave Mitch a kiss and sent him to his mother, as he smiled brightly at her and positioned himself to lead her in the dance. I marveled at the way he moved with her, as if he had been dancing with her for a hundred years, and smiled at how much the two of them resembled each other. She was a very attractive woman and time had been kind to her, aging her gracefully. They were lost in conversation and I wondered what they were talking about, but I knew I would never ask. I thought of my own mother, and how I wished she could be there to dance with him, too. She would love him so much, I knew she would.

"So, Mitchell, how does it feel to be married?" Olivia asked her son.

"So far, fantastic. If anyone would have told me even six months ago this is where I would be right now, there is no way I would have believed them. It's so amazing." Mitch said, smiling at her.

"Like I told you, time doesn't matter. Mitch, it's just so hard for me to believe that you are all grown up. I can remember you being little, just like it was yesterday. And now look at you, a married man." Olivia gave Mitch a gentle hug. "I'm so proud of you, honey."

Mitch smiled at her as the song ended. "Thanks, Mom, I love you." He said, hugging her.

"I love you too, Mitchell. Always." She said.

"Ok, gang, let's get this party started!" Ty said, and the band began to play some more upbeat songs. Suddenly, as if a town were being evacuated, the dance floor was taken over by people. Mitch found me and grabbing me, pulled me to him.

"Come on, Mrs. Mitchell Tarrington, dance with your husband." He kissed me, and began to dance with me.

Although I already knew he was a good dancer, I was once again amazed at the ease with which he moved. He wasn't awkward or clumsy looking like some of the other guys who were pretending they knew how to dance. He didn't have to pretend, because he really did know. I smiled at him, just having fun and dancing like no one was watching. He enjoyed life so much, and most everything was a game to him. I decided right then that he had the secret to happiness, and I couldn't wait to have him share that secret with me for eternity.

We danced for what seemed like an endless amount of time, and Mitch finally pulled me off to the side. "Well, my love, it's almost ten thirty. Are you ready to make an exit?"

I looked at him timidly, knowing in my mind and heart what he was actually saying. He was ready for the next phase of the evening.

"We should say goodbye to everyone first, don't you think?" I said, deciding to stall just a little longer.

Mitch smiled. "Ok, we can do that, I guess." He took me by the hand and one by one, we hugged and kissed his family and our friends goodbye. As we made it to the band at the end of the song they were playing, Ty handed Mitch the microphone.

"Everyone, Dana and I would like to thank you all for helping us celebrate and for all your love, friendship and support. Please keep us in your prayers as we travel to and from Hawaii, but now, we'd like to say goodnight and it's off to the Tarrington love nest!"

I blushed as he said it, and before I knew what was happening, Mitch had swept me up into his arms and was heading out the door with me, everyone applauding behind us. Our limo had gone, and we were now standing beside his car that Chris had brought for us earlier, which was all decorated with pink and blue pom poms. A sign on the back said 'Just Married'. Mitch smiled.

"Cute, huh?" He said, unlocking the door, and opening it for me.

"Very." I answered, as I attempted to pull my dress inside the car.

Mitch ran around to the other side and hopped in. He turned to me and smiled.

"Well, my love, that was a lot of fun. But, now, it's time for just you and me." He started the car and after pulling out, took me by the hand.

I looked out the window at the big bright moon and the sky filled with endless stars. I remembered back to Christmas night when we had gone to Chris and Trudy's and how the sky had looked very much like this. It was so romantic just to stand with Mitch beside the car and look up at the sky, so peaceful. Mitch saw me gazing up and smiled at me.

"The stars are pretty, aren't they?" He asked.

"There must be a million of them." I replied.

As I gazed out the window, I began to feel a little nervous in anticipation of what I knew was to come. I looked at Mitch. I did love him, more than anything, and in my heart I knew he loved me, too. I tried to dissect my fears, to analyze why someone in love would be afraid of the one act that epitomized the pinnacle of sharing that love. I decided that it could only be that I was afraid my inaptitude would disappoint him somehow, or that I would when the mystery of me was finally revealed to him. Mitch looked at me thoughtfully, and squeezed my hand.

"You're awfully quiet all of a sudden, sweetheart. Something on your mind?" he asked.

I looked at him and managed a smile. "No, not really." I replied softly, trying to keep my voice from shaking.

Mitch pulled me to him, and kissing my forehead, he put his arm around me. "Just relax, baby, it'll be alright, I promise. Nothing to worry about."

It amazed me how well, in such a short time, he could read me like that. I hadn't said a word, and yet he knew.

Mitch pulled up to the door in front of the apartment building to let me out, coming around to open the door for me. "Wait right here while I go and park." He said. A minute later he was standing next to me, taking me by the hand.

"Good evening and congratulations, Mr. and Mrs. Tarrington." Pete said, opening the door for us.

"Thank you, Pete." Mitch said. As we stepped inside, Mitch turned to me. "Would you like to walk up, or take the elevator?" he asked.

"Let's walk, it's not that far." I said, thinking that would stall us a few minutes more.

Mitch took my hand and we walked up, stopping at the door. Pulling out his keys, he unlocked the door, pushing it wide open. "I think I'm supposed to do something here." He said, and he picked me up in his arms again, to carry me across the threshold. I smiled as he kissed me and pushed the door shut. "Lock that, will you?" he asked me, not putting me down. I did as he asked, and he carried me through the apartment, setting me down in the bedroom, closing that door as well. He quickly moved to the nightstand, and turned the light on low. Then he came to stand back in front of me.

For just a moment he stood there, not saying a word, just gazing into my eyes as if he were trying to hypnotize me. It was working, and I felt the love he was radiating from himself to me. He smiled at me sweetly, his eyes shining with love and passion. Then, very softly, he kissed me, pulling me to him gently.

"I am so in love with you, Dana." He said softly. "You are so beautiful."

I caught my breath with his next kiss, and he pulled away from me, smiling. "Don't be afraid, love, it's just me. Just relax and kiss me like you always do."

I slowly put my arms around his neck and started to kiss him, and he started to rub my back with his hand, in an attempt to calm me even more. He continued to kiss me, each kiss soft and purposeful, but not forceful. Without pulling away from me, he took off his jacket, then his tie, and began to undo the buttons on his shirt, slowly letting it fall with the other things. He pulled away from me and smiled, taking off my veil and laying it on the chair, taking me back in his arms.

I found myself lost in the pleasure of his kisses, and as he moved from my lips to my neck, I felt him starting to unzip my dress, slowly taking it off my shoulders. I pulled away and looked at him, and he looked at me with love and compassion.

"Are you frightened, Dana?" He asked. I nodded timidly, casting my glance down from his. "It's ok, just relax. It's only you and me, and I love you." He said softly.

I looked up at him. "Can we wait? I mean, until later or something?" I asked shyly.

Mitch chuckled softly. "No, sweetheart, we aren't going to wait. Everything will be ok, we're married now, and I want to be with you, Dana. I want to be with you now. Don't be afraid."

Mitch took my hand and leading me to the side of the bed, he sat down and pulled me to him, still kissing me with all the love he had in him. I was so mesmerized by the look in his eyes that I didn't think about the fact that we were both undressed now, and he pulled the covers over us, then drew me in close. Mitch was making love to me now, his hands expertly exploring places previously unknown to him, his every move precise. His kisses were stronger now and more passionate, and I knew that any inhibitions he might have had were now gone. He was giving himself to me completely, and with each moment I felt my own inhibitions fading more and more. I opened my eyes for a moment to catch him looking at me, his face full of emotion like I had never seen before, his eyes full of love. I knew we were now husband and wife, one together, no longer separate. The touch of his fingers against my skin sent sensations through me like nothing I had ever felt before, and I could feel his heart pounding wildly as if it would surely explode under the pressure of his passion. He pulled me closer to him, and I could feel the hunger he had for me growing stronger in the way he was holding me. Suddenly, as if some force unknown to us both had taken over, we were swept away in a flood of emotions so strong that it was almost hard to breathe. A moment later he kissed me again, then pulled me to him and held me gently, brushing the hair back from my face. I opened my eyes and he smiled at me lovingly.

"Wow, that was incredible." He said, looking at me, waiting for my reaction.

I smiled. "Really?" I said, as if I were needing to reaffirm his approval.

"Yes, love, really." He chuckled softly. "Were you expecting me to say something else?"

"I guess not, I mean, I don't know, I'm not sure." I said, making circles on his chest with my finger.

"Well, if you thought I'd say anything less, I'm sorry to disappoint you." He replied.

He lay there just holding me for a few minutes, allowing me to become comfortable with this new state of affairs. He looked at me lovingly. "Are you ok, sweetheart? I mean, I didn't scare you, did I?"

I held him tighter and shook my head. "No, I was already scared. But not anymore." He smiled.

I put my head on his shoulder and he kissed my forehead. "Ready to go to Hawaii?" He asked.

"I guess so. I just wish I didn't have to fly to get there." I told him.

Mitch smiled at me. "You certainly are a fearful little thing, aren't you? I guess I've got my work cut out for me, getting you over all this." He kissed me softly.

Mitch set the alarm, turned out the light and snuggled up to me. Soon I could hear his slow and steady breathing and I assumed he was falling asleep. I closed my eyes and in my mind, replayed the events of the day. As is usually the case with fears, all mine were unfounded. Mitch and I made it through the wedding, and the reception without passing out or running away. And with his love and tenderness, we had come to know each other tonight in a totally new and special way, something that would bond us together for the rest of our lives. I started to unwind, and softly kissing my husband, I drifted off to sleep, exactly where I wanted to be.

Mitch slowly turned over, looking at his new bride sleeping peacefully next to him. Contentment filled his heart as he watched her there, her breath falling softly on his skin. How he loved her, he thought, how he wanted to be everything for her that she needed him to be. Today they'd begun a new journey, a journey that was sure to be nothing less than wonderful. He knew that this was just the beginning of a lifetime of happiness, but not without responsibility. Responsibility. That thought, for some reason, captured him, and he turned to face the nightstand. Slowly opening the drawer, he took out his unopened purchase from the day before. Sighing deeply, he gently shook Dana awake.

"What is it, honey?" I asked sleepily.

He held up the box before me, biting his lip nervously. "Surprise." He said sarcastically.

And he hoped there wouldn't be.

Will a wedding night blunder, a groom's confession and a bride's unsettled past spell turmoil for the young Tarrington's or will their love be enough to see them through? Find out in Book Two of the 'Forever Love' series, coming soon!

Thank you for purchasing this book. If you enjoyed it, please let us know by contacting the publisher or placing a review on Amazon.com. Please know that a portion of the price you paid will be donated to the American Cancer Society.

About the Author

Debbie Alferio is a lifelong resident of Northern Ohio. Her interest in writing this novel came after a dream she had one night involving the character of Mitch. Feeling inspired by this dream, she began to write and now views it as her passion. Feeling it important to write in a way that readers could easily relate to, she made each character very realistic and down-to-earth, instilling her own importance of high moral and family values into each one. The relationships between characters, the surprises revealed throughout the story, and the humorous and heartwarming approach to each situation they face makes Debbie's writing both interesting and entertaining. This is her first novel in the series.

Debbie feels that long stories are the best stories. "When you are absorbed in a good book, you don't want it to end. I like to give that satisfaction to my readers by keeping the excitement going just a little longer."

Having lost several relatives to cancer as well personally knowing many others touched by the disease, Debbie chose to donate a portion of her profits from the sale of each book to the American Cancer Society. In doing so, she hopes that her novel will not only bring enjoyment to those who read it, but will aid in finding a cure for this deadly disease.

Printed in the United States
62459LVS00003B/19-27